FOREVERLAND BOXED

TONY BERTAUSKI

BERTAUSKI STARTER LIBRARY

Get the
BERTAUSKI STARTER LIBRARY
FREE!
Click link below.

bertauski.com

BOOK 1

THE ANNIHILATION OF FOREVERLAND

ROUND 1

LOCAL COMPUTER GENIUS ARRESTED ON FEDERAL CHARGES

SUMMERVILLE, South Carolina. – Tyler Ballard, 37, was apprehended by authorities of the Federal Bureau of Investigation for practicing federally banned computer technology.

Ballard is best known for inventing the controversial technique of Computer-Assisted Alternate Reality (CAAR) that induces lucid dream states. The program requires a direct connection with the user's frontal lobe by means of a needle-probe piercing the forehead that results in a realistic computer-generated environment. Users reported no difference between their CAAR experience and flesh-body experience.

The controversial technology was later banned in most countries when all users began to suffer irreparable psychological damage that resulted in vegetative states.

Ballard was practicing CAAR in his basement with his wife, Patricia Ballard, 36. Patricia suffers from bipolar disorder and, Tyler Ballard claims, was responding well to CAAR treatments. Authorities dispute this claim since Patricia has been unresponsive to physical stimuli since the arrest.

Harold Ballard, 12, their only son, was placed in the custody of his grandparents.

1

Click-click-click-click.

The walls inched closer. Reed gripped the bars of his shrinking cell.

His legs, shaking.

The cold seeped through his bare feet. The soles were numb, his ankles ached. He lifted his feet one at a time, alternating back and forth to keep the bitter chill from reaching his groin, but he couldn't waste strength anymore. He let go of the bars to shake the numbness from his fingers.

He'd been standing for quite some time. *Has it been hours?* Occasionally he would sit to rest his aching legs, but soon the cell would be too narrow for that. He'd have to stand up. And when the top of his cage started moving down – and it would – he'd be forced to not-quite stand, not-quite sit.

He knew how things worked.

Although he couldn't measure time in the near-blackout room, this round felt longer than previous ones. Perhaps it would never end. Maybe he'd have to stand until his knees crumbled under his dead weight. His frigid bones would shatter like frozen glass when he hit the ground. He'd fall like a boneless bag, his muscles liquefied in a soupy mix of lactic acid and calcium, his nerves firing randomly, his eyes bulging, teeth chattering

Don't think. No thoughts.

Reed learned that his suffering was only compounded by thoughts, that the false suffering of what he *thought* would happen would crush him before the true suffering did. He learned to be present with the burning, the cold, and the aches. *The agony.*

He couldn't think. He had to be present, no matter what.

Sprinklers dripped from the ribs of the domed ceiling that met at the apex where an enormous ceiling fan still moved from the momentum of its last cycle. Eventually, the sprinklers would hiss another cloud and the fan would churn again and the damp air would sift through the bars and over Reed's wet skin, heightening the aches in his joints like clamps. For now, there was just the drip of the sprinklers and the soft snoring of his cellmates.

Six individual cells were inside the building, three on each side of a concrete aisle. Each one contained a boy about Reed's age. They were all in their teens, the youngest being fourteen. Their cells were spacious; only Reed's had gotten smaller. Despite the concrete, they all lay on the floor, completely unaware of the anguish inside the domed building.

They weren't sleeping, though. Sleep is when you close your eyes and drift off to unconsciousness. No, they were somewhere else. The black strap around each of their heads took them away from the pain. They had a choice to stay awake like Reed, but they chose to lie down, strap on, and go wherever it took them. They didn't care where.

In fact, they wanted to go.

To escape.

Reed couldn't blame them. They were kids. They were scared and alone. Reed was all those things, too. But he didn't have a strap around his head. He stayed in his flesh.

He took a deep breath, let it out slowly. Started counting, again.

1, 2, 3, 4, 5, 6, 7, 8, 9...10.

And then he did it again. Again.

And again.

He didn't measure time with his breathing. He only breathed. His life was in his breath. It ebbed and flowed like the tides. It came and went like the lunar phases. When he could be here and now, the suffering was tolerable. He counted, and counted and counted.

Distracted, he looked up at the fan. The blades had come to a complete stop. The air was humid and stagnant and cold. Around the domed ceiling were circular skylights that stared down with unforgiving blackness, indifferent to suffering. Reed tried not to look with the hopes of seeing light pour through them, signaling an end. Regardless if it was day or night, the skylights were closed until the round of suffering was over, so looking, hoping and wishing for light was no help. It only slowed time when he did. And time had nearly stopped where he was at.

1, 2, 3—

A door opened at the far right; light knifed across the room, followed by a metallic snap and darkness again. Hard shoes clicked unevenly across the floor. Reed smelled the old man before he limped in front of his cell, a fragrance that smelled more like deodorant than cologne. Mr. Smith looked over his rectangular glasses.

"Reed, why do you resist?"

Reed met his gaze but didn't reply. Mr. Smith wasn't interested in a discussion. It was always a lecture. No point to prolong it.

"Don't be afraid." The dark covered his wrinkles and dyed-black hair, but it couldn't hide his false tone. "I promise, you try it once, you'll see. You don't have to do it again if you don't like it. We're here to help, my boy. Here to help. You don't have to go through this suffering."

Did he forget they were the ones that put him in there? Did he forget they made the rules and called the shots and forced him to play? Reed knew he – himself – he had gone mad but IS EVERYONE CRAZY?

Reed let his thoughts play in his eyes. Mr. Smith crossed his arms, unmoved.

"We don't want to hurt you, I promise. We're just here to prepare you for a better life, that's all. Just take the lucid gear, the pain will go away. I promise."

He reached through the bars and batted the black strap hanging above Reed's head. It turned like a seductive mobile. Reed turned his back on him. Mr. Smith sighed. A pencil scratched on a clipboard.

"Have it your way, Reed," he said, before limp-shuffling along. "The Director wants to see you after this round is over."

He listened to the incessant lead-scribbled notes and click-clack of shiny shoes. When Mr. Smith was gone, Reed was left with only the occasional drip of the dormant sprinklers. He began to breathe again, all the way to ten and over. And over. And over. No thoughts. Just 1, 2, 3... 1, 2, 3... 1, 2—

Click-click-click-click.

Reed locked his knees and leaned back as the cell walls moved closer. Soon the fan would turn again and the mist would drift down to bead on his shoulders. Reed couldn't stop the thoughts from telling him what the near future would feel like. How bad it was going to get.

He looked up at the lucid gear dangling above his head.

He took a breath.

And began counting again.

2

"DANNY BOY!"

Danny's aunt's voice was muffled. She was calling from his bedroom with that thick Irish accent, obviously thought he was still in bed. Eventually, she'd come up to the attic where Danny was hunched over the keyboard, eyes on the screen. His mother had cleared a space out of the corner just for him, no one else, and even when the weather was too hot or too cold, Danny would sit up there all day.

"Danny Boy! Where are you, darling?"

He couldn't be interrupted now. He'd been acting sick for two weeks and got behind in school work. His mother trusted he was getting the homework done but he'd spent all his time modding the computer to do exactly what he was doing now.

People are stupid.

They used easy passwords and repeated the same one over and over. *Who thinks the word* password *is a password? Morons.*

It wasn't difficult to get past the school's firewall. Danny broke the encrypted password – using a program *he* wrote, thank you very much. In two seconds, he'd be a second grade, straight-A student. Once again.

Thank you very much.

Wait. I'm 13, not 7.

"Danny Boy?" The steps creaked. "Are you up here all ready? It's not even six o'clock in the morning, sonny boy."

Danny's fingers danced over the keys.

"Danny Boy... what are you doing?"

One more stroke and—

CRRUNNCH!

Danny fell out of the chair. The sound was deafening, like a metal pole plunging through the roof, smashing wood and shingles. Dust swirled in the new light. The steps creaked again, but something had changed. There wasn't insulation hanging from the ceiling anymore and there was a pile of boxes that wasn't there before.

The house changed.

"What are you doing in the attic?" A man was on the top step holding a golf club.

Danny blinked but it wasn't his aunt. And he wasn't in front of a computer anymore. He was lying in a crib. He was a thirteen-year-old kid in a baby's crib. In someone else's house.

The man's golf shoes sounded funny on the wood floor. He stopped short of the crib with his hands on his hips, the club teetering in his left hand. "Son, what in the hell are you doing? You think you're still a baby?"

Danny didn't move. Then the man smiled like a proud father.

"Well, if you want to do the baby thing again, let's give it a try."

He dropped the club and started tickling Danny's ribs. His fingers hit the funny spot and Danny gave out a chuckle. The man was all smiles, making happy-daddy sounds as he tortured him with loving grabs. Danny tried to knock him away but the man was too strong. Danny was about to piss his pants he was laughing so hard.

"Come here, you." The man snatched Danny up by the arms with a strong grip, but it wasn't strong enough. Danny slipped out of his clutches. He heard the man gasp as Danny fell out of the rickety crib, thought he'd land on his feet but the drop was farther than he expected. He crashed, all right; not on the floor, but on grass.

The sun was over him. The house was gone.

A crowd cheered. Danny was wearing a baseball uniform with a glove on his left hand. He'd never played baseball in his life, but there he was in center field with a cap pulled down just above his eyes.

Somewhere, an aluminum bat went *ting*.

The players on the infield turned around. The ball was high in the sky. The sun was in his eyes. He lifted the glove but couldn't see it. He tried squinting, tried covering the sun with his right hand but it was blinding. And the ball was going to hit him smack in the face. But he couldn't let the team down. He had to catch it. He had to—

And then he was swimming in the ocean. The waves crashed around him. There were other kids, too. Danny had never been to the beach, but there he was, swimming in water that churned at his waist—

And then he was coloring Easter eggs. There was a lady at the sink with an apron and some little girl across the table. He'd never seen her before—

Opening birthday presents and people were singing. People he'd never—

Playing Hide and Seek. He was hiding behind a bush with someone he'd—

Baking cookies—

School bus—

The scenes stacked on top of each other until he couldn't tell where one began and the next ended. It was all a blur. All a blur.

All a blur.

The throbbing.

That was the first thing Danny noticed before he cracked the seal of his sleep-crusted eyelashes. The head-splitting throb. His forehead felt like it had been punched with a dental tool.

"Don't sit up just yet, young man." A soft hand was on his arm. "Give it a few seconds."

He did what the man said.

When he opened his eyes, the light seemed bright. It took a minute of rapid blinking to adjust. He was in a doctor's office, on a patient's table. The paper that covered the table was bunched up under him, crinkling when he moved. There was an old man sitting on a stool next to him. His face was plenty wrinkled and his hair as white as the coat he wore.

"I'm Mr. Jones." The man broke out in grin worthy of a father looking at his newborn.

"Wa..." Danny's tongue was gummy. "Water, please."

"Sit up first, all right?"

When Danny was up, Mr. Jones passed him a paper cup and watched him chug it.

"More, please."

"Let that settle for a moment, okay. There's more when you're ready."

He wrapped a band around Danny's arm and took his blood pressure. Then took his temperature and pulse. He did some scribbling on a clipboard, occasionally looking up and humming.

The room, now that Danny had a chance to focus, was less like a doctor's office and more like a lab. There seemed to be large equipment attached to the wall that could be pulled out and centered on hinged arms. And behind him, the room went back another twenty feet with a treadmill and monitors and more machines.

"You go by Danny Boy?" the man asked.

"I'm sorry?"

"You were dreaming before you woke up and mumbled Danny Boy. I thought maybe that was what you preferred to be called. Danny Boy."

"My aunt... she called me that..."

"Ah, yes. Aunts are special, aren't they?" He grinned, again.

Danny reached for his head that felt so full of... stuff. But Mr. Jones caught him by the wrist. "Just relax a second, Danny Boy."

"I was having this weird dream... like it was a bunch of dreams all crammed into one."

"Dreams are like that." Mr. Jones quickly looked at his clipboard.

"Where am I?"

"You've had an accident, but you're okay now. Would you like some more water?"

"Yes, please."

He downed a second paper cup and wadded it before handing it back.

"Um, Doctor..."

"You can call me Mr. Jones."

"Mr. Jones, am I in a hospital?"

"You're somewhere much better than a hospital, my boy. You're in a special rehabilitation center that is unique for your condition. You'll have the best care that money can buy while you're here and you'll get to do things no other kid on this planet has ever tried. You'll also... ah, ah, ah... don't touch."

Danny reached for his forehead. There was a round band-aid the size of a Bull's eye right in the middle where it hurt. He tried to remember an accident, anything that he would've been doing that would've knocked him on the head, but all the memories were gibberish. He couldn't remember his home address or phone number. If his aunt hadn't been calling for him, he wouldn't remember his name.

"Is this why I'm here?" He tried to touch the bandage again.

"In some ways, yes."

"Did I fall on an ice pick?"

"No." Mr. Jones snorted. "You've been asleep for a long time while you've undergone treatment, so you may feel a bit woozy when you stand up. Be careful, all right? I want you to lean forward and let your toes touch the ground... good. Now stay just like that a second." Mr. Jones spun on the stool and coasted to the computer behind him. "And don't touch your forehead."

Danny's toes were tingly. Just the little weight that was on them, he could tell standing wasn't going to go well. He left his forehead alone, reached for his stiff neck, instead. It was sore, too. And there was a knot between the vertebrae. It felt like a band had been inserted just under the skin about the width of a wedding ring that made it seem like one large neck bone. Mr. Jones had one bulging on his neck, too.

"What's this?"

"That's part of your treatment," Mr. Jones said without looking. "It's new technology meant to stay in touch with your nervous system. We'll talk more about that later."

"Okay," was all Danny could think to say. He was thirteen. When an adult said something, he listened and that was that. But nothing was making sense, not the strange lab or Mr. Jones and his proud grin like everything was normal. His head was just so full.

"Where are my parents?"

Mr. Jones took several moments at the computer before he stood up with the clipboard over his stomach. "They want you to get better, Danny Boy. And that's what you're going to be... better."

Smile.

"When will I see them?"

"Can you put all your weight forward?"

He held out his hand and Danny took it. His weight was a little wobbly, but he felt better on his feet than he thought he would.

"Where are we?" Danny asked.

"Take a step for me and I'll tell you."

He took one step, then two. They reached the door and Mr. Jones opened it without letting go. The hallway was long and white.

"We're going that way." He pointed to the left. At that end was a glass wall.

Danny dragged his feet the first couple of steps. He was already breathing a little hard. Mr. Jones was slightly hunched over next to him. Danny put his hand on the wall and traced it with his fingers. His knees were weak but Mr. Jones watched him with a smile like every-thing was just okie-dokie. His touch became lighter as Danny's foot-steps became more confident. When he let go, Danny still touched the wall but was walking closer to normal when they reached the end.

The glass wall was slightly curved like the building was a giant cylinder. They were a few stories above ground. A little ways away was the back of a horseshoe-shaped building. Beyond that was a large green field with people.

"You're going to love it here, Danny Boy," he whispered.

The field looked like a college campus lined with tropical trees and palms with giant white birds. Danny was smart but he wasn't college-smart. Unless something happened to his brain. He reached for his forehead. Mr. Jones gently caught his arm before he could graze the band-aid with his fingertips.

"I'm going to be your Investor while you're here. I'm invested in your future, Danny Boy. If you ever need anything or have any questions, I'm the one that will help, all right?"

Danny nodded.

Mr. Jones smacked a sticker on Danny's shirt. *Hello, I'm Danny Boy.*

"I'll be by your side the whole way, Danny Boy. That you can trust. We have a deal?"

They shook hands and watched the activity below. It looked like one big summer camp on a tropical island. Danny's parents weren't rich, they couldn't afford something like this. At least he didn't think so. He couldn't remember them at the moment. But he wasn't going to ask questions, even though Mr. Jones said he could.

"Let's go down to the Yard," Mr. Jones said, gesturing to the wide-open field, "and meet your fellow campers."

By the time they reached the elevator and selected the ground floor, Danny had already forgotten about the doctor's office and the dream and the confusion. He stared at the doors inside the elevator; the reflection of a red-headed kid with a slight body and freckles looked back. He looked like a stranger with a name tag stuck on his t-shirt.

"I'm Danny Boy," he whispered.

3

THEY WALKED through the woods for ten minutes. The path was mulched and the trees thick above them with dangling vines and scrubby palms. Mr. Jones was sweating through his shirt and had to stop midway to catch his breath and wipe his face. He was all hunched over. Danny found a stick and Mr. Jones said thank you.

They came out of the trees at the back of the horseshoe-shaped building that had no windows. It was a huge blank wall tinted green with algae and one door right in the middle. They went inside.

Danny's room was smack in the middle of the building. Unlike the back wall, this side of the building faced the Yard with plenty of windows. Danny could see to the other side. It was big enough to hold five or six football fields.

Mr. Jones sat on the bed wiping the sweat from the folds of his neck. He gave Danny a feeble smile and pointed to things. "There's your sink and the bathroom is next to the closet. Your drawers already have clothes folded in them. The hamper chute is down the hall." He took a few wheezy breaths. "You can get new sheets once a week."

Danny opened the closet and thumbed through the shirts and pants that were all brand new and all pressed and ready to wear. All exactly his size. Mr. Jones attempted to stand but the mattress drew him back down. Danny offered a hand but he ignored it, doing sort of a side roll to one buttock before throwing himself onto his feet. He nodded with a pained grin.

"Out there, Danny Boy," he said, sweeping his hand at the window, "that's where most of the boys hang out in their spare time. The Yard is where you'll find them."

The Yard sounds like a prison.

The area near the dorm was crisscrossed with sidewalks forming an X with – from what Danny could tell – a giant sun dial in the middle. Tables were in between the sidewalks but the Yard beyond was grassy.

"But you're not limited to the Yard. You can go wherever you want, I mean it. You're free here, Danny Boy. Go climb a tree, hike the trails, fishing... whatever. Well, you can go anywhere," he lifted a finger, "except where I live. None of the campers are allowed in the Investors' quarters."

"Where's that?"

"We have accommodations back where we came from, only a little further. Besides that, the sky's the limit, my boy."

"Can I go home?"

Chuckle. "Not unless you're a real good swimmer. We're on an island, Danny Boy. It's about five square miles or so, but there's nothing but water as far as the eye can see. Even if you're a good swimmer, I don't recommend it. Sharks and ship-eating coral and the like will tear you up."

He wanted to call them, but there wasn't a phone in the room and Mr. Jones didn't have one on his belt, either. There wasn't even a clock. Besides, Danny was having a hard time remembering what his folks looked like and that disturbed him, so he tried to forget it.

"Where are we?"

"Let's just say we're plenty isolated." Mr. Jones shuffled closer to the window. "Now, this isn't all recess, just so you know. You see over there on the left is the library where you'll be taking classes, but don't get nervous. They're not like high school. You don't get grades, they're just fun classes to keep your brain active and strong. And next to the library is the gym to keep your body active and strong." Mr. Jones flexed his biceps and said with his best Russian accent, "Strong like bull!"

He lifted Danny's arm, smacked his bicep like he was trying to wake it up.

"Listen, Danny Boy. We just want you of sound body and mind when you're ready to graduate. Only the best, only the best, my boy."

The cafeteria, Mr. Jones said, was on the west wing of the dormitory. As long as Danny was here, everything was free. Games, food, classes, all of it paid for. By who, he didn't say. He might have some limitations on food because, Mr. Jones said with a chuckle, "I don't want you getting fat on me."

"They're all boys," Danny Boy said.

"Pardon me?"

Danny pointed at the field. "This is a boys' camp, right?"

"Well, it's easier that way, Danny Boy. Girls can be a distraction and we want all your attention on improving your body and mind. But just between you and me," Mr. Jones winked and nudged him with an elbow, "you'll have plenty of chances to meet girls when you're ready. Nothing wrong with that, if you ask me. Nothing wrong, indeed. By the way, see those boys down there?"

He pointed at a group sitting at one of the many picnic tables.

"That's your group. You ready to go meet some of your fellow campers?"

Danny didn't know what to say. Didn't seem like he had much of a choice. Mr. Jones walked a little easier to the door this time. He stood a little taller and started to open the door.

"What's that building over there?"

Mr. Jones answered without looking. "We'll talk about that later."

It was past the far end of the field buried in the trees. Its dome-shaped roof was just above the forest canopy. Sunlight reflected off the circular skylights.

"Come along, Danny Boy. There's nothing to worry about."

Danny followed him, reluctantly. He was thirteen years old. When an adult says there's nothing to worry about, there's usually plenty.

4

EVERYONE STARED.

Mr. Jones walked damn near zero miles an hour. Danny kept his eyes straight ahead. They cut across the grass. Everyone seemed pretty tan, but the sun bit into Danny's fair skin. They were aimed at the group at a picnic table near the sun dial. Four of them were playing cards. The fifth was watching. When they got close, the game stopped and they watched the painfully slow approach of Mr. Jones and his sidekick.

"Well, lookie there," one of them mumbled. "We got ourselves a new poke."

Mr. Jones leaned one hand on the table.

"Boys." He took a long breath. "This is your new camper. I'd like you to meet Danny Boy."

"Hey, *Danny Boy*," one of them said.

Most gave a head nod. Danny sort of smiled, waiting for Mr. Jones to either leave or die.

"This is your group, or camp," Mr. Jones finally said. "You'll be going through your work with them for the next couple months, so you'll get to know them pretty well."

"We love pokes," someone said.

"Now be nice, boys. You remember what it was like when you first got here, extend some courtesy to this young man. I don't want to hear about any funny business. You remember that, now. I've got my eye on you. Anything happens to my Danny Boy I'll come down here and tan your hides, you understand?"

My Danny Boy?

The card dealer with a shag of black hair waggled his bushy eyebrows and those around the table smirked.

"I'm not kidding, boys. You try me and see how fast I can reach into my pocket."

Danny wondered what was in the pocket. A notepad or a laser beam?

A golf cart silently pulled up while Mr. Jones eyeballed each of them. The driver was older than Mr. Jones. His gray hair looked wet and parted on the right. The white line of his scalp showed through the part as straight as a razor. He set the brake and made an attempt to get out but his belly was rubbing against the steering wheel. He got it on the second try.

"Mr. Miller," Mr. Jones said.

Mr. Miller acknowledged Mr. Jones with a nod but ignored the rest of them. He walked to the other side of the table to speak with a gangly kid with an Adam's apple the size of a walnut. His cheeks were pasty and he stared vacantly at the table while Mr. Miller spoke quietly into his ear, occasionally nodding. The walnut bobbed up and down. Mr. Miller patted him on the back and waddled back to the cart without making eye contact with anyone, again.

"Remember, I'm watching, boys." Mr. Jones pointed two fingers at his eyes, then at the rest of them. Danny needed him to leave for a whole lot of reasons. If the rest of the Investors were as decrepit as Mr. Jones, they would be as much help as a box of kittens.

And when he thought it couldn't get any worse.

Mr. Jones waved him over to the cart. He stopped a couple steps away. Mr. Jones pulled him closer and put his hand − soft with lotion − on Danny's cheek, lovingly. "You call if you need me. All right, my boy?"

He did not.

Do.

That.

Danny jumped back and shook like a wet dog. Mr. Jones looked a little hurt, but then nodded like maybe he realized and understood that you just don't do that TO A THIRTEEN YEAR OLD BOY!

Unless you wanted him to die of embarrassment, of shame and humiliation.

The entire world would have to be on fire before he called Mr. Jones for help.

The card game was more important than Danny. That was a good thing.

He walked away to get some space. If he was going to hang out with them, he needed to make a new first impression. He shoved his hands in his pockets and turned his back, looked around the Yard. There were maybe a couple dozen boys out there, but they were a mix of race and nationality. He heard someone speaking French. Regardless, they were all boys. Every last one of them.

But you'll get your chance.

There was only one loner. He had his shirt over his shoulder. His long hair was dark. He walked slowly, one foot in front of the other, like he was just soaking in the sun with nowhere to go. Even from where Danny was standing – about fifty feet away – he bet he could count the kid's ribs.

"Hey, I'm Zin." A kid about Danny's height stepped next to him. He was plump, brown skinned with a shaved head and a mean looking zit in the middle of his forehead. "You're Danny Boy, huh right."

"Oh. Yeah." Danny peeled off the nametag.

"Ain't much of a welcome wagon, but that's the way it goes around here. You'll figure it out soon enough."

"How soon is that?"

"It'll feel like home in a day. Two, tops."

Danny had transferred to a new school when he was ten (or was it five?). His dad was a teacher (or was he an engineer?) and got transferred to the mountains (or was it the beach?). Danny got in a fight the first day (or did he run away?). The biggest of the bunch got up right in the middle of class and slapped him while the teacher had her back turned. They duked it out after school.

(Or was it lunch?)

"How long you been here?" Danny asked.

"Long enough. I can tell you one thing, I didn't get a welcome half as warm as you got. As soon as the Investors left they threw me in a trash can."

Yep, there it is. This was prison because he was standing in the Yard and there were no girls, just boys. No need for barbed wire when you were surrounded by "sharks and ship eating coral and the like".

He remembered a time he got in trouble, something about a computer. Danny knew that if he was right – that this really was some sort of prison enclosed by water – then there had to be rape. He'd watched enough *Locked Up* episodes to know the weak got it good and these guys were going to bust into his room for a little midnight snack and who was going to stop them? Mr. Jones and his team of geriatric superheroes?

"Listen, it's a little intimidating the first day," Zin said, picking up on Danny's expression or the pale color of his cheeks, "but you get used to it in no time. And these guys aren't going to do anything to you, so don't worry. We all look out for each other."

"How'd you end up here?"

"Same way as everyone else." He shrugged. "Woke up with my Investor staring at me and couldn't remember a damn thing. I take that back, I remembered too many things and nothing made sense. You?"

Danny wanted to just forget about the dream and the weird feeling in his head and Mr. Jones touching his cheek.

"That's what I thought. Listen, don't sweat it." Zin lightly punched his shoulder. "This place has its ups and downs, but it ain't so bad... look, that's the library over there... and the game room is behind the gym..."

Another orientation, but this one felt better coming from Zin without the creepy grin Mr. Jones was wearing when he did it. The buildings were all dome-shaped besides the horseshoe-shaped dormitory. Zin pointed everything out and then named everyone in their camp.

"And if you want to know what time it is, there you go." He pointed at the sun dial. "It's never wrong."

"What's that?" Danny pointed at the round building across the Yard, the same one he'd seen from his room.

"That's the Haystack. You'll find out about that in a few weeks when we start a new round. I don't want to spoil the surprise."

"That much fun?"

Zin thought about it. "Yes and no."

"He looks like he had a blast." Danny nodded to Mr. Miller's kid, still staring. Saliva glistened on his lip.

The kid with a mop of black hair dealing the cards had been listening. "Yeah, old Parker here is about to get smoked, ya'll." He smacked zombie-Parker on the back and rattled his head. Parker didn't seem to notice so much. Or care.

"Sid means that Parker's about to graduate," Zin said. "We all graduate at some point."

"From what?"

"From the island. You're here because you got problems, Danny Boy. You'll learn that problems start with your mind, that we assign concepts and requirements to life that create friction and chaos. If we want to heal, we start with the mind. Or at least, that's what the Investors tell us. Who the hell knows."

Zin's smile was infectious.

"You believe that?" Danny asked.

"Sure, why not? Don't you see, Danny Boy, the universe is perfectly imperfect." Zin wiggled his hands in mysterious-fashion. "There are no problems, you just think there are. And you believe what you think, and that's why you're here. We're going to fix you."

Zin jabbed at Danny's forehead.

"And once you're fixed, you get smoked. And once you're smoke, you're out of here."

Zin pointed at the cylindrical building rising up from behind the dorms. Bands of glass windows alternated with bands of metal. Five floors. One of those glass floors was where Danny woke up and walked down the hall. The top floor was black glass. At the very top was a long chimney.

"That's right," Zin added. "Once you go to the Chimney, you leave the island. It's graduation time, kind of like how they pick a new pope, when someone graduates the Chimney puffs and then it's sayonara, baby."

"Where do we go?"

"Home, I guess. Where else?"

The thought of going home wasn't as comforting as it should've been, mainly because Danny couldn't quite remember it.

"Come on." Sid slung his arm around Parker's shoulders. "Let's have some fun before they smoke you, pal. What'd you say, huh? Old times?"

Parker was glassy-eyed.

"That's the spirit. Let's go, ya'll." They chucked the cards on the table and left the mess behind. "Zinski, bring the new poke. We'll need him to take Parker's spot on the team so let's get him to the game room. We got a match in an hour."

Zin pulled Danny along. Sid walked with his arm around Parker. It didn't look like he was going to make it unless someone kept him propped up. A cold feeling crept into Danny's stomach. He had a feeling what happened to him.

"What's a poke?"

"That means you're a rookie, a virgin that just got popped." Zin pointed at the round band-aid on Danny's head. "You got poked, Danny Boy."

Danny touched the bandage. He felt a little guilty after Mr. Jones told him not to, then he noticed the zit on Zin's forehead. When he first saw it, it looked like a deep blackhead. It was a little red and puffy around the edges, like maybe he was squeezing it. *Is that a hole?*

A cold feeling trickled into his legs.

Danny noticed the loner kid with the shirt over his shoulder. He was hardly a kid, looked like he was nineteen or twenty. Easily the oldest one around. An old man (there seemed to be an endless supply of them) limped toward him. There were a few words exchanged.

"Yo, Danny Boy!" Zin was calling. "Don't get lost on day one, hurry up!"

Danny watched the long-haired kid follow the limping old man. Maybe he was going to get smoked.

5

MR. SMITH DIDN'T TALK MUCH. Reed expected that.

The old man limped along with a small grunt whenever he heaved his bum leg forward.

The elevator was in the center of the first floor. The inside was curved like a big tin can. There were only buttons for four floors. Nothing for the fifth. The doors remained opened while Mr. Smith looked at the numbers and the small camera staring back. A few seconds later, they closed and the elevator made the gut-dropping rise to the top of the Chimney.

Mr. Smith put his hand on Reed's chest. "Wait here."

The elevator opened. There were no walls on the top floor. Just one big room. One section had bedroom furniture, another office furniture; there was a bar with liquor bottles. But nothing in-between.

On the far side, by the dim windows, a large man wearing a flowery shirt was looking through an oversized telescope. Mr. Smith limped over. His words murmured across the room. The Director never looked up from the eyepiece but occasionally muttered back.

There had been other boys that failed in the Haystack for whatever reason and they just disappeared. No graduation or farewell just *poof* –

they were gone. Didn't matter if they went mental or the needle lobotomized them, it was game over.

Move on to the next contestant.

But they had been patient with Reed. He was nineteen. He'd be twenty in a couple months. And twenty – for whatever reason – was a magic number. *Poof.*

Mr. Smith didn't look happy.

He was trying to hold his voice in check and kept stealing glances at Reed when he got too loud. The Director never bothered to pull off his telescope while Mr. Smith waved his arms and smacked his fist. And then he was dismissed. Mr. Smith came back like a peg-legged pirate that dipped his hair in a bucket of ink.

His cheeks were flush.

"The Director would like a word."

"Reed, my boy, come here." The Director was still hunched over the telescope when Reed approached. "You don't want to miss this, take a look."

Reed hesitated. The Director stood up and stretched his back. "Well, do I need to mail you an invitation? Come on, you must see this," he said, happily. "Nature is happening, son."

The Director was a large man with a scraggly beard and squinty, smiling eyes. He was wearing baggy shorts and flip-flops. Reed stopped short of the telescope, peering out the window at the back side of the island – a view rarely seen by any of the teenage campers. Rarely was one of them brought up to the Director's office. The Investors' living quarters hundred yards away, right on the edge of the island – the Mansion with stately palms. Beyond that was endless water.

"Reed, unless you can stretch your eyeball out of your head, you're going to have to bend over to see what I'm talking about." The Director smiled. "Take a look."

Reed did so. Slowly. He adjusted his eye around the lens. It was focused far out into the ocean. Everything shimmered blue.

"You see it?" the Director asked. "Don't touch the scope, just look with your eye. Just stay open and you'll see it."

There was nothing. Suddenly, there was a spray of water. A hump-back whale broke the surface, its slick body rolled over and the white speckled tail slapped the water. He wanted to see it again.

"Magnificent, right?" The Director slapped him on the back. "Nature."

Reed stayed perched over the telescope. Moments later, another one came up for a breath and disappeared beneath the waves, free to go as deep and as far away as it wished.

"How many rounds have you been through, Reed?"

Reed stood.

The Director was at the bar near a section of plush furniture. Ice rattled in a couple of tumblers and the Director poured drinks. One with Coke, the other whiskey. He brought the Coke to Reed, handed it to him with a stiff smile, the eyes still crinkled.

"I've lost count," the Director said. "Twenty-five, would you say?"

"Sounds a little high."

"Math wasn't my strong suit, but twenty-five times you've been through the Haystack, Reed." The Director took a drink and grimaced. "You like punishment?"

"I've discovered my inner masochist."

"Well, then, how about I punch you in the face and we'll have a ball." He smiled wide and laughed loud. Reed joined him. They were both in on the joke for several moments, although the Director laughed a little hard.

The Director leisurely strolled away. He swirled the glass. He stopped at a large cage behind the expansive mahogany desk. It reached up to the ceiling, inside were a pair of large white parrots. He looked up at them, said, "Why won't you take the lucid gear, Reed?"

"I'm not crazy about getting punched in the head with a needle."

"It's not a needle, Reed. It's lucid gear, and it doesn't hurt, you know that. The other boys have told you so. Hell, I'm telling you." He pointed at the neat little hole in his forehead.

"Forgive me," Reed said. "The *needle-like* lucid gear goes through the skull. It can't feel good."

The ice rattled. The Director sipped, nodding. He looked over, head cocked. A grim smile. He jerked his head, signaling Reed to come over. The glass of Coke was still full, soaking in his hand. *Sweat or condensation?*

Together, they watched the birds.

"This is my island, Reed. It's my program, my vision that happens here. These..." He waved his drink toward the Mansion. "These Investors fund it, but it's my vision to use cutting edge technology – revolutionary ideas – to help people like you, Reed."

"I didn't ask for help."

"Yes, you did. You just don't know it."

"I don't know much of anything, thanks to you."

The Director ignored the insult. "You're a kid, Reed. You don't know anything about life and your place in it. And it's a damn shame to see a kid like you with so much potential just waste away to nothing. I can't accept a world that turns its back on people that need help, Reed. I can't. I won't."

Reed realized the floor was slowly rotating. His view of the Mansion was slightly askew from when he arrived. Eventually, they'd be turning back towards the dormitory and the Yard.

"Why do you think I brought you here, Reed?"

"You know I don't know that."

The Director was nodding. He knew that Reed couldn't make sense of the multitude of memories that crowded his mind; memories they both knew were implanted in Reed's head to keep him confused, to keep him from remembering his past.

The Director put his drink on a small table and opened the doors beneath it. He pulled out a small cage squirming with oversized cockroaches. The parrots flapped madly, squawking. Feathers floated out of the cage.

"You think I brought you here to torture, mmm?"

"It's crossed my mind."

"You think I get my jollies by filling an island with young boys to torture?" He popped the lid and reached inside. The cockroaches hissed. "You think that's me?"

"I don't know who you are, Director. Like you said, I don't even know who I am."

A wingless cockroach clung to the Director's finger, blowing air from the spiracles on its abdomen to hiss loudly. He held it close to his face. The cockroach hunched over and went quiet.

"I like you, Reed. You remind me of myself, all full of piss and vinegar. For all I know, you're refusing the lucid gear just to spite me, to spite Mr. Smith. And I can respect that. I mean, Jesus lord, you've withstood some discomfort, son. I don't think I could've done it when I was your age and I was one tough son of a bitch. You believe that?"

There was a long pause. The Director turned his hand over; the cockroach clung to it upside-down.

Reed answered, "Believe what?"

"That I was a tough S-O-B?"

"Again, I don't know you, sir."

"Yes, you do, Reed." The Director glared, intensely. "You know me."

Reed turned away. He didn't know the Director, but that look told him everything he needed to. *You know what I do.*

The Director plucked the cockroach off his hand. It threw a fit, hissing and scratching for a grip. He pinched it by the abdomen. The birds jumped to the branch nearest the cage, their beaks jawing open and close, open and close. The Director dangled the cockroach just out of their reach. Feathers flew.

The cockroach hissed and hissed, and then it ended with its exoskeleton crunching loudly in the curved beak of the larger bird. The Director took a sip of his drink, watching the bird pull half the insect's body, legs flailing, out of its mouth with its claw, chewing on it like popcorn.

"What makes you so tough, Reed?"

"I don't know, sir. Maybe my father was a Navy SEAL."

The Director stepped directly in front of Reed. They were eye to eye, only inches apart. Scotch was on his breath. "Every single boy that's been to the island has taken the lucid gear the very first time they go to the Haystack. Not one has resisted, and you've done it... how many times, Reed?"

Shrug.

"Twenty-five," the Director said. "You get it wrong again, I'll slap you."

He stayed uncomfortably closer, staring. The bird grinding the insect into bite-sized pieces.

Reed knew how he resisted, but how did he tell the man responsible for all the misery around him that it was a dream that told him not to take the needle? *Sounds crazy, but what doesn't?*

It happened when he woke up in the lab with Mr. Smith staring at him. He clung to a memory as he opened his eyes. It was a girl with long red hair. She told him – as if she was talking to him – to resist. She told him that if he did, they would be together again, one day. It wouldn't be easy, but he had to resist. If anyone could do it, he could.

He didn't know what resisting meant until he entered the Haystack.

And when his resolve faded, when he considered reaching for the needle because he just couldn't take it anymore, when he just wanted it to end, he would have another dream.

Resist.

The Director, looking as far into Reed's eyes as he could and seeing nothing, stepped away. He sipped, thinking. Reed noticed the lump on the back of his neck when he bent over for another cockroach, the tracker imbedded between the C4 and C5 vertebrae. No one went unchecked on the island, not even the man at the top.

"I can't accept watching you piss away an opportunity, Reed. Do you know what's right in front of you? The effort Mr. Smith and I made to bring you here, to offer you freedom from your problems, to give you a nobler life. Do you know what it costs every day we keep you here and watch you deny the healing we offer?"

He squeezed the cockroach in his palm, crunching inside his closed fist.

"Do you know how hard we work TO GIVE YOU A BETTER LIFE?"

The birds jumped. So did Reed.

"We're pioneers, Reed," he said, softly. "We're forging into new ground of healing the world. You're a pioneer, do you understand that?"

Reed nodded, slowly.

The Director held his gaze, then offered his hand to the unfed bird. It pushed its beak between the bars and snatched the cockroach out of his palm. The Director flicked the slimy remains on the bottom of the cage and walked away wiping his hands with a paper towel.

The Director went to another telescope at the perimeter of the room, this one aimed over the Mansion. The floor had rotated. Reed was looking at the dorm and the Yard beyond.

"You have a shot at a second life, but I can't make you take it. All I can do is offer you healing. No one can make you go lucid, you have to want it. Don't you see, that's why we make you uncomfortable before it's offered? Your mind detaches from the body when it's in pain, yet you continue to stay. You won't take what I offer, Reed. And I can't understand that."

The Director spent a few minutes focusing on a new target. He stood up, hands on his hips. Staring out, pensive. Struggling with a thought. A decision. "Five more rounds, Reed." The Director looked at Reed over the couches and tables and space in between. "I'm giving you an opportunity to help me help you. This is your last chance to take my outstretched hand. I can't help the unwilling, son. You understand?"

The Director smiled, eyes squinting.

"If you don't, then I've failed you, son. And I'm sorry for that."

The Director went back to the telescope. The birds licked their beaks. Reed looked at the Yard below, wiping his slick forehead where the needle hole had long since healed.

6

DANNY REMEMBERED GOING to summer camp... or something like that. The more he thought about it, maybe it was just camping. They went fishing. It seemed like a really fun time in his life.

The island was even better.

No one assaulted him in his sleep. No one dumped him in a trash can or even so much as gave him a wedgie. It was ten days of non-stop fun.

It started in the game room which turned out to be a game *building*. Flat screen monitors were positioned around the perimeter showing on-going games or flashing team standings of various competitions. Most of them were small capsules where campers could experience three-dimensional action while some were simple screen games for one or two people.

On the first day, Sid led them through the crowd. There were about twenty-five people – all boys, no old men – watching or playing. They made their way to center stage: a twenty-foot wide circular platform enclosed by a clear dome. Inside was a small scale layout of a war-torn city with smoldered buildings and overturned cars. Digital troops strategically stalked the cityscape and miniature helicopters rained bullets and missiles into clouds of smoke and fire.

There was a group on each side that controlled the tiny figures and with each explosion and each death, numbers changed on the four-side scoreboard hanging from the ceiling. Names repositioned in the standings. An hour later, one team stood victorious.

Zin smacked Danny in the chest. "We're up."

The taunting started when they stepped onto the small stage vacated by the losers, a group of Middle Eastern boys in their early teens. Danny saw the other team on the opposite side of the dome – they were Russian, maybe – pulling on black gloves. Sid was trading insults with the crowd, pointing at the scoreboard and thumping his chest. Zin gave Danny a pair of gloves and knee pads.

"No time for instruction. You'll figure it out."

The gloves slid on like silk embedded with fine wire mesh. The knee pads strapped on without anything special. Sid passed out yellow-tinted goggles with embedded earbuds and miniature microphones. Danny was still playing with the goggles when he was assigned to a tower and told to keep his head down.

"Watch and learn." That was the only time Sid addressed Danny. "And try not to get killed, poke."

The game started.

Instead of watching the action like the spectators, Danny saw it inside the goggles. The view was first person, like he was inside the dome, shrunk down to size. The goggles absorbed his vision. When he turned his head, the view changed.

He was in a tower with a two-ton bell. For the first twenty minutes, he did what he was told, experimenting with the controls and not getting killed. He learned his movements were controlled by bending his knees. The gloves controlled his hands and weapons. After that, he watched half of his crew get slaughtered on one of Sid's stupid ambushes.

When there was nothing to lose, he went to the ground.

He felt the rubble under his feet, the heat of burning automobiles. He ran from building to building and by the time he neared the action, Zin was the only one left. He was hiding inside a bunker that was about to be flamed.

When Danny was later asked how he slaughtered the opposing

team, he didn't have a good answer. He just said that it made sense, that he didn't realize he was intuiting the enemy's moves and shot them with effortless accuracy and moved with the grace of a veteran assassin. He just did it.

He sniped the last enemy from three hundreds. After that, everyone in the game room knew his name.

There were classes, too.

Although, like Mr. Jones said, it wasn't really class. They talked about economics and geology and philosophy, but it was just talk. There was no homework, no tests. The instructors were the old men, of course, that insisted they exercise their whole brains when they thought about various topics, so they kept the discussion lively. The boys debated loudly, acted out their passion and shook hands when it was all over. It wasn't bad, Danny had to admit. Without the busy-work of homework, he was interested in class.

Sort of. Kind of.

Strange thing, though. There was no Internet, no email, text messages or phones. There weren't even computers. There was plenty of time for worldly things, the Investors said. Just not now.

Occasionally, Danny would hear a bell ring three times like a gong. Then he'd see boys heading for the Haystack and sometimes leaving it. Once, someone was carted away from it. An Investor was driving a utility vehicle and another old man was on the flatbed with the boy lying down. No one said much and the Investors stared straight ahead as they drove around the dormitory toward the Chimney.

In the first couple weeks, Danny saw the Chimney smoke three times.

Danny sat with his camp at lunch. He didn't know anyone else.

He half-listened to Sid layout their next game strategy and watched people move through the line. Another group returned from the Haystack, this one Hispanic. They hardly spoke.

One of them was a new poke. *The band-aid.*

Mr. Jones took Danny's band-aid off within the first week. He was a little more chill after the hand on the cheek incident. Danny decided if it happened again, he was swimming for it, screw the sharks. But Mr. Jones was cool. He just wanted to make sure Danny was getting everything he needed and followed his schedule. He had a knack of always finding Danny, but then he remembered the tracker in his neck. Mr. Jones could probably count the number of turds Danny dropped in the morning.

Danny peeled the band-aid off. Beneath it was a neat little hole. It wasn't red, wasn't sore. Just a hole. Mr. Jones wiped it with some alcohol, said the stent was healing just fine. He sensed Danny had a question – as anyone who woke up with a hole in the head would have – and said the hole was for healing. And not to worry.

Don't worry, my boy. He said that a lot.

"You listening?" Sid snapped his fingers in Danny's face. "Come on, man, you need to pay attention. This next battle is our last before we go to the Haystack. That's when it gets real, son. You're good with the gloves but things change when you get inside."

"Danny Boy isn't going to be any good the first round," Zin said, swallowing the last of his milk. "He shouldn't even be on the squad until he gets a few rounds inside the Haystack, you know that. You forget, he's a new poke."

"Yeah, just in case, Zinski."

"That's what we do in the Haystack?" Danny asked. "More games?"

Long silence.

Silence, every time the topic of the Haystack came up – and what the needle was. Danny knew what was likely to happen, it didn't take a genius. There was a needle and there was a hole in his head. It didn't take an engineer. Still, it was hard to imagine a needle going through his skull, so there had to be other explanations. He didn't want to think about that.

When everyone was on another topic, Zin leaned over. "We're going inside the Haystack in two days. Everyone gets a little edgy, but don't let them worry you. It's all cool."

"So what happens, exactly?"

"It's a good time. You won't remember much, though."

"What are you going to be doing?"

"Uhhhh..." Zin looked around then smiled, mischievously. "Well, I don't know about the rest of these war mongers, but I'll be hooking up with my lady. If there's time, I might join them for some shoot 'em up, but that ain't my priority. I promise you."

"Girls?"

"Oh, yeah." Zin looked around again but no one was paying attention. He mouthed the word with a smile.

GIRLS.

They were going to see girls? There had never been one on the island – coming or going from the Haystack – unless they were dropped off on the back side of the island and snuck into the back of the building. Danny thought of the possibilities. Boys were in the Haystack alone for half a day or longer. If there were girls in there, too, then all kinds of things could be happening. So far, the island was a summer camp, but the way Zin was smiling made him wonder if it had some real-life sex education.

Just keeps getting better.

The last people in line were grabbing their trays off the dessert table. The last one was all alone, something Danny rarely saw. Everyone travelled in packs. There were no loners on the island, except for the guy at the end of the line – the long-haired kid Danny saw his first day. He moved slowly, carefully. Occasionally, he turned his head listening to something, looking around the cafeteria. Then he slid his tray along the service line.

"We're going to be down three men," Sid was saying. "Parker's going in with us but he ain't going to last long. He'll be smoked, after this. Am I right, Parker?"

Parker breathed through his mouth, holding an empty spoon over his tray. His food was untouched. He shrugged his shoulders when Sid snapped his fingers.

"Easy money," Sid said. "Anyway, Zin's right about Danny Boy clumping up like a vegetable, so we'll be short-handed. We'll have to play some defense."

"Who's the third person?" Zin asked.

"Oh." Sid twitched his chin at the loner in line. "Forgot to tell you, we got the freak."

There was a collective moan and some pissing to go along with it.

"Who is he?" Danny asked.

"That's Reed," Zin said. "Guy's been through, like, 100 rounds or something like that without taking the needle." Zin shook his head. "One tough dude, man. Someone said his head got all scrambled when he first got here. Ask me, I think he's just some badass that wants to piss in the Director's cereal."

"Where's he been?"

"He goes to the beach on the north end, stands there looking at the water all by himself. No one goes out to the beach, man. The bugs and the wind and no one's going swimming. There are a thousand better things to do, trust me."

"That makes him crazy?"

"You wait and see, no sane person would do what he's done. He just doesn't have any friends and no one wants to get near him, afraid his crazy will rub off. Can't say I disagree."

Reed stopped at the dessert table and held still like someone hit pause on him.

"See what I mean?" Zin said. "He's an odd dude named Reed, the kid that bends but don't break."

"What's that mean?"

"You'll see."

Reed nodded. He was either agreeing with himself or with the voices Zin said he was hearing. Reed left his tray on the dessert table and grabbed an apple. He left the cafeteria.

"I rest my case," Zin said. "Whack-a-do."

Reed didn't walk like he was crazy. Danny didn't exactly know what a crazy man would walk like, but it didn't seem like it would be confident, slow and steady. Just because someone doesn't fly with all the birds doesn't mean he's nuts.

The flock could be going in the wrong direction.

7

DANNY WOKE up two hours before the sun rose. His eyes opened and refused to shut. He stared at the ceiling. The unknown was terrifying. Everyone else seemed excited. Danny rubbed his forehead, making a tiny circle around the hole. *No way they stick a needle in there.*

There was a soft knock.

Danny pulled the sheet up to his chin. Mr. Jones opened the door. Danny realized he looked pathetic, but he couldn't will himself to get up anymore than he could make himself sleep. Besides, he was in his underwear and even though Mr. Jones wasn't so creepy, there was no need to roll the dice.

"Good morning," Mr. Jones said.

Danny didn't answer.

Mr. Jones, usually cheery that time of the day – usually throwing open the curtains and welcoming the morning and telling Danny it was a great day to be alive – this time he went directly to the chest of drawers and began to fold Danny's clothes. When his shirts were orga-nized, Mr. Jones put his hand on the desk. His cheeks moved like he was chewing on his tongue.

He sat on the bed, sinking into the mattress and rolling Danny closer. Thankfully, he placed his hands on his own lap.

"Danny Boy," he started and let out a sigh. "Today is a big day. It's a big day, my boy. You can't imagine what it means to me. The journey you're about to take will be revolutionary. You should know that, so that in your darkest hour you have something to hold onto. The Haystack is critical to what we do here on the island, you understand? We wouldn't do anything to hurt you, but sometimes you have to go to the dentist to stay well, am I right?"

Danny pulled the sheet just under his eyes. He wanted to pull it over his head but that wouldn't make the bogeyman go away.

"Here." Mr. Jones held a pill between his finger and thumb. "Put this under your tongue, it'll boost your immunity. I don't want you catching cold while you're in there, it just makes things harder."

Danny didn't move.

Mr. Jones had to pull the sheet down and put it on his lips. His fingers smelled like old leather. Danny let the pill fall into his mouth just so he'd get his hand away. It dissolved like candy.

Mr. Jones sighed again, looked at the ceiling. His eyes looked a little wet. It was times like this Danny thought he might be regretting something. He squeezed Danny's knee. "You're a hero, son. A real hero."

And then he got up, after two attempts, and went to the door looking more hunched over than usual. He put his hand on the knob and, without turning, said, "You go on and get dressed now, you hear? I'll be back up in an hour to escort you over to the building. No one goes into the Haystack alone, my boy."

The door clicked behind him. Danny stayed in bed with the sheet pulled up. He remained there for a while and only got dressed because he didn't want Mr. Jones in the room when he did.

All modesty was about to disappear from Danny's life.

Danny walked the Yard with Mr. Jones. This time he had no problem with his slow and steady gait. The others were walking with their Investors, too. They were all spread out, heading in the same direction:

the multi-eyed round roof peeking above the distant trees. Their paths converged the closer they got.

They got in line as they entered a narrow path. There was little talking. But the silence was more than that; it was the sort of intense concentration that spontaneously happened before a big game, before surgery or some other life-altering event. Even Sid, walking a few bodies ahead of Danny, was quiet.

Suddenly, the path ended in an opening. The Haystack was at the far side. Its concrete wall was painted dark brown, stained with algae and sucker-cups that remained from vines stripped away. A man stood at the entrance with a clipboard in his folded arms. He was old, but kind of young among the old men. He had gentle gray eyes inside folds of skin. He began checking off items on his clipboard as they entered.

A bell rang three times.

Danny didn't look around but once. Zin was to his left. He lifted his eyebrows in mild celebration. Just past Zin was Parker as glassy-eyed and slack as ever. He wasn't looking around. He didn't even look like he knew anyone else was there.

"Welcome, young men," the man at the door suddenly said. "My name is Mr. Clark. I'll be supervising this round. Most of you know the drill. I know some of you are nervous, as would be expected, but I assure you that your experience will be just as exciting as the previous ones have been. For the newcomers, you will follow your Investor inside and he will orient you on what to do. But there's nothing to worry about, things are very simple inside."

Mr. Clark looked at his clipboard.

"Before we enter, are there any questions?" He looked around with the same welcoming smile. "Very well, then. Let's begin, shall we?"

He pushed the door open and stood to the side. Mr. Jones's hand fell on Danny's shoulder and squeezed reassuringly. Danny immediately tensed, but noticed every Investor was doing the same move with the hand on the shoulder, guiding their kid into the Haystack in some sort of ritual. Danny got in line. When they stepped inside, it was cold and dim.

It was the last time he would see the sun for quite some time.

Danny clenched up, a full-body seizure.

His knees locked and he pushed his weight against Mr. Jones's hand. It wasn't the dim light coming through the skylights or the giant steel fan that waited to chop them up or the smell of urine or the dank dungeon cells that lined both sides of the aisle that made Danny step back. It was a sense of panic, of fear, that saturated the atmosphere like an electrical current, tingling in his bowels. The boys ahead of him didn't seize up, but they stutter-stepped. Like the end of a ship's plank was dead ahead.

Danny felt this type of fear spreading through his groin like cold fingers once before. A memory emerged in the soupy sea of memories inside his head. He remembered getting pulled out of the back seat of a car with his hands cuffed behind his back by someone. But then like everything he tried to remember, there were gaps.

There were FBI shirts, and big doors—

"It's all right, Danny Boy." Mr. Jones gently urged him forward.

Danny's knees refused to unbuckle. The cages were open and waiting. The boys ahead of him each walked inside one without resistance and their Investor closed the door.

"Come on!" someone shouted from outside. "We're waiting, Danny Boy!"

"Come along, my boy." Mr. Jones pressed forward, pushing Danny ahead. "It's all right. It's all right."

Danny walked with his weight leaning into Mr. Jones's hand. The old man showed surprising strength. His hand was like a talon. It guided him past the open cells. No cot or toilet or window on the walls. The boys were stripping off their shirts. That's when Danny realized the cold wasn't just fear eating away his innards but the humid cold air dimpling his skin.

They stopped about halfway down the aisle. Mr. Jones turned Danny to the left. He tried to squirm away but the old man's claw shoved him inside the open cell. The door latched closed before he could turn around.

Mr. Jones grabbed the bars.

"Why are you doing this?" Danny suddenly wanted to be back in his bed. He didn't mind if Mr. Jones sat on the bed and patted his knee. He would let him touch his face, if that's what he wanted.

"Danny Boy, trust me. Everything will be all right. It'll be better than okay, you just trust me now, son. These boys have been through this already and they're doing better, I promise."

No one else needed to be pushed inside a cell. They knew the deal and didn't seem to mind. They didn't look happy, but they weren't freaking out.

"We're about healing the world," Mr. Jones said, quietly. "This is the work that we ask you to do. As with any work, it is not always easy. But it will be rewarding, my boy. Richly."

The Haystack was silent except for the somber mutterings of a few Investors. The rest of the boys were taking off their clothes. First their shirts. Then shoes, socks and pants. And finally underwear.

Completely naked!

Mr. Jones held out his hands. "You need to hand me your clothes, Danny Boy. We enter the work like we enter life, completely exposed to the world. We are reborn into our flesh, revealing our humility for everyone to witness."

Danny backed up. The others were folding their clothes and passing them between the bars, neatly stacked. They stood unabashed with various amounts of pubic hair. The cold had shriveled most of them to embarrassing sizes, but no one seemed to care all that much. None of them were looking around like Danny.

"No one can touch you, Danny Boy."

Mr. Jones was right. There was a gap between the cells on each side. Even if he reached all the way through, he wouldn't be able to touch the person imprisoned next to him. He noticed the walls were set inside slots that could slide but it only looked like the cell could get smaller.

"You're safe inside the cell. No one will bother you."

"But... but why? Why do we have to do this?" Danny's voice cracked with an embarrassing whine.

"You'll understand. You'll just have to trust me."

Danny hugged himself. "I just don't want to. You can't just expect me to... I'm not just going to get naked because everyone else is. I'm not doing it."

"Stop pissing around, Danny Boy!" Sid shouted from across the aisle. His penis had shrunk into the bush of pubic hair that crawled up and around his belly button. "The longer you go on like that, the longer it takes... NOW GET NAKED, BOY!"

Investors were already leaving. Mr. Jones stood with his hands around the bars. His expression was silent and sympathetic. Sid was growling and pacing inside his cell. But Danny couldn't break the grip the cold hand of fear had on him. He just wasn't going to do it. He just wanted to close his eyes and disappear. He wished this would all go away, that he could somehow escape his body and go somewhere nice and warm and safe.

"Hey." Zin was pulling his shirt over his head in the cell next to him. "Listen, you got to do this. I know it's all weird, but it's no big deal. It's like showering in the gym. I can tell you, nothing happens."

"Then why do we have to do it?"

Zin shrugged while he stepped out of his shorts. "To make the first part more uncomfortable, I guess. To humiliate us, to make us want the needle. I don't give two craps either way. All I know is that we got to get this thing going or it's going to suck being here even longer."

Zin folded his shorts and shirt into a stack and placed his flip-flops on top. His Investor gave him a nod and left.

"Danny Boy," Mr. Jones said. "You should understand that in life, there is joy and there is suffering. Your work includes everything. The Haystack is designed to allow you to experience suffering safely, to learn to let go of your physical body so that you may experience another level of your existence. But I can't make you, Danny Boy. I can't make you do it. You'll have to do it on your own." Mr. Jones held out his hands. "You'll have to walk naked alone."

Others had joined Sid in the taunting. Danny could see there was no way to escape. And the others had been through it and they didn't seem to mind. Zin, too.

Danny's shirt came off, first. The cold air pulled his skin tight and his nipples were like BBs. He was shaking when he took off his shorts.

Despite Sid screaming to go faster, he took his time getting his shoes off.

His underwear was last.

He took a long shaky breath before pulling them down. Unlike Sid and Zin, he didn't have much hair downstairs. What little he did have was bright red and barely covered his boyhood that looked more like a mushroom cap.

He threw the clothes at Mr. Jones' feet and cupped his hands over his genitalia.

"I'll need you to fold the clothes, Danny Boy." Mr. Jones didn't stoop to pick them up. "It's our attention to every moment of our life that matters. To make room for this very moment, to allow it to unfold. To care for life. Now, please, hand me your clothes properly."

Danny squatted down and did his best to put his clothes in order like Zin had done. Mr. Jones didn't seem completely pleased with the quality of his stack, but he nodded and stepped back. He nodded again and without another word, exited the Haystack.

The wrath of the others didn't stop. Danny backed up until he pressed against the bars, wishing it was dark enough to hide him. He kept his hands over his privates. The room had become loud with anger, vibrating inside Danny's head. Even Zin had his hands on the bars, shouting obscenities until finally one Investor was followed by another until they were all gone.

Sid tried to shake the solid bars on his cage, shouting, "Come on! Come on, already! LET'S GO!"

It seemed to go on forever. Danny's shoulder blades had numbed on the cold steel when a loud clank erupted from the ceiling. Everyone cheered as the dim light began to fade. Shutters inside the skylights were turning. What little light was available disappeared.

Danny shivered in the dark.

"Danny Boy?" Zin called.

"Yeah?"

"Welcome to the Haystack."

8

DANNY MOVED to the center of the cell. It was so dark that it didn't matter where he stood, no one would see him. The worst part was the concrete, slick and cold. Danny began to pace to keep warm.

"Save your strength."

There was a lump in the darkness to Danny's right. Slowly, the details of the room began to return with grainy, gray detail and fuzzy edges. The lump was Zin, sitting in the center of his cell with his knees pulled against his chest and his arms wrapped around his shins.

"You want to protect your core, Danny Boy," Zin said. "Do whatever you can to conserve your body heat. Walking around is only going to waste it. It might feel good now but you'll pay for it later."

"Why are they doing this, Zin?"

"Sit down and do what I told you," he snapped. "And use your legs to keep your balls from touching the floor. You don't want those getting cold."

He didn't have to worry about his scrotum touching anything. It had shriveled up like a mummified prune. The floor felt like a glacier. He stopped rocking back and forth before Zin snapped at him again, but he couldn't control the shivering.

"You good?" Zin asked. "Now, get into a breathing rhythm. Slowly, take in a breath and let it exhale on its own. In." Zin sucked air through his nostrils, loudly. "Out," he said, letting it leak out. He did it again, and again.

Danny followed his example. The chattering continued, but he felt less scattered. A little more settled. The fear that was strangling his insides had subsided to mild warmth. The muscles that were bunched around his shoulders released.

In.

Out.

He continued.

The room was mostly silent. Some of the others were talking. There was subtle laughter. Someone was whimpering.

"Here's the deal," Zin finally said. "We come here every two weeks, get naked and wait for the needle."

"What's that?"

"You'll find out. After this round, we'll screw around for two weeks like we've been doing until the next one. You get the picture."

"How long do we do this?"

"Don't ask that question. Just count your breath, that's all you need to know."

Laughter crackled through the room. Someone said to shut the hell up, then added, "God, I hate this freaking part."

Danny went back to breathing like Zin. It wasn't helping, he was getting colder. But there wasn't much choice. Danny could make out more details, could see that Zin was sitting with his back straight and legs folded beneath him, his hands in his lap. His chest rose and fell.

Danny didn't know who was in the cell on the other side, but he was standing and shrouded in darkness. He hadn't uttered a word.

Across the aisle, Parker had not moved. He stood in his cell hunched over. He looked disconnected already. He didn't seem to care whether it was hot or cold, whether he suffered or not. Like some spirit from another world.

The seconds stitched together and became minutes. Zin told him when to get up and walk around, when to rub some feeling back into his buttocks, and when to sit still and breathe. Danny was still shivering. There were moments when he swallowed the knot in his throat that threatened to break out sobs.

Danny lost count of how many times he and Zin walked, how many times he rubbed the feeling back into his buns, and how many breaths he'd counted. But he would remember for the rest of his life the sound the fan made when it engaged.

It started with a buzz. The long blades began to crawl in a circle. After one rotation, they picked up speed and the breeze came down with a slow helicopter sound.

Wop-wop-wop-wop-wop.

Then came the hiss of the sprinklers. A fine mist swirled in the current and settled on the floor and everything else.

"I won't talk after this, Danny Boy, no offense," Zin said. "This is where the real work begins. Just remember when the needle drops, push your tongue against the roof of your mouth."

"Why?"

Zin began to pace. "Or else you'll bite it off."

And that's when the lump in Danny's throat broke. He tried to smother the sobs but failed. No one said anything.

No one laughed.

The fan would stop. So would the mist.

Then start again.

Danny stopped the breathing exercise. He hadn't done it since the fan began. He was curled up on his side with his legs drawn up to his chest. He had cried out all his tears. His stomach ached.

He found strength watching Zin. He sat so still. He was getting up more often and walking back and forth with a steady, measured pace; his hands folded over his stomach. His head was slightly bowed.

And on and on, it went.

On and on, it went.

There were large patches of forgetting.

Danny wasn't sure if he'd fallen asleep or just blanked out. The floor had begun to grind into his hip and his neck hurt from lying down. He started to walk like Zin but didn't talk to him. It was just back and forth, back and forth.

The guy in the other cell turned out to be Reed. Danny only guessed from the long hair. He faced the other direction. He didn't fidget. Didn't much move. He just remained steady.

The fan finished another cycle of turning and they were in for a short reprieve. The following silence was interrupted by shuffling and a cough or a moan. Droplets of water condensed on the bars until they fell with a heavy drip.

But there was a new sound.

Above Danny's cell, a tiny mechanized motor turned.

The atmosphere changed. A heavy pause, like a collective breath.

Everyone stared up.

Danny saw a black box fastened in the center of the barred ceiling of his cell. Something was moving inside it. He didn't see the tiny door open, but heard the wire and straps fall out.

A jubilant roar shook the room.

The others were on their feet, calling to each other. There was laughter. They all reached up.

Zin stopped pacing. He paused for one final breath before reaching for the black box and pulling down a gaggle of straps and wire. He sat down and pulled the line from the box until there was plenty of slack on the floor. Then he took the straps and fastened them over his head like some sort of wrestling gear, but instead of ear protection there was a single knob that centered over the middle of his forehead. He didn't look at Danny, only took a deep breath and lay on his back.

His body convulsed once, his back arching off the floor for a long moment.

Then it went limp.

Everyone was in the same position. It was suddenly silent. No labored breathing. No groans or whimpers. Just complete silence.

He reached for the mess dangling from his cell. His joints ached. The straps were cold leather; the wire a thick cable. The knob was hard. He was reluctant, despite the agony. There was a needle inside the knob, he knew it had to be. It would plunge into the hole.

The thought was as cold as the floor.

He sat down, unable to put it on. But when the fan began to whir, Danny was in motion. His body moved on its own. He couldn't stand the cold, wet air anymore. Not when everyone around him was so peaceful. He just wanted out.

Away from this body.

The strap fit snugly around his head. He pulled extra cable from above until it pooled at his side. He shifted the knob over his forehead. If there were any tears left, Danny might have squeezed out a few. Instead, he just squeezed his eyes shut.

The knob began to squirm like flagellating lips, like the bottom of a snail. It numbed the skin beneath the knob. A cold fire spread into his forehead, like a river of icy water gushing inside his brain. His bladder released; a warm puddle grew between his legs. It was embarrassing, but he didn't care.

He just wanted out.

The cell walls shifted. The one next to him got smaller. Reed had turned around, staring down at him.

Then came the needle.

9

DANNY TASTED STEEL.

The needle plunged into the frontal lobe. The pain was minimal, but his body thrashed on the concrete, scraping his elbows and cutting the back of his head.

All Danny felt was the dull blunt force of metal and the crunching sound of the hole reopening. He no longer felt the cold floor or the frigid mist blowing over his naked body or the warm blood seeping from the back of his head. He was in another type of darkness.

Bodiless. Sightless.

Somewhere else.

Once he'd ridden a three-story water slide. He flung himself into the dark tube and plunged into the unknown where turns tossed him left and right and the water surged over his head. His stomach twisted with fear and excitement until he was shot out the bottom of the ride.

He remembered that. The whole thing.

The memory seeped into his mind from somewhere in the dark.

Danny was on another sort of ride that caused his stomach – if he still had a stomach – to buck and he was thrown through a series of twisting turns. But this ride swirled up and down and side to side, and it kept going and going. Until, finally, he fell through the bottom into a soft pit that was still black. Still nowhere.

There was a sense of floating. It was amniotic, thick and fluid. He tried to shout but had no lips, no throat. He was just somewhere, and that somewhere was better than his flesh.

He was seven years old. He slept in tee-pees and ran through icy streams and shot arrows and threw knives. He didn't change his underwear once. It was the best week of his life.

That was summer camp. He remembered! The memory was whole again. It was him.

A small man with a badge on his belt put his hand on Danny's shoulder and walked him up wide concrete steps that led to big wooden doors.

He had done something seriously wrong. He and some friends got caught writing computer code and hacking into websites. They did it as a goof, didn't think they'd get caught. And if they did, they were only seven or eight years old at the time. What were they going to do, put them in prison? They were kids. But the men and women waiting for Danny inside the wooden doors wore FBI t-shirts.

The needle was bringing back his memories. He felt more like himself.

There were sounds. It was distant, as if coming through a long pipe stuffed with towels. At first, it didn't sound like much, but then it took form. It sounded more like... laughter. The kind that comes from a playground.

He tried to swim towards it, but he was just floating, just listening. But it got louder. Words were popping up, now and then. They seemed to be running past him.

"Danny Boy!" It was right in front of him, just on the other side of the darkness. On the other side... of... his eyelids?

"I knew it," the voice said. "He ain't worth crap and in the middle of the field. Someone get him out of the way!"

There were footsteps. More voices. Some very far away, others going past him. Someone was nearby, out of breath from running.

"This is Danny Boy."

Zin! He's right there, just out of reach.

"That's him?" There was a girl with him. A *girl*. Colors swirled in the dark when Danny had the thought. "I thought you said he was some big deal," she said. "He's barely old enough to be here."

"Yeah, well you never saw him in the game room. The kid's some kind of prodigy with the computer sticks in his hands. I mean, there are kids on the island that have been here longer than me that aren't half as good as Danny Boy."

"Video games?" She sighed. "Seriously, who cares, Zin?"

"You want to help me move him, Sandy?"

The darkness shifted. Danny had a sense of the ground below him, the open sky above. Zin hooked his arms under Danny's armpits and Sandy took his feet. He felt the jostling of their footsteps. The breeze whistled past him and the grass was soft on his cheek when they put him down.

"Zin!" Sid called. "Don't get lost, I want you at the sundial when it hits noon, you got it?"

"Aye—aye, Capitan!"

"You're not really going to play that game again, are you?" the girl said.

"Naaaaaw."

"Seriously, Zin. We don't know how many rounds we have together and you're going to waste time gaming?"

And they went back and forth. Danny imagined the wry smile on Zin's face, what he usually looked like when he lied right in your face but still made you laugh. The image looked so clear and vivid, like he was looking right at it. Then he heard someone laugh.

Zin and Sandy were quiet. There was laughter again, and this time he felt it.

It was him.

"Danny Boy! Holy crap, did I tell you this kid was a winner, Sandy?"

Zin was very close, his voice soft but loud.

"Open your eyes, kid. Get here, man. Get all the way inside?"

Danny didn't know how to open his eyes. It was like telling a quadriplegic to move his legs when he didn't even know where they were. But then he felt pressure from the outside and recognized his face. There were hands on him. Once he knew where his cheeks were, he followed the pattern to his eyes.

They opened with a crunch, like years of sleep were crusted on his eyelids. There were blurs of color. A few blinks and smudges merged into a face. Zin was inches away, a big smile warping his lips.

"Danny Boy, you did it, man. You went fully lucid on your first round. How about that?" Zin looked back at Sandy. "Did I tell you? Who goes lucid on the first round? No one does, that's who. No one except Danny Boy. Freaking all the way inside on his first round."

Danny felt a smile on the inside, but he was still completely numb. His eyelids were already too heavy to keep open. Zin lightly slapped him.

"Not yet, don't go to sleep yet."

"Let him go down, Zinny," Sandy said. "He's not going to be able to move and I want to spend some time with you. The clock is ticking."

"I know, baby. I know. I just want to keep him lucid as long as possible. That will make the next round a lot easier."

Zin reached under Danny and propped him against a wall so that he was looking across a green field. He blinked and thought he was dreaming. He was sitting against the dormitory looking at the Yard and it didn't look a whole lot different.

"You see that, Danny Boy? We're inside the needle, somewhere between your mind and the Haystack's network. The needle is sunk inside your brain right now, boy. It's realigning your synapses so the computers can link directly with your frontal lobe. You're about as useful as a bowl of pudding, but you can see, Danny Boy. You can see, and the next time you'll be moving around. Next time, you'll be able to do this."

Zin lifted a boulder above his head. He tossed it over the distant trees.

"Peter Pan went to Neverland, but this is Foreverland, Danny Boy! We can do anything here. ANYTHING! There are no rules, no laws. Where gravity doesn't exist if we don't want it to. Where magic is limited only by our imagination."

Zin opened his hand and a long-stemmed rose grew from his palm. He took a knee in front of Sandy and kissed her hand. She rolled her eyes. She pointed over her shoulder and a truck squeezed out of her finger like a cartoon, but bounced on the ground like a ton of steel.

"It's not magic if everyone can do it," she said.

"Magic is not defined by the number of people that can perform it, but by the manner in which it is done."

"Okay, Socrates." She wrapped her arm around his neck and whispered. "Can we go?"

She whispered something else. Zin smiled wide.

He twirled his arm in front of his stomach and half-bowed. "I must bid you adieu, Danny Boy. There's only so much time and we work so hard to get here." He began to backpedal while Sandy pulled at him. "But don't give up hope. The first round sucks because you suffer without a payoff, but you'll see, Danny Boy. The next one will be better, you'll see!"

And they were off, running across the field, gleefully trotting like long lost lovers.

Danny didn't stay awake long. He managed to keep his eyes open to see the magic Zin was talking about. What seemed so ordinary when he first opened his eyes quickly turned into Foreverland. People were shapeshifting into lions and tigers and eagles. A mastodon thundered past with a horde of spear-chucking warriors that jumped off and floated away with their arms spread out.

It was everything that made dreams. But it was so real.

A long blink and the sun was lower. The field was nearly empty. There was half a spaceship buried a hundred yards away, its back half was on fire. It looked like the Millennium Falcon. There were distant explosions and gunfire. Someone shouted orders nearby. Another person went flying past on the back of a dinosaur.

Another long blink and it was night.

The ship was gone, replaced by an empty crater. Two moons were high, one full and the other half-crescent. There were several campfires in the field. Some people were singing, others laughed loudly while chasing each other. Girls squealed. It looked a lot like summer camp. Except for the people flying past the moon.

Dawn arrived.

The Yard was empty, except for the crater and dead campfires.

The sun was rising somewhere behind him. The shadows were long and dusky and the sunlight turned the trees a weird shimmery magenta. The quiet was disturbed by an occasional frog. Danny closed his eyes again. He was going to sleep when he felt someone very close. It was a girl.

She was inches from his face. Her eyes were green and her hair red, like candy. Her nostrils flared and her eyes searched his face. There was desperation in them, the eyes wide enough to expose the whites around her irises. She leaned in and pressed her cheek to his. She smelled like a beautiful flower.

"Find him," she said. "Tell him we found you."

And then she was off.

Danny hadn't even blinked. She moved so fast, it was like she hadn't been there. Maybe he would've believed he imagined it if not for the lingering scent.

He went to sleep for the last time. The next time he would wake, it would be in his bed, back in his body. But he would wake with her smell upon him and her words.

Tell him we found you.

ROUND 2

ONE-CAR ACCIDENT. ONE DEAD, ONE MISSING

HOBART, Oklahoma. – A blue Ford F-150 hit a tree off route 55 and caught fire. Both occupants were ejected from the vehicle. One was a female in her late teens and pronounced dead on arrival. The other occupant is a male, also in his late teens, and severely injured. Neither person had identification on their body.

The female was Caucasian, 5' 7", 130 pounds, long red hair and green eyes. The male is Caucasian, 5' 10", 180 pounds, shoulder-length black hair, and brown eyes. He was taken to Elkview Hospital but was mysteriously missing shortly after being admitted. He was last seen wearing denim jeans, work boots and a brown t-shirt.

If you have any information regarding their identification and the male's whereabouts, please contact local police.

10

DANNY STARED at the popcorn texture of the ceiling. His face was fat; his lips rubbery. Every joint in his body ached.

The curtains were closed. A sliver of light etched the dusty air, falling on a plastic cup on a tray next to his bed. Danny reached for it, winced when the scabs on his elbows cracked and his entire head throbbed, front to back. The crown of his head was crusty and bruised. He leaned on one elbow and took the cup, drinking the water in three swift gulps, noticing the medical equipment on the tray, the blood pressure cuff, thermometer, and bandages.

Mr. Jones's smell was all over the place. Danny threw the covers off and sat up, the floor cold on his bare feet. *Nothing but underwear.*

He didn't want to think about Mr. Jones putting him in bed. Problem was, he couldn't remember anything. A cloud filled his head. He dropped his face into his hands to think a moment but it was hopeless. There was a strange taste in the back of his throat and all he could think about was more water.

He took the cup to the sink. There, in the mirror staring back, was a circular bandage in the middle of his forehead. He touched it, gently.

The fog cleared.

The Haystack and the fan and the mist. *The needle.*

Vertigo smacked him. He held onto the sink. It got worse. He sank to his knees and crawled to the bed while the memories settled. It was strange how his mind was like water and the memories swirled like grains of sand. There was something he was supposed to remember but it was so hard. Summer camp? FBI? Damn, he couldn't remember it now.

He had journeyed through the needle to some... dream. *Foreverland.* It was torture to get there.

The taste still lingered, but it wasn't just in his mouth. It was in his head, too. *Metallic. The taste of the needle.*

The price to pay for reality limited only by the imagination. Danny looked at his hands, turned them over and studied the creases in his palms. *Is this Foreverland, still?*

He decided it wasn't. But it was hard to tell.

When the doorknob slowly turned, Danny threw the covers over his lap. The door cracked open. An eyeball slid into the opening and the door closed again. Before he could decide if it was Mr. Jones's eyeball, the door flew open and banged on the wall, followed by a mob.

"Danny Boy!"

Zin was the first one in the room. The others were right behind him. Danny curled up under the covers just before they piled onto him. They were slapping his back, his legs, his butt, shouting his name and whooping loudly.

"What a player!" Zin threw open the curtains, stabbing Danny's eyes with light. "The kid went lucid on his first round! ON HIS FIRST ROUND!"

There were high-fives and another dog pile on top of Danny. Zin mercifully pulled them off. The celebration continued in the center of the room.

"You all right, Danny Boy?" Zin asked

"A few aches."

"Yeah, but you did it," Zin said. "You did the impossible, you opened your eyes. No one does that."

The room got quiet. They stood like they were posing for a group photo, waiting for Danny's words of wisdom. He had none. They looked at him, expectantly. Everyone was there, except Parker.

"Poof."

That was Sid's explanation for Parker. He snapped his fingers, said, "Ole Parker is a puff of smoke, Danny Boy. He's gone on to bigger and better, my friend. Bigger and better."

No one explained it much beyond that, other than Parker graduated and was likely on his way back home, all healed up.

Bigger and better.

The slam dance of celebration began again. "And now you need to get out of bed, son! You've been sleeping for two damn days while we've been back in the real world. We need you, Danny Boy. We've been holding your slot open in the game room and we're about to drop in the standings. We can't wait any longer."

"Relax, Sid." Zin stood between them. "The kid hasn't eaten in two days, either."

"Then let's eat," Sid said. "Get dressed, we'll eat. We'll game. Daylight's burning, son."

Danny put his hand up to pause the ceaseless slam dance. It was hurting his head.

"Give him some privacy," Zin said. "Kid's in his underwear."

"He was butt naked two days ago. Underwear is a step up," Sid countered.

"All right, well, give him a second. We'll meet down in the cafeteria, right, Danny Boy? When you're ready, you come down. What do you say?"

Danny nodded with his eyes closed. He listened to Zin push them out. The chaos faded down the hallway. Danny dropped his head on the pillow. He needed some silence, just enough space to let the sand settle in his head. The last grains were falling into place.

We found you.

Mr. Jones was the happiest Danny had ever seen him.

No more hunching over. He walked upright and smiled all the time. He was proud of Danny, he said so every day. Looked like he was about to cry once or twice. Even the other Investors took notice. They shook

Mr. Jones's hand and congratulated him, like he'd done something himself. Mr. Jones stood up and shook their hands back vigorously. Once, when he was walking with Danny to the cafeteria, another Investor stopped to congratulate him. The old man didn't pay much attention to Danny when he shook Mr. Jones's hand and said, "You got a good one there, Jonsy. Lucky you."

"Maybe he'll graduate in five rounds," Mr. Jones said.

"Wouldn't that be something."

They parted ways and the old man didn't look back. Danny kept thinking. *Got a good one there... lucky you.*

Like the pick of the litter.

Danny didn't feel special. All he did was follow everyone else into the Haystack, put the needle on his head and wake up two days later. It wasn't like he did anything.

Evidently, others thought different.

He got high-fives in the game room, and those that didn't raise their hand were staring. Zin was out front, making room for them to walk to the central game dock where Sid and the others were waiting. Danny strapped on the gear and felt the pressure of half the game room gathering around to watch.

"Word gets around," Zin said, pulling on his gloves. "Don't disappoint."

And he didn't.

Danny took control of the game and Sid let him. Like before, he didn't feel like he was doing anything special, it just happened. He thought faster and clearer. He knew where his enemy was going, like he knew their thoughts. He'd operated with the efficiency of a computer, and when he snuck into the enemy camp and put a bullet through the last one's throat, the entire game room erupted.

He forgot they were even there.

Danny had discussed the first round with Mr. Jones, how he opened his eyes and what he saw. Mr. Jones listened, jotting down the details on a clipboard. When Danny was finished, he asked him to start from the top and go through it one more time, just in case there was something he was missing. "It's sort of like dreams, Danny Boy," he said. "The more you think about them, the more you remember. So one more time, my boy."

The more he remembered. That was the strange thing. Danny had the sense he got a bunch of his memories back when he was inside the needle, but now he couldn't remember them. Just something about summer camp and the FBI.

Danny got the feeling Mr. Jones just wanted to hear about it again. He added a few more details about people flying and the weird creatures that spawned from the ground (*Oh, yeah, and the Millennium Falcon had crashed; weird, huh?*).

"That's good. Good." When Danny stared at the floor, twisting his fingers, Mr. Jones said, "Anything else?"

"No," Danny said. "No, that's it."

But there was something else. He left out the girl. That felt secret and a gut-feeling decided to keep that part to himself. He waited another week before he did what the girl asked him to do.

Danny went to the beach.

11

DANNY FOUND the narrow path somewhere near the Haystack.

It meandered without apparent direction. Clearly one less traveled.

Palm fronds hung across it like soft arms blocking the way. He was wet from the dew and eventually found a stick to push them out of the way while knocking down spider webs.

The path eventually turned sandy and ended on a wide dune. He climbed over the soft mound of sand to the hard-packed beach. The wind was strong on this side of the island. The surf drove towards the shore in ten-foot waves, crashing hard only thirty yards out and leaving foamy residue on the beach. Danny could see the jagged edges of coral just under the surface, too dangerous to surf.

A lone figure was far down to Danny's left. He sat in the loose sand of the dunes. Danny started in that direction. His stomach tightened with nerves. And even though the sun was biting his white skin, he felt shivers the closer he got to him.

Reed didn't look up, not even when Danny was a few feet away. He sat with his arms resting on his knees, staring at the ocean. His bare chest was red. The edges of his shoulders poked out like his skin was hanging on him like an old shirt. The tracker bulged on his neck.

Danny started to say something but the sound of the surf blotted out his hesitant words and then he just didn't know what to say, so he swallowed the lump and looked at the water, too.

"What do you think's out there?" Reed finally asked.

Danny squinted, shading his eyes to search the horizon but nothing disrupted the flat line. No ship or island or rock, just water.

"Home," Danny said.

Reed didn't tell him if he was wrong or right. He got the feeling he was wrong.

Danny continued to search the horizon. Just because he couldn't see it didn't mean it wasn't there. He came from someplace and it wasn't the island. Out there, somewhere, were his parents and a place he called home. And when he graduated, he would see them again.

"Tell me what home looks like," Reed said, without looking up. "Better yet, tell me about your favorite Christmas. Think about the best Christmas you ever had, when you got everything you asked for and the world was the greatest place to be. Tell me what it was like."

Easy.

It was the time he got a skateboard half-pipe. He came down the stairs rubbing his eyes and his little brother was opening these big boxes from Santa and all Danny had was a green envelope. It was a message to look out the kitchen window. Danny pressed his hands on the cold glass. There, standing six feet tall and filling the back yard was the thing he wanted most in the world.

The half-pipe was covered in all his favorite stickers – Fallen and Zero and the fiery red head of Spitfire. His mother, wearing her pink robe with dyed blond hair hanging in her eyes, went onto the back deck with him.

But when Danny went through the back door, he stepped in three feet of snow. His mother was wearing a coat and her hair was black and short and she was smoking a cigarette. And his dad was there, too. He was fat and unshaven with a cigarette stuck in his lips. He handed Danny an air rifle and said Merry Christmas and aim for the cans he set up in the back yard. The yard was empty except for a dozen Budweisers.

Danny looked back to his mom because he had a half-pipe, not a rifle, but now she was shorter and wearing a tank top and the snow was gone and there were palm trees next to the house.

"They didn't erase our memories, Danny Boy." Reed still hadn't looked up. "They filled us with random ones, layered them one on top the other until we don't know which ones belong to us, which ones are false."

He was right. They didn't feel like his memories. And they were never the same parents. But Foreverland, that was different. "In the Haystack... I remembered..."

"They put your memories inside the needle. Every time you go inside, you get more of them back but you come back to the flesh, they get mixed with an ocean of random ones that aren't yours."

"Why?"

"The more you go inside the needle, the more you feel like yourself. The more you like it."

Danny tried to remember Christmas again. He knew who he was, he remembered getting what he wanted. He remembered the half-pipe covered with stickers and the sound of the skateboard clapping on the metal coping. But then he couldn't actually remember skating.

Then he realized he didn't know how to skate.

"She sent you," Reed said. "She told you to come find me, didn't she?"

There wasn't a hole in Reed's forehead, only a scar where it used to be. He went into the Haystack and endured the suffering without taking the needle. After Danny went to sleep, Reed stayed in that dreadful room. He'd done it before, Danny had been told. Reed was a sick puppy, he was told.

"How do you know that?" Danny asked.

Reed remained still and quiet. "You can trust her," he finally said.

"Do you know her?"

"I did, once upon a time." Again, quiet. A slight shrug. "Or maybe I just think I do. It's an ocean of thoughts, Danny Boy."

Danny wanted to ask him a hundred questions. Everyone on the island was buying everything the Investors were selling, gobbling it up like a bunch of hungry fish, and here was a kid that seemed to know something. Danny wanted to know why they were on the island and why Reed didn't take the needle and who the girl was...

But then a cart came over the dune and began driving down the hard-packed beach, the water skimming beneath it. Reed never looked at it, just continued staring. The cart stopped in front of them. Mr. Jones rested his hands on the steering wheel and stared at Reed. It was the first time since Danny had come out of the Haystack that the old man didn't look happy. He patted the empty seat next to him.

"Come along, Danny Boy. Your camp is looking for you, they've been waiting at the game room. You don't want to disappoint, now do you?"

Mr. Jones's eyes flickered at Reed when he said that. Reed didn't notice. Or seem to care. He just stared at the ocean, not looking for anything, almost like he was waiting for a ship to arrive. The girl said to tell Reed that they found him. He did that.

Now what?

Danny got on the cart. They left Reed behind. He'd stay there the remainder of the day. Maybe longer.

The next time Danny would see him was through the bars of his cell.

12

REED HAD SPENT time on every section of the island. Most were sandy beaches; a few sections were cliffs. At first, he explored these areas in search of an escape while all the other boys wasted time in the game room. It didn't take long to see the futility of the choppy surf and rocky coral. Of course, he hadn't seen the south end where the old men lived where hope may still exist.

But hope was no longer in Reed's vocabulary. He extinguished it. Twenty-five trips – now, twenty-six – through the Haystack will scrub that out of any person. Boy or man.

Reed spent his time on the north end because no one else did. He would remain on the beach for days while the sun spread warmth deep into his bones where the cold torture felt unreachable.

He rarely saw anyone on the north end. Not even Mr. Smith, especially since he wasn't talking to Reed anymore. Mr. Smith didn't show up when the last round ended. Reed walked back to his room and curled up under the covers, chattering in and out of fitful sleep where he dreamed of turning blades and endless rain.

Reed came to the beach just before the sun rose, when the sky was glowing orange and purple. He sat, watching the waves come in. There was a time when he decided escape was impossible but still looked for a sign that he was wrong.

Not anymore.

Now he just watched the waves crash, reminding him of the one sustaining lesson: *hopelessness.*

Reed had given up hope that he would one day find a way off the island, to discover home somewhere out there, to be rid of the cease-less random thoughts churning in his head. Because to hope was to reject the present moment, the only thing that was real, regardless of its misery. Reed clung to the present moment like a buoy. Reality had frayed. He didn't know who he was.

He hadn't given up, only the hope that things would be different. He found his suffering was bearable when he did so, that he accepted the totality of life, regardless how he felt about it, whether he liked it or not.

And like it, he did not.

Reed couldn't look at Danny. If he did, he would risk clinging to hope again.

He wasn't surprised he'd come. He had an intuition that he would seek him out. Reed's intuition didn't come in words or thoughts, it came in dreams. The only consistent thing about them was the image that followed them: red hair.

He didn't know who she was. He sensed her presence the day he woke up in a lab staring at Mr. Smith's hopeful grin. Her essence warmed him. At first, he thought he'd imagined it like all the other random thoughts, but the essence that accompanied her was different than all the others.

It was fragrant.

He didn't know her name. Didn't know if she meant anything to him or if she was real. He may have given up hope for escape, but he wasn't able to expel hope concerning her, hope that she was real, hope that he meant something to her. When things were darkest it was hope that he would see her one day that warmed him.

But that was as far as he hoped. That was it.

He couldn't look at Danny because he'd see the hope in his eyes. Danny needed to accept and understand where he was. This was the island. It was the end of the world. Home didn't exist, not anymore. If he hoped to find something better, he would eventually look inside the needle. But the answer wasn't in there.

But he would go inside. They all did.

Reed wasn't disappointed when he did. Danny confirmed what he suspected. *She's in there, too.*

It was harder to know that she was in there than suffering through the Haystack, knowing that if he took the needle he would find her. But he would have to stay strong. In his dreams, she told him to resist. She told him that someone would come for him and show him the way.

And then Danny appeared at the beach and he knew it. He just knew it. Maybe he was the one that would put an end to all the suffering. Maybe he would give them hope.

That was why he couldn't look at him.

13

CLASS WAS IN SESSION.

About thirty of them in small desks arranged in tidy rows and the teacher discussing the world economy. He was propped on the corner of the desk. He was mostly bald and his bottom lip glistened when he took a moment to gather his thoughts.

Some of the guys in the back row were asleep, carefully hiding their faces behind the people in front of them. Danny was up front and had taken to doodling on a piece of lined notebook paper. It started out as a tapestry of curly lines, but then a face took shape in the middle of it all. First the eyes, then the petit nose. He began to darken the hair—

"Danny Boy?" The teacher had crossed his arms, scowling over his glasses. "Art class is not today. I'll advise you to join the discussion or I'll be forced to report you to your Investor for tutoring."

Danny folded the paper.

After a long, uncomfortable pause, the teacher continued in the same droning tone about the recent flash crash of the New York Stock Exchange. Millions of dollars were lost in a matter of moments. The market closed early that day and all trading suspended. A week later, the culprit was found: some dopey day trader that lived in his parents' basement that hacked his way into the market and over reached.

"You don't mess with money, boys," the teacher intoned with a gurgle. He cleared his throat. "Money is power and it will find you."

The teacher asked for questions. He was answered by the sound of soft snoring somewhere in the back but didn't hear it. He had no idea why everyone started laughing.

"Okay, I understand this is not a stimulating topic," he said, finally standing up with a grunt, "that's why I got special permission to do an exercise today."

Their interest piqued.

"We're going to use tablets for our class discussion today."

There was no buzz, no excitement. There was a fully-loaded game room in the next building, why would anyone care about a tablet?

The teacher unlocked a cabinet in the corner of the room. He pulled a box off the bottom shelf and slid it across the floor. The guys sleeping in the back continued sleeping. The others looked bored. Danny listened.

They were going to begin a business in a simulated program. It could be anything: services, goods, investing, whatever. All they had to do was show they could create a fake business that made fake money in the fake world inside the tablet and that would prove they had some understanding of economics.

A few of the guys started taking them out of the box. The teacher stopped them by holding up a knobby finger. "And remember, these tablets are not allowed out of this room. The repercussions of such an infraction will be severe."

Ass = grass.

When he dropped his hand, Danny was the first one to the box. He found a seat next to one of the Sleeping Beauties. The tablet felt warm in his hand. It fit nicely.

The teacher got stern with the rest of the boys barely making an effort.

"We'll be here all day," he said. "Until you finish, I swear to God."

Every second in the class was a second away from the game room. They began breaking down into small groups. Even woke up the sleepers. The teacher advised them on how to begin. Danny, though, stroked the smooth glass as instincts bubbled inside him. He ignored the instructions and, with all the excited chaos, called up a virtual keyboard on the touchscreen.

His fingers raced over the keys with the tablet snuggly cradled in his left hand. He swiftly hit a combination of keys to override the operating system. The screen went black. A cursor blinked in the upper left corner. He began typing again.

The commands came from somewhere deep in his subconscious. He didn't stop to think about the letters or the meaning of what he was writing, he just let it flow through his fingertips until line after line of code began scrolling rapidly from top to bottom. He was looking for a combination of words that would give him an encrypted password. He didn't know what it was, just trusted he'd know it when he saw it.

AW34uT!69fEW&8990.

There it is.

He tapped the glass and stopped the word flow, then dragged his fingertip over the password and dropped it into the upper right corner. The screen went black again. One second. Two. Three.

And then color swirled into focus.

A light blinked in the upper right. He had hacked into the network. That blinking light meant he had access to the Internet. To the world outside.

Danny began to download a browser from an FTP site that popped into memory—

"Aw, what?"

Every single tablet went blank.

Danny looked up. The class was moaning, some of them trying to shake their tablet back to life. "What happened?" someone whined.

"Class! Class!" The teacher held up his hands. "I need you to hand the tablets back to me in an orderly fashion..."

Danny quickly slipped into the middle of the room and exchanged his tablet with one of many abandoned on a desk. Then he switched with another one, careful no one was watching.

"Class, please!" The old man cleared his throat. "Please! It's important you give me your tablet so we don't lose your data. Line up, keep orderly, please. Keep orderly."

Danny did what everyone else did and began moaning. He told the guy next to him about the idea he had for a lemonade stand. When he was checked off and dismissed, he left the classroom smiling.

We're not alone. There is an outside world.

14

THEY HAD a match in the game room in an hour.

It had only been a week since Danny woke from his first round and he'd put them firmly in first place. In fact, they were so far ahead they would still be in first after the second round. Sid didn't even pretend to be running the crew anymore. When they talked about strategy, he got everyone quiet and then looked at Danny.

They were in the cafeteria, talking about the second round only days away. Most had met new girls in the first round and Sid was having a hard time getting them to agree on another match once they were inside the needle.

Danny pushed his tray away and checked out of the conversation. He looked around for Reed. He had to come back to eat but maybe he did it at night when everyone was sleeping.

Danny pulled a sheet of paper from his back pocket. He had continued the doodling he started in economics class and fleshed out the details of the girl's hair, added plump lips and eyebrows. He hoped to see her again once he was inside. Danny didn't know what he was supposed to do and craved some direction. Craved some answers.

"What's that?" Zin plucked the paper out of his hand. "Ooo, you're a Michelangelo *and* a war hero, huh? Who would've guessed?"

Danny snatched it back. Zin didn't seem alarmed by the over-reaction.

"That your girlfriend?" Zin asked.

"Yeah," Danny said. "I meet her every night in my dreams."

Zin opened a box of juice and sipped, absently. When no one seemed interested in what they were doing, Danny unfolded the paper and smoothed out the wrinkles.

"You ever see her, Zin?"

He glanced. "No. Why, you?"

"No, no. I was just wondering, you know, for the next time we're..." Danny stumbled over his directionless conversation. Again, Zin took no notice.

"Where do they come from?" Danny asked.

"The girls?"

"Yeah. I mean, are they real or just part of Foreverland?"

"No, they're real all right."

"How do you know?"

He shrugged. "Sandy describes a camp kind of like ours. They do the same things we do, only they don't call it the Haystack. I think they call it the Vase, or something girly."

"How do you know it's real?"

He shrugged, again. "I don't, but it makes sense. We're a boys' camp and they're a girls' camp. Why not?"

Danny looked at the face in the doodle. She was different than the rest. Maybe she wasn't real.

"But how do you know?" he said. "Who says that this, right here, isn't real? Maybe this is the dream."

Zin shook his head, took another sip and grimaced.

"I mean, what proof do I have that any of this is real? Maybe this is just another Foreverland that we think we woke up in and we're really still in a dark room somewhere freezing our asses off while we wander around another Foreverland—"

"Look! This is real!" Zin slammed his juice down. "It just is, so get that through your little punctured skull, all right? This is real, Foreverland is real, it's all real." He grabbed the paper and held it up to Danny's face. "She's real, too, Danny Boy. You know why?"

Danny backed off.

"Because we got nothing else. It's just this, and that's all. My girl is real, you got it? Stop pissing all over my party, why don't you?"

He finished the drink in one long sip and crushed the carton on the table. His leg was shaking. Then he got up and left.

Sid didn't see any of it, just figured Zin was making an early exit for the game room. In seconds, all of them followed Zin out. Everyone on the island had a nerve, Zin once told him.

Danny just stepped on Zin's.

15

DANNY WOKE early for the second round.

Mr. Jones walked him to the Haystack. They walked inside without introductions from another clipboard carrier as the last bell faded.

Danny wasn't nervous until the air inside hit him and the steel fan loomed overhead and the smell of dank misery crawled up his nose. By the time he reached his cell, his insides had turned to jelly. Mr. Jones had sensed his hesitancy and placed a firm comforting hand on his shoulder. Danny turned quickly into his cell to get away. He waited until everyone was inside their cells before getting undressed, doing it quickly and folding everything neatly so that Mr. Jones would leave.

"Hey, Danny Boy," Sid shouted. "I want you fully lucid this time and get to the sundial, my man. You hear? Once you're inside the needle, none of this exploring crap like a new poke, you stay in the Yard and meet us at the sundial. We need to clock some real kills in the game, son. We only need to stay in first place another week!"

Someone whooped and shouted, "FIRST PLACE!"

And then everyone joined the seemingly random celebration.

"Zin, you, too!" Sid shouted above the melee. "You be at the sundial, boy, or I'll dot both your eyes. You're screwing with my time if you get lost inside the needle."

And the chant continued. *FIRST PLACE! FIRST PLACE!*

"What's the obsession with the game?" Danny said.

Zin was already sitting on the floor with his back straight. "There's a reward for any team that captures first place for three straight weeks. They drop the needle as soon as we get here. No getting naked and no suffering."

"Why didn't anyone tell me?" Danny grabbed the bars. He wanted to pull them apart and throttle Zin sitting so composed and unmoved. *No suffering? I'd be in that game room every waking second!*

"Bad luck to tell you," Zin said. "It's a jinx."

Danny wanted to argue, but he was right. They were in first.

"Don't fight it, Danny Boy." Zin took a deep breath. "Suffering is part of life. Either way, we go inside the needle."

"You mean you like this?"

"Hell, no. But it doesn't matter how I feel." Another deep breath. "Be here, no matter what."

"Fine." Danny crossed his arms and began pacing. "If you want to freeze your ass off, be my guest. I want out."

Reed was standing in his cell with his back to Danny. He was as motionless as Zin was sitting. The skylights began to turn, followed by another round of cheers. Light faded. Darkness settled like thick soup. Forms disappeared. Voices became bodiless chatter.

The second round had begun.

———

"Danny Boy?"

Zin's voice was soft, blending in with the docile conversations that were beginning to trail off into the silence of impending pain.

"The game, it's a waste of time," he said. "We're going to explore once we're inside the needle. I'm going to give you the tour, show you Foreverland."

Danny resumed breathing like Zin had taught him. He finished his count to ten. "Sid's going to be pissed."

"Good thing he's not running the show."

"Then who is?"

"You are, Danny Boy."

"Me?" He cringed, hoping Sid didn't hear him. "Dude, I'm a poke, I'm not running anything."

"Don't be a clown, you're the whole reason this place was cheering about a half hour ago. They're all watching you, Danny Boy. Not Sid. He's just a cheerleader."

"You're cracked, man," Danny hissed. "Sid will put a black mark under my eyes after he's done with you."

"You think the old men are going to let him do anything to you or me or any kid in this place? Nothing's going to happen, Danny Boy. This place is locked down tight."

Danny imagined a mob of old men charging through the Yard wielding stun guns. It wouldn't matter if they were carrying nuclear weapons, they'd throw a hip before they got anything under control.

"What about when they threw you in a trash can?"

"It was a trash can, who cares. It was funny. Even I laughed."

"So how's a bunch of crypt keepers going to keep us from getting pummeled?"

"Right here." Zin's dim figure tapped the tracker on the back of his neck. "They got some sort of remote in their pocket. They put their hand in there and they can kick a volt or two into your spine and you're sleeping, my friend. And Sid knows it. The geezers load you on a cart and it's over."

"What're you saying over there?" Sid's voice carried from across the dark aisle. "You got something to say about me?"

"Nothing, Cap-i-tan," Zin said. "Just girl talk over here, that's all."

Sid grunted. His teeth ground together. He said, "You just make sure—"

Click. Hmmmmmmmm.

The fan engaged. The blades began to crawl.

Conversation died.

"Let's get on with the suffering," Zin said.

Danny was already counting his breath. He glanced at Reed, still standing, still facing the other direction. It would be long and hard for him. Maybe if they held first place, he'd get a reprieve.

But he wouldn't take the needle, so then what?

Danny thought about doing the same. He could talk to Reed when everyone was out. He could tell Danny more about the underlying secrets of the island, the red-headed girl, and why he resisted. Maybe they could talk long enough to sort through each other's memories, figure out which ones were their own without having to go inside the needle.

But then the sprinklers began to hiss.

Moments later, Danny looked at the top of his cage. He knew he'd reach for the needle as soon as it dropped. Just like everyone else.

16

REED SETTLED into the rhythm of breathing.

The wet cold had reached his bones, but he found peace with it. Even the shivers seemed to fall into rhythm. He was at peace with misery.

He didn't like the suffering, didn't prefer it. If the gates opened, he'd gladly leave. But he didn't resist it.

He found space for it.

Mr. Smith's familiar walk-shuffle came down the aisle. Reed could smell him.

In-out, he breathed. *In-out.*

"Reed, look at me."

Reed saw a haggard face that was losing the battle with time and gravity, the cheeks sagging like an old dog that needed putting down. The eyes were hidden in the shadows.

"You've put me in a very difficult position, my boy. In an effort to convince you what's best, the Director and I have decided to alter your experience. We hope you'll make the best of your opportunity."

Reed drew a long breath through his nostrils.

"You understand we put you under duress to facilitate your progress. It's not meant to harm you, you see. Only to propel you forward. But you refuse our guidance, Reed; therefore, we'll need to push harder."

The back of the cell began closing. It did not stop until the bars were pressed against his chest and back. Reed was sandwiched tightly in place, barely able to move. The lucid gear dropped from the top of his cage and brushed the top of his head. He would only need to lift himself onto his toes to let it slide into place.

Mr. Smith clamped something on the bars, turning the wingnuts with his arthritic fingers. It was a metal frame, box-like. An empty bracket was centered twelve inches from Reed's face.

Mr. Smith remained a few seconds longer, then headed for the exit.

Reed closed his eyes. He squirmed against the bars and panic threatened to overwhelm him. He just wanted to move.

The lucid gear touched his head. They were making escape easy.

Each breath was forced to be shallow and quick as his chest was constricted by the bars. He wasn't able to turn his head. Thoughts of being buried alive piled up. Trapped, he focused his efforts on breathing, again.

Mr. Smith returned. He was dragging something long and snake-like.

Reed wouldn't look. He barely controlled his breathing.

Mr. Smith fastened it onto the metal bracket, turning wingnuts to hold it into place. He left the Haystack, the heavy door clicked shut. Locking the darkness inside.

Reed was tempted to lift up and take the needle. *What if it's a box of rats?*

Water hit his face.

He choked. Struggled to breathe. Unable to turn his head, he was forced to swallow too much of it, choking on the rest. He managed to hold his breath until it stopped. He coughed up excess liquid.

Drowning.

A hose was locked into the metal frame.

When he had regained his breath, when the burning subsided in his chest, when the bars weren't pressing as hard, the water came again.

And again.

17

Floating in darkness.

Not exactly floating, that implied motion.

Danny was just nowhere. There was no sound, smell or flesh. No nothing.

When the needle had dropped, Danny couldn't pull it down fast enough. He didn't bother looking at Reed. He was shivering too much to care about anything but escape. The suffering was worse than the first time. Felt longer, colder. He welcomed the needle like a savior.

The strap numbed his forehead. The needle hit the stent with a dull thump. His back arched. And then he went to the dark place.

And it was better than the Haystack.

Boundaries formed.

What felt like an endless void shaped into arms and legs and a body. He had no sense of up or down, just a feeling of being curled up in a fetal position.

Slowly, there was something hard beneath him. Gravity pulled the weight of his body against it. A rhythmic beating throbbed distantly, got louder. *Heartbeat.* Blood rushed past his ears.

The ground thundered beneath him.

The world spun and pain struck his arms—

"Don't challenge me, son." The voice was modulated and robotic. "Wake up."

Danny's head bobbled and neck popped. His eyes began to open. First, light. Then color. Then the details of a mechanical face. Danny was twenty feet off the ground, in the clutches of giant mechanical hands.

Danny's world shook violently, again. A word vibrated in his throat but didn't make it out.

"You ever have any delusions about who runs our camp, let this be a reminder," the thing said.

Danny's arms filled with sparking pain. The monster squeezed until they were painfully numb.

"You might be a hero in the game room, but you're a little thirteen year old bitch. You got that? Life on the island is short, and I've been here way longer than you, so get in line, son. I don't care what Zin told you about the tracker volts, I'll stuff your head up your cornhole before they konk me out. You'll be tasting last night's dinner for weeks."

The lower jaw jutted out. Flames ignited on the incisors like pilot lights.

"Try me again and I'll set your head on fire. You hear?"

When Danny didn't respond, his world shook. The popping in his neck was louder.

"You hear—"

"Whoa, whoa there, Sid. You're going to turn him into a jellyfish if you're not—"

Danny crumpled on the ground. The mechanical beast's enormous hand clamped around Zin and lifted him up. The fingers squeezed so hard that Zin bulged like a water balloon. Then he melted, dripped to the ground like mercury, coagulating and reforming. Zin was whole again.

"I'm not kidding, Zinski! You start putting ideas in Danny Boy's head and I'll cook you both."

"Sid, you got to remember that he just got here. He's still a poke, man. He needs a little introduction to the needle before you start throwing him in the Foreverland game room. Just give him a second to get used to it, will you? You remember what it was like on your second round?"

Zin was engulfed in a cloud of fire. He was unfazed when the fire died, pinching off a small flame dancing on his sleeve.

"Both of you." Sid pointed back and forth. "Don't jerk off all day, you hear? If we lose and you're MIA, then it's cornhole time. Got it?"

Danny nodded. Zin gave him a thumbs up.

The ground shuddered as the monster trotted across the Yard. Danny bounced with each step.

How'd you do that? Those words were stuck inside Danny.

Zin grabbed his arm and lifted him to his feet. "Lean against the sundial and stand there a minute."

It vibrated beneath his hand, penetrating into his chest until he was filled with warmth. The aches from Sid's punishment faded. He noticed other sensations, too. The breeze brushed his cheeks. The grass tickled between his toes. He noticed the shouting and laughter from across the Yard. People running. People flying.

"Welcome to Foreverland, Danny Boy." Zin let go of his arm. "You're all the way inside this time, my friend."

A body began to appear in the empty space only a few feet away. It first appeared translucent and ghostly, slowly solidified into one of the new pokes that came to the island shortly after Danny. He was sucking his thumb, eyes closed.

"That's what most people look like on the second round," Zin said. "Don't tell Sid, but I heard he sucked his thumb for five rounds." He looked around, suspiciously, whispered too loudly, "Even sucked his thumb inside the Haystack."

Danny laughed.

"How'd you do all that?" Danny asked, weakly.

"What? Turn to water? Old trick, man. Sid was just trying to scare you. He knew you'd be lucid enough to feel it but not enough to control the pain. After this round, Danny Boy, you'll be able to do anything. You can feel as much pleasure or as little pain as you want."

Zin splayed his hand on the sundial. He pulled a meat cleaver from his pocket and rammed it through the back of his hand. No blood. He didn't even flinch.

"See?" Zin held up his hand, the tip sticking through his palm. "If I wanted to feel that, I could. But I don't."

Danny felt dizzy. The blade sticking through the flesh and people flying like birds and the ground swaying and—

"Whoa, hold on there." Zin placed Danny's hands on the sundial before he fell over. "Hang on a bit longer, Danny Boy."

Feelings of seasickness subsided. The ground held still. The alternate reality felt normal again and the urge to vomit disappeared.

"You good?" Zin asked.

Danny nodded.

"All right, give it another minute. The sundial is the center of Foreverland, where we feel most solid when we get inside. It helps to touch it when you first get here. After while, you'll just hit the ground running."

"Where are we?"

"You mean you don't know?"

Danny shook his head.

Zin laughed. "We're inside a computer, Danny Boy! This is a program, a digital environment. Our identity has been sucked out of our heads, and the needle is doing the sucking. Hell of lot better than freezing your ass off on that concrete floor, right?"

Danny smiled. *Yeah, it is.*

"Once you're fully here, fully present, you'll figure out how to control this body. You can dial up pleasure, push out pain, turn yourself into a baboon or swim to the bottom of the ocean... whatever you want to do. The sky's the limit, Danny Boy. And the sky has none."

Zin pulled Danny from the sundial. They walked around the poke curled on the ground. Danny felt shaky the further they got from the sundial, but he was still solid. He had a new body, one he could control with a thought.

"So what do you want to do, Danny Boy? What'll it be?"

Danny stepped away from Zin. The Yard was exactly like it was on the island. The same buildings, same trees. Even the Haystack. But it was different. It all felt interconnected. Danny could feel the grass shifting in the wind. He could feel it crush when a footstep landed. He sensed the birds singing and the crackle of heat as a fire erupted in the trees. He was one with everything.

Not separate. But one. And the sky was the limit.

"That," Danny said. "I want to do that."

Zin looked up. "All right."

The island was lushly shaped like the state of South Carolina, dominated by trees with a bald spot of turf in the middle.

Tears streamed down Danny's cheeks in the cold wind. He kept his arms out for balance, like walking a tightrope for the first time, 3000 miles above the ground. Zin flew next to him on his back with his hands laced behind his head. For him, it was as thrilling as riding a bike for the thousandth time. For Danny, it was everything he imagined.

The ocean was choppy, but the distant horizon disappeared in a gray haze. Even the sky above them looked more gray than blue, like they were inside a fuzzy dome.

"What's all that?" Danny shouted above the wind.

"The Nowhere." Zin made hardly any effort to speak, but his words resounded clearly across the whistling wind. "You can't go out there, it's the edge of the program. Where your memories are."

"Wait. What?"

"Your memories." Zin put a finger on Danny's forehead. Inside Foreverland, there was no hole. "Haven't you noticed?"

Danny concentrated on flying straight, but he was remembering the time he stepped on a nail when he was six and had to get a tetanus shot; the time he got caught smoking his mom's cigarette and had to finish the pack in front of her as punishment. The time he kissed a girl behind the garage on a dare—

He began to wobble. Zin grabbed his arm to straighten him out.

"I don't get it," Danny shouted.

"It's part of the reprogramming, Danny Boy. The healing. They sucked our memories out so our bad habits get fixed. You know, like addiction and stealing and whatever else the bunch of us lowlifes did wrong before we got here. Inside the needle, we get them back until we're whole again."

"Reed said we'll get sucked inside the needle."

"Yeah, well, he's not exactly the voice of reason." Zin resumed his relaxed posture. "But he might not be all that crazy."

"Why?"

"You might not want to remember everything, Danny Boy. There's a reason we're here."

He didn't have a chance to ask for more. Zin floated farther away, eyes closed. Not so happy. If they were a bunch of screw-ups before they got to the island, it wouldn't be so rosy to remember.

They soared over the beach. The waves were just as angry as the day he went to visit Reed but the beach was empty. Reed was still back in the Haystack, forced to stand in the blowing cold. *How would he know what was going on if he'd never been inside the needle?*

Danny liked the way it felt, remembering his life. He wasn't sure it made sense, how it was fixing him, but if he was broken then maybe he shouldn't know how it worked. Just because he was regaining memories, though, didn't make him more of who he was.

Is that what I am, memories? Or am I something else?

It was too confusing to think about. He was perfectly fine with the thrilling sensation of flying, of being so far off the ground without the fear of falling. If they just did circles all day, it would be a good one.

There were no girls on the ground. Zin was flying with his eyes closed. Danny wanted to ask about them, even about the redheaded one, but then a squad of boys blasted between them in v-shaped formation and tossed Danny head over heel. He went tumbling.

I'm going to crash, I'm going to die!

Zin steadied him. "You got to watch it. If you let your thoughts get a hold of you, you'll divebomb out, man. You crash, it's going to hurt. You're not ready to control your pain so if you split a bone, you're going to feel it. Remember, they're just thoughts. *You* are not your thoughts. Stay focused. Sometimes it helps to imagine a dot in the middle of your brain. Breathe in and out of it until there's nothing left but the dot. You'll get the hang of it."

He did that. First, with his eyes closed. Next, eyes open.

They did a complete circle around the island. The second time around, he felt a little more in control. In fact, he put his arms down and did a Superman pose. Zin was pretending to swim.

They were over the south end of the island where the Investors' Mansion divided the trees from the coast. They soared around it and cut across the middle of the island. Zin turned on the jets and did loops around the Chimney.

The Chimney, where everyone woke up and everyone disappeared. Graduated. *Smoked.* But no one knew what really happened. Would Foreverland really show them what was inside?

"Get to the ground, Danny Boy," he said. "I don't want you crashing and burning, my man."

"Where you going?"

Zin pointed down. Danny could see the girls popping into existence near the sundial. "Girl plus boy... you do the math."

They landed safely. Danny didn't see Zin after that.

The two moons had fallen below the tree line. There was a castle in the Yard with smolder holes in it. The moat was on fire. Danny watched Vikings carry out chests of gold. They celebrated around a fire with pre-historic turkey legs and vats of beer, wine or whatever was slurring their speech. Apparently, they won.

Danny had gone to the beach. It was empty. No sign of the redhead. He explored the island, messed around inside the castle and went swimming. He even went to the game room and helped the team win.

(They were getting slaughtered before he showed up.)

DA-NNY! DA-NNY! DA-NNY!

Sid was all happy.

Danny looked for the redhead some more. He ended up where he first met her on the Yard. The castle had crumbled into dust by then. The moat continued to burn with eerie red flames. Campfires were all around it. When the moons began to fade, they were hugging and saying goodbye. Some of them were crying. Danny watched from the edge of the trees, alone.

Someone walked toward him.

"You Danny Boy?" It was one of the girls. "Someone found this by the fire."

She handed him a gift. It was wrapped in red paper that sparkled in the dimming light. He opened the card taped to the top.

Merry Christmas, Danny Boy.

He could hardly see his hands as he ripped the paper from the box. The fires were nearly gone when he pulled the top open. He put his hand inside.

Sand.

ROUND 3

FIRE TAKES LIFE OF MOTHER AND SON

GILBERT, Arizona. – The Gilbert Fire Department responded to a call at 4:22 AM where a two-story house belonging to Allison Forrester was engulfed in flames. Fire fighters were able to keep the blaze from jumping to neighboring houses but unable to rescue the occupants. Once the fire was extinguished, two unidentified bodies were discovered inside. One is believed to be Allison Forrester, 47, and her son, Daniel Forrester, 13.

The cause of the fire is unknown.

18

SHE NEARED the edge of the gray boundary, dared not go any closer.

But she could see... all of Foreverland.

Danny flew by with the other boy. He was quite... good.

Quite.

She... she was right. He was who she needed. She needed someone to watch Reed. Needed someone to help her... to put an end...

She watched, she watched.

He would need the practice. He would need to learn the ways of Foreverland. He would need to be stronger. She couldn't wait long, but she... she needed to wait for now. To give him time to get stronger.

She left him a present. A gift. A clue.

He would use it.

To find her next time.

In the...

Nowhere.

19

LIGHT SOFTLY FLOODED THE HAYSTACK. Danny shivered.

The boys were slowly coming to life. Zin was still on his back. Reed's cell was empty. Danny didn't bother wondering where he was or if he was alive, he just needed to get out. The others were already ahead of him, scurrying for the exit. No one spoke.

Danny's clothes were near the opening of his cell, the door slung open. He quickly got dressed and hurried for the outdoors, to get heat into his bones. They exited into the shade of the trees, but the air was so much warmer than inside the Haystack. They trotted down the path to the end. *Sun.*

Danny stopped as he entered the Yard, savoring the warmth on his face, the smell of green grass and the sound of birds.

Something flashed.

He shaded his eyes and picked up a small twinkle in the top floor of the Chimney behind the black windows. He gave it little thought. Instead, he started for the dorms to get some rest. He hadn't moved all day, but all that healing was exhausting. He couldn't exactly remember what had happened.

Danny crossed the Yard.

Zin was still inside the Haystack, shivering on the floor.

20

THE DIRECTOR SCRUBBED his hair with a towel.

It had been days since he'd showered. Work was demanding. Sometimes he forgot what he smelled like. But when a man stays locked away on the top floor of a luxury penthouse-style apartment, it didn't matter what he smelled like. But a shower was in order. He needed to get outside and stretch a bit, see his island. Reconnect with the reason he came to it in the first place.

Things have evolved so quickly.

He saw the line of boys emerging from the trees.

The Director threw the towel over the back of a chair and aimed one of his telescopes. He dialed the knob until the faces came into focus. They were exhausted and shivering. Eight hours of bone-chilling cold would make a polar bear chatter. Those boys had no idea what their bodies were enduring while they were away.

Foreverland, they called it.

The Director couldn't have come up with a better name. Then again, he never could have envisioned what his island had become. Not in a million years.

These kids had no idea what a gift they'd received. If they knew what their lives had been like before he brought them to this paradise, they'd break down like rag dolls. Then again, if they knew the price they were paying for such freedom, for the unadulterated alternate reality, they might not exactly drop to their knees in thanks.

Evolution works that way. The weak feed the strong.

The boys continued to exit the trees, crossing the Yard toward their warm beds. They'd stop for some food but then they'd sleep the night away. The Director kept his telescope focused on the trees until he came out. The kid stopped, shaded his eyes and glanced in the direction of the Director.

Danny Boy.

He was filled with the urge to mix a drink.

The Director questioned that acquisition, the young little redheaded hacker. He wasn't the typical candidate for his program. He was too smart. Too skilled. He needed kids that were physically fit. Not necessarily retarded, but he didn't need a genius, either. Just an ordinary kid that would follow the pack.

But that Mr. Jones persuaded him it was the right choice. Said the kid had enhanced brain activity that would open new avenues in the program. The Director knew Jones was only in it for himself, but he made sense.

The Director was reluctant because the program was delicate. There were so many unknown factors that a risk was dangerous. But if he didn't push into the unknown, the program would stagnate. In fact, if the problem – *the problem* – hadn't already started, he would've told Jones to go slam his head in the sand. But he needed some solutions, and, damnit, Jones made sense.

Reed created the problem. The Director needed to keep him around to solve it. So far, that wasn't working. He couldn't make Reed take the needle. It just wouldn't work if he didn't want it, if he wasn't open to it. If the Director punched it through his skull against his will, it would do more harm than good.

Danny Boy, though, could be the key. He'd already reached out to Reed on the beach. The Director knew it had something to do with the girl that confronted him in the first round.

She is the problem.

She was still hiding in the Nowhere. She was careful, sent the kid a clue. The Director didn't know what she had in mind, but he would keep following. And like all his enemies, she would be destroyed in the end. He rubbed the small hole in his forehead. After all, she couldn't escape. He knew where she was, he just couldn't reach her.

"Director?" the intercom squawked.

"Yes," he answered.

"We're ready."

The Director watched Danny cross the Yard. He was too sleepy, too damn cold, to do anything else. He'd go to his room and sleep off the experience for the next day. That would give the Director some time to figure out something for the next round.

He decided he'd mix that drink after all. Tomato juice and vodka mixed over three ice cubes. The Director stirred it with a stalk of celery. He took a swig, hit it with a dash of pepper. He crossed to the other side and stood over another telescope, this one pointed over Geezer Mansion. He munched the celery and looked at the water beyond.

He focused on the horizon. There was nothing but the sharp edge where water met the sky. He often imagined he could see land beyond it. But that was too far for a telescope. He hadn't seen it in many years.

"Director?" The voice was impatient. "We would like to begin—"

"Don't interrupt, Mr. Jackson."

The intercom remained silent.

The Director finished his drink. When he was good and ready, he went to the elevator to assume his position as Director of a revolutionary program.

The world would remember him long after they forgot Jesus.

21

PARKER LAY ON A BED. Mouth open. His lips were dry and cracked; his hair springing out in all directions.

A needle in his forehead.

A bald old man pulled aside a curtain that divided the room in half. "We're clear, Director."

"Thank you, Mr. Jackson."

The Director stood at the foot of the bed. The room was hospitable with soothing blue walls and the white curtain. There was a large glass window with half a dozen old men staring at them. At one time, the Investors stood in the room with the Director. Now, they were sequestered in the sound-proof booth. The Director needed peace and quiet when he worked his magic.

The Director would've banished them altogether, but these old men funded the project. The Director had proven to be a smart man in science and politics, so he let them watch. They didn't like it, but they were smart men, as well. They eventually stopped complaining and the Director eventually forgot they were there. Besides, he wanted them to see him perform the miracle. The Director was not a magician.

He was a savior.

Parker's eyes began rapid eye movement. The Director moved next to the bed. The eyes danced beneath the lids.

"Come on, now," the Director said, gently. "Come on."

Sometimes he lost them in the final leg of the journey; they just needed to connect the mind with the body. The sound of his voice gave them guidance. Previous patients said it was like a beacon bringing them home. It was very dark and directionless where they were; the mind drifting in unknown territory.

He cradled Parker's head, careful not to bump the wire protruding from the end of the needle that connected to a bedside computer. He brushed the wild hair back and stroked his cheeks, anything to stimulate the nervous system, give the mind direction.

"You're almost there." The eyes bounced faster. "Almost. Come on, now."

The eyes stopped.

Opened.

Parker stared at the Director without seeing him. Slowly, they came into focus. The Director pulled the needle from his forehead and stood back, gave him space. Parker sat up like a spring. He jerked his head around, surveying the room, eyes wide with wonder. He looked at his hands, turning them over, palm to back to palm.

"You did it," he said. "I've never felt... this good."

The men in the booth were waiting for a sign. Parker lifted his hand and waved. He saw them silently clap. The Director stopped Parker from standing.

"The password."

Parker jittered like a kid hopped up on energy drinks. He watched the men in the booth, mouthing out the words, *He did it, he did it!*

The Director squeezed his arms. "Password."

Parker focused on him. His lips moved but the word wouldn't come. He searched the Director's face for the answer. Mr. Jackson appeared from around the curtain, hiding a syringe behind his back. The Director glanced at him.

The old men settled.

"Last time," he said. "Password, please."

Panic jittered in Parker's stomach. The Director gave him a password before the journey to ensure he had made it. Without it, he couldn't be sure.

He knew the moment was about to pass by and he was about to lose everything he worked for. The Director let go of him and sat back. Parker sat still, thinking. A word was coming. He felt Mr. Jackson take a step and held up a finger to give him more time. He knew there was a needle behind his back. He knew if he didn't give the Director the word they would put him out and try it again. Next time, he might not return from that dark, drifting place.

He looked up.

Eyes bright.

"Foreverland."

The Director nodded. Smiled. "Foreverland, indeed."

He grabbed Parker's arm and held it up. They turned to the booth and the expectant faces inside.

"We've saved another one, gentlemen!" the Director shouted.

The old men entered the lab with cheers, shaking Parker's hand vigorously and patting him on the back. The Director stood back and watched. It was his favorite moment. The fruit of his labor. They brought Parker a glass of water and – in between sips – listened to him describe the details of his journey. They listened with bright eyes.

Mr. Jackson sheathed the syringe and stepped next to the Director.

"Check his vitals," the Director said. "And run him through cognition testing. If everything checks out, put him on the standard quarantine for six weeks. His body's in good shape, but we don't want him slipping away after all this hard work."

Parker touched his forehead, tenderly.

"Wait to remove the stent until the quarantine is complete," the Director added. "Just in case we need to go inside again. Otherwise, he won't need that anymore." He smiled at Mr. Jackson. "At least not for quite some time."

"And the garbage?"

"Hold it in the freezer for a few days, then the oven."

Mr. Jackson went behind the curtain.

The Director put his arm around Parker's shoulders and shook hands with all the men.

"We're saving the world one life at a time, gentlemen." He smiled through the scraggly beard. "One life at a time."

22

"Boom!" Sid slammed down the Jack of Spades. "That's game, you hole-headed freaks!"

The others threw their cards down. Sid swept them up. They were two days out of the Haystack and the damp cold was still inside them. Lying in bed just wasn't the same as letting the sun heat them up. They sat around the table killing time while they slow-roasted their bodies in the mid-afternoon heat.

Danny had been to the beach. He was expecting Reed to be warming up on the dune, but it was empty. He wanted to tell him.

Merry Christmas, Danny Boy.

It was from her. The red wrapping, the same bright red of her hair. The sand, he figured, maybe that meant the beach. *Meet her at the beach inside the needle? Was that it? Or meet Reed at the beach when he got back? And Merry Christmas?*

"Zinski!" Sid slapped Zin. "Wake up, boy. It's your deal."

Zin had his elbows on the table, staring at the mess of cards. He was yawning. Danny caught him shivering, earlier. Zin slowly unraveled the cards, stacking them all in one direction. He attempted to shuffle but they sprayed over the table.

"I think Zinski's heading for the Chimney, boys," Sid announced. "You feeling a little foggy, son? A little muddled in the noodle?"

Zin batted his arm away. "I'm waking up, fool."

"Oooooo..." Sid poked the cards out of his hands. "This dog's got some bite."

Zin carefully picked them up and began putting them back together. He was sluggish. Maybe he was tired, but he was breathing through his mouth. Vacancy lingered in his eyes now and then. How long before the Chimney took him?

Danny didn't want to think about it. He just got here and now Zin was looking more like Parker. Danny got up and stretched.

"Where you going?" Sid scooped up the cards as Zin dealt them.

"A walk, I guess."

"Maybe you're going to the beach with Reed."

"Why would I do that?" Danny snapped.

"I don't know. You been there a couple times, I thought maybe you two were dating."

"Give him a break," Danny said. "Who on this island is normal?"

"That's my point, you lunatic. He's standout crazy on an island of crazies. Right, Zinski?"

Zin blocked Sid's attempt to rustle his hair.

"Reed's in his room," Zin said. "I heard him in there before I came down."

"Well, good," Sid said. "Maybe they finally broke through his granite skull and he'll pop the needle like the rest of us." Sid played a card. "He thinks he's too good, that's his problem. He's special or something, all high and mighty that he can't damage his royal head. Friggin idiot, is what he is."

"You hit it right on the money." Danny stepped closer. "He's so stuck up that he would rather suffer than go inside the needle. All this time I thought he was trying to work something out or maybe he was just afraid we're all doing the wrong thing, but now you've made so much sense, Sid. He's an asshole! Why didn't I think of that?"

The game stopped. Sid tapped his cards on the table. "What's your problem, kid? You got a crush on Looney Tunes?"

"You ever stop to think why we're here, Sid?"

"We're here because we're sick." Sid nodded at the others. "This is a revolutionary method of healing, or did you miss orientation?"

"You buying that?" Danny looked around. "We've all had our memories sucked out and scrambled and we're marched into a prison cell and forced to get naked before they torture us until we stick a needle in our brains... that's what you're buying, no questions asked?"

"It's revolutionary, dummy."

"Or something else," Danny said.

Silence settled.

Sid tapped his cards into a neat stack and placed them face down. He was thinking. They all were. It was the line of questions that was always ignored. No one wanted to think about it. Even Danny.

But it was out there like the Ace of Spades.

"Okay, hotshot." Sid was expressionless. "Why don't you do something about it?"

Danny clenched his fists so no one would see him shaking. He didn't have any more balls to do something about it than any of the rest of them. He was reaching for the needle just like they were; swimming towards a bone-crushing waterfall.

Danny opened his hands. His fingers trembled.

"That's what I thought." Sid picked up his cards. "So why don't you shut your little cake hole and play some cards."

Sid shouted for the next play. Zin was staring, mouth open.

23

DANNY WENT to the beach a couple of times that week. Always empty.

He avoided Sid and company and they didn't seem to care. They had locked up first place so they didn't need Danny anymore. They went to the game room without him while he was lying in the middle of the Yard with an unobstructed view of the Chimney. The smoke stack was leaking fumes. It was hardly noticeable, just a thin discolored wisp.

Danny dozed off. It felt good to be so warm and alone. Sometimes when he felt that good, he forgot about the island. He thought about a time when he was sitting in the kitchen at home when a warm breeze made brightly colored curtains dance in the windowpane. It smelled like cut grass. And his mom was there with macaroni and cheese in a plastic bowl.

It didn't bother him that it probably wasn't his memory. He enjoyed it, nonetheless.

"Danny Boy?" A shadow passed over. "You all right, my boy?"

Danny refused to open his eyes. He was sick of being Mr. Jones's *boy*. "Yes, sir. Just enjoying the weather, that's all."

"Okay." Mr. Jones's laugh was grating. "Well, your camp is going to the cafeteria. I thought maybe you'd be with them."

"I'm not hungry."

"You're not sick, are you?" Mr. Jones's took a knee and his old-smelling hand landed on his forehead. It was soft, untouched by manual labor. "Perhaps you should get some rest in your room so you don't get sunburned."

"Maybe I'll do that." It was best not to argue. "I'm waiting for Zin, though."

"Isn't he in his room?"

"He's coming." Danny lied.

"Are you boys going to the game room?"

"No, sir. I think we'll do some exploring. Maybe hike over to the beach or something."

"That's a fine idea, Danny Boy. A little exercise is good for you. Maybe you could grab an apple before you head off. You know what they say, an apple a day..."

"Keeps the doctor away," Danny finished.

And Mr. Jones laughed. He grunted as he stood up but kept on laughing. "At a boy," he said. "You're a good boy, Danny Boy. A good one."

Mr. Jones smacked the grass off his hands. There was an awkward silence. Danny hadn't opened his eyes. Mr. Jones finally said, "Well, I'm going to turn in for a nap and sleep for the both of us, my boy." That was punctuated by a short laugh and Danny cringed. "If you need anything, ask one of the Investors and they'll be in touch with me."

"Yes, sir."

And the shadow was gone.

Mr. Jones was halfway across the Yard before a cart picked him up. It looked like Zin's Investor (Danny was getting accustomed to the subtle differences in gray hair). A few minutes later, another cart pulled up to the dormitory and the Investor (he didn't recognize this one) went inside.

Zin's curtains were closed. Only one other room had the curtains drawn: two to the left of Zin's. *Reed.* He was sleeping, too. Or hiding.

Danny could get at least one of them to go on a hike.

Or a ride.

"What are you doing?" Zin stopped short of the golf cart.

Danny shoved him onto the seat. The Yard was mostly empty. He swung around to the driver's seat and stomped on the accelerator. The cart jerked forward and Zin nearly fell off. He went around the dorm at full speed. Zin grabbed onto the roof.

"Hold on!" Danny shouted. "We're out of control, Zin! We're out of control!"

Zin's eyes were wide open for the first time since they'd finished the last round. A smile had returned, too. Danny saw it. They made the next turn even faster and Zin held on to keep from sliding off. No one saw them hit a narrow path and disappear into the trees.

Danny was breaking the rules. He was doing something bad. It felt *gooood*.

The wooded turns were hard to manage at full speed. They side-swiped a couple branches, gouging the side of the cart. But the laughter never stopped. They drove past the Chimney where, luckily, no one was around and they got to the path on the other side without being seen. Several minutes later and a close call with a tree, Danny slammed the brakes. Zin nearly went over the dashboard.

"There it is." Danny huffed.

The path ended a hundred yards away at steps leading to gigantic palms that framed doors at the top.

"Geezer Mansion?" Zin said.

Danny smiled wide. "Let's storm it."

"Reed's rubbing off on you."

"What are they going to do? Ground us? Stick a needle in our head?"

Zin thought about it, then was overcome with laughter. "Let's ditch the cart and ambush these old bastards."

Danny started up the cart again. They each hung a foot over the edge as they approached the end of the path. Just before they hit the opening, he gunned it and they leaped out, rolling into the scrubby palms. The boys crawled out in time to see the cart come to a stop at the bottom step.

Perfect landing.

"What are we doing?" Zin asked.

They were crouched just inside the tree line, watching the front doors. "We're going to see what the old men got inside there."

"No, I mean why are we hiding? It's not against the rules to be here."

"We hijacked a cart. There's a really pissed-off Investor back at the dorm."

They waited another five minutes.

When nothing happened, they stepped into the opening. The Mansion was more intimidating in the real than it was flying overhead when it was Foreverland. It was only one story tall. The walls were white and smooth with a wide soffit that would keep anyone from climbing on top. The trees were kept twenty feet away, preventing anyone from climbing up one and leaping to the roof. The infrequent windows were a hundred feet apart, interspersed with single garage doors for the golf carts.

But it was long.

In both directions, the building was a solid barrier that extended all the way to each coast, cutting off the southern tip from the rest of the island. That much he had seen in Foreverland, and it was dead-on.

"You believe this?" Danny said. "It looks like a prison wall to keep us out."

"Or keep them in. You got any ideas besides bum-rushing the front door?"

They stared at the doors. There was nothing but the sounds of the jungle all around.

"If we time it right—"

"I'm kidding. That idea sucks," Zin said. "They'll jolt our trackers before we're two steps inside."

"How do you know?"

"You want to try it?" Zin stepped to the side and gestured.

Danny hadn't given it much thought. He wasn't serious about

getting inside, but now that they were on the doorstep, it didn't sound so bad. Danny looked in both directions. He started to his left.

"Where you going?" Zin asked.

"Looking for a mouse hole. What else?"

"You scared of getting smoked?" Danny asked.

They'd been walking for twenty minutes. Zin faded in and out, not like he was deep in thought but more like he was just absent, staring at the ground while his body was on autopilot. Then he'd come back and they'd be talking again. Danny wasn't all that sure Zin even knew it was happening.

He didn't snap his fingers or clap. That was something Sid would do. Danny just gave him space because Zin always came back and then they'd pick up where they left off. Most of the time, they just walked. The Mansion was nothing but a long wall with an occasional window and not one of them accidentally left open.

Danny was about to ask the question again when Zin answered.

"No," he said. "I'm not. I just want it to be over."

Danny gave that answer a good twenty steps. "You giving up hope?"

"Since when was there hope? Like it or not, Danny Boy, we all get sucked into the needle. You want to swim against the current, you're just going to get tired. Just sit back and enjoy the ride, that's all you can do, son. And hope you come out the other side."

"Where's that?"

"The Chimney, where else?"

They reached the end of the building. It dropped off a sheer cliff about thirty feet. The Mansion was built flush against it. And just in case someone figured out a way to get down, tangles of barbed wire extended down to the water.

"Figured as much," Zin said.

"Man, they don't want us in there. Think there's any reason to go to the other side?"

"Not unless you want to see a mirror image of this."

The breeze was nice. They stayed there until the sweat evaporated from their cheeks. Five minutes back down the trail, they were wiping sweat off their brows. Zin seemed present, although he wasn't talking.

"What'd you think they're doing in there?" Danny asked.

"Healing, I guess."

"How, though?"

"Who knows?"

"That's what I mean," Danny said. "They tell us they're healing, but we don't see anyone after they've graduated."

"Maybe we're all infected with something, it's a quarantine."

"You believe that?"

"Hell, I don't know, Danny Boy. You think salmon wonder why they're swimming up stream?"

"They should. Bears eat them."

Zin shrugged. A few seconds later, he glazed over. He'd been on the island much longer than Danny and asked all the same questions, made all the same arguments when he first woke up in the Chimney. But you bang your head with a hammer long enough, you come to realize it only hurts when you swing. He'd put the hammer down long before Danny arrived. Explanations only made his head hurt.

"What's it like?" Danny asked.

Zin still seemed absent, but then coughed. "What?"

"Fading out like that, what's it feel like? Where do you go?"

He thought about it. "It's like... becoming hollow."

"You mean like a log?"

"Kind of," Zin said. "I'm tired, but not the regular tired. It's more like I'm just not connected with my body like I'm supposed to be." He swung his hands around like his identity was a ghost floating around him. "I am out there and I'm attached to this body by these invisible filaments, like a puppet." He began to zone. "And they're breaking, Danny Boy."

"What happens when they all break?"

"I guess I go to Foreverland."

"Why do you say that?"

"Because that's where I want to be. I don't remember much of anything when I'm back here. When we go inside the needle, that's when I feel like myself. I get my life back and it feels good. You know what I mean."

"But that's a computer program, you said so yourself."

"So, what's the difference?"

"It's not real. And if you're not real, you're dead."

"Like I said, Danny Boy, why fight it."

Zin went into the zone and didn't come back out, almost like the argument exhausted him. Danny could see the cart still parked at the steps, exactly where they left it. He couldn't stand the look on Zin's face, remembered how the joy ride brought him back. Maybe joy rides would reattach those filaments and Zin wouldn't go away so much. Maybe he just needed to live life in the real world and make some new memories. He could reverse the tide.

He was about to ask Zin if he wanted to drive the cart this time when the front doors opened.

Danny yanked Zin into the trees.

Just as the garage door to the left of the steps began to open, someone came down the steps. He didn't take them one at a time and he wasn't hunched over a cane. The kid went three at a time, hit the ground with both feet and sprang into a somersault!

Danny didn't recognize him because he'd never seen him with that much energy. He'd been a zombie from the day Danny woke up.

But Zin knew him.

"Parker?"

The kid was climbing onto the driver's seat.

"Parker, dude." Zin said. "Is that you?"

Parker stood, slowly. The boundless energy dissipated. He looked from Zin to Danny and back again. The knot in his throat bobbed up and down.

"Danny Boy, look. It's Parker! He's right here. Oh, man." Zin grabbed Parker's hand and shook. "Me and Danny Boy here were just talking about never seeing anyone that graduated and here you are... man, it's good to see you!"

The handshake shook Parker's whole body. The zombie look that Danny associated with Parker was gone. He was confused but completely focused. He looked exactly the same, except for the hair. The wild shag was gone, replaced by a proper haircut above the ears and combed to the side. The part was so sharp and neat that it looked like a white line on the side of his head.

"I almost didn't recognize you, man." Zin tried to muss up the hair but Parker jerked away. Zin didn't notice the rage that flashed across his face. "Are you living inside the Mansion? Is that where the graduates go?" Zin turned to Danny. "Holy crap, you know what that means? They're not lying, Danny Boy. They're really healing us, I mean look at Parker. I never seen this kid so... alive."

One thing Danny couldn't argue with, he looked good. Half an hour ago, Danny thought there was a chance they might be chucking the graduates into an oven that smoked out the top of the Chimney. Now, there was proof they weren't.

"Can you get us inside?" Danny looked inside the open garage. "We'll hide in the garage until night, what do you say?"

"Oh, hell yeah," Zin said. "How about it, Parker? Maybe you can give us a sneak preview?"

Parker's eyes widened. The knob was bobbing non-stop. He started backing up the steps and tripped backwards.

"I don't know, Zin." Danny watched Parker crab-walk his way up the steps. "Something isn't right."

Zin was catching on. "You remember us, Parker?"

When Zin took a step towards him, he crawled faster.

"That's enough."

The deep authoritative voice sent shivers through Danny's guts. A round old man was at the front doors. He stepped aside and two old men came out to help Parker inside. The round old man kept Danny and Zin frozen in place with a baggy-eyed stare.

"Danny Boy?" Mr. Jones came out. "What are you doing here, son?"

The gentle, grandfatherly look that distinguished Mr. Jones from all the other old men quickly darkened. Danny experienced another familiar feeling.

Getting caught.

24

DANNY LIFTED the desk onto his bed and sat on top of it. It was midday and most people were in the game room or the cafeteria. Only three guys were in the Yard playing catch with a long-distance disc.

Danny hadn't been outside in three days.

Mr. Jones put him on room-restriction for two days and threatened to send him to the Director if he got to misbehaving like that again. None of that bothered Danny. To prove it, he volunteered to stay in his room a third day. Who knows, maybe he'd stay there until they dragged him to the Haystack for the third round.

He spent the day staring at a spot on the ceiling and counting his breath, practicing his focus like Zin taught him. *You'll need it to control yourself when you're inside the needle. Find your point of existence and breathe into it.*

There were a dozen old men that were eventually lured out of the Mansion when they got caught. When Mr. Jones got the full story – how they hijacked the golf cart and conspired to break inside – his face turned dark red. A jagged vein throbbed on his right temple. Danny thought it might wriggle out and explode.

Zin's Investor, Mr. Stevens, didn't change color. He arrived ten minutes later and calmly took Zin aside while Mr. Jones ushered

Danny down the steps with a stranglehold on his arm. Anger transformed his feeble task-master into a thundering disciplinarian. They went to the dormitory on the very same cart that Danny swiped.

"You love trouble, Danny Boy," he said. "You have to have self-control. Chaos leads to anarchy, my boy. It'll lead you down the wrong path. It led you here."

Thought I was here for healing.

Mr. Jones strangled the steering wheel. "There are much worse places than here, I promise. You go back to trouble and you'll find out."

Mr. Jones was telling Danny more than he should've and Danny knew it. Most thirteen year old boys would've been reduced to a trembling mess under the glare of those father figures, but not Danny. It was thrilling. And the more Mr. Jones frowned – the more he shook his finger – the more fun Danny was having. He was forced to look away before he began laughing. Mr. Jones thought it was because he felt shame and, out of compassion, left the boy alone. He was hopeful Danny was punishing himself and that maybe, just maybe, he was mentoring this boy to a better life.

But authority doesn't scare me, Mr. Jones.

And neither did Sid.

Self-preservation should've instilled some fear in him since all the above could cause a great deal of pain. Maybe worse. Danny knew he was good with computers, that perhaps he'd been arrested for hacking a federal agency, and that he loved trouble. It was a start.

He also knew something else: Parker was alive and healthy. Maybe a little confused but, besides the creepy haircut, he looked good. That ended speculation that the old men were using them for firewood. But Parker didn't look excited to help them out.

Something had changed.

Danny had a future date with the Director, he was sure of it. And it might be sooner than later if he didn't curb his behavior and he had no plans to do that. He was just starting to flex his muscles and he liked it.

The boys had stopped throwing the disc and headed inside. Someone else was crossing the Yard.

Reed finally left his room.

Danny's self-imposed restriction came to an end.

25

REED FELT SMALLER, frailer. Vulnerable.

I'm breaking.

Reed stayed in the room because he didn't trust himself. He craved the sun's warmth but the ocean would be so near. If he went to the beach, all he'd have to do was step into the water and let the undertow sweep him out. It was moments like this – moments that revealed cracks in his will – that made him ask the question.

Why?

Why keep going?

Sleep came in short bursts. His body continuously ached. Dreams were fitful. He had delusions of falling, of shattering, of dying. He dreamed of drowning, over and over and over. Sometimes waking up gulping air. He didn't find a restful night.

Until she came.

He was in a field of soybeans. The rows ran over the hills like a sea of green. He walked them and picked the heads off foxtail and stripped the seeds to chew on the bitter stalks. When the sun had peaked, someone appeared in the row ahead of him.

Her hair was below the shoulders, a halo of cherry red. She walked toward him in a fluttering white summer dress. She took his hand and led him to a lone elm tree in the middle of the field. Her smell was like a dewy morning. Her laughter, pure joy.

It was a dream. A long one. A safe one.

He lay back on the grassy knoll. The grass tickled his shoulders. "If I take the needle, we'll be together," he said. "I won't have to dream anymore."

"If you take the needle, you'll never see me again."

"Why?"

"I don't know." She looked off. The dappled shade mottled her complexion. "I just know that you must wait. You must resist."

"I don't think I can anymore."

"You must. Not for you and me, but for everyone on the island and everyone that will come. This is bigger than us."

"But this is just a dream. Maybe I'm imagining this. Imagining you. Maybe none of this is true."

She ran her finger over the bridge of his nose, touched his lips. "It's all a dream. We just need to wake up."

He took her hand and traced the blue veins on her wrist.

"If any of this matters," he whispered, "then why can't I remember you?"

"You will, Reed."

"But I don't even know your name."

She took his hand and pressed it to her chest. Her pulse beat steadily into his palm. He slid his hand into her hair. The sun was low and the shadows hid her face as he drew her closer. Her cheek was warm against his.

The sun set.

Reed didn't understand dreams. He might be delusional. All his bravado misguided. His suffering, useless.

But it was all he had.

When he woke, he returned to the beach.

The water lapped against his ankles.

He walked the length of the north shore until he reached the rocky outcroppings. He went no deeper into the water, just enough to keep his feet wet. He turned back, his footprints washed away.

His life was like his footprints: no trace of his past. Everything he could remember he disregarded as chatter. None of it was true, there was no reason to give it space. He just walked and walked, one foot in front of the other. The footprints dissolved behind him.

Up ahead, Danny was on the dune. He looked different. His chest was out, his gaze patiently set upon the horizon. He paid no attention to Reed's approach.

Reed plunked down and leaned back on his elbows. He was tempted to take his shirt off and let the sun warm him but didn't want Danny to see what had become of him. His appetite had waned and it was beginning to show.

Danny sat next to him. The wind scoured their shins with sand.

And the waves rolled.

"They're healing us, Reed. Just like they promised."

He told him about Parker, how he looked, how he acted. He wasn't dead, not a zombie. He was vibrant, happy to be alive.

"You believe that?" Reed spoke just loud enough to be heard.

Danny took a breath, started to answer. He picked up a shell, instead, rubbing the shiny backside with his thumb. He wanted to say yes, he believed it. They were doing exactly what they told us and there was the proof. Parker was alive. *He's alive! They're not killing us.*

But are they healing us?

It was what they all wanted to believe. And he saw it with his own eyes.

He started to say *yes* again, but stood up. He walked to the water and threw the shell sidearm, skipping it on the thin water racing over the hardpacked sand. He remembered throwing flat rocks on a pond and counting the number of skips when he was a little kid. He was fishing with his dad.

Someone's dad.

Someone's memory.

He'd come to the beach to bring good news: they were being saved.

Reed shattered it with three words. Cut right to the heart of Danny's doubt.

He picked up another shell, this one as big as his hand, and carried it back to the dune. He rubbed the inside of the shell, the pearly white inside. Half a clam.

Where was the other half?

Danny picked up sand, let it sift between his fingers. It scattered in a gust of wind.

"I remember hiking," he said, grabbing another handful. "Hunting and fishing and fighting. Once, I got stuck on a trail without water for a day and nearly dehydrated before I got back. My ankle was twisted, too. Lost ten pounds on that trip."

He smacked his empty hands, the grains of sand lost on the dune.

"The thing is, I know none of those memories are mine. I don't hike and I don't fish."

Reed nodded.

"What I'm trying to say is, maybe you don't know her. Maybe she's someone else's memory and you're just hanging onto it and you're wasting your time resisting."

"I *don't* remember her."

"Then what are you doing?"

Reed looked far away. "I dream about her."

Danny hadn't dreamed once since he woke up on the island. In fact, he always woke up with a buzzing noise, like static. And it had gotten louder since the second round. Was the needle killing their dreams?

"I didn't see her in the last round. But she gave me something. She left a gift just before it ended, or at least I think it was from her. It was wrapped in red paper, the same color of her hair. It said *Merry Christmas, Danny Boy.* And inside was sand."

Reed tensed.

Describing her made him cringe.

He didn't like to think of her inside Foreverland. Not when he was outside.

"What do you think it means?" Danny asked.

"It's a clue."

"A box of sand, but what does it mean?"

"You need to find her. It'll make sense the next time."

"Why don't you go with me and help find her?"

Reed didn't bother responding. He'd been through enough pain and suffering that a bit of guilt wasn't going to get him to take the needle.

"Why is she hiding?" Danny asked.

"I don't know," he said, quickly. "But you need to find her."

Danny played with another shell, sifted more sand. Reed didn't have anything else to tell him so he got up, whacking the sand off his legs. He started back over the dune without saying goodbye.

"Danny Boy!"

Danny turned around but Reed was sitting still, facing the ocean. Maybe Danny imagined him shouting his name. The waves were so loud. He left him on the dune, all alone. But even when he was sitting next to him, he seemed so alone. Hollowed out by the suffering, a shell of a boy.

And the waves rolled.

26

"KEEP YOUR CLOTHES ON, GENTLEMEN," Mr. Clark said. "You've earned a reprieve for your masterful skills in the game room."

The boys gathered outside the Haystack and gave a rousing cheer. The Investors applauded. Sid lifted his arms and strutted around. He stood next to Mr. Clark, jutting like a rooster. Mr. Clark pushed him gently back toward the boys.

"Yes," he said. "Your appetite for killing in a virtual environment was unparalleled."

The Investors chuckled but the boys didn't catch the sarcasm. They were still slapping hands.

"As you know, you will be ineligible for another hiatus until the fifth round, so I encourage you to enjoy the reprieve. Please, take advantage of this gift bestowed upon you by the Director."

Again, only the Investors noticed the sarcasm.

"You may enter the Haystack and your prospective cells." He opened the door.

They lined up single file, as usual, but there was no need for the Investors to guide them with a hand on the shoulder. The damp cold was nothing to fear, only a temporary nuisance.

Danny found his cell and Mr. Jones closed it for him with a curt nod and a quick exit. Danny blew into his cupped hands watching the others find their place. He wasn't going to lie on the concrete until the skylights went out. Zin entered his cell with his head bowed. He dropped to the floor and crossed his legs, falling into his typical breathing pattern. Reed stepped into his cell alone. His Investor wasn't with him.

"Zin." Danny bent down. "Zin, hey!"

Zin took a long breath and turned to Danny. A slight smile curled on his lips. That was all Danny wanted to see.

The Haystack door closed and the room became a shade darker. Only one Investor remained inside. Mr. Smith paced the aisle and stopped in front of Reed's cell.

"Reed, you are ineligible for the reprieve, son. I'll need you to—"

"Wait a second," Danny said. "He's part of this camp, he gets the same treatment as the rest of us."

Mr. Smith waited for the interruption to end. "I'll need you to hand me your clothes."

"Listen to me, dammit!" Danny screamed. "You're being unfair!"

Mr. Smith was unperturbed. His gaze was trained on Reed like crosshairs.

"He deserves it, Danny Boy," Sid chimed from across the aisle. "What the hell has he done to get reprieve? I'll tell you what: *squat*. He's done nothing, Danny Boy. He's a waste of time. They should put a bullet through his skull instead of a needle."

"Mr. Smith, please." Danny hugged the bars. "Reed needs the reprieve, sir. You're going to break him. He's not going to take the needle, you know that. There's got to be another way. Have a heart, man."

Mr. Smith's stare did not waver.

Reed stripped off his shirt. His shoulder blades knifed from his back and every one of his vertebrae could be played like a xylophone.

"Mr. Smith..." Danny said.

"Ah-hah-hahaha!" Sid bellowed. "Look at the goon! It's Halloween in cell six, boys. Reed's got an eating disorder, the crazy mutt!"

Reed slipped off his pants. His pelvis poked from his hips.

Danny couldn't watch. He'd sat with him on the beach, but seeing him bared to the world told of every second he'd endured since he'd been on the island. Even his face looked like a barren skull in the shadows.

Danny took off his shirt.

"Hey, look at Danny Boy!" Sid laughed. "He's copying his boyfriend. I knew the two were gay for each other."

Mr. Smith finally looked Danny's way. He muttered something. By the time Danny had his pants off, the door to the Haystack swung open and a crowd of Investors rushed inside.

"Danny Boy." Mr. Jones grabbed the bars on his cell. "What are you doing, my boy? You don't need to do this, you have a reprieve. You can't worry what the others are doing, you need to keep yourself in line, son."

Danny removed his underwear and began folding his clothes.

"You're a good boy, Danny Boy. You're a good boy. This is so..." Mr. Jones looked at the other old men. "Danny! Look at me! LOOK AT ME, BOY!"

Danny turned his back.

"Stop this madness, son. This is just so unnecessary... I mean, you don't need to go through the suffering. You don't need..." He chuckled nervously, then reached through the bars but Danny was out of reach.

The other Investors murmured. "It'll be all right," they said. "He'll get right, Mr. Jones, don't worry. The kid will get right. Let things go at their own pace, you can't make him do it."

Reed placed his clothes at the foot of the cell door. Mr. Smith retrieved them and left. The Investors consoled Mr. Jones until he let go of the cage. He muttered on the way out, leaving Danny's clothes behind. When the door closed, the Haystack was quiet.

"You're as crazy as he is, Danny Boy," Sid said. "You're a pair of cracked pots, son. A pair of them."

Reed turned his back on Danny and started a breathing routine.

The skylights began to close and darkness settled.

Danny began pacing to combat the chill running up and down his body. The camp began talking in half-hushed tones. He didn't care.

It was impulse. He didn't plan on joining Reed, but he just didn't

want to follow the rest of them into the needle. It was too much celebration, they were embracing it too happily. *Someone needs to resist.*

But the lights had gone down and he was already shivering.

The cages whirred. The needles began to lower. The excitement
had been dampened by the weirdness of Danny's voluntary nudity, but
it didn't slow any of them from reaching. The lines whined as they
were stretched to the floor.

Zin was still sitting, unaware that the needle had dropped into the
cage until it lowered to the top of his head. He reached up, mechanically, and began to fit it around his head.

"Zin," Danny said. "Come back, all right. Don't... just come back."

Reed still had his back to Danny. And Zin was reaching for the
needle and Danny realized it might be for the last time. If he got
smoked on this round, Danny would be completely alone.

"Zin!" Danny just wanted him to hear it, to make sure. "You
hear me?"

"Isn't that lovely, boys?" Sid's voice echoed in the dark. "Danny
Boy's afraid for Zinski. Hot damn, I'm tearing up over here. It's
breaking my heart."

"Zin." Danny tried to keep it quiet, but it was impossible. "Just
look at me, man. Just, don't smoke out. Not yet."

"He's a goner, Danny Boy," Sid said. "Say goodbye."

"Shut up!" Danny rushed the front of his cell and reached into the
dark aisle. "SHUT THE HELL UP, SID!"

Silence fell as heavy as the cold air. Faint rustling told Danny that
none of the boys had gone inside the needle, yet. They were listening.
A drop of water fell from one of the sprinklers.

Sid laughed. "You think you're a man, now? You're Danny BOY,
son. You better mind your manners."

"I quit, Sid. I ain't never stepping foot inside the game room
again."

"I don't need you."

"You were nothing before I got here. You and the rest of these
clowns were just running around in circles until I saved your asses
again and again because you're an idiot. It's over, now. All you dumb-
asses, you're on your own. I'm done."

The silence grew heavy, again. It was undercut by growling.

"I hope you learned how to control the pain response, Danny Boy," he said. "Because when you get inside the needle, I'm going to pull you apart like a bug, son. I'm going to pour acid in your eyeballs and piss in the holes." Sid laughed, but no one joined him. It was as dark as the room around them. "You think it's torture in here, wait until I get a hold of you in Foreverland."

Danny was grateful for the cloak of darkness, but it couldn't hide the shivers in his voice. "I'm not going inside the needle."

"Of course not." And Sid laughed again. It carried down to the floor and faded off. Soon, the entire room no longer moved except for the heavy mouth-breathing. They were all inside the needle.

It was just Danny and Reed.

"Danny Boy?" Zin's voice was scratchy, just above a whisper. "I'm coming back."

Danny leaned his head against the bars.

The big fan clicked.

And the breeze came down.

"What are you doing?" Reed had turned around. Danny couldn't make out his expression in the dark but he could see him latched onto the bars facing him. "This is my fight, not yours."

"I'm not letting you do this alone."

"It doesn't prove anything."

"Then follow your own advice!" Danny shouted. "You're not doing anything by staying here."

Reed remained at the side of his cell. He dropped his hands and went back to the center. Danny could hear his breath fall back into rhythm. He was not going to waste words.

Danny began pacing again. The cold crept into his ankles. The fan was on but not the sprinklers. With the rest of the camp wearing clothes, maybe they didn't want to keep them soaked. Still, it was plenty uncomfortable, especially since Sid promised something much worse on the inside. Danny wasn't sure he could control the pain response. He hadn't even tried.

Zin will protect me.

But would he even remember Danny? Parker didn't seem to know anything near the end. Perhaps his memory completely evaporated.

An hour elapsed.

Danny was cold but without the mist it was easier to stay in rhythm. If it remained this way, he could tolerate the suffering like Reed. Maybe the hole would even heal. Maybe the others would see the wisdom in fighting the system and they could form a revolt. If everyone refused the needle, they could make a difference.

That's when the door opened.

He knew it wasn't Mr. Jones, unless he hurt his knee in the last hour. An old man appeared in the darkened aisle dragging a bum leg. Mr. Smith passed Danny's cell. He was carrying tubes attached by a cord that dangled and swayed between his hands.

"Reed." The old man stopped at his cell. "I need to see your hands, son."

Reed took a deep breath and turned.

"What're you doing?" Danny said. He was ignored.

Mr. Smith held up the tubes. "Put your hands through the bars."

"Don't do it, Reed," Danny said. "They can't make you."

But Reed voluntarily went to the front of his cell and offered his hands. Mr. Smith slipped the tubes over his thumbs and adjusted clips on the sides. He stepped back and watched the cell begin to collapse.

"The pressure will increase over time, Reed. Please don't be stubborn. You're not accomplishing anything by the needless suffering."

The cell continued to shrink until it sandwiched Reed, pressing deeply into his chest and back. Mr. Smith stared at Reed. They were unflinching in their hatred. Until the pressure clamped down on his knuckles and pinched the webbing between his thumb and finger, pressing on a nerve that buckled his knees. He would've fallen had the bars not held him tightly.

The lucid gear dropped just inches from the top of his head.

"Stop this," Danny said. "This isn't fair, he doesn't want the needle. You can't do this. YOU CAN'T DO THIS!"

But they could. They did.

Mr. Smith began to take his leave.

"Come back here, you old bastard!" Danny reached through the bars, losing sight of the limping man. "YOU HEARTLESS BASTARD!"

Light cut through the Haystack as the door at the end of the aisle opened. Danny turned away as it hit him in the face, but for a moment he saw Reed's quivering hands and the shackles squeezing his thumbs. He didn't see the expression of agony. But he heard it.

Danny paced back and forth. Reed's pained breathing was worse than anything inside the Haystack. He'd rather they come put the thumb shackles on him.

There was nothing he could do.

He had to find the girl.

Danny pulled the lucid gear from the top. It whined as the cord unreeled to the floor. He dropped hard on the concrete and pulled it quickly over his head. The needle numbed his forehead, searching for the stent.

Before it jolted inside his brain, before he arched off the pavement, he muttered something to Reed. He doubted he would hear it.

"I'm sorry."

And then the needle took him.

27

DANNY VISUALIZED A SPOT.

He imagined it was a glowing dot floating in the darkness where he was drifting. He put his breath into it. *One. Two. Three.*

It abolished thoughts.

It brought focus. Presence.

And when he felt his body forming near the sundial, he willed it to become numb. There would be no pain when Sid pulled out his intestines. He would melt like water and blow like wind. Nothing would hurt him.

The grass was beneath him. Sunlight and wind. And the screaming of engines.

Danny opened his eyes.

An asphalt racetrack circled the Yard and rocket-shaped cars roared around it, disappearing into the trees. The engines called from the jungle and soon wound around him before reentering the Yard behind him and making another lap.

He was alone. Sid was nowhere to be seen. Maybe he got bored. Or perhaps he was setting a trap. Didn't matter. Danny needed to get to the business of finding a Christmas present. And it would be much easier if he was invisible when he did it.

He put both hands on the sundial and felt the power vibrate through his arms. He pictured the focal dot and willed transparency to enter his body. What was his body other than data, really? Danny knew how to handle data. It helped to think of it that way, that he was computer code that needed to be manipulated. He breathed in and out, in and out.

Opened his eyes.

He was still there, but he could see the sundial through his hands.

"Translucency. Okay, close enough."

He wasn't invisible, but he'd faded enough that no one would notice unless they were looking right at him. He crouched down and – as the rocket cars came around – leaped into the sky.

Danny hovered just inside a cloud.

The gray haze on the horizon seemed closer than it did the last time. No one would see him, especially being half-faded. As long as no one flew into him, he could stay there all day. Since it seemed everyone was part of the race, he took his time.

The track serpentined around the entire island – through the trees and over the cliffs. The rocket cars even made a loop into the water. Occasionally, one would fire a weapon and there would be an explosion and parts flying.

The only other oddity about the island was tiny lights twinkling on top of random trees. He floated around the cloud and willed his vision to zoom on one of the trees. It appeared to be a star set on top, along with smaller lights strung from the branches.

Christmas trees. They're all Christmas trees.

It would've been an easy clue to follow, but there was easily a hundred of them scattered over the island. Even one that appeared to be floating out at sea. He cloud-hopped around the sky, zooming in on several trees but couldn't make out any substantial differences.

"I'm going to have to go down," he muttered to no one. Then said like he was the one answering, "Yep, going to have to go down."

The sun was already falling toward the horizon. Time in Foreverland went faster than it did in the flesh. He had wasted half of Foreverland's day in the Haystack. Maybe he already blew it.

He dropped from the sky and hit the ground like a stone. He was able to quell the pain from the impact. He was getting the hang of it. He dusted off the dirt and stared at the twenty foot tall Christmas tree that shaded a dozen red-wrapped gifts. Nothing else was around. There was no time to waste.

Danny began ripping open presents.

He had been to nearly fifty trees. Each one had a pile of gifts that he tore open to find more sand. By the time he got to the tree in front of the Mansion, the sun had dropped below the trees and the sky had turned orange and was quickly dimming. He wasn't going to get to all the trees, but he couldn't sit around and think about it.

This tree was near the entrance. A golf cart had been abandoned exactly where Danny and Zin had left one a week earlier. Seemed odd, but Danny was focused on the tree and the dozen gifts beneath it. He tore through them, sifting sand from each one, finding nothing new. He crouched down to bounce back into the sky to find the next one when lights inside the Mansion caught his eye.

One of the double doors was open. An enormous tree glittered inside the dark entrance.

Danny climbed the steps. The doors had been vandalized with spray-painted graffiti and skateboard stickers. The hinges creaked as he pushed the door open. The tree stood beyond the foyer against the far back window with a view to the ocean where lights twinkled. More trees.

He sighed. He'd never get to all of them. She was killing him. And yet he couldn't forget what Reed must be going through. He opened the dozen presents to find more sand. Danny threw the last one across the room. He grabbed the tree and launched it through the window. Shards of glass exploded.

His curses echoed down the empty halls.

But he was wasting time. Every second that was wasted was a second that Reed endured needless suffering.

He went back to the front doors. There was a narrow closet door on both sides of the foyer, both closed. But the one on the right had a sticker. Danny stopped.

It was a Spitfire sticker; the flaming head smiling at him.

One sticker. The rest of the room was in order, just the one sticker.

Merry Christmas.

Sand.

Christmas on the beach.

Tell me your favorite Christmas.

Reed asked Danny on the beach and Danny remembered the thing he wanted most in the world: the half-pipe covered in stickers. But no one would have known that, he didn't tell anyone about it. He wasn't even sure it was his memory. But there it was, a Spitfire sticker in an otherwise pristine Mansion without a half-pipe in sight.

Danny put his hand on the door knob. He turned it slowly and cracked the door open. An odd grainy light spilled out. It crept out in misty tendrils. Danny tried to slam it closed but the foggy light wrapped around him. Liquefied him.

And sucked him inside.

28

THE MIST HAD TEXTURE.

Grainy particles, scratching.

Momma?

A boy. He sounded sad, crying for—

First! I'm first!

On the right. Someone excited, someone—

You go first!

Where am I?

How long until we eat? I'm hungry.

The voices bunched together, above and below. They were everywhere, but nothing came out of the gray mist. The bodiless words whizzing by like passing trains.

The mist thickened.

The grains pelted his face like sand. He looked at his hands, saw his feet and realized he was standing on something solid. The wind began pulling away, revealing a white floor.

A spot of color developed ahead of him. It was soft and faded, like a beacon appearing in a blizzard. It was pink.

Then red.

Bright red.

The mist swirled out like an ever-widening hurricane. And then it was gone. He was in a round room, walls white. And she was sitting in the center, hands on her lap. The bright red hair cut below the shoulders.

"I'm sorry for the inconvenience," she said, softly. "But you couldn't know where you were going. He would've known, he would've followed... he was watching."

"Who?"

"Whoever runs... Foreverland."

"The Director?"

She shrugged.

Her eyes were large, the pupils engorged and the irises brilliant green. She was almost cartoonish, the colors saturated.

The room was barren, except for the chair she was sitting on, legs crossed, hands on lap. She stood up, her bare feet touched the floor silently; toenails the same color as her hair.

Olly-olly-oxen-free! The voices soared through the wall.

"Where are we?" Danny asked.

"The boys call this the Nowhere," she said. "It's outside... the eyes of Foreverland. Outside the reach of he who... is Foreverland."

"Those are memories?"

"In a way..." Her cheeks suddenly matched the color of her hair and toenails. "I know you have questions and I'll answer them the best I can, but the truth is... I don't know much and we don't have much time..." She wrapped her arms around her chest like she was hugging herself. "I'm sorry. It's just... he hurts so much... and you're our only chance... and I never..."

She trailed off. She had difficulty finding words, like she had to search for them.

"You mean Reed?" Danny asked.

She nodded, hugging herself again.

"Who are you?" Danny shook his head. *That sounded rude.* "I'm sorry, I just don't know much about Reed. Or you."

She thought, staring blankly. "I don't really know, Danny Boy. I just woke up here..."

Danny remembered the confusion of waking up on the paper-covered table and Mr. Jones staring at him with his white lab coat. He didn't know anything before that moment. She had the same experience, only she woke up in Foreverland.

Is she real? Definitely rude. *But is she a memory? Reed's memory? But she's here, alive. She had to be something other than a memory, right?*

"If you're in here, how do you know about Reed?" Danny asked.

"I see the boys' thoughts. I see what they bring in from the island... I know the suffering they go through... before the needle."

That's how she knew about the half-pipe at Christmas. She saw it in my thoughts.

"Then you know Reed is—"

She began shaking her head and rocking in her self-hug.

Damn.

She was still muttering about Reed. Danny stopped her. "How can I help?"

Her oversized eyes were glassy. Her brow furrowed when she pointed at the chair.

"Sit."

Danny went to the chair. When he sat down, a desk appeared from the floor and circled all the way around him. Several keyboards appeared.

"You don't really need the keyboards or the monitors... but you're familiar with that medium... so that's what you'll start with."

She glared at him.

"You need to understand... I'm as much a prisoner in here as you are out there."

"But Foreverland is a computer program."

"I don't know what this is, Danny Boy. You need to help us find out... what it is."

"How?"

She lifted her arms and the walls flickered like the entire room was a monitor. The walls were blue with white puffy clouds, like the wallpaper of a computer desktop. Danny brushed his fingers over the keyboard and felt something for the first time since arriving.

A familiar thrill.

A bead of sweat trickled down his cheek. Strange, this was an illusion but his body believed it.

It took several minutes to get familiar with the 360-degree monitor and multiple keyboards, but the keystrokes were the same as any computer. He accessed the mainframe and was soon sneaking around the security firewalls. The system was like one he'd never encountered. The code seemed to evolve like a living organism. Maybe it was a program that believed it was alive, just like he was sweating.

He synchronized several programs and let them run like digital wrecking balls smashing holes in databases and security code. He spun on his chair to unravel the next layer of the firewall. The security system operated like a virtual vault that continued to change the combination. Danny learned its tendencies and began to solve the complex code. His fingers blurred across the keyboards but it wasn't fast enough.

I'm inside my head. I don't need the keyboards.

He began to call out commands instead of typing and they were executed just as if he'd pecked them on the keyboard. He swiveled around to watch geometric shapes of computer code connect, shift and reconnect like organic chemistry. He stopped seeing the numbers and letters and began to see the computer language in three-dimensional objects that began to float off the walls. He shouted at them, made them change direction, change form, merge or divide. He was looking for the arrangement that would open the door to the system that was driving Foreverland.

Still, he was behind the evolving firewall that was always half a step ahead.

In the mind.

He focused inwardly, forming his next command into a sharpened thought instead of a spoken word. Then he created another one. And another. The shapes began to move again. Silently, Danny looked around the room and sent the thought-commands out. The room was in continuous movement, washed in morphing shapes and colors. Danny stopped looking at what they were doing so that he wasn't limited by his eyes. He connected with his mind; he began to construct the code, predicting outcomes, glancing only to verify what they were becoming. He was in the center of another universe that operated on numbers and formulas and colors, looking for the right combination—

The room went black. Something clicked.

A spot of light hung over his head.

"What is it?" the girl said.

He'd forgotten she was there. "The firewall cracked."

"What's that mean?"

More clicking, like blocks were stacking and pieces latching and uncoupling. The spot of light shrunk to a pinpoint and began to dim. The clicking ended. Something fell into place like a key sliding into a lock. And turning.

The point exploded in blinding light.

And then they were flying above planet Earth.

"We're through," Danny said.

"Where?"

Danny stood up. "It's the outside world."

It exists.

There was an outside world. The desks and keyboard had disappeared. Danny walked on clouds, looking at the blue ocean thousands of feet below.

"We're seeing the world through satellites," he said.

"Where's the island?"

Danny put together a few thought-commands, requesting the location of the portal he'd just hacked. The view spun like the planet rotated below. They were in the middle of the South Atlantic Ocean, halfway between South America and Africa.

Nothing but water.

[Enhance,] he thought.

The view zoomed toward the water and two tiny islands came into view. The southern one was very small and narrow. There appeared to be an airstrip the length of it. The larger island to the north was shaped like South Carolina.

"That's it," Danny muttered. "That's where we are."

"It's in the middle of nowhere."

"Exactly."

He began pacing around, observing the two islands. The details were sharper than what he'd seen in his flying sessions in Foreverland. There was the Yard in the center of the larger island and the horseshoe-shaped dormitory and the top of the Haystack nestled in the trees.

That's where I am. Right now.

He scrolled the view to the south end, over the Mansion. He enhanced the view until he was walking right over the roof. The area behind the Mansion was a resort with swimming pools and lounging areas. There was a large pier attached to the shore with a yacht.

He looked at the smaller island, now off in the distance about five miles.

"They must fly into that island." Danny took a few steps and the view scrolled beneath him until the airstrip was just below their feet. There was a hangar at one end and an empty pier on shore. "And then bring people over on the yacht."

The girl stood next to him. "What do you think they're doing?"

The view returned to the Mansion. Someone was swimming. One of the Investors was taking long, smooth strokes to the end of the pool before turning to backstroke in the other direction.

"Looks like they're on vacation," he said.

After scrolling over the rest of the Mansion yard and finding nothing unusual, he began to look at the rest of the island. The view – directly overhead – looked like a privately owned tropical island. If someone flew over it, there would be nothing out of the ordinary.

"There's not much time." The girl had been walking along Danny's side, looking where he was looking but watching for his reaction. "Is there anything here that helps?"

He grunted. "Not really."

Danny continued walking, looking for anything that would be of interest. The Yard had a few people in it. The Chimney was highest in the sky, the stovepipe quiet. The waves were crashing violently on the north shore. The beach was empty, of course, because Reed was still in the Haystack with those vicious looking things on his hands.

Danny turned.

The girl was standing in the middle of the room, her hands clutched in front of her. She saw his thought and her eyes were big but not glassy this time.

"How do you know Reed?" he asked.

"It's hard to know... my memories..."

"They're mixed up?"

She shrugged.

"But you're stuck in here?" Danny asked. "You can't get out of Foreverland?"

"I don't know... I just remember suddenly being here... something was after me when I woke up..."

Danny waited, but she seemed more confused than before. "So you escaped into the Nowhere?"

Quick nod, again. "No one can come out here. Not even him."

The Director.

"You know that Reed dreams about you. He thinks you're telling him not to come, that he has to—"

"I know... I just... want him to be okay."

She turned away so Danny couldn't see her face. Her shoulders tensed. He thought she might be weeping, but when she turned back around, Danny thought it was anger fading from her expression.

Her fists were clenched. "What are we going to do... to make all this end?"

An old man was getting out of the pool. He wrapped a towel over his shoulders and waved to someone back at the Mansion. A young man ran down the wide, curving steps off the balcony. *Parker.*

"I'll figure something out before the next round," Danny said. "Can you bring me back here?"

"Yes, but it'll have to be like the last time... just look for a fight and I'll get you back."

Danny looked across the island at the Haystack where Sid's body was twenty feet away from his. "That shouldn't be too hard."

The random voices began penetrating the walls and the grainy mist twisted across the floor, obscuring the view below.

"There isn't much... time. You need to figure something out... fast."

"I know," he said. "I know."

The light began to fade.

"Goodbye, Danny Boy."

The fog swirled around him. Her red hair faded to pink. "Wait! What's your name?"

The voices were louder, one after another. The gray fog thickened, wrapping him in a cocoon of silky darkness. The voices got farther away. Danny slid back to the space between Foreverland and the Haystack.

Just before he felt his flesh and the hard concrete on his back, he heard one last word from far away.

Lucinda.

ROUND 4

REAL ESTATE TYCOON MISSING AT SEA

LAS VEGAS, Nevada. – Local real estate and business billionaire, Franklin Constantino, 82, was reported missing after taking his yacht for a solo excursion out of San Francisco into the Pacific Ocean.

Constantino had been diagnosed with lung cancer two months before his disappearance. According to one of his staff, he rarely boarded his 70' yacht without a captain and crew, but insisted on a lone journey for some "soul searching".

The Coast Guard received distress calls about fifty miles off the coast but were unable to locate the ship. Evidence suggests the ship may have sunk but nothing has been confirmed.

29

THE TOP FLOOR of the Chimney hummed as the electric motors began winding up the shades. Evening light – diffused by the window's tint – filled the room.

The Director was stretched out on a comfortable recliner. His lips began twitching before his eyes fluttered open. He stared vacantly at the black ceiling for a few moments before reaching up. He slid the needle out of the stent. He quivered. The sensation of the lubricated needle was a queer one that tickled the inside of his brain.

He rubbed salve over the hole and sighed while the Foreverland world faded. It would take a few minutes before he felt all the way back in his body. He drummed his fingers on the cushiony armrests while the chair's internal rolling pins massaged his back, legs and buttocks. Circulation was important after lying still for so long. When the tingling faded, he put his feet on the ground and slowly stood.

He hadn't eaten since he'd gone "inside the needle" (another term the boys invented) but he wasn't thinking of food. He was thinking of what he just saw.

He found her.

The Director mixed a drink.

He stooped over a telescope aimed across the empty Yard. The boys would exit the Haystack in a half hour or so. It always took them a bit longer to return to the flesh when a round had ended. After all, the Director had been doing it for years, one of the few people to master the ability to go inside the needle. They were still rookies.

Only Danny Boy's third round and he'd already managed to get control of his body. Maybe she was helping him, but he somehow doubted that was it. The kid was brilliant. The Director secretly wished he could somehow cryogenically freeze him for about twenty years; he could save the kid for his own personal use. But he didn't have that technology. Not yet.

The drink warmed him.

She was clever, of course. He continued to underestimate her. She left that Christmas present as a clue and then sent the kid on a wild chase throughout the island. The Director already had a lot of responsibility keeping Foreverland stable, so keeping track of Danny Boy racing around was difficult. Somehow, she managed to construct a trapdoor in the Mansion and the kid found it without knowing it. By the time the Director realized what had happened, she'd collapsed the tunnel that led to the outer perimeter of the Nowhere. Out of his reach.

She's learning, that's what's happening.

And learning was a problem.

Before she infected Foreverland, it was an expanding universe that started at the sundial and extended hundreds of miles past the shoreline. The Director envisioned it encompassing the planet, the solar system, and eventually the universe. The growth was exponential and the system operated flawlessly. He had great plans for humanity's next evolutionary step. Foreverland wasn't just an imaginary place where the kids went to play.

Everything was right on schedule. Until they inoculated Reed.

He appeared to be a healthy, normal subject. As he lay in a medically induced coma – after his body healed from the car accident – they strapped him with the initial needle-piercing for false memory infusion, but when they drew his memories out, this girl had slipped out of his subconscious. Memories always ended up floating around the Nowhere like bits of chicken in a bowl of soup.

But the girl was conscious!

Initially, she was merely a nuisance, a cockroach that would eventually run into the bottom of the Director's heel. But she found cover in the Nowhere where the Director was blind. And ever since then, Foreverland had been collapsing.

The misty Nowhere was less than five miles off the shore, shrinking every day. He predicted that it would take a month to collapse all the way back to the sundial. If there was no Foreverland, the program would come to a screeching halt. The Investors would not be pleased. Not with the sums of money they were putting up.

But Danny Boy found her and that wasn't necessarily a bad thing.

It was the first time she'd stuck her neck out of the Nowhere. The Director missed it, this time. He wouldn't the next. She wanted Danny Boy and that meant she would do it again. If he caught her – no, not if... *when* he caught her, he would put a stop to the collapse. And then he could continue with the original plan: get Reed inside. He knew that once Reed was inside Foreverland, he would absorb her like a memory. Because that's what she was. She would go back inside his mind and leave Foreverland.

And Foreverland would grow, once again.

Why Reed had resisted all this time he still couldn't understand. Somehow, the kid seemed to know he was the antidote to the Director's problem. That's why he needed Danny Boy. He needed him to tell Reed about what she was doing, what she looked like, how much she needed him. Danny Boy would apply the pressure the Director needed, he would help bring him to Foreverland.

He swallowed the drink and mixed another.

Someone was crossing the Yard. Reed was the first one out, clutching his hands to his stomach. There were Soldiers of Fortune that didn't have balls half the size as his. The Director would have to get medieval, very soon. Reed would discover that every human had a breaking point.

"Director?" the intercom called.

"Yes?"

"At your convenience, could you come down to the network floor? I think you'll find this interesting."

He finished the drink. He was tired and already a little buzzed. But there was data to observe from Foreverland.

30

Lucinda watched Foreverland recede.

She knew everything about the Nowhere. She knew all the thoughts of the boys that had been there. Knew all the... suffering, too. But it was Danny Boy that cracked the system open. He showed her how to work with the code, how to see into the network that helped operate... Foreverland.

The Nowhere fog circled the sundial as the boys went back to their bodies. And Foreverland went to sleep. Until the next round.

31

DANNY WOKE ON THE FLOOR, shivering. His clothes were still piled up where he left them. The door of his cell was open. A sharp pain gouged his ribs as he sat up. He couldn't remember falling before taking the needle. He got dressed and wiped something off his cheek, like snails raced across his face.

The Haystack was empty, except for Zin.

He was awake and sitting with his arms propped on his knees. His throat bobbed up and down like he was trying to swallow something that just wouldn't go down.

"Zin." Danny squatted in front of him. "You all right?"

A string of saliva dangled from his lip.

Danny pulled him onto his feet. At least he didn't have to dress him. He threw Zin's arm over his shoulders and guided him out of the Haystack and through the woods. Zin continued to swallow at nothing until they emerged into the Yard. When daylight hit their faces, Zin looked up. Focus returned.

"Thanks, Danny Boy."

They went straight to their rooms. Danny helped him crawl in bed and then went to his own. He was asleep as soon as his head hit the pillow.

There were no medical trays when Danny woke up. As far as he could tell, Mr. Jones hadn't been to his room. At least, he couldn't smell him.

He did come to his room a couple days later. He was apologetic, at first. He stood in the middle of the room with his hands behind his back like he was addressing the press.

"I'm sorry I lost control in the Haystack, Danny Boy. I understand you're under a lot of stress and it can be confusing about what to do. It's easy to become irrational, I know. We're all under a lot of stress."

Danny wondered what kind of stress Mr. Jones could be enduring. Did he have to swim three laps in the luxury pool instead of two?

"But what Reed is doing is borderline insanity. No, it *is* insanity." That was about the time the apology ended and the finger-waving began. "The fact that he's been allowed to remain in the program this long is unconscionable, Danny Boy."

And that was another first. *Program. He called this a program.*

"He's a terrible example," Mr. Jones said, pointing at Danny. "Refusing the lucid gear is an insult and a travesty and sabotages everything we strive to..." His tone softened. "Everything we strive to give you boys. It makes no sense, and I don't want to see you contaminated by his actions. You understand, Danny Boy?"

"I'm sorry, too," Danny said with his most convincing doe-eyes. "I just lost it in there, Mr. Jones. It didn't take long to realize my mistake, trust me. It won't happen again."

Mr. Jones smiled. He sat on the bed, permeating the sheets with his Mr. Jones smell.

"You know, I can't forbid you from talking to him. I just want you to understand how damaged he is. I don't want that to happen to you. You're a good kid, Danny Boy. You know what they say about spoiled apples."

"You don't have to worry about me, Mr. Jones."

Danny stopped from adding, *Golly gee. I love this place.* Mr. Jones would've bought it even if he did. He scrubbed Danny's head.

"A good kid, you are."

The camp was at the table, again, soaking up the sun and tossing cards. Danny mostly stayed in his room for a couple days and only snuck down to the cafeteria when they weren't there. Sid didn't seem to be looking for him but Danny wasn't taking any chances. He just needed some peace to sort through his thoughts.

Lucinda.

She woke up in Foreverland, but what was she? Part of the program? Something real?

It didn't matter. They all had the same goal: get off the island. He just needed to come up with a solution. He'd established contact with the outside world and no one that ran the place seemed to notice. But that didn't mean he wasn't being watched. He'd slipped through the firewall and he was sure he could do it again, at least once. And if he only had one chance, it needed to work.

He couldn't send for help, it would just look like a hoax. *We're a bunch of kids held on a tropical island given everything we could ever want and we go into a barn and get a needle shot into our heads so we can experience an alternate reality. Please help.*

The island was a slick operation. Surely they'd have a plan for visitors. Danny needed something that would get the world's attention, something that would piss off some important people and make them come looking for them. The next round wasn't for another week and a half. He had time to think and no distractions. He had to go into the fourth round with something ready to go.

And look for a fight.

The card table was empty. Sid and his band of merry men had gone to lunch. Zin hadn't left his room. His Investor was bringing up food and closing the door quietly on his way out. Danny had been checking up on him, too. He was tired, but at least he was alive. Maybe when this was all over, he'd find the old Zin in the Mansion. Or maybe a new and improved Zin.

Danny opened his door. The hallway was empty and Zin's door was closed. He lightly tapped on it. He was going to try the door knob and peek inside the room when someone said, "Zin's looking for you."

It was James. He was a fourteen year old kid that never gave Danny any crap.

"Where is he?"

James opened the door to his room and said, "I saw him going out back, said something about a joyride."

Danny went to his room and threw on clothes and started for the stairs. *A joyride?* Maybe the old Zin was putting up a fight after all.

He never bothered opening Zin's door.

（32）

"PREPOSTEROUS." Mr. Jones threw his arms up. "You'll have a real problem on your hands if he's hurt, I promise you, Director. Something happens to my Danny Boy..."

Mr. Smith stood next to him. They were looking out the tinted windows of the Chimney's top floor. Mr. Smith calmly kept his hands latched behind his back, while Mr. Jones folded and unfolded his arms making a small sound each time he did, like he was choking on words until he had to spit them out.

"There will be hell to pay. I've invested too much time and money to take such a risk, you should've consulted me." He looked over his shoulder. "This is absurd!"

The Director was throwing a floral red and white shirt over his head. "Mr. Jones," he said, his flip-flops slapping his feet, "I don't consult my clients. You pay me to do the thinking."

The Director stood next to Mr. Smith. They were looking at the back of the dormitory.

"Besides," he said, "you don't exist, so don't make idle threats."

Mr. Jones's face went red. "You're punishing him for what? For going in the Nowhere? I'm a fair man, Director, and this has nothing to do with fairness."

The Director looked at Mr. Jones. His beard did not conceal the smile. *Fair man? His delusion knows no bounds.*

The program thrived from the self-centeredness of these old men, the infection of false entitlements that comes from money and power. Their universe revolved around their petty concerns and anything that affected them. They couldn't see the bigger picture, they couldn't see opportunity when they looked in only one direction. *Stay open to life, gentlemen. Let it unfold and the universe will provide you with endless paths on your journey.*

Fact is, they got lucky.

The Director expected Danny to be risky, but he never would've guessed the kid would *hack through the security firewall and spread across the world!* He did it through a vast web of communications. He didn't attempt any communication because he was smart. Any other frightened kid would've shouted out to the world, *Help! Help!* The Director had answers for that, but that wasn't what Danny Boy did. He was patient, scoping out his potential. He would do something the next time, something the Director might not be able to stop.

But, more importantly, he showed the Director how the world's vast communication network had become a living body that just needed a soul to breathe. Danny Boy merged his identity with the network. He became the network.

Danny showed him just how short-sighted he had been all this time.

"We're making him stronger," the Director said. "He needs this to push through his psychological barriers."

"On what basis do you make these assessments?" Mr. Jones said. "Those barriers were put in place by us! He's not supposed to remember his past in the flesh, Director. Like every boy on this island, he only recovers them inside the needle, and now you want to remove the barriers that prevent him from remembering in the flesh? Director, I must question your motivations—"

"Question nothing, Mr. Jones," he snapped. "Every boy on this island is different, each needs the program tailored to his individual needs. May I remind you that you were the one that argued to recruit this young man against my better judgment, that he would bring problems that would be dealt with in an unorthodox manner. Do you recall that conversation?"

Mr. Jones folded his arms, once again. "You are introducing anarchy. I hardly see how that will benefit those involved."

"Sometimes death provides life, Mr. Jones. I believe that is something we can all agree upon."

They watched the scene unfold behind the dormitory.

"I've had enough. I'm putting a stop to this now."

The Director didn't stop him from going to the elevator. The event was over.

Mr. Smith was nonplussed. It didn't involve his boy. In fact, it was for the benefit of Danny Boy *and* Reed. Therefore, Mr. Smith watched with great interest.

"Danny Boy is Reed's salvation," is what the Director told him before Mr. Jones had arrived. "He's our best chance to draw him inside the needle."

And the needle was what Mr. Smith needed him to take. Otherwise, he would have wasted his time and money. Money, he had. Time was what he was trying to buy.

So the Director's argument was very compelling. The pressure they had put on Reed still had not succeeded. The Director and Mr. Smith agreed that Reed was likely to die before succumbing to it. His health was already on the decline and his time was very short. It wasn't going to benefit Mr. Smith if he destroyed him. He was willing to try anything.

The Director twisted the curly whiskers on his upper lip. The event behind the dormitory was taking an unforeseen turn, but Mr. Smith didn't flinch. He watched as it unfolded. This made the Director smile. *He trusts me.*

"There's hope yet, Mr. Smith. The two are bonding. Keep them close, let them continue to develop a relationship."

"What about Mr. Jones? He will not be pleased with this approach."

"I'll handle Mr. Jones. Danny Boy made contact with Reed's 'problem' inside the needle. We can't let that opportunity go to waste."

The Director didn't lie. There was a problem. The extent of that problem, however, was not fully explained to any of the Investors. Reed's problem was a threat to all of them. Mr. Jones, included. If Danny Boy was part of the solution, there would be no discussion about how to handle it.

The boys behind the dormitory fell to the ground as Mr. Jones and other Investors arrived on the scene. Mr. Smith took his leave to attend to Reed.

"He's worth saving," the Director said, as Mr. Smith boarded the elevator. "They're all worth saving."

Not a lie. But not exactly the truth.

33

DANNY RAN towards the only door that opened to the back of the dormitory. Zin must have come out of it to swipe a golf cart. His Investor was going to flip. And Mr. Jones was going to drop a nuke. *That's right. Danny is not a good boy.*

Maybe they could scout the other end of the Mansion but this time take the cart, drop a brick on the accelerator and send it over the edge. It was a horrible idea, but he'd run it by Zin, see what he thought. If he was game, Danny wasn't going to stand in his way. May as well have some fun destroying personal property.

He threw open the door—

CRAAACK!

Danny tumbled with lights in his head and the side of his face numb, the tang of iron on his tongue.

"Booooom!" Sid shouted. "Where I come from, that's called a boom-shot, son!"

Danny touched his fat lips, pulled back bloody fingers. He spit a dark red pool into the dirt.

The camp was throwing high-fives at Sid. One of the guys was down at the corner on the lookout for Investors. James nearly tripped over Danny on his way out of the back door.

"Did I miss it?"

"Hell, yeah, you missed it." Sid shook his hand like it was hot. "I broke up his damn face. You should've seen the look he gave me right before I landed the boom-shot." He high-fived James. "That's what we call it where I come from."

Danny got on his hands and knees and spit red. "You don't know where you come from." He spit out a chunk of skin. "None of you morons do."

It got quiet. Sid squatted down. "I don't care where I'm from, that's what we call it."

He kicked Danny onto his back and got another round of hand-slapping.

"I'm king of this island, Danny Boy," Sid called. "And you're the trash. You and Reed, a couple of crazy bastards getting naked. What's wrong with your brains, son? Did the needle drive too deep? Did it suck the noodle out of your skull?"

"Maybe I've seen the truth."

"Yeah, the truth of your mental illness. What is there not to love about this place, idiot? We got everything we could want, we don't pay for a thing, and we got the best games in the world. I mean, sue me for not wanting to stay here forever."

"We get smoked, Sid," Danny said, spitting. "You forget?"

"Yeah, well we all got to die. That's a fact, brain surgeon. May as well do it happy."

The clowns around him agreed. A pack of lemmings.

"The Director is a genius," he said. "You should be kissing the man's feet."

"Excuse me for wanting to know what they're doing to us," Danny said.

"Who gives a flying fart?"

Danny was on his hands and knees, again.

"And another thing." Sid was back down at face level. "You're getting your ass back in that game room to put us back in first place. I got a taste of that freebee and I like. We want another pass, you hear?"

"Forget it."

"You might want to think about it because there's more where this came from." Sid kicked dirt in his face. "You got to sleep sometime."

"So do you."

They laughed. Sid led the way toward the corner of the building where they'd sit their fat asses on the card table and yuck it up. Danny just needed to sit it out until they were gone. He was going to need stitches, but what would he tell Mr. Jones? The truth would probably help the most, but that seemed boring. Besides, Danny sensed the thrill beneath the throbbing in his face. And that's what made him stand up.

"You forgot something!" He took a shuffle-step to catch his balance then threw up his middle finger. "Take this to the game room with you."

Sid thought about it. It would be easier to let this one go, but everyone was watching and Danny hadn't learned his lesson. And that was the whole point. How could Sid really be the king if a little punk gave him the finger and got away with it? If he walked off, Danny wins no matter how many stitches it takes.

Danny sealed the deal when he threw his hands out to the side. *Still standing, bitch.*

Sid got a running start.

Danny bent at the knees, balled his fists. He was going to start swinging before Sid got too close. He had no plan after that. But it didn't matter.

Sid launched himself – feet first.

Danny went flying like a limp doll. Before his wits returned, Sid was on top. He tasted gritty blood, now. Sid planted his knees on Danny's arms, grinding them into the dirt and sat on his chest. Danny's legs flailed behind Sid. He grabbed a handful of Danny's hair and held his head still. A bubbly glob of spit hung on Sid's lower lip, then fell.

"How's that, munchkin?" Sid said.

The others gathered around. Their shadows loomed.

"That loogey matches the one I dropped on you in the Haystack. That was from me and you're welcome."

The snail slime when I woke up.

The pain radiating from his arms had extinguished the thrill and replaced it with rage. But he was too small to do anything, helpless beneath 180 pounds of Sid. He tried to spit on him but it only landed on his own face.

"Listen, you crazy dwarf. What I say goes. You'll game and shut your bloody mouth or I'll spit in your eye every day you wake up. You'll be begging to get smoked when I'm done with you. You think you can out-crazy me? Well, I got news for you, I'm the real deal. I'm a psychopath. I'll climb inside you and eat your damn gizzard."

Danny started laughing. *Gizzard. What an idiot.*

This caught Sid off-guard. Danny's cheek lit up with a loud smack. But it only made him laugh harder. He didn't care about pain. Sid would have to break his teeth out to get him to shut up. And that's what he was about to do, pulling his fist behind his ear—

Sid went rolling across the ground.

Elbows flying.

Danny was back on his hands and knees, catching his breath, listening to grunts and the slap of skin-on-skin. Sid was on feet, dragging someone with him.

Reed.

His shirt was pulled over his head, revealing his bony chest. Sid pushed him into the group and two of them pinned his arms behind him. Reed's face was gaunt. Yellow-darkness hung beneath his eyes. He was out of breath.

"A hero, huh?" Sid paced closer. "Hold him still, let me show you what we do to heroes."

He pulled his fist behind his ear, again, lined up a shot that would break Reed's entire face—

They all dropped on the ground.

Sid, Reed, and all the rest. They fell like dead bodies.

"It's all right, Danny Boy." Mr. Jones was on one knee. "We got things under control."

Golf carts pulled up and old men unloaded, each one of them going to their camper. They rolled them over, cradled their heads. Their eyes were rolled back and the Investors talked to them. Slowly, they came out of the tracker-zapping stupor and their Investors – each with his own look of disapproval – guided them away.

"Come along." Mr. Jones helped Danny up. "Let's get you to the doctor to have a look. Don't worry about those boys, it's all right now."

Each of them was up and being cared for, tended to. All of them, except one.

Reed was alone and still unconscious.

34

I<small>T WAS</small> Danny's second time inside the Chimney.

Mr. Jones took him to the big, silver elevator shaft in the center of the first floor. He held Mr. Jones's handkerchief to his mouth. It was white with major splotches of blood. They went to the second floor. Danny didn't see a stairwell. Either Mr. Jones was too tired to walk or this was ultra-security. The only way up was in the elevator.

Five floors in the Chimney. The third one was where I woke up. The second one is the doctor's office. The fifth one is the Director's penthouse. What's on the fourth?

The second floor was silent. Four hallways radiated from the center like spokes. They went down one of them and stopped outside an office door with a row of chairs against the wall.

"Would you have a seat, Danny Boy?" Mr. Jones asked. "I'd like to speak with the doctor."

Danny grunted through the handkerchief. Mr. Jones helped him into one of the chairs and went inside the office. Danny couldn't hear them talking. He flicked his tongue over his bottom lip, felt the hole carved out of it when Sid's fist crushed his face against his teeth. Mr. Jones assured him that would never happen again. If Sid got within fifty feet, an alarm would sound on his tracker. If he got closer than twenty, he'd get knocked out.

Danny wouldn't mind testing the system. Maybe sneak up on him while he was in the bathroom, watch him crumple up on the toilet. He'd be in trouble – major, big time – but it would be so worth it. So, so worth it.

He laid his head against the wall and closed his eyes. He was sinking in the chair, exhaustion weighing him down. He was breathing heavily when the elevator doors broke open. Two sets of footsteps came down the hallway. One was dragging a foot.

"Hello, Danny Boy," Mr. Smith said. "How's your mouth feeling?"

Danny shrugged. He could answer, but the bloody rag was a good excuse not to speak without being rude.

"Listen, son. You'll be all right. We've got a real sharp doctor on the island that will have you back to normal in a snap." Mr. Smith snapped his fingers to illustrate his point. "No one hurts for long around here."

Mr. Smith turned to Reed, mumbled something about sitting. "Let me go inside and talk with Mr. Jones and the doctor, all right?"

He winked at Danny, smiled, and went inside.

Reed hunched over, hiding his hands in his lap. The silence was enormous.

"You didn't have to do that back there."

Reed didn't respond. Danny took that as a sign to shut up. He said thanks. Move on. Danny pushed his tongue into the hole in his lip. The bleeding had stopped but he kept the handkerchief to his mouth.

"He's a psychopath, you know that," Reed mumbled.

"Yeah, he told me."

Reed sat back, holding his hands beneath his shirt. "Next time you'll get more than a bloody lip."

"There won't be a next time. Sid gets a warning if he's within fifty feet of me. Twenty feet and the tracker knocks his ass out. I might sneak up on him just to watch him twitch."

"You're playing with fire."

"We all are, Reed. May as well have some fun."

Zin would've liked that line; he'd tell him when he woke up.

"Why are you here?" Danny asked.

Reed hesitated. He unveiled his hands. The thumbs were purple and doubled in size. They stuck out like useless pegs. "To put Humpty Dumpty back together."

"So they can push you back off?"

"That seems to be the pattern."

Reed put his hands beneath his shirt, again. His breathing was a little shaky. It hurt just moving them. Danny couldn't imagine what it took to tackle Sid.

"Why don't you go inside the needle?" Danny asked.

Reed chuckled, smiled at the floor.

"What's so funny?" Danny asked. "It doesn't make sense, going through all this suffering when you know we're going to end up in Foreverland anyway. Come on, Reed, give yourself a break. You've suffered enough, you've proved your point. You can take a beating."

Reed was quiet. He drew a long breath and let it out, thoughtfully. Then threw his head back with laughter. It echoed up and down the hallway.

Danny watched him unravel. "You're losing it, Reed."

"What's so funny?" Reed said, wiping his eyes. "This is exactly what they want."

"Who?"

"Them." Reed gestured with a nod at the doctor's office. "They want us to be friends so that you'll talk me into taking the needle. And you're biting, Danny Boy. You're biting hard on the bait, son."

"I'm not biting on anything, I'm just making sense."

"You don't know what you're making."

"I saw her, Reed." The fits of laughter trailed off, quickly. "Want to know what she said?"

Reed hunched over, quietly.

"She sees you, Reed. She sees you in everyone's thoughts when they go inside the needle. She knows you're staying in the Haystack and suffering and refusing to come for her. She's alone and something is after her. You got to tell me why you're not going inside to help her."

Reed bowed his head lower like he barely had the strength to hold Danny's words.

"She's in your dreams," Danny added, "but that's a dream, man! Lucinda's alive, I'm telling you."

Reed jerked. He turned away. No sound came out of him. Just quiet convulsions.

"It's a trick, Danny Boy. The Director's got you fooled."

"It was no trick. She was—"

"YOU THINK I LIKE THIS?"

Reed shoved his hands in Danny's face. They weren't just swollen, they were misshapen and three different colors of purple, parts of them black. Thin red lines streaked down his wrists.

"You don't think I want to see her? That I just want to dream about her, that I don't want to touch her, smell her? That I don't want to be with her, Danny Boy, to know she's okay? To know she's alive? Is that what you think?"

Danny pulled his head back.

"It's hopeless, Danny Boy." Reed walked away. "It's all hopeless."

Lucinda.

Her name opened a memory.

Reed suddenly remembered, with fine clarity, a time he was driving a truck – a twenty year old pickup – with torn seat covers. He reached for the stick shift between her knees.

"We're doing it, Reed!" Lucinda said. "We're really doing it!"

The landscape rolled past them with long legs of corn and bushy fields of soybeans, dotted with silos and lonesome houses. The wind blew her red hair around. Lucinda grabbed Reed's face and planted a kiss. Her lips wet, warm and full.

Bip. It ended. Memory, over and out.

But it wasn't a dream, it was a memory. He remembered her.

He remembered that he loved her.

She's real.

———————

Danny stepped next to him. They were at the end of the hall, standing at one of the glass walls that overlooked the dormitory and the Yard. And, beyond that, the Haystack.

"The world, it's out there, Reed." Danny told him about hacking the firewall, locating the island through the satellite system. "There's hope."

"Can you do it again?" Reed asked, staring out.

"I don't know, it was some wild code. It was evolving like an organism, never seen anything like it."

"You can't just send for help. They'll have that figured out."

"I know."

"It has to be something the whole world will see, Danny Boy. You got to give them a reason to search for us."

Reed hung his hands inside his shirt like a hammock. He couldn't fold his arms and it hurt too much to let them hang at his sides. Besides, hiding them kept Danny from staring. Reed just wanted to get to the beach where he could be in the sun alone with the memories. He wanted to drive down that country road, again. He wanted to kiss her.

Lucinda. You're in there and I'm out here. The Haystack is nothing compared to that.

"Danny Boy?" Mr. Jones called from the doctor's office. "Son, the doctor would like to see you now."

Danny waited a bit, turned and nodded at the old man. He started to say something to Reed then went on his way. Mr. Jones closed the door behind them. He'd get his lip fixed and be ready for the next round. Reed only hoped he could do it again. Yes, he hoped.

Because he wouldn't be able to resist much longer.

35

THE CAFETERIA WAS FULL. But the table Danny was sitting at was empty.

He was in the corner, far away from the windows. The compartments on his lunch tray were filled with pudding, Jell-O and noodles. No chewing required. The doctor patched the gaping hole with a gel adhesive, but it didn't relieve the swelling. Pressure on his teeth hurt. His smile was lop-sided, but there wasn't much to smile about.

He slurped a spoonful of pudding and looked at the lined sheet of paper in front of him. He chose the corner of the room because it was the farthest spot from the rest of his camp eating at their regular table. They were in last place in the game room. Without Danny, they'd have to suffer every round they went inside the Haystack until they all got smoked. That gave him a little satisfaction. A few guys asked him to come back.

You've got to be kidding.

Danny glanced up and Sid flipped him the middle finger.

He also wanted privacy and the lighting was weak in the corner. He wrapped his arm around the paper to cast a shadow over his notes. It was stupid to write these things down, but he had to organize his thoughts. He was just writing bullet points but they were still clues:

- *Mutual Fund*
- *FBI*
- *Mt. Rushmore*

These were the three ideas he'd come up with to get the world's attention. The first one, mutual fund. Get control of the largest mutual fund in the world and sell all the assets. The stock market suffers a flash crash and people lose money.

Money is power and it will find you. If they found the rogue trader holed up in his parents' basement, they would find an island in the South Atlantic.

The second idea—

"Danny Boy." James flung a folded sheet of paper into his pudding. "Message."

Danny turned his notes over. James looked back. They were watching. And laughing. Danny wiped the chocolate smudge off and spread the note open.

Turdbrain. You die in the needle.

Sid was standing on the table with both birds flying. James nodded and smiled.

"Hey, you're a pal," Danny said. "Hang on a sec."

James waited for him to finish writing, watched him fold it back up.

"Don't peek now," Danny said. "I want it to be a surprise."

James opened it anyway. He carried it back to Sid still holding up middle fingers and still getting laughs. James handed it to him and Sid opened it. He sat down.

I'm running at you in five minutes.

Sid was sixty feet away. If Danny rushed him, he'd be less than twenty and pissing his pants. He could curse him all day long, but all it took was minus twenty feet and he'd be catatonic.

Second idea: destroy the FBI's database. Danny was drawing on previous memories. Crime-fighting agencies, like the FBI, were touchy when it came to their data. If he got inside their network, he could detonate everything digital. That was like kicking a hornet's nest. They wouldn't come to the Chimney asking questions, they'd kick the door down.

The third idea: blow something up. Destroying a national monument was surely going to set off a worldwide manhunt. If he dropped a building with a couple thousand people in it, they were as good as rescued, but Danny wasn't a killer. And there was the problem of getting explosives to detonate. It could be done; he could redirect a couple of military bases but that would get complicated.

It was down to the first two ideas. He was only going to get one chance. It had to work. But he wouldn't know until he was back inside the needle and tested the system. First, he had to find Lucinda.

Pick a fight.

Danny took his tray to the return window. Sid was in a conversation with someone across the table, but kept an eye on Danny as he filled a to-go box with food. Danny closed the lid and held up his hand for Sid to see, all four fingers and thumb.

He had Sid's full attention as he dropped one finger at a time. When he folded the last one into a fist, he started walking right at their table.

Sid was out the exit before twenty feet.

36

DANNY TAPPED ON THE DOOR. He didn't expect an answer. He turned the knob, poked his head inside, slowly. There was a lump on the bed. The curtains were closed. Danny didn't bother closing the door quietly. Zin had been asleep for two days.

"Zin, my man." Danny pulled one of the curtains open. "Let the sunshine in, brother."

The light fell on his face with no effect. His head was half-buried in the pillow, mouth open. His complexion was lighter, a grayishness mixed with mocha. But still dark beneath his eyes.

"Hey, man, wake up." Danny shook him. "You got to eat or you'll shrivel up like a leaf."

Zin moaned, smacking white slime between his lips. Danny sat him up. Zin's head lolled around. "What time is it?"

"Daytime," Danny said. "You need to join the living while you're still alive. I brought you some food, here." He doled out an apple, a turkey sandwich with spinach and tomato, a bag of chips and a container of pudding. "Get some of this in you before you fall asleep again."

Zin was beginning to collapse.

"Hey, come on." He shook his shoulders. "Throw some water on your face or something. Wake up."

Zin rubbed his eyes then shuffled to the sink. When he turned around, his eyes were at least open. So was his mouth.

"The mouth-breathing is starting to annoy me, you know," Danny said.

"Then look the other way."

"Can't you just breathe through your nose or something?"

"I'm too tired."

Zin started for the bed.

"Ah-ah-ah." Danny pulled the hard chair from the desk. "Have a seat, my friend. You're eating and then we're going to the Yard. If your skin gets any lighter, you'll officially be Caucasian."

"I didn't realize it was that easy."

"You see yourself lately? You're a ghost."

"Well, that's how I feel." He fell into the chair and limply unwrapped the sandwich. He leaned back and chewed with his mouth open. "This sucks, dude."

"Sorry. I would've taken your order but you were busy snoring."

"Not this." Zin held up the sandwich. "I feel like I'm barely here, like a puppet down to one string. I can barely remember anything. It's like everything that was me is still in Foreverland."

"Right now, get some of this highly nutritious food in you and stop complaining. We can get to the Yard and if we got time we can chase Sid around."

Zin was still awake but the distant gaze fogged over his eyes while he stuffed chips in his mouth. Danny had learned not to push. It was better to let him zone out from time to time. He was more responsive afterwards. As long as he was awake, he'd eventually come back. Danny pulled his notes out of his pocket. It wasn't much and he didn't need anything written down. It would be better to destroy it. He took a pen from the desk drawer and blacked out all the words.

"What's that?" Zin shot food out with the words.

"Nothing, just ideas."

Danny wadded up the paper and tossed it in the air, playing catch with himself. He couldn't decide which idea to go with. Maybe he could bounce them off Zin, he would know what to do, but it wasn't worth the chance. He was going to disappear after the next round and who knows if he talked in his sleep. He might blab the whole plan to his Investor and Danny would be screwed to the max.

Zin finished the sandwich and opened the pudding. "Maybe I can help."

He was behind on the conversation.

"You want to see these?"

Zin shrugged.

Danny went into a wind-up – an exaggerated kick – and threw a fastball right at him. It was a trick throw. When he brought his arm back, he flipped the paperball behind his back and threw an empty hand. Zin still didn't flinch.

Instead of a fastball hitting him square in the face, it gently lobbed from behind his back and bounced off Zin's chest.

Danny stared at it. Something happened. It was déjà-vu, he'd seen someone do that before. He learned it... from his father? He used to do that when he was a kid and it scared him the first time. The fake fastball, he called it. And when Danny's cousins came over, he'd do it to them and they'd laugh when they flinched. The fake fastball always tricked them. Always hit them right in the face. They never saw it coming.

It wasn't Danny's memory, but it didn't matter.

"That's what I'm going to do," Danny muttered. "Only I'm going to hit them right in the face with the fastball."

"What?"

"Nothing, nothing." Danny nodded at the empty desk. "You finished?"

"If you say so."

"Let's go, then. First, the Yard. After that, Sid-city."

Zin pushed himself out of the chair and took his time getting dressed in auto-pilot. Danny picked up the paperball. *Was it my father, really?*

Didn't matter. Danny was going to hit the island with something the United States military would notice.

37

THE MOON WAS JUST A SLIVER.

Danny didn't sleep that night. He lay in bed, working through the details of what he'd need to do when he got inside the needle. He'd have one chance. If he blew it, he'd be headed for the Chimney, and probably not to graduate.

No pressure.

He got dressed, stopped at Zin's room. It wasn't locked anymore, not unless Danny locked it on the way out. Danny didn't bother turning on the lights. He sat on the edge of the bed, felt a little like one of the Investors. Zin was on his back, mouth open, ripping wind through his throat.

"Zin." He shook him, over and over. "Zin, wake up."

Zin's eyes opened but remained unfocused. Danny gently slapped his cheek. He ended up dripping water on his face. "What the..." He looked around the room and couldn't see Danny right next to him. "What're you doing?"

"Two things." Danny held up two fingers. "First, I got to fight Sid when we get inside the needle so don't get in the way."

Zin nodded, sleepily.

"Repeat it," Danny said.

"You got to fight, got it. What's the other thing?"

"Let me in the Mansion when you get there."

Zin was thinking about it. Moments later, he got it. He nodded. *All right.*

Danny went to the door. Zin was still up on one elbow. It was the longest he'd stayed lucid in the last days. He watched Danny leave.

Danny stepped onto the dune. Black waves roared onto shore with white foam on top. The tide was high; the water skimming across the hardpacked sand.

He gripped the paper sack against the tug of the wind. It was too dark to see down the beach. Reed was usually on the left end. A hundred yards proved him correct. His knees were pulled up to his chest, hair fluttering.

Danny had been on the island almost two months. In that time, Reed had become a withered camp survivor. Every bone was visible from the waist up. Danny sat next to him and pulled out two bananas and passed one to him. Reed took it. He held it for several moments before peeling it.

"You got to eat, Reed."

Reed chewed, slowly. "It only makes me feel better."

"Yeah, that's the idea."

"And that makes it harder."

When the bananas were gone, Danny handed him an apple. "You know what they say about apples."

"They don't say that here, Danny Boy. Besides, I don't think it's a good idea."

Reed pushed up his lip, revealed the black gap of a missing tooth. Danny hadn't noticed it when they were at the doctor's office. His teeth were falling out.

Danny bit a chunk and handed it to him. "Yeah, it's gross but there are worse things. You got to eat. I can't have you petering out before the next round ends."

Reed eyeballed the slice. Danny swore he could see him smile before taking it. Danny took another bite and held it out. He ate the entire apple that way.

"I'm going to drop a satellite, Reed."

Reed didn't respond.

"I'll hack the United States Air Force, direct one of their Milstar satellites to make an emergency landing in the middle of the island. The government will be here before it lands."

"You think you can do that?"

Danny recalled the processing speed and the ease at which he maneuvered through the global communications network the last time. It had become more an effort of will than skill.

"I can."

Reed just nodded.

They listened to the ocean, to the rise and fall of the water.

Danny leaned back on his elbows. The sky was filled with a thousand points of light. He located the Big Dipper and Orion's Belt. He put his head down and closed his eyes. And the water lulled him to sleep.

A bird woke him. The waves glittered with morning light.

Reed was gone.

The fourth round was near.

Mr. Jones was waiting at the Haystack. The gongs had already passed.

He led Danny inside with a few encouraging words. The rest of the camp was in their cells, still dressed, waiting for Danny. They were glad he arrived but not happy to see him.

Reed was already nude with his back to Danny. He could count all the vertebrae.

Mr. Jones took Danny's clothes. Zin was the last to arrive. His Investor guided him inside with a hand on his shoulder. He was vacant, spastically swallowing. The Investor asked him three times for his clothes before he caught on. The boys grew impatient.

When the doors closed and the skylights darkened, Zin stood in the middle of his cell, shoulders slumped. Head down.

"Bye, Zin," Danny whispered.

He wasn't sure he heard him. But didn't expect him to.

38

THE DIRECTOR WATCHED the sun set.

He awoke completely refreshed. He had not slept well until recently. He never slept well in the face of uncertainty. That was over now. He knew what needed to be done. And how to do it.

"Director," the intercom said. "We'll be dropping the lucid gear in thirty minutes."

"Thank you."

He changed into a clean shirt and settled into his reclining chair. The kneading rollers adjusted to his shifting weight, allowing him to settle into a comfortable position. The Director stared at the ceiling. Deep breath.

The network technician that monitored Foreverland showed him how Danny had somehow circumvented the security like some sort of science fiction mind meld. He became one with the environment and rode it into the Ethernet, around the world and all the way to the satellites.

He wouldn't do it again. They were ready for him.

In fact, he was hoping he would try.

He would watch closely this time. Even though he couldn't see into the Nowhere, there were ways to watch how Foreverland was being manipulated. It was a risk to let the kid's mind run free, but they were ready. But it was still a risk. *A risk worth taking.* The reward was far beyond his imagination.

Danny Boy was a jewel.

There was still the girl and there was Reed. They would be dealt with. For now, he needed to discover the potential Danny Boy had unveiled.

The Director reached for a tray next to the chair with two glass tubes. One contained a needle – two inches long – soaking in a solution with a thin cable extending from the end of it that went all the way to the third floor where rows of computers would help transform his mind into Foreverland. The boys – when they took the needle – would come to the Director's mind. Foreverland wasn't a computer program, that was too artificial. It had to be organic. But the Director needed the assistance of his computer network to keep his mind stable, so that he could create the world of Foreverland, where the boys would find their thoughts. *Where he would eat their souls.*

Well, to say he ate their souls was a little dramatic. Their identities – whoever they are – were absorbed by the Director's mind. It made him bigger, stronger. It made him *more.*

And he liked that.

And his mind would continue to expand. Once the girl was gone.

The Director pulled the needle out and punctured the second glass tube that greased it with electrolytic salve. Careful not to touch it with his fingers, he lifted it to the hole in his forehead. The tip made contact with the stent just below the skin.

The Director took a deep breath. He pushed it through the stent and into his frontal lobe.

His vision quivered.

His body quaked.

He laid his arm at his side and closed his eyes.

Foreverland.

39

THE GRAINY WORLD was all that Lucinda knew.

There was no land to walk, no object... for her to lay her head. She existed in its endless vacuum. In the swirling gray of... voices.

The sound of static.

It was continuous in the Nowhere.

It was lonely.

Until a shockwave began.

It rippled outward, stimulating the grains of gray... excited atoms. The voices began to chatter, fleeing from an object that began to take shape. It was the color of sandstone, a pedestal with a triangular fin atop a circular disc. It was always the first to appear before Foreverland was reborn.

The gray scattered around it like insects. Colors bled from the base of the sundial. Lucinda hid deep in the Nowhere as... grass and trees and buildings and sky was born. She prepared to find her savior, hoping that he might bring her peace.

That he might bring them all peace.

40

DANNY FLOATED in the bodiless darkness. He escaped the suffering, forsaking his body for the needle. But he carried the image of Reed's naked body shivering in the cold.

The fan would blow on him. The sprinklers would mist.

But Mr. Smith would arrive with something much worse.

Danny couldn't fail.

Solid ground formed beneath him. He was next to the sundial. The entire camp had arrived, forming a half-circle around him.

"Welcome, dirtbag." Sid was a monster of fleshy muscle and blue, snaky veins. "I'm dedicating this round to your misery. I'm going to invent ways of torture, invent things even the Director wouldn't dream of doing to another human being, Danny Boy. There's going to burning, there's going to be cutting and ripping... just, all sorts of fun stuff."

He popped his knuckles like snapping timber.

"I'm going to do those things to you, Danny Boy. I'm going to do them all night long."

Foreverland was quiet. No one flying in the blue sky or miniature warriors racing across the Yard. They were all around the sundial to watch Sid perform surgery. Whether they wanted to watch or Sid told them to, they were there.

"Try to run, Danny Boy, and we'll catch you. Call for help, we'll shred whoever shows up."

Does he mean Zin?

"It's going to be the longest day of your life, my friend. You'll beg me to stop, but you missed that chance, son. You already sold your soul to the devil." Big toothy grin. "And I bought it."

He paced around the semi-circle, rolling his head like a mixed martial artist warming up for a big fight. He glared down at Danny. He was nearly twenty feet tall, and growing. Muscles writhed like snakes. He pulled a long breath through his nostrils. It came out like exhaust, blowing hotly in Danny's face.

Danny looked around.

"No one's coming, Danny Boy." Sid's voice dropped an octave, filled with gravel. "No one is here to save you, it's just us, punk. Just us."

Sid filled his chest with another deep breath. His shoulders bulged, his arms rippled. His skin turned a shade redder. Talons emerged from the tips of his fingers with razor edges.

"I'm really going to dig this," he blurted with a slight lisp as sharpened incisors bit into his lower lip. "I only wish Reed was here to make it double-dip ass whipping."

The others were growing, too. It would be like a pride of lions feeding on the lone antelope. Danny was not a lion. He closed his eyes, focused on a tiny point.

Stay numb. Until she comes.

Breathe, in and out.

"I love this place, Danny Boy," Sid stated, deeply. "I'm afraid you're really going to hate it."

Sid took one more long breath and let out a roar. He lifted his tree trunk arms, flexed the dagger-tipped claws, and slashed downward. He would dice Danny into cubes. He would put him back together and do it again. And again.

He was going to do it all night.

But then Lucinda arrived.

She emerged from the ground like a ghost.

She smacked the edge of the sundial with her fist. It rang like a gong struck with a hammer. The vibrations shook Foreverland.

Danny staggered. His vision doubled.

Only Lucinda remained in focus, unaffected by the tremors emanating from the sundial. She had let loose a never-ending earthquake.

"If you love this place," she said, "then you will never leave it."

Lucinda walked toward Sid as he lost his balance. She plunged her hand into his chest. He continued to convulse, but slowly – very slowly – he began to settle like a bell reaching the end of its ring until he was as unaffected as Lucinda.

His eyes were wide. His mouth was open.

He shrank back to normal-size. When she gently placed him on the ground, he had become Sid, the gangly kid back in the Haystack. His expression was not angry or scared.

It was vacant.

She took Danny's hand. Warmth penetrated his arm and filled him. And then they fell through a trapdoor that opened on the ground.

Into the grayness of the Nowhere.

Danny was on his knees when the circular room appeared.

His hands were splayed on the floor. Twenty fingers were jiggling out of focus, the sundial ringing between his ears. His stomach turned and twisted. He thought he might vomit, then thought it weird since he was a digital body and hadn't really eaten anything.

He closed his eyes, focused on the tiny dot. In and out, he breathed until things settled. When he opened his eyes, he had ten fingers again.

"He's a bad kid." Lucinda was sitting in the lone chair, center of the room. "I saw what he was doing... in the others' thoughts."

"I thought the fight was a clue. You just wanted Sid."

"He tortures Reed," she said. "He deserved what he got."

"What'd you do to him?"

"I gave him what he loves." She crossed her legs. "I gave him Foreverland."

It sounded like a bad thing.

Danny sat up, allowed a few moments to adjust before standing.

The floor swayed a bit. He felt like he just stepped off a roller coaster. A chair appeared. He grabbed the back but didn't sit.

"What's that mean?" he asked. "How'd you give him Foreverland?"

"He'll never leave."

"You can do that?"

She glanced away. "You're all coming here, Danny Boy. You all join the voices in the Nowhere."

"I don't understand, Parker was better. He couldn't have stayed here."

She shrugged.

He'll join the voices? She couldn't have that right. Parker was there, he was back. It had to be some mirror image that remained in Foreverland, perhaps the ghosts of ideas and thoughts that weren't real to begin with. Perhaps that's what the program was about, cleansing our minds of impurity, erasing the habits of self-destruction and reprogramming us with desirable thoughts.

But then who would be deciding what to program? And who decided what was desirable?

Zin might already be scattered in the Nowhere.

"He is not," she said, sensing his thought. "But he's close."

"How do you know?"

"I just know... he's with his girlfriend. He's a good person, Danny Boy. I like Zin."

But none of that would matter if Danny couldn't do something because she was right. They were all heading for Foreverland. If they were really helping them become better people, then a satellite landing on the island wouldn't harm anything.

But if they weren't helping...

"Are you ready?" she asked.

Danny let go of the chair and nodded. She stood up and the chair disappeared. He took his place in the center.

Thought-commands lit up the room.

He was in the eye of a data storm.

The colors swirled around the room. Sometimes they appeared as shapes that connected with other shapes, sometimes merging, sometimes snapping together. Other colors were blurs or streaks or dots that interweaved and interlocked and became something larger.

Danny stood still, eyes closed.

He forgot he was in a room. Forgot he once inhabited a body. He had become the data, swimming through the ethereal universe of networks on the island, searching for the conduit that would let him leak out and spread across the outside world—

The colors stopped.

He opened his eyes. The room looked like the inside of a kaleidoscope.

"What's wrong?" Lucinda asked.

"It's too easy."

Danny walked the perimeter, thinking. He wanted to be sure. If he fell into a trap, everything ended. Game over. He made one loop around the room, started another. By the end of the second one, he was positive.

A bubble appeared in the middle of the room, hovering off the floor. Its surface swirled with colors reflecting from the walls.

"That's like the firewall that seals the island from the rest of the world," Danny said. "Last time, I exploited a line of communication."

He put his finger on a black dot floating on the surface.

"They only stay open for a millisecond because snoopers scour the entire firewall a thousand times a second looking for these inconsistencies and closing them. I was able to slip through one before they closed it."

"So? Do it again."

"But I shouldn't be able to. Snoopers are learning programs, they would fix the gap. It shouldn't be there."

The lights from the bubble scattered over her face, glimmering on her electric red hair.

"I think it's a trap," Danny said. "They might know what I'm doing."

"Then why set a trap?"

Good question. "I can't chance it. If I blow this, it's all over."

Lucinda gazed at the bubble. She gave him the space to think as the clock inside Foreverland ticked closer to the end of the day. Closer to his return to the Haystack.

"Is there another way to get out?" she asked.

A red dot began glowing in the center of the bubble. It took the form of a building with five floors and a smokestack. Danny reached inside and touched it.

"I'll go deeper."

Danny had become the colors, again. He had become the data streaming through the network pipelines like blood through the body's arteries. He swished through the Ethernet web, spreading out and observing the flow of data, reading its content, following multiple directions and destinations, searching for the center of activity. He experienced the sensation of shooting across space.

Lucinda watched quietly.

Many times, he disguised himself as quantifiable data as the security snoopers trolled the network for potential intruders. And then he'd be on the move again. But the closer he got to the center of activity – the mainframe processor – the slower his progress became. He spent long chunks of time idle. One slip and the security snoopers would trace his presence back to an identity known as Danny Boy. He had cloaked his identity, but they would eventually unravel it. And then everyone would know what he was up to. And on an island, it was hard to run and hide.

He began to doubt his intuition about the outer firewall, but he knew it was just wishful thinking. His new path was slow and tedious and dangerous, but he couldn't take forever. At some point, the needle would withdraw from his body and he'd return empty-handed.

His senses adjusted to the new reality of colorful data. He began to *see* it and feel it. The room reflected his experience. Lucinda watched as his experience reflected a recognizable reality in the room. They soared through slippery tunnels and past doorways and stopped inside empty rooms. They flew down hallways, beneath doors. Sometimes they went so fast it was just a blur. Something silver formed ahead of them. It was down a long hallway. It came into focus.

An elevator opened.

Danny moved for the first time in hours. He walked toward the elevator and then appeared to go inside it. The doors closed.

Lucinda wouldn't see him come back.

The Milstar communications system consisted of five satellites – each weighing approximately 10,000 pounds – positioned around the world to meet wartime requirements with a price tag just under $5 billion.

They'd notice one missing.

Danny went up to the fourth floor of the Chimney where the bulk of computer activity operated and streamed through a major conduit of data that was transferring updates to the outside world. He did a quick search of the Milstar program and found it linked to three locations: Los Angeles Air Force Base, Hanscom Air Force Base in Massachusetts, and Schriever Air Force Base in Colorado.

He was careful not to set off any alarms while snooping around each location. Since he resembled data, it only took seconds to cross the country for preliminary observations. Once he was certain, he penetrated Schriever Air Force Base.

There were very few gaps to exploit and the multi-layered security system was covered with alarms. But it wasn't evolving like the Chimney. Danny easily disguised himself as a top-secret document and streamed onto a secretary's computer in one of the outer offices. From there, he leaped into the network and passed through encrypted firewalls as a variety of updates and system maintenance. He avoided any sort of forced entry that might trigger a lockdown. He needed things to be open and fully operational.

Once he cleared security, he migrated to the central command processor and located the geosynchronized orbit of the satellites. He could take complete control of all five, if he wished, shoot all of them at the island like falling stars. But that was risky. Alarms would be triggered and there was a chance that a system override could derail his actions. They would know the coordinates and likely investigate, but that wasn't as sure a thing as dropping 10,000 pounds of metal on the Mansion.

Danny tucked Trojan horses into the system that would lay dormant until one of the satellites was positioned over the island. Then they would send the satellite hurtling toward the South Atlantic. At that point, there would be nothing Milstar could do to restore power in time to alter the $1 billion belly flop.

Estimated impact: ten hours, twenty minutes.

Danny double-checked his work. When he was satisfied, he drifted back into the network. He took his time reentering the same portal inside the Chimney, trailing an email that was downloading onto the server. He ended up in the middle of the main database that contained phone calls, emails, and documents. He filtered through the information disguised as system maintenance, integrating with the content.

There were lists of clients, none of which Danny recognized; surveillance video showing "prospects" of teenage boys that were sometimes in hospitals, alone in poverty or abandoned in remote areas. Prospects had psychological evaluation documents attached to them, evaluating them as either viable candidates or not.

Nothing explained what they were doing with them.

Danny ventured out of the system, past highly secure compartments that controlled all the buildings, food storage, power and security features. He could shut down the island, if he needed to. But that wouldn't do any good without someone coming to the rescue.

He was about to return to the Nowhere when something stopped him. It was a large database called "Records".

Danny hesitated. Records would mean histories. The past.

Who I am.

Night had arrived in Foreverland.

Danny hurried inside the Records.

41

THE ATMOSPHERE TRANSFORMED INTO IMAGES. He was no longer amorphous data that streamed along the colorful conduit. The Records database took shape of something that resembled an enormous library with vaulted ceilings and hanging lights. The floor was hard and shiny and the walls covered with bookshelves. But there were no tables or chairs; there was no need to reach for the symbolic books that held the records of the island. Danny only needed to think and the information streamed into his consciousness. He could absorb and comprehend the data about everyone, but he was only interested in one person.

[Search for Danny...] he thought-commanded, suddenly realizing something he had been missing every since he woke up.

I don't know my last name.

It didn't seem important before. He was Danny and that was all he needed. It didn't even feel like he had a last name, like it had been erased.

The walls shifted. The bookshelves rotated and changed positions. Three books floated off the shelves and levitated in front of him, each with the name *Daniel* on the cover. He didn't recognize any of the last names, but two of them had two small words lettered in red just below the name.

Crossover Completed.

Danny sent them back to the shelves. The third one centered in front of him.

"Daniel Forrester," he said. "Let's see what you got."

He touched the cover. The book opened. There were no words on pages, only the colors of raw data. He put his hand on it and knew.

I'm Daniel Forrester.

Daniel Forrester was born in Gilbert, Arizona.

A healthy boy and an only child. His parents were John and Maggy Forrester. They were both only children, as well. The grandparents all deceased. The only extended family was a great aunt that lived in Rockford, Illinois. She was in her eighties and suffering from dementia.

Ideal candidate, it said.

That's what Danny was labeled, an ideal candidate for the program. He didn't know if that referred to his health or the dementia. Or maybe the lack of extended family.

His father was a finish carpenter.

Memories emerged of his father coming home when it was dark. Danny would be parked in front of the television when his truck pulled into the driveway. His father smelled of sweat and cedar. Sometimes he'd lug his double-saddle tool belt into the house loaded with every tool ever invented and work on a project at home, fixing a doorframe or building a new room. He knew where every tool was located in the tool belt, finding it without looking. And when he was done, he always slipped it back where it belonged, without looking.

He was very good.

Until he fell from a roof and severed his spinal cord.

Danny was nine when it happened. He was on the computer in the attic when his mother took him to the neighbor's house. She was crying and didn't tell Danny anything. She didn't come back to get him for three days. She didn't talk much then, either.

His father died on the operating table.

Danny held her hand at the funeral. It was cold. When he squeezed, she didn't squeeze back. Her eyes had become blank. No family attended, only neighbors and woodworkers. The house was very quiet that night.

His mother was not home much. She worked a lot. She had a prescription drug problem and washed it down with gin. She often never made it off the couch. This suited Danny's lifestyle just fine.

Danny learned how to hack computers when he was six. It started with online games. He and his friends hacked Xbox and PlayStation databases, rewriting the code for unlimited weapons. They downloaded free music, movies, and games. Sometimes they had games before they were released.

By the time he was nine, it wasn't even a challenge. After his father died, he stepped up the stakes.

They hacked into the school and planted porn in the principal's inbox. They changed all the jocks' grades to Fs. They set off fire alarms ten times in a month.

They hacked their first bank when he was 10.

They set up a dummy account with false ATM deposits. They never let the balance go over five hundred dollars and they never withdrew the money as cash, simply used it to pay for things online. Because his mother was never home, they had clothes, shoes, computers and software shipped directly to his house.

It was a parole officer that busted him.

Danny skipped school, sitting up in the attic on the computer for days at a time. The cops came to the house and wanted to speak to his mother. It pissed Danny off, so he swiped the officer's identity, repossessed his car and foreclosed on his house. The man's credit was trashed. They couldn't prove he did anything.

He had all the money an 11 year old would want, but he wanted more. He began trolling Las Vegas casinos. At first, it was just jacking accounts and hacking online poker games. But the real money was in Vegas. His friends came over. It took a weekend and a case of Red Bull, but they managed to set up a dummy account with three million dollars and a penthouse timeshare waiting for them at the top of a resort. Their biggest problem was the fact that they were a bunch of eleven year olds.

But they ended up with bigger problems.

At first they thought they'd been discovered by Vegas security and they'd lose all the bones in their thumbs. They were relieved that it was just the FBI. They'd be in trouble, but at least they wouldn't be hung from a hook through the tongue.

The rest of them wanted to stop, but Danny wasn't going to lie down. He planted a data bomb inside the FBI network and wiped it out. Their evidence disappeared. But not all of it.

They came to the door disguised as the UPS man dropping off another package. Danny answered the door in his sweatpants. They put him in the back of a black Suburban. His friends sat next to him.

He was back home by the time he was thirteen.

Despite the federal shadow watching his every move, he went back to his Vegas accounts and set up two more. He could retire when he turned eighteen.

That's when the house burned down.

That's when Danny's life – as he knew it – ended.

Danny Forrester was acquired by Franklin Constantino.

The file said he'd been acquired by this man.

Acquired.

Franklin Constantino made his money in real estate and other businesses. He had lung cancer and had not been seen in public for quite some time. Some reports stated he had died in a boating accident.

But Danny knew he wasn't dead. Franklin Constantino stood in front of him as the record book projected his image before him.

Mr. Jones.

The house had burned down. The police found two bodies. One was a woman and the other was a boy. Each was beyond recognition but assumed to be the bodies of Danny and his mother. The fire started when she fell asleep on the couch and dropped a lit cigarette. Danny was asleep in the attic and couldn't escape.

None of it was true.

He didn't fall asleep in the attic. On the nights he did sleep, he went to his room. It was too cold upstairs and there was nowhere to lie down. But to the world, Danny was dead.

And there was no family left to care.

No family left to look.

Like the database at the Federal Bureau of Investigations, he had been erased from the world.

He had been *acquired*.

The record ended there.

No explanation how he got to the island. Only when he got there and who he belonged to.

Danny closed the book. It flew back to the shelf. So many books, each someone that had been acquired. And every one of them boys, each of them brought to the island, fed and cared for, each marched to the Haystack where they gladly stuck a needle in their head. Every one of them doing what they were told to do and the world would never know.

All of them following this trail to Foreverland. All of them but one.

[Reed...] Danny thought-commanded.

The room shifted. One book came out, front and center.

———

Reed Johnston, born in Wooster, Ohio.

He was an only child, too. Grew up on a farm. His mother had died when she delivered him.

He was raised by his father. He stopped going to school before he graduated so that he could help with the crops. Reed planted the fields and helped harvest at the end of the season. He also cleaned out the bottles of vodka that rolled from beneath the seat. When his father went on a real bender, he'd be the only one in the fields. He was the one that answered the door when the creditors came knocking and he was the one that called the bank when they needed money for seed.

Reed didn't socialize much. He wouldn't talk to anyone at school except for a girl that sat behind him in most of his classes. Her name was Lucinda Jones.

Lucinda lived with her aunt and uncle and their twelve kids. They weren't thrilled about it; they had enough mouths to feed. She was given custody over them when her father died serving in the military and her mother died of breast cancer two years later. Lucinda was only five.

She made plenty of trouble by the time she was ten.

Reed spent years watching her. He even went to church just to see her walk back from communion. He'd sit in the back row while his dad was sleeping off a long one and slip out before mass was over. But she knew he was watching.

She would meet him out in the field and they'd find the shade of a tree to sit and talk. She would sometimes sneak out after midnight and meet Reed waiting on the road in his father's old pick-up. They would drive the deserted country roads and look at the stars until she fell asleep in his arms. He would take her home and help her back through the window.

There was no mention of Reed being an ideal candidate.

When Reed was seventeen, he finished the morning rounds. The tractor needed parts. He ate lunch before heading into town. When he got back, his father was still asleep. At supper, he finally checked on him, found him dead in his bed.

Reed didn't bother calling an ambulance.

He buried his old man in the soybean field out behind the silo. No tombstone, no cross or words. He put him in the ground still wearing coveralls, his mouth slightly agape, and covered him with dirt. When he was done, he dropped the shovel and went inside and called Lucinda.

The next day, they were hundreds of miles away from home. Lucinda's suitcase was in the back. Reed's few belongings were in a paper sack. They were driving south. They didn't know where, they were just going to drive until they felt like stopping. They wanted to get married but they'd have to find someone that would wed seventeen year olds without parental consent. There was always Vegas.

Their truck went off the road somewhere in Oklahoma. The bumper wrapped around an oak tree.

Both of them went through the windshield.

Reed survived. He saw her body next to a tree. She wasn't moving.

He tried to get to her, to help her, to breathe into her lungs, to touch her once more...

The record ended.

Reed Johnston was *acquired*.

And woke up on the island.

42

THE NOWHERE ROOM WAS EMPTY.

Lucinda wasn't there when Danny returned from the Records. He was relieved. He considered staying in the Records until the round ended but it was too risky. Lucinda would know his thoughts the moment he arrived. She would know that she was dead.

Lucinda is a memory.

When Reed arrived on the island, somehow she slipped out of his memories and came to life in Foreverland. She didn't know that she didn't exist outside in the real world.

She thinks she's alive. Does that make her real?

Did Reed know?

No, Reed was just as confused as she was. He dreamed of her, didn't know her name. Only Danny knew they had a real past. He knew they had parents, they were real people before they woke up on the island. But their parents were gone. There was nothing left of their lives.

No one would look for them.

Danny drifted back to his body, back to the Haystack and cold reality. He sat up, groggily. The cells were open and empty. Reed was gone. Zin, too. A few Investors were standing outside his cell. They were looking across the aisle. They didn't pay attention to Danny quickly getting dressed.

Two more Investors came inside with a stretcher. They placed it next to Sid. He was still lying flat on the floor. The Investors began to dress him. His eyes were open. His mouth, too.

"Let's go, Danny Boy." Mr. Jones reached for him. "There's nothing to watch."

Danny pulled his arm away. *Mr. Constantino.*

"Come along, son." Mr. Jones blocked the view into Sid's cell. "Why don't you get to your room and get some rest. This was a long round."

"What happened to Sid?" Danny said.

"He just progressed a little faster than expected, nothing to worry about, son. Come along."

Danny hurried into the aisle so that Mr. Jones wouldn't touch him. He went to his room alone and looked across the Yard. A flatbed cart emerged from the trees. Someone was lying on the back of it, covered with a sheet and his Investor riding next to him. They went around the dormitory. Toward the Chimney.

You can stay here.

Lucinda pulled him into Foreverland, like she ripped his identity from his body.

Where was he now?

It didn't matter.

A satellite would soon be punching a crater in the Mansion.

FINAL ROUND

FOSTER PARENTS ARRESTED FOR NEGLECT AND ABUSE

CHICAGO, Illinois. – Cynthia and John Halner were arrested for neglect and physical abuse of twelve foster children living in their home. The Department of Child and Family Services investigated claims of children complaining at school about being punished with belt buckles, bamboo sticks and screwdrivers.

Eleven of the children have been placed in the custody of other families. The oldest child, Eric Zinder, 16, was reported missing. Cynthia and John Halner claimed he had run away several months earlier and failed to report it, although they continued to receive support for his care.

43

IT FELT like his brains got pulled out of his head.

The Director had to yank the needle out. His hands were still shaking. He lay in the chair, his breathing shallow, staring at the needle in his forehead for too long. Foreverland had closed but he was afraid to reach for it. Each time he did, his hand quivered violently. It would be dangerous if the needle shook inside the stent and scrambled his frontal lobe like a lobotomy knife. He took a deep breath and ripped it out like a loose tooth.

It was several minutes before he stopped seeing double.

She shook Foreverland.

He'd never seen anything like it.

The boys were gathered around the sundial where the Director could see them very clearly. He didn't even sense her nearing, she just appeared out of nowhere. Before he could act, she struck the sundial and let loose tremors that never ended. They were still inside his head.

The Director threw the needle on the floor.

He put his feet down. He needed some water, maybe something to settle his stomach. He'd already been on the recliner far too long. The room felt like it was turning ten times as fast as it should've been. He was imagining it.

He stood slowly, hand on the armrest. He let go, took a step and another, quickly leaning over. The floor felt tilted. The Director went several more steps and crashed into the telescope. He rolled to his back, swallowed back bile bitterly surging upward.

Relax, you idiot. This will pass.

Foreverland needed to be shut down for awhile. He had to admit, that would be the best thing after what he saw. It was getting too risky. He'd never become paralyzed inside the needle. Not only had he lost track of Danny and the girl, he didn't see anything after she belted the sundial. He didn't know where they went or what they were doing. He was half-baked until the day finally ended and he returned to the chair.

But he couldn't shut things down. That would require starting everything over. He'd lose the confidence of the Investors. He might not get it back up and running. Besides, the girl... she was out in the open.

She was getting too strong. For that reason, Foreverland needed to continue, full speed ahead.

The Director decided right there – staring at the ceiling, swallowing foul gulps of saliva – he would follow Danny into the next round and put an end to this madness once and for all. He'd set a trap for the little bitch and be done with it. He had to do something. Soon.

But who's trapping who?

"Director?" the intercom called. "Is everything all right?"

"Yes." He rolled to his side and spent some time on his hands and knees. He decided to sit on the floor a bit longer. "I want Jones and Smith up here."

"They are with the boys right now."

"Well, send for them."

"I think we have bigger problems, Director."

Oh, you have no idea. "What would that be?"

"You'll need to come down to the network floor. I think we need to consider suspending the program until we can—"

"No."

The Director pulled himself up. He saw the cart driving away from the Haystack with someone lying in the back. He assumed the boy Zin had finally crossed over for graduation and was being transferred to the Chimney.

"What would you like to do?" the intercom spoke.

"Right now, I want Smith and Jones in my office." He filled a glass with water and drank. "Afterwards, I want to see what Danny Boy was up to."

"I'm not comfortable with the risk you're suggesting."

"Life is a risk."

"You're risking everything."

The world settled around the Director. He smoothed the front of his floral-designed shirt, brushing away the fear that, seconds earlier, churned inside him. He poured Scotch over the water.

"Get Smith and Jones up here. Now."

44

DANNY WOKE IN HIS BED.

His room was lit up. He pulled open the curtain. The sun was high enough to be noon. The Yard was active. Dozens of campers were playing soccer. Others were hanging out at the tables.

Something is wrong.

When the sleep-fog cleared, he remembered. The satellite!

It should have landed. The impact would've been like a bomb. There wouldn't be much of the Mansion left and there sure as hell wouldn't be a soccer game. Unless it was off the mark, landing a mile or two in the water. That was possible.

Maybe the Trojan horses were quarantined. Possible, sure. There was always a chance a security scan picked them up while they lay dormant. Still, they would find him. Eventually. One day.

He cursed.

Stupid. Stupid, stupid, STUPID. He should've pulled the trigger while he was there, sent them all hurtling toward the island. That way, at least, he could battle off security snoopers and if they caught him they would trace him back to the island.

Stupid.

He needed to get dressed, get over to the Mansion and see if anything had landed. Maybe there would be some debris that would indicate an off-target crash. Even if the satellite was fifty miles off, the military would cruise by the island. There was still going to be an investigation.

He threw on some clothes and noticed someone sitting at the card table. The camp wasn't down there throwing cards like usual. It was just one person. One he didn't expect.

Zin was lying on the table, hands folded over his stomach. Taking in the sun.

"Zin?" Danny approached, warily. "Is that you?"

Stupid question. But after seeing Parker not recognizing them, he worried that Zin would be absent. But then he turned his head and smiled. His eyes were bright and focused.

"Danny Boy," he said.

Danny wanted to hug him. They slapped hands, instead. Zin sat up, stretched. "Man, the sun never felt so good."

"What the hell happened?"

"I woke up in the Haystack before you did. You should've seen the look on my Investor's face! He looked like he dropped a ten pound load in his trousers when I stood up and hugged him while I was still full on naked. The old man was speechless. I wanted to wait until you woke up but the old men were running everyone out of the Haystack."

"I don't get it. What happened?"

Zin rubbed his face, looked out to the Yard, thinking. "I don't really remember anything about the last... week, I guess. I mean, I don't even remember going inside the needle. It just felt like I was... floating, I suppose. Like, I was out in the Nowhere just floating around and coming apart."

He stalled.

"It's weird, I don't know how to describe it. I just felt like I was being pulled in a hundred directions, like I was being stretched. It didn't hurt, really. It was all rather numb. And I just didn't care."

Zin looked good. He was more present. Healthy, somehow.

"The weird thing? I remember everything, Danny Boy. You know how we remember more when we go inside the needle? I'm Eric Zinder. My parents died when I was little and I ended up in foster care. I ran away and lived on the streets. I was homeless, dude. I was some street rat jacking cars and... and... no good, man."

He looked sick.

"I was no good."

Zin recalled robbing some tourists on their way to the theater, some old man and a woman way too young. He remembered getting hauled into a van and a sack over his head. Something over his mouth and vapors in his head.

And then he woke up in the Chimney.

But the weird thing was, Danny was remembering, too. He didn't know his whole life, not like Zin was reciting. But he remembered the stuff he knew inside Foreverland. He forgot things when he came out before, but now he was remembering it.

"She did it," Zin said.

"Who?" Danny said. "Your girlfriend?"

"A girl with this..." He chopped at his ears. "She had long red hair, these big eyes. She sent me back."

"Lucinda?"

Zin shook his head. "She didn't say her name, she just came out of the fog and then she was standing in front of me."

He put his hand on Danny's shoulder and bowed his head.

"'You don't belong here' she said to me, Danny Boy. And then I felt all pulled back together. The fog lifted and I woke up in the cell."

She sent him back. Zin was fading from his body, he was heading for Foreverland and she had the power to send him back. Of course, she did. And maybe that's what she did to Danny, gave him the ability to remember in the flesh. She did the opposite to—

"Sid!" Danny said. "What happened to him?"

"You didn't hear?" Zin threw his arm over Danny's shoulders. "Our man Sid set the record for smoking out, brother. He went into that round all normal and came out empty. The Investors were more baffled by Sid then they were watching me walk out of there. I think the rest of our camp thinks I'm possessed, they think maybe I did something. They're not talking to me."

They had to know it wasn't Zin. They saw Lucinda come out of the ground and hammer the sundial, stick her arm in Sid's chest. Right? Or did they not see any of that? Maybe they didn't even see her.

The sky was nothing but blue. No clouds or streaks or smoke.

Untouched.

There was no point going to the Mansion. Nothing was coming. The good guys would never arrive. They were truly alone, now. The Director would figure out what he did in the last round, there was no way they were letting him inside the needle again. Maybe they already knew.

"What's going on, Danny Boy?" Zin calmly said. "You expecting someone to parachute into the Yard?"

Danny shook his head.

"None of this was supposed to happen," Zin said. "I shouldn't be here and Sid shouldn't be wherever he is. Did you do something?"

"No. Not really."

"Well, what did you do?"

Danny sat down, rested his elbows on the tabletop. All the dorm windows were open except Reed's. The curtains were drawn. He was probably curled up in the dark recovering from God-knows-what they did to him. And now Danny had to tell him that he had another round to go.

"I blew it, man."

"Ah, yes. You've got the world by the balls here on the island. You can do whatever you want, as long as you go to the Haystack and let them drill your head. Yeah, how could you blow that?"

"You really want to know?"

"I'm all about knowing." He held out his hands and smiled, typical Zin fashion.

Danny sat nodding and thinking. He got up, walked around. The sundial was fifty feet away. It was the center of Foreverland. Maybe it meant nothing in the real world, but he didn't like being that close to it, not when he was about to tell Zin everything.

"Let's go see Reed," he said.

45

THE DIRECTOR DRAPED his floral shirt over the back of a chair and buttoned up a beige long sleeved one. He had not been for a walk on his island for quite some time. Lately, it had been all work, work, work.

When he first arrived on the island some thirty years earlier, he hiked every day. He could also see his abs. Now he couldn't see what color flip-flops he was wearing. It was the price of intelligence, he often told himself. That, and becoming a lazy slob.

It was an abandoned resort when he first arrived. Most of the buildings were in severe disrepair. The jungle was taking them back. It wasn't worth much. So he bought it.

He didn't know why he was so hasty. At the time, he just wanted to escape the world. He'd seen his share of heartbreak (his fiancé was having an affair) and disappointment (his business partner died of a stroke at the age of 41) and wanted to heed the advice of a famous philosopher, one Henry David Thoreau.

Simplify.

He planned on living out his life on that island. But nothing stays the same. That was the only guarantee life gave you: things change.

Yes, they do.

He needed to get out. He was nearing the most critical point of the program, of his life, and he needed to be thinking with a clear head. He had just returned from the fourth floor and had seen what Danny had done.

He spent some time contemplating it, but his penthouse was suddenly suffocating. Now he was lacing up snake boots to get outside for awhile. He shirked the flip-flops and shorts. He wasn't opposed to risk, just not when there wasn't a payoff. And what he'd seen on the fourth floor was a risk, indeed.

But the payoff was worth it.

The boy became data.

The fourth floor analyst, Mr. Jackson, advised him to remove Danny from the program. When boys went inside the needle, they needed a digital body. Once that was gone, the identity would scatter into the Nowhere, bodiless. Lost. Nothing.

But Danny didn't need a body. He became data, floating through the system like a ghost. He had done something no one had done before. Something the Director didn't know was possible. He had no idea what kind of power he had. It came too easy.

He could bring everything down the next time.

Danny had sensed the trap. The Director made it obvious, rigged it so that Danny would suspect it was too easy. He knew the boy was brilliant, and with brilliance comes patience. He wasn't hasty. He would look for another way to escape the island's network to get into the outside world, and the only other way was to infiltrate the heart of the Chimney.

Right where they wanted him.

Danny moved inside the Loop Program: a digital environment that simulated the outside world. There was a chance he would recognize it was a mock-up, but he didn't. Danny thought he had escaped again and went right through the United States military firewall like it was a video game.

His infiltration of Milstar was all inside the network of computers on the fourth floor. If he had actually been in the real world, there would be a satellite-filled crater somewhere on the island.

Brilliant.

Mr. Jackson suggested Danny be removed from the program permanently. *What if he knew it was the Looping Program and slipped out?*

Well, he didn't.

Mr. Jackson didn't understand what the Director saw. He didn't see the potential. He knew that Lucinda was an anomaly that escaped from Reed's mind and haunted Foreverland. He knew that she was getting stronger and more troublesome. But he wasn't looking in the other direction.

They were on the threshold of mankind's next great discovery. Freedom from the body. *Enlightenment through technology.*

The Director would go down in history ahead of Edison, Einstein and Jobs.

He would become the 21st century Buddha.

———

When the Director was young – in his 20s – he travelled to Third World countries, places like Ethiopia and Rwanda. He went there to help people with suffering. He brought them medicine and food; he worked with government officials to curb corruption. He educated them. But there was nowhere to go. And the more he helped, the more he saw their suffering.

It wasn't just the physical suffering. It was the suffering of the mind.

He decided, after only two years of service, the world needed a revolutionary way of healing the mind. If the mind operated clearly, physical suffering could be tolerated, even avoided. Nothing in the last thousand years brought relief to the mind. People weren't going to the mountain tops to meditate for twenty years, they were plugging in smartphones and tablets. They needed easier access to real freedom.

The record number of prescriptions for depression was proof we were doing something wrong.

Life is suffering.

The Director came to the island to save humanity because God wasn't helping. He meditated on the cliffs and explored the wild. He rebuilt the island, renovated the buildings and created a paradise that would heal the body and nurture the soul. His father – just before his death – had developed alternate reality and the Director used it to rewrite corrupt minds and correct bad habits. He would do what the Buddha failed to do: bring enlightenment to the masses.

Such an endeavor wasn't free. He would need money. Lots.

But the Investors would need a reason to spend that kind of money. They weren't interested in altruistic endeavors like the Director; they needed a return on their investment that would be worth the risk. The Director gave them one. He gave the old and dying Investors what they desired most. He gave them the only thing their money couldn't buy.

More life.

The Director holstered a machete to cut through the overgrown paths. He carried a sitting cushion to the elevator. He decided that he would sit meditation on the cliff to further contemplate the future of the program. His thirty years had culminated at this very moment. He did not want to be rash.

Mr. Clark waited in a golf cart outside the front doors of the Chimney.

"Director," he said, "the Investors would like a word."

"I see." The Director started around the cart. "I will hike first, Mr. Clark."

"They request your presence immediately."

"Mr. Clark, I am not prepared for a meeting. I have a schedule. Presently, they're not on it. But I'll make room later today."

The Director started around again and Mr. Clark bumped the cart in front of him. "I think now, Director, would be an appropriate time to alter your schedule. Impatience can fester, you see. I suggest you come along."

"I see." The Director balanced the tip of the machete on the front of the cart. "Mr. Clark, what is it that cannot wait an hour?"

"Your future, Director."

He laughed. "I don't attend those meetings."

"Today, you do." Mr. Clark patted the seat. "We're all in this together. And we don't care how silly you look."

The Director didn't mind the insult to his hiking gear. He didn't like meeting on their terms. And certainly not on their grounds. But he slid onto the seat. Without the Investors, there was no program. And he was so close.

They took the wider path, heading for the Mansion.

46

DANNY STEPPED BACK into the cover of the trees. He had been hiding outside the Chimney, trying to figure out how to get around Mr. Clark and through the front doors. Danny assumed he was there to pick the Director up, but the minutes dragged on.

The Director looked like he was going on safari. Danny had never seen the man in person. There was a picture of him in the cafeteria posing with a bunch of happy boys like they'd just won the lottery. He was smaller in person and sported a pot belly. He was wearing long sleeves and rugged pants with boots laced up to his knees.

He wasn't happy to see Mr. Clark, the way he jabbed the machete into the cart. After a few words, he got on the cart and they started in the direction of the Mansion.

Danny went to the front door but it was locked. He wasn't sure what he was going to do if he got inside. He just figured it was time to talk with someone in charge.

He had gone to Reed's room earlier that day. He began to open the door—

"Son!" Mr. Smith shouted. "Don't go in there."

Danny backed away. Mr. Smith walk-limped as fast as he could. He was carrying a lunch bag.

"I just wanted to say hello," Danny said.

"He's in no shape to talk with anyone." Mr. Smith huffed.

"Yeah, I wonder why."

"Don't take that tone, my boy. Have some respect when you talk—"

"What did you do to him this time? Did you poke sticks in his ears or rip his fingernails off? Did you break him in half? What was it this time, Mr. Smith?"

Zin pulled him back. "Danny Boy, come on. Let's come back another time."

"No, he needs to answer me!"

"Now, relax a second, son." Mr. Smith stopped Danny with a hand on his chest. "None of the treatments are permanently damaging. He'll recover just fine, he's just a little uncomfortable. It's for his own good. All of this is for his own good."

"Treatments? You're torturing him, admit it!"

"I'm going to call Mr. Jones."

"I don't care if you call God."

Danny pushed open the door.

The room was dark. Reed was curled up on the bed. He tried to roll over but convulsions shook him like he'd been struck by lightning.

Mr. Smith reached inside his pocket and then Danny went down. Everything went black.

He woke up on his bed with Mr. Jones.

It took several moments to realize Mr. Smith hit his tracker. *Mr. Smith. That wasn't his real name.*

When Mr. Jones finally left, Danny snuck out. And now that he saw where the Director was going, he could find plenty of trouble.

All the bastards will be together.

47

MR. CLARK DROPPED the Director off at the front steps of the Mansion and took the golf cart through the slowly opening garage door, closing just as slowly behind him. The Director stroked the flat side of the machete, contemplating the front doors and brass knobs. He despised going inside their fortress. It smelled old. Smelled like dying.

The Mansion was built upon the remnants of the resort's hotel. He had no input of how the original Investors would build it, only that it needed to keep the boys out. He envisioned a fence, but the Investors and their mountains of cash built a damn fortress that dissected the southern tip in gaudy, institutionalized fashion. There was enough square footage to hide a small village.

He stopped at the top step and knocked with the backside of the blade. He stepped inside the foyer, patting the machete in his open palm for all the old codgers to see. He thought it might be over the top, but it wasn't. They were on the veranda waiting for him. He saw them through the glass wall. Beyond their gray and balding heads, he could see the ocean.

All forty of them were in attendance.

They had pulled chairs onto the expansive veranda that jutted out from the back of the building. A few of them had canes leaning against their knees; others had oxygen tanks parked next to them. It looked like the Board of Directors for the AARP.

A podium was set in the center. In front of that, facing the committee of Investors, was a lone chair. Ceiling fans blew down on the Director as he stepped out to greet them, still handling the machete.

"You may shield your weapon, Director." Mr. Black, a fat Arabian with a checkered headdress, stepped to the podium. "Threats are not necessary."

"What, this? It's for brush cutting. You thought I was going to chop you up?"

These old bastards, so used to their former lives as CEOs and business titans with their formal rules and procedures, had to have a freaking podium just to talk. Now the Director regretted not changing back into his flip-flops.

"Please." Mr. Black aimed his best glare at him; a glare that worked well with employees.

The Director sheathed the blade with a flurry of sword-fighting moves. "I'm not sitting, gentlemen. This will be a short meeting. You've all signed contracts agreeing to the terms of the island and I have final authority of how to proceed. The fact I'm even here is a modern day miracle, so make it quick."

"I speak for everyone in attendance," Mr. Black said. "And we have had enough."

The Director rolled his eyes.

"We have sacrificed much, Director. But we are powerful men and we do not take risks without contingency. We will replace you if changes are not made."

The Director rumbled with laugher.

"Mr. Black, with all due respect to you and your gang," he cleared his throat, "I AM THE PROGRAM! You can't replace me, gentlemen, I am every reason you are here today. I brought you here because I have proved, over and over, this program works. You didn't risk everything because I made a promise, you did it because I deliver. I am the way, gentlemen. I am the Alpha and the Omega. Without me," he tapped his forehead, "there is no program, I suggest you understand that."

The men did not stir.

"Be that as it may," Mr. Black said, "there are reasons for concern. Eric Zinder has fully recovered from his progress with his memories intact. At the same time, Sidney Hayward has become completely unresponsive. And now we are hearing reports that Danny Forrester has circumvented security."

"Where'd you hear that?"

"We are not ignorant, nor will we sit back and be taken advantage of, Director. You are taking unnecessary risks that could impact all of us."

"You're not qualified to judge the program." He fingered the hilt of the machete. "None of you know what it takes to run this island, to do what I do. It cannot be done, it cannot be understood by anyone else but me, gentlemen. You should not speak where matters do not concern you."

"On the contrary, they do concern us. And, despite what you believe, *we* are the program, Director. We fund this operation. Without us, you are nothing. You are playing a game that you won't win. I suggest you listen."

The Director nodded along with the accusations. He let go of the chair, meandered around the Investors and leaned against the railing. The ocean breeze was warm but cooled his face as it filtered through his beard that was becoming itchy with perspiration.

"Director, please come back to the chair. Some of the Investors cannot see you."

"And what game would that be, Mr. Black?"

Chairs scuffled.

"Director, please."

"What game, Mr. Black? What game am I playing? The game that extends your lives another 80 years, is that the one you're referring to?"

"We are not barbarians, Director. You are torturing one of the boys. We did not agree to the inhumane treatment of them, that was in the contract. Perhaps you should review it, yourself."

"I see." The Director didn't want to leave the edge of the balcony, took his time doing so. He returned to the chair that was on trial and sat this time. Mr. Smith was sitting on the far left side of the semi-circle, arms crossed and tight-lipped.

"Gentlemen," the Director said, loudly and slowly, "you bought these boys. You arranged for them to be delivered to the island. You're not barbarians? What is it do you think we're doing to them that is not barbaric?"

"We agreed to discomfort, not torture."

"We have to make adjustments for abnormality. Mr. Smith has invested as much as the rest of you, I believe he has every right to collect on that investment. As would the rest of you."

"The boy is in agony."

"He won't be for long."

"You're not being honest, Director. These are more than minor incidents."

"Every science has its wrinkles, Mr. Black. We have to adjust. I assure you, the program is well. We are analyzing the current state of these abnormalities and will act accordingly."

Quiet settled, interrupted by the hiss of an oxygen tank.

"Now, if we're finished—"

"We want to suspend Daniel Forrester, Reed Johnston, and Eric Zinder," Mr. Black stated.

Mr. Smith stood up. "That was not what we discussed!"

In-fighting broke out.

The Director sat back, twirling the curly whiskers on his chin. Let them tear each other apart. They had no alternative, they knew it. They were all accustomed to having control and that rarely made for good teamwork. Especially when you add the desperation of impending death. They were all dying and that would tend to make anyone impatient, especially power-hungry old men.

THUD!

The front door cracked loud enough that almost all of them heard it on the veranda. The Director turned to listen while the argument began to lose steam. When the second one hit—

THUD!

—he was the first one to the door. He opened it, saw the fist-sized dents about eye level. Carefully, he looked outside.

48

DANNY WAS HALFWAY to the Mansion when he picked up the first rock. He didn't know why, but then he picked up another. He held the bottom of his shirt and cradled them like a hammock.

He launched the first one as he arrived at the bottom step. A direct hit, head-high. It went bang off the metal door like a gunshot. The stone skipped down the steps. He grabbed another one from his stash, yearning to hear that satisfaction again. He reached back—

Felt it ripped from his hand.

"What the hell you doing?" Zin tossed the rock into the trees. "You want to get killed?"

"They're already doing that, Zin."

Zin knocked his hand off his shirt and the cache of stones crashed on the bottom step. He grabbed Danny by the shirt. "Come on, before someone comes out."

He let Zin drag him a couple steps and pulled. "No."

The second rock sunk a dent as deep as the first and not more than six inches to the left. He was reaching for a third when Zin knocked him down.

"I'm not letting you commit suicide."

Zin was on his knees, chucking the rocks into the underbrush.

They were going to get caught, but two rocks looked a lot different if there wasn't ten more waiting to be fired. He had just enough time to grab the two that rebounded off the door. The last one rolled out of sight just as the door opened.

The Director appeared in the doorway, wearing some kind of desert scouting outfit. His left hand rested on the hilt of a small sword. A fat old man pushed past him, followed by more.

"JUST KILL HIM!" Danny screamed. "He's not going to take the needle, so just go ahead and kill him, already! Put us all out of misery!"

Danny started up the steps. Zin caught him on the third one. He wasn't going to slip away again.

"I know what you're doing to us," Danny shouted. "You're a bunch of fat, selfish bastards!"

"What are you doing?" Zin hissed in his ear.

"If you don't want to just kill us, I will! I'll throw all of the boys over the cliffs." Danny jabbed at them. "We're all going over, anyway. We'll do it on our own!"

"DANNY BOY!" Mr. Jones stumbled down the steps. "Stop this foolishness, right this second. What has gotten into you?"

Another ten Investors were out the door, exchanging knowing glances. The Director's steely gaze never wavered.

"I'll tell you what got into me, go see Reed. Mr. Smith knows, he's doing it to him. He's breaking him. He doesn't want to take the needle, all right? Are you so desperate that you're going to kill him slowly for it?"

"He's just trying to help him, Danny Boy." Mr. Jones helped Zin restrain him. "You don't understand what's happening, you must trust us."

"Trust you?" Danny turned on Mr. Jones. *Constantino* was on the tip of his tongue. *Acquired,* too. He was about to spit them like darts. Had he, it would've changed everything. The Investors would've known their privacy had been breached. They would've condemned the Director without question. The program would have failed. Nobody would escape, ever.

But the Director's hand gently fell on Danny's shoulder.

"It's all right, son," he said.

Danny stopped struggling. Everyone said *son*. But the Director said it differently. It wasn't an expression, it meant something. And it fell quietly on Danny.

"Mr. Jones." The Director turned to him. "Let me have a word with Danny Boy."

All three of them – Zin, Mr. Jones and the Director – kept their hands on him, slowly letting go. Danny stared at the Director. He wanted to hate him, but there was calm in his expression.

"Gentlemen." The Director turned to the crowd inside the doorway. "We will proceed as usual. Remember why we've come together."

He turned to Danny.

"We're here to help," he said to the others. "Let's remember that."

No one moved.

The program teetered on that moment.

And then the Director led Danny away from the Mansion.

A man doesn't achieve that level of power without knowing how to handle pressure.

49

It was a narrow path. An overgrown one.

Danny trampled on leaves and fronds sheared cleanly by the Director's blade. The Director didn't turn around when Danny caught up to him. He was grabbing with the left hand and swinging the machete with the right. The jungle bent to his will as they made their way through it.

Sweat drenched the back of his shirt. Danny could hear his breathing between each swing. When they reached a small clearing where a tree had uprooted – its roots bare and dead – the Director wiped his head with a handkerchief and leaned against the massive trunk.

"Whew!" he said. "This trail hasn't been used in awhile, wouldn't you say, Danny Boy?"

Danny kept a healthy ten feet between them.

"It reminds me of the time I first discovered this place. Nothing but trees in this part of the island, nature taking back what mankind put in its way. Can you believe that was 30 years ago?" The Director looked up, shaking his head. "Goes by in a flash, Danny Boy. Cherish that youth, my boy, while you can. One day you're going to be fat and out of shape like me, son."

The Director pulled a drink from the canteen on his hip. He wiped his mouth with his sleeve and offered it to Danny. He didn't even bother shaking his head. He just stared.

The Director screwed the lid back in place and smacked his lips.

"Yes, sir," he said. "Thirty years ago, this was a dying resort for the super wealthy when I got here. I was going to resurrect it, turn it into an extreme vacation island resort with hiking and meditation and snorkeling. Maybe import some animals so it had a real jungle feel." He slowly moved his hand as if reading a banner. "Discover Your Inner Tarzan."

He laughed.

"Wouldn't have worked, Danny Boy. Stupid idea. The rich don't want anything to do with Tarzan and that's when I heard a higher calling. That's when I decided to help the world, to heal it one person at a time. This is a revolutionary program, Danny Boy. We're on the verge of taking mankind to another level in its evolution..."

He stared at Danny.

"But you've heard the pitch, I'm sure. I don't need to tell you. Right?"

The Director wiped his whole face, again, tucked the handkerchief in the upper pocket of his shirt. He leaned back and waited.

"That's hard to believe," Danny finally said, "after what you've done to Reed."

"I see." The Director nodded, thinking.

Danny clearly didn't understand what was going on. He was a kid. He needed an adult to explain the world to him.

"The brain operates like a computer, wouldn't you say?" the Director said. "It's got connections and information that form concepts and ideas. And computers are susceptible to corruption, like malicious code. Something that will disrupt its ability to operate normally."

"I've never fixed a computer with torture, Director."

"No, but you have reformatted one. Am I right? Of course, I am. You are a computer genius, there's no denying that, Danny Boy. You know that when an operating system is corrupt, sometimes it needs to be erased and reprogrammed from the beginning. It needs to relearn the right way to operate."

"There's nothing wrong with me."

"You don't know that, Danny Boy. You can't change and stay the same. In order to heal, you have to be willing to let go of the past. Be willing to let go of the programming that corrupted your soul to begin with. All you boys have a chance to be new again."

"Reed's almost crippled. He's broken. You're destroying him."

"Some are more damaged than others. I can only offer him salvation, Danny Boy. Only offer the healing, he has to take it."

"So you torture him?"

"It sometimes takes a strong hand to get people to let go of their past. People aren't willing to give up what tortures them. Every time Reed goes to the Haystack, he has the power to heal himself but refuses. I can't make him, I can only encourage him. He's got to trust what I'm doing for him, you see. Trust, Danny Boy."

"I don't trust you, Director. I don't know you."

"How do you know?" He raised his eyebrows, questioningly. "I could be the father you need to forget."

"No one on this island trusts." Danny tapped the back of his neck. "That's why everyone has a tracker, just in case. Including you."

"We're dealing with the human condition here, Danny Boy. Corruption, sin. People cheat if given the opportunity. These little things in the neck take that away. Makes everyone feel a little better. Good thing Sid had one, wouldn't you say?"

The Director smiled.

———

They walked for a long time, in silence. Their path was serpentine. The Director seemed to go out of his way to cut giant leaves when he could've just ducked under them. Eventually, the trees began to thin out. The soil turned to stone. A breeze howled down the path, rustling the leaves above them.

They stepped onto the barren ledge of a cliff. The ground was gray with granite and green with lichens growing in the cracks like whiskers and fuzz. It was the highest Danny had ever been on the island. None of the paths led to this spot. He figured if they continued to the right, they would eventually descend until they reached the beach on the north end.

The horizon was flat in both directions. The water deep, dark and blue. The Director wedged his hands on his hips and closed his eyes. He inhaled the ocean's scent.

"Don't you wish you could just be that, Danny Boy?"

He inhaled, again.

"The ocean, my boy. The smell, the sight... the life it contains. All of it, don't you want to be that?"

"How would I know?"

"What do you want, Danny Boy? If you could have anything in the world, what would you ask for?"

"I'd start with knowing who I am, but you took that away."

"I didn't take anything away, you didn't have it."

"Only I would know that."

The Director stepped closer to the edge. A half-step forward and he'd go a hundred feet to the bottom. He walked along the edge to a boulder that jutted up from the ground – flat like a table.

"This is where I had the epiphany, Danny Boy. I would come up here to sit every morning and this is where I received the calling. I knew what mankind needed. We needed to harness the power of the mind, the most powerful weapon a man possesses. If we can control the mind, Danny Boy, we get what we want. That's your answer, son. If you could have anything in the world, it should be the power of the mind."

The mind is a weapon.

"How can you torture us and call that healing?"

"Your body is a prison, my boy. You need to understand that through experiencing its misery. The Haystack is the best teacher you'll ever have. It forces you to face the body's desire, and the suffering that results. You take the needle, you see the freedom of the mind. That's all we're doing, son. Setting you free."

Danny wanted to flee. Everything about the island was wrong, but in the presence of the Director, it all made sense. The body was a prison. The mind was freedom. When he was inside the needle, there was nothing he couldn't do. Why was that less real than his flesh? He was still Danny Boy.

The Director picked up a handful of rocks and pitched them one at a time over the edge. "You went out into the Nowhere with the girl. She's been teaching you to be bad, Danny Boy. She gave you access to our mainframe and you escaped."

He peeked back.

"Didn't you, son?"

Danny didn't answer. There was no need to make it any worse. Now for the punishment.

"You're a true pioneer, Danny Boy." He threw the last rock as far as he could, grunting. "I tell all the boys they're a pioneer, but you are true-blue, Danny Boy. Amazing."

The Director smiled and laughed.

"You did something I never knew possible. You transformed yourself into pure mind. You became data without losing your identity. You were still Danny Boy. And I never thought that was possible, son. Always, I believed, the mind was rooted in the brain, it needed the physical body or it dispersed into random thoughts."

"The Nowhere. Is that what became of the boys before me?"

"Some of them. But you, Danny Boy. You went into the Nowhere and remained Danny Boy. She knew, didn't she? She knew you'd survive being out there, and once you did, you embraced it. You became it. And you were set free."

"How do you know her?"

"I know everything." He nodded, slowly. "Everything."

Danny walked back to the scrawny shade of trees and leaned against one, bending it with his weight. The waves crashed far below.

It's over.

"Is that why you brought me here? To throw me over the edge? Is that what you do with people like me and Reed, throw them in the ocean?"

Laughter. "Son, you don't understand what you've done. You've created an inner reality beyond the needle. Until now, all the boys were limited to Foreverland. Danny Boy, you created a new reality. A new dimension. I want to follow you out of the flesh. I want you to lead us to a new dimension of existence. Show us Nirvana, son. Bring us to the world of pure mind."

"You're wrong," Danny said. "I'm just a hacker. I just created an illusion, no different than a video game."

"We make our own reality." The Director touched his head. "With our minds."

"The reality you create with your mind, Director... that's the definition of delusion."

The Director shook the handkerchief out of his pocket and wiped his forehead, wiped his mouth. He went back to the ledge and put his hands on hips, losing himself in the view.

The cloudless blue sky.

Deep blue water.

Violent collisions on the boulders.

"They want you out, Danny Boy." The Director didn't turn around but said it loud enough for him to hear it. "You, Reed and Zin... you know what that means, don't you?"

Danny didn't want to answer. A lump swelled in his throat. Despite the anger burning his spine, fear had the trump card when it came to survival.

"The program is a delicate thing, Danny Boy. It has balance. When a candidate is rebellious, it tips the scales. These men have a lot invested in you boys. A lot of time, a lot of money. They don't want to see the program come down, a lot of people will get hurt. And sometimes it makes sense to sacrifice a few to save many."

Danny was sure that he had thrown people from the cliff. There was no doubt. It was neat and clean to crush them on the rocks and let the fish destroy the evidence. Not that anyone would find a body even if it was staked to the side of the cliff. This was the Director's island. He was judge and jury.

The Director strode away from the ledge in a meandering sort of way, head down with his fingers buried in his beard, scratching the hidden chin. He knelt at the edge of the trees and broke off a branch, twirled it.

"But I see something in you and Reed." He looked up. "Something this program needs, Danny Boy."

He walked over, looked down.

"I need you to show us what it can become."

The stem spun between his fingers like a helicopter stick with green blades. He plucked one of the leaves and crushed it in his palm, cupped it over his nose and inhaled with his eyes closed, savoring the fragrance.

"Take this." He put the leaves in Danny's hand and closed it. "Steep it in hot water for five minutes and give it to Reed. It'll relieve his suffering. He'll find peace."

"How do I know it won't kill him?"

The Director bit the tip off one of the leaves and chewed. "If I wanted him dead, I wouldn't send you to do it."

Danny put the leaves in his pocket.

The Director went back to the tabletop stone where he had his epiphany and leaped up. He stretched back with his hands on his hips, once again gazing at the view.

"This is your last chance to get Reed inside the needle, Danny Boy. The Investors are powerful men. I can only do so much."

He sat down and crossed his legs into a pretzel. His back was straight, his hands in his lap, he closed his eyes. Breathing, in and out.

Danny left him there so he could become one with the view. He had some tea to make.

50

DANNY SAT at the picnic table. A plastic cup was in front of him. The water had turned light green with shredded foliage floating on top. He fished them out – one by one – with a stick, steam wafting out. Occasionally, he'd look at the door at the end of the dormitory where an empty golf cart was parked parallel with the building.

The tea smelled like diluted turpentine. He put the cup to his lips, not too hot to drink. The aroma made his eyes water. He didn't sip. He wanted to save all of it.

The dormitory door opened. Mr. Smith limped to his cart and slid on the seat. Danny waited a few minutes before going inside, taking the cup with him.

The door was locked.

He should've known it. Mr. Smith knew he was coming back. Danny tried the door knob again, turning it with both hands, then put his shoulder into it. There was nothing in the hall, nothing like a fire extinguisher or a baseball bat to bash the knob off.

He went back to his room, looking for something heavy. The only thing was the sink. He could get that off the wall and drive a hole through the door big enough to crawl through. But that was only going to make things worse. Reed would be locked away in vault. Danny would never see him again. Maybe a rock on the doorknob could get it open without too much notice. There would be something at the beach.

He left his room—

Zin was on his knees, poking wires into the lock. It clicked. The door swung open.

"I told you I remembered everything," he said.

The room smelled like dirty socks rolled in bacon. The lights were out. There was a lump on the bed.

At least it wasn't convulsing.

Danny closed the door, quietly. He knelt next to the bed and put his hand on the lump.

"Reed." He shook him. "I need you to drink this."

No response. He shook him harder. Maybe he was finally sleeping and Danny was messing him all up. But he shook, anyway.

"Come on, man. Wake up."

On the fourth try – one more and he would quit – Reed rolled over. His hair, matted to the side of his face. His face, caved beneath the cheekbones.

"It's Danny Boy," Danny said. "Drink this, man. It'll make you feel better."

The tea was still warm. Reed tried to lift his head.

Danny reached under the pillow and picked his head up. Reed's hands were somewhere under the blankets. Danny lifted the cup to his lips. Reed was on the edge of convulsions. He winced and tried to pull away. Danny wouldn't let him, pouring the astringent water into his parted lips. It spilled down his chin but he swallowed – against his will – until it was all gone.

He dropped back down, breathing heavy. His eyes closed.

Danny could've stopped this from happening to Reed if he just called for help. It was his fault they were still on the island. His fault they might never leave. Reed could be in a proper hospital with medicine and doctors, not sunk into a sweaty mattress. He'd die on the next round.

If he makes it that long.

He sat there a while longer. Reed slept.

"Hey, come on." Zin stuck his head in the room. "Let's go already."

Danny left. He looked back. There was no more quivering.

Danny followed the path out to the tabletop cliff for more leaves, then remained there until the end of the day. He snuck into the cafeteria late at night and stocked up on food, eating in his room. He was back out to the tabletop cliff before the sun was up, watching the water catch fire beneath the sun's burning rise.

He returned with more tea. Reed didn't shake as much. He lifted his head on his own, drank more than he spilled. The room still smelled like a corpse. Reed still looked like one.

It was the third day he brought tea that Reed was sitting up.

"Get me out of here."

Zin and Danny walked across the Yard. Reed was between them, a hand on each shoulder. His shirt fluttered like a sheet thrown over bones. His skin was something like the yellow of old parchment.

People stopped what they were doing to watch.

"Mind your own business," Danny shouted. That only made it worse.

It was a relief to reach the beach. Reed was exhausted. He sat back, the sun on his face.

"Give me some time," he said.

So they did. When they came back to get him, he was still in the same spot. They walked back to the dormitory. He draped his arms over them, dragging his feet. They carried him to his room. The window was open. The stink still lingered. They carried him over to Danny's room so he didn't have to sleep in the smell. It had sunk into his clothes.

Mr. Jones was inside. "Where have you been, Danny Boy?"

"Helping Reed." They dropped him on the bed. Zin picked his legs up, put them on the bed.

"This is not appropriate. Mr. Smith will want him in his own room."

"The bed is ruined. He needs some rest before they kill him."

Danny arranged the pillow so Reed's head wasn't at an odd angle. Zin pulled the sheet over him. Mr. Jones watched them close the curtain.

"I'll be in Zin's room," Danny called.

Mr. Jones followed them out, stopped them from closing Zin's door. "Danny Boy, I don't like what's going on."

"Yeah, neither do I."

"Is there something you want to tell me?" Mr. Jones said.

"You go first." Danny held onto to the doorknob, waiting. Mr. Jones had the sense that someone much older than a thirteen year old boy was looking back. "I'll see you when the next round starts," Danny said.

The door closed.

Mr. Jones suppressed the urge to pound on the door. The insolence. The disrespect.

He tried to have compassion for these boys' plight. They were confused and distressed. They needed space to process everything. But something was going on and he didn't like it. He felt the need to slap Danny, knock some sense into him. But he didn't want to upset the program. Any more stress and it would only slow things down. Besides, there were signs Danny was wearing down. Soon, he'd come close to graduating.

He just had to be patient.

Reed was different.

Perhaps he needed to consult with Mr. Smith. He'd been here longer than Mr. Jones. He'd know what to expect from Danny. Besides, he should know what they were doing with Reed.

51

MR. JONES LIVED on the west wing. His penthouse was an apartment with enough square footage for a family of four. Even so, he only lived in a small portion of it to cut down on cleaning and cooking.

He walked down the empty hallway, rounding the corner in the foyer onto the veranda. The chairs were still arranged in a half-circle from their meeting with the Director. There would be another soon, he believed.

Mr. Smith paddled on top a floating board in the swimming pool. Mr. Jones went to the end of the pool. Mr. Smith grabbed the ledge and looked up.

"I would like a word," Mr. Jones said. "I don't trust what's going on. The Director, the boys... they have things on their mind."

"You believe they're planning an escape?"

Mr. Jones shook his head. "I think we should cancel the next round and call another meeting. Maybe the boys need to be reset."

"Everything is back on track. They have Sid ready to graduate. Besides, I don't have time to start over, Mr. Jones. The clock is ticking for this old man. It's now or never."

Cancer is an impatient foe.

"Have you seen Reed?" Mr. Jones said. "You might live longer than him."

"He's young, Mr. Jones." He floated on his back, spitting water. "His body can recover once he gives it up. There's nothing I can do about this body."

He drew a long breath and went underwater. He frog-kicked to the steps and pulled himself out. Mr. Jones handed him the towel. Mr. Smith dried off and collapsed into a lounge chair.

"Do you ever feel guilty?" Mr. Jones asked. "What we're doing to them."

Mr. Smith draped the towel over his neck. "They had their chance at life, Mr. Jones. The mind is a terrible thing to waste. And so is a perfectly good body."

He put on sunglasses and laid his head back. Mr. Jones watched him. He was lightly snoring within a minute.

Mr. Jones left him.

He's right. They had their chance.

52

Danny went out to the tabletop cliff with a bag of food.

He wouldn't return to the dormitory. He had enough food to sustain him until the next round started. Reed had enough leaves, too. He could make all the tea he needed. Danny just wanted to be alone. He needed to think. He needed a plan. One that would make it their last round, ever.

There were rumors that Foreverland was getting smaller. It still worked, but they couldn't get out to the water or fly as high into the sky without running into the Nowhere. Lucinda had something to do with it. Danny knew it. And the Director did, too.

There was only one way to stop him. Only one way to be sure. They couldn't wait for someone to save them.

Danny knew what he had to do.

The trees rustled behind him.

Danny was sitting on the tabletop, legs crossed, practicing his breathing when Zin emerged from the forest.

"It's almost time," Zin said.

Danny unfolded his legs. "Where's Reed?"

"He's on the beach."

They started back down the path. Danny looked back at the view.

It would be the last time he would see it.

Reed was sitting on the sand dune.

He wanted to get up, walk the beach. His body began to ache again. He reached into his waistband and pulled out a long leaf. He stopped bothering with tea. He chewed the leaf, instead, spitting out the coarse fibers and swallowing back the acrid flavors that stuck in the back of his throat.

The healing compounds surged into his blood. His muscles let go. Nerves relaxed. A mellow cloud drifted through him and he tingled with pleasurable numbness. The ocean seemed to surge through him, each wave pulsing in his groin. He sat there, smiling.

Life is beautiful.

He wanted to try the water, feel it on his ankles. One more time. He might be flying high, but he was lucid enough to know this could be the last time he'd ever get a chance. They would come for him, take him to the Haystack again.

He wouldn't be leaving it.

He rolled onto his hands and knees. He would straighten his legs first then try to throw himself upright. He started with the right leg—

"It won't work."

She was there, to his left.

Her hair glowing fire.

Reed blinked, shook his head. But she was still there, her butt planted in the sand. Her hair fluttering.

"You can't do it, Reed," Lucinda said. "You don't have the strength. You don't have much of anything. It's just about over."

He collapsed back to the ground. A pile of mashed leaves was between his legs. *How many did I eat?*

"I think it's time you went inside the needle," she said. "You've waited long enough."

He closed his eyes and covered his ears. His heart thumped inside his head.

But she was still there.

"I'm serious." Her eyes were big and green. "There's nothing to lose now. May as well come to me, Reed."

"I thought..." he started. No. He wasn't going to talk to her. She wasn't sitting there. He was alone on the beach. She was in his dreams. She was in Foreverland. She couldn't be sitting there next to him. He wasn't going to acknowledge it.

"I agree." Another Lucinda said on the other side of him. There were two of them. "You should come inside, Reed. You're not leaving the Haystack. You may as well come to Foreverland."

"But..." He dropped his head into his hands. *No. No, no, no...*

"I know about the dreams," the first Lucinda said. "I know we told you to stay here, but now that's over. The end is here, baby. I think it's time you come inside."

"No." He clamped his hands over his ears, eyes tightly closed. "This isn't happening."

"We've waited long enough." He could still hear her.

"I'm not going." He shook his head. "I'm going—"

She touched his arm.

He fell back, pushing away from her—

"Reed." Danny stood over him, his hand out. "You all right?"

He looked around. The Lucindas were gone. Danny and Zin were there. That was it.

"I think..." he said. "Yeah, I'm all right."

He relaxed, melting into the warm fuzzy euphoria of the leaf juice. He wanted another.

Danny and Zin heard him talking.

They thought he'd fallen asleep sitting up, but he was shaking his head. He jumped back like he'd seen a ghost. Green flecks stuck to his chin. Half-chewed leaves were scattered at his feet. *Good.*

They helped him stand. "Can we walk to the water?" Reed asked.

His legs were sticks. They stopped just where the foam skidded over the firm, black sand, splashing over his bare feet. He smiled a strange smile, a dreamy one. Closing his eyes.

"I'm going to miss this," he said.

"Not me," Danny said.

"I'm with Danny," Zin added.

Reed hummed to himself, wiggling his toes into the sand. Danny and Zin let their shoes become soaked, propping Reed up as he began to slouch.

"She wants me to go inside the needle," he said, slurring. "After all this, she said I should come inside."

"You can't," Danny said. "That's what the Director wants you to do."

"You said she was alone."

That was before I knew she was a memory.

"Reed," Danny started, "I was wrong. She's not..."

He stopped. It was better not to tell him.

"Listen, I'm taking the island down. I'm going inside the needle first and stopping everything. The Director has to be stopped. I'll bring down the power and ignite all the trackers. It's all coming to a stop, we're going to hijack the island. It'll all be over. Foreverland is going to disappear and everyone has to be out of it when I do it."

Reed nodded. A moment of clarity. "You're right."

"You won't suffer anymore." Danny tucked a handful of leaves into his waist. "Eat these, man. Zin and I will go inside the needle and be out before they can do anything to you."

"Are you sending for help?"

"If I can send for help, I will."

Reed wasn't going to recover no matter. Danny would send for help, but it wouldn't get to the island in time to save him.

The Haystack bell sounded.

Reed began chewing another leaf. Danny thought about telling him the truth about Lucinda. She *was* real Reed. And she *loved* you.

But she's gone.

53

THE DIRECTOR OPENED THE CAGE. The birds squawked. They were rarely let out. On occasion, he would reach in and let one perch on his arm. If he set it down, he'd leash its foot to a stand. This time, he carried them both to an open window. He set them on the ledge and walked away. They turned around, watched him pull the floral shirt off and drop it on the floor.

He scratched at the curly brown and gray hairs on his chest, stepped out of his flip-flops, then his shorts. Naked, he went to the bar.

A Bloody Mary for the road.

It felt so good to be free of clothes. It would feel even better when he was free of the skin.

Today was the day he transformed. Today was the day he shed his flesh and soared to higher planes. It had been thirty years in the making, and now it was here. He swirled the tomato juice into half a glass of vodka. It would be the last time he would need a drink. From that day forward, euphoria would be on tap.

"Director," the intercom called. "We're ready down here."

"Very well, continue. I'll be down after the round is complete."

He lied. They could get started, but they'd never finish.

His plans were carefully laid out. He wouldn't need them anymore. Wouldn't need anyone.

The Haystack bell rang.

The Director finished his drink while the group walked toward their final round. He waited until a trio of boys crossed the Yard – one propped in the middle of the other two. Once they entered the path leading to the Haystack, he placed the drink on a table and slid onto the chair. The material stuck to his skin but was soft and warm. The rollers whirred beneath his buttocks. He sunk into the cushions.

The needle was greased and ready.

It entered his brain.

Here I come, world. Ready or not.

54

REED'S HEAD BOBBLED.

Danny and Zin walked sideways to get down the narrow path. Reed was throwing a lazy step for every two steps they were taking. They were almost carrying him by the time they reached the Haystack.

Mr. Smith was standing at the entrance. Reed's lips were tinted green. He wouldn't feel a thing. Danny wanted to give the sadistic old bastard the finger, standing there with his hands behind his back, waiting patiently for Reed.

Danny and Zin began turning to walk Reed through the door. "Stop there, boys."

"He can't walk." Danny cleared his throat, tried to take the venom out of his tone. "Mr. Smith, he can't walk on his own. He's messed up, as you know."

"You won't be going inside." Mr. Smith didn't hide the smirk.

"What are you talking about?" Danny said. "The Director told me we were all going to do this round, you can ask him."

"I don't need to, son. He changed his mind. You and Zin will be sitting out this round."

The other boys were going to their cells. Reed's chin was touching his chest.

"I don't believe you," Danny said.

"I don't care." Mr. Smith put his hand in his pocket. "You can ask the Director, but right now you're going to let go of Reed. If you don't, I'll drop you on the ground. You're familiar with that feeling, aren't you, son?"

Smile.

Danny pulled Reed back. The old bastard would have to zap him, if that's what he wanted. He wasn't giving him up. Zin got between him and Mr. Smith, like that would stop the tracker. The old man smiled bigger. He was going to enjoy this.

"Danny Boy." Mr. Jones came out of the Haystack. "It's true, son. The Director gave us new orders to postpone your round until this one is over. It's only temporary, my boy. I promise."

He reached out, but Danny jerked away.

Mr. Smith took a step forward, reached deeper in his pocket. Mr. Jones put up his hand to stop him. He looked sad. Remorseful. Pleading with Danny to stop the foolishness. Mr. Smith would drop him if he didn't.

Danny took Reed's arm off his shoulders. Mr. Smith ducked under it and took Reed's weight. He needed Mr. Jones to help with the other side. Together, they walked into the Haystack.

Reed's feet were dragging.

Just before the door closed, Mr. Clark could be heard announcing from inside. "Clothes on, gentlemen. The Director has granted you reprieve."

"Something's not right." Danny paced outside the door. "None of it makes sense. No suffering, clothes on. Something's not right, Zin."

He looked at the closed door.

"He knows."

"Who?" Zin said.

"The Director. He knows I was going to blow up the island. He locked us out and now something big is going down. I got a bad feeling, Zin. I got a bad feeling Reed isn't going to hold out. He's going inside the needle."

Zin took a knee at the door, inspected the lock. He could pick it. They could go get Reed as soon as the Investors were gone. But that would only delay the inevitable. And make it worse. The Director would toss them over the cliff for sure.

There were no needles anywhere except the Haystack. Even if they could find them, they wouldn't work. Putting a needle in his brain wouldn't automatically take him to Foreverland. There had to another way to access the island, another way to hack into the system.

"I got it."

Zin turned around. "What?"

"We got to get to the classrooms."

Zin didn't know what he was thinking, but he didn't bother asking. They were running across the Yard.

55

"STAND UP, SON." Mr. Smith sagged under Reed's weight. "You're not helpless."

Reed's feet flopped behind him. Mr. Smith and Mr. Jones struggled to get him in the cell and lower him to the floor. His arm slipped from Mr. Smith's grasp and his face kissed the concrete.

"Goddamnit." Mr. Smith put his hands on his hips, huffing. He looked around the cell, deciding how to make it work. "Let's push him against the cell door and then we can hold him from the outside."

Mr. Jones helped pick up Reed. It was difficult. He flopped against the bars, knees buckling. They maneuvered around him. Mr. Jones went to the aisle first, holding Reed under the armpits. Mr. Smith quickly jumped out next, catching Reed as he slid down. They were able to hold him up and close the door.

"Go on." Mr. Smith pushed Mr. Jones out of the way, harnessing Reed by wedging his arms beneath the armpits and grabbing the bars. "I'll hold him until the round starts."

"You sure?"

"Yes, yes! Now go, I'll be out in a moment."

The boys in the other cells watched the spectacle silently, fully dressed and waiting. Mr. Smith looked at the empty cells next to his. There were two of them.

Danny Boy and Zin are gone. The Director made the right decision, those boys would be a distraction. They'd be trying to keep Reed from the lucid gear. This has gone on too long.

Mr. Smith met with the Director the day before. The slob stood over his damn telescope sipping whiskey while Mr. Smith – for the thousandth time – made suggestions.

"It's now or never," the Director said. "Let's make it happen now."

Mr. Smith, if he was honest, was shocked. The Director agreed to everything Mr. Smith asked to do. He'd leave Reed in that cell until he either took the lucid gear or died.

And that was fine with Mr. Smith. He had grown weary.

Sweat ran on both sides of his face. When Mr. Jones closed the door, the skylights went dark and the lucid gear dropped. The boys quietly pulled their gear to the floor and slid it over their heads. In moments, the only sound was Mr. Smith's labored breathing.

Then the cell walls began to click.

The back wall continued moving until it pressed against Reed's back. Mr. Smith heaved him up one more time before removing his arms to avoid being pinned. The wall pressed him tighter. Tighter. And tighter.

Reed let out a groan. His eyes opened.

Something popped in his chest before the pressure eased.

"Last chance, Reed."

56

THE FLOOR WASN'T STABLE.

It was like walking on a platform that was balanced on the end of a pole. No matter which way Reed leaned, it was too far. He tried to compensate but couldn't find the tipping point.

When the old men got him to his cell, he crashed.

He tasted blood and the acrid tang of green leaves. His chin was numb.

"He's a pig. He wants you to die."

She was in the next cell. Her hair was long. Red. He couldn't make out the features, his eyes too swollen, but he recognized Lucinda's voice.

She squatted so she was eye-level. Grabbed the bars.

"Disgusting pigs."

Hands grabbed him, again. Heaved him against the cold bars. His knees refused to lock. His arms, noodles. Old breath was in his ear.

Door slammed.

Lights out.

And then the clicking of the cell. And the squeezing. The pressure.

The pain.

It cut through the leaf-induced fog.

A rib popped.

He couldn't breathe. His breath burned in his chest. And the cell squeezed. It would crush him.

And then it relaxed.

Reed sucked in air that sliced inside his broken chest. He tried to stop, but he had to breathe. And each one hurt so bad.

The cage remained tight enough to hold him up.

Mr. Smith, his old spotted face, was inches away. His eyes relaxed, limp and uncaring. He told Reed *last chance*. This was his last chance. Reed knew what that meant. He knew he would die in the Haystack this time.

Grateful it would finally end.

"Don't let them win." Lucinda was behind Mr. Smith. "They want to keep us apart. If you die, they win. This old, rotten bastard... wins."

Reed tried to speak, but there was only enough space inside his chest for a ragged breath before he needed another.

"Don't fight it," Mr. Smith said. "There is peace inside Foreverland, Reed. There is no need to suffer."

A breath.

Pop.

"I..." Reed ran out of wind.

Mr. Smith was unsympathetic. Unmoved. Eyes of grey, uncaring.

"I hate you." Reed whined with the next breath that cut deeply into his rib cage. His eyes streamed tears. Not sadness. *Hatred*.

"I want..."

"Stop, son. I didn't do this to you. You have steadfastly refused to help yourself. You have no one else to blame. You can put a stop to it right now. Let's end it, my boy."

Mr. Smith put his hand on Reed's cheek. Meant to comfort, it was stiff and cold.

Reed quivered. Head convulsing. He kept his breath shallow and braced for the pain.

He spit in Mr. Smith's face.

"Get... out." He squeaked. "Get out."

Mr. Smith stepped back. He wiped the pink saliva off his face, unable to control the stern anger that pinched his brows and hid his eyes in shadows. Stiffly, he marched away, pulling his dead leg along.

Lucinda remained in the aisle. Smiling.

Reed closed his eyes. A sob escaped. He tried to control it. It only hurt inside. But when she reached out, when she touched his face, it was warm and loving and kind.

His tears grew hotter.

57

THE DIRECTOR WAS NOT surprised to see that the sky had been consumed by the Nowhere. He felt it getting smaller. Foreverland was disappearing into chaos. It wouldn't be long, but he wasn't too late.

He assumed a body that, for all intents and purposes, looked like the one lying on the chair at the top floor of the Chimney. Minus the belly and wrinkles, he looked like the Director in the flesh. Perhaps a little more youthful and glowing. A body worthy of an immortal.

He walked across Foreverland's Yard. It had not changed much since the first day he had visualized it. In the very beginning, he decided that his alternate reality environment would look like the island. It didn't really matter what it looked like. When he invited the boys into it, they didn't seem to care since they could do anything and be anything.

After this trip, he would escape the confines of Foreverland and burst into the universe like the Big Bang. He would be much bigger than his own little mind. He reached the edge of the Yard and leaned against a tree. Then melted into it. He became the tree. He waited patiently for the boys to arrive. And one at a time, they did. Until they were all there. Just about all of them.

The Director had a change of heart.

After much thought, he decided Danny was, indeed, too dangerous to let free inside Foreverland. He had progressed much too quickly. It was too much of a risk that he would control everything this time. And if he got control of Foreverland, he would control the Director. There was a chance he might even crossover into the Director's body and abandon him in the Nowhere, lost in his own mind.

All would be lost.

The Director formed a thought-command. He learned that from watching Danny. He willed all the boys in the Yard to disperse. He willed them into the Nowhere. He felt their identities loosen, watched them scatter like molecules set free. They drifted like vapor into the gray fog where their identities would unravel never to be what they were before that. Their bodies would remain vacant in the Haystack. Some might call it murder.

When the Yard was clear, he waited.

And when the time was right, he willed himself into another body, this one in the likeness of a red-headed boy with freckled cheeks. And, next to the sundial, he appeared as if Danny Boy had returned. The Director walked around and looked surprised.

The girl fell from the sky like the Goddess of the Nowhere.

She meant to snag Danny and pull him into the Nowhere. Instead, Danny grabbed her.

She had taken the bait.

Danny turned into a bearded man. He smiled at her.

"At last, we meet."

She squirmed but it did no good. The Director wrapped his mind around her and squeezed.

The first of many screams rattled in her throat.

58

DANNY AND ZIN took the steps three at a time and threw the door open.

The library was quiet and empty. Lights hung from the vaulted ceiling, softly illuminating the rows of bookshelves.

The main desk was to the right. Mr. Campbell – one of the oldest looking and slowest moving men on the island – was straightening a pile of papers. He looked up with a stiff neck.

"Hello, boys," his voice rasped. "I'm closing the library. It'll be open tonight sometime."

"Mr. Campbell." Zin took a second to catch his breath. "We just need to get a book for a... for a report that's due... soon."

"Well, you'll have to come back tonight when we open."

"Please, sir. We've fallen behind on our studies and just want to make sure we do things right this time. We're serious about our studies, sir. We'd like to better ourselves, our minds and bodies. We'd—"

Danny elbowed him. "Just five minutes, Mr. Campbell. And then we're out of here."

Mr. Campbell carried the papers to the shelves behind him. It took so long they thought he might have forgotten they were there.

"Five minutes, boys."

Danny and Zin took off.

"And no running," Mr. Campbell said, forcefully. "This is still a library."

"Laying it on a little thick back there, don't you think?" Danny said. "We just want to check out a book, not rewrite the Constitution."

They turned down an aisle, the shelves towering over their heads.

"You know these geezers, they love it when we do our best."

They turned right at the end of the aisle, moving along the wall with the classrooms along it. Danny stopped at the one in the corner. He could see the cabinet in the corner of the classroom.

"That's the one. Do your dirty work."

Zin took a knee, pulled wires from his pocket and inserted them into the lock. Danny walked away, looking down the aisles. He could hear Mr. Campbell sorting books at the front desk. The wires were clicking in the doorknob.

"What's taking so long?" Danny whispered.

"I can't get it."

"I thought you were an expert."

"I never said that."

Zin dropped the wires and went to the nearest aisle, looking quickly through the books.

"What are you doing?" Danny ran back to the door. "We don't have time..."

Zin reached to the top shelf and pulled a thin, spiral-bound book down. He slowly ripped the plastic cover off the front and pushed Danny out of his way. The cover was flimsy but stiff. Zin inserted the corner between the door and doorjamb. He moved it up and turned the knob.

It clicked open.

"I take that back." Zin stepped out of the way. "I am an expert."

Danny quietly closed the door. Zin stood outside. He moved through the room, plowing into one of the desks up front. He stopped, moved more slowly this time.

The box of tablets was on the bottom shelf.

He grabbed one and moved to the wall next to the door so no one could see him. He turned it on.

His hands were shaking.

This is it.

If he screwed this up, they were all dead. He had to hack the Chimney's security system, find the power grid to shut down the island and the trackers to knock everyone out. He had two minutes.

Maybe three.

59

Mr. Jones waited patiently outside the Haystack.

He heard groaning inside.

It was the sound of a tortured young man.

When Mr. Smith opened the door, he was followed by hoarse cursing. Mr. Smith was told that he could go to hell and burn forever. He closed the door behind him. His eyes were dead.

He shook his head.

"I'm sorry," Mr. Jones said. "Is this really necessary?"

"It is his end. He has a choice."

Mr. Jones did not reply. He did not care to think too deeply on the subject. He had agreed to come to the island. He knew what they did and he agreed to be part of it. He could not judge.

Not now.

"Mr. Williams is prepping Sid to crossover," Mr. Smith said. "We should go witness. Perhaps we will be next."

"Your method may destroy your investment, Mr. Smith." Mr. Jones couldn't stop himself. "What good will he be to you then?"

"Bones can heal, Mr. Jones." He looked away. "Much quicker than mine."

They climbed onto a golf cart and cruised down the path. As they crossed the Yard, they both noticed the white parrots flying out of the top floor of the Chimney.

They stopped the golf cart next to all the others.

The Investors had all arrived at the Chimney to watch Sid's graduation and crossing over. If they were lucky, they wouldn't have to wait for the Director to finish the round. Sometimes the crossover took place without him, when there were no issues. They needed to have very few problems. They needed to be assured everything was on course, that when it came their turn to cross over it would happen without a problem. Mr. Jones didn't like the way things had changed.

He didn't like a lot of things.

They stepped onto the elevator and held the door for late-arriving Investors. They arrived at the fourth floor. There was only one hallway. Halfway down, there was a door on the left, another on the right. The one on the right was the network computer room. Mr. Jones had never been in that room. There was no need, he knew very little about that part of the program.

He followed the others to the one on the left.

They passed Sid lying motionless on a bed, a needle protruding from his forehead. A cable was attached to the needle, plugging into the equipment that was beside the bed. The technician, Mr. Jackson, pulled the curtain across to hide Sid's Investor, Mr. Williams, lying on a bed parallel to Sid's. A needle protruding from his head as well. Eyes closed.

Mr. Jones averted his stare.

He did not like thinking of the needle. He imagined it would feel like a cold, steel nail when it came to his turn. He hoped it would be quick and numb, that he wouldn't remember it. That when it came his turn for the crossover, he wouldn't remember any of this. That he could leave all the memories in the past, start a new life.

He followed the Investors into the side room where they would watch the progress. It would be quite boring. Many of them resented being forced to sit in the waiting room like outsiders. Mr. Jones didn't mind it so much. He could sit in a way that he didn't see the needle sticking from the boy's head. And he didn't have to smell the antiseptic that clung to the back of his throat.

He got comfortable in one of the chairs at the back, happy to let the others sit in the front row. Besides, the air vents were on the ceiling and aimed at the back wall. It was a relief to have fresh air on his face. The room was so stuffy.

He leaned back and folded his hands over his belly. He thought, maybe, he might take a short nap. It could be hours before there was any progress. It was like waiting for a baby to be born. It was like that in more ways than one. And sometimes, when the crossover was slow, they went back to the Mansion. You never knew when the delivery would take place. You just hoped you didn't miss it.

His eyelids became heavy.

60

"OKAY, MY BOY." Mr. Campbell's voice was muffled outside the door. "It's time to lock up. I hope you boys found your books because I have a meeting to attend."

Danny's hands were slick with perspiration.

He stopped to take a breath in order to steady his hand. It quivered over the scrolling text and he needed to be touching with accuracy. He had circumvented the security without setting it off and located the power grid. It would be simple to overload the power distribution and cause a blackout but he needed to find the tracker net before he did that or he wouldn't be able to activate them and there would be a horde of old men looking for them.

"Yes, sir," Zin answered. "We got them, thank you for letting us find them. You know, we don't want to waste any more of your time, but you know how important it is that we do well in our studies. They say that a brain that is active in studies is one that will be stronger and healthier. In fact, research has shown that higher brain activity increases the—"

"Where's Danny Boy?"

"I'm sorry?"

"Son, you're playing games. Where is Danny Boy?"

Found it.

The tracker net wasn't difficult to open. He had gotten past the hardest part of the security system, but the database of trackers was large. He did a quick search for names, located his own tracker. Now he need to find Zin... Zin...

Brain cramp. He couldn't remember Zin's real name.

"He had to take a dump, sir," Zin said. "He ate some spicy food at the cafeteria an hour ago, I think it was a bad burrito or something. Anyway, he was—"

A shadow passed in front of the window. Danny moved down the wall, all the way to the corner, squatted behind the last desk. He did a global search for...

The cabinet is open!

Keys jingled outside. "Son, you better locate Danny Boy in the next five seconds."

Metal connected with metal as the key slid inside the lock.

The knob turned.

Danny crouched down as low as he could, inputting a global search for *Zin*. Dozens of names scrolled over the interface. He went down the list. Everything with a Z was showing up. No time for another search. He went through the names.

The light went on.

Cameron. Nicholas. David.

Mr. Campbell stepped inside. Shuffled over to the cabinet.

Anthony. Benjamin. Theodore.

Closed the door. Looked around.

Hayden. Dane—

He saw him, stooped in the corner. Cheeks flushed, Mr. Campbell moved his hand quicker than Danny thought possible.

ERIC ZINDER!

Mr. Campbell's hand reached inside his pocket—

Danny punched the tablet.

The classroom went dark.

Desks slid and tumbled. Mr. Campbell fell into a heap of over-turned chairs. He laid motionless, hand buried in his pocket.

Eric Zinder was still highlighted on the tablet.

"Cut that sort of close." Zin leaned inside the room.

61

HE HAD DRIFTED AWAY – how long, he couldn't say – when the rattle
of the air handler went quiet.

The air stopped blowing.

The lights went out.

The room was pitch black.

"What the hell is going on?" someone said.

Mr. Jones felt a tingle on the back of his neck. He had never had
the sensation before. He was told that the tracker was installed for his
own protection, that everyone had one in case something went wrong.
Even the Director had one. But, he was assured, no Investor ever had
experienced the unconsciousness brought about by the tracker voltage
that shocked the nervous system and overloaded the senses.

But they all felt it.

It was sudden. Like a hot wire spiking the back the head.

The old men dropped like sacks of meat.

Mr. Jones's foot twitched in the dark. He would never experience
pain that intense again. He would never feel anything again.

None of them would.

His last thought. *We deserve this.*

62

THE DIRECTOR WALKED around the sundial, taking his time to let the grass slip between his toes. The gray Nowhere had blotted out the blue sky, descending like a plague of locusts.

She thought she could take his world.

Not anymore.

The girl was on her hands and knees inside a circle of dirt. She wouldn't escape the ring where the Director focused all his attention. He willed her to experience her flesh curling off her bones, willed her to sense the smell of fried hair and boiling bones. None of it actually happened to her.

But she felt it.

He took a knee. Her red hair hung over her face, shimmering as she convulsed. He lifted her chin. Her face contorted. Eyes filled with tears.

"It's all over, *Lucinda*."

She lunged, snapping her teeth at his hand. He pulled back, laughing.

She cried out, curling into a ball.

Now that she was out of the Nowhere and into the open, he knew everything about her. *Everything*.

"You know what you are, don't you?" he said. "You're just a thought. A memory. You're nothing different than data. You are a reflection, a shadow, of a girl that once lived. A girl that is now dead. Your body has long since fed the worms. How does that make you feel?"

He waited.

Her skin fluttered in waves. Her nervous system fired uncontrollably. It appeared her flesh was trying to strip itself from her body.

"I am Foreverland, Lucinda. This whole existence," he stood up, waving his arms, turning in a circle, "that you've been trying to destroy is me. It is my mind that creates this. That's why I'm a little bitter you've been pissing on it."

He wiped the hair from her face so she could see him.

"You're one dimensional, darling. You can't understand what I've done to help people. You don't know what I've sacrificed to give them a new life. I pulled their memories from their damaged minds to heal them.

"At first, Foreverland was just a computer program but it didn't work. It was too scripted, too artificial. Their identities didn't survive and they turned into vegetables. I discovered they needed an alternate reality that's organic. I became that, Lucinda. They plug the needle into their brains and transfer their identity into my mind where they can live their fantasies. Where they can heal their lives. I am the beautiful mind that heals them. I am the new dimension of existence."

He leaned closer.

"And you tried to take that away. Shame on you."

Another wave of pain. She shook, bouncing on the ground. This made the Director smile. He began pacing around the circle, observing the trees barely visible in the gray fog.

"I gave you life when I pulled you from Reed's mind, Lucinda."

He breathed the sweet air.

"You're dead, but I made you live, again. And how do you repay me? A thank you? Maybe a kiss on the cheek?"

He looked down on her trembling body.

"You're an ungrateful little bitch. But not for long."

She was inferior. He could control her, but he couldn't destroy her. And as long as she was inside Foreverland – inside his mind – she would be a distraction. But any moment now, his solution would arrive and absorb her, take her out of Foreverland—

"I know what... you are." Her words scratched her throat. "I know... what you hide... from yourself."

Something vibrated in the Nowhere.

"Your true memories..." she said. "The ones... you want... to forget... I know what you are."

Something buzzed around the Director.

He closed his eyes, but a thought still entered him. A boy's voice, pleading. It came from above.

No! No, please, please don't! Please! PLEASE!

"You are not who you believe. You try to forget..." She sat up. "What you've done."

The thought he heard was more than a voice. It was a vision. A young boy, his African skin was black. His arms skinny.

His eyes, empty.

A needle in his head.

Stop. Stop, stop, stop... STOP!

The Director spun and pointed. "WITCH!"

Lucinda was lifted by invisible hands. A stake emerged in the ground, her hands bound behind her back. Kindling at her feet.

"You will poison me, no more," he said.

He refocused his efforts, pushed away the thoughts of dead and dying children, willed them back into the Nowhere. Pushed them far away until he forgot them, until he was strong again. Sure of who he was. He was a man that brought healing to the world.

The 21st century Buddha.

A body began to form near the sundial. Translucent and fetal.

The Director smiled. He released the girl from the witch's stake. She collapsed in a pile. *Pathetic.*

"Your end has arrived."

63

REED TRIED TO COUNT A BREATH. Tried to be with the pain.

He could not.

The bars were crushing him; his chest had no room to inflate. His breaths were shallow, quick and stabbing. When he supported some of his weight, the bars would relax. He had more room to breathe. But that brought more pain. And there wasn't much feeling left in his legs.

The lucid gear brushed the top of his head.

"They want to keep us apart." Lucinda stepped out of the dark aisle. "They'll win."

"They—" He grimaced, took a dozen tiny breaths. "They want me to take the needle."

He went limp. The bars squeezed. He whined.

"Why do you think they brought you to the island?" She reached out.

The room was darker.

Reed couldn't see the ceiling. Or the fan.

But he could see her. Like she was in a spotlight. Her fingernails candy red. Like her hair.

She reached for him.

"They want to keep you away from me. They don't want us together."

Her fingers touched his ribs. Cold numbness spread across his ribcage. She traced up his side, to his arm, numbing a path as she went. It was cold and freezing and pleasurable.

He took an easy breath. It came out smooth.

Her hand was on his shoulder.

Touched his collarbone.

Erasing the pain.

"I can't," he said. "I won't—"

"You die. They win."

A black tunnel closed around him, ate up the cells across the aisle. Closed in behind Lucinda as she leaned closer. Her lips were full. They touched his ear.

"Bastards," she whispered.

The pleasurable numbness spread across his face.

Down his neck.

"I miss you," she said.

Her fingertips touched his lips. His upper lip frosted over.

"I miss you, Reed."

His lips fluttered.

"Tell me," she said. "Tell me."

"I..."

She hooked her finger beneath his chin. Sensation left his bottom teeth.

"I miss you." He closed his eyes.

Let her lift his chin.

Let her lift the crown of his head into the lucid gear.

The strap tightened around his scalp. The knob snugged up to his forehead. He was losing feeling in his head, but could feel the coldness of the needle searching for the hole that had healed long ago. It sensed the stent embedded in his skull and centered over it.

Lucinda's lips hovered over his.

The needle shot through.

Cracking the skin. Piercing the frontal lobe.

His head snapped back. He saw a bright light. His body stiffened against the bars. Crackled. Then let loose.

He went inside the needle with his eyes open. Head cocked to the side.

Body, limp.

He went to Foreverland.

64

DANNY AND ZIN LEFT MR. CAMPBELL in the classroom. They didn't bother to check his pulse.

They stood outside the entrance of the building. The sun was up. The sky was blue. It was like any other day, except for the four bodies in the Yard.

"How long did you put them out?" Zin asked.

"I don't know. I just activated every tracker in the system, besides ours." He looked at the tablet. "I think I hit them pretty hard. And I crashed all the solar and hydrogen power systems, so everything's off. Well, everything except the building with a backup generator."

"Which one is that?"

"Guess."

The Chimney was pouring smoke.

"We can stop him," Danny said. "This is our chance. Maybe our only one."

"What about Reed?"

Danny looked at the tablet. There was no telling how much time the trackers would keep the Investors unconscious. He could always zap them again, assuming the system didn't lock him out this time.

They sprinted toward the Haystack.

The Haystack smelled like sewage and piss.

Maybe that was how it always smelled during a round, they weren't used to it. But it was stronger, more pungent. Danny's eyes watered when they entered. It took a few moments to adjust to the darkness. They went down the aisle, past their empty cells—

Reed was crushed.

"Oh, no." Danny got there first. "Oh, no, no, NO!"

Zin was on his knees, working the lock. Danny could tell, even in the dim light, that Reed's face was blue. His tongue swelled in his mouth.

"HURRY, ZIN!"

Zin fumbled with the lock, but it was taking too long. Danny reached for the lucid gear—

"Don't take that off!" Zin shouted. "It's too soon, he might be in there and won't be able to come back if you take it off."

"It doesn't matter." His hand brushed Reed's cheek. It was cold. "He doesn't... he shouldn't have died like this."

Danny slid the black strap off his head. The needle was wedged firmly in his forehead. It came out like a cork. Watery fluid leaked from the hole.

The lock clicked.

Reed's dead weight threw the door open. Danny caught him before he hit the ground. Zin helped lay him down and started to arrange his hands in a dignified manner.

"Not in here," Danny said. "I don't want him staying in here anymore."

His body was limp, but not as difficult to carry as it should've been for someone his age. He weighed less than Danny. They stopped outside the door.

"Let's take him to the beach," Danny said.

Zin shaded his eyes, looked at the sun. "We don't have time."

Danny retrieved the tablet. He was right. There was no telling when someone would recover. Once the island was back to full power, there would be nowhere to hide.

They left Reed's body outside the Haystack, hands folded over his chest.

Eyes closed.

Dozens of golf carts were parked around the Chimney.

Danny and Zin hid in the trees, just in case someone was watching. No one was in sight, awake or unconscious. Danny started out first. Zin made a lot of noise.

He was holding a stick the size of a bat. "Just in case."

Together, they crept to the front door. Still no one. Nothing.

Danny took a deep breath. "We're in deep, man. There's no going back, now."

"So what are we waiting for?"

Zin started to inspect the lock. Danny yanked the handle and the door opened. No jokes, this time. They moved cautiously inside. The ground floor was open floor space with bunches of comfortable furniture and tables for informal meetings. Large monitors were mounted on the large cylinder elevator, showing an overhead tour of the island on a continuous loop. It looked like an area to entertain company or tourists. Or potential clients.

They stepped inside the elevator. There were four buttons.

"Where's the fifth floor?" Zin asked.

"Fifth floor is the Director. No one goes there, he brings them."

"Where then?"

Danny dragged his finger over the tablet, rearranging data and tapping commands. He searched the Chimney for clues. "Most of the power consumption is on the fourth floor."

Zin pushed number four. "We have a winner."

The doors closed slowly. The floor shifted. The elevator began a slow ascent, the numbers ticking off above the doors.

Second floor, we have the doctor.

Third floor, where we wake up.

The elevator eased to a stop. Number four appeared. The doors jerked a bit, then began to slide open. Zin cocked the stick. Danny stood off to the side. They waited.

The hallway was reflected on the back silver wall. Empty.

Tentatively, they looked out.

One hall. Nothing branching out, just one long hall. Near the end, there was a door on the right, one on the left.

Someone was on the floor, halfway inside the left door. Legs in the hall.

"It's Mr. Lee."

Zin gently rolled the old Asian man onto his back. He felt cold. Zin put his fingers on his throat, looking for a pulse. He didn't really know how to do that, so he put his ear next to Mr. Lee's mouth and listened.

"I think he's dead."

"Oh, man." Danny looked at the tablet like it would tell him what happened. But he knew. "Oh, man."

"It's not your fault, Danny Boy. You weren't trying to kill him."

Danny shook his head. He didn't want to hurt anyone, despite what the old bastards had been doing. He just wanted off the island. He wanted his life back.

"What the hell?" Zin went inside the room. "Is that Sid?"

Danny followed.

There was a hospital bed with white sheets and a curtain next to it. Sid was on his back, hands folded over his chest and a needle poking from the center of his forehead. Danny approached with the tablet at his side. Zin cocked the stick back, ready to swing.

Sid looked skinnier than usual. Sort of gray. His mouth was open, breathing. At least he was alive. Danny followed the wire from the end of the needle to a machine next to the curtain.

"What the hell is going on?" he said. "I thought he already graduated."

Maybe that was the last step, one last trip to Foreverland where they download the rest of the memories, all reprogrammed for a better, more efficient mind.

Danny reached for the curtain—

"Take a look at this, Danny Boy."

Zin was looking inside a large window with the stick at his side. It looked like a waiting room. Danny could see the old men piled on the floor as he stepped up to the glass. They must have been standing there, watching, when Danny ignited their trackers. Some of them had knots on their heads where they hit the floor.

Mr. Jones was in the back, laid back on a lounge chair. His fingers laced over his belly. He couldn't tell if he was breathing.

Zin tried the door. "Want me to pick it?"

"No."

He didn't want to find out if he killed all of them. Especially Mr. Jones. The guy cared about Danny in his weird way. He didn't want to live with the thought that he accidentally murdered him. Even if Mr. Jones did *acquire* him.

Even if his name was really Constantino.

"What's over there?" Zin asked.

It appeared that the room was fairly large, separated by the curtain. Zin snuck up to it with the stick ready for action. Danny grabbed a handful of the fabric and yanked it to the side—

A flash of silver.

Zin wasn't fast enough to stop the aluminum table leg from cracking Danny's hand. The tablet hit the floor, the glass screen spiderwebbed. The old man jumped back, table leg back and ready for another swing. Danny got behind Zin, his hand already tingling.

"You all right?" Zin asked, faking a swing at the attacker.

"What the hell you kids doing up here?" the old man said.

"None of your business!" Zin shouted. "What the hell you still doing awake?"

The old man huffed, his eyes darting around. "You did this? You knocked out the power and killed the Investors? You did this?"

He shook his head.

"You boys are done, you hear me? You're done, out of the program. You had your chance but you're finished now. The Director will be down any second."

"Why is he still awake?" Zin muttered back to Danny.

"I don't know. Maybe he wasn't on the tracker net."

"And neither is the Director," the old man said. "You can say goodbye any second now. Any second."

He stepped behind the hospital bed that was on the other side of the curtain, this one parallel to Sid's. An old man was on it, same position as Sid and a needle in his head that was attached to the same machine. They had never seen an Investor with a hole. They never went to Foreverland.

"Isn't that Mr. Williams?" Zin asked.

Yeah, thought Danny. *Sid's Investor.*

Side by side, same machine. Needles in their head.

That's how Parker graduated. And when he was done, they never saw his Investor again.

After that, Parker began parting his hair on the left.

"What the hell is going on?" Zin said.

"I think I know."

65

Reed felt nothing.

Saw nothing.

And liked it.

He'd been trapped in a broken body for too long. He couldn't remember the last time he was without pain. *If this is death, then it is sweeter than imagined.*

But it wasn't death.

He drifted in the black nothingness, his identity drawn inside the needle, drifting toward Foreverland. He only knew the sweet release.

But another body formed around him. This one firm and pain-free. Curled up. Fetal.

He clutched at tufts of grass with his eyes tightly closed. There was wind in his ears. Light on his face. There was sound—

"Reed."

Her voice. It was feeble. It was near.

It was not a dream.

He blinked. A blurry layer of fluid smeared over his eyes. But he could see her. She was out of reach. She was on the ground, curled up like he was. Her head turned so that she could see him.

Blink. Blink, blink, blink.

Her lips quivered. Her body shook. She was in pain.

He tried to move his hand, tried to reach for her, but he couldn't feel his body enough to control it. Barely felt the ground below him. But his heart ached. He couldn't reach her. Couldn't help her.

Couldn't save her. Again.

She managed to crawl out of the circle scratched from the grass. She pulled her body over the ground, dragging her legs behind her. Her breath was labored. Tears in her eyes. She stopped to gather her strength, then pulled herself closer. One handful of grass at a time.

Until her breath was on his face.

"Where am I?" he asked.

"You're with me, my love."

Her hand, convulsing, reached out. Gently cradled his cheek. Warm and soft.

And he remembered.

Lucy.

He knew her when he was very young. He stopped a boy on the playground from pulling her hair when they were seven. She watched him in church, leaning forward and smiling at him from the end of the pew. He watched her at basketball games, with her friends.

They held hands in the back of a friend's truck on the way home from a concert. Their fingers interlaced like broken pieces that belonged together.

Their first kiss was on the couch when her family was gone.

He remembered her smell.

The memories returned, and filled him. All the joy. All the pain.

She put her arms around him. In a full embrace, they merged. His body became light. It became sweet.

He was home.

The bitch is a liar.

She manipulated the memories in the Nowhere to fool the Director, to make him forget who he was. He was not those things. He was not a murderer, he was a savior.

He felt Reed arrive near the sundial. His body appearing like a full grown baby, naked and curled up. So helpless.

And the Director felt such happiness.

He's here.

The air shifted. Suddenly, it was not so heavy. The gray seemed lighter.

Reed couldn't move. He was lucky to open his eyes, to see his memory – the bitch – in front of him. The Director released her from the confining circle so that she could crawl to him like a wounded animal.

Specks of gray flitted from the sky, penetrating them like tiny bullets the closer she got. And when she touched his cheek, it rained gray pellets. They had become a magnet the Nowhere could not resist. When they embraced, they absorbed the lost identities that filled the Nowhere.

And in a burst of light—

An explosion—

A thunderous clap—

Foreverland expanded into infinity.

The Director closed his eyes, shielded his face from the burst. And when he opened them, they were gone.

Not a hole in the ground, not a depression, no sign they ever existed.

And the blue sky reached into the heavens.

And the ocean reached the horizon.

In that moment, he realized how puny Foreverland had become. Now it was all existence. He was free. For the first time in his life, he was free.

Enlightened.

He was these things. He created them. He was a god, after all.

And it was finally time to act like one.

To stretch out, let the world know who hears their prayers.

He reached out, feeling a connection with all of Foreverland. His body, back in the Chimney, was of no use to him now. He was free to be his mind, to be whatever he wanted. He dissolved into the air, his identity drifting like vapor, like the data Danny Boy had demonstrated.

The Director moved his identity into the Chimney's network where he would slip out into the world, melt into the vast web of data that inhabited homes and businesses and governments. He would know everything. He would be everywhere.

I'm God.

The computers bent to his will, the network did what it was told. And as he streamed through the Chimney network, as he passed through his last portal, just before he graced the world with his omnipresence, a room formed around him. He didn't recall this avenue.

It was a large room. There were shelves all around, filled with books.

A pedestal in front of him.

A book slid off one of the shelves near the ceiling, floating like an invisible hand had pulled it and brought it to the pedestal. There was a name on the front.

Harold Ballard.

He willed the book to be gone, for the room to disappear. He was ready to leave. But none of that happened. The book remained. And it opened.

And the Director witnessed Harold Ballard's past.

Foreverland faded into sunbleached colors.

First the sky turned lighter blue, then white. Then the ocean followed. Whiteness crept over the trees. It was a different kind of nothingness, not filled with random memories of lost identities but the void of non-existence.

Foreverland was ending.

Reed walked out of the trees just before they evaporated.

He crossed the Yard with the white void nipping away the ground behind him. He went to the sundial. Put his hand on it. Just like she told him.

And he was absorbed by it.

He left Foreverland as it ended.

Forever.

66

WHY DIDN'T we see this before?

It seemed so obvious, now that the answer was lying in a pair of parallel beds. An old man and a young kid, their brains wired to the same machine.

"Don't you see, Zin? They kept us physically fit and exercised our brains. They let us doing anything we wanted so that we were happy. They put our memories inside the needle and made us go after them. You said it yourself, you just wanted to leave. You belong inside Foreverland."

Zin was squeezing the stick with both hands. His face relaxed but his hands didn't.

"It's a body farm," he said.

"Every Investor has a kid," Danny said. "And when the kid graduates, we never see the Investor again, do we?"

Zin stepped toward the old man. "Oh, we saw one of the Investors. We saw one inside Parker's body."

"How are we doing so far?" Danny asked the old man.

He backed into the door, slid all the way into the corner, the table leg held in front of him like a four-sided long sword.

After Danny went inside the needle the very first time, the old men were telling Mr. Jones that *he got a good one.* Yeah, he got a kid that would graduate soon. A smart one. And Mr. Smith was so desperate because Reed refused to cooperate. The amount of money it took for them to *acquire* one of them had to be a lot. These were billionaires from all over the world that refused to die. The Director showed them a way that they could live another 70 years. All they needed was a kid that no one cared about and bring him to the island so they could lure him out of his body, scatter his identity into the Nowhere until his body was empty.

So they could take it.

"The rich old bastards?" Danny said. "None of them are using their real names. It's all regular names like Jones and Smith. None of them really want to know who each other are. They aren't helping us, Zin. They're just kidnapping kids that no one will miss, kids with a troubled past and no connections. Like you and me, Zin. No one's looking for us. No one will notice when our bodies return to the outside world. Without us in them."

"You're done," the old man said. "You'll go right in the oven for this."

Danny grabbed the back of Zin's shirt before he charged. The table leg was shaking in the old man's hands. Zin tried to get loose.

"WHY ISN'T HE KNOCKED OUT?" Zin shouted.

Danny shook his head. "Doesn't matter. Tie his ass up, we'll figure it out later."

"Don't come near me." The old man reached behind him while holding his table leg in the other hand. He scattered the items off the table, swung his arm around with a syringe in his hand. He pulled the rubber cover off with his teeth.

"There's enough in here to kill one of you," he said. "Come after me, and one of you dies."

"If someone has to do, then I vote for you." Zin raised the club over his head.

Danny stopped him, again. "Don't hurt him."

"Are you kidding me?" Zin didn't drop the stick. "Weren't you listening to your own story? He's one of them... he's some rich old bastard that's going to kill one of those kids out there and steal his body. If we ace this old bastard, we save the kid. Eye for an eye, Danny Boy."

He poked the stick at him. The old man hit it like they were dueling.

"Who's your kid?" Zin asked. "Which one of us were you going to steal, you sick bastard, huh? Did you import a nice little Kenyan for your next life?"

The old man's head was shaking as bad as the table leg. Danny's grip loosened. Zin stepped closer.

"A Kenyan too dark?" Zin said. "How about a Canadian, they got nice white skin, you might like that better, you know with racism and everything. It might make things easier."

The old man pointed the needle at Zin, then Danny. Back to Zin. His eyes darted back and forth with the needle.

"We didn't hurt you boys," he said. "No one got hurt."

"Oh, no. That Haystack was a blast," Zin said. "We loved freezing our balls off."

"But you didn't get hurt, we just make you uncomfortable so... so..."

"So you could what?" Zin said. "So you could kill us with kindness. You're demented. You're the ones sick in the head. You're the ones that deserve to die."

"You wasted your lives!" The old man dropped the table leg and held the syringe with two hands like he was going to squirt it at them. "Maybe it wasn't your faults, but it didn't matter. You were going nowhere, your lives were a waste of time, you didn't need your bodies to continue a life of misery. Trust me, you were heading for a lot more suffering than that Haystack. You would've ended up in jail or killing someone or something worse. The Investors have lived good lives, they've helped a lot of people, and they deserve your bodies a lot more than you."

"It's murder, and you know it," Danny said. "I don't care what you say."

"You choose to leave your body," the old man said. "You reached for the needle, you went inside it. We didn't make you, it doesn't work that way. You have to want to leave your body. All we did was make it uncomfortable and you did the rest."

Danny thought about the two splotchy purple lines down the front of Reed's chest where the bars had crushed him. He wouldn't cooperate. So they killed him.

Danny pulled Zin back and shoved the corner of the bed against the back wall, pinning the old man in the corner. "Knock the needle out of his hands, Zin. Just don't hurt him. Not yet."

"Are you kidding, I'm going to knock the brain out of his head."

"No, don't. I want him tied up and alive. He doesn't deserve to die, not yet. I want him alive when the authorities get here—"

The old man genuinely laughed. "Stupid kids. No one's going to find this place. It's been operating for over thirty years, you think a couple rogue teenagers are going to bring it down? There are trillions of dollars that protect it. The rich stay rich, son. And they stay alive."

Zin swiped at the needle, narrowly missing. The old man tried to back up further but continued to smile. They couldn't charge him with that needle and they'd wasted enough time. Danny wheeled the bed back a few feet, put his weight into it and shoved it like a battering ram into the old man's gut. He picked his leg up to absorb the blow at the same time Zin took a full swing. He caught the old man on the hand, knocking the syringe into the wall. It skittered across the floor.

Danny pulled the bed out. "Grab some of those wires, Zin. We'll lace his ass to the bed—"

"That's enough, boys."

It was the one voice that could freeze them.

The Director stood in the doorway with his hand in his pocket.

67

"I NEED you boys to step over to the booth." The Director pointed to the observation window. "Just do as I say."

Danny didn't move. Zin was fingering the stick like he was deciding if the next pitch would be a strike.

"Boys, you realize I'll knock you into next week." He wiggled the hand in his pocket. "And it won't be any kinder than what you've done to the Investors. Now step away from the bed and plant your backs to the wall. Do it, now."

The Director stared them down.

The man had exceptional skills, some sort of hypnotic spell he cast just by looking. It didn't matter if it was a rich, power-hungry oil baron or a juvenile delinquent, he knew how to get people to do what he wanted them to do. And the boys did just that.

Zin lowered the stick and followed Danny. Neither one of them turned their back on the Director. It wouldn't matter, all the power he needed was in his pocket, the miniature controller that activated trackers. And the boys knew it.

"Are you all right, Mr. Jackson?"

Was he all right? The island was filled with troubled youth. An occasional uprising wasn't surprising, but when half the Investors drop dead and two little maniacs show up with a stick to knock his brains out his ear? No, Mr. Jackson was a little less than all right.

But the Director had arrived. He would put things back in order. He always did. You don't run an island like that for thirty years without ironing out a few wrinkles.

"We've had some problems, Mr. Jackson. I'd like to start in the network room."

Mr. Jackson cradled his hand against his chest. It was probably broke. The Director moved the bed out of his way. He wasn't concerned about the Investors or the aborted crossover lying in the bed.

"Problems," Mr. Jackson said. "Yeah, I think we need to start in the observation booth, Director. Some of the Investors don't have a pulse."

"Yes, we'll get to that. First thing's first. Let's have a look at the network room."

The boys watched them cross the room. Mr. Jackson kept his distance. *Why doesn't he just knock them out?*

The Director was barefoot. He let Mr. Jackson lead the way. They stepped over Mr. Lee – spread-eagle in the doorway – and crossed the hall to the only other door on the fourth floor.

There were endless racks of servers in the network room that went up to the ceiling in aisles that paralleled the curvature of the building. The network room took up half of the fourth floor. Midway around the semi-circular room was a large monitor with continuously scrolling data.

Mr. Jackson sat down. His left hand took the majority of Zin's stick. He couldn't move his fingers. *Broke, for sure.* He placed it gently on his lap and worked the mouse with his right.

"What the hell happened?" he asked. "Power is out on the entire island. The Chimney only has about three hours of charge left in the backup generators. And the Investors..." He looked back. "How could this happen?"

The Director stood behind him, arms crossed, staring at the monitor.

"Something unexpected happened, Mr. Jackson." He fiercely scratched his beard. "Call up the Looping Program, please."

"Looping...? That's not active. We shut that down after Danny Boy hacked into it and thought it was the outside world."

"Humor me."

The Director was acting weird. He was an odd-ball, but none of this seemed all that alarming. Things went wrong, but never at this magnitude. And now he was concerned about some insignificant computer program.

"All right, well, let's see." Mr. Jackson executed a few commands, the screen went blank. More data came up. He leaned closer and squinted. "That's strange. It's been activated. How did you..."

"What's in there? Tell me what you see."

Mr. Jackson wasn't aware that the Director couldn't decipher the data.

He used his good hand to peck out a few more commands to interpret what he was seeing. It didn't seem possible, but there was an identity inside the Looping Program that was often used to mimic the illusion of Foreverland, but they didn't use it that often. An identity could be damaged if it spent too much time solely in the artificial circuits of the network. That was why the Director had become the interface between the boys and the network, serving as an organic "computer" that became Foreverland.

But now there was someone in there. Someone got left behind. Everyone should be out of the Haystack.

Mr. Jackson leaned closer. He could see just fine, the monitor was six feet wide. He leaned closer because he couldn't believe what he was seeing. Couldn't believe who it was that was inside the Looping Program.

"Tell me what you see," the Director said. "Tell me."

Mr. Jackson turned slowly. His lips were moving, finally uttered, "Password, Director. Give me the password."

The Director stared back.

Mr. Jackson waited.

And waited.

He knew what he had seen inside the Looping Program. He saw the identity that was trapped inside it.

And then he saw the Director put his hand inside his pocket.

Mr. Jackson didn't flinch. Didn't try to escape. He just waited for the darkness of unconsciousness to arrive.

It was painless, when it did.

Mr. Jackson crumpled in the chair, falling to the floor in a heap.

He didn't see the Director watching him. Didn't see the Director look at the meaningless data on the monitor. The Director couldn't interpret it, but Mr. Jackson's expression told him everything he needed to know. Asking him for the crossover password to confirm who the identity was inside the Director's body.

Mr. Jackson also didn't see the Director go to the window and begin to weep.

68

"Something's not right," Zin said. "That guy has no mercy and he tells us to just hang out after we just brought the whole island down? No sense, Danny Boy. It makes no sense."

They leaned against the wall like they were told. They looked through the window at the Investors, still motionless. Some of them were breathing. Occasionally, they'd twitch like the tracker was still hitting them with a low dose of voltage to keep them out. Danny didn't feel so sad about Mr. Jones, not after putting it all together. Maybe he did care about Danny, maybe he did want the best for him while he was here. It didn't matter. In the end, the old bastard brought him here to steal his body.

And that could not be forgotten.

Zin was hunched over Sid, looking closely at his open eyes. Danny walked around the bed toward the back wall.

"Where you going?" he asked.

"I'm not waiting around to get zapped." Danny put his hand on the doorknob.

"Hell, if you're going to do that, let's just get out of here."

"And go where? We can't outrun this." Danny smacked the back of his neck. "Let's see what else these old bastards are up to."

Zin thought for a second. He was right behind Danny.

The room was fairly dark, lit only by a few backlights beaming up the wall near some of the desks and the faint glow of tiny lights flashing on computers and various machines.

The room was dominated by a large stainless steel table in the center with a big lamp hanging from the ceiling. A number of shelves and steel carts held more computers or medical equipment.

"Think they did surgery in here?" Zin asked.

"I don't know."

It didn't look like surgery. There was just the one table and too many computers. If anything, it was an autopsy room.

There were nine doors on the wall to the right arranged in three stacks of three. Like a tic-tac-toe board. The doors were only three feet by three feet. Danny had seen doors like that on TV. They were used to store bodies. Pull the handle and the bed would slide out just like a filing cabinet with a plastic bag and a body inside.

He touched the handle on the one in the center. *Did they deep freeze a new candidate until they were ready to suck out his memory and scramble his mind with random ones? It would be so claustrophobic inside. And what if they woke up?*

He yanked the handle. An empty slab rolled out with a cloud of frosty air. It was a freezer. They were storing bodies in sub-zero temperatures. Nobody would survive that. *Did they just hold the old men in these things after they crossed over into the candidate's body?*

He had his hand on another handle—

"Danny Boy."

Danny jumped. Zin scared the hell out of him.

"Come here." He had his hands around a small window on the other wall. "You need to see this."

Zin stepped aside to let Danny have a look. The window was on a heavy-duty door. There was a slab inside but it wasn't like the freezers on the opposite wall.

"Watch this." Zin punched a button next to the door.

The interior lit up with blue flames. The room flickered with an eerie glow.

"A crematorium," Danny said. "They burn bodies in there."

"You thinking what I am?"

Danny nodded.

Once the Investor crossed over, their body was empty. They had no use for it. So they cremated it. That's why the Chimney smoked whenever someone graduated. It was the Investor's body they were destroying.

"Boys."

They jumped back. The crematorium's blue light illuminated the Director standing in the doorway. His eyes flickered with strangeness. Danny and Zin backed up.

"I need to show you something." He turned around and left.

Danny and Zin waited for him to come back. After a minute or two, they found him across the hall in the network room. He offered the chair in front of a large monitor to Danny. They moved slowly, suspiciously. The Director stood several feet away from them, but distance didn't matter. Not with the controller in his pocket.

Danny sat down. The Director told him to tell them what he saw on the monitor.

It took Danny a few minutes to understand what he was seeing. He was able to interpret the information and it became apparent who was standing next to him. The Director was inside the Looping Program, even though his body was standing next to him—

"It's me, Danny Boy." The Director held out his arms, displaying his new body. Tears brimmed on his eyes. "I made it out."

Zin was a little shocked to watch Danny hug the Director.

69

Harold Ballard's mother was a beautiful woman. She was tall and slender and – given the right breaks in life – could have had a career as a model. Instead, she was committed to a psychiatric hospital. She received electric shock therapy on three separate occasions. Each time she returned home, things were better before they got worse.

Harold's father was a genius. He was an unassuming fellow with glasses that sat crooked on his nose. He was nothing close to model-quality. Seeing him with his wife at a party, one would guess he had tons of money.

He did.

He was recruited by every computer manufacturer's research and development department. He was, arguably, the most sought after man in the computer industry; that is, until he was fired for unethical practices. His crimes were never made public, but the word behind the scenes had tainted his reputation enough to make him untouchable.

No matter. He didn't need to make money, not with the number of patents that belonged to him. His basement had become his laboratory.

Harold was their only son. He was not pretty, not ugly. Not brilliant, not stupid. What he lacked in looks and raw intelligence, he made up for in cunning.

He was never allowed in the basement. Instead, he spent his nights looking at the stars through his telescope. But during the day, he shot squirrels with a pellet gun. He'd put birdseed on a plate in the middle of the yard and hide in the bushes. He'd lie there sometimes for an hour, pretending the enemy was coming over the fence, and then he'd plug the first squirrel that dared to grab a sunflower seed right through the eyes. Sometimes he'd nail them to a tree, put them in poses of the crucifix. The yard stunk like death, but his parents never went back there.

He was a loner at school. He was the weird kid with weird parents. His mom was crazy and his dad a nerd. The jocks put rotten food in his locker and the burnouts tripped him in the hallway. At the bus stop, Blake Masterson got on his hands and knees behind Harold and John Lively pushed him over. They laughed, all of them. Even the girls.

That night, Harold climbed on the roof with his pellet gun and a high-powered scope. He was up there until his fingertips were numb from the cold. When John Lively – who lived two doors down – walked outside, Harold put a pellet in his left eye. It was an amazing shot.

The doctors saved his eye. No one ever found out who did it. But John knew. Off the record, everyone knew.

They caught him getting off the bus.

Even though Harold wasn't physically fit, he got away by swinging his book bag and losing his jacket when they grabbed it. He bound up the steps of his house and through the safety of the back door. But John and Blake didn't stop there. They went inside after him. Harold threw the kitchen chair at them and ran through the basement door.

He stumbled down the steps, falling all the way to the bottom. There was a sharp pain in his wrist. He rolled into the corner and watched John and Blake stalk him. But, halfway down the steps, they stopped.

Across the room, there were two bodies lying side by side. One was his mother. The other, his father.

Needles sticking out of their foreheads.

Harold's father was arrested after John and Blake told their parents what they saw and the FBI showed up with search warrants three days later. The computers were confiscated. The needles, too. Harold went to live with his grandparents. He rarely saw his parents after that.

But he picked up where his father left off.

Computer-Assisted Alternate Reality (CAAR) had been banned from all developed nations as cruel and destructive to all forms of life. No animal would be subjected to the debilitating effects that plagued the users of such technology, invented by his father.

But a dictator will look the other way when the bribe is big enough.

Harold used his trust fund to begin CAAR research. He set up labs in Mexico, Ethiopia, and Somalia. He went through thousands of unwilling subjects. None of them were healed in any way. They all died. All destroyed. Sometimes, tragically. Sometimes, horrifically.

The body continued to live, even though the person – the identity – was destroyed.

While some would view his research as a failure, as a crime against God, life and humanity, Harold saw it as an opportunity. The world was run by a small percentage of very wealthy people. The only thing these powerful men and women could not purchase was more life. Death was non-negotiable.

Not any more.

Harold found the island. He found the money.

And he continued destroying.

Eventually, he used his own technology to rewrite his life, erasing all his memories and the atrocities he'd committed. He came to know himself as a good-natured man that served the best interests of humanity. A man of God.

He even shed his name.

And became known as the Director.

The Director knocked the book from the pedestal.

His rage burst out like a telekinetic tidal wave, wrenching all the books from the walls and ripping out their pages and setting them on fire. The room shook and cracks opened on the ceiling, raining bits of concrete on the marble floor. He searched for an escape, a way to dissolve back into data and escape the library, to slip back into the network and find a way back into the world. He might even go back to his body and DESTROY THE BITCH THAT DID THIS TO HIM!

But then he found himself standing in the library, again, the shelves reassembled, the cracks repaired, the books back in order. And a pedestal in the center with Harold Ballard's book opening to play out his history.

He experienced it again.

And again.

And again.

70

LUCINDA LAID THE TRAP.

The Director was right, she was getting smarter. His only mistake, he had no clue just how much she knew. In the end, she knew everything.

When Danny was caught in the Looping Program, she knew he was not in the real world. But it gave her access to all of the Chimney's data. Danny was only able to see a few of the records – his and Reed's – before he returned to the Nowhere. But Lucinda absorbed it. She knew the real purpose of the island, she knew all the Investors, and she knew the Director's true past.

She knew everything.

She also knew that the Director would eventually get Reed to go inside the needle. And when he did, she would cease to exist. She would return to being a memory. She was not sad about that. After all, it was her true identity. In fact, she yearned for it. Being away from Reed had been... difficult.

But what she couldn't accept was the future of Foreverland and all the boys it would continue to destroy to satisfy the gluttony of men.

While the Director ruled Foreverland – he *was* Foreverland – Lucinda ruled the Nowhere. She knew all the random thoughts, all the lost boys. She knew, also, the Director's thoughts and his desire to be free. She knew the Looping Program was a dead-end, a virtual cul-de-sac with only one way in, one way out.

She laid the trap.

He attempted to leave the island through the only data conduit to the outside world and, like Danny, mistook the path into the Looping Program as the way out. Before he recognized his mistake, the door closed behind him, trapping him inside. Lucinda had programmed the loop with the data of all the island's records, most importantly that of Harold Ballard. He would see his true identity, his authentic past. He would exist in the loop until he knew what he had done. As long as there was power on the island, the Director would live in the hell he created.

Lucinda also knew that Reed's body was beyond repair, that he would likely be physically dead. With the Director's identity in the Looping Program, his body would be abandoned and vacant. When they embraced, he absorbed her. No longer conscious, she was part of him. Her thoughts and memories of her time in the Nowhere became part of Reed.

He knew everything, too.

Including her best laid plans.

When the Director exited Foreverland, Reed couldn't go back to his dead body. But he made his exit, as well. And entered the Director's body at the top of the Chimney.

My body, now.

71

DANNY WAS on one end of the bag. Zin on the other.

They let it rest on the floor of the elevator until they reached ground level. Zin was blowing on his hands to warm them up. Ice crystals had formed on the bag.

They managed to get it outside without dropping it. They slid it onto the bed of a cart. They both began blowing on their hands. Zin took the wheel. They drove away from the Chimney.

The Yard was bustling.

It was another day in paradise and all the boys were outside, playing cards, throwing discs and everything else. Not an Investor in sight.

Danny checked the tablet. A few strokes of the finger told him the old men were all exactly where they were supposed to be. The Mansion.

About half of them survived the prolonged blackout. Mr. Jones was not one of them. Most of their bodies were sick with disease or just broken down with age. They didn't tolerate the voltage. They relocated the survivors to the Mansion and left them a note that the island was under new management and they would be staying inside the Mansion until further notice. Then they locked the doors from the outside and had not heard from them since. Danny occasionally checked the location of their trackers, just to be sure.

The only indication of the old men that was outside the Mansion was concentrated inside the Chimney. The Investors that died were put inside the freezers, some stacked two high. They could have cremated the bodies but it made sense to preserve as much evidence as possible. Someone would have to sort through everything.

They drove the cart through the Yard. No one paid much attention to the body bag. The boys were told that the Haystack was closed until further notice. Until then, it was unlimited game room and no suffering.

No one argued.

They drove over the sand dune.

A man was in a hole about waist deep, shoveling a pile of sand next to him. He had a round belly and shoulders red from the sun. His face was clean shaven.

"Slow down there, old timer." Zin pulled up behind the man. "You're not a teenager anymore, you know that."

Reed tossed a shovel full of wet sand off to the side and leaned on the handle. He was breathing hard. His cheeks red with exhaustion.

"Got to get this fat ass in shape," he said.

"You can't do it in one week, son."

Reed rubbed his smooth chin. The beard was the first thing to go. It was smelly and itchy. How the hell the Director walked around with those long, curly hairs around his mouth Reed couldn't understand.

Danny and Zin pulled the body bag off the cart and dropped it next to the hole. Reed climbed out and pulled the zipper down. His former body was inside. Frost had accumulated on the eyelashes. The lips purple. He pulled the zipper to the bottom. The chest was bruised and bony.

"You sure you want to bury yourself on the island?" Danny asked. "Not a lot of good times here."

"That's not me," Reed said.

It made sense to put it on the beach. That's where he spent most of his time while he was on the island. The body should remain part of it.

They rolled the stiff body into the hole.

It was strange to throw sand on the face. It was hardly recognizable, but it was the only thing Reed had known until a week ago. He was breathing harder with each shovelful of sand. It wasn't so much the exertion anymore. *That's not me,* he kept telling himself. *That's not me.*

But he didn't resist when Danny took the shovel from him. Reed went to the water while he and Zin finished the job. He listened to them pack the sand over the body's final resting place.

Finally, it was at peace.

The sun dropped below the horizon. The sky was a myriad of purples and reds and oranges. They stood on the hardpacked sand, the water wrapping around their ankles. Home was out there. The outside world was within reach.

For the first time, Reed embraced hope.

Zin leaned on the shovel. "You know, they were right, the old men. There's not much for us to go back to. I don't know about you guys, but I got nothing out there. I'm not saying I want to stay here, but there's nothing great waiting for me in the real world. My life sucked. I got no parents, no home... I got nothing."

"That's why we're not going back there, Zin." Danny put his arm over his shoulder. "We're starting a new life."

Slowly, the sky went dark.

They left the golf cart on the beach and walked back. They crossed the Yard and went around the dormitory. For the first time ever, the Chimney was dark. They passed it on their way toward the Mansion.

Danny was on the back of a yacht.

The foamy water rippled in deep-cut waves as the ship's motors churned the water. He held onto the railing and watched the island recede into the night. A few lights twinkled on the back of the Mansion. Danny informed the old men that he would be passing through and they needed to be in their rooms. He reminded them that he had control of their trackers and that he would put them to sleep on sight.

They were old and harmless. Still, the three of them walked cautiously through the building and across the back yard to the yacht. He saw them watching from their windows. They would see the Director with them (without the beard) and would want to talk to him, to find out why he was keeping them imprisoned after they paid a fortune. They would want to tell him that he would not get away with this. But they wouldn't get the chance.

They would never have the chance.

The Director, as they knew him, was no more.

Reed had shut down the Looping Program, ending the identity known as the Director.

Even if the old men knew the Director had passed, there was nothing they could do. There was no communication with the outside world. That was the terms of their contract. They signed their life over to the Director. They had purchased a younger body when they acquired a young man, but had to sell their soul in order to do so.

Once they were on the yacht, Reed took the helm. Zin stayed up front to watch the way to the other island. The rest of the boys were back on the island and would never know they were gone. They would keep playing games, find food in the cafeteria and sleep in the dormitory. They probably wouldn't even know something was wrong.

Until help arrived.

"There it is!" Zin called. "Straight ahead!"

Reed waved from the helm. Danny joined Zin at the bow. The water was black and the island invisible in the dark except for a single light at the end of the dock. There would be someone waiting to help them tie off the yacht. Reed had called ahead, telling them to prepare the plane. He would be bringing the boat over soon.

They sounded surprised. The Director, flying?

Of course, he told him. *Vacation is long over due.*

It took some research, but Danny discovered the Director was a billionaire many times over. He had so much money that if they split it three ways, they would all still be billionaires. For the time being, they were going to stay together. The Director had an estate in Italy.

That seemed like a good place to start a new life.

MISSING SATELLITE UNCOVERS HUMAN TRAFFICKING RING

ASSOCIATED PRESS. – The Military Strategic and Tactical Relay (MIL-STAR) reported the sudden crash landing of one of their satellites in the South Atlantic when their network was infected with a malicious virus. The virus will likely cost the government millions of dollars to recover and reestablish communication.

However, the recovery of the downed satellite was near a remote island previously thought to be unoccupied. Authorities of the United States have reported a sophisticated human trafficking ring. Preliminary reports have identified wide-spread use of banned technology called Computer-Assisted Alternate Reality (CAAR), though it is unclear how the organization was using the technology.

In addition, dozens of previously reported dead or missing people were being held captive in a resort located on the island. All the people are male and worth billions of dollars. None have agreed to cooperate with the investigation until they have consulted their legal counsel.

However, many have admitted the leader and creator of the island's society was missing. Currently, his name has not been discovered but he went by the nickname, The Director.

BOOK 2

FOREVERLAND IS DEAD

AUGUST

Now I lay me down to sleep,
  When I wake,
  Who will I be?

72

The rising sun on us, day beginning.
The sky collapses.
And consumes us all.

A ROOSTER CROWS.

Over and over and over.

He wants her to wake up, to get up. But the girl is stuck in a dream where she's screaming, submerged in a cloud of fear, unable to move. Unable to see.

Everything, just gray.

She can't escape, buried beneath the snowy sleep that buzzes like the inside of an anesthetist's mask. Holding her down.

And the rooster crows.

The girl claws to escape, scratches through the cloth of sleep, follows the rooster like a beacon, a lighthouse on the rocky shoals of the living. She rises to the surface—

The seal of crusty sleep breaks.

She blinks to stay awake, to clear her sight, staring into darkness.

Her head is nestled in a pillow, covers pulled up to her chin. The gel-like mattress fits perfectly to her body. Still, her body aches.

Her eyes adjust. Forms bleed from the darkness. First, there are lines...lines scratched on a wooden wall only inches away. They are bundled in groups of five, organized in rows.

She can smell her own breath, thick and rank. A film glues the corners of her lips together. She swallows. Her tongue sticks to the roof of her mouth. Hunger growls in her stomach, perhaps expecting something now that she's awake.

"Mmmm."

She jerks her head around, sinking into the pillow. Eyes wide. She listens to her pulse.

It's a cabin.

There are more beds with lumps beneath the covers, not moving. She can't tell where the moan came from, but she hears slumbering breath.

She breathes slowly, silently, until it hurts. She tries to remember where she was before she woke, but nothing has ever existed before this moment except for fleeting dreams, like whispers of another world. She dreamed of someone else.

A boy.

The sky falling.

And screaming.

Something flutters on the back of her neck.

She runs her hand over her scalp, her hair bristling on her palm, and feels a lump. It's marble-sized and quivers beneath her touch, sending electric tingles through her head, all the way to the back of her eyeballs. She jerks her hand away. A wave of nausea fades.

She tries it again, this time starting at the crown of her head and rubbing as close as she can to the lump until the tingling warns her.

Fear balls up in her throat.

The faint sound of a helicopter is nearby, interrupted by the sound of an insistent rooster.

The girl pushes up on one elbow, waits and listens. She sits up, moving silently. Her bare feet meet a cold, wooden floor. It's brisk outside the blankets. Her bed is in the corner. With her back to the wall, a door is to her right and a window to her left.

She walks to the window.

The floor creaks, and she waits to take another step. Her reflection looks back from the dark glass like a ghost, an unreal apparition: white skin smudged with dirt. Perhaps her hair is blonde. It's definitely a buzz cut. Body odor wafts up from her long T-shirt, her legs exposed from the knees down. Outside, the jagged edges of distant mountains.

A gust of wind slams the cabin. The window crackles. The helicopter gets louder. She can't see anything in the sky, though. It's hard to see anything except her reflection. And she doesn't recognize that.

Coughing.

The girl spins around. Chills creep into her chest, fear and cold. Another girl whimpers, stifled by a sucking sound. Maybe a thumb.

There's a can on the small table in front of the window. The side has been cut out. It's fastened onto a saucer with a short candle. A box of matches next to it. She pulls one out and holds the wooden stick in her fingers, trembling. She looks around, not really seeing the back of the cabin. There could be monsters.

The girl strikes the match. The flame quivers but finds the black wick curled at the top. The tin can reflects the firelight like a lantern.

Oh my.

It's a small dormitory.

A total of six beds with a window and table between them. There are boxes beneath the beds. The tables each have a hooded candle like the one she's holding, surrounded by a variety of knickknacks.

The lumps beneath the blankets come to life, rolling over and lifting up. Their heads are shaved, each with a fuzzy crop of black or brown or blonde. Some of them rub their eyes, waking from a long sleep. One of them throws the covers over her head and whimpers.

"Who are you?" A skinny girl sits up, her skin smooth and brown. She can't be more than fourteen years old.

"Where am I?" another asks.

The girl shines the candlelight on each bed. The one in the back corner looks empty, but the rest are filled with young girls, all about the age of puberty, maybe a little older. The girl with the candle isn't sure how old she is. Her breasts are loose beneath her shirt, no bra. She's definitely past puberty. She feels older than the others but isn't sure. She can't remember her birthday or where she was born.

I don't know my name.

There has to be an adult somewhere, someone that knows where they are and how they got there.

And who they are.

She takes the candle to the front door and steps outside. The wind quickly snuffs out the flame and almost knocks the candle from her hand. The sun isn't visible, but morning light bleeds through the sky from her left. She quickly notes which way is east.

She feels the helicopter's whoop-whoop-whoop in her chest. To her right, near a barn, there are three windmills, each with big white blades spinning on a post. Grit blows into her eyes and she drops the candle to shield her face. Knee-high grass waves in a wide-open pasture.

Hooves stampede up to a five-wire fence near the windmills. A horse rears up and neighs. Two others join it, stomping around when they see her. Just past the horses, the barn looms, the doors swinging on rusty hinges that sing in protest.

One of the girls comes outside, followed by two more. They crowd together. The early morning chill has them hugging themselves, teeth chattering.

"Who are you?" one of them asks.

"Go back inside," the blonde girl says.

She looks to her left, away from the whoop-whoop-whoop of the windmills and rampaging horses, to see a big cabin built from logs like the bunkhouse.

"Hello?" the blonde calls, walking toward it.

There are no lights inside it. She steps onto the empty porch, the boards creaking under her bare feet. Some of the girls follow from a distance. The blonde cups her hands over one of the windows. It looks like a dining hall of sorts: a long wooden table with chairs on both sides and an elegant candelabrum in the center. Empty and lifeless.

Her breath fogs the glass.

There's a large garden on the other side of the building, filled with sprawling vines and rows and rows of vegetables. Compost bins are at the far end, and maybe a hundred yards past that is another cabin. Not really a cabin.

More like a two-story modern brick house.

One of the youngsters climbs onto the porch. Her hair is black, her skin dark. The other two follow. Two more are still inside the bunkhouse.

The blonde steps quickly past them. She just wants to find someone who knows what's going on. These are just kids.

Grassy stalks stab the soft bridges of her feet. She folds her arms over her chest, hunches against the chilly wind and shuffles past the garden. Near the compost bins are ten black-dotted faces of solar panels that are turned towards the east, where the sun is due to rise at any time now.

"Where you going?" someone shouts.

She doesn't know. She doesn't know where she is, how could she know where she's going? But someone does. Someone has to be in that house, and they would know. Someone knows why there's a bunkhouse of filthy girls running around in bare feet and long T-shirts in the middle of nowhere.

Someone has to.

She's halfway there when the back of her neck starts to tingle again. She's not touching it this time. It's a low vibration. It tickles at first. Makes her skin itch. She reaches up to scratch it and remembers what it felt like the last time she did that. But each step makes it worse.

Electric lines extend out from the lump, tiny bolts of lightning crawling along her jaw and the back of her head. She looks back. The girls are watching from the front porch of the dark and empty dinner house.

She starts for the brick house again. One step.

Two.

Three.

The tingling begins to sting. Tears well up in her eyes, blurring the house. She's twenty steps away from the front porch with ceiling fans and bench swings and glass tables. There's a lamp in one of the windows, illuminating the front room.

"Hello?"

She's ten steps away when her ears begin ringing. Someone will hear her. Someone will come out. Someone will tell her where she is.

Tell her who she is.

"Is anyone—"

An electric shock shoots from the lump in the back of her neck; her teeth snap together. Her jaw clenches. Black shutters drop over her eyes.

She doesn't feel the earth slam into her face.

73

SKY. Sky. Sky.

And boys.

They're laughing. One of them, his hair is brown. He has dimples when he smiles. There's a gap between his front teeth that's more endearing than goofy. He grabs her hand—

Screaming.

The look on his face.

And the sky falls, and it's over. Over.

Over—

The girl is nowhere in particular, but feels the dull grind of grit on the back of her head, the bumpy ground beneath it—

She sits up, sucking in air like she's drowning.

Sun-sting on her cheeks. She tries to open her eyes, breathing greedily. Things are a bit blurry. Her face is numb on the left side. Her bottom lip is swollen, the taste of blood.

This time, though, she remembers something. She remembers that it was cold when she awoke in a strange bed inside a bunkhouse; she remembers a dinner house and windmills. The brick house is behind her.

A few girls are on the dinner house porch. They're watching

another girl walk toward her. She swaggers along the garden, where bell peppers swing in the breeze. Her skin is pasty white, her hair jet black and shaved near the scalp. She's wearing denim jeans and a stained white shirt. Her boots are heavy.

She carries a bundle beneath her arm. She stops a few feet away and tosses a pair of jeans at the girl on the ground. Drops a pair of boots.

"Thought you might want these, Cyn," she says.

The girl on the ground squints, not sure what "sin" means. The black-haired girl smiles, sensing the confusion. It's a "been there, done that" sort of smile. She crouches down and flips the waistline of the jeans inside out, revealing a white tag and block letters.

"Cyn."

That word means nothing to her. It rings no bells, brings no memories. It's just a word.

"These were under your bed," the black-haired girl says. "At least, we figure they're yours. Everyone else had clothes under their bed, their name tagged on the inside. I'm Roc."

She holds out a clear plastic bottle.

"Water?"

Cyn doesn't hesitate, and the water spills over her lips. It washes down her throat, bringing small relief to her empty stomach. She tips it up, chugging it all. Roc holds out an apple.

"Hungry?" she asks.

Cyn takes it without a word, biting off most of one side. The sugars hit her tongue like a drug. She barely chews before swallowing and takes another bite. It's nearly gone before she looks up.

"Figured you were starving," Roc says. "Everyone is. Found a stash in the middle cabin."

The white windmills rotate in the distance, slower than before. The wind has slowed, not nearly as cold. She recalls the odd sensation on the back of her neck when she neared the brick house.

"How long have I been here?" Cyn asks.

"A while. We couldn't get near you without this going off."

Roc turns around and points at the lump. She's got one, too. And she's careful not to touch it.

Cyn remembers something electric wrapped around her face. It feels like days ago, but it was just this morning. Now the sun is overhead.

"I woke up last," Roc says. "Everyone was already outside; the sun was up. You were on the ground; we thought you were dead. The girls told me what happened, said you started wobbling when you got close to the house, did a face-plant right about there."

She points a few feet behind her.

"We tried to get you, but the lump gets strange the closer we get." Roc scratches her throat like it's starting to buzz. "There's like an invisible fence around the place. You could draw a line in the dirt right where things get weird, like we're dogs with invisible leashes."

Cyn notices the scar on Roc's throat. The raised white line slashes just below her jaw.

"How'd I get here?" Cyn asks.

"You mean outside the fence?" She lets loose a humorless smile. "The little one walked out of the brick house like nothing at all, like her leash ain't working. She got the lump, it just doesn't do anything. She says she just woke up. We were all standing around trying to figure out if you were breathing or not, and she comes out the front door and stares at us. We told her stop gawking and drag you out. She did, but you kept on sleeping. Thought you were dead, but I checked your pulse." She shrugs. "You just got knocked out."

"Where is she?" Cyn looks around. "The girl, where is she?"

"With the rest of them."

Nothing makes sense. Roc looks the same age as Cyn—sixteen or seventeen, if she had to guess. The girls, as far as she can tell, are younger. They're still on the porch, watching from a distance. She can't blame them. The brick house is spooky, even without the fence. The light is still on, but nothing moves inside.

It's almost noon. Cyn's cheeks feel sunburned, maybe a little wind-scorched, too.

"Want to tell me what the hell is going on?" Roc asks. "'Cause none of the other dipsticks have a clue."

Cyn shakes her head. "Where'd you get the food?"

"There's a stash in the dinner house, in the back room. All sorts of stuff—eggs and fruit and milk. You put that there?"

"I don't know."

"What's that mean?"

"That means I don't know."

Cyn pushes herself up, pausing until her balance is right. Roc watches her knock the dust off her bare knees. Cyn's only wearing a T-shirt and underwear that look like they've never been washed. Smell like it, too. She puts the jeans on and they fit just right. The boots are worn leather, cracked along the seams. There's a hole in the right one, but they fit. Without socks, though, they chafe.

"Maybe we should get everyone together," Cyn says. "Meet in the dinner house around the table, find out what everyone knows. See what's around here."

Roc heads back while Cyn tucks her shirt inside her jeans, flipping the waistband one more time, reading her name stitched inside. It feels strange.

Everything does.

The solar panels had raised their mechanical faces to follow the sun. The garden is mostly free of weeds. The houses all face a large, grassy meadow interspersed with swaying yellow flowers.

White-capped mountains are in the distance.

The middle of nowhere.

The girls are on the porch. Three of them stand next to the door, shoulders hunched against the slight chill. Or maybe it's fear. Their filthy shirts freshly stained, their chins glistening with the sticky juice of apples or oranges. Their eyes, though, are still hungry.

The one girl that doesn't belong is in the corner. Her blouse is clean, her shorts pressed. Her socks have little frilly edges. She leans into the railing, blonde hair hiding her eyes.

Roc tells one of the girls to fetch her an apple.

Cyn walks past the porch for a closer look at the bunkhouse. The cabins look different in the daylight. Even older than she would've guessed, like they were built with an ax. The horses gallop to the wire fence, one of them rearing up. They snort and stomp dust clouds.

The windmills stand in contrast to the dilapidated barn. Wind harvesters. That thought pops into Cyn's awareness, like she knows it's not some ordinary windmill but a wind turbine that converts kinetic energy into electricity.

Yet the barn is missing planks.

The girls watch her, all except the blonde. She's hiding in the shadows.

"Let's go inside," Cyn says.

Roc pulls the door open and lets it slam behind her. The others watch Cyn, waiting for her. She opens the door and waves them in. Cyn looks around like she's not sure if someone else will show up. The horses whinny.

The walls and furniture look like something from pioneer days, all hand-carved and primitive. A cold black woodstove is in the back, a pipe running straight up the wall, through the rafters and ceiling. But the windows are triple-pane insulated.

The girls shuffle around the table but don't sit. There are plenty of chairs—twelve of them. There are only six girls. Roc drops into the chair at the head of the table and throws her boots on it. She rips into the apple, juice dribbling from her chin.

Cyn examines the rough surface of the table and the candleholders, which appear to be iron rods crudely welded together. Wax puddles on the table. The walls are barren and the wood floor scuffed. There are two doors on the back wall, one on each side of the stove.

The girls' heads are shaved, all except the blonde. Roc's laughter breaks the silence. "You're looking at them like cattle."

Bits of apple shoot from her mouth.

"What are your names?" Cyn asks.

No one speaks. She points at the one with black hair and dark skin. Indian, maybe.

"Jen."

"That's what it says inside your pants?"

She nods.

"Okay. How about you?"

Kat's hair is bright red, her cheeks freckled. The other one is Mad.

She has black skin, tight curly hair. The blonde has found the corner again, looking for a mouse hole to climb inside.

"What about you?" Cyn asks. "What's your name?"

"Miranda." She rattles the bracelet on her right hand. She doesn't have a tag inside her designer clothes, just a fancy bracelet, her name engraved on a gold plate.

"You're the one that pulled me out of the fence."

She nods, eyes cast down.

"You woke up in the brick house. How come you were in there?"

Miranda shakes her head.

"Why doesn't the fence bother you?"

Again, she shakes her head.

"Well, what's in there?" Roc interjects.

Shrug.

"You don't know?" Cyn adds, softer.

No response.

Cyn looks over her shoulder. Roc says, "Told me she woke up in a bedroom and came down some steps, came right outside. Don't think she looked around, but how should I know? She hasn't said two words since. She ate the hell out of a can of beans, though."

Roc tosses the apple core into the corner.

"So no one knows anything?" Cyn asks. "I mean, where we are or how we got here?"

They shake their heads.

"Does anyone remember anything?" Cyn looks at Roc. She's picking her teeth. "Because I don't. I couldn't remember my name when I woke up. I don't know if we're in the United States or Russia or on another planet."

All she gets is Roc sucking on her teeth.

Cyn goes to the window. *Yet I know those are horses. I know the garden has been weeded and the wind harvesters are generating electricity. Am I dreaming?*

"I remember something," Mad says. "I remember a dream."

Cyn turns. "What was it?"

Mad describes a tropical island. She was flying over the palm trees and soaring over the ocean. She says there were boys there, like it was some sort of Neverland, only they didn't call it that.

She stops.

"Then what?" Cyn asks.

"Something happened...but...I don't remember."

The sky falls. That's what.

"What about you?" Roc points at Miranda. "You have any dreams?"

Miranda dips her shoulder. Her face is completely hidden behind her hair.

Roc rubs the scar along her chin. There's a tattoo on the inside of her right arm. The fuzzy blue lines look like a long dagger from the inside of her elbow to her wrist.

"Come over here, Miranda." Roc pats the chair next to her. "I don't bite, girl."

Cyn doesn't care about the dream. She'd rather forget it. As dire as things feel, it's better to be inside the cabin than inside the dream. The screams sounded like people were being pulled apart.

"They're hungry," Kat says.

Cyn didn't realize she was staring at the horses. They're still romping along the fence, craning their necks over the wire, but the grass is out of reach.

"How do you know?" Cyn asks.

Kat shrugs. "Isn't it obvious?"

Not to Cyn. But now that Kat said it, Cyn can tell they're anxious. Have they been without food as long as the girls? *How long have we been asleep?*

"I don't remember." Miranda is next to Roc, hugging herself.

"I'm not asking what happened before you woke up," Roc says. "What's inside the brick house, girl? Is there a phone or a computer? You know, something that could save our lives, that sort of thing?"

Cyn walks past Roc's interrogation. The kitchen is to the right of the woodstove. The door is cedar plank, but there's an electronic lock on the silver handle, one that requires a programmable keycard.

The shelves are stocked with canned goods and jars of fruits and vegetables. The food has been shoved around; empty cans lie on the floor. A half-empty bottle of water. Bruised bananas hang from a hook but are still yellow.

There are two stoves: one wood burning and the other electric. The industrial-sized refrigerator is polished silver with a pantry next to it. A nail is bent on the shelf above the sink, holding two cards on strings, each about the size of a credit card.

Cyn retrieves them. She slides one in the kitchen lock. A green light goes on and gears turn. The light turns off and the gears go back.

"I DON'T REMEMBER!"

"Don't give me that!" Roc towers over Miranda. "You walked through that house, you're not blind, you had to see something, now what's in there?"

"She's right." Cyn steps between them, kneeling down. Miranda is shaking. "If there's a phone, we could call someone."

"That's genius," Roc says.

"Let's go over there." Cyn rests her hand on Miranda's. "We'll go with you. You could be the one that saves us."

Miranda stops quivering but doesn't lift her head. Cyn pats her knee. Roc reaches over her head and yanks the chair back. Miranda has to stand to keep from falling. Cyn stands between them. She holds out one of the keycards.

"Here."

"What's this?"

"It unlocks the kitchen. If there's not a phone in the brick house, we need to start rationing food."

Roc puts the keycard around her neck. "Why?"

She doesn't look at Roc. She stares at Miranda. "Because we're going to run out."

Miranda looks up. Her eyes are blue, her face clean and free of scratches. Cheeks puffy. She lacks the gaunt tug of hunger.

———

Miranda waits on the front porch while Cyn and Roc lock the kitchen.

Kat, Mad, and Jen venture off the porch towards the garden. They don't want to be around Roc and she can't blame them. But they didn't ask Miranda to come. They couldn't care less about her.

She doesn't care, either.

She wouldn't hang out with them anyway. She doesn't like to mix. She's not sure what that means, but it seems to have to do with race. Blacks, Irish, and Indians—that sort of thing.

Miranda's the one quaking on the porch while they walk through the garden, but they're the dumb ones. If Cyn hadn't said something about the food, those pea-brains would've plowed through those shelves like rats led by the Dagger Queen. They wouldn't listen to Miranda. No one would. She's too small and...different.

Thank God for Cyn.

Miranda can't remember any more than the rest of them, only she didn't wake up in the bunkhouse. She saw where they woke up; it looked like a redneck cellblock that smelled like an armpit. The stink was in them and they didn't smell it. Miranda breathed through her mouth when they were in the same room.

"You ready?"

Cyn comes out of the dinner house. The shoestring is around her neck, the plastic keycard dangling between her breasts. She needs a bra. The rest of them don't.

Miranda least of all.

"Let's go see what's in the brick house." Roc puts her hand on Miranda's neck, guiding her off the porch.

Miranda breathes through her mouth.

The house is a two-story home with Old Georgetown brick, functioning shutters, and a green metal roof. The cabins look like they were built two centuries ago. The brick house, last year.

They slow at the end of the garden. Roc still has her hand on Miranda's neck, gently squeezing.

"Circle around," she says. "If we stand where the tall grass starts, we'll be able to see into the front door."

Cyn doesn't know much about the fence. The others tested it from every angle, knowing where their necks would start buzzing and how close they could get. They walk along an invisible line but only they can feel it. Feels like nothing to Miranda.

They stop twenty feet from the house. Double doors are between large windows. There's a lamp in each one, the one on the right still on.

It's no accident the house faces south, not that any of the others would know. The southern exposure allows the light inside for warmth. The other end faces north. They're protected from the winter wind by trees. Miranda doesn't know where they are, but it doesn't take a genius to know winter is cold.

She's not really sure how she knows.

"Open both doors," Roc says. "Open them real wide so we can see."

"Find the kitchen," Cyn adds. "We need all the food out of there, first thing. We don't want anything to spoil if no one's in there."

"Yeah, that's great," Roc adds, "but if there's a phone, you forget the food and start dialing 9-1-1."

Miranda wants to get away from them—she doesn't like all the attention—but the other direction doesn't feel any better. The brick house is so quiet. The lamps look like eyes, the steps like teeth. As much as she hates the attention and body odor, she remembers what the inside of the brick house smells like.

It's not body odor.

Roc pushes her.

Miranda's legs are stiff. Roc shoves her again. Miranda steps safely inside the fence. Roc can't reach her, but now she's stuck between them and the brick house. She wants to chew on her finger, bite the skin from the sides, but stops herself from that bad habit. Perhaps she'll just sit down, right there, inside the fence.

The first step is the hardest. The second one isn't much better.

The grass is worn away near the bottom step. Miranda looks down at her shoes. They aren't boots, aren't made for roughing it. These are casual flats. And she feels the pebbles through the thin soles.

She puts her foot on the first step. It feels like the house is pushing back. She wonders if that's what it feels like to the others. She doesn't want to go in there, she doesn't know why.

"Come on!" Roc says. "We're going to starve before you get there."

Miranda grabs the railing. She pulls herself up—a high-pitched scream.

It's somewhere toward the dinner house. Cyn and Roc turn toward it. Miranda backs off. The girls aren't in the garden. Cyn starts walking, careful to stay outside the fence. It's hard to tell where it's coming from.

They hear it again. This time, two girls are screaming.

Cyn starts running. Roc follows, but she goes straight through the garden, plowing a path through the rows and snapping plants off at the base. Miranda is all alone, one foot on the bottom step. The lamps stare at her—one on, one off—like the house is winking.

Or got punched out.

She leaves the safety of the fence and runs around the garden. Right now, the pack is safer than the unknown. The screams are coming from the trees.

74

JEN STUMBLES OUT of the woods before she falls. She scrambles to her feet.

Roc is there first, rushing to the trees. More screaming. Kat and Mad come out a little farther down. Cyn puts her arms around Jen. She clings to her. Her chest heaves with sobs.

"What is it? What happened?" Cyn says.

Kat and Mad fall behind Cyn. Their arms and faces are scratched and bleeding. Mad hides her face.

"Settle down, settle down." Cyn peels Jen off of her, brushing away tear-streaked grime. Long welts line her face. "What happened?"

"We were..." Jen swallows a sob, taking a deep breath. "We were just looking around. Mad saw it first and then...then I saw it, too."

Mad's still hiding her face.

"What is it?" Cyn asks. Neither of them answer. She looks at Kat.

"I didn't see anything. I hauled ass when Jen started screaming. There's a little path in there, but we cut through the trees; limbs tore us up."

"Where is it?"

"Go down a bit; you'll see the opening. Mad's the one that found it—"

"I'm not going back there." Mad's shaking her head.

"Me neither," Jen adds.

The girls sit closely, huddling behind Cyn. Miranda stands several feet away. They're watching the trees. Limbs begin cracking. Cyn creeps closer, her heart thumping.

Something rushes through the thicket.

Cyn backs up, arms out, like a mother fencing off her cubs.

Roc jumps out, wiping spiderwebs off her head and arms, spitting.

"What's in there?" Cyn asks.

"There ain't a trail, I can tell you that. But something's back there. Something dead."

"Down there." Jen points at the bunkhouse. "You'll see down there."

There are black plastic cisterns on the back of the bunkhouse and the dinner house. They're as tall as the roof and are connected to gutters to collect rainwater. Each must contain thousands of gallons. There are no windows on the back of either cabin, but there's a door on the bunkhouse, right between the cisterns.

Cyn wanders over, warily looking at the trees and back to the girls. There's a narrow path starting at the bunkhouse door that cuts to an opening.

Cyn's guts feel twisted, her eyes unblinking. She points at the opening and Jen nods. Cyn ducks under a low-hanging branch and enters the cool shade. Branches have been cut away. A dirt path swings around the tree trunks and, up ahead, turns to the right.

Roc breathes loudly behind her.

Cyn pauses, looks and listens. The wind rustles the tops of the trees, but the air is dead beneath it. She reaches the turn and stops. The smell hits her. Something foul, something spoiled. It's not a skunk. More like road kill baking on summer asphalt. She leans around the corner and pulls a branch down.

Twenty feet away, right where the path turns, there's something on the ground. Tan and ragged.

Cyn takes a step and waits for it to move. Deep down, she knows it won't. *Pants. Those are tan pants.*

Two legs lie across the path, both mired in dirt and dried blood. There's only one shoe. The other foot is bare, the sole caked with mud.

"It's a body." Cyn says it louder than she intended to.

Roc looks over her shoulder. "Told you."

Cyn covers her face with the bottom of her shirt. Roc does the same. The smell penetrates the fabric. Even when she holds her breath, she still feels it.

The torso is off the path, buried in the undergrowth. The pants are shredded on the back side, exposing muscles and tissues. Looks like the work of scavengers. Hopefully, long gone.

They'll be back.

Cyn stops short of the body. The odor saturates her face. A knot swells in her throat. She blinks away the tears and tries to hold her breath again. Vertigo spins in her head, but she wants to make sure.

An adult.

The woman is heavyset, facedown in the weeds. Her hair gray and matted. The shirt has been clawed away, the bra strap still intact. The flesh isn't.

"The hell happened?" Roc asks.

"I don't know. Wolves, maybe."

Maybe.

"Think we need to bury her?" Roc asks. "Keep the wolves away?"

Cyn is thinking the same thing, but she doesn't want to touch that body to roll it into a hole even if they dig it right next to her.

"Let's leave it," she says. "Keep the girls out of here for a while. No one comes down this path, not until we're sure it's safe."

Roc is already backtracking.

Cyn kneels down for a closer look. She dry-heaves once and pinches her nose. If there was more than an apple in her stomach, she would lose it, but she's not coming back anytime soon. She wants to be sure she's not missing anything. Perhaps if she sees the face, it will remind her of someone. Maybe jog loose a memory, provide a clue.

But there's nothing familiar. Not the clothing or the body or the hair. And she's not about to roll her over to see the face. She's certain it's beyond recognition.

There's something in her hand. Cyn pokes it with a stick, but the fingers are stiff. Looks like a plastic bag.

Cyn backs away. She'll come back much later to investigate.

Or maybe never.

75

MIRANDA DOESN'T SLEEP much that first night.

There's an open bunk in the back. The clothes in the box are her size, but they're filthy. She sleeps in the clothes she's wearing. They're dusty, but at least they don't smell like wet animal.

She's the first one in bed. There's no way she's going back into the brick house, even if there's clean clothes and a soft bed in there. She just wants to go to sleep, wants to wake up from this dream. Because it has to be a dream.

The other girls wander into the bunkhouse once it's dark. Miranda peeks from under the covers, just a sliver of an opening. They look drunk, sort of staggering to their beds and getting undressed, eyes half shut. They're breathing heavily, softly snoring.

Somewhere out there, a wolf howls. It sounds like outside the cabin. Others join. It's getting hard to breathe beneath the blanket, but she's not about to look. She's trying not to think about an animal getting inside.

They're probably coming back for the body.

She didn't follow Cyn and Roc into the woods. She stayed back. She wanted to run, but then she would've been all by herself, so she waited outside the trees. She never saw anything, but she caught a whiff.

Cyn didn't talk about it, but Roc did. She said it was an old woman, half-eaten. Said the head had been gnawed off and the spine stuck out like a chewed corncob.

Miranda didn't believe her, but still...she tries not to think about it.

She doesn't fall asleep until the wolves finish howling. But then, in the middle of the night, someone gets up and goes out the back door. Miranda figures someone's going to pee.

She has to pee, too, but decides to hold it. Doesn't matter if those wolves stopped howling, they could still be out there. The bathroom is a little outhouse near the trees. She doesn't know what's worse: walking outside at night or peeing in that bathroom.

It's a tie.

Half an hour later, the girl comes back. She must've delivered a number two.

Even grosser.

76

Not day.
Nor night.
Endless gray. Forever and ever.
It cannot be grasped.
Cannot be let go.

CYN TEARS AT THE FOG. It slips between her fingers, yet clings to her skin. She tries to swim, tries to run, tries to do anything but be there.

She hears them cry. The boys are out there. They're crying for help. The rooster crows.

Sleep is like death, bottomless and heavy. Her head is a rock sunk into the pillow; her body gently cradled in the gel-like mattress. Feels like she's hovering in its embrace. Cyn opens her eyes and stares at the lines carved in the wall. She can't remember getting into bed.

They fed the horses and chickens before sunset. The girls wanted to pet the horses. Kat knew what food they ate and how much. The barn had a feed room with tack and barrels of oats.

They straightened up the kitchen. Dinner was pickles and boiled potatoes. The brick house sat in the distant dark, one eye lit on the front porch.

They went to bed, but she doesn't remember doing it.

Cyn quietly sits up. Her feet hurt like she'd been walking barefoot. She doesn't recall taking off her boots. She's wearing the same T-shirt. The smell of death clings to it like smoke. Or perhaps that's the dead body still staining her sinuses.

She reaches under the bed and slides out a box. She digs blindly through a stack of shirts, finds a pair of socks near the bottom and something else. Something leather.

It's curved at the bottom with a smooth, cold handle. There's not enough light to see, but she knows what it is. She lights the candle. Buck knife.

She unsnaps the latch and slides it out of the leather case. The blade is silver, heavy. She flicks the end and listens to it ring. The edge is sharp, but the tip is dull.

The lines on the wall.

Are those days? Has she been marking how long she's been there? There are so many. She pulls the bed from the wall, the legs grinding. The lines go all the way to the floor.

More than a year.

Cyn snuffs the candle out and gets on her knees. She reaches under the bed, feeling one of the boards that support the mattress. She unsnaps it one more time and reaches over the bed, gouging a line in the wall.

A new row begins.

There are plenty of tools in the barn, but no buckets. A dozen eggs fit in the cradle of Cyn's shirt. It's more than they'll eat, but she wasn't going to leave the eggs to rot. The cisterns stand like black sentinels drinking from the roof. There's a door to the kitchen on the outside of the dinner house.

Cyn slides the keycard into the slot and listens for the gears to turn before pushing it open. She flips the light switch, turns on the griddle, and looks for butter.

There's a list of daily chores tacked to the refrigerator. She puts it in her back pocket. The refrigerator is stocked with milk, fruit, and dried strips of meat. The meat could be from a hunt—there's probably elk and deer—but milk and fruit? Oranges don't grow where there are snowcapped mountains. Someone had to bring those.

They'll be back.

No butter in the fridge. There's a cabinet below the sink but no food, just hundreds of plastic bags containing clear liquid. They look like IV bags. The shelves on the door contain brown bottles of peroxide and iodine.

Medicine, good.

She grabs one of the IV bags. No label. Maybe medicine or nutrients. If things get desperate, they might be drinking them.

Half the eggs get burned.

Mad finds a tub of lard and turns the heat down, salvaging the other eggs. Cyn scrapes the blackened bits onto a plate. They each get two eggs and a banana. Cyn's eggs look like they were cooked with a hammer.

They eat in silence.

Kat's the first to finish, licking her plate. She starts scraping the inside of the banana peel. Miranda picks at her food, pushing the crispy parts to the edge. Roc pinches them off her plate. Miranda doesn't complain.

Grit gusts against the windows. It sounds cold.

Roc takes her plate to the kitchen and returns with a jar of preserved apples. The top pops. She dips two fingers inside like chopsticks.

"We need to start rationing," Cyn says.

"There's enough food for months," Roc says.

"We might be here longer."

"I don't plan on being here that long."

"Where you going?"

"Out there." Roc points at the front door. "I'm not waiting around to die; I'll hit the hills and take my chances."

"That's not smart. Grizzlies are out there."

"How do you know?" She plucks out another apple.

"We're in the mountains. This looks like Wyoming or Montana. Either way, bears live here."

"She's right," Kat adds. "This is the wilderness. You won't survive two nights out there. Plus, we're at the end of summer. That means it's going to get colder."

"And we need to conserve food." Cyn reaches for the jar.

Roc slides it away. "Maybe I'm Daniel Boone."

"You don't know who you are." Cyn looks around the table. "None of us do. And until we know more, we need to work together. We need to survive until someone finds us."

"That's your plan? Hang around until someone finds us?"

"Look, oranges and apples don't grow here, someone brought them. Someone built these cabins."

Roc laughs. "Maybe the dead lady did."

"That's not funny!" Miranda stands up. Her chair falls over.

Her chest heaves, fists clenched at her sides. Her lip starts trembling and she crosses her arms, turning her back.

The wind hurls another gust of sand.

"Look," Cyn says, "there's a lot we don't know. We don't know anything, really. We have to play it safe. We need to conserve food. We have to eat to survive, and that means staying hungry, eating little. We need to make it last."

"Maybe the world ended, is that what you're saying?" Roc says.

"First, we need to survive. So would you put the lid back on that jar and put it away?"

Roc wipes her chin, staring at Cyn. They're all watching.

"How about this?" She lifts the jar as if to make a toast. "We go ahead and divvy this up since it's already open. After that, we tighten the screws. I promise."

Roc doesn't wait. She walks around the table, giving everyone a portion. The pieces plop onto the plates, cinnamon syrup spilling over the plump slices. Cyn watches the keycard dangle from her neck.

The girls pause, but their appetites take over. They clear their plates and slurp up the syrup. They don't look at Cyn. She doesn't eat the fat chunks mellowing in a puddle of sugar water, even though her stomach fights her. Roc drops her boots on the table while running her finger inside the jar.

"I found this." Cyn pulls the paper from her back pocket. "It's a chore list. I think we need to start doing it."

She spreads it on the table.

"It makes sense, seems like things we should be doing." No one objects. "Someone needs to be in charge of the garden, like weeding and harvesting. Who knows how much longer that stuff will grow; we need to get as much food out of the garden as we can. We've got at least one empty jar to fill."

Roc licks the rim.

Jen raises her hand. "I'll do it."

"Then there's the barn, and feeding the horses and chickens—"

"I'll do that." Kat stands up.

"Okay, good. I saw tools in there, so you and Jen can get that figured out. Someone also needs to manage the kitchen, clean stuff, and plan the meals, do all the cooking—that sort of thing. Mad?"

She nods.

"That leaves chopping wood." Cyn drops her finger on the chore list. "There's a stack on the other side of the barn. I think we need to stock up all the wood we can. If we're here all winter, we'll need to keep the stoves burning. I don't think the bunkhouse will stay warm enough without a fire. We have to plan for the worst, start searching for dead wood or fallen trees. There are axes and wheelbarrows in the shed."

Cyn looks at them.

"Stay off the path in back. We'll just leave the body alone for now." It gets quiet. Time slows.

They're all wishing Cyn didn't remind them.

"What do you think happened?" Jen asks.

"I don't know." Cyn shrugs. "We just have to survive. We have to hope."

"What about her?" Roc slides the empty jar in Miranda's direction. "What's she going to do?"

Miranda remains distant. She grabs a lock of hair from behind her ear and puts it in her mouth. She hasn't touched her preserved apples.

"She'll have to do what none of us can."

The others don't say anything, either.

Cyn takes her plate to the kitchen and eats the apples. She rinses her plate. Roc drops her plate in the sink, still chewing. Miranda is already on the front porch, her plate still on the table.

The apples gone.

77

"I DON'T WANT to do this," Miranda says.

"Who the hell wants to do any of this?" Roc snaps.

Miranda looks at the meadow and the faraway trees, the mountains beyond. She thinks about running, not turning back, just going and going and getting as far away from this place as she can. The wolves are out there. Bears, too.

Maybe that's safer.

"Look." Cyn touches her shoulder. "We've got to know what's in the brick house. We need to know if there's a phone or a computer. And if there's not, we need food."

She gently squeezes.

"You're the only one that can do it."

Miranda looks at the wooden planks. She nods and starts for the brick house without them. She doesn't like to be touched, even if Cyn is the nice one.

The lamp in the window is still on. Miranda's legs begin to lock up as she nears the fence.

"Go on." Roc shoves her. "We ain't got all day."

Miranda trips ahead and stops. She's inside the fence and Roc can't touch her. Stuck between two rocks—the brick house and the Dagger Queen—she pauses.

Anger balls up in her belly. If she was big enough, she could drag that bitch through the fence and watch her go unconscious. But Miranda's a waif. A fairy compared to Roc.

A skinny little Barbie.

"Come on, let's go!" Roc claps. "Everyone's working and you're standing."

"Take it slow, Miranda," Cyn says. "One step at a time. Open the door, look inside, and go in, nice and easy. No one's going to hurt you, we're right here. Go on."

Like they can do anything if something happens.

She pulls herself up the steps with the help of the railing. The floorboards are painted. There are glass tables and rocking chairs at both ends. One of the tables has a tall glass on it, half-full of diluted tea.

There are twin doors. Miranda drops her hand on one of the brass knobs. The hinges creak. She decides to push both doors open.

The smell hits her.

It's dull and rotten, sticking to the back of her throat, clinging to her tongue like gluey vapor. It's the smell from the woods.

"What is it?" Cyn asks.

"It smells. Bad."

"Smell ain't going to hurt you," Roc says.

"Cover your face." Cyn demonstrates with her shirt. "Breathe through your shirt."

Miranda does that. It helps.

The first step inside makes her dizzy. It's not so much the odor, more like déjà vu, that strange sense she's been here, done that. She braces herself against the doorjamb. Roc's voice is distant. Miranda's ears are ringing.

The front room is immaculate, the couches pristine. The coffee tables are arranged with magazines and framed photos of the mountains and trees. Elk grazing in the meadow. There's a TV set in a cherry hutch and a grandfather clock ticking in the corner.

No computer, though.

No phone.

There's a hallway down the center of the house with a metal door at the end. Everything is homey and nice: there's crown molding, the wood floor looks polished, and the lamps have frilly lace on the shades. But the door at the end of the hall looks thick and heavy.

The staircase is halfway down on the right. That's where she came down only a day earlier. Seems like forever. She didn't pay much attention to the house then. Too consumed with what was going on outside. Now she wishes she had looked around. Then she wouldn't have to be doing this.

All the doors along the way are closed. *Thank God*.

The odor, though, gets worse. It seems to be clinging to her clothes. She'll smell worse than body odor. She continues, one step at a time, just like Cyn told her. There are frames on the wall, photos of grandmothers and grandchildren. Sometimes they're photographed out in the meadow or on the porch of the dinner house. There's another one in the woods next to a small cabin.

Miranda swallows a lump.

She stops for a moment, pulling a deep breath through her shirt, closing her eyes. She feels funny. Maybe she's hyperventilating.

She should probably open a few doors, look for a phone. Roc and Cyn are watching, expecting her to do something. She gets halfway down the hall. The stairwell is to the right, but there's an open door to the left. It's the kitchen.

There's a sink below a window that overlooks the garden. Jen is on her knees, plucking peppers and storing them in the bottom of her shirt.

All the cabinets are closed and the island countertop wiped off. The sink is empty. There's no sign of a phone. There's a door to the right. Miranda reaches out with her free hand, tears building on the rims of her eyelids. She rests her hand on the knob, suddenly battling thoughts of dead bodies stacked inside and tumbling down when she opens it.

She stifles a sob and her hand slips from her face. The swampish odor wafts inside her head. She bends over. A tear splashes onto the linoleum.

She has to take something out there, something that will satisfy them. Miranda closes her eyes, and before her thoughts seize her arm, she yanks the door open—

Food.

Lots of it. Cans of beans, beets, corn, beans—a culinary treasure chest. The shelves are deep and loaded, enough to feed them all winter.

There's a hamper on the floor. She holds her breath and lets go of her shirt so she can scoop the contents of one of the bottom shelves into the plastic hamper with the crook of her arm. She dry-heaves once.

She drags the hamper across the floor, backing into the hallway with the food in tow. She feels dizzy again. The smell has worked its way past her throat and into her esophagus, staining her senses.

But she keeps going, despite the tears... She closes her eyes, backing out of the hallway and into the front room. She backpedals until she feels the cool breeze and the sun. She steps off the porch, the hamper banging on the steps and cans falling out.

She keeps going.

One foot after another.

Until she backs into something soft. Arms wrap around her.

"You did it." Cyn has her.

Miranda collapses. The tears, this time, are different.

She never wants to go in there again.

78

"This is good stuff." Mad holds up a can of black beans. "Everything on our shelves is generic, but this is brand name. Is there more?"

"Miranda said the entire pantry is stocked," Cyn added.

"Where is she?" Mad asks.

"Puking." Roc's laughter sputters.

Cyn walks away from the back corner of the dinner house. The outside door to the kitchen faces the garden and brick house. Mad slides the hamper inside and starts stacking the goods. Roc follows her, pulling out random items and setting them to the side.

"Get all that inventoried," Cyn says. "I want a list of all the food we have in stock."

"You an accountant now?" Roc says.

"We've got to plan our meals, know what we have. Then we'll know how long it'll last."

"There's a crapload in the brick house, you said so yourself."

"We won't know how much until we get it. Until then, we work with what we have."

Jen arrives from the garden, a pile of green peppers cradled in her shirt. She puts them in the sink. "We're going to eat like queens tonight," she says.

"No, we're not," Cyn says. "We're only going to eat what we need."

"Well, these peppers aren't going to last forever."

"They'll be just fine for a couple of weeks. We prioritize what needs to be eaten first. We'll eat what comes out of the garden until the cold gets here." Cyn looks at the sky like the color tells the season. "After that, we start on canned goods."

Roc's pile is two cans high. Cyn grabs the can of cherries, the pie-filling kind. Roc drops her hand on Cyn's wrist. "What're you doing?"

"Helping."

"I've got a system here; you're messing with it." The dagger tattoo ripples. "Why don't you start writing stuff down?"

"Your cans are out of order. They need to be organized with the others."

"They will. I'm just looking, seeing what we've got. No need to be getting your hands on everything."

Roc stares. She doesn't let go until Cyn looks away.

"Look at this." Jen digs to the bottom of the hamper. "Soap."

Cyn had forgotten what clean smelled like. She's afraid to take the soap, nervous that if she gets clean, she'll just be more aware of the filth. Maybe it's better to just wallow in it.

At least for now.

Miranda comes around the cistern, head down, hair in her face.

"You all right?" Cyn pushes the hair away. Her skin is clammy, the color sort of yellowish.

"Well, look who's here." Roc peeks out of the kitchen. "Don't tell me you fed your breakfast to the outhouse. That's a waste. Give her a demerit, Cyn."

"You need some water?" Cyn doesn't wait for her to answer and whispers to Mad to bring a cup.

"What'd you see in there?" Roc says.

"Give her a second," Cyn interrupts.

"She's had twenty minutes. What'd you see in there, Shiny?"

Miranda hides her right foot behind her left. The shoes are scuffed but still reflective. She can't hide them both; instead, she backs up.

Mad hands a plastic cup to Cyn. "Here, have a sip. You don't want to dehydrate."

Miranda holds the cup with both hands. She takes a drink.

"Look, I know you're traumatized." Roc steps outside, getting between Miranda and Cyn. "It's a big, scary house, but we could use a little help here."

"I brought the food," she mutters.

"Yeah, thanks. But boiled yams ain't going to call for help. Did you even look around?"

Miranda shuffles her left foot behind her right.

"Give her some space." Cyn gently grabs Roc's elbow. She pulls away, eyebrows wedged together. "Just give her a minute to think. Go count the food—she's not going anywhere."

Roc continues staring. She doesn't want to do what Cyn says, but she does it anyway. The cans slam together. Mad and Jen stand back.

"Something's dead in there." Miranda doesn't look up.

"Did you see it?"

"I could smell it."

"Where was it coming from?"

She shakes her head. "The doors were all closed."

"Was it coming from upstairs? Downstairs?"

"Downstairs. I think."

There's a dead body in the woods; no surprise there's one in the brick house, too. Cyn feels sad for the old women. She knows she shouldn't, because they were apparently living in luxury and the girls in filth, but she doesn't like to hear that people are dead.

"What else did you see?" Cyn asks. "Besides the kitchen."

The cup is shaking in Miranda's hands. "It just looked like a nice house. The front room has a television and coffee tables with magazines. It was all very clean. The davenports aren't faded—"

"The hell is a davenport?" Roc asks.

"It's a couch," Cyn answers. "What about a phone or a laptop or tablet? Did you see anything electronic besides the TV?"

She shakes her head.

"Did you open any doors?"

The water lightly splashes inside the cup. Cyn takes it before she gets wet.

Metal cans tumble across the kitchen floor.

"You didn't even look." Roc comes out again. "You just went straight to the kitchen and didn't even—"

"I looked!" Miranda screeches. "There's no phone, all right! There's no one to call. It's just a house with no one in there but a dead body, all right?"

"Yeah, a house *you* woke up in. A house only you can go in. You didn't look around, Shiny. You walked your little white ass in there and clicked your heels, hoping you'd be back in Kansas when you opened your eyes. And when that didn't happen, you grabbed some food. Well, good for you, you're a hero. We should all kiss your ass that we'll starve to death in three months instead of two."

"I looked."

"No, you didn't. You didn't go upstairs, you didn't open a single damn door. You didn't look, Shiny."

"Don't call me that." Miranda wraps her arms around herself, rocking.

Roc goes inside the kitchen. A can of green beans ricochets off the sink and rolls out the door. Mad and Jen get out of the way. More cans crash. Cyn reaches out, but Miranda jerks away. She bows her head, quivering. Her sobs are silent thumps inside her throat.

"You're going back in there." Roc comes out and points a can at Miranda, the label hanging. "You're going back in that big-ass house and opening those doors, and you're going to find out what the hell is in there—"

"NO!"

Miranda runs.

Roc swipes at her. Cyn flinches, wanting to stop Roc from chasing her, but she doesn't have to. Instead, Roc rears back and throws the can. The label shears off, flapping to the ground. The can misses, wide left. It rolls into the tall grass.

"You need to go get that," Cyn says.

"Yeah, I'll get it when that little bitch goes back in the house."

"She's scared."

"Who isn't?"

Roc watches Miranda sprint deep into the meadow, swallowed by swards of wildflowers and grasses, disappearing on the other side of the slope. For a second, Roc tenses. She might give chase. Cyn would have to stop her if she did. She couldn't let her go after Miranda. She's just a little girl. And their only hope.

But then Roc kicks an errant can toward the garden and curses. She stomps around back, out of sight.

Mad and Jen start cleaning up.

Cyn considers going out there. If she goes too far, if she doesn't come back, she's a goner.

She'll never survive the night.

79

In the formless gray void
Lost forms appear.
Two distant lumps
Coming closer.

THE WIND HARVESTERS lift her out of dead sleep. That's what sleep feels like: death. Cyn lies beneath her warm blankets, listening to the *chop-chop* of the wind harvesters and the soft breathing of her bunkmates.

The last thing she remembers is eating. If she concentrates, she recalls walking through the grass, her hand on the door...

And then gray.

Something's out there. Something's coming.

Someone.

It's just a dream, but it's not the random images of dreams. She feels like she's somewhere else when she sleeps. Somewhere, but nowhere. It makes no sense.

She reaches under the bed without letting the cold air inside the covers; rolling over, she scores another line on the wall.

Day three.

She tries not to look at the endless bundles that are stacked like sticks below her puny new lines, too many to count.

Cyn slides the box out from under the bed, blindly pulling out a second heavy sweatshirt and jeans. She pauses for a moment, bracing for the morning chill.

The boots feel like reinforced cardboard. It'll take several steps to loosen them up. The soles bang against the wood planks. She walks to the back door and sees the lump beneath the covers of the last bed on the right, blonde hair splayed on the pillow.

She made it.

Cyn smiles. Miranda must've snuck in when they were asleep. Good.

She runs to the dinner house. The wind smacks her, grit biting her cheek. The egg collection will have to wait. The dinner house creaks. Cyn considers firing up the woodstove, but doesn't want to waste wood. She has no idea how much wood it's going to take to survive the winter.

Cyn rubs her hands for warmth. The scent of fresh vegetables instantaneously reaches deep inside her. She's tempted to sneak a bell pepper, maybe one that's half rotten, one they wouldn't likely use. No one would know.

She distracts her senses while she waits for Mad and starts taking inventory of food. Black beans, garbanzos, corn, and tomatoes on the top shelf. More of the same on the second shelf. Canned fruit is on the third shelf, with a gap on the far right.

No cherries.

Cherries.

She shifts the cans around to fill the hole. She'll bring it up at breakfast, see if anyone has anything to say. Maybe making everyone aware that she's watching will put a stop to it.

Tap-tap-tap.

Cyn jumps. The pencil rattles on the floor.

The sound on the outside door is small. She opens it. Miranda is outside, her arms wrapped around herself. Her clothes are smudged with dirt and grass stains.

She's shivering. "Sorry."

"For what?"

Miranda looks down, still shaking. She doesn't have to say anything else. Cyn knows she feels bad about not going back into the brick house. She's their only hope to see what's in there. But she's so meek. So scared.

She goes back to the inventory. Cyn gets down to the bottom shelf with Miranda watching her, grateful there are no more gaps to hide.

"Can I help?" Miranda asks.

The dinner house groans against the wind. "You can get the eggs."

"I don't know how."

"It ain't hard. You just go in the coop and pick them up and bring them in here."

Cyn fires up the griddle. Mad should be waking up soon. Miranda stands next to the door, shuffling her feet. She's not asking to help so she can really help; she's just asking to be polite. Or maybe she's waiting for Cyn to help.

"Look." Cyn pulls plates out of the cupboard. "I didn't make you go back in the brick house yesterday, but things have got to change. You can help out. Those shoes ain't made for working, but we ain't got the luxury to do what we want, understand? It's cold out there and maybe you're scared of chickens, but those eggs need collecting."

The door shuts. Miranda's gone.

Maybe she thought Cyn would take care of her, protect her. Well, maybe so, but that doesn't mean she's going to hang around while everyone else carries their weight.

Cyn eyes the shelf with the missing can of cherries.

There are enough problems already.

80

THE CLOUDS ROLL over the sky like a lead blanket, blotting out the sun for a week. Rain leaks from the dreary sky, the wind throwing it against the buildings like pellets. The wind harvesters churn ceaselessly.

Miranda stands inside the barn. The doors are wide open, but the wind and rain can't reach her. The cold, however, always finds its way in.

She looks puffy, wearing three sweatshirts. If there were more, she'd be wearing them, too. She doesn't care that they're stained and slightly damp, or that they smell like mold. The barn smells better. If she hand-washes them with water from the cisterns, they'll never dry. She'll never be warm.

She shivers beneath layers of grimy cotton.

Filthy. Just like them.

Jen and Mad spend their time in the dinner house. The kitchen is clean and orderly. The cans are stacked in straight lines and the inventory posted. They found a pack of playing cards in the back of the pantry. Sometimes Kat joins them.

They never ask Miranda.

Roc hardly ever leaves the bunkhouse. Except to eat.

And steal.

Miranda hears her leave the bunkhouse at night when everyone is sleeping. Miranda hears the back door open, hears her come back thirty minutes later. No one seems to care that she's stealing.

Cyn doesn't.

She's out in the meadow. Despite the bitter rain, she paces across the open field, counting her steps. If she's not chopping wood, she's out there. Doesn't say what she's doing. No one really talks about what they're doing. Not anymore.

"Chickens need fed." Kat drops two steel buckets on the dirt floor.

Miranda leans over, looking inside: seeds mixed with food scraps from the garden. The wire handles are cold. She carries them through the breezeway and braces for the weather as she steps outside. Mud sloshes beneath her rubber boots. No more shiny shoes. Kat lets her use the work boots as long as she helps with the animals. It's the price she pays to keep her feet dry.

The chickens come out squabbling. Miranda quickly heaves the contents through the wire fence, a pathetic attempt to spread the food, but she's not going inside. Chickens freak her out, the way they peck. She's afraid one will pluck out her eye. Chickens can do that, they can fight.

She runs back to the barn.

"Wash them out," Kat says before Miranda can put the buckets down.

She knows, but she wouldn't have cleaned them and Kat knows that, too. The water from the cistern is cold—always cold. She dries them with a damp towel, her hands stiff and slow.

There's a horse in the breezeway when she's done. He jerks his head in her direction, nostrils exhaling like exhaust. Kat puts a brush in her hand.

"Brush Blackjack while I tend to his hooves."

"How do you know his name?"

"I don't."

Kat's got a dingy rag tied over her head, covering her red hair. Probably full of lice. She digs through a plastic toolbox.

The horse's coat is matted in patches, what Kat calls rain rot. She minds not to get behind him, in case he kicks. "He can snap your bones," Kat had told her.

Kat begins digging into the bottom of the front left hoof with a tool.

"Doesn't that hurt?" Miranda asks.

"Keeps the thrush out."

"But it doesn't hurt?"

"Not any more than if you cut your hair."

Kat reaches for a pair of long-handled pliers that pinch off the end of the hoof like nail clippers.

"How do you know how to do all this?"

Kat shrugs. "Thinking about it don't do you no good. Like Cyn says, we got to survive until we figure something out."

Her dialect had changed. She sounds so country.

"How come everyone gets to be good at something? You got horses, Mad's a cook, and Jen does the garden."

"And Roc does the stealing."

Kat drops the hoof and goes to the other side. Miranda looks down the breezeway, hoping no one is around. She walks a safe distance from Blackjack's rear end and starts stroking his right flank. Kat digs the packed dirt out of another hoof.

"You know about that?" Miranda says.

"Don't take a genius."

"I thought I was the only one that heard her getting up at night."

"I don't know anything about that, but I see her hanging around the kitchen when no one else is around. She's got that key around her neck, what do you think she's doing?"

"Why don't you say something?"

"Like that's going to do anything."

"Tell Cyn."

Kat snorts while reaching for the hoof trimmers. "Cyn can't do anything. I mean, she's trying to be a leader and everything, but what's she going to do about Roc? Seriously."

The rain patters louder on the barn roof. Cyn's still out in the meadow with a sheet of plastic over her head. She looks lost.

"What about me?" Miranda runs the brush through the horse's tail. "What am I good at?"

Kat stifles another laugh.

"What?"

"I ain't going to say."

"Go ahead. I can take it."

Kat finishes filing the hoof and stands up. Straight-faced, she says, "Ain't it obvious?"

Miranda shakes her head.

"You're nice enough and I appreciate the help, but I think there's something missing in you. Something fake. You're a beauty queen."

Miranda picks the long hairs from the brush. She tries not to let her lips flutter. "That's mean."

"You asked."

Kat taps the horse's back leg and gets to work on the next hoof. Miranda drops the brush into the bucket. She doesn't feel much like helping anymore, even though it proves Kat's point.

She's a beauty queen.

The rain sounds like falling rocks.

81

THE PENCIL ISN'T WORKING.

The paper is limp in Cyn's hand. She can't hold the sheet of plastic up and write without the rain falling on her notes. Maybe she'll just walk to the east end of the meadow and make observations; she doesn't necessarily have to write everything down. So far, there's nothing but trees and grass.

She'd already determined that the house and cabins faced south and the trees were approximately six hundred feet away if she walked straight out of the dinner house. If she went west, the land rolls for quite a while—maybe miles—before the next dense stand of trees. It'll take a full-day excursion to explore that. Once she gets a feel for the surrounding area, they'll do that. The only thing left to explore is the trees behind the cabins.

Where the body lies.

Cyn studies her notes where she's sketched the outline of the meadow. She puts the point of the pencil in the middle, about where she's standing, and twists back and forth to mark where she's starting when the hard rain comes, hitting like cold bullets, running down the plastic, marring the world around her.

She runs for it.

The puddles seep through the holes in her boots. She splashes a path straight for the bunkhouse, smelling smoke. She rushes inside. The bunkhouse is warm and dry. *Warm?*

One of the beds is only a few feet away from the stove, the seams glowing.

Cyn strips off the wettest layers of sweatshirts and wrings them out near the door. Her feet slap across the floor. She sits as close to the stove as possible, hands out. Heat is welcome. She drags the blanket off of her bed and strips the rest of her clothes off, the fleece rough on her skin.

"Cold as a witch's tit." Roc's head appears from the bed.

"I'm going to need help cutting more wood," Cyn says.

Roc settles back inside her blankets. They sit in silence, absorbing the heat. Cyn doesn't move. She can't put those clothes on. It'll take hours for them to dry.

"You having dreams?" Roc's voice is muffled. "About the gray?"

Cyn doesn't answer.

"You see the lumps coming for us?"

A shiver runs through her. *We're having the same dream.*

"Someone's coming," Roc says.

"Don't say that. It's just a dream."

"That we're all having. I talked to the others; they saw it, too. Someone is coming out of the fog, coming to save us."

"We don't know that."

"I do. And I ain't freezing my ass off while all this wood sits out there."

"Bad idea."

Roc wraps the blanket around her face. Her lips glisten. Cyn smells peaches.

She doesn't say anything.

"When the weather breaks, we're going to start exploring what's out there. I've mapped the surroundings, but it's time to go farther out. I'm planning a day-long hike in two directions, far enough out that we'll be back by sunset."

"Good luck," Roc says.

"You're going, too."

The covers slide up Roc's face, leaving a sly eye peeking out.

Cyn scoots closer to the stove. Her skin is hot, but her bones are still frigid. She puts her head inside the blanket teepee, breathing the warm, rank body odor.

Welcome to the cold, she thinks. *Here to stay.*

82

"MIRANDA!" Mad waves her hand in front of Miranda's face. "Yoo-hoo, girl. You going to eat, or do I need to feed your breakfast to the chickens?"

Miranda looks at the plate in Mad's hands. "Thank you," she mutters.

All the girls are sitting and waiting, spoons in their hands. Everyone is there except Roc. Once Miranda sits, they dig in. That's Cyn's new rule: eat together, like a family.

Except Roc. No one seems to mind.

A dysfunctional family.

Cyn is at the head of the table, fingers steepled in front of her. She watches the others eat. Eggs and hominy. And prunes so slimy they race past the tongue and down her throat before Miranda can properly swallow. She doesn't want to taste them.

"This sucks." Mad looks at the cold woodstove.

"This all sucks," Cyn adds. "But we've got to save the wood for the real cold."

Cyn promises not to light another fire. Roc lit the one yesterday. *No more*, Cyn promised herself.

"As soon as the weather breaks, we're hiking into the countryside.

I've got some routes planned to get as far out as possible and be back before sunset. Maybe there's a trail out there or a sign of civilization."

The wind blows, and the roof crackles in protest, reminding them how cruel the weather is.

"What if it never breaks?" Kat asks.

The door slams open. Roc throws a square of wet plastic onto the floor and stomps mud into the floorboards. "Started without me?"

Miranda hunches over her bowl even though it's empty. She feels Roc's shadow pass over her. The kitchen lock beeps. Roc slides the keycard out and puts it around her neck.

Cyn stares ahead.

Roc makes just as much noise coming back, grabbing the chair next to Miranda. A poison slick of fear coats her stomach. She hides within her blonde locks.

"That's not what we're eating," Cyn says.

Roc pops the top off an extra-large can of baked beans. She dumps them into a pile and shovels in two spoonfuls. "Well, you shouldn't have started without me."

Mad walks loudly to the kitchen, using Cyn's key to open the door.

"She seems pissed," Roc says around a fourth spoonful.

"Give her your keycard," Cyn says. "She's running the kitchen; you don't need it."

"Give her yours."

"I'm first up every morning, getting things ready. Mad needs access."

"Yeah, well, I'm making sure no one is thieving."

"And who's watching you?" Kat says.

Roc stops chewing. Lowers the spoon. She glares from beneath her hooded eyes.

"You better watch your mouth."

"I'm keeping an eye on Mad," Cyn interrupts. "There's nothing to worry about. It'll go easier if she's got the key, Roc."

Roc hunkers over the plate, pushing the final bites with her dirty fingers. Every last bean eaten. She drops her heavy hands on the table and exhales, looking around.

"It's food you're worried about?" she asks.

"We're conserving."

"Well, I know where there's more. How about you, Shiny?"

A rancid flavor crawls into Miranda's throat. She feels Roc's weight lean closer, smells her musky odor. Cold beans on her breath.

"You know where we can get some food?" Roc kicks the back leg of Miranda's chair.

"Stop," Cyn says.

"Stop what? Stop getting more food? I thought that's what this was about—getting food. Make up your mind, fearless leader. You want food or not? Because if you do—and I think we all do—I know where to get it."

Roc slaps the tabletop. The dishes rattle.

Miranda squeaks.

"I don't want food, Shiny. I want...the hell...out of here!"

"STOP!" Cyn's chair tips over. She hangs on to the table's edge. "Stop threatening her, Roc. She'll go inside when she's ready. There's probably nothing in there but food that's not going anywhere. We've got to focus on conserving what we've got."

Roc hovers in place. A fearful shiver trickles down Miranda's neck.

"Whatever you girls want." Roc tosses her plate in the middle of the table. "Call me when you've had enough of this crap."

"We're splitting wood after cleanup," Cyn says.

"Good. We need some."

"You're helping."

Roc shakes the water off the plastic, drapes it over her head, and leaves the door open. The rain patters on the front porch.

They sit quietly. Kat is the first one up. They begin clearing off the table. Cyn is still standing, eyes cast down.

She never finishes breakfast.

83

MIRANDA SNUGGLES UP IN BED, warm and smoky.

Roc started a fire that afternoon and no one said anything. Not even Cyn. They spread their wet clothes on chairs. The fire was wrong, but they were warm.

Roc did nothing but take.

Miranda feels the decay of cowardice in her backbone.

They all do.

When the back door clicks shut sometime in the night, she comes out of her sweet slumber. She has learned to ignore the nightly raids while everyone slept. Everyone else slept right through it. Miranda could stop her, but not by herself. But if they all come together, if they're all sufficiently pissed off, if they all taste the foulness of their cowardice, they'll rise up together.

Miranda can do that. She can bring them together.

If she can wedge a few slivers of wood between the door and the doorjamb, Roc will be locked out. She'll have to pound on the door to get back inside, waking everyone up. And if they don't wake up, she'll stay out there in the rain.

Maybe she won't survive. That's how nature works.

She quickly finds three long slivers that are thick on one end, like custom-made shims. She starts for the door—

Something's not right.

Roc's bed isn't empty.

It has to be her. Who else would do that?

There's a pile of clothing in the center of the cabin, like someone had undressed, stepped out of stiff jeans, and tossed shirts and socks next to them.

Her ears prick to attention, primed to grab any sound out of the ordinary. She walks softly, stopping each time a board creaks. Miranda squats low to the floor and grabs the pants, but it's too dark to read the tag inside the waistline.

She goes from bed to bed, all of them occupied except one. The one to the right of the front door. The blanket is turned back, a dirty sheet exposed. Lines carved into the wall.

Miranda covers her mouth.

She runs to the bed and pats the covers like Cyn must be in there somewhere. She has to be. She can't be the one. She just can't.

Miranda runs to all the beds, no longer concerned about noise or who might return from the midnight run, because it can't be Cyn. She identifies them all and they're all there, sleeping soundly.

All except Cyn.

Miranda rubs her face, pinches her arm. She has to be dreaming. There has to be an explanation, has to be a reason.

She's not a thief. Can't be.

Miranda looks out the window. The dinner house looms. Nothing moves. No ghosts. No Cyn. She considers going out there, but what's she going to do if she runs into her in the middle of the night while everyone else is sleeping? What good will it do?

Instead, she crawls into bed, hiding beneath the heavy blanket. Staring at the crackling stove. Listening to the bunkhouse resist the rain. She doesn't move.

Until the doorknob turns.

Her heartbeat thumps in her ear against the pillowcase. In her throat. Miranda nearly closes her eyes, peeking through a crack. She spies the form walking slowly past her bed and around the stove.

The fuzz on Cyn's head is orange in the stove's glow. Her clothes drip water onto the floor. She strips them off, slapping them over a chair until she's completely naked, her hair matching the hue of her pubic hair. Despite the orange glow of the fire, her skin is pale as moonlight.

The body of a mature woman.

Cyn pulls one of the dry sweatshirts off of a chair and wipes down. She rubs the scruff on her head. Her ribs push from beneath her skin, her pelvis knifing out.

She dresses in the center of the bunkhouse. Miranda pushes down the blanket, observing her sluggish, mechanical movements. Watches her put the finishing touches on a perfect crime. When everyone else is dead asleep, she can do what she wants.

But Miranda's not like them.

Now she knows.

Cyn climbs into bed and doesn't move. Miranda's skin crawls. So exposed. So betrayed. Cyn pretends to be one person, but she's another beneath the surface. She's a thief and no one knows it. At least Roc is honest about her darkness. *It's the wolf you don't see that's dangerous.*

Miranda lies awake for most of the night. As the embers die and the bunkhouse cools, cold penetrates the walls and slithers beneath her covers. It's a different kind of cold, one that a woodstove can't cure.

Before morning, she crawls out of bed. She's tired of being scared and hungry. Tired of the cold.

She has to act now, while they're all still asleep.

84

CYN NOTCHES ANOTHER LINE.

She doesn't count them, just sees the bundles. Funny how minutes become hours, hours become days... *Will it become years?*

The dream hasn't changed. Something is in the gray, but it doesn't mean someone is coming for them. Dreams are thoughts, not reality.

Cyn plucks her clothes from the chair around a cold stove, still damp. She pulls her boots out from under the bed. She stitched the holes in her socks, but they won't last. They already have the color of chocolate.

Her feet are caked with mud. She needs to do a better job of washing them, especially before getting into bed. A bad case of jungle rot will only make things worse.

The wind harvesters are relatively quiet. The patter of rain is gone. She runs to the dinner house, her stiff boots squeaking. Cyn gets an old-fashioned coffee percolator set up. There might be enough coffee to brew for another couple weeks. No one else drinks it. *Coffee is for adults.*

Enjoy it while it lasts.

She checks the shelves while the percolator burps. Everything is in order. No gaps, nothing shuffled around or apparently missing. That's good. Cyn will update the inventory list after breakfast.

The coffee is strong. The caffeine surges into her head, clearing out the cobwebs. She holds the mug with both hands, the steam warming the tip of her nose. She'll collect the eggs when she's finished.

Cyn stands at the window, occasionally sipping, watching the sky lighten over the trees. The brick house is brighter. The windows are lit, like another lamp has been turned on.

Something's changed.

She almost drops the mug, coffee splashing on her chin.

In a second-floor window, a shadow passes.

SEPTEMBER

Biting the hand that feeds.
Blaming the one that bleeds.

85

"Cyn!"

Cyn looks up with a log in one hand, the ax leaning against her leg. Jen's running alongside the trees, waving as she approaches the barn.

"She's come out!" Jen's shouting.

Cyn drops the ax and sticks her hand in a bucket of frigid water, cooling the blisters. Sweat tracks down the sides of her face even though she can see her breath.

The brick house is still lit up. All the lights have been on since Miranda disappeared. They haven't seen her in days and thought she was dead. Cyn saw a shadow pass by a window from time to time. The girls had seen her ghost.

Cyn walks through the garden; several rows have nearly defoliated to the soil, weeds already crawling over their withered leaves, rain resting on the waxy surfaces. Drizzle drifts down in tiny droplets.

The girls are in front of the brick house.

"What's going on?" Cyn asks.

"You ain't going to believe this," Kat says. "Beauty Queen dumped a whole bag of winter clothes for us. We're talking coats and pants, socks and shoes. We're set for winter, boss."

Jen holds up a sweater. "So long smelly rags, hello Versace!"

It's a travel bag, something a hockey player would lug onto a bus if he were hauling designer gear for women. The girls pull out sweaters and coats, shoving them back to the bottom in search of something better, thicker, and warmer.

"Take it to the bunkhouse, keep it from getting wet. And take inventory of what's in there, see what we've got."

Roc snorts. Inventory doesn't exist in her world.

"I've got something for you, Cyn." Jen holds up a white sweater, white pearls attached evenly across the front. "Match your hair."

Cyn laughs. She wouldn't mind getting all dressed up, but there's a time and place for that. It isn't now.

They drag the oversized luggage through the grass, giggling. *It's like Christmas. In Hell.*

Roc hasn't moved off the fence that is clearly defined by the trampled grass. Her arms are stiff, each hand latched onto the opposite bicep. She's staring at the door, which is slightly ajar.

Is that music?

String instruments moan in concert. At first she thought it was the wind but, no, it's violins and cellos calling out long, mournful tones. Cyn hadn't spent much time near the brick house since Miranda had gone in.

Roc hardly left.

Cyn pulls a square plastic sheet out of her back pocket and unfolds it over her head. The rain tracks off the edges. It's dripping from Roc's furrowed brow.

"Want under?" Cyn lifts the corner of the plastic.

Roc's eyes set deeper.

"That winter gear is nice."

"Can't eat it," Roc says.

"What she doing?"

There's a loud *bang* somewhere deep inside the house. Cyn stands on her toes, as if four inches will give her a better vantage point to see through the windows. A few steps in either direction doesn't help.

Something is sliding. The door opens. Candlelight flickers against the walls. Classical music bellows.

Miranda backs out with something behind her. Her hair is radiant, pinned above her ears. The jeans are new. The coat, too. And the outdoor Merrell hiking shoes—those look new.

She looks up at the gray and dimming sky, pulling the fuzzy-edged hood over her head.

"Jesus," Roc mutters.

Miranda pulls a travel bag out of the house. It thumps down the steps, scratching the wet grass. She stops a few feet from the fence line, the tall grass on the inside. She goes back to the porch and fetches a bamboo stick with a plastic hook attached to the end.

"Use this." Still not looking at either of them, she offers them the bamboo. "Drag it across the fence. I stuck rain gear in there if you want to put it on."

"Princess," Roc says.

Cyn hooks the handle of the travel bag, sliding it well past the fence. There are shoes and boots, tons of socks and rain slickers. Roc ignores the one Cyn holds up. Rain drips from her chin and brows, eyes dark and deep.

Cyn shimmies into a green poncho and throws the hood on. The material sticks to her skin.

"Thank you."

"I'll send out food tomorrow, once I get it sorted."

"What you mean is pick out the best food and give us the rest," Roc says.

Miranda pulls at the strings dangling from the hood.

"I thought you were scared?" Cyn says.

"Not so bad."

"Find any phones?"

"No."

"You checked all the rooms?"

"Yes."

"Even the one with the dead body?" Roc adds.

Miranda's lips twitch. She flicks a dark glance at Roc. "If there was a phone, don't you think I'd call someone?"

"So you haven't checked them all?" Roc says.

Miranda holds her glare and turns to Cyn. "I can wash the clothes and dry them when you need it."

"There's a washer and drier?" Cyn asks.

"It's like a regular house. Looks like six or seven people lived here."

"What for?" Cyn asks.

Miranda shakes her head.

"Isn't it obvious?" Roc says. "What else do rich people have to do with their money besides build a house in the middle of nowhere? Huh?"

Roc leans on the bamboo stick.

"Probably too noisy in the city to hear Mozart. And all those poor people get in the way, too. That's why we're out here, right, Shiny? We're here to chop wood and weed the damn garden. We're in the servant quarters, getting the horses ready and serving up meals. We're slaves, Cyn."

Roc elbows her in the ribs.

"They got a shower in there?" Roc pokes the ground with the stick. "Hot water? You got that, too? I know you do because that hair is shining under that hood, girl."

Miranda dips her head.

"Probably have a toilet to tinkle in, too. You tinkle, right? We piss, you tinkle. And you sure as hell don't fart. You fart, Cyn?"

"Why are you doing this?" Cyn says.

"How are you going to wash those clothes for us? I mean, if we can't get in there to do it, how are you going to figure it out, Shiny? While you're sitting in the hot tub, filing your nails—"

"I gave you clothes!" Miranda shouts. "I'll give you food! Can't you have an ounce of appreciation?" Miranda shakes her fingers as if she were pinching a walnut. *Just an ounce.* "It's not my fault you're out there and I'm in here. Why are you blaming me?"

The bamboo squeaks in Roc's twisting hands. "Because tonight, when I go to bed hungry and dirty and cold, I'll know you're in there curled up on the couch with vanilla-scented candles. And I can't take that."

"You wanted me in here."

"Now I want you out."

"I didn't have to share anything, you know. I could stay in here until you're all cold and dead, when you've all cheated each other out of food and clothing."

Roc shifts her weight. Her hands grip the end of the stick like a bat. Miranda is too close to the fence. Roc turns as if she's going to walk away, fed up with the injustice, disgusted with looking at a clean and comfortable young girl who is providing them with clothes and food.

The stick settles on her shoulder, both hands still firmly grasping the end. She plants her right foot, the bamboo levels out and begins to arc—

Cyn strikes out with rigid fingers, catching the tendon in Roc's elbow.

Roc's left hand opens. The bamboo cane falters in her right hand. She loses momentum, accidentally striking Cyn across the back instead of cracking Miranda on the side of the head.

Roc is stunned.

It all happened so fast. It would've been easy to knock Shiny out, drag her across the fence line. Her lips thin out. The bamboo cane lands softly in the grass. She grabs two fistfuls of Cyn's poncho.

"Touch me again, I'll throw you into the fence."

Rain spits off her lips, spattering Cyn's face.

"This time you'll never wake up, bitch."

Roc throws her close to the fence. Cyn feels it in her neck.

"And if I even see you again," she says, pointing at Miranda, "I'll throw a rock through every window. You'd better hope that fence stays up."

Roc walks off. Her form blends into the rain and gray dusk. She goes inside the dinner house through the kitchen door. Cyn will have to correct the inventory in the morning.

"Thank you, Miranda." She zips up the bag.

Miranda nods. She goes inside, closing the door behind her.

Cyn lugs the bag through the rain, the strap cutting into weeping blisters.

86

MIRANDA PRESSES AGAINST THE DOOR, mouthing the lyrics to Carl Orff's "O Fortuna". The words are Latin, but she knows them. The poem of fate and tragedy. The string instruments draw her out of her body, out of this world, away from these feelings.

The music is her source of sanity, masking the haunting sounds in the house. It smothers her thoughts, transforms her emotions. Allows her the strength to stay inside the brick house. Without it, she'd be out there, with them.

And she can't do that.

Not now.

Miranda's hands tremble over her lips, brush the hair from her face. She cups them over her mouth, trying to slow her breathing. She's hyperventilating.

Why does the Dagger Queen have to be such an ungrateful, ragged bitch? Miranda went through every bedroom, searched every closet just so they wouldn't freeze. The two downstairs bedrooms are the largest, but there are four more upstairs. She doesn't go up there at night, not anymore. Too many strange sounds.

She spent days picking out clothing that will fit them, coats to keep them warm. They think they'll survive a real winter in those dirty rags? If they want to live, they need Miranda.

Why do I have to suffer?

"O Fortuna" ends with a flurry of applause, followed by "Ode to Joy".

She peeks between her fingers, staring down the end of the hall. The one room she hasn't explored. The room with the smell. It took every bit of Miranda's courage for her to climb the stairs during the day, but there wasn't enough courage in the universe to open the metal door.

If she hadn't found the shelf of candles, she's not sure how long she would've lasted. It takes six Yankee Candles of evergreen, vanilla, and apple-cinnamon to battle the odor. *Smells like the Gingerbread Man's corpse.*

Miranda crawls into the kitchen, candles on the counters, and leans against the industrial-sized refrigerator to the left. Her breathing has slowed. She lets Beethoven finish "Ode to Joy" before eating something.

87

CYN ISN'T the first one awake.

Kat is stoking the fire. Jen and Mad sit cross-legged, sorting through clothes. It looks like they just struck gold. Cyn curls up beneath the blankets. The windows are dark. Rain patters the roof. The rooster is quiet.

Jen snatches a fuzzy sweater from the pile, holding it up to her chest. "Liz Claiborne. You like?"

"The fuzzy collar will drive you nuts," Mad says.

"But what will the boys think?"

Mad's laughter is punctuated with a snort. The first time she's ever done that. Maybe only the third time she's laughed.

There's a stack of clothing next to Cyn's bed. It's like Santa brought sweatshirts and coats and balled-up socks. On the bottom, thick and puffy, are tan coveralls.

"Those are yours," Jen says. "We thought you could use them when you explore the countryside."

"It's cold out there," Mad adds. "Plus, you're not getting new boots."

"Nothing's going to fit *your* paddles, Cyn," Jen says. "Unless Miranda finds snowshoes."

The girls laugh. Cyn joins them. She's got wide feet for a girl.

Her body odor wafts out, permanently stained and eternally damp from the sheets. Cyn shucks her clothing, dropping each piece at the foot of the bed. Her soft, warm skin contracts in the frigid air.

"Whoa!" Mad hides her face. "Decency, girl!"

Kat stares, smiling. "Panties in there. On the bottom."

Cyn never thought she'd be excited about underwear, but denim has about rubbed her parts raw. She craves cotton. The fabric snugs against her hips and feels nice between her legs. She pulls a padded sports bra over her head and quickly puts a new Ralph Lauren on.

Lastly, she steps into the Carhartt coveralls. It's all baggy, but so warm, so comforting, like a mother's embrace. Exactly what she needs.

Thank you.

The stove throws orange light against the walls. Shadows stretch over the floor. Jen struts to the front door.

"You like?"

She's wearing jeans cuffed at the bottom with sequins stapled to the outer seams and a cardigan that hangs to her knees. The girls clap. She stops at the front door and turns, lips pouty, and catwalks to the stove. Kat puts her fingers in her mouth and a whistle splits the bunkhouse.

"Shut the hell up!" Roc flops over in bed.

They look at the lump in the corner bed and stifle their laughter.

"Let's grab some breakfast," Cyn says. "I'll get the eggs."

88

A GUST of wind splashes against the window. The brick house creaks under the assault.

Miranda takes the sweet honeysuckle candle into the bedroom to the left of the kitchen. *Adagio for Strings* plays in the front room. She sits at the desk and sorts through the tubes of lipstick and lotions, humming along with the music, imagining the conductor's steely glare and fluid hands.

The upper desk drawer is full of office supplies. The second drawer is a mess of papers and envelopes. There's a box at the bottom. She pulls an oversized pair of binoculars out of it.

Mighty powerful ones.

She steps to the window, lifts them to her eyes, and scrolls the middle dial. The wind harvester comes into focus. Kat is pulling on the barn door. The hinge must be damaged; the door only gets halfway closed before the wind snatches it back. Cyn helps push while Kat gets the latch into place. They run for cover.

Binoculars just armed Miranda in the battle against boredom.

She puts them on the bed, digs through the middle drawer for more treasure, and strikes gold again. This time, a fat manila envelope full of photographs. They're old and scratched, bent at the corners, mostly shots of the ocean, yachts, beach houses. The sorts of things wealthy people photograph.

The bottom drawer is mostly junk. A few more photos and a box of necklaces. She starts to shut it when she notices a leather-bound notebook, scuffed and tied with an elastic band, at the very bottom.

The pages are rough-cut. The script is beautifully written in blue ink. She flips the pages, captivated by the handwriting. The words are a work of art.

There's no name inside the cover. The line on the first page reads

They call this place the Fountain of Youth. I call it Hell.

Miranda sits on the bed, flipping through the pages. No dates or page numbers, just line after line of lovely script.

Everything arrived. Some of my possessions, though, were sent back. Not enough room, I was told. Perhaps they're right. There really isn't a need to make this place a home. But I'll be here until the end, so forgive me if I want it to feel like home.

Until the end? Is this a place for dying? Miranda adjusts the pillows and leans back. She reads more, but it quickly becomes mundane. Three pages on learning to saddle a horse isn't riveting. Still nothing about why they're here.

Miranda begins speed-reading.

Until...

My girl arrived.

Miranda sits up. She adjusts the journal to catch the waning sunlight.

. . .

My husband is completely opposed to her. But she's so much like me in my younger years, when I was hardheaded and tough. He just wouldn't understand. I can't sponsor someone I can't relate to, and she's perfect. I understand his reluctance, though. She's a risk.

In fact, she's dangerous.

Her background is quite alarming, but she's the perfect candidate. If she weren't, they wouldn't allow me to sponsor her.

I didn't greet her when she arrived. I was supposed to; that's what all the sponsors did—they met their girls when they arrived. I just wanted to see her from afar. She just reminds me so much of myself, it's quite distressing.

Her hair—it's just like my hair when I was that age. I can't quite believe my luck.

There's a space. As if the journal skips a few days. Maybe weeks.

They're scared of her. That's good. My husband had no idea of just how frightening I could be when I was growing up. Nothing got between me and what I wanted. She exhibits the same attributes.

Sweet Jesus, I like that.

I know that she's capable of getting what she wants. A trained fighter. Perhaps a murderer. She grew up in the roughest parts of the city; she did what she had to do to survive. I respect that.

And I look forward to seeing just what she can do. After all, I wouldn't be here if I hadn't done the same.

Miranda drops the journal onto her lap and looks at the photos on the desk. She spreads them out on the bed. It looks like vacation photos, water and sand and boats. But there's one. It looks recent. This one isn't on a tropical island; this one has snowcapped mountains in the back and open meadows. It features a group of old women dressed like ranchers.

Six of them. Four wear cowboy hats. They have their arms around each other, grinning and laughing. Four of them have gray hair, one of them has dyed brown hair.

The sixth has black hair. Jet black.

My girl has been very disruptive, although I would disagree. She's demonstrating amazing leadership qualities. She picked out the toughest of the bunch and asserted her dominance. It was quick and decisive.

I watched her from my bedroom, how my girl took her behind the cabin. How she took her down in a split second, with minimal effort. It was exciting, if I'm honest. To see someone with that much power, that much aggression. She would've killed her if she had to. That's not what I want, but I like having that as an option. I like knowing that others' lives are at my discretion.

I must admit that I was a little nervous that she would go too far, but she's smart. And that's why I sponsored her. She knows exactly how hard to push.

I think I will introduce myself to her soon. We will get along very well, I believe. She needs some guidance. If she continues, she'll discover why she's here.

Sweet Jesus, that would not be acceptable.

Miranda drops the book.

She pushes the photos around. If it wasn't clear already, it is now. The girls will need more than warm clothing to survive.

89

THE WIND HURLS a gust of rain against the dinner house like a bucket of water. Jen and Kat race along the garden, hiding from the weather beneath their hoods. They grab onto the handle of a bag. They lug it like it's a dead body, having to stop halfway to adjust their grip.

The garden is a sopping mess. The roots have drowned. The landscape is an eternal shelf of misery. If Cyn is waiting for the weather to break before she escapes, she'll be here too long. Maybe this is always the way it is. Maybe clear skies are rare.

The wind hurls the front door open. Kat grabs it while Jen drags the sack inside. There's a zipper down the length of the brown plastic bag. Cyn has never seen a body bag, but the sack could pass for one. She doesn't say anything, doesn't want to put that thought in the girls' heads. No one wants to believe there are body bags in the brick house.

"Oh my God. My boots are filled with ice water." Jen sits down and pries her rubber boot off. Her socks splatter the floor with water. "I swear to God, there's a gallon in here."

"I done told you, tuck the boots inside the pants." Kat peels her jacket off.

"No, you didn't."

"Did so."

Mad comes out of the kitchen and they slide the bag in front of the hot stove. Cyn looks away while the zipper is drawn to the bottom.

Just in case it is a body bag.

Mad plants her hands on her hips. "I thought she was sending food?"

"You got something against warm clothes?" Kat says.

"What good are they if we starve?"

"Maybe we can eat the gloves." Jen holds up fur-lined leather gloves. "Looks like rabbit skin on the inside."

For the third time in a week, they unload Gucci and Ralph Lauren. Jen pulls out a full-length fur.

"Oh my God. It's so soft."

"Take that off," Kat says. "You look like an idiot."

The bag is nearly empty. Cyn starts sorting the gear into piles.

"Looks like this one's for you, Cyn." Kat lifts up a North Face coat.

"Why me?"

"Got your name on it." Kat flicks a white piece of paper folded and pinned to the front. "Says to meet Miranda up at the brick house, she wants to talk."

"Secret meeting, huh?" Jen says. "Better hope Roc doesn't find out."

Cyn takes the coat and looks inside as if there might be more. She slides her arms inside, zipping up the front. It fits wonderfully.

"Nothing secret," she says. "You can come if you want."

"Pass."

"I'll watch from the window," Mad adds.

Cyn puts on the rain gear while the girls continue sorting, discovering another load of insulated socks. She's watertight when she leaves. All except for boots. Still, nothing fits.

Miranda unfurls a red and white umbrella. The black rubbers are up to her knees. She stops a few feet from the matted grass, where the invisible fence still works.

Cyn has the hood pulled over her eyes, standing in a shallow puddle. "Why haven't you sent food?"

"It's coming, I promise." She sniffs, glancing behind Cyn. "I'm just sorting through the inventory, that's all. There's a lot."

Cyn doesn't blink. "We're hungry, Miranda."

"We all are."

"Are we?" She tips her head.

Another glance behind Cyn. "I'm scared that everyone is in danger."

Miranda reaches inside her coat and pulls out the leather book. She looks around, steps over to the fence, and hands it to Cyn.

"What's this?" Raindrops spatter the cover.

"A diary."

Cyn quickly stashes it inside her coat before the pages swell.

"Most of it is just regular, everyday stuff—riding horses and hiking. If you ask me, it's like this place is some sort of dude ranch for old, rich women, like one last thing for them to do. I think they move here; I think they're sick. They end up dying out here."

"What about us?"

"They sponsor us, but that's all it really says. Like we're a bunch of poor kids they bring out here to save, maybe bring us closer to nature. I don't know."

"You're not poor, Miranda. You never were."

"You don't know that. Maybe they're training us to be better, maybe that's why I'm in here. Maybe I graduated and moved into the brick house and all the rest of you will, too."

She had never considered that until just then.

Cyn nods, but not in agreement. "Why are you giving me the book?"

"The lady that wrote all that," Miranda says, looking around, "sponsored Roc, and she talks a little bit about her. Says she's from the street, that she's dangerous."

"I figured that out."

"She killed someone."

Cyn nods again. Now she looks behind her, like something might be crawling through the weeds. "That's what it says in the book?"

Miranda nods. "In so many words. I just thought you should know that she's more than just a bully. I think she's a murderer that someone wanted to rehabilitate. I think those things in our necks are to protect the old women from us."

"Why doesn't yours work?"

Miranda rubs her neck. "Like I said, maybe I passed a test and they turned it off. It doesn't say."

"Anything else?"

"Just don't let her see the book."

"She can't get to you, Miranda. You're safe in there."

"I'm not worried about me. She starts reading that, and who knows what she'll do. Maybe she'll start stealing food right in front of you."

Miranda doesn't look away this time. She wants to see a reaction. Cyn doesn't blink.

"I'll keep it safe. Let me know if you find anything else."

"I will."

"You've searched the rest of the house, right?"

Miranda sniffs and doesn't answer.

"Because we're cold and hungry, Miranda. You're warm and full and clean. The least you can do is open all the doors. I don't want to be out here for months and find out a phone is behind a big, scary door."

Miranda turns without another word. She makes it to the porch, flapping the water off of the umbrella. Her hand is on the doorknob.

"Thanks for the clothes," Cyn says. "I'm exploring tomorrow, no matter what. The coats and stuff will make all the difference."

Miranda looks at Cyn's rotten boots. There's nothing she can do about that. She kicks off her boots and goes inside, where the air is warm and dry.

Bach's Toccata and Fugue plays ominously. She kneels down and taps the stereo to skip that song. The foreboding pipe organ cuts off, leading into the soothing sounds of Pachelbel's Canon in D Major. She basks in the uplifting tones, imagining lakes of glass and open fields with laughing children.

90

CYN HOISTS the backpack off the bed. Her back sags under the weight of clothing, a tent, and a sleeping bag. Her knife is stashed near the bottom, next to a leather-bound journal.

"You sure about this?" Jen helps Cyn adjust the straps.

"First thing in the morning."

"What if it's raining?"

"Then it's raining."

The backpack is surprisingly balanced. Cyn walks around the bunkhouse, her bare feet slapping the boards. She bends over to pick up a wet sock that's fallen off a chair near the stove, just to see how it feels.

She locks her thumbs beneath the straps.

"Here." Jen twists wires around the buckle, a slim strip of dangling aluminum. "I made it."

"What is it?"

"Good luck."

"I'm heading straight south, uphill to find a vantage point. I figure I'll be able to see into the valley in all directions after a half-day hike. I'll be back before nightfall."

"You're taking a lot of food for a day hike," Roc mutters from bed.

"Something goes wrong, I may have to camp."

"We should vote on it."

"You can come." Cyn pulls her arms out and lets the backpack bounce on her bed. "I can pack enough for two."

"You don't know what's out there." Kat sits backward in a chair, leaning toward the stove. "You should be taking one of the horses."

"I don't know how to ride."

"I can teach you."

"We don't have time."

"It's a bad idea, Cyn."

"Surviving isn't enough."

Roc pops her head out of the covers. "I thought that was the whole point of starving ourselves—to survive long enough for someone to find us."

Cyn points at the marks on the wall. "I got tired of that."

"So now you're rushing out to die?"

"Who says we're not an experiment, that maybe we'll wake up again and not remember anything, like it's the first day?" She yanks the bed away from the wall, exposing all the marks. "Maybe we'll wake up tomorrow and the whole wall will be filled because all we're doing is lying in bed and waiting."

"I hope so. Then I won't remember how miserable I am now."

"You'll still be miserable."

"I won't remember it," Roc says.

"I don't want to fill the wall, that's all I'm saying."

"Maybe you need to run these things by us, stop making all the decisions on your own."

The windows are dark. Night has descended. Cyn already feels the weight on her eyes. The girls do, too, making their way to bed. Kat throws a few more logs on the fire before crawling under the covers.

Cyn strips off her pants and socks, stuffing them beneath the covers where they'll be warm in the morning. She takes the keycard from around her neck, crosses the room, and presses it into Mad's hand.

"Take care of that," she whispers.

Mad puts it around her neck and tucks it inside her shirt. Cyn pats her shoulder. She should have the keycard, especially if Cyn doesn't return.

Soft snores are already drifting up from the bunks.

Cyn pulls the blankets over her shoulder and snuggles into her pillow. She begins to drift off, carrying a guilty weight with her. She'll be leaving the girls alone with Roc. But she'll be back. She won't abandon them. Even if the girl in Miranda's journal is real, Roc is more interested in sleeping and eating.

The girls won't get in the way of that.

91

THE LAST CRACKER.

Miranda shakes out the crumbs and licks them off her palm. It's past midnight and she's still hungry. The food for the girls is almost loaded and ready, just a few more items to think about. She's got to be careful. Can't give away too much.

The photos from the bedroom are scattered on the coffee table. She pushes them around like playing cards, endless tropical scenes that make her feel colder.

Hell.

That's what the woman wrote in the leather-bound journal about this place, like she didn't want to be here. *Why did she come here? She's got all those boats and houses and she comes out here until the end?*

Miranda's stomach whines. She takes the binoculars to the window. It's something to do, to help her forget about food. There's not much to see at this hour, but there's nothing else to do. The day is a better time for spying. She spotted Jen inside the dinner house, picking her nose and wiping it under the table.

She scans the horizon, looking for a wolf or a marauding grizzly bear. Maybe she'll spot a truck or an airplane—wouldn't that be nice? She'd be the one to save them, laugh right in the Dagger Queen's face.

Sometimes she catches Roc sneaking into the kitchen when the others aren't around. She hasn't seen her at night, though. Not yet. What's she going to do if she does see her? Tell the others? They already know and do nothing. How long will it be before Roc just steals right in front of them?

If Miranda had a gun, she could make things right. Problems go away in a hurry when someone has a bigger stick. Miranda would do it, too. Why not? She's the runt. A gun would level the playing field.

Time for a little payback.

Something moves.

Miranda's heart thumps. "Our Father, Who art in Heaven, hallowed be Thy Name..."

The prayer leaps to her lips like a talisman. She aims the binoculars at the garden. *The kitchen is open!*

There's no light, but the door is clearly open. The shelves are easy to see in the moonlight. She turns the knob, watching the open doorway—

Someone comes out.

Cyn's skin is bluish-white. Her legs are bare from her pointy hips down to her naked feet. She's wearing panties and a T-shirt and it's freezing. She must be carrying the keycard. Cyn closes the door and heads around the back of the dinner house.

Miranda keeps the binoculars trained on her.

Cyn doesn't turn toward the bunkhouse. Miranda fumbles the binoculars, losing sight of her. She presses them against her eyes, refocusing, scanning. *Where'd she go?*

There. Right there near the trees.

Miranda races to the kitchen for a better vantage point. Her pale skin flashes in the shadows.

She almost drops the binoculars this time.

"Our Father..."

Cyn just went down the dead-body path.

92

Where once there was floating,
Now there is ground.
Where once there was nowhere
Now there is land.

THE ROOSTER.

Cyn rises from sleep, her head still in the clouds, listening to the wind harvesters thump and the rain patter. She hooks the clothes at the bottom of the bed with her foot and dresses without breaking the warm seal of the blankets. Her feet are sore.

She sits up and inspects the scratches on the soles and the dirt around her ankles. Doesn't notice the smell anymore. Mud flakes on the floor. She doubles up on socks.

The sole is breaking away on one of her leather boots. It won't last ten more miles. The old boots probably can't make it to the chicken coop and back. She could duct tape it, but a new pair of L.L. Bean duck boots is under her bed.

Cyn shoves her feet inside and laces up. The soles rap the wood planks. They're damn snug, but dry. She rolls the pant legs over them and tosses the old leather boots under the bed.

The knife is already packed, so she uses the edge of her candle-holder to make a thin scratch on the wall. The girls snore on.

Outside, the sky is a colorless tarp. Rain taps the hood of her coat. The windows in the brick house are lit. Cyn fantasizes Miranda will wave from the front porch, tell her she found something, anything, so she doesn't have to hike.

False hope brings false suffering.

She takes her first step. Due south.

Her feet already ache.

There was a dense stretch of forest at about the half-mile mark, but it didn't last long. It's hard climbing after that, mostly hills with boulders and grassy clumps in between conifers. There's easier ground if she goes around, but she stays on a southern course. It'll be easier to map, and she won't get lost.

The sun is a hazy circle. Cyn unzips her coat, letting in the cool air. She doesn't want to break a sweat. Too late for that.

She takes a swallow of water. If she can reach the next summit, she'll have a look around, stop for a snack. She hoists the backpack and grinds ahead.

She hasn't been at it long and her legs are weak. Hopefully, she'll find a second wind by noon when she turns back. Maybe she'll glimpse a column of smoke before that, or a road or town. Something.

So far, nothing but God's country.

The back of her right foot is on fire. She limps along, taking easier paths that put her slightly off course. She stops often to correct her path. Her breathing falls into rhythm with her stride, head down. One step at a time.

One after another.

Her head feels light. There's a buzziness behind her eyes. She's breathing heavily, maybe the air is thinning. She can't dehydrate, not out here.

There's a large boulder at the summit next to a dead tree. If she can make that, she'll rest. She'll eat. She's been hiking for an hour, maybe longer. Each step forward is another step back.

She figures she's about a mile out from the cabins when she reaches the top. Cyn throws the bag down, collapsing against the stone. The aluminum strip dances around. She's winded, can't catch her breath. So dizzy. *So thin.* The sensation is sort of like a fence, but slightly different. Not so much in the neck, more in the gut.

She chews a bite of jerky and leans her head against the boulder. The tree, its gnarly trunk long dead, the bark flaked off and blown away, exposing the smooth weathered grain beneath, is wedged inside a fracture, as if it broke the stone but couldn't survive.

To her right, far to the west, is a large lake. The water is glassy and blue. It looks like a day or two away. Where there's water, there are animals. People, too. To the east, open valley.

She peels off her right boot. The heel of her sock is soaked red, a hole worn through the outer sock. She strips them off. The skin is stripped off her Achilles. What was she thinking, hiking in brand-new boots?

Stupid. Head back before things get worse.

She leans her head back, working on the last strip of jerky, staring down the slope. It'd be nice if the rest of the trail were that easy. The grassy hill goes down a mile or so to a line of trees. May as well go back, there's nothing but grass and rocks, a scraggly tree here and there. Unless there's someone in a hole, she's not going to find anything.

She washes the jerky down with a swallow of water and chases that with the yams. A nap would be nice. Kick the boots off and rest an hour or two. She'd still be back by lunch.

Even though she already ate it.

The aluminum strip rattles against the backpack. Her eyes get heavy, but she's not going to do it. There's work to be done back at the cabin. And she'll need to treat the sores on the backs of her feet.

She hoists the backpack.

At the bottom of the slope, there's an opening. A peculiar one. All these trees and just a blank opening. If she had binoculars, she could see if it's anything. It would take half an hour to get down there.

But it's so cleanly open. So clear-cut.

Cyn drops the backpack by the rock. It'll go faster without the weight, and she'll return to get it, anyway. It'll be easier on her feet. She considers hoofing it barefoot, but forces her boot back on, wincing.

Cyn half-steps her way down the slope, focused more on the topography than the destination. The buzzy, good feeling in her stomach dissipates as she descends, replaced with fatigue. She stops halfway, shading her eyes.

Looks like an opening.

A bit farther down the hill, she sees a pair of depressions coming out of the trees and fading into the patchy grass. Tracks.

She hobbles along a little too quickly for comfort, but she's going downhill. The impact on her heels burns; she's paying no attention to the increasing lightness in her head.

The buzzing in her neck.

The numbness in her fingers.

Cyn trots to the opening, more sure than ever that those are tracks. Someone drives through here! Maybe they deliver supplies along this route. Maybe someone lives nearby, or this is a hunting road.

It's something.

Has to be.

Cyn reaches the shade of the tall spruce when darkness falls on her. She leans back, but her momentum carries her forward.

She can't stop.

She tumbles into the clearing, recognizing the warning too late, remembering the sensation rattling along her neck, reaching around her face.

Dragging her into darkness.

Two miles from the cabins, Cyn passes through another fence.

93

CYN STARES DOWN. She's looking at something, seems like she should know what they are.

Ah, yes. My feet.

She wiggles her toes, scratching at the bed of pine needles. Pine needles that are gray and grainy.

The world is gray.

No black.

No white.

Just every shade of gray in a pixelated world.

The air is heavy, pressing all around. Her arm moves in a strangely slow manner, like animation trying to catch up with real time. She wiggles her fingers, dirt packed under her nails, as close to black as anything around her.

She's breathing sand.

I'm in the dream. In the gray.

She doesn't recall the needles below her feet, though. Not in the dream. She reaches out, running her fingers through the branches that suddenly appear from the fog, prickly, short needles that poke her numbly.

She doesn't remember how she got here, only sees the light ahead.

She follows the path. Trees on both sides, branches crisscrossing overhead. The dense light is closer.

An opening.

Her hands out, she quickly steps ahead, almost running, as if there's something on the other side—

She skids to a halt. Her foot slips, hanging over the edge where the ground ends.

A sheer drop-off. No bottom. Just fog.

Never-ending gray.

The trees continue to her left and right, growing up to the ledge, where they, too, fade into the gray. *Do they go on forever? Or does the gray consume them?*

Cyn kicks a rock and watches it silently evaporate into the mist.

Gone.

The distant nowhere of homogenous gray swirls.

Voices are distant.

Too distant to understand. Close enough to recognize.

Like children on playgrounds.

She reaches out, as if fairies will poke their heads out. The particles of gray begin to shimmer. A low thrumming bass rattles somewhere out there like thunder, reaching inside to shake her intestines. She feels something.

Something coming.

Stalking her.

It's coming!

She turns, steps—

Like a wave swelling from the deepest part of the ocean, something curls over her, driving her to the ground—

Color.

The world lights up with color.

There are paisley flowers on the walls and a soft comforter beneath her arms. The sun shines brightly in her eyes. She covers her face, recognizing the bare light bulb in the ceiling fixture.

"You're a bad girl."

He's heavyset, standing in a doorway. His head is closely shaved. Black and white whiskers cover his face.

He unbuckles his belt and slides it from the loops. Cyn pushes back on the bed and grabs a pillow. The man folds the belt over and snaps it. She squeals.

He grins. "You deserve this."

The belt stings the tops of her toes. She crawls back, hiding behind the pillow. He snatches her foot before she can yank it away. Grips her ankle like a vise.

She hears the zipper.

Feels the full weight of the man. His chest in her face. The smell of his armpit. He uses his knees to open her legs. She feels so small.

So young.

She feels the pressure as he pushes inside her. Like a pipe.

"You deserve this." He thrusts.

She tears.

Screams into the hand cupped over her mouth.

The gray moves in and she's back in the woods.

She scuffles across the soft needles, back into the world without color. Her eyes wide with panic, afraid to look down, afraid to see a red stain spreading between her legs.

A memory.

Her stepfather had done that to her in a trailer outside Cleveland. He raped her for years...until she left. She wasn't old enough to go out on her own, but she was smart enough to leave.

Why do I remember that now? Where the hell am I?

It's coming back.

She feels it rumbling like electricity, a storm stampeding from out there, a battering ram plunging forward. She starts to get up and begins to run deeper into the trees, away from the cliff—

Asphalt scuffs her cheek. Something drips and echoes.

Her face is fat and numb. Her body like wood. There's pressure in her arm.

"You did it," someone whispers. His voice echoes. "You killed her."

Somebody weeps.

Footsteps splash away.

Cyn bats open her eyes, heavy like coins. She wants to run, too. She can't feel anything. Her chest rises and falls involuntarily. She wants it to stop. There's something bad, something rotten inside her. She wants to flush it out, to get away.

For it all to end.

She moves her arm, the pressure spikes at her elbow.

A syringe. A needle filled with red. Stuck in a bulging vein.

She just can't get away—

Cyn sobs into the ground. The memory is a dead weight on her chest. She starts crawling away from the memories. Away from her life. I don't want to remember, I don't want to know! Stop this...please, stop.

The needles begin to thin. She feels a clump of grass.

She's beneath an underpass—

Running from the police—

Swings her fist, her knuckles meeting the soft flesh of collapsing nose—

It's so hard to crawl.

The memories pile into her, filling her like liquid metal, sluggish in her veins. Heavy on her heart.

Cyn closes her eyes.

She crawls deeper into the trees, further away.

Clutching more grass, fewer needles. Hand over hand, like pulling out of a hole. She feels a breeze. The wet tickle of grass on her cheeks.

Her legs are dead.

She rolls onto her back. The gray turns to black. And stars sparkle. The moon brightly smiles in a clear night sky.

Cyn lies on the slope, the trees below her.

She made it out of the clearing. It's not an escape, just another fence. Another nightmare.

But the entire day has passed. Night has arrived.

She doesn't attempt to get up. Sleep, as it always does, arrives like a hammer. She hears herself whimpering, fearing not the wolf's howl, but her return to the gray.

94

MIRANDA SITS BACK, binoculars up. Her eyes ache, but she continues to scan the horizon, a landscape void of life beyond trees and grass. The snowy mountains pale in the setting sun's dying light, appearing after so many days behind gray skies.

Cyn has been gone all day.

The girls have been outside. Jen cleaned out the garden, harvesting the last of the vegetables. Kat's in the barn, Mad is in the kitchen. And Roc came to eat.

But no Cyn.

It's getting late.

Candlelight flickers inside the dinner house. Miranda turns the binoculars to one of the windows, adjusting the focus. She sees Jen with a plate in front of her. She bows her head for a moment before scooping up food with her spoon.

Dinner is over in less than a minute.

Jen licks the plate. Miranda imagines the others are doing the same. The girls move past the windows, wiping the table and gathering the plates. Except Roc.

She goes back to bed.

Miranda slices off a piece of cheese she found in the back of the pantry. She was eating it with crackers earlier, but she needs to save those. There are only four boxes left. She figures if she eats ten a day, they'll last four months. It's been hard holding back. Sometimes she wonders if it's easier to have nothing.

Miranda lifts the binoculars again.

Kat and Jen are on the front porch, looking at the horizon. A candle warmly lights their faces. Miranda adjusts her focus across the meadow to the sparse trees on the hillside. Cyn has been plundering the kitchen, but if she doesn't return, things will get worse.

Our Father, Who Art in Heaven...

Roc returns to the dinner house.

Kat and Jen step aside. She nudges them, not bothering to say a word. Not bothering to look to the horizon.

Miranda tastes something bitter in the back of her throat. She grinds her teeth, wishing the binoculars were attached to a weapon.

Roc walks through the dinner house, passing both windows on her way to the kitchen. Kat and Jen are watching her through the windows in the front. Several minutes pass.

The kitchen door bursts open.

Roc stomps through the garden, dragging one of the empty travel bags behind her. Mad watches from the kitchen. Kat and Jen come around the front. Roc points at them, obscenities streaming out in all directions, no one spared.

Bile rises in Miranda's throat.

The big bad wolf is coming.

Miranda crawls off the couch, staying close to the floor so that Roc won't see her. She leans against the front door and pulls her legs against her chest. There's a box in the hallway half-full of food. She keeps filling it, plans every day to put it in the front yard, but every day she pulls items back out and swaps them with others.

Sometimes she eats them.

She just can't decide. Once her food is gone, she'll have to leave. They just don't understand.

The front window rattles. Miranda jerks toward the sound.

"The hoarding ends now, Shiny!" Roc shouts. "Time to share or time to burn."

Miranda squeezes her legs tighter. She swears she heard her say "blow your house down".

"I know what you're doing in there. I know you're sitting around eating all the food. I'm not letting that happen. Get out here."

The window rattles with debris again.

"Now!"

Miranda lowers her head. Roc is throwing something at the window. She'll keep throwing it unless she goes out there. Miranda squeezes her legs until her arms hurt. The back of her head thumps on the door.

She messes up her hair, pulling her shirt out. She stands, her legs cold and weak.

Pebbles pepper the front of the house.

Miranda puts her hand on the doorknob, turns and pulls.

The door cracks open.

Roc stands on the fence line. Staring.

"Fill it up." She tosses the bag onto the steps. "I'm not playing."

"It's almost ready. There's not as much food in here as I thought."

"Liar."

"I'll bring it out tomorrow. I promise."

"You'll bring it out now."

Miranda looks back. "It's not ready."

Roc bends over and picks gravel from the dirt. "You're a greedy pig."

"Stop it. It's not my fault."

"Shower all you want, but you can't wash the pig off. A pig smells like a pig." Roc sniffs. "I can smell you from here."

"That's not true."

She tosses a pebble. It plinks off the door. "Like a pig in slop."

Miranda almost closes the door. She doesn't stink. If she does, it's because the house smells. If she does, it's because there's something dead, but it'll wash off. If she could come outside, it would wear off. But she's stuck.

The Dagger Queen.

Another pebble hits the door and bounces across the porch.

"You should behave yourself." Miranda yanks the door open. "You need to learn manners; you are acting like a spoiled brat. You! You're the brat! I come inside the house and I give you all the clothes and you stand out there calling me names, throwing rocks at me... Have you no appreciation? No scruples?"

"Who the hell do you think you are?" Roc pokes at the rocks in her hand.

"You're the bully, Roc. You are. I know more about you than you do. I read something about you. I read that you're trouble. That you're dangerous."

Miranda glances at Kat and Jen, who are standing not far away.

"You're stealing from them. You're going to hurt them. And when they're starving and you're not, I'll be safe in here. I'll keep my food; otherwise you'll take it all from me like you'll take it all from them. I'm not the pig. You are."

Miranda steps onto the porch. The fence protects her—she knows this. But the step is an act of bravery, of defiance. And Roc knows it.

She's not hiding anymore.

"I'll tear you apart," Roc says.

"You're scum."

Miranda goes back inside and closes the door. She's not shaking. Roc is a thief and now they all know it. And until they do something about it, she's not giving them her food. And if Cyn doesn't return, they never will.

Miranda's not selfish. She's smart.

"You're dead!" Roc shouts. "When I get to you, you're dead!"

Gravel scatters against the house.

Miranda smiles. She hit her good, where it counts. Right on the pride. Her anger is fully lit. It hurts and this gives her pleasure.

Miranda looks out the west window. Kat, Jen, and Mad are watching from a distance. Roc might take it out on them.

What have I done?

Boom.

Miranda jumps, a squeal popping out of her. Something thumps the door and rolls on the porch.

"The party's over, Shiny!"

Roc pushes the tall grass around, searching for something larger.

The pleasurable confidence leaches away from Miranda, leaving twisted, toxic fear in the pit of her stomach.

She can't get in here. She can't get to me.

And she has to sleep. The sun has dipped below the mountains. Darkness is near. They'll fall asleep like they do every night. No one will wake up until morning, no matter what. She just has to survive this and then Miranda could do something. She can end this.

Permanently.

It's Roc or us. If it wasn't for Roc, Miranda would be out there with the girls. It's Roc's fault. All her fault. If Miranda gets through this, she can sneak out at night, smother her with a pillow. Put a knife in her throat, a stick through her eye—

"You're dead, bitch!"

Roc heaves a stone, this one purple and angular. The size of a softball. Miranda instinctually leaps away from the window—

The window spiderwebs into a thousand lines. But it doesn't break.

SHHHHHT-THOOM.

SHHHHHT-THOOM.

SHHHHHT-THOOM.

Metal shutters slide in front of the windows. The room dims as light is cut off from the outside one window at a time. Dust trickles from the ceiling as shutters bang closed over the upstairs windows.

Miranda falls against the door and hides her eyes.

Roc's voice is muffled. Distant.

Another stone bangs harmlessly off the shutter to the right of the door. A distant curse punctuates it. Miranda crawls away from the door and curls up in the middle of the floor, listening to shot after shot land harmlessly against the house.

Classical music plays softly.

Something is beeping in the back of the house. An alarm is going off, a steady, even droning. A mechanical warning.

The metal door is cracked open.

A red light is flashing.

95

THE BRICK HOUSE IS A TOMB.

And each time the back room beeps, a nail is driven deeper into its lid, shutting it tighter. Darker.

Miranda feels the weight of the shutters sealing in the sound, shutting out the light. She tries to open the front door. She raps on the windows. She's safely entombed, away from danger. Roc will never hurt her.

But she's haunted by thoughts.

The beeps bounce around the walls, driving deep inside her head. She presses pillows to her ears, buries her head beneath couch cushions and blankets. Still, it's out there.

The incessant warning.

She heaves a candle at the metal door. "Shut up!"

The door eases back. The crack widens. And the alarm seeps out louder. Fiercer.

Miranda weeps with her ears covered. Hours go by, trapped with her worst fear. There's no avoiding it.

The back room is calling.

Exhausted, she turns off the music. She stands in the hallway, red light pulsing. Each beep perfectly spaced, exactly pitched.

"You win," she whispers.

Miranda wipes her face. A wave of serenity passes through her. No more avoiding it. Hate it, but embrace it.

She takes a step. Then another.

Her fingers against the door, she pushes it open.

Unbelievable.

A chuckle rattles her throat. She shakes her head. Ten feet, straight ahead, there is another metal door.

But in between, there's a room. The flashing and beeping are coming from her right. Miranda takes a half step forward, peering slowly inside. A countertop runs along the right wall with several monitors mounted above it, computers below. All the screens are blank except for the largest one in the corner. A red square blinks in time with the beeping.

The smell is not any worse. Whatever is dead, she tells herself, is behind the next door. Relief rises again with a trace of dread.

Another door.

There are chairs along the clean countertops. The computers have flashing green lights, indicating hibernation.

She looks to her left before entering.

The furnace and hot water heater are in the corners. Generators and battery banks, all stacked and wired: power storage for the solar panels and wind harvesters. With all the computers, the power consumption must be considerable. Three wind harvesters still seem like a lot, but some could be backups in case of failure.

Or whatever's behind the next door.

Miranda flips the light switch and goes to the large monitor.

BREACH. The word flashes over and over.

Roc had shattered the window and activated the security system. And if she can't turn it off, she'll go insane and may never escape.

She touches the spacebar on the keyboard—

It stops.

The screen sputters to life. A program opens. An interface scrolls with numbers and words, nothing that makes any sense. She's afraid to click anything that might start the alarm again. Besides, Roc is probably still stalking the brick house; it's better to keep the windows covered up for now. Despite the claustrophobia.

The computer below the counter whirs. The other computers answer the call, spinning awake, green lights flickering.

The generators kick on. All the monitors light up.

Miranda backs up.

Images appear on a dozen screens. The far left monitor displays a view from the front porch. Evidently floodlights have been activated, illuminating far out into the meadow.

The monitor flickers to another view, this one overlooking the garden. Several seconds later, it goes to the back of the house, eventually cycling around to the front.

The other monitors are glowing with eerie green light.

Night vision.

The inside of the dinner house and the kitchen are displayed in infrared. There's another monitor showing the inside of the bunkhouse, the views focusing on each of the beds. Four beds are filled. The fifth bed—the one tucked in the corner—is Miranda's.

The sixth is also empty. *Cyn.*

Miranda watches it cycle through again. She'll never survive out there. Not in this weather.

Not in the wild.

The next monitor illuminates views from another building. At first, she thinks it's the barn. But there's no pasture, no fence. And none of the other buildings are around. Just trees.

It's in the woods!

No one really goes back there. Three of the views are just trees, but the fourth shines brightly on a path leading up to it. Miranda leans closer; something is at the end where the path turns sharply.

A ghostly chill passes through her. *That's a leg.*

The dead body. It's there. That's the body down the path. None of the girls have ever gone past it to discover the cabin in the woods. The four views—presumably from four different cameras—are frightening. But the fifth one is shocking.

Miranda jumps back, covering her mouth to hold back panic. Tension holds her eyes wide, and her jaw clamps shut.

An old woman.

She's inside a tiny room, lying on some sort of hospital bed. She stares at the image, a ghostly green visage of a comatose old woman. And then it's back to the trees.

Miranda watches the cycle. The path. The body. The woman again.

Suddenly, the brick house feels much less like a tomb and more like a fortress. The last place she wants to be is outside. Something's in the trees.

The generators kick off.

All the monitors go green. The floodlights must have turned off to conserve power. The cameras switch to infrared.

She glances at the unopened door. The last frontier. Her last hurdle of fear. She's had enough, though. The adrenaline is wearing off. Exhaustion takes its place.

Miranda goes to the couch and curls up beneath the blankets, still hearing the beeping in her head. She falls asleep.

Much later, the generators start up.

Miranda lifts her head, staring at the clock. It's almost one o'clock in the morning.

The candles have burned out. The hallway appears brightly lit. Maybe the floodlights have turned on, but she doesn't care. Miranda closes her eyes and goes back to dreaming.

Dreaming that final door leads to oceans and beaches and yachts.

96

CYN HANGS in that place between sleep and wakefulness, disconnected from her thoughts and body. She's rudely yanked into the world by fiery spikes deep in her feet.

Ceiling. Wall.

Daylight shines through a window, late morning.

She's wearing her coat, boots, and stocking cap in her bed beneath the covers. Sweat soaks through her thermals and cotton shirts.

Her memories are fragmented and cluttered, like a junk drawer dumped onto the floor, each piece unrelated to the next. Each piece broken.

Something inside her had died.

She throws the blanket off, her joints stiff. There's a full-blown fire in her boots. Slowly, she slides her legs off of the mattress, placing them gently on the floor. Her pulse slams in her heels, her feet swollen and snug inside the rubber.

She doesn't think, just reaches down and pries off the right one, ignoring the slivers of pain that bore through her heel and into her thigh.

She stifles a scream. Her breathing is shallow, rapid. Awareness hangs tenuously on each breath. She opens her eyes.

The sock is red. The back of it completely worn away, revealing scorched tissue, red and angry, as if a belt sander had been laid on her heel.

She wedges her finger under the sock, hand quivering, and peels it away. It sticks on the floor. The cool planks bring little relief.

Ten more breaths and off comes the left one, not as bad as the right. The sock not as red.

She waits until her pulse stops hammering in her heels. Now that her feet are out, the pain recedes and they swell without constriction.

I walked through the night.

That's how she got back to the bunkhouse; she trekked through the midnight hours until she crawled back in bed. There's no memory of it. Like every night, there's only falling asleep and waking in the morning.

She didn't expect this.

She didn't expect to sleepwalk to the bunkhouse. It would've been better to sleep on the hillside than mangle her feet. Infection could be the end.

Her backpack isn't in the bunkhouse. It must be out there, on the hilltop next to the split boulder and dead tree, where the slope leads to the trees where there's an opening and tracks and...

And memories.

That's why she feels dead inside. She remembered her past in that place, the memories forced inside her. A past she wants to forget.

She stands, welcoming the pain to blot out thoughts, erase the guilt and rot and ugliness. She has to stay present, be in the here and now, not there.

First, she must tend her wounds.

She knows where to find medicine.

"You're up... Oh my God!" Mad shouts, stepping out of the kitchen.

Cyn hobbles past the dinner table. Mad gets out of the way, staring at bloody streaks, the shiny wounds on her heels. Cyn falls onto the stepstool next to the sink and lets out a troubled breath. Pain crawls through her legs and into her stomach.

"We thought you were a goner." Mad reaches into the pantry. "When you didn't come back last night, I didn't think we'd ever see you again. You must've walked all night."

She's holding a white metal box, staring at Cyn's feet.

"How'd you do it?"

"I don't remember." Cyn takes the box from Mad.

"That came with Miranda's last batch of clothes. There's ointment and gauze and enough wrap that you can get those covered." Mad bends over, grimacing. "Those get infected, you'll be in a world of hurt."

The box is filled with small amounts of iodine and triple antibiotic and other low-dose pain meds. She'll go through all of those before it's over. Cyn opens the medicine cabinet beneath the sink and looks at the brown bottles with pills. She's not sure what they're for or how much to take. *Last resort*, she decides. *If I start a fever.*

She begins to close it. "What the hell happened?" she blurts.

Mad steps back. Cyn's tone is direct. *Harsh.*

"This thing was full, but now there's a bunch missing." Cyn pulls out a clear plastic bag. "Where are they going?"

"I don't know. I don't use them. I don't even know what they are."

Cyn doesn't know, either. But they're missing. And the shelves of food are half empty. They shouldn't be, not by her estimates. She looks at Mad.

Mad shrugs and looks away.

"Where is she?"

"Up at the brick house, I think." Mad takes the keycard off of her neck. "Here's your key."

"Keep it."

Cyn slides an empty pail from under the sink. "Fill this."

Mad brings her fresh water. She helps clean the blood from her feet. Cyn winces when she comes near the wound. Mad doesn't stop. She cleans it, scrubbing away the dirt and dead skin. She applies the iodine and triple antibiotic. Cyn does the wrapping, though. She weaves the ACE bandage over and under each foot until they're fully wrapped.

She tests her weight. It's manageable.

She opens the kitchen door. There's a small fire on the other side of the garden, near the brick house. The windows are all covered with metal shutters, like a fortress under siege.

Cyn doesn't ask. Barefoot, she walks outside. Her gait is slow and methodical.

"Glad you're back." Jen stands in the garden. "I didn't want to wake you..."

Cyn doesn't answer. Eyes ahead.

Roc stacks wood on the growing fire at the fence line. There are smoldering branches on the porch. She squats down, rubbing her hands.

Cyn stops several feet behind her. Adrenaline numbs the pain, lubricates her joints, and pumps into her arms and back.

Roc feels someone watching and turns around. "Believe this? Bitch is hiding in a bomb shelter. I'm going to smoke her ass out."

She returns to rubbing her hands.

"Nice shoes," she adds.

"Give me your key."

Roc pretends not to hear. She looks over her shoulder, eyeing Cyn's stance. The calm expression.

"You find a bunch of bravo berries on your vision quest?"

"The key." Cyn holds out her hand.

"Not happening." Roc laughs, shaking her head. Her hand moves to a branch.

"Last chance." Cyn removes her sweater and wraps it around her forearm. "The key, Roc. And it goes easy."

Roc stands, thick branch in hand, the opposite end glowing embers. "You're about to make the mistake of a very short life."

"Come on," Jen says. "Don't do this. It's hard enough out here."

"Back up." Cyn points to where Kat and Mad are watching near the edge of the garden. "This is going to happen quickly."

"I'm going to set you on fire." Roc circles around, getting her back away from the fence. "Throw you on the porch and burn the little piggy's house down. You won't go to waste, Cyn. You'll smoke out the little princess; then I'll have fun with her. Take my time."

She grips the branch like a smoking club.

"I'm tired of playing nice," she says. "We're in the bush where the alpha dog eats."

Cyn watches her eyes, keeping her peripheral vision on the branch, and adjusts her stance as Roc circles. She stays loose, hands open.

Fingers twitching.

"You ready?" Roc fakes a swing.

Cyn remains relaxed.

Roc smiles, laughs. Her grip strengthens, forearms tense. She stops walking sideways and pauses for a moment.

Reaches back for the big swing—

Cyn shoots.

She doesn't feel the bite in her heels when she launches her shoulder into Roc's midsection. The branch comes down on the back of her thigh, but the collision with the ground knocks it out of Roc's hand.

Cyn throws her leg over Roc, mounting her, keeping her head buried against her collarbone. Roc curses, throwing weak punches into the side of her head. Cyn reaches up without exposing her face, interfering with the strikes while she hooks her heels around Roc's legs.

Pain is irrelevant.

She's patient, tightening her grip each time Roc bucks. Every twist allows Cyn to gain more control, immobilizing Roc with a full-body clench. She doesn't know how she's doing it. Maybe it's the memories. Maybe, out there in the gray, something downloaded into her psyche.

This is who I am.

Roc growls. Tries to pull her hair. Her strength drains quickly. She throws glancing blows off Cyn's shoulders with no leverage, no power. Cyn remains clenched.

Waiting.

Roc goes limp, struggling to catch her breath. Resignation sinks in. She's helpless, back to the ground.

Now she strikes.

It's quick and surgical. She pops up just enough to bring her elbow into the side of Roc's head before hunching over again to ride out Roc's short burst of fury. Once exhausted, Cyn lands another elbow, this one slicing from the left, gashing open her scalp.

Blood drains into her ear.

Confusion glazes her eyes. Concussion symptoms already in effect. Two more elbows and Cyn sits up, heels hooked.

Blood is smeared across Roc's forehead, pooling around her eye. Cyn's knuckles crack against her jaw. Another hook from the left. Roc's head limply rotates, blood streaming from a hole in her lower lip.

"Stop!" Jen shouts. "That's enough!"

Cyn sits upright, all of her weight bearing down. She's hardly winded. Roc gasps for air, head rolling back and forth, a distant gaze, no focus.

Jen pulls at her, cheeks glistening with tears. "You're going to kill her."

"Get back."

Roc shakes her head, spittle building at the corners of her mouth, struggling to breathe.

Cyn gets up. The burn on the backs of her legs throbs worse than her heels. She paces around the gurgling mess and yanks the keycard from around her neck.

She turns around, facing the meadow, looping the keycard over her head. She grinds her teeth, hardening against the soft emotions rising in her throat.

Roc spits blood.

"I don't know where we are," Cyn says, "but two miles out there is another fence."

She rests her hands on her hips, turning to the others.

"Do you know what that means? Do you?"

She waits.

"It means we're never escaping."

"Why?" Jen asks.

Cyn doesn't answer because it's obvious. They all know; they just don't want to say it. There's a fence surrounding the hills, an enormous dome over this world like some science experiment. Only they can't see the gods' microscopes or what they're looking at. Or what they're doing to them.

She knows one thing they don't, though: bad things are beyond the fence.

"I don't know why we're here, but I know this." Cyn points at Roc. "You're poison."

Roc attempts to sit up. The tip of her tongue pokes around her lower lip, assessing the damage.

"You have two choices." Cyn holds up two fingers. "One, we tie you to your bed and feed you like a cripple. You don't ever leave it. You understand?"

She looks at the girls. They're still speechless.

"If you don't like that, you're banished from this camp. You go out there on your own. We give you enough gear and food to last a couple days, but you never show your face here again. If you do, I'll throw you through the fence and you'll sleep forever. You understand this?"

"Cyn, don't say that," Jen says.

"She would've killed you, Jen! She was trying to kill Miranda, and she's eating all the food and contributing nothing. You know it—all of you know it. She was going to end us. I'll do the same to her." Her eyes are so relaxed, so convincing. "I won't hesitate."

Jen covers her mouth, her voice muffled by her fingers. Mad puts her arm around her. Kat watches impassively.

"We'll vote." Cyn holds up two fingers. "I vote number two."

Roc pushes up on her elbows. Head down.

"Kat?" Cyn says.

There's a long pause. Kat stares at Roc. "Two."

Cyn points at Jen. She shakes her head, refusing to answer.

"Mad?"

Roc turns a hard stare, focus finally returning with vengeance. The cook looks at the ground, then back at her.

"I can't do it, Cyn."

Cyn nods. Roc spits at her feet, flecking the bandages with blood. The backs of her feet are already soaked with her own.

"Get up." Cyn waves her to stand. "You try anything and I knock you. Now get up."

Roc takes her time moving to her knees, slowly standing. Her shoulders slump. Cyn puts her finger on her chest and begins pushing. Roc backs up a step, slapping her hand away.

Cyn points. "Keep stepping."

Roc steps backwards, glaring beneath furrowed brows. Cyn shadows her steps until she feels the fence in her neck. Roc stops.

Jen is sobbing.

"You've stolen food. You do nothing to help us survive—"

"I helped pull you out of the fence on day one."

"You tried to burn down the brick house. You're nothing but a threat, and you don't deserve to stay. But you can thank those two you won't freeze tonight in the wild."

"Kiss my ass."

"Step backwards."

Cyn is within striking distance, dangerously close, daring her to do something. Roc doesn't take the bait, the last of her dignity falling away.

"Step back or get knocked back."

They stare.

The battle is over.

Roc steps across the fence line. Her eyes roll back as the fence lights up the knot in her neck. She collapses, unconscious. Cyn stands at her feet, close enough that her vertebrae shiver.

"Get something to bind her," she says.

Jen's sobs fade.

The leather-bound book spoke of a dangerous girl.

It wasn't Roc.

OCTOBER

I dreamed a dream,
  And it was you.

97

CYN CHOPS WOOD until her feet are numb. She keeps them heavily wrapped, but it'll be weeks before she can wear boots. She doesn't mind the cold. It soothes the wounds. She changes the bandages frequently, keeping them clean.

Her knuckles ache. Gripping the ax for hours at a time doesn't help, but they need wood. And she needs something to do. She refuses to sit still.

If she does nothing, she thinks. She remembers.

The brick house is still locked tight, with no word from Miranda. Roc occupies the bunkhouse, and she'd rather not be near her. Cyn walks her to the outhouse. She doesn't trust the others.

Be easier if Roc was dead.

No other way to put it. She's a threat, a waste of food. If she loosens her bindings, if she catches Cyn by surprise, the others will pay dearly. Cyn is comfortable with the idea of killing her. She could do it. She could cut her throat, this she knows.

And she hates that. She hates that she could do it. Hates that she wants to.

Hates that she remembers.

She doesn't like the memories. They feel foreign and wrong. She'd gotten used to a fresh start, even if it was a miserable one. Now she's dragging the past with her, each step heavier than the last.

Even when she doesn't think, the gray dream returns at night to find her. She walks to the edge, the trees rustling behind her. She trembles, fearing what will come out of the fog, what heinous memory will force itself upon her. She stands frozen, toes over the ledge.

Trembling.

She wakes as if someone has their hands around her throat, as if she's drowning. It takes all her effort to force down the sobs. The backpack is still on the hill with her knife. She reaches under the mattress for a spoon and puts a light scratch on the wall.

Marks another day.

Another day she hasn't died.

Do we die?

Mad is the last one to sit down for breakfast.

They bow their heads, allowing a moment of silence before plowing through eggs and pinto beans. Breakfast doesn't last long. Hunger doesn't go far away. They scrape their plates, listening to the wind.

Cyn grips the edge of the table, staring at her plate while the others wipe their mouths and lick their fingers. The scabs are thick on her knuckles, the tendons popping up as she squeezes harder.

It's been days. No one asks about the trek; they don't want to know what happened to her, why she returned... *different.*

They hardly talk to her.

But she can't hold it in. Closing her eyes, her tongue won't work. Her lips clamp shut.

Mad scoots her chair out from the table.

"I remember who I am."

Silence.

Mad sits back down. Cyn doesn't look up. She can't, not yet. But she started. Something she hasn't been able to do yet.

"How you know that?" Kat asks.

Nervous energy constricts around her chest. She stands too quickly, knocking her chair over. The girls are staring.

Waiting.

Cyn paces back and forth, searching for the courage she had only moments ago, courage that has drained into a pool of quivering fear. Strange how easy it was to destroy Roc, how helpless she feels faced with emotions.

Memories.

She stops at the window, the glass cold. The brick house is shuttered and quiet.

"The fence that's out there—it's different than the one around the brick house. When I fell into it, I just started remembering...things."

Long pause. "How did you get out?" Kat asks.

"I crawled out." Cyn shakes her head. "At least I think I did; it's all a little cloudy."

There's nervous shuffling. But she's stuck again. She wishes she'd never started talking about this, just wishes they would eat and clean up and chop wood and go to sleep. Keep it simple. No need to dredge up these—

"I want to remember," Jen says.

"No," Cyn says. "No, you don't. You don't want to remember. I wish I could put the memories back in the gray. Wish I could forget them."

"Memories don't make you who you are," Kat says.

Cyn steadies her hands on the windowsill so the girls don't see them shaking.

"But memories tell you what you've done."

Something drifts over the garden. Snowflakes are falling. Cyn feels them inside her, cold and drifting.

What the hell is this place?

"We've got names, too," Kat says. "How can we go forward if we don't look back?"

"What if the memories drag you down?" Cyn says to the window. "Trap you in your past?"

"I'll take my chances."

"Really?"

"Better than this. You said so yourself just before you hiked off. You said it's better to take a chance, to explore, than sit around waiting to die. You said that, Cyn. You regretting it?"

Cyn presses her forehead to the cold window, snow spitting on the ground and resting on the brown grass. She involuntarily claws the windowsill. She can't fight this, not the way she beat Roc.

Can't hide from it, either.

Her throat knots up. The sadness just won't go down this time.

"You want to remember?" she asks.

They agree.

"I was raped," she says. "My stepfather did it until I was ten. What if that happened to you? You want to remember that?"

She closes her eyes, swallowing.

"That's not your fault," Jen says.

"That ain't you now," Kat says. "I know you, Cyn. You ain't memories."

"But they're in me now. I did bad things—you saw what I did out there." She points to the garden. "I remember what I've done. I'm no better than Roc."

"Yeah, you are."

"And neither are any of you." Warmth dissipates. "You're just as bad, and that's why you're here. That's why we're all here. This is Hell, and we're paying for what we've done."

"You don't know that," Jen says. "You don't know that."

"Those memories might not even be real," Kat says. "Maybe they're not even yours."

"You think I can just remember to fight and do that to Roc? No, that was me out there, and you know it."

"None of this makes any sense. This whole place is playing tricks on us; maybe those things you think you remember are fake. They're just thoughts."

"No. They're real."

"Yeah, and you know what? I don't care," Mad says. "You came back and saved us from Roc, so if you're some evil demon, then I'm on your side. We need you."

Cyn shakes her head. Her heart is beating in her throat now.

"I want to remember," Kat says. "It ain't your decision to make, either. If you think those memories are real, then I want to know. I want to understand. Even if bad things happened to me, they're still part of me."

"Me too," Mad says.

"Me too," Jen adds.

Cyn nods at nothing in particular. She licks her lips, which are suddenly dry. Her hands are no longer shaking. She stares out the window again. Snow is already dusting the ground and the brick house's roof.

"When I can wear boots again, we'll go out there. You can get your memories. Just remember what I said: you don't want them."

Another long pause. The chairs slide out; plates scratch across the table. Mad begins cleaning up in the kitchen. Kat goes out the front door.

And the snow continues.

98

STEAM RISES FROM THE BOWL.

Miranda blows across the broth, mouthwatering. She made herself wait until late in the afternoon to have lunch. She's been eating five meals every day, and it's time for some self-control.

Down to three meals. Plus two snacks.

She wraps a blanket over her shoulders and continues to blow on the soup. The monitors are blank. Several cups and wrappers are scattered on the countertop. She sits in the chair, careful not to spill the soup. She taps the spacebar, lighting up the monitors.

She navigates the main screen while the soup cools. The first pop-up box asks: Deactivate Security?

The cursor moves over YES and stops on NO.

Click.

It's easier that way.

Since the brick house was shuttered, the girls stopped asking for food. They don't know if she would open the door or not. And now that she's learned to work the cameras, being inside the brick house is almost as good as being out there.

Without actually being out there.

The bunkhouse shows up on the big monitor. It's empty except for the bed in the back corner. No one hangs around the bunkhouse anymore, not with Roc tied up. Miranda missed what happened, just woke up and Roc was cursing from her bed and Cyn was out back chopping wood.

Miranda scrolls the mouse-wheel and the view zooms in on Roc. *Asleep again.* Mouth open. The swelling has gone down, but that front tooth is definitely brown, killed at the root.

If only I could've seen that.

At some point, Mad will drop some food within reaching distance. Roc already looks gaunt.

Miranda slurps a spoonful and cycles through the cameras. The dinner house is empty. Kat is in the barn, shoveling crap out of the stall. *I don't miss that.* The unmistakable thumping of an axe is near the barn.

Cyn is swinging it. That's all she does. Her feet are wrapped in thick wads of cloth that often hang off the ends of her toes like loose socks. Miranda isn't sure why she's doing that, especially with an inch of snow everywhere.

The garden is dead, so Jen helps drag wood out of the woods and stacks it after Cyn has split it into stove-size chunks. They'll have enough to burn for three winters.

Miranda eats a few bites of soup and clicks over to the last camera view.

The old woman.

Not as shocking as the first time, but still creepy. Sometimes there's a blanket over her, sometimes she appears to have adjusted her weight, but she's always lying down, eyes closed. She must be awake sometimes, but Miranda never sees it.

For a while she thought the old woman might be in the very back room, behind the locked door. But she decided against that. The old woman isn't dead. Her nostrils flare, her chest moves up and down. Very much alive, very much asleep.

She's in the woods, in a small cabin. No doubt. She wants to tell the girls, but then they'd ask for food. Miranda likes things the way they are. Besides, the old woman is out there.

Miranda is safe.

She slides the bowl onto the desktop and goes to the kitchen. She counts out ten crackers, heats up a cup of tea, and returns to the back room. The monitors are now cycling through the views of the countryside. She doesn't need the binoculars anymore; the cameras have excellent zooming capacity as well as night vision. She could see gnats humping on a log if she wanted.

She crushes up half the crackers, stirs them into the broth, and eats them before they're too soft. She's scooping out the noodles—

Something moves.

She taps the keyboard, backing up to the last view.

There.

There's an unnatural color in the meadow. In a landscape of browns and greens, something bright red and yellow is approaching.

She scrolls the wheel.

Zooms in.

Can't be.

She's hallucinating, has to be. Maybe the tea has peyote or the crackers are laced with LSD or—

"Cyn!" Jen's voice calls from behind the barn.

She sees it, too.

99

THE THIN LAYER of snow is more sloppy than frozen. Cyn's feet slosh in mud. She can't feel much. She'll go inside, warm up. Just one more swing.

She's said that ten times. *One more swing.*

With the log balanced and pointing at the sky, she swings—

"Cyn!" Jen shouts.

The axe ricochets, burying the blade in the ground.

"Look!"

Cyn wipes her eyes, the sweat smudging the landscape. Something's in the barren meadow, like wildflowers. She lets go of the axe and continues walking and wiping.

Kat comes out of the barn, dropping the brush in the snow.

Jen is running.

Cyn blinks her vision into focus. She's not sure what she's seeing. It can't be. It just can't...

She starts running, too.

Her legs are like cold stumps. She feels the skin splitting on her heels but powers through the pain, into the meadow, toward the brightly clothed people staggering across the field.

One of them collapses. The other stumbles forward aimlessly, falling to his knees.

Jen drops down next to the man on the ground, putting her arm around him. Cyn puts her hands on her knees, ignoring the pain cutting through her feet, biting deep into her bones.

She touches the old man on the ground.

They're real.

Jen turns him over, putting his head in her lap. His receding gray hair exposes most of his scalp. His cheeks are pale, lips blue. Teeth chattering uncontrollably.

"Get him into the bunkhouse," Cyn says. "Wrap him in blankets."

He's dressed for the beach: a bright red shirt with yellow flowers, white shorts smudged with dirt. His arms and legs are covered in scratches, the worst on the top of his head, blood trickling down to his chin. They sit him up. The old man doesn't see anything. He's staring off into nothing, just trying to breathe.

"We're picking you up," Jen says. "Can you help?"

He doesn't respond. Kat and Jen wrestle him to his feet and heave his arms over their shoulders. He flops along with them, his breath heaving in and out.

Cyn leans over the teenage boy. He's taller than her, about her age, and isn't dressed any better than the old man: just a T-shirt, shorts, and flip-flops.

"Can you walk?" she asks.

He's staring at the ground, mouth hanging open. Daydreaming. Or so far into pain, he's receded to the safety in his mind.

"Come on." Cyn hooks her arms under his armpits. He doesn't help and she can't lift him.

"Hey!" She slaps him. "Wake up!"

It shocks him back to the present moment. His shaggy hair falls over his eyes, but he looks at her, sees her. His cheeks are rosy.

"You hear?" she asks. "You need to stand and walk, you understand?"

He nods once.

Cyn lifts again and up he comes. His legs are scratched like the old man's; big toe split open, the nail missing. *How did they survive?*

She puts his arm over her shoulder, more for guidance than support, not sure if she's helping him walk or he's helping her. Kat and Jen are picking up the old man, who's stumbled face-first into the ground.

Eventually, they get inside.

"Take these." Mad holds two white pills in her palm. "There aren't many left."

Cyn works up enough spit to swallow them dry. Her heels are screaming all the way to the top of her head. She rests on the edge of her bed, keeping the weight off her feet.

Two beds have been pushed in front of the stove, which is stocked with flaming logs. The old man and boy hunker beneath the blankets, still dressed in dirty, wet beachwear. No one wanted to undress them.

Kat and Jen watch them shiver.

More mouths to feed.

Cyn calculates the number of weeks these two just took out of their stock. If they stay, they might not make it through winter. Then again, maybe these two know something.

Something that will get them out of here.

"Put them in the same bed for the night," Cyn says.

"They barely fit," Jen says.

"It's our wood, our food, and our beds. None of us are sleeping on the floor."

"But that's mean—they're hurt. I'll sleep on the floor. Let them be comfortable."

"No, you're not sleeping on the floor. They'll be fine."

"They'll share body heat," Kat adds. "That's what men did in the Civil War—slept together. Hell, the old man needs it."

The old man rolls back and forth, moaning. Jen pulls the covers back over his shoulder. The scratch over his head is caked with dried blood. He needs to be cleaned up, but at least he's not bleeding.

"I wish something would make sense," Cyn mutters.

"Why start now?" Kat says. "I'm just getting used to it."

"We need to find them clothes for tomorrow. If they survive the night."

"You want to move them into the same bed now?" Kat asks.

"After dinner."

Kat tosses another log onto the fire. The old man starts rambling again. Jen kneels next him and puts her hand on his forehead, her face etched with concern.

"Don't..." he mutters. "Don't leave us out here."

"We won't." Jen strokes his head. "You're safe now. It's all right."

A moan rattles his throat. More angry than pained. "I paid good money, damn you."

Jen looks up, confused.

"Delirious," Kat says. "His brain probably froze."

"I'm staying," Jen says. "Can someone bring dinner to me? Maybe they'll want to eat, too. Are you hungry?"

The old man remains quiet.

The boy's eyes are still unfocused, like he sleeps without closing them.

"They're from the dream," Roc says from her bed.

The girls look at Cyn. She doesn't say anything. She remembers the dream they've all been having, the one where someone's coming out of the fog. She also remembers falling into the fence, hearing the voices beyond the cliff, like speeding apparitions on a carnival ride.

She has the same thought: that there are people out there.

But that's a dream.

And two men just walked into their lives dressed for the beach.

100

THE OLD MAN and boy eat chicken noodle soup for breakfast, spilling broth down their Christian Dior sweaters and furry Forzieri coats. The old man is still shaking.

They don't talk, just eat. The boy mechanically lifts the spoon to his mouth like he's running on autopilot, his body programmed to eat, methodically moving the spoon in timed increments.

The old man, however, looks around after each bite, studying what he sees. He doesn't look at the girls, as if he's already figured them out. He's just trying to figure out where the hell he is.

He lifts the bowl to slurp out the last of the noodles and wipes his mouth with the back of his hand.

"My name," he says, "is Mr. Williams."

"If you want to stay, you'll have to pull your weight," Cyn says.

"Cyn!" Jen glares at her. "Mr. Williams, we're just happy you're feeling better. My name is Jen."

"Yes. This here is Sid." He pats the boy on the shoulder. Sid keeps eating, one spoonful at a time. "Do the rest of you want to tell me your names?"

Mad and Kat respond. Cyn only stares.

"How about you?" he asks.

Cyn nods. Finally relents. "Cyn."

"Yes."

His eyebrows rise. They're bushy, unwieldy and wild. He looks around the room, out the window.

"Sufficiently unpleasant here."

"You were expecting a beach?" Cyn says.

"Hoping, I suppose."

"What's that supposed to mean?"

Sid appears stuck, his spoon dipped in the soup. Mr. Williams nudges him. He begins eating again.

"There something wrong with him?" Cyn asks.

"It's been a long trip. He's still...adjusting." He looks out the window. "Tell me a little bit about this place."

Mad comes out of the kitchen and slides a bowl in front of Mr. Williams. Steam rises from the soup. "That's enough food," Cyn says.

Mr. Williams avoids looking at her. He takes a moment and looks up when his expression has softened. Smiles again.

"If you're annoyed," Cyn says, "you're welcome to give back the clothing and be on your way."

"Not at all, my dear." His smile is wide enough to expose a gold molar.

Cyn's back stiffens. She bites her words.

"My apologies," he says. "Please, tell me about where we are and what you've been doing here."

The girls look at each other. Cyn doesn't know why she's so tense. She's afraid she'll snap at him. Perhaps it's watching them eat their food, the way he's looking around, judging the room.

"We don't remember," Jen finally says. "We just woke up here. We don't know...anything."

Cyn stares at Jen, getting her attention. *No more.*

"I see," he says.

"What does that mean?" Cyn says.

"Thank you for your generosity." He takes Sid's bowl, pouring the remains into his bowl. "I see you all are very hungry, and we don't want to be an imposition. Or eat food we haven't earned."

He stands up, holding the chair for support. Sid stands so that Mr. Williams can hold on to his shoulder.

"Let an old man rest, if you don't mind. So that I may gather my thoughts. Come along, Sidney."

Sid leads the way, still wearing flip-flops. Socks cover his bloodied and bruised feet. The old man stops him at the door.

"Would you mind if we rested in separate beds?" Mr. Williams asks. "There's not much room in one bed."

"During the day." Cyn folds her arms. "Not at night."

Mr. Williams's teeth are straight. His smile, hollow.

101

MIRANDA WATCHES the girls bring the men into the bunkhouse. They sleep in separate beds next to the stove until night; then the girls shove the younger one in the same bed with the old man. They barely fit, but they seem too exhausted to care.

She zooms the camera, but their faces are buried in the blankets. They hardly move.

Miranda wakes the next morning in the back room, curled up on the office chair and wrapped in a blanket. The bunkhouse is empty except for Roc, who is waiting for someone to bring her breakfast.

Miranda doesn't bother with breakfast or tea. She flips through the cameras and finds everyone except Roc in the dinner house. The men are dressed like women. They were dressed like cruise-ship tourists before that. *How did they even survive?*

The boy is strange. He's skinny and tall, would be cute if he wasn't so zombie-ish. She zooms in on his face. He's yet to really look at anything. Hasn't smiled or frowned or anything. Not even sure if he knows he's hungry and cold.

The old man, though, he's sizing things up. He doesn't react to Cyn being a bitch. He's looking around, learning who's in charge. He's not biting the hand that's feeding him.

But he looks familiar.

He says his name is Mr. Williams, but that's no help. The boy's name is Sid, but she's never seen him before. She's positive. They go back to the bunkhouse. Mr. Williams has Sid push a bed in front of the stove and climbs into it. Sid goes to the corner where Miranda slept and lies on top of the covers, staring at the rafters.

She focuses on the old man. *Where have I seen him?*

She flips back to the dinner house, listening to the girls argue. Cyn is adamant about survival. They don't know these people, they could be dangerous, there's only so much food. Jen just wants to help.

Miranda prepares a cup of green tea, stirring in a dollop of honey. She paces the hallway while steeping the bag. She listens to a piece composed by Richard Strauss, closing her eyes and letting her thoughts fall into the music's flow.

Vacation clothes.

She puts down the teacup.

There's hardly space on the coffee table. She stacks empty plates and pushes trash onto the floor, but it's not there. She goes to the bedroom next to the kitchen.

The photographs are scattered on the bedspread. She pushes them around, sorting through images of oceans and beaches and boats. She picks up the photo of a couple standing on a balcony, the sharp line of the ocean behind them.

More hair, fewer wrinkles.

She takes it to the back room and holds it up to the monitor.

102

CYN FALLS ON THE FOOTSTOOL. The walk from the bunkhouse to the kitchen has become a long one. She stopped chopping wood and now spends more time next to a stove, but still, her feet hurt.

Especially in the morning.

She unwraps the dirty bandages. The wounds are red and weepy. She's resorted to folding clean patches to cover her heels, wrapping them with strips of cloth ripped from T-shirts.

We need clean clothes.

The brick house is still shuttered and quiet. Not a crack of light penetrates the shielded windows. No sound, no movement.

Is she even alive?

"I don't like the way that looks." Mad leans into the kitchen.

"I don't like a lot of things."

She's used half the ointment and nearly all the bandages. There won't be much left if someone else gets hurt. Cyn opens the cabinet beneath the sink, picks up one of the brown bottles, and shakes it. Pills rattle inside.

"Don't know what's in there," Cyn says. "It could be poison."

"That gets infected, it won't matter."

"How many should I take?"

Mad shakes her head. "Hell, I don't know."

Cyn pops the top and dumps several capsules into her palm. They're blue and white. *Why don't they have labels?*

"No." She snaps the lid back on and puts the bottle away. "I'm holding off."

Mad nods. She's not sure she should take the pills, either. Downing a bunch of unknown pills isn't great advice. At least not yet. She goes back out to the dinner room and returns with tree branches.

"Use these," she says.

Crude branches are tied with twine, with handles about halfway down. Wide braces are fastened on top to fit beneath her underarms, and a wide bottom is formed to keep the branches from sinking into the soft earth.

"Jen put them together," Mad says. "These, too."

She tosses a pair of boots on the floor. The backs are cut out.

"They're not waterproof, but at least you won't go barefoot."

Cyn holds them up. She laughs.

"Told her you'd be pissed."

"They're brilliant."

"Okay. I was wrong."

Cyn stands, balancing with the sticks under her arms. They're not the most comfortable support, but with a T-shirt or two wrapped around the tops, they might be all right. Mad's right: an infection is the end. There's no CVS, no Doc in the Box to wipe out a blood disease.

Game over.

Mad kicks the cabinet door with her toe. Cyn pokes one of the crutches in the opening, bouncing it back open.

"More of those bags are missing."

"Forgot about those," Mad says. "How many?"

"You serious? This thing was half full."

Mad leans over. "I'm not taking them. Honest."

They're definitely missing, no doubt about it, no need to get an exact count.

Point is, who's taking them?

"Here." Cyn yanks the drawer open next to the stove and pulls out a pen. She breaks it in half and hands the ink-filled tube to Mad. "Cut that with scissors, smear it on the handle. Blue fingers are guilty."

Mad stares at the tube. *A good pen wasted.*

She digs a pair of scissors out and begins to lay the trap.

Cyn sits down on the footstool, spreading a layer of salve on her heels while Mad smears the inside of the handle.

"Good morning, girls."

Cyn nearly jumps off the stool. Mr. Williams pokes his head inside the kitchen. She didn't hear the front door open. He smiles with all of his crooked teeth. His cheeks are fleshy, not pale. His eyes clear, not glassy. And he has ditched the frilly Christian Dior coat.

"Feeling better?" Mad stands, ink on her fingers.

"Your soup is a miracle worker, Ms. Mad." A gold cap twinkles. He tugs on the collar of his coat. "I'm a Ralph Lauren man. Makes all the difference. How are the ankles?"

"Beautiful."

"How did you hurt them, if I may ask?"

"Too much walking." She makes the final wraps and tapes the cloth in place. "How did you get so chipper?"

"Sleep works wonders."

Again, the gold cap.

"Ms. Cyn, I'd like to request your assistance in a tour of your camp. I'd like to know exactly how Sid and I might contribute. The last thing we want to do is become leeches. You've been so kind. That is, if you're up to it."

Cyn looks at Mad. She shrugs.

Clearly, he knows who's running the camp.

"Where's Sid?"

"Resting." His expression is slack. "Can we talk?"

He doesn't wait, going out the front door and standing on the porch. Cyn gingerly slides her foot into the altered boot. It hurts going in, but the opening along the back keeps the pressure off. She pushes up on the crutches.

"Keep an eye on us," Cyn says. "Just in case."

Mad watches from the front door. Cyn hobbles out with the old man to the meadow.

The sky is a thin slate of gray, bleaching the sun like tissue paper. The wind harvesters barely turn.

Cyn rests on the crutches, pointing out the houses, the barn, the garden, and everything they've done since waking up. She leaves out the hike, something he doesn't need to know.

"The girl you have tied in the bunkhouse," Mr. Williams says. "She was assaulted?"

"She's trouble."

"I see."

"You don't belong here." Cyn looks at his summer loafers. "Where'd you come from?"

"Hmm." He locks his hands behind his back, lips mincing on thoughts. "Did you realize those wind turbines and solar panels generate enough power to run ten or twenty houses?"

"Not ours." Cyn points a crutch at the bunkhouse. "No heat, no lights. Just the kitchen."

"And the brick house?" he asks.

"I don't know what's in there."

"You don't know?" He lifts his eyebrows. Inquisitive, but not really.

"There's an invisible line around it, something we can't go past."

"What happens if you do?"

"A thing in our neck." She bends her head, exposing the lump. "It knocks us out."

"You mean like this?"

He has one, too.

"Yeah. Like that. Why do you have one?"

All he says is, "Hmm. Is there anyone inside the brick house?"

"Miranda's in there."

"I see."

"Do you know something?" Cyn turns to face him. He's far too calm for someone that was nearly an icicle a few days earlier.

"I suppose," he says, turning with his hands still behind his back, surveying the grounds like a land developer, an eye for value. "But is that all? Is that everything around here, or is there more?"

She wants to poke him with the crutch, double him over so he gets to the point. A few days ago they could've left him for dead, now he's looking left and right with his bottom lip plumped out like he owns the place.

"There's a dead body," she blurts.

The eyebrows rise. "Sounds interesting."

"You see it, you answer my questions. All of them."

"I'll answer all your questions, Ms. Cyn. Undoubtedly. But I am very intrigued by a dead body. If you're up for it, perhaps we could see it now?"

"In the woods."

"Very well."

Mr. Williams isn't shocked. And it's beyond gross. The stink has waned, but the sight of the deflated clothes and discolored flesh is almost too much for Cyn.

She stops halfway down the path, letting him go the rest alone. He shuffles along like he's out for a Sunday stroll, a speed bump up ahead.

At first, he bends over with his hands on his waist, studying the lower torso. He crosses over and does the same with the upper. Then he takes a knee and pokes the skull with a stick.

She almost vomits.

"The only older woman, you say?" he asks.

Cyn moans.

"Do you know her?"

She shakes her head. "You?"

He drops the stick and stands. "The wolves have eaten well."

Cyn turns around, leaning heavily on the crutches. A knot the size of a softball has formed in her stomach.

"Have you gone beyond?" he asks.

She takes a moment before looking. He's pointing over his shoulder. She shakes her head.

"Down the path?" he asks. "You've been here all this time and haven't ventured beyond the body?"

"We're a little freaked out."

He waves his arm. "She was going somewhere; let's take a look. Come on, she hasn't moved in weeks. You'll be all right."

Cyn pivots. She holds her breath, sliding her crutches along the wet snow until she reaches the body. She tries not to look but notices the flesh is mostly bone. The fingers, like leathery sticks, are clenched around a clear plastic bag.

Like the bags in the cabinet.

She follows Mr. Williams.

His hands are in his pockets; she swears he's humming. The path bends left and then right, weaving deeper into the forest. She's not sure how far he wants to go, but her arms are aching. This path could go on forever. She's about to turn around, to call ahead, when he stops.

And she sees it.

A dark alcove in the trees. And a small cabin covered in leafless vines and silver lichen. It's not much bigger than a closet, ten feet by ten feet at the most. Mr. Williams waits for her. She leans on the crutches.

"You didn't know this was back here?"

She shakes her head.

"Well, someone does."

He points at the tracks in the snow leading from the front door. Someone has been in and out—many times.

A cold chill rises in Cyn's stomach.

Someone has been watching them. Have they been coming out at night? Are they hiding?

Mr. Williams walks up to the door. Cyn follows—

"Oh!" She stops.

Puts her hand to her neck. The tingling wraps around her face; darkness threatens her vision.

"What's wrong?" he asks.

Cyn backs up slowly. First one step, then two. She rests on the crutches until the feeling goes away.

"There's a fence around it."

He's immune, like Miranda.

He smiles and tries the door handle. It's locked. He twists it up and down, but it refuses to open and looks plenty thick to resist persuasion. There are no windows to peek through. Mr. Williams walks around the right corner. A few minutes later, he comes around the other side, dragging his fingers along the wall, looking up and down, like he's expecting a secret door to open.

None do.

He locks his hands behind his back and stares at the front door. "I'd like to speak with Ms. Miranda," he says without turning.

"Tell me what you know. Why were you in beach clothes? What is this place?"

He turns. One eyebrow raised. "None of this is what you think it is."

"Tell me. You said you'd answer all my questions."

"I will, Ms. Cyn. I promise. But first, I need to know a few things before explaining our strange arrival. Trust me, it will benefit all of us if I understand everything before explaining."

Cyn squeezes the crutches, clenching her teeth.

He faces the cabin, teetering on the balls of his feet. She doesn't stop him from walking past her.

103

MIRANDA HASN'T SLEPT MUCH.

She spends most of her time watching the old man, even when he's sleeping. At first, he and the boy slept like they were dead, lying in bed all day, only getting up to eat.

Cyn still makes them sleep in the same bed at night. Miranda thinks it's rather cruel. The men are sick. One of the girls could make a bed in front of the stove. The way they sleep, they'd never know the difference between a mattress and a plank floor.

Miranda has been so consumed with the monitors, she stopped playing music days ago. She moves only between the kitchen, bathroom, and back room, her obsession blotting out fear.

He knows something.

It's the way he looks around, studying his surroundings, taking it in, digesting it. Sometimes she catches him nodding, affirming some thought or feeling, and then hiding behind a smile.

Finally, he's ready to talk. That's what Miranda thinks. He's been biding his time and now he's feeling better, ready to make a move.

He gets out of bed and sorts through a pile of clothes, switching out some of the things the girls put on him when he was too weak to dress himself. He instructs the boy to remain in bed. The boy does as he's told, curled beneath a fleece blanket, doing what he does: staring and drooling.

Ignoring Roc's pleas for help.

The old man goes into the kitchen. He thanks Cyn for her gratitude because he knows she's in charge. She couldn't care less. Cyn doesn't stand, doesn't make eye contact, just sits there with the permanent scowl.

Miranda turns up the sound, but they don't say much in the kitchen. Cyn and the old man go out to the meadow, where Miranda can't hear. And she can't read lips. They're pointing around the camp. Cyn must be giving him an update about how they woke up and what they found.

Miranda feels a cold sensation crawl up her back when Cyn points at the brick house.

She pulls her legs onto the chair. The old man nods as Cyn explains how Miranda's hiding from them, denying them food, telling him lies about her.

They finally look away. They walk around the buildings, toward the woods. Toward the path.

Miranda reaches out, tapping keys and directing the mouse, changing the views. She loses them in the trees. She flips back and forth, finally finding the view from the little cabin in the woods.

The old man walks along the path with a slight hitch in his step. He stops and surveys the front of the cabin, looking left and right. Cyn hobbles not far behind.

The old man comes up to the front door and, without hesitating, turns the knob. It doesn't open. He's adamant, twisting in both directions and pulling with both hands like perhaps the hinges are rusty.

Cyn suddenly backs up.

The old man turns around. She explains something. Miranda turns up the sound. She rubs the back of her neck. The old man isn't distracted. He walks around the east corner of the building, looking up and down, as if a secret crevice might reveal itself.

Miranda punches a key. The old woman is on the monitor.

The old man and Cyn's voices are muffled, but they're out there, right outside the small building.

The old woman is still motionless, but in a slightly different position than the last time. The pillows have been rearranged beneath her head, and a different blanket covers her. She's sure of it. Last time it was a brown fleece blanket, but now there's one with woven Native American patterns. But she's still asleep, her chest gently rising and falling.

Her gray hair is pulled off her face, kinky strays poking in different directions. It's too dark to tell how old she is. Old enough.

The voices are gone.

Miranda switches the view outside the cabin. No one is there. She cycles through the outside cameras and finally sees the old man crossing the dead garden.

"Ms. Miranda?" He raps on the shutter over the front door.

Miranda wraps the blanket more tightly around herself, sinking into the chair.

"My name is Mr. Williams. I'd like to talk with you."

She jumps out of the chair before fear holds her down, and paces back and forth, mumbling. Looks down the hallway. It feels so much longer, so much darker.

"Ms. Miranda?"

Rap, rap, rap.

Miranda takes a long breath. She tiptoes through the house, listening to his gruff and muffled voice call her name. She leans against the door, careful not to bump it or scratch it.

She feels his knuckles through the protective shield.

"I know this is all very confusing," he says, "but we have a lot to talk about. Perhaps you could open one of the shutters?"

It's been so long since she's seen daylight with her own eyes, not the camera's eye.

She slinks to the back room, dropping the blanket near the kitchen. She taps the spacebar, activating the main monitor. The cursor speeds across the screen and centers over the same question it asks every time.

Deactivate security?

The cursor hovers over YES.

She looks to the other monitors. The brick house camera is focused on Cyn standing beyond the fence, leaning on sticks. *She'll know I've been hiding. She'll be pissed.*

She releases the mouse like a hot coal.

"Ms. Miranda?"

Miranda switches the view on one of the smaller monitors to the front porch, swinging it around to focus on the old man. He has a slight hunch near his shoulders. His hair is wispy around the crown.

He knocks again. Turns his head.

Looks right at the camera.

He knows!

He drops his hand to his side, still looking. A nod of resignation. Perhaps a brief smile.

"Perhaps she's trapped." He turns to Cyn. "We need to find a way to communicate. Maybe there's a crack in one of the shutters; I can slide a note inside for her to see."

He looks at the camera again.

"She needs to know she can trust me. That I can help."

They walk back to the dinner house. One slowed by injury, the other by age. Miranda watches them go through the front door and sees them sit down at the dinner table. But she doesn't switch the view to look and listen.

Instead, she runs to the kitchen.

She begins hiding food around the house.

104

The ledge is sharp.
The fog shifts. Beckons.
The fall, bottomless.

SLEET PECKS THE WINDOWS.

Cyn's breath curls in column after white column, each fading into nothing. The stove is lifeless.

Pain greets her. *Good morning.*

Her heels throb. Each pulse pushes pins into her legs. She pulls the covers up to her chin, closing her eyes, wishing it away. But it doesn't. Nothing goes away, no matter how many times she asks.

The girls are waking. The bed in the far corner is missing. Cyn lies still, hoping her heels will forget she's awake. She scratches another day on the wall, ignoring the endless lines behind it. They are her challenge, each line a brick in a wall that she's building up to the sky, one she can crawl over, where the sun shines and birds sing and pain does not exist.

Each day a brick. Heavy and solid. Each day she carries a brick to the wall and puts it in place.

"Good morning," Jen says.

Kat and Mad mutter back, dressing quickly.

Cyn throws the covers off and reaches for the stack on the floor. The undergarments are dingy and already reek of dead skin. The bottoms of her socks are black and damp. She peels them off and replaces them with another pair that are soiled but dry.

The girls walk past, asking how she's feeling, if she needs any help. Except Jen. She won't look at her.

Kat turns the block of wood nailed into the wall—a rudimentary lock cobbled together from parts in the barn—and opens the door. They brace for the weather and start the morning trek to the dinner house.

The girls run. Cyn walks.

The sleet stings like frozen sand.

The dinner house is warm.

The table is pulled away from the stove. Miranda's bed—the one she was sleeping on before retreating to the brick house—is in front of the roaring stove. Mr. Williams is sitting on it, fully dressed, hair slicked back.

"Good morning," he says.

Sid is curled up on the floor, a blanket serving as his mattress.

Cyn goes to the footstool to dress her wounds. She folds a piece of paper until it's thick and narrow, wedging it between her teeth like a bit, and begins to unwind the grimy wrappings. The bandage is soaked with watery discharge and slimy pus.

She bites harder.

Pills.

The time has come. The wounds aren't healing. She reaches for the cabinet—

She jerks her hand back like the cabinet is hot, slowly looking at the smudges on her first two fingers. She didn't touch the ink trap yesterday, hadn't gone near the cabinet... It can't be.

The dirty socks. The sore feet.

"I don't like the way those look." Mad starts up the griddle, looking down at Cyn.

Cyn quickly opens the cabinet, hiding the blue smudges. She pops the lid on one of the bottles and shakes out two white pills.

"You sure?" Mad asks.

She pops them in her mouth, dry swallowing. They stick in her throat. Mad hands her a cup of water. The kitchen door opens. Kat carries four eggs in one hand and puts them on the counter.

"That's it?" Mad asks.

"Feed's almost gone. Surprised we're getting any eggs at all." She blows into her cupped hands. "Need to think about eating those chickens before they go to waste."

Mad shakes her head, cracking the eggs on the griddle.

"Can you give them horse feed?" Cyn asks.

"Not much of that, either. Can't imagine they'll make it through winter in the pasture—grass'll be gone. Maybe it's best to let them go, fend for themselves."

They'd been preparing wood and food for winter, but what if nothing else survived?

Cyn smears ointment on her heels and dresses them up for another day. Ink smudges the wrappings.

"No breakfast for them," Cyn says.

Mr. Williams and Sid sit at the far end of the table near the door. The old man looks at Cyn at the other end, next to the stove.

"No, you won't do that!" Jen slams the table. "You're not going to take away their food!"

"This ain't a camping trip, Jen! Mom and Dad won't pick us up before it's over, so let's get clear. We *will* run out of food; we will get sick."

Jen keeps her fists balled on the table.

"There's no room for manners, Jen. Unless something changes, we die. All of us."

"I hardly think we're a threat, Ms. Cyn," Mr. Williams says. "We've agreed to sleep in separate quarters, but it's not fair to deny us food when we've offered to help."

"You didn't agree to anything. We made you leave the bunkhouse at night. You're lucky we let you sleep in the dinner house."

"You did, Cyn," Jen says. "You made them leave."

"And you'll get food when you talk. You arrive like tourists and haven't told us anything. I've got a feeling you know plenty. Begin with him." Cyn nods at the kid with the blank stare, the wet lip. "What's his problem?"

"It's complicated," Mr. Williams growls.

"Start talking or start starving."

"You going to starve me, too?" Jen says.

"You threaten us, damn right I will."

"Or if I just threaten you."

Kat and Mad have already finished eating. Jen's plate is still full. She'll sneak them food later.

Not if I can help it.

"Well, Mr. Williams?" Cyn says. "You hungry yet?"

He stands up. Sid gets up automatically. Mr. Williams looks out the window at the brick house still battened down tight as a tank.

"Okay." No gold cap glittering this morning. "In private, Ms. Cyn. We'll talk in private. I'll leave you to finish your breakfast."

They go out the front door.

Jen looks at her plate, the food completely untouched.

"Eat your breakfast." Cyn forks eggs into her mouth. "If not, the rest of us will. But they won't, Jen."

She eats.

105

CYN LIMPS TOWARDS THE BARN, trying to keep the crutches from chafing her underarms. The sleet is sticking to the walls, wet on her face. Kat waits in the open breezeway. Mr. Williams is at the other end, looking at the mountains.

"Want me to stay?" Kat asks.

"No. Watch the boy, he's in the bunkhouse."

Kat steps aside. Cyn slows, careful not to slip. She leans the crutches against the stall. One of the horses pokes his head out, nibbling on the end of the crutch; his eyes are large in his skull.

Cyn takes a moment, then slow, limited steps down the middle of the breezeway.

"You did the right thing," Kat says.

Cyn stops and looks back.

"He's up to something and we ain't got time," Kat adds. "Hunger'll make anyone talk. You did the right thing."

She leaves her to go alone. Cyn doesn't want to admit it, but she's relieved someone understands.

"Quite a sight." Mr. Williams doesn't turn around. "Rich and detailed, not a thing missing. It's beautiful."

Cyn refuses to sit on the bench. She stands next to him. She's already sweating.

"You're cold and hungry." He looks at her, nostrils flaring. "You have an infection; you'll have a fever. It's all very convincing."

"No more games."

"I wanted to see the brick house before having this talk. It'll make more sense once I see the inside."

"I get the feeling you won't come out."

He looks across the pasture again. A gust of wind hits the wind harvesters.

"None of this is real." His expression is flat. He's no longer enamored with the view.

"I thought you would take this seriously." She turns around, wishing the crutches were closer. "Let me know when you're hungry."

She makes it to the first stall.

"You dream about the gray world at night."

She stops, hand on the wall.

"You dream of static, of fog and haze. You dream that something is out there in that nothingness, but then you wake up. You realize it's just a dream."

His voice is stronger.

"But then you went to the edge and discovered it wasn't a dream. You stepped out of the cold, out of this world, and saw the nothingness that is in your dreams. You went there, you peered into the gaping gray sky, the world of the Nowhere."

Cyn scratches the old wood. Not finding something to grab, she collapses on a bench, leaning back.

Exhaling.

"Where did you go?" he asks. "Where did you find the edge of this world?"

"Two miles out, straight south," she mutters. "There's another fence."

"That's not a fence, not like what's around the brick house. That is the limit of this world. You stepped out of it and into the Nowhere."

She turns her distant gaze to him. He's a fuzzy silhouette, the snowcapped mountain a bright, white backdrop. Her stomach turns.

"That gray void of nothing used to be another illusory world like this one, only it was tropical and lustrous and exotic. You won't remember this, but you and the girls would come visit it, but that was a long time ago, before it collapsed and Sid and I became homeless souls."

He steps closer.

"Our...*identities*...if that's what you want to call them—our true Selves—are frayed and dissolving. I don't think there's any way to truly express what it's like to be lost in the gray, Cyn."

She twitches. He smiles.

"You only came for a visit; we live out there. Imagine what it feels like to be pulled apart, piece by piece, and set loose on the wind, randomly mixed with so many other disintegrated souls. Sid and I were doomed to waste away, becoming thinner. Becoming less. Our souls bleached lifeless."

He laughs without mirth.

"But then you peeked into the Nowhere, you shone like a beacon. Suddenly, I knew this world still existed, that there was something out there besides the Nowhere. We were able to draw out of the miasma of despair."

He looks at his hands, turning them over like he still can't believe it.

"Sid, my boy, didn't transition as well as I did. Part of him is still out there."

"The world doesn't end, Mr. Williams. You don't walk two miles and drop off the edge."

"In this one you do."

"No, but someone did insert something in our necks that gets triggered by an electrical fence. I ain't saying I know how they do it, but it's possible. It ain't magic."

"No. It's a dream."

She chuckles, turning her head. "It's not magic, it's a dream—that's what you're saying?"

"You're asleep, Cyn, but this isn't your dream. Someone else is dreaming this world. And you're in it. We're *all* in it." He waves his arms, gesturing at the grand view beyond. "Your *real self*, whoever *you* are, is real, Cyn. You're somewhere, just not here. You think you're real, but you're asleep. You need to wake up."

"And you?"

"Me too. Sid, the girls...we're all real."

"But asleep?"

"We're part of an...experiment, so to speak. It's hard to explain, you'll have to trust me."

"Whose dream world is this? I mean, if it ain't mine, whose is it?"

"That's irrelevant. The point is, we can escape. We can wake up in our bodies, wake up in reality where the world exists beyond the edge, where there is no Nowhere. Where we can escape the suffering, get back to living."

"And you expect me to believe this?"

"No." What little joy had filled his eyes quickly drains. "You don't realize this is a dream, so you'll hang on to it to the very end. Only you can discover it's false. This is not how I wanted to tell you."

"Why are you still here? If you know this is a dream, wake up, then. Go ahead, disappear or say the magic word, whatever you've got to do, you do it and I'm a believer."

"Knowing the truth isn't enough, child. It's hard work to escape."

Cyn throws her head back, thumping the weathered wood. There are old nests and white streaks on the rafters, holes in the roof and cobwebs in the corner. These are not the details of dreams.

And she's never had a dream she couldn't wake up from.

Sweat forms on her forehead. She swallows the nervous swelling in her throat. "We're out here starving and freezing and you say just wake up."

"It was summer where we were." He holds his arms out. "That's why we arrived in those clothes. We're lucky we survived."

Her laughter is as empty as his. She rolls her head on the wall, eyeing him with a shallow smile. "You're a liar—you're up to something. And you can starve, for all I care."

She throws her weight forward. Her steps are small. Her heels are cracking.

"What's your plan?" Mr. Williams calls. "To survive long enough to see your feet rot off?"

"If it's a dream, I'll get new ones."

"Just because it's an illusion doesn't mean you won't suffer. You're invested in the dream, child. You don't want to give it up, no matter how much it hurts."

Cyn uses the wall to slowly turn around.

"What happens when I die, Mr. Williams? If this is a dream, won't I wake up?"

He sinks his hands in his coat pockets. "You already died; you have the marks on the wall to prove it."

The end of the breezeway tilts. She blinks the world back into focus, but the floor wobbles. She needs to get out, get some air, get away from the nonsense.

"You're saying we start over? We wake up in a cabin without memories?"

He nods. *Isn't it obvious?*

Cyn doesn't want to believe it. He's convincing, but that doesn't mean he's right. The squeeze of hunger will bring him back to his senses. He'll talk.

He'll tell the truth.

She just wants her crutches, wants to go lie down.

"We need to find the gate," Mr. Williams says. "It's the center of the dream. In our world, it was a sundial. If we find the gate in this world, we can use it to wake up."

Cyn reaches the other end. The crutches stab beneath her arms. She's panting and sweating. Nausea swirls inside her stomach, reaching for her throat.

"Tell me." Her voice echoes in the stalls. "What was your tropical world called?"

She feels him smiling. "Foreverland," he says.

"Foreverland is dead. If you don't tell me what you're up to, so are you."

She starts for the bunkhouse, where she can rest. Her mouth begins to water. She gets a few steps before vomiting. On her hands and knees, she throws up her breakfast onto the ground, melting the sleet.

This is not a dream, she thinks, heaving again. *Dreams don't hurt.*

106

"I CAN DO IT." Cyn tries to prop herself up on her pillow.

"Just lie down and shut up." Mad wipes Cyn's forehead with a damp cloth. "Eat the soup and take those."

Cyn looks at the oblong pills. "I'm not taking these."

"Those are from a bottle," Mad says. "The other pills must be old or you're allergic to the medicine. That's why you puked. Girl, you've got a fever and your wounds smell like road kill. You're going to take every medicine in that cabinet if you got to."

Cyn can't get warm. Can't stop sweating. This could be it. It's all over. *If the old man isn't lying, then I'll just wake up wondering what all those lines on the wall are for.*

She puts the pills on her tongue, chasing them with chicken broth. Mad brings another spoonful to her lips and sneaks a look toward the back where Roc is sleeping. "More of those clear bags are gone," she whispers. "I started a count."

"What bags?" Kat asks.

Mad tells her about the plastic bags in the cabinet. Chills storm Cyn's body with renewed force. Now she wants to forget about them, wants to forget the ink. *I'm stealing them. I'm the one who's been going to the little house in the woods, taking those bags with me. And I don't remember doing it.*

The dead woman on the path—she'd had one in her hand. Was she the one taking them before they awoke? What's in the cabin? What could make Cyn sleepwalk almost two miles through the night until the flesh wore off of her feet?

I wish this would end.

"Is the old man crazy?" Mad tips the bowl for the last couple spoonfuls. "He thinks this is all a dream and you believe him?"

"You ever go hungry in a dream?" Cyn says.

"He said we were part of an experiment," Kat says.

Kat admits she went around the barn and listened, and heard all the nonsense. Cyn wishes she didn't do that; now she's got to explain everything when all she wants to do is sleep.

"This ain't a dream—we'd know it," Cyn says. "He's just saying things, Kat. He's crazy."

"Maybe we're crazy," Roc says. "We just don't know it."

"Shut up," Kat snaps.

"You'd better hope I don't get loose, horse girl." The bed creaks. "You're the first one I'll break in half."

Kat shakes her head, arms crossed.

Cyn rests with her eyes closed. At first, she'd wanted to punch the old man in the throat for such a lie. Their days are numbered and he thought they'd believe anything, like children. But she's sleepwalking plastic bags to a little cabin, so he could say anything and it might be true.

"I'll talk to him," Kat says. "Figure out what he's up to."

"You do that," Roc says. "I feel better already."

"Get some sleep, Cyn." Mad runs her finger around the bowl and licks it. "More medicine later if you don't puke those pills up. There's plenty more soup, too. Miranda probably has more."

"Miranda?" Roc chuckles. "Proof you are dreaming."

The girls go to the door, ready to get away from Roc, whose only enjoyment is getting under their skin. She's good at it.

"Mad." Cyn, already half-buried in sleep, croaks out her name. She holds out her keycard. "Take this. I don't need it."

"I'll give it to Kat."

"No. Just...for now, hang on to it. Keep it safe. All right?"

Mad puts it around her neck, tucking it under her shirt. She puts her hand on Cyn's forehead, her palm clammy and cold.

Cyn fades into a soft haze. *I can't steal the bags if I don't have a key.* The front door closes. The bunkhouse is quiet except for the creaks and pops as the wind pushes against it.

"You asleep?" Roc says.

Cyn couldn't care less if Roc talks. They're just words. Besides, stampeding elephants couldn't keep her from sleeping.

"I lied to Kat," Roc whispers, cackling like she's lost her mind. "If I get loose, you're the first one I break in half."

"You'd better kill me if you escape," Cyn mutters. "You're a dead body if you don't."

The dark laughter follows Cyn into the gray.

107

THE DREAM IS ENDLESS.

Feverish.

As always, she's on the ledge, staring into the abyss of eternal fog. Where the memories are. Memories of the lost boys from Foreverland, dissolved in misty gray. Reduced to thoughts scattered in space.

But how did my memories get into the gray?

She feels them coming for her. She runs every time. She turns, racing from the chasm into the trees. She'd rather suffer in the dream than face life.

Rather than have those memories inside her.

Sometimes she wakes long enough to feel someone put dry pills onto her lips, cool water washing them down.

Feels the sweat on her pillow.

And then it's back to the ledge.

Back to running.

Wondering, who's the dreamer?

Who am I?

108

CYN SITS UP. "How many days have I been in bed?"

"Seven," Kat says.

"A week?"

"Ain't lying."

Kat points at the wall. New scratches are on the wall. The girls kept track of the days while she dozed. The days blend together. *Those pills are sledgehammers.*

The shivers are gone. The sheets are dry.

She throws the covers off, the stench of dead skin and infection wafting out, and gently puts her feet on the floor. The wounds are oozy, but the swelling is down.

Kat rattles the bottle. "Last of this bottle. Hope you don't relapse or we've got to experiment with another bottle and hope we get lucky."

Cyn works up enough spit to swallow them. There's fresh snow on the ground, about six inches on the dinner house. The old man and Sid are visible through the window. Jen, too.

"You want to eat?" Kat asks. "Mad's almost got supper ready."

"No. I think I'll go for a little walk. I need to get out of this nasty bed. If I don't make it over to eat, tell the old man I want to talk in the morning."

"Why not now?"

"Got to think about some things."

Not a lot made sense in the delirium, but maybe Cyn needs to hear more about this dream experiment. She doesn't want to even think about listening to that crap, but unless a helicopter drops into the meadow, Prince Charming isn't coming.

It can't hurt to hear more about this gate.

"Jen's feeding the old man and the kid," Kat says. "They wait in the barn and she takes food out when she thinks we ain't looking."

"Figured she would," Cyn says.

"That's what I said. Now we're just letting them eat with us, Cyn. Hard to watch them starve, you know."

Cyn doesn't answer. Kat leaves her at the window.

She watches them through the windows. They eat supper, but it's not much. The old man looks up from the table and sees her. Cyn moves a little too quickly, pain lancing her hamstrings. She probably shouldn't be walking, but she's got to get out of the bunkhouse, even for a little bit. Her body is sore.

She moves slowly, walking out to the barn. The horses are anxious, their hide pulled between their ribs. She sits on a bench, admiring the mountains, recalling what he'd said.

Rich and detailed. Not a thing missing.

Can this really be a dream? She turns her hands over and rubs them on her thighs. Her pulse bounces in the backs of her feet.

She comes back to the bunkhouse when she's shivering and climbs into bed as her fever rises. She throws the covers over her head, pretending to be asleep when the girls come back. The stove crackles with heat. The last person in fastens the homemade deadbolt on the door, knowing that even the old man could kick it open if he wanted.

They wouldn't wake up if he did.

In the morning, Cyn's feet ache.

Her socks are wet.

Fresh ink on her fingers.

She gives up. *Please, let this be a dream.*

If the old man is right, there's hope that they can wake up. And maybe waking up is their only hope. If not, she's doomed. They all are.

Cyn struggles to get out of bed, wincing while getting dressed, but she sweats through the agony. The crutches creak under her weight. She opens the door without waking anyone, which is good. She wants to talk with the old man alone, still not convinced that he's sane. If there's a gate out of here, they can find it.

She limps through the snow and stops on the front porch, catching her breath. It's completely dark inside the dinner house.

The stove is cold.

The brick house is lit up.

The shutters are open, lights illuminating every window both upstairs and down. She holds on to the post and knows, before even opening the door, that the old man and Sid aren't inside the dinner house.

109

SHE'S SEEN ENOUGH. Heard enough.

Miranda waits until dark. She turns on the cameras, watches their eyes grow heavy, and checks each of them twice before rolling the chair to the keyboard.

She punches a button. YES or NO.

Miranda takes a deep breath.

Clicks the mouse.

A rumble rides through the house. She flinches each time a shutter slides across a window, snapping inside the brick wall. Like dominoes, they clack one by one until it's quiet. Dust floats down from the ceiling. String instruments bellow from the front room.

The girls haven't moved, eyes dancing in REM. Floodlights illuminate the dead garden. Nothing moves but the wind.

Miranda shuffles through the hallway, exposed and alone. She looks out the window. The moon and stars are crisp. The glass is cold. A light flickers inside the dinner house. A hunched figure looks out the window.

Miranda has the urge to duck.

Too late.

A minute later, the candle appears at the front door, quickly blown out by the wind. The floodlights, though, show him the way. Miranda watches the old man plod through the snow, followed by a gangly figure. They pass through the fence, unflinching.

Their footsteps on the porch.

A knock at the door.

Mr. Williams stands in the front room, hands behind his back, looking around. Sid is behind him with shaggy dark hair and a slack lower lip, waiting while the old man drinks in the details of the home.

The old man breathes deep, closing his eyes. Miranda isn't sure if the house still stinks, her senses long dulled to the odor.

"Who are you?" She holds out the photograph like a gun.

Mr. Williams cranes his neck, squinting. He slides his feet toward her, reaching out, plucking it from her hand. He caresses the photo. His eyes are glassy.

"I can explain," he says meekly. "Perhaps some food first?"

Miranda taps her foot, her stomach clenching. Cans of food are stashed all over the house, enough to last her a year. He'll know she's lying if she says she's out.

And she can't starve him. That's what the girls were doing.

Miranda goes to the kitchen and returns with two plates. They're sitting on the couch. Sid attacks the food like a dog, smacking with his mouth open. *Can't he do anything with his mouth closed?*

She fetches a teapot and pours cups for all three of them. The old man has more self-control, but he leaves little room for talking, keeping his mouth full until the plate is nearly empty.

"What's wrong with him?" Miranda asks.

Mr. Williams pushes his plate toward Sid and sits back on the couch, crossing his legs. "He's incomplete."

"What does that mean?"

"It's like a file that hasn't completely downloaded. It's just not entirely there."

Sid nabs the remaining squares of cheese from Mr. Williams's plate and pushes them into his mouth, chewing with his lips open.

Wide open.

"It's safe in here." Mr. Williams lifts his cup of tea toward the spider-webbed glass.

"Roc doesn't like me. The others probably don't anymore, either."

He sips. "Don't apologize, Miranda. You belong here; they don't."

He tips his head like he's catching the notes floating out of the speakers. He hums along with the refrain, closing his eyes, savoring the moan of a viola, bouncing his chin along with the pluck of violin strings.

He slides the stack of photos across the table and leans over. "Barbados. We had our honeymoon there. Barbara loved the place so much we bought a condo."

He picks up a photo.

"She was always so white, she couldn't be out in the sun with her fair skin. She'd had skin cancer twice, but she never listened. Loved the sun, she did."

He drops it on the other photos.

"Not all blondes are ditzy. Some are tough as nails."

Miranda twitches. *Blondes?*

She grabs the pile, shuffling them like cards. There's the group of women. The one with black hair is up front, the same color as Roc's. "That's not her?"

"No." He chuckles. "Always a blonde. Of course, she grayed as she aged." He drops his finger on one of the other women. "Gracefully, I might add."

Barbara was talking about Cyn.

"Where did you find these?"

She points at the room while staring at the picture and hardly notices Mr. Williams get up. Miranda flips through the other pictures, looking for another group photo. Maybe the woman that sponsored her is in the group. *Will I recognize her?*

She goes to the bedroom. He's at the dresser, turning a glass Buddha figurine in his fingers.

"This was her favorite, had it when she was a kid, attached it to all her backpacks by a string. When she was nervous, she'd rub the belly."

Mr. Williams looks around the room, his thumb circling the glass belly.

"This place is perfect," he says.

"What's perfect?"

He opens the top drawer and picks through brightly colored scarves. Smells one and smiles.

"Mr. Williams? What's perfect?"

He closes the drawer. "Let me see the rest of the house and I'll tell you what I know."

Miranda backs into the hallway, crossing her arms. "That's what you told Cyn."

He smiles, turning his head slightly.

"I promise, Miranda. I just need to understand a bit more, get my mind around this place; then I'll tell you everything." He holds up his hand. "Swear."

She taps her foot. "Bedrooms upstairs. Some strange stuff in the back."

He palms the Buddha and goes upstairs, pulling his weight along the railing. Sid sits on the couch, mouth-breathing.

"I was scared of this room at first." Miranda ventures into the back room. "The smell was coming from here and the door was different, so I just ignored it. But when Roc broke the window, everything automatically closed up."

She turns around.

"And the door opened."

Mr. Williams steps inside tentatively. He looks left, leans over the batteries, and rubs dust off the stickers. He inspects the furnace and water filters.

"I notice you leave all the lights on. You need to start turning them off." He pushes a button on the furnace. "And turn the heat down, put on a sweater if you're cold."

"It's been fine so far."

"Winter's coming and the solar panels won't harvest as much power."

He seems satisfied with that side of the room and takes a moment to survey the monitors before sitting in front of the large one.

"Cameras are everywhere." Miranda wraps the blanket around her. "I figured out sound, too. I can see inside the buildings. Sometimes I feel a little guilty watching them."

"Don't. It's for your protection."

"I saw you walk into the woods, around that little house."

He's afraid to touch anything. She had felt that way at first, too. Instead, he looks from monitor to monitor. The girls are still asleep, some already snoring. She taps a few keys, advancing the views on the monitor to the little cabin in the woods. It rotates around the back and then inside.

The old woman lies peacefully.

Mr. Williams rolls the chair over and leans closer. "Patricia."

He touches the screen.

"The dreamer becomes the dream," he mutters.

"What's she doing in there?" she asks.

He sits back, gazing at the screen, as if seeing something else. He mutters something unintelligible.

"Is what you told Cyn true? That this is a dream?"

"There must be..." He pulls open a drawer beneath the desktop, rattling through the office debris. His thick fingers are bent, the skin spotted.

"Mr. Williams?"

He mutters again and goes to the next drawer.

"Mr. Williams!"

He snaps out of the trance, sits up, and looks around like he's forgotten where he is and how he got there. His gaze settles on the doorway. Sid blocks their exit, a hand on each side of the doorframe. His eyes are big, his breathing heavy. Chest heaving.

"It's all right, my boy. She's just getting my attention." Mr. Williams calmly waves him away. "Why don't you go lie down in Barbara's bedroom, get some sleep. Miranda and I have much to discuss."

Sid's hands slide down the doorjamb and fall against his legs. Mr.

Williams nods again. Sid saunters down the hallway and goes into the bedroom.

"Tell me. Is it true?"

He sighs. "We are in a dream, Miranda. But we're not dreaming."

"I don't understand."

He takes another deep breath, starts to say something, but changes his mind. The old woman is still motionless, still sleeping. *The dreamer becomes the dream.*

"Perhaps you could prepare more tea while I visit the men's room?"

"What are you looking for?"

He takes the cup and sips. "A key fob. One of those little black remote controls, only this has one button, a red one. Have you seen anything like that?"

She shakes her head. The teacup rattles on the saucer. "Tell me what's going on, Mr. Williams."

He leans his elbows on his knees, staring into the black tea like the future is hidden somewhere inside. A smile touches his lips. He's seeing a memory.

"Harold Ballard was a visionary," he starts. "If you ever met him, you'd be overwhelmed with his charisma, charmed by his love of life. His mind was a true gem."

He shakes his hands, as if he can't find the words to express something so large, so special.

"It contained a universe, another world, an alternate reality where anything was possible. The boys, like Sid, called it Foreverland. It was truly magical, an island in the ocean, warm as the tropics."

He pauses again. Contemplating.

"I suppose he could've just lived there, inside his mind, for the rest of his life. But he wasn't like that. He wanted to share it with others, for the good of mankind. So he conducted these...*experiments*. I was part of them."

"Sid, too?"

He nodded. "But something happened, I don't know what. Everything was as normal as possible. Sid and I reached a critical juncture in the process when the world collapsed. Just one second it was there, and the next..."

Snap.

"We were disembodied, lost in a soupy dream, the gray place the boys called the Nowhere. We were ghosts." Mr. Williams looks at her. "It's the place in your dream."

"I don't dream, not like them."

"I see."

She curls the teacup against her chest. "What does any of this have to do with us?"

"Patricia Ballard is Harold's mother."

"The old woman?"

"Yes. She ran a sister program, an experiment like Harold's Foreverland."

"What kind of experiment? What were you trying to discover?"

"It's hard to explain." He avoids looking at her. "Let's say we were exploring expanded consciousness, living life outside the physical body. My wife, Barbara, volunteered to participate in Patricia's experiment, which only allowed females." He chuckles. "I was on a tropical island, and she was in this place."

"So you're saying this place, right here and now, is like Foreverland?"

"In a way. You see, the girls in Patricia's program—"

"The Fountain of Youth."

"Um, yes," he stammers. "I believe that's what they called it. How did you know?"

"I saw it somewhere." She sips her tea. "Go on."

"Okay. Whatever happened to Foreverland also affected Patricia, only she didn't crash. She rebooted. Your experiment started over."

"Then where's your wife?"

"I don't know." He pauses with a grimace, although it looks forced. *Fake.* "Maybe they got out before it crashed."

"But why didn't we get out?"

"Look, Miranda, I don't know everything, just where we are. I do know this, we don't want to stay here."

She pulls her legs onto the chair, throws a blanket over her lap and sinks into the cushions. Mr. Williams sits back quietly.

The music soothes the moment.

"It's not fair." She holds the teacup with both hands below her chin. "Foreverland was nice."

"It was utopia, Miranda. Patricia's world is an exact replication of reality. This place is exactly where my Barbara lived, all the way down to the pictures. I don't know how Patricia did it. It's almost like she absorbed the details of reality around her and created this alternate reality in her mind. Patricia made this world exactly like the physical one. There's almost no difference."

She hides half her face behind the blanket. "I want to wake up."

"There's no waking up." His eyebrows shade his eyes. "She didn't create this world to last, there's only so much food, only so much time. The only way out is to escape."

"And then what? If we die, we wake up?"

"In Patricia's world, you start over, you wake up without memories."

"How do you know?"

He sighs. "This isn't the first time you've been through this." The corners of his mouth turn down grimly. "We have to escape."

"A gate." Miranda pulls the blanket down. "You told Cyn in the barn there was a gate."

"It's like a doorway between reality and this world, the epicenter of Patricia's mind."

"What does it look like?"

"I don't know. Maybe it's another sundial. We'll know when we get near it, feel reality begin to quiver. There are several square miles to search and the weather is getting worse. It should be in the middle, but I don't even know where that is."

He rubs his face, yawning. His eyes are red. His cheeks hang like dead skin.

"I'm old and tired, Miranda. Old and tired. I can't take much more of this."

"We've got plenty of food, Mr. Williams. There are elk in the countryside, I've seen them. It's not as bad—"

"No!" He launches to his feet. Miranda sinks into the chair. "We can't wait, this won't last. And I won't go into the Nowhere again, do you understand? I can't do it, Miranda."

He points at her, his finger knobby and hooked.

"We have to find the gate. And when we do, I have to be the first one out."

She pulls the blanket up higher.

He downs the remaining tea and puts the cup on the table. He rubs his face again. "I need some rest. Would you mind if I take one of the beds?"

She nods, cowering.

Without another word, he slips into the bedroom next to the stair-well. Miranda doesn't move from the chair, curled up and shivering. It's very late. She is scared and awake, but sleep eventually comes.

At some point, she hears drawers opening and closing.

110

THE WIND HARVESTERS' blades are locked in place against the punishing wind. Mad stops in the kitchen. Cyn looks up from the footstool.

"It's me," Cyn says. "I'm the one."

"What?"

She holds her head like she's clamping it together, hair tufts sticking out between her inky fingers.

"In the mornings..." Cyn starts, trailing off. "In the mornings my feet are cold, my bandages wet and muddy. But I don't go to bed like that—I just wake up that way."

"What're you talking about?"

Cyn holds up her hand, exposing the ink stains. "I'm stealing the bags."

"You're not making any sense."

"I know!" She squeezes her head, rocking back and forth. "I'm sleepwalking in here, stealing the bags, but I don't remember. I don't know why."

"And doing what?"

"Taking them to that..." She waves her hand at the wall. "That cabin in the woods, I think."

She doesn't tell her how she ruined her feet, walking all the way back the night of the excursion, not remembering a thing.

"But you don't have a key." Mad holds two keycards, both around her neck. "How are you getting in here?"

Cyn's eyes sit in deep, dark pockets. "I don't know."

She stares at her feet. The toenails are cracked and caked with mud, her skin slightly off-color. Throbbing.

Mad's hand is cool on her forehead. "I think the fever is back. We need to try another bottle. And unwrap your feet—"

The outside kitchen door opens. The wind spits sleet inside. Kat backs into the room, hood over her face. She hugs herself, stomping her feet.

"The chickens are dead."

"What?" Mad says.

"Chickens. They're dead."

"All of them?" Mad says.

"Yeah, all of them. Something got inside, feathers everywhere."

Kat pushes the hood back, looking at Cyn, who is hunched over. "What's up with her?"

"Sleepwalker," Mad says.

Kat waits, rubbing warmth into her arms. The chill creeps into Cyn just under her sternum. She shakes all over and looks up, her face about to cave in.

"I walk at night," she says. "I get up, I steal one of the bags, and I take it to the cabin in the woods. That's what the old woman was doing when she died on the path—I saw the plastic bag in her hand."

"So you took her place?"

"How the hell should I know? Does anything make sense?"

Cyn shakes her head. No one has an answer. The more they know, the less they understand.

The front door slams; someone stomps their feet, humming a little tune and flapping their lips. Jen is dressed in enough clothes for two Eskimos. She turns her head left and right, aiming the long snorkel at each of them, her face deep inside the hood.

"Anyone come out of the brick house?"

No one answers.

When the long, fuzzy hood points at Cyn, a deep breath is sucked in. She pushes the hood off, kneeling in front of her.

"You don't look good," she says. "And the bandages are wet and nasty, why aren't you wearing the boots? Get those off. We need to start a new medicine. Right, Mad? She looks flushed. Someone get some water."

Jen opens the cabinet and grabs one of the three brown bottles still left. Kat reaches in before the door closes, snatching a clear bag.

"You're feeding someone," she says. "This ain't medicine, I bet. These are nutrients; you're feeding someone through the veins."

Cyn takes pills from Jen and water from Mad. She sits up and lets Jen begin unwrapping her right foot, trying to remember taking the bags. But it's the same, always the same, every night. Blank. Empty.

How would she know how to fix an IV? How could someone force her?

The dreamer.

She doesn't want to believe the old man, doesn't want to think about the dreamer hiding away in the woods, making her sleepwalk to care for her.

"Ooh." Mad turns away, covering her nose. "Don't look, Cyn."

The odor is obscene.

The wound is pitted, the edges inflamed, the center white with pus. Her ankle is stiff and achy.

"That's not good," Kat says. "Double up on the pills, I say."

"Okay." Jen backs away. "All right. Mad, get a bucket of water and a rag. We're going to clean this up, get it wrapped. Then we're taking you back to bed and bringing you some soup. You got more soup, Mad?"

Mad drops the bucket and rag next to Jen. They stare at it.

"Kat," Jen says, "get behind Cyn."

"Why?"

"You'll need to hold her."

Jen's gentle at first. But Kat does have to hold Cyn. She wraps her arms around Cyn's chest, each dab of the cloth like a hot poker knifing through her leg.

The room starts to turn.

They carry her out. She doesn't remember that.

The storm pelts her, but she doesn't take cover. Her face is numb before they reach the bunkhouse. They tuck her in her bed. Kat stokes the fire. Cyn feels Jen lean over and hears her scratch the wall.

Adding another day.

111

THE SHOWERHEAD DRIPS.

Miranda backs away from the mirror, the edges fogged. She pulls her hair up and clips it into place with a small barrette in order to show off her ears and the dangling pearls. Mr. Williams found the earrings in Barbara's room and asked her to wear them.

Don't sink to their level, he said. *Don't be afraid to be who you are.*

They're going to hate her, think she's showing off, rubbing it in their faces. But she likes them. They complement her complexion.

So does the necklace.

She brushes her teeth and rubs a splash of perfume on her wrists. One last look.

She feels good, like herself. Who she is.

Mr. Williams is standing at the window in the front room, hands in his pockets, staring at the dinner house. His hair is slick with comb lines. He found a yellow collared shirt and white sweater vest. Gender neutral.

Sid is on the couch, doing the usual.

Mr. Williams turns. Smiles. "You are a beautiful young lady."

"Thank you." She straightens up despite the tension in her chest. "I don't think this is a good idea, though. I don't want to go with you."

"We cannot allow our *wants* to be the compass of our lives, my dear. Life demands. We answer, like it or not."

"That doesn't make me feel better."

"How you feel is irrelevant." He wraps a wool scarf around his neck and holds a coat out.

She can't move. "They hate me. They'll hurt me."

"Of course they hate you. But they can't hurt you."

He lays the coat over the arm of the chair and reaches into his pocket. He dangles a black key fob.

"What is it?"

"Stay near me."

He holds the coat up again. The gold cap twinkles. He looks from beneath shaggy eyebrows with cold blue—almost gray—eyes.

She's compelled to move.

Miranda slides her arms into the sleeves. Mr. Williams zips it up and hands her a scarf.

"It's cold out there."

Sid puts on a frilly coat over multiple sweatshirts, sliding leather gloves over his hands, his wrists still exposed. Mr. Williams pulls a thick stocking cap over his head and buttons up an overcoat. He slides his hand over the back of Miranda's neck, his palm soft with lotion. His thumb caresses her hairline.

"Sid," he says. "Lead the way, my boy."

The wind whistles through the doorway.

Miranda steps onto the front porch and turns her back to the west, losing her breath in the frigid gale. She gulps at the air. Painful as it is, the air feels clean and fresh. Purifying. Only then does she realize how bad it smells inside the house.

"Come along!" Mr. Williams holds out his hand.

They walk single file, Sid leading the way. His lean body is hardly a shield, but bears the majority of the weather. Miranda shuffles along, head down, plowing through their tracks. Snow falls into her shoes, packing against her socks. When they reach the dinner house, the path widens.

They stop outside the bunkhouse.

Snow is melting into puddles near the door.

Kat and Mad are gathered around the stove. Jen sits next to Cyn's bed. They look up, their cheeks sunken, their listless eyes dark. They don't look emaciated on the cameras.

In person, they look like refugees.

Miranda's legs threaten to buckle. Her skin is cold from the weather, but her insides are numb with fear. She stays behind Mr. Williams.

He looks around, observing the quarters. Hand in pocket.

"You bring food?" Kat stands.

Mr. Williams pulls a chair up next to Cyn's bed and sits with a groan. Miranda goes with him. The blanket is pulled up to Cyn's chin. He feels her forehead.

"She'll be dead in a week," he says. "Maybe less."

"We're giving her medicine," Jen says.

"It won't matter. What I have to say is more important."

"You said this is a dream." Kat stands over him.

Mr. Williams is unfazed. Miranda steps back. She never should've trusted that thing in his pocket. The girls might be starved, but desperation can be dangerous.

Sid stands near the door.

"It is a dream, Ms. Kat." He leans forward, using his momentum to stand. "And the dream is ending. We need to be out before it does."

He walks to the stove and warms his hands. Miranda follows him. Kat tells her she looks pretty. She doesn't mean it.

"There's an exit out there," Mr. Williams announces. "I don't know what it looks like. Where I came from it was a sundial, but it could be anything. Whatever it is, it'll be located in the center of this world."

"You mean *dream*," Kat says.

"I don't have time for this." Mr. Williams's eyebrows lower. "You can believe me or not; you can stay here when it all comes to a halt. I don't really care. But what you will do is help me find the gate. I would assume these cabins are in the center of this world, but I have my doubts. That means it's out there. Somewhere."

He sweeps his crooked finger around the room.

"We'll need to find it. All of us."

"Ain't going out in this weather," Kat says.

"Yes, in this weather, Ms. Kat. You will go out and so will the rest of you." He nods at Jen and Mad. "We'll also untie the young lady in the back; the more feet on the ground, the better."

Miranda grabs the back of his coat. "I don't...that's not a good idea," she whispers.

"There will be five of you searching. You will go in five directions, walk for an hour, and return."

"You're not going?" Kat asks.

"I'm far too old to be out there." A dangerous edge sharpens his tone.

"If it's a dream," Kat says, "why do you care how old you are?"

He stares at her until it's uncomfortable, his hand working inside his pocket.

"You'll look for something interesting, like a sculpture or waterfall. I don't know. More importantly, you will feel it when you get near it. It will vibrate inside you, a tingling sensation at the very core of your existence. Do *not* touch it."

He takes a long moment to look at each of them.

"If you encounter it, do not touch it. Come back for the rest of us and we'll all leave this dream together. That's how it works."

He walks to the back of the cabin, Miranda attached to his coat. His footsteps clop on the wood floor. Roc is a dark lump in the corner. Miranda closes her eyes, both hands grasping his coat. She wishes Sid was with them.

"Miranda and I will bring all the food out of the house," he says. "We'll eat until our bellies are full, give us strength."

Roc rolls over at the mention of food.

He nods at her. "Can you behave yourself?"

She doesn't answer.

"If you can't, you will never leave this place. Answer me."

She nods. Miranda isn't convinced.

"This isn't a dream," Jen whimpers. "I can feel and see and hear. I hurt. This is real, Mr. Williams."

He walks over.

Mr. Williams kneels next to her with much effort. He reaches out, runs his hand over Jen's black scrub of hair, and cups her cheek. Her eyes are big, imploring. And they roll back.

She slides out of the chair.

Mr. Williams places her on the floor.

"What'd you do?" Kat says.

"I'm in charge, girls." He looks down at Jen, brushing something off of her lips. "There is a device imbedded in your neck. It will deliver a jolt to your nervous system if I want. It will render you unconscious. I have this control."

He holds up a fob and hands it to Miranda. It fits nicely in her hand, her thumb snug in the button's indention.

"And so does Miranda."

He reaches up. Sid is there to help him.

Mr. Williams's knee has stiffened. He limps to the door and waves Sid and Miranda to his side.

"I'm trying to help all of you, you understand. Without me, you would rot inside this dream for eternity. I don't ask for thanks, just a little help so that we all can escape."

"Bastard," Kat mutters.

Mr. Williams doesn't hear it, or chooses not to acknowledge it.

"We'll eat in an hour," he says. "Be dressed and ready. We'll plan our search."

"What about me?" Roc says.

Mr. Williams doesn't bother smiling. "Sid will come for you."

She mutters something, too.

Miranda holds the fob. Both hands shaking.

Sid opens the door for Mr. Williams. She hurries after him.

112

SHE CAN HEAR the weather battering the windows.

Doors open and close. Logs pop in the stove.

Coughing.

Cyn swims through watery delirium, a spirit paddling against the current, rolling beneath the surface, attempting to keep her head above sanity.

And failing.

Often she finds herself landing on the ledge, fear screaming her name from the chasm. Turning—always turning to run. To get away.

And she always returns. Never escapes.

She's caught in the current of thoughts and tension and contraction. Back to the ledge. Toes hanging over.

Nothing she ever does works. She never gets away, always comes back.

So she stops.

She stays on the edge, staring into the abyss. Gray swirling like lost souls. Loneliness howls inside her, but she doesn't look away this time.

This time she doesn't run.

Doesn't resist the discomfort.

She remains there, on the edge, with the tension. The fear. Without pushing it away, without grasping. Just there.

Just there.

No more running.

This time, she finds home on the edge.

"No stealing tonight."

Cyn is jostled from slumber. She hears the voice, different from the ones that whisper from the gray. This one is over her, near her.

She opens her eyes.

"Here." Mad puts something against her lips. "Swallow."

Cyn lets the pills fall under her tongue and swallows the water poured in after them. Feels like she's drowning.

Her head falls onto the pillow. So hot. So achy.

Mad and Kat are dim outlines in the failing light. It must be late.

"We got rid of them," Kat says.

Kat dangles something. The plastic bag catches a little light coming through the window, clear nutrient solution dripping through a tear on the bottom. Tubes wrapped around her wrist.

"No more stealing."

113

MR. WILLIAMS and Sid are waiting outside the brick house.

Miranda pulls on her gloves and tucks her scarf into the gap under her chin before stepping outside. The sun is rising. Fresh snow glitters like a blanket of diamond dust.

It smells so fresh, so clean.

Mr. Williams smiles, throws his arm over her shoulders, and draws her tightly against him. He inhales deeply, feeling the clean air, too.

His hand finds its way onto her neck, thumb circling on her flesh. Goosebumps flash down her back.

"If all the days were like this, I wouldn't mind staying."

Another deep breath.

"Sid," he calls.

It takes Sid a moment to process this. He slides his hand down the railing, scraping a two-inch layer of snow onto the ground. Mr. Williams keeps his hand on her neck. She's too afraid to move, wondering if he can make the fob work on her.

The garden looks like a graveyard of fallen soldiers, old stalks beneath lumps of snow. An arm here. A leg there.

He stops at the first solar panel, wiping off the snow. He uses his arm like a wiper, exposing the black glass to absorb the light once the sun is up.

Miranda watches.

"A good start, yesterday," he says. "We'll find it soon enough, Miranda."

"How long do we have?"

He goes to the next panel. Sid is working his way towards them. Mr. Williams winks. "Plenty of time. Don't tell them."

They finish cleaning the solar panels and plod their way through the snow, around the garden. The outside kitchen door is cracked open. Mr. Williams discovered he could unlock all the doors through the computers, except for the small cabin where Patricia sleeps.

"Plenty of food," he says. "We don't have to go hungry, it'll last us."

Again, arm around her.

She walks stiffly, head down. Funny how they're still hungry in a dream. Still breathing. They don't really need food or air.

Not in a dream.

Sid walks through pristine snow piled at the foot of the kitchen door. He pushes it open and steps aside. The shelves are full of food. Mr. Williams chuckles, in the best of moods. He kisses the top of Miranda's head, gives her a squeeze, and steps into the kitchen.

Stops.

She and Sid wait outside.

Nothing looks out of place. But his cheer dies. Mr. Williams's hand slips into his pocket. He lumbers through the small kitchen, poking at something in the sink.

Miranda's afraid to follow. She backs up a step, feeling her chest contract. It seems as if his posture swells, that he fills the room with anger.

He holds something up.

It's plastic and limp.

It slaps onto the floor.

Mr. Williams grasps the edge of the sink, hunched over. Head bowed. Sid doesn't move.

"Dammit!" He swings his arm.

A stack of bags scatter, each smacking against the wall. He kicks through the debris, stomping outside. His face a shade darker.

Miranda flips on the light. The clear plastic bags ooze on the floor.

114

THE SILENCE WAKES HER.

She's accustomed to the bunkhouse creaking, the wind pushing against the windows, through the cracks. Now there's not even the *whump, whump, whump* of the wind harvester.

Just the silence.

Cyn opens her eyes, staring at the rafters. Her pillow still wet from fever, but her forehead cool. Legs no longer on fire.

Such a wondrous moment.

She falls back to sleep.

She wakes to the rustle of coats, to boots hitting the floor. The stove is fully stoked, embers popping against the metal belly. Trays sit on chairs, a few on the floor. Food, uneaten.

The girls are pulling on winter gear.

Roc is cursing from her bed.

Cyn's lips are glued together with slime. She pulls them apart, smacking them to work up saliva.

"How you feeling?" Jen asks.

"Water." Cyn pokes her hand out.

Jen brings it. It's a cold rush down a hot pipe. She hands it back. "What's going on?"

The front door slams open.

A Russian bear fills the doorway. His nose is ruby red. Cheeks scuffed by winter. He steps inside. The bear transforms into an old man scuffling into the bunkhouse. A fur cap is forced onto his head, the fuzzy edge resting just above his eyebrows.

"Do you realize what you've done?" He shakes plastic at them. "Do you?"

Sid comes in. Miranda after him, wearing knee-high boots and a flawless white coat, plus pearls and new earrings. Jealous anger stirs inside Cyn. *She's a thief.*

"Untie the one in back." He points a hooked finger.

Sid marches to the back corner. The bedsprings creak.

"What are you doing?" Cyn sits up. "Wait, you can't untie her. Do you know what you're doing?"

"I ask the questions." He spikes the bags on the floorboards, droplets spraying in all directions.

He pulls the hat off, grinding his teeth. He walks toward the stove, thoughtful steps. Head down.

Hand in pocket.

Kat and Mad step aside.

"We had months to survive." He turns around, shaking his head. "All winter, probably. Now we might only have days!"

He finishes pacing to the door and swings around.

"Do you understand? *Days!* You don't know anything about this world, none of you. You stumble around in the dark like children. I am your light. I am the one who will lead you out of here. And you!"

He crosses the room with large steps, shaking his finger at Cyn.

"You had one purpose: you were chosen to keep the dreamer alive. She chose you to bring those bags to her, allowed you inside her sanctuary to feed her, and you destroyed it. This is your fault!"

He stands over her, balling his fist, restraining himself from striking her. Cyn is unmoved, unblinking. If he decides to cave in her skull, she can't stop him.

"Thought you said this was a dream," Kat says.

The rage dissipates. His eyes blink heavily. He straightens, looking down at Cyn, nodding.

And then the pulse, the electric prod ignites a thunderstorm in her neck, lightning flashing behind her eyes. A thunderbolt in her throat.

Her body is like a steel plank.

And blackness falls like a marble slab.

Consciousness lifts like a fuzzy shade.

Her body buzzing. Teeth numb.

"Listen to me," a disembodied voice calls. "And do what I say."

Footsteps echo.

Moans follow.

Forms creep from the hazy light. The girls are on the floor. Mr. Williams walks across the room, his shoes grind at a turn, stepping in the other direction.

"Patricia is the dreamer. We are inside her mind; she creates the rules. And the rules mirror reality. That means her body, back in the woods, needs to be cared for, needs to be fed. That old woman on the path was the caregiver. When she died, Patricia chose Cyn to take her place."

He picks up the limp plastic bag.

"When Patricia dies, so does this world."

The girls sit up.

"Get dressed," he says. "Meet me in the dinner house. We will eat and plan routes. You will explore this land until nightfall. I would leave you out there half the night if Patricia didn't put you in the dream."

The girls sleep like the dead. They all dream the same. *Patricia's doing that to us.*

"Why?" Cyn croaks.

He turns toward her.

"Why does she do that?" Cyn asks.

"You're her children. She wants to share the dream."

"And you?"

His head shakes. Perhaps he's contemplating the button.

"You," he says with stiff lips, "are useless. Stay in the bed and die there."

He punches the door open. Miranda flees behind him.

There's a scuffle in the back. Sid drags Roc by the arm, her coat open, bootlaces whipping around her feet. She yanks her arm out of his grasp. His reaction betrays his slack posture: a lightning-quick slap to the nose. He twists her arm behind her back, bending the wrist until her fingers tickle the back of her head.

He marches her through the doorway, slamming it shut. Roc's curses are heard through the closed door.

The girls get dressed. Cyn is just getting the feeling back in her fingers.

"We'll bring you something to eat," Jen whispers.

"Where are you going?" Cyn asks.

"He's got us searching for the gate," Kat sneers, not bothering to whisper.

Cyn throws the blanket off, squirming to move her legs. "I'll come with—"

"Stop her," Kat says. "He'll freak out. Besides, you won't make it to the door, not on those rotten-ass feet. Last thing we need to do is dig a hole for your body."

Mad inserts pills in Cyn's mouth. "Here's two more"—she pushes pills into her palm—"and take them if we don't come back."

"We'll be back," Jen says, wrapping her face in a scarf.

They leave Cyn with the silence and a medicinal haze.

Then the gray.

115

MIRANDA STAYS OUTSIDE, where the air is brisk and renewing. The cold washes away feelings of heavy dread. She imagines she's a filter, the pores plugged with dust and grit and decay.

The air blows it out. Makes her new again.

She opens the front door, where the air is dry and warm and unwholesome. Somehow she dies a little every time she goes inside.

Mr. Williams stands at the window, a cup in hand. The smell of coffee mingles with the stagnant odor of the brick house. Miranda stomps the snow off of her boots and steps past a fully loaded backpack. He holds out his arm, beckoning. She pretends not to notice, unzipping her coat.

"Come," he says, wiggling his fingers.

She's frozen in place again. He knows she heard him. She's looking right at him.

It's easier to just go to him. He's old.

Miranda comes within reach. He pulls her against his body, squeezing tightly. Perfume emanates from his wrist.

Kat, Mad, and Jen exit from the outside kitchen door and begin their trek through the woods out back. Roc and Sid exit the front door, walking west. Together. Even though Miranda never lets the fob out of her grip, she's relieved Sid is staying near her.

And if he causes her pain, she enjoys that.

"Don't worry." He pulls her tighter. "We'll find the gate."

"Is it true?"

"Of course, it's out there."

"No, I mean about Patricia. Will she die?"

His grip stiffens. He pulls a sip from the cup, smacking his lips and letting go of Miranda. He pulls a sheet of paper from his back pocket, unfolding it.

Miranda moves away, not wanting to be near him if she doesn't have to. She goes to the rack next to the door, pulling the coat off her shoulder—

"No."

Mr. Williams holds the paper out while continuing to look out the window. Miranda reluctantly takes it. The letter N is at the top. There's a small square drawn in the middle labeled "camp". Five arrows point out from it in different directions.

Miranda's name is penciled over one of them.

"You go east," he says. "You go until the sun is high and then return. Write down everything you see."

He sips the coffee.

"You want me to go out?"

"You're young and able, darling. In this body, I wouldn't make it past the meadow. You can walk all day."

She stares at the paper. It starts quivering.

"We all have to pitch in, Miranda."

He looks over his shoulder. She still hasn't moved. He puts the cup on the windowsill and begins to slowly zip her coat up.

"There isn't much time."

He tucks her scarf around her neck, sliding his hands over her shoulders, pulls the hood over her head and ties it below her chin.

"I've prepared a pack for you with food and water."

He puts his hand on her cheeks, a slight smile. He reaches out with the other hand—

Miranda breaks the ice in her knees, jerking away.

She pulls open the door and slams it behind her. She stomps through the snow, leaving the food and water, keeping her face in the wind, hoping it will shear away the smell of perfume.

116

A GENTLE HAND WAKES CYN.

Her eyes, slightly crusted, open with effort. Mad is there, her face scratched with red lines. Her hand is on Cyn's shoulder, pills pinched in her fingers. She doesn't ask, just puts them between Cyn's lips.

Cyn lifts her heavy head high enough to chase the pills without spilling water. Not that it matters; the pillow is damp with sweat.

It's light outside. There's a lump in Jen's bed. Roc is making noise in the back.

"What's going on?"

Mad puts the cup on the floor and hands her a bowl of cold grits. She pulls the covers off the foot of Cyn's bed, inspecting the bandages. They feel dry, but a stench rises.

Kat limps to the stove, poking the dying embers to life, throwing another stick inside. She begins undressing.

"Jen hit a fence," Kat says.

"What?" Cyn gets higher on her elbow. "Where?"

"Went through the woods, the three of us. Went to that small cabin and split up. Jen went straight north and I went northeast. Must've walked about twenty minutes but didn't get far. Trees are thick and there's no path. Mad went the other way, same thing."

Kat's face is scratched as bad as Mad's.

"Right about the time I saw the end of the forest, I started to feel the buzz," Kat continues, sitting on the edge of her bed to shuck her boots. "I slowed down, but kept going. It got more intense the closer I got to the end of the trees. I could see the clearing right where they stopped, like I could just step out and walk into another meadow. I got all the way to the edge and felt like I was going to drop."

She leans on her knees, rubbing her face.

"Then I heard screaming."

"Jen?"

"She was a long ways off, but it sounded like she was set on fire. Took about ten minutes to get to her. She was just outside the trees, squirming in the snow, wouldn't stop."

Mad pulls the covers over Cyn's feet, tucking them in. Won't look up.

"How'd you get her out?" Cyn asks.

"It took a while," Kat says. "We reached in and grabbed her foot, damn near blacked out doing it. Once we got her, though, she stopped screaming."

"She ain't talked since," Mad says.

What memories are in her now?

"It was a road, Cyn," Kat says.

"What do you mean?"

"There were tracks in the ground, just like you saw. Mad and I think she ignored the feeling in her neck, just walked out of the trees and right through the fence."

"And started remembering." Mad goes to the stove. "Ain't that right, Cyn?"

"It's like the road was taunting us," Kat says. "Pretending there's a way out, but then we just start remembering."

"I don't want to know," Mad says. "Not anymore."

Their eyes are cast downward.

Their spirits will starve long before their stomachs. There's no escape.

No hope.

They feel the cage, too. Sense the walls. The illusion of freedom is crushing them. There was a world beyond the mountains, but not anymore. *Hope is the dream.*

"How far did Jen get?" Cyn asks.

"What?" Kat looks up.

"She walked straight north, how far did she go from the bunkhouse before she reached the fence?"

"I don't know, three hundred yards or so. Hard to say with all the trees."

Cyn visualizes the bunkhouse from a bird's-eye view. She trekked due south about two miles, give or take. Jen went in the opposite direction only three hundred yards or so.

She reaches under the bed for her coat and searches the pockets. There's a pencil and a tattered square of paper in the pocket. She unfolds it, holding it up to the light.

If Jen walked three hundred yards to the north—she puts an X on the paper—and Cyn went two miles to the south, then she could identify the perimeter. And if the fence is an enormous circle—Cyn sketches an outline using the two points as a reference—that would mean that the center would be...

"Got it."

Kat and Mad are at the stove. "Got what?" Kat asks.

Cyn circles the tiny X in the center of her notes and holds it up.

"I know where the gate is."

117

MIRANDA'S ELBOW wakes her at three o'clock in the morning.

She had slipped on an icy rock during her exploration. Every muscle in her body aches, the blisters on her feet throb. And the pain relievers are wearing off.

There's a light on somewhere in the back of the house.

Mr. Williams is adamant about conserving energy. Lights get turned off, the heat turned down. Even the music. She lies on the couch, beneath three heavy comforters, listening to the office chair creak.

He's up.

Miranda doesn't want to move; it took forever to get warm. Mr. Williams wouldn't let her take a hot shower—too much power to heat the water. Everything needed to be conserved for the back office.

But she has to pee.

She wraps one of the blankets around her and waddles down the hallway like a human burrito. Sid is snoring in Barbara's bed. She put the necklace and earrings back; she doesn't plan on wearing them again. She saw the jealousy in Cyn's eyes. Doesn't want to see that again.

She's forced to drop the wrapping to sit on the toilet, holding it on her lap while she does her business. She doesn't flush, and she stops when she sees the mirror. The night-light casts yellow light on her face, illuminating the long red line across her cheek. A branch had nearly poked her in the eye earlier.

Miranda heads back for the couch, but Mr. Williams is exiting the forbidden door, the eternally locked one at the very back. He doesn't notice her looking out from the bathroom.

The office chair creaks.

Miranda looks inside. The monitors are lit up. The inside of the bunkhouse is on the main one. The girls are unconscious.

"Still up?"

Mr. Williams slowly spins the chair around, hands laced behind his head. "Too excited to sleep."

"Something happen?"

"Tomorrow will be a good day, I believe."

"Did someone find it?"

A sly smile. "Don't worry. Go to sleep, get some rest."

He leans back, sinking into the chair's depths. He hasn't slept in a bed for days. The chair has molded to his bottom.

One of the monitors is focused on Cyn. No more midnight runs. She can hardly get out of bed. She lies there, rotting.

Dying.

Aren't we all?

Miranda yawns, turning to leave. The back door is cracked open. The odor is a bit more noticeable. Now that she's been outside, she notices it more.

Fear pushes her back a step, but she holds her ground.

Mr. Williams notices. He throws his weight forward to lean out of the chair. He gently pushes the door. It clicks.

"Nothing you want to see," he says. The smile is gone. "Get some sleep."

He's right. She doesn't want to see what's back there. She just wishes he didn't go back there, that the door would stay closed forever. Instinct tells her that she never wants to know what's back there.

Miranda lies awake on the couch, listening to the chair creak and pop for quite some time.

118

Spreading her arms,
She tips like a statue.
Over the edge she falls,
And lets the chasm take her.

———————

A SHARP POINT pierces the soft tissue beneath her chin.

Cyn opens her eyes. It's too dark to see the face in front of her, but she can feel someone's breath. Taste the stink.

"I promised to kill you," Roc hisses. "To stick this wire through the top of your brain, but I want out of here. I want the old man to kiss my ass."

Cyn pushes her head into the pillow, but the point just follows her. The sheets are too tight. The weapon will be in her sinuses before she gets free.

"What are you talking about?" she says without moving her lips.

"You know where the gate is."

"You believe that crap?"

"What else is there? If the old man gets to it, he'll screw us—you can count on that."

"And if it doesn't work?"

"Then we die in Hell."

Cyn struggles to move her head. The tip of Roc's weapon is breaking the skin. "Back that off."

Roc leans closer, pushing it deeper. It's about to go through when she puts it against Cyn's throat. She relaxes her head. The spot under her chin burns.

"It's too far to walk," Cyn says.

"We've got horses."

"Then we'll need Kat."

Roc plants her free hand on Cyn's face and presses her lips to her ear. "Mess with me and you die with a rusty twig in your eye. You don't stand a chance against me, not anymore. You smell like dead ass."

She's right. Cyn doesn't have the strength to fight.

Roc springs back. Despite Cyn's decrepit condition, she's still wary. It's hard to forget a thorough ass whipping. She backs into the dark, barely an outline. It's still night, but morning must be close or they wouldn't be awake.

"Surprise," Roc whispers.

Kat wakes, startled. A hand clamps over her mouth.

There's unintelligible whispering, all Roc.

"Cyn?" Kat calls.

A loud slap. "I'm not playing," Roc says.

"It's all right," Cyn says. "Just do what she says."

"Get dressed before the sun's up," Roc adds.

She's thinking about the fob. Maybe they get all the way out there and get knocked out. Maybe not. One thing's for sure: they'll get knocked out if the old man comes to the bunkhouse.

"Wake up the others." Cyn reaches under the bed.

"No." Roc stands in the middle of the room. "Just the three of us."

Cyn drops a sweater on the floor. "I'm not going, then."

"You can come back for them."

"I'm not moving."

Roc bounds across the room and slams Cyn's head into the pillow, squeezing her face with one hand. The point presses against her temple. Spittle flies with each angry breath, like a dragon contemplating the next move.

"We can ride double," Kat says. "Cyn's going to need help staying on the horse anyway."

Roc presses down, her breath hot and humid. Cyn sees the whites of her eyes.

She leaps off. "Hurry, then; go."

Kat scurries to the other beds. The girls moan. Roc yanks them up. They protest, but not for long.

Cyn slowly puts on clothes. Sluggish. Sore. Her body full of sand. The others scuffle to get dressed, whispering back and forth. Roc's anger wanes; there are fewer threats and more action.

Maybe Roc is saving us.

Cyn puts on three pair of socks and looks down at the last thing.

Boots.

Even with the backs cut out, they're tight.

"Here." Mad drops four pills into her hand. "Take all of these."

Cyn rolls them in her palm. She just wants the pain to go away. Dream or not, she wants it to end.

She swallows them dry.

And shoves her feet into boots of hot, broken glass.

Somehow, she chokes down the scream.

119

MIRANDA WAKES EVERY TWENTY MINUTES, spinning on the couch, searching for the comfort zone. Finding none. She wishes for a little music to mask the sounds of the house, the creaks of the office chair.

It's the door.

She can't stop thinking about it. She's positive she doesn't want to see what's back there, but now that it's been opened, her curiosity nibbles.

It's almost six o'clock.

The sun will be up very soon. She doesn't want to hike, not today. Not ever. If only she could run a fever, she could stay on the couch all day, listening to her favorite composers. Just her and the comforter and Mozart and Brahms. That would be a good day.

Mr. Williams won't be happy. *Can he work that thing to zap me?*

There's nowhere she can hide, not inside the house. He goes everywhere and knows how to work everything.

She goes down the hall, dragging the blanket, giving the thermostat a little bump. The air handler kicks on. Lifeless dry air blows from the vent. Miranda leans into the back room; the monitors are lit up.

Light snores rise and fall from the office chair. Mr. Williams is slumped out of view. The monitors flicker with green light, one of them focused on an empty pillow. The others pan around the bunkhouse. All the covers thrown back, beds empty.

All of them.

She steps into the room.

Mr. Williams snorts, jerking in the chair. He spins around, eyeballing the blanket-clad blonde standing in the doorway. It takes him a moment to process, and then he remembers where he is and why.

She's looking at something.

Mr. Williams attacks the keyboard, cycling the monitors around the buildings. They're not in the dinner house. The floodlights illuminate the area with white light. Not in the garden, not outside the brick house. Not in the woods or at the small cabin—

The barn door is open.

Horses gallop into the open, free at last. Their legs stretching out, clopping the ground, snow powder tossed in their wake. Kat's on the first one, gripping the mane with both hands, hunched over, bouncing with the horse's stride.

The other horses bear two riders each.

"Sid!" The office chair flies across the room.

Mr. Williams limps toward Miranda, almost losing his balance. He fumbles his way into the hallway.

"Sid!"

Their footsteps hammer the hardwood. The door slams.

Miranda watches the monitors. Watches the girls ride out of the floodlights and into the early morning, hugging each other.

Sid sprints past the garden in his socks. Mr. Williams isn't far behind, aiming the fob at the distant riders. They remain on the backs of the animals, not breaking stride.

Fading into the snow-laden meadow.

They left me. Her head knocks against the doorframe. *I deserve it.*

120

THE HORSES RUN ON INSTINCT.

Cyn squeezes Mad from behind, pressing her head against her back. "Hold on to the mane like it's your life," Kat had told them.

Cyn told them which direction to run, and to run as fast as they could. They have to get out of sight, as far away as possible. She'll figure out the rest once they can't see the cabins. The horse's backbone slams into her each time the hooves hit, sending painful waves through her.

She holds on.

Closes her eyes.

They're in the trees within minutes. The horses work their way between the trunks, ducking beneath the limbs. The slow pace eases the pain, but Cyn doesn't look up until they're out of the trees.

It's still dark. And she doesn't know where they are.

The horses walk the easiest routes, going around rock outcroppings and steep hills. But they don't stop. Cyn wonders if Mr. Williams will send Sid after them, if he'll run until he drops from exhaustion.

The sun breaks the horizon. Cyn gets her bearings and has them turn more to the left, hoping this will put them back on track. They can go in circles all day to find it if they have to.

They're not going back.

They reach a shallow valley. The horses dig in and scale the steep slope. Cyn hangs on, almost sliding off the back of her horse. They gather on the ridge, the ground gently sloping down the other side. The horses paw at the snow, tossing their heads.

Snorting.

The girls slump over. Tired and hungry. Spirits bending.

Cyn recognizes nothing. It's just an endless stretch of trees and hills and rocks, all covered in snow. Immoveable mountains in the distance.

Something flashes further up the ridge.

She wipes the tears from her eyes. It's a beam, a mirror, or something reflective.

"There!"

The boulder and dead tree are too far to see with any clarity. Cyn taps the horse with her toes, the pain receding in the numbing cold.

The others follow.

"You feel that?"

Cyn holds up her hand. The others trot to a stop. The boulder and tree are still fifty yards away.

"It's a fence," Kat shouts.

"Not a fence, it's different."

Cyn rubs her stomach where the quivering has begun. She felt that last time and thought the same thing, but a fence starts in the neck. This begins somewhere in the core, at the center of her being.

The horses walk closer. The backpack is still there, tattered and sun-bleached. The strip of aluminum rattles in the breeze.

Kat pulls up next to Cyn and dismounts. The others do, too. Roc stomps to the front, clutching a rusty bedspring. The end is bent outward.

Mad slides off while Kat and Jen reach up for Cyn. She leans over, falling into their outstretched arms. When her feet touch the ground, fiery sparks lance her dead legs, spraying pins and needles throughout her body.

She collapses.

Kat and Jen carry her closer. The vibrations in her stomach increase, beating back the pain, filling her with warmth and goodness. They lie on the ground.

Together, they stare at the dead tree, its branches worn smooth by harsh weather. Beautiful and ancient.

"What now?" Roc says.

"I don't know," Cyn says.

"Start by putting that away." Kat points at the bedspring.

"Not until this is over."

The horses are restless, wandering over to the nearest trees, nibbling at shoots poking through the snow, lichens on the trunks. The girls stare at each other. Jen hasn't said a word.

"Touch it," Mad says.

"She already did that," Kat says. "The backpack is against the rock."

"Don't tell me we wasted our time." Roc waves the weapon. "And don't tell me we need the old man for some secret word."

"Not the tree." Cyn takes a few breaths, her chest shrinking. "I didn't touch the tree."

There's a moment where she doesn't hear anything, the pain too large to process. She breathes so small. When she opens her eyes, they're looking at her.

"Someone," she says, "touch it."

"You go." Roc points the bedspring at Kat.

"You wanted to ride out here, you go."

Roc starts at her—

"I'll go." Mad jumps between them. "I'll touch it."

Roc wipes the sweat from her forehead, exposing the skin between the glove and sleeve. Her wrist is ringed with raw flesh where the restraints cut into her.

"Go, then," she says.

The horses look up from the trees, grinding lichen in their mouths. Mad strips the gloves from her hands and tucks them in her pockets.

The snow is piled on the boulder.

On the branches.

And the wind hardly moves as she reaches out. Her hand pauses a moment and then grips the trunk.

She goes stiff.

Like electricity coursing through her. The branch is like a live wire.

Her eyes go wide. Her arm stiffens.

She's not convulsing, just staring into nothingness.

"Do something!" Jen shouts.

Kat runs up—

"Stop!" Cyn shouts. "Give it a second."

Kat's only a step away, hands out. Mad is a statue. Catatonic. Transported to another world.

"Maybe she's gone," Kats says. "Maybe the dream body stays here."

"I'm sick of this." Roc pulls off her glove. "I want out before that grisly bastard shows up."

Roc lumbers forward—

Mad collapses.

She draws a deep breath like she's been held under water, starving for air. Kat and Jen pull her away. Mad's eyes are crazy. She's gulping like a fish.

"It's all right," Jen says, stroking her head. "It's okay."

They wait, giving her time. Soon she calms. Sanity returns. She looks around, wondering where everyone came from, like she's been all alone.

"The dream." She clutches Kat's coat, pulling her close. "As soon as I touched it, I was in the dream, standing on the ledge...there were things out there, in the fog."

She inhales, squeaking. Eyes wide.

Mad points at Cyn, like she knows. "The memories are out there."

Jen scurries away, like she's infected. She turns over and crawls past Cyn. She gets to her feet, stumbling down the slope, spooking the horses. The horses gallop away from her mad scramble into the trees, and she collapses on the ground in a heap of sobs.

"I'll get her." Kat is on her feet, sprinting down the hill.

Cries echo through the valley.

Mad crawls away from the stone. Roc clutches her weapon, staring down the slope. She swings her hand at Cyn, shaking. "This ain't, this is just some..."

"This is what?" Cyn says. "It took her back to the dream, what do you think it is?"

"You go." She gestures at the monument. "Grab it, see what happens."

Cyn dips her head. She finally found a level of relief, the cold embracing her legs with numbing comfort. She doesn't want to move, doesn't believe this will be anything. She welcomes death.

Just lie down and go to sleep, let winter have me.

"Get up." Roc gets a handful of her coat, dragging her through the snow. "Get over there and grab it."

Cyn winces at the sudden feeling. She knocks Roc's hand away and gets to her hands and knees. She's drooling. Snow is packed inside her gloves.

She begins crawling.

Hand in front of hand.

Knee after knee.

Until she bumps into the boulder. She stares up at the dead branches; the undulating trunk ripples like muscle. Smooth like polished wood.

Kat is holding Jen.

Mad watches blankly.

Roc's knuckles are white around the weapon.

You can have me. All of me.

And Cyn reaches; her fingers crawl over the boulder, contact the trunk—

Gray.
The edge is there. Her toes hang over.
And the haze swirls in the Nowhere mist.
Beckoning.
Body ringing like a struck bell.
The girls behind her.

Watching through a tunnel.
And below her,
The abyss.
She stretches out her arms,
Inhales the senseless mist,
Teeters on the brink.
And falls like a statue.
Falls into the unknown.
Her belly swirls,
Toes curl.
Head over heel, she tumbles.
Disintegrates,
Into the Nowhere.

The wind harvesters thump.

Cyn feels the coarse pillowcase on her neck. The embrace of the mattress. Smells the woodstove.

She feels pressure in her forehead.

Her eyelids crackle, tearing apart the crusted seal. The rafters are blurred. She blinks but can't focus. Her eyes aren't responding.

Something is between them.

There's waxy balm on her lips. And pressure in her arms. Arms she can't move. She licks her lips in slow motion, blinking heavily. Trying to will her hand to lift, to remove whatever is stuck between her eyes—

A face.

Her brown hair hangs down. She's leaning over Cyn, obstructing her view of the ceiling. Her lips move.

A sound comes out, slurred and long.

She looks to the side and says something. Looks back. Tries again.

Her lips move. A single word.

"Cynthia?"

She reaches for Cyn's forehead and takes hold of the object

between her eyes. It slides out like a sliver, a cold metal sliver, sending a queer sensation between her ears, down her throat—

There's sound.

Objects.

She turns her head. There are people in the bunkhouse. Adults. They're all watching.

They've come.

We're saved.

The woman's hand touches Cyn's arm. There are needles in her arms, tubes running to IV bags on a stand over her head. Across the room, Kat is tucked into bed with IVs in her arm, too.

A needle protruding from her forehead.

"Can you tell me the password?" the woman asks.

Cyn has no idea what she means. She asks her the question twice. Cyn shakes her head, confused. Lost.

The woman squeezes her hand and smiles. "You made it out,

NOVEMBER

Peel an onion, layer by layer.
What's in the middle?

121

THERE'S dull pain in her arm matched only by the sensation in her forehead. Both are persistent.

Nauseating.

She rises into consciousness against her will, harpooned by discomfort and dragged to the surface. Her eyes crack open, not really seeing anything. The lids are weighty, wanting to close, wanting to sleep.

Pain denies her, pushing them open.

The beige ceiling is low and curved. It appears to be canvas held up by hoops. It smells like new fabric. The wind breathes against the walls.

Somewhere, someone is tapping a keyboard.

Cyn's lying in a bed, a dark green blanket up to her chest. Just beyond her feet, a brown curtain is drawn for privacy. She turns her head. On the other side of the narrow room is another bed, the covers turned back, the pillow dented.

She lifts her arm, pain radiating from inside the elbow. There's a tube sticking out of her vein, the plastic port taped down. The skin around the insertion point is yellowish.

She tries to lift her head—

"Ooh."

She drops back into the pillow. Didn't expect that dull pain to bite. She takes several quick breaths, bracing to roll onto her side.

The curtain slides open.

A slender woman stands at the foot of the bed, holding the curtain. Her teeth are very straight. Cyn holds still, examining her, deciding whether to see what happens next or try to make an escape, despite the pain.

"Are you thirsty?" the woman asks.

Her throat is hot. She nods once.

The woman comes back with a water bottle, bending the plastic straw and putting it to Cyn's lips. She draws a few swallows. It puts her at ease.

"Take these if you can. They'll reduce the discomfort."

She puts two pills between her lips and follows it with water. Cyn swallows them, recalling someone giving her pills before, but not quite remembering whom.

Or why.

The woman's hair is straight, cut at the shoulders and graying. "I'm Dr. Mazyck. Call me Linda."

"Doctor?" The word scratches its way out.

"I'm a psychologist. I work for the military. Do you know where you are?"

Again, Cyn looks around. Nothing is familiar. A four-wheeler drives somewhere out there, changing gears and speeding off. A generator starts up. In the background, there's a thumping of propellers, steady and low.

I should know what that is.

"You've had a long journey." Linda gently squeezes her shoulder. "You're safe."

Cyn takes another drink. Her forehead has cooled. She touches it without considerable pain. Her back and legs ache terribly. She moves her arm.

"Do you want to sit up?"

Linda pulls off the covers, puts her arm beneath the pillow, and uses it to slowly lift her into a sitting position. Her clothes are beige and clean, like hospital scrubs. Cyn puts her feet on the ground, expecting it to hurt. When the nausea settles, she reaches halfway down her shin, her fingers walking the pant leg up to expose her feet.

Her clean, perfect feet.

"I don't understand," she half-whispers. "There was something wrong..."

"What do you remember?"

Confusion obscures a thousand thoughts. She can't pick one of them out of the mental storm, the memories swirling around and around.

"I was lost." She looks around. An empty bed across from her. "There were others."

Linda nods, her light blue eyes sympathetic, understanding. But it just doesn't seem real, just something she's imagining, not remembering.

"You have been dreaming."

Cyn touches her forehead, very tender around a circular bandage. Tubes dangle from her arm. "What's happening?" she whispers.

A door opens at the far end of the room, letting in a draft. Linda stands and walks briskly towards the man hustling inside.

"Not yet," Linda says in a semi-hushed tone. "She just woke up. It'll take a little time for her to understand what's happened."

"There's no time," the man says. "The others are still inside."

"Don't push it, Thomas."

"Now's not the time to be cautious, Linda."

"Now is *exactly* the time to be cautious!" She stops him from going around her. "Give me an hour, that's all. She needs time to adjust to reality. If you go too hard, she could lose her grip. She'll be no good then."

The man stares at Cyn, listening.

"Trust me, Thomas. I saw it happen on the island. Some of the boys were caught between two worlds and fell apart. You could destroy her."

He's thinking. Puts his hand on her shoulder. "I'll just talk."

"Let me—"

He's too quick this time. He snags the folding chair from a desk just past the curtain and plunks down in front of Cyn. No smile from him.

"I'm Agent Carlson. You hungry?"

Cyn looks at Linda.

"I wish there was more time for pleasantries, but time is very short. I'm a federal cyber-terrorism agent. What's happened in the last month is all new to us. Quite frankly, it's the stuff of science-fiction movies."

Blankness moves into her eyes. He pauses, giving her a moment to comprehend, holding up a hand when Linda takes a step.

"Cynthia," he says, touching her knee, "you're part of an identity-theft conspiracy. You were kidnapped months ago, brought out here, and inserted into a dream. We are very close to finding the people responsible, but we need your help. Tell me what you remember before waking up."

Cyn looks back and forth between the two. She tries to say something but keeps forgetting what it is.

"Thomas." Linda steps up.

He leans forward, holding Cyn's gaze. "Tell me," he whispers.

But she's stuck. She's got nothing.

Linda gives his shoulder a firm pull. He stands reluctantly, not looking away. Linda guides him with her hand on his arm, whispering as they go.

"What did you mean?" Cyn calls.

They stop halfway across the room.

"When you said I was adjusting to reality, what did you mean by that?"

Linda comes back and sits in the chair. Thomas stays back.

"You've been immersed in an alternate reality," Linda says. "We're not sure how long."

"Weeks, we think," Thomas says without moving any closer. "Maybe a month."

Cyn focuses on the sound of the distant thumping, like a slow-moving helicopter. She closes her eyes, imagining white blades churning at the end of a long post.

Three of them.

Next to a barn.

It was so cold. So white and cold.

And hungry.

There was pain and fear, a brutal fight, marks on a wall, other beds—

"Where are they?" She opens her eyes and notices that the bed behind Linda is empty. "Where are the girls?"

Linda takes her hands. They're soft and warm. She looks like she's going to say something just as soft, just as warm and supportive—

"They're still in the dream," Thomas says. "We need your help."

Linda's lips tighten, but her expression shifts to something pained, sorrowful.

"Is that true?" Cyn asks.

Linda nods.

Cyn tries to stand but feels too dizzy. Her legs, too weak.

She left them behind. She didn't mean to do that, didn't want to abandon them. Why didn't they follow her? Why didn't they do what she did?

I left them in Hell.

"We need to take this slow. Let's talk about where you are, right here and now, and get a good grip on physical reality before we start investigating the dream."

"No." Cyn grabs Linda's arm. "Take me to them. I want to see them."

"You heard her," Thomas says.

Linda sighs, searching for a reason to stop her. Cyn squeezes tighter, hoping to look strong and confident. Hoping to hide the fear and her fluttery grip on reality.

"Please," she says.

"Leave, Thomas," Linda says. "Let the young lady get dressed."

Thomas leaves as quickly as he entered. Linda remains seated for several seconds before retrieving clothes for Cyn, closing the curtain for privacy. She has to rest once she's dressed.

She's not accustomed to moving.

Linda holds the door open.

Cyn is greeted by sunshine and warm air. The tent is set up near the woods, behind the garden that's full of blossoming vegetables and overgrown weeds. She expects to see Jen pop up from one of the rows, hauling out a bundle of green peppers or eggplants.

Beyond is the meadow, wildflowers swaying in a gentle breeze. There was snow out there before. They crossed it on horseback, the bitter cold bringing tears to her eyes and aches to her ears.

Now there's a helicopter nestled in the grass.

"Are you all right?" Linda asks.

"It was...colder." Her knees wobble. She licks her lips and swallows, her chest fluttering.

Linda carefully pauses, allowing Cyn to look around, before saying, "We believe time goes faster in the dream."

Two red ATVs are parked in front of the brick house. People are inside, passing by the windows. They look more like Thomas than Linda.

"You don't have to do this."

"Where are they?"

Linda holds her elbow lightly and lets Cyn take the first step before guiding her around the garden, toward the dinner house. The outside kitchen door is closed. Cyn watches as they pass, expecting Mad to open it and shout at Jen to fetch the eggs.

The chickens are dead.

Cyn allows Linda to steer her around the front of the dinner house. They approach the bunkhouse. Thomas is waiting by the door. White trucks are next to the barn. The horses trot around the corner, along the fence. Cyn's breath catches in her throat, waiting for Kat to call them into the barn for trimming.

The wind harvesters turn like ornaments.

Thomas opens the bunkhouse door.

Cyn slows her gait, her breath coming in short bursts. Linda allows her to go at her own pace, half steps that occasionally stutter.

She steadies herself on the doorway.

Steps inside. Her balance betrays her; she reaches back to find Linda's outstretched arm. Her heart slamming.

The beds. The rafters.

The girls.

They lie on their backs, blankets up to their chests, arms at their sides. A wire protrudes from each of their foreheads, extending to the black box on the small table where there used to be candles and matches. Metal stands are posted at the end of each bed, decorated with a clear plastic bag and tubes attached their arms.

"It's exactly the same," Cyn whispers.

Linda lifts a hand at Thomas, stopping whatever he's thinking about doing. He walks past an empty bed and stares out the window at the barn, arms crossed.

Cyn lets go of Linda and goes to her bed. The blankets are piled on the mattress. She pulls them back, revealing marks etched into the wall. She thought she scratched more than that, but then she realizes.

The dream days aren't there.

But there are scratches. She put those there before they were trapped in the dream.

The small table holds a black box like the others. A wire is coiled next to it, a needle submerged in a glass vial. Cyn holds it up to the light. The gel holds tiny bubbles around a needle that's almost two inches long.

She touches her head. Remembers the queer sensation when she awoke. When they slid the needle out.

The floor teeters. Linda is by her side.

Kat looks so peaceful, like a young girl waiting for Prince Charming. Her brown hair is only an inch long. Cyn runs her hand over her own head, her hair the same length.

"Kathryn Landon," Linda says.

Of course her name isn't Kat. Those tags were just abbreviations. Like property.

"Kathryn was born in New Mexico. Her family worked on a ranch. Her mother died when she was young. Her father never reported her missing."

Mad is positioned in the same way as Kat, hands at her side, that disturbing wire protruding from the middle of her forehead.

"Madeline Foreman, born in Florida, lived with her grandmother. When the grandmother died, Madeline's whereabouts became unknown. And there's Jennifer. That's all we know about her. No last name. We suspect she was kidnapped in India, transported to the United States."

"She didn't have an accent."

Thomas scribbles something. A clue, perhaps.

Roc is lying on her side. Someone is massaging her legs with lotion.

"We have a nursing staff tending the bodies to prevent bedsores."

Cyn winces. *The bodies.*

"Every couple of hours, they'll get turned. Those beds are made of some special gel that helps reduce the risk, but lying for three weeks is a long time."

Roc's arms are like the others, her tattoo partially visible. She's bigger than Cyn recalls. Or maybe Cyn just feels smaller.

"Her name is Rochelle Dandoval, last known whereabouts Los Angeles. Her parents kicked her out of the house after she beat up her mother a few years ago."

The final bed is empty, the sheets tucked in and the wire coiled on the black box. Miranda woke up in the house, not the bunkhouse. She's probably still up there.

"Why'd you ask me for a password?" Cyn asks.

"Just to be sure it was you."

"But I didn't know the password."

"Exactly. But someone from someplace else would've given me one when I asked." She glances at Thomas. "The men used passwords to identify each other when they returned from the dream. We were just guessing you wouldn't know it if it was really you."

"Guessing?"

"We don't have much to go on, Cynthia."

"He said this was an experiment, what did that mean?"

"Who did?"

"The old man."

Linda and Thomas exchange looks. "There aren't any males here, Cynthia."

"He said he was from someplace *else*." She shakes her head, staring blankly at the floor. "I can't remember."

"Foreverland?"

"How'd you know?"

Thomas scribbles something in a notebook. "Did he tell you his name?"

She has to think about it. "Mr. Williams. He brought someone with him, a boy. About my age. I don't remember his name, though."

"That's all right," Linda says. "How are you feeling?"

"Why don't you just pull the needle out of their heads?"

Linda holds her arm, just above the elbow. Cyn's not sure if she looks as weak as she feels.

"Think of the body as a vehicle," Linda says. "You are not your body, Cyn. None of us are. Whoever we are—the soul, the identity, whatever you want to call it—resides in the body. Right now, the girls are there."

"If we pull the needle out," Thomas adds, "they'll end up like human vegetables. Empty bodies."

Suddenly, the girls look like machines wired to a small computer, these organic humanlike things used to power an alternate world. It's the motionlessness, the lack of expression, the lifeless repose that clearly illustrates whoever they are—whoever Jen is, Mad, and Kat, Roc—whatever or whoever they are is not the body.

They're not in there.

"Where are they?"

"You were transported somewhere else."

"Where?"

"How did you escape?" Thomas interjects.

Cyn looks at him, searching for an answer. Finding none. "Where did they go?" she repeats.

"If we know how you escaped," he says, "maybe we can help them."

Cyn yanks her arm away from Linda. "Tell me where they went."

Linda gives her space and doesn't try to force comfort on her. She pauses, considering whether Cyn really wants to know the answer. But she already does. She knows where they went.

The image of an old woman suddenly forms. "Patricia," Cyn says.

Linda nods.

Cyn wishes Linda was holding onto her, keeping her from falling. Or maybe she just wants someone touching her, to let her know this isn't a dream anymore. This time it's real.

Because she's just not sure.

122

The next morning is brisk.

Cyn sits on the front porch of the dinner house, watching the morning sun streak over the meadow. Dew glitters on the helicopter, the blades sagging.

She dreamed that night. She dreamed a normal dream, one with random images and illogical scenarios, the way dreams are supposed to be. No fog, no gray.

No cliff to perch upon.

It seems so obvious now.

This is real. This physical world feels different, feels real. The colors more vibrant, the air more fragrant. The sensations deeper. The experience denser.

Is that what defines reality? Is the human experience in the physical world the gold standard for truth? Do our five senses separate illusion from enlightenment?

She shivers, not from the cold but the questions.

She can't ask them, not now. Not yet. She has to be here, has to be present. Those thoughts make her doubt.

Maybe this is a dream, too.

Linda steps onto the porch, a thick beige coat to her knees, carrying two steaming mugs. She hands one to Cyn.

"I'm sorry, tea is all I have. Would you rather have coffee?"

Cyn shakes her head.

Linda takes the chair on the other side of the door, cupping the mug with both hands. She inhales.

"Beautiful morning," Linda says.

Birds are chirping. Cyn doesn't remember hearing birds inside the dream. Maybe they were there in the beginning. Not at the end. Not when it was so cold.

"Oh, I almost forgot." Linda pulls an apple from her pocket. "If you're hungry. You haven't eaten much solid food, so it may take some time to adjust."

Cyn examines the apple. So red and firm. Shiny. She rubs the skin with her thumb and takes a bite.

The taste is explosive.

"We had fruit when we woke up."

Linda sips and listens. Cyn studies the apple after each bite, like each one is a new experience.

"I thought someone would come for us."

"We did," Linda says.

Another bite. Another look. "Not like I thought."

"Did you do that assignment?"

Cyn pretends like she doesn't hear, but Linda doesn't look away. Finally, she reaches in her pocket and hands her a folded piece of paper. Linda flips it over.

What do I remember? Nothing.

"You have lovely handwriting." Linda hands it back.

Cyn wads it up.

It's that question again. Over and over, they ask it. She's not pissed at Linda; it's just that the answer doesn't come to her—it only muddles her brain. Frustrates her. Like she doesn't want to remember.

And she does.

Suddenly, she's full. She puts the apple core on the porch railing and leans against it with the sudden urge to vomit.

She can't remember specific things. She just knows what they feel like. Heavy and thick and wet. Whatever memories she has, she doesn't remember them, but they weigh her down.

"No one cares," she says.

"I care."

Cyn spits. "No offense, but that's your job. You don't know me."

"I don't have to know you to care."

There's thumping in the distance, like wind harvesters coming down from the sky. A black dot approaches from the east, the chopper blades echoing off the trees.

"This might be a dream. Ever thought of that?"

"This is not a dream, Cynthia. You woke up, you're here and now. Trust me."

"Why should I trust anything?"

"You can trust me."

"Saying it don't make it true."

The mug hovers beneath Linda's chin. "No. It doesn't."

Cyn feels the helicopter in her chest, the percussion banging inside her, stirring up anxiety. She wants to run, but where would she go?

It hovers in the meadow, slowly dropping the landing skids into the grass, thrashing the wildflowers in the downdraft. A few people jog out to meet it, one of them Thomas. They help a man and woman out of the back door and shake hands, shouting to be heard. They half-duck until they're clear of the blades.

"More experts?" Cyn asks.

"There's a lot of evidence. This camp was abandoned when we arrived. The people who brought you out here had escaped, leaving you and the others behind. We need to know what's going on, how it works. Are there other places like this?"

A truck goes out to the helicopter; supplies are loaded into the back. Once that's finished, the pilot salutes and, when it's all clear, lifts off. Cyn feels the downdraft this time.

The new guests stand in front of the brick house. Two people come out to meet them. There's a meeting on the front step. Thomas gestures toward the dinner house and they all turn.

Pretty soon, he's walking toward them.

"How did you escape?" Linda asks. "They're going to want to know."

Thomas doesn't wave them over. He's going to make the trip all the way to the porch.

"You don't have to go, Cynthia. If you're not ready, you don't have to see everything, not yet. You can rest, get yourself grounded. I'd prefer you remember more so that you know who you are."

The helicopter is far above the trees.

The girls still have needles in their heads. Still in the dream. Cyn's not going to sit on the front porch sipping tea while they starve.

"Remembering doesn't make me who I am," Cyn says distantly. "My soul ain't memories."

Linda sips. They watch Thomas approach.

"Some people want to talk to you." He puts his hands on his hips.

Cyn steps off the porch. He leads the way.

Linda puts her mug down and follows.

123

CYN STOPS at the tall grass.

There's a faint line, a subtle difference in how the grass grows, that crosses in front of the house, circling around it. Not one these people would notice.

Cyn stands at the line, the end of her boots almost touching.

"You okay?" Linda is almost to the steps.

She rubs her neck, wondering. When she woke up, she was the first one to hit the fence, like a cattle prod to the back of the head.

"Cynthia?" Linda's next to her. "We don't have to go inside."

She shakes her head. Takes a breath. "There's this thing in our neck."

"We know. They used it to track your location. It shouldn't be hard to remove, once you're back."

"It did other things."

Linda gives her space to sort through the thoughts.

"There were places we couldn't go or it would go off."

"How?"

"Like a jolt to the nervous system. If we crossed that line"—she points at the soft line, following it around the corner—"we were knocked unconscious. We called it a fence."

Linda's nodding. "I'm sorry, Cynthia. The boys from the island had something similar, but it wasn't activated by a fence. Are there other fences in the dream?"

She shakes her head, remembering something else that ignited the lump. Something the old man had, like a remote control. "I'm not sure. I don't remember."

She doesn't remember other fences. It seems like there was another place around there that initiated the lump and knocked her out. She's sure there is. And she doesn't want to go back there.

"Do you want to go back to the tent?"

"No. I don't think this is on." She rubs her neck again. There's no tingling, no sensitivity. "There was always a warning when we got near one, I'm not feeling it."

Still, she has trouble breaking the hold on her knees. She puts a hand on Linda's shoulder. She doesn't mean to close her eyes—it's more like a long blink during that first step.

And then she's on the other side.

"Nothing?" Linda asks.

Cyn shakes her head. *Nothing.*

Dead things are inside.

Cyn stands at the front door, impulsively sniffing the foul air. The hairs on her arms bristle. "Where is it?"

"In the very back," Linda says.

"Old woman?"

"Yes. The body was removed weeks ago. The smell probably won't ever go away."

They look around the front room. The couches are spotless; the tables clean. The front window is intact. The stone that Roc threw was in another dimension.

In the dream, she reminds herself.

"We're still trying to determine how they built this?" Linda says. "It's a gorgeous house."

Cyn cringes. *Gorgeous.*

She can see the paltry shelter through the window. She feels left out, ignored. Banished.

"It's built like a fortress," Linda adds. "Retractable shutters, security cameras. Quite an architectural feat."

"What were they doing in here?"

"Well, it's mostly living quarters. The upstairs is all bedrooms and a bathroom. There are a few bedrooms on the first floor, a kitchen down the hall."

There are voices in the back of the house.

They stop at the first bedroom on the left. Cyn is filled with the odd sense of comfort, peeking into someone else's bedroom without their permission. She's not supposed to be in here, but no one can stop her.

The bed is large enough for three people. Probably only slept one. Plastic containers are stacked on the bedspread. The desk drawers are open and empty. So are the dresser drawers. The closet still has a few items.

Cyn walks past the desk. The perfume smells expensive.

"Her name was Barbara Graham." Linda's voice sounds more distant than it should. "She mostly lived in the San Francisco area but had houses all over the world. She was married to a man named Michael Graham."

Cyn is careful not to touch anything, afraid she'll never want to leave if she does. There's a set of crystal figurines gathered on the dresser. She leans in closely. The Buddha looks like it's made of ice.

"Michael went by another name," Linda says. "Mr. Williams."

Cyn looks back. Linda is still in the hall.

"The men from Foreverland used aliases. It was on a tropical island, and when it failed, we discovered this one."

"He said he was lost, that Foreverland collapsed."

"He was still plugged when it did. He's dead."

Cyn's chest contracts sharply. "No, he's not."

"Cynthia, we're still not sure what's going on. We were surprised when you mentioned him yesterday. What we do know is that his body is dead. And so is the body of a boy who was in the bed next to him."

"Sid."

"Yes." Linda's not shocked to hear the name. "Maybe their identities were in Foreverland when it failed and they couldn't get back to their bodies. We assumed that since the body was dead, so were they. But obviously there's more to this than we know. Somehow there was a connection between Foreverland and the world you were trapped inside."

They were lost in the gray for a long time. How long? There's no sense of time in the gray. Just eternity.

And suffering.

Files are stacked in one of the open containers on the bed. A leather spine sticks out among the manila folders. Cyn doesn't ask, just digs it out. Miranda gave that leather-bound journal to her in the dream.

But she remembers what she told her. She warned her that one of the girls is dangerous and to be careful. Miranda was sure it was Roc.

The Fountain of Youth... This is Hell.

Cyn almost laughs. Even surrounded by this posh palace, she has the nerve to comment on suffering. This book will burn nicely in one of the woodstoves.

"How did she do it?" Cyn asks. "How did Patricia recreate a world exactly like this?"

Linda shakes her head. "We don't know. Her brain activity is nothing like we've ever seen. Maybe she's triggered something in the human mind that can just absorb the details around her."

"Miranda gave this to me." Cyn shakes the book.

"Who?"

"The girl with blonde hair—she's upstairs, I'm guessing."

Linda nods slowly. "And she gave you that book?"

"One exactly like it. I never read it, though."

"Why?"

She had lost it, but where?

Cyn thinks, overcome with foggy blankness. That's where those memories are: lost in some inaccessible part of her mind where it's rainy and cloudy.

Gray.

Photos slip out from between the pages. Oceans and boats,

beaches and homes. Old people smiling at the camera, having the time of their life. The photos are glossy, developed from film long ago. One of the photos is older than the others. The woman is younger, her hair not so gray.

Blonde.

"She brought me here."

Linda doesn't answer.

"Do you know where she is?"

"There are some leads."

Cyn traces the outline of Barbara Graham's face, wondering if she ever spoke with her. Of course she did. Her face is so familiar; they probably became friends, probably rode horses and hiked trails. She likes to think that she and Barbara ate dinner together.

She thinks she'd like to meet her again one of these days. And she hates herself for having that thought. But she can't stop. She drops the book and photos in the box, all except the one that shows her blonde hair. That one ends up in her back pocket. If she ever sees her, she's not sure if she'll hug her or knock her out.

Or both.

If she ever sees Mr. Williams, she knows exactly what she'll do. Tell him that he's dead.

Laughter in the back of the house.

They walk past the kitchen, the cabinets open and empty. Boxes on the counter. Everything bagged and tagged for analysis, as if the old women were hiding in coffee cans.

Linda passes Cyn and looks into the back room. "Gentlemen."

The laughter fades off.

There's muttering.

Linda glances back down the hall. The foul odor is stronger, mixed with the fumes of a scented candle. Cinnamon. It doesn't do much to mask death. She breathes through her mouth, but then she can taste it.

Cyn steps inside slowly. *The body is gone.* She wonders if it was back here, sitting in a chair, dead from a heart attack or a guilty conscience. There's another door in the back wall, this one closed.

Monitors wrap around the right side of the room, the largest in the corner. Two men sit in chairs, keyboards on the counter. Thomas is next to them.

Thomas slaps their seats. "Give us five minutes."

The techs tap a few keys, shutting down their work before leaving without looking at Cyn.

"What is this?"

"Headquarters," Thomas says. "These computers monitor the entire camp. It's a lot smaller than the island; that's why the old women only managed half a dozen girls at a time. Still, it may have cost a billion dollars to set it up and maintain its secrecy. Cameras are everywhere, constantly recording and backing up."

Thomas taps on the keyboard. The monitors begin cycling through views. She sees the tents on one monitor, the inside of the bunkhouse on another. She remembers the floodlights but never thought there were cameras. That means Miranda could see them. Before that, the old women had watched them.

They knew everything.

He points at the batteries and generators on the other side of the room.

"That's why there are so many power generators. If you think about it, one wind harvester would be enough for normal living. Their demand was much more than that."

"Patricia," Cyn mutters. Something tugs at her stomach.

Thomas looks at the big monitor. An old woman lies in a very small room with electrodes taped to her head, face, and chest; wires are bundled and connected to machines in the corner, where there's barely enough room to stand.

He looks at Linda, then Cyn. "Yes," he says slowly. "How do you know that?"

"Mr. Williams said she was in that cabin in the woods. We couldn't get inside, though."

And I took her IVs. And now they're gone.

"He said she was the dreamer," she says. "Are the girls inside her? Is that what he meant?"

"We don't really know," Thomas says. "Her brain activity is remarkable. Based on what we've learned about Foreverland and what you said, we're assuming that she's operating like a host computer—an organic server, so to speak. I don't know if you know what that means—"

"I know what that means."

Her emotions boil up. She's tired of this victim crap. She isn't a stupid kid.

"Instead of watching a movie, I was in it. She created a world in her mind and the old ladies sent me there."

"That's right."

"So that's where the girls are right now."

He's nodding. "We believe so, yes."

"Why?"

Thomas balks. Linda's hand is on her shoulder again. "Cynthia," she says in her softest, most supportive therapist voice, "we think they sent you there so you wouldn't come back."

"Come back where?"

Cyn knows, but she asks anyway. She doesn't hear Linda answer. Doesn't need to. The old women bring the destitute, the hopeless, the dregs of society out here to the middle of nowhere. Old women spend millions to sponsor a perfect young woman with a twisted mind in a healthy body.

They don't heal the mind. But they don't waste the body.

Old women unwilling to die.

Yeah, she gets it.

She knows why Barbara Graham brought her out here. And she hates herself even more for hoping that Barbara was nice, that maybe she was trying to help her.

That maybe she was good.

Not a murderer.

"Where is she?" Cyn asks. "Where's Patricia?"

124

THE WHITE TRUCK is next to the helicopter. The men are loading boxes onto it this time, presumably full of evidence for analysis in a real lab.

The techs watch Cyn come out of the brick house. One of them smokes a cigarette. They stare. She looks right back at them, jonesing for a drag.

Do I smoke?

They call Thomas over. Maybe they're talking business. Maybe not. They watch Cyn and Linda walk toward the tents while chatting.

The wind harvesters are still turning, the solar panels following the sun as it peaks. All that energy going to the brick house, powering all that equipment, all those toys. Only a slice of it goes to the cabins, enough so that the girls don't die. They already had a miserable life, just more of the same out here.

That's the point. They made it miserable to be here, which made Foreverland even more inviting. Once the girls got a taste, they wouldn't want to leave.

Desire. Best drug there is.

Important people are in front of the tent on the far right, nearest the brick house. They watch Cyn and Linda approach. Popular for all the wrong reasons.

"Dr. Mazyck." A young lady wearing camouflage approaches. "Mr. Erickson would like to speak with you."

"Certainly."

They follow her to the third tent on the left, the one closest to the dinner house. Camouflage Lady opens the door.

"Wait here, Cynthia," Linda says. "I'll be right out. If you're hungry, you can go to the mess tent. There's a cooler in our tent, too. Help yourself."

Cyn's not hungry. Even if she was, she's not walking closer to the important people still outside the tent. Enough with the staring and wondering.

Cyn hears a deep voice from inside the tent. "How's she doing?"

A generator starts up, eating up the conversation before Linda responds. The important people point at the brick house. Thomas comes around the corner of the garden, shaking hands. They talk a bit, a few heads turning toward Cyn.

Dammit.

It feels like a bear is standing on her chest, a spotlight sizzling on her skin. She steps around the corner of the tent. The generator is too loud to hear anything inside. She's not sure she wants to hear it, anyway.

They're discussing what they're going to do with her—that's what they're doing. *How's she doing? What is she saying? What does she know? Does she remember? Does she remember?*

DOES SHE REMEMBER?

They should be talking about the girls. Not Cyn.

An ATV coasts out of the wood and parks behind the bunkhouse. The rider turns the key off and goes through the back door with an armful of IV bags. *Time for lunch, girls.*

The voices inside the tent rise above the hum of the generator.

"We can't keep her here," he says.

"You can't send her back," Linda says. "Not yet."

The voice fades into the background noise; perhaps they have realized that the walls are only fabric. They want to send her back...where?

Home?

The guys are finished loading the helicopter, sitting on the tailgate and talking to the pilot. It's too far away to know if they're looking at her, but she doesn't wait around.

The path to the little cabin is right around the corner.

She knows the way.

The trees soften the noise from the generators and all-terrain vehicles. Dried sticks break beneath her boots. Up ahead is the turn where the body had lain. Much of the undergrowth around that spot is trampled or uprooted.

The body was here, too.

They probably already know her name, where she came from. What she was doing. At least she's dead. *Good.*

A green tent extends over the front of the cabin, the flaps tied open. There are tables of equipment and computers with bundled cables running through the open door like black snakes. A skinny tech slouches on a folding chair, tapping on a keyboard.

A generator is grinding away behind the cabin, loud enough to mask her footsteps. He doesn't see her until she's in front of the tent.

"Whoa." He pops up, the chair falling over. "You're not allowed back here, not without permission."

He holds up his phone like somehow that's proof no one called to give her permission.

Cyn doesn't pay attention. She sees through the open door. She sees the body lying on an elevated platform. The hands are curled over the chest like dried claws. There's mild pressure building inside her head, the odd sensation that comes with bizarre and unlikely events. The impossible.

If what they say is true, there's a god in there. She contains a universe.

And the world slowly begins to turn. And tilt.

"Hey. You hear me?"

A shadow passes between her and the god.

A hand snatches her arm—

She pivots, raising her arm and twisting, kicking the back of his legs, using leverage to drop him. A fist glances off the side of her head, but she's on top of him. He bucks, but she hooks her heels behind his legs, limiting his range—

Footsteps.

Someone wrenches her arm behind her back. She loses her grip and the tech throws her off, scampering through leafy debris. A knee punches her between the shoulder blades, grinding her cheek into the earth.

"Stop!" Linda comes around the corner. "Get off her! Now!"

The man twists her other arm. Doesn't budge.

"She's all right, Henry." Linda kneels down next to them. "I promise, she won't do anything. Will you, Cynthia?"

She tries to nod, but her head is pressed into the ground.

"I'll take responsibility. Please, just let her up."

The knee eases a bit, testing her. Cyn holds her position and doesn't fight even though the strain on her shoulder aches. All at once Henry jumps back.

Linda helps her sit up. Cyn rubs her wrist, swinging her arm to relieve the pain. Linda rubs the mud off her cheek. "Are you okay?" she whispers.

Cyn nods.

"She didn't have to do that," the skinny tech says, rubbing the back of his head. "She's not supposed to be back here, and she wouldn't answer me. All I did was touch her and she went off."

"I understand, Jeff," Linda says. "We just came back to look at Patricia and she got ahead of me. It won't happen again. Will it?"

They wait for Cyn to respond.

She shakes her head.

Henry crosses his arms. Jeff continues rubbing his head where it was planted in the dirt. They're not moving. Linda places a call. A few seconds later, Jeff's phone buzzes. He answers the call from someone with more power than Linda.

The men stalk off.

Jeff explains how the hell a girl beat his ass.

The room smells like antiseptic.

Cyn stands on the threshold, listening to the hum of machines and the grind of the generator. There's enough room to slip between the wall and the platform.

Her wrinkled skin is like tissue paper wrapped around bones. It's hard to guess her age. A wire protrudes from her forehead, the needle completely embedded. A clear tube runs beneath her nose, her chest slowly rising and falling. Nothing else moves, not even the eyes beneath the lids.

So frail, so brittle and small. A dried-up body on the outside. A universe inside.

Are the girls still cold? Hungry?

Cyn abandoned them, left them to suffer alone. "She was in a vegetative state when her husband experimented on her decades ago. It's controversial technology, one that creates an alternate reality by directly connecting the brain to a computer, transporting the person's identity into a program. The technique is illegal."

"Why?"

Linda considers how much to say. "Too many side effects."

"Like what?"

Another pause. "Reality confusion, for one."

Sure. Which one is the dream?

"Patricia spent many years in a psychiatric ward before her son, Harold Ballard, took her. There are no records of where they went, but Harold is the one that created Foreverland. We can only guess that he used her to develop another alternate universe."

Linda strokes the blanket over the old woman's leg.

"She suffered from a split personality before her husband's experiment. He claims that he was attempting to heal her mind, to place her in a supportive alternate reality before waking her back up. Unfortunately, it locked her inside of her mind."

"You think she's a victim?"

"I don't know. Maybe she doesn't know what's happening; she's just trying to survive, trying to make sense out of her reality like the rest of us. Imagine being the only person in the universe."

Cyn feels like that now. She bends over the old woman's face. It smells like mold.

"We hope to begin interpreting what's inside her, to see her world, like pointing a camera inside her mind. If we can do that, we can communicate with her and the girls. Guide them out."

The wire is right in front of her. It would only take a second to rip it out, to end the girls' suffering. Would the universe turn off? She can't do that. As much as she wants the suffering to stop, she can't take the chance that she'll make it worse.

"How did you get out, Cynthia?" Linda says, sensing her thoughts.

Cyn shakes her head. What good would it do if she knew? They can't tell the girls. All they can do is wait.

And waiting helps nothing.

125

THE GENERATORS CYCLE on and off all night. Cyn hardly notices them anymore. Like the rooster.

But there's no rooster here. No horses.

Just lots of people. Lots of food.

And guilt.

Linda's gone. Probably an early morning meeting. When she's not prodding Cyn to remember, she's talking to the important people. She hasn't said anything about home; maybe they were talking about sending her somewhere else. Like a lab for experimenting. For some reason, this place feels like home, not somewhere else. That should alarm her.

There's a chill this morning, enough to make her hurry getting dressed. She digs a yogurt out of the cooler and peels the foil off the top while stepping outside. Her breath is foggy.

The two helicopters are still in the field. The ATVs are lined up at the dinner house. She sees people sitting at the table through the windows, more of a meeting than a meal. Cyn dishes out the peach-infused yogurt and goes around the back. The back door to the bunkhouse is unlocked.

The inside smells clean.

The nurse isn't there. The door clicks behind her. Nothing moves. Clear bags hang on metal stands, empty tubes running inside skin. She rubs her arm where the stent was removed—still sore.

She's smothered by the silence. *Four bodies, but nobody here.*

The front door opens. A young man sets a box on the floor, washing his hands at the dispenser set up on a small table. He's smaller than Cyn by a few inches, maybe a few pounds, too. He pulls the blanket off of Kat's body, bunching it at her feet, and turns her onto her side, careful not to disturb the tubes and wires.

And needle.

He does the same to Jen and Mad.

"Oh good gracious!" He jumps back. "Have you been standing there the whole time, young lady?"

Cyn doesn't answer.

"Scared the hell out of me." He strips the blanket off of Roc. "Grab her feet."

He doesn't ask if she wants to help, just tells her. And that's enough to get her going. She approaches the foot of the bed, nervous to be that close to her. For some reason, touching her makes it real.

Feels like meat.

"Go wash your hands," he says. "I could use some help setting up bags and rubbing them down. Jackie is still taking care of Sandy and we're a little behind."

Sandy?

Cyn goes to the dispenser and rubs the sanitizing gel on her hands while he opens the box, pulling out five bags. Each contains separate packets that need to be mixed. He sets those aside.

Cyn hangs them on the stands. He connects them.

He shows her how to rub their legs, focusing on the pressure points where bedsores are likely to fester, including the buttocks. The beds, he says, are specifically designed to relieve pressure, but can't prevent sores indefinitely.

"If we weren't doing this, it'd get real smelly in here."

He lets her massage Mad's heels. Cyn rubs the lotion in a circular motion, her eyes following the wire from the girl's forehead to the black box on the table. Cyn's bed is on the other side, the needle still stuck in the tube.

When they're finished, he hands the extra IV bag to Cyn.

"I thought Jackie would be over here by now. Take this over there while I finish up."

"Where?"

"The big house, second floor. I assume she's taking care of Sandy still. I hope she is. The poor girl needs the IV changed."

"Who's Sandy?"

"The little Sleeping Beauty."

"You mean Miranda?"

"No." He flicks the IV bag hanging on Mad's hook. "I mean Sandy. She was in the brick house when we got here, second floor. Maybe she was in that empty bed before that, I don't know."

He points at Miranda's bed.

"All I know is that she's upstairs. Trust me, it'd be a lot easier if she was over here, but there's no way to move her. So if you'd be a dear and take that up to Jackie, I can get this finished."

Cyn stands there, holding the bag.

Miranda could be her middle name. She's just a kid; it wasn't her fault she woke up in the brick house.

But she did.

"You all right?" he asks.

Cyn's breathing loudly, exhaling through her nostrils like a bull pawing the dirt.

She can hear the techs talking in the back room, the keys tapping. The office chair popping. No one stops her from going upstairs.

All the doors are open. Boxes and folders are stacked, the beds stripped, the dressers empty. All except one.

She lies on top of the king-sized bed, hands folded over her stomach. Her blonde hair is splayed on the pillow, eyes closed. She's wearing loose-fitting clothing, rather plain. Probably not what they found her wearing when they discovered this place.

The IV bag is empty.

Cyn walks to the side of the bed. This piece of meat smells better than the others. Looks better.

She was so frail and timid when she woke up, curling up in the corner like a mouse. But she was the one who pulled her out of the fence that first morning. She was the one who sent out winter gear and warned her about Roc. Cyn wanted to protect her.

But then she went inside and never came out.

And neither did the food.

Not a mouse. A rat.

She was so different from the rest of them. It wasn't just her hair or the clothes; it was the way she spoke, the words she used. Once she was safely inside the fence, it was the way she looked at them. The way she wrinkled her nose when she was near, the way she turned her head. Kept her back straight; walked like what came out of her didn't stink.

And the thing in her neck didn't work.

"Miranda Myers is a seventy-seven-year-old woman." Linda is at the door. "She was diagnosed with cancer and was given about six months to live before she relocated out here. When we arrived, we found her body in the back room—the one behind the computer room. Sandy Bell's body was up here. At first, we couldn't understand why she wasn't in the bunkhouse."

Miranda's slender hand is limp. Cyn takes it, a lump rising in her throat. The heavy bracelet slides up her bony arm. *Miranda* is engraved on the gold plate. Before it looked like expensive jewelry. More of a dog collar now.

Cyn massages her hand, kneading the palm with her thumbs.

"We think Miranda was crossing into Sandy's body when Foreverland collapsed."

Sandy.

Is she as scared and meek as she looks right now? Or maybe she was scrappy, mean, and nasty like the rest of them. *I'll never know.*

"Did she introduce herself as Miranda?" Linda digs softly with the therapist voice.

Cyn brushes the blonde hair from the young face while rage and sadness tangle inside. She resists the urge to yank the hair from her pretty little head.

It's just a body. Sandy's body.

"She came out of the brick house when we woke up, like this innocent, scared little girl that didn't belong out here. Didn't belong with us."

"Do you belong here?"

"That's not what I mean. She didn't know anything about this. She was afraid of Roc. She was cold and hungry, like the rest of us. She went inside the brick house and sent out clothes for us to wear."

Linda takes the other hand, massaging it like Cyn.

"Her name is Miranda," Cyn says. "That's all I know."

"Where do you think Sandy went?"

Cyn shakes her head. "How am I supposed to know?"

"Right now, we think Sandy—her identity or soul, whatever you want to call that true nature—was pulled out of the body and replaced with Miranda's identity. It's a body swap, but we don't know where the girls go once they're pulled out of their bodies."

Where do you go when you don't need a body?

That's the question everyone wants answered. Just because you have an answer, though, doesn't mean it's right. Maybe Miranda knows. Maybe she knows where she sent Sandy once she pushed her out of her body for good.

Yeah, Miranda knows.

The sleeping girl's lips begin to quiver.

Linda doesn't notice; she doesn't see the wisp of smoke leak from the corner of Miranda's mouth. She doesn't feel the frigid grasp of misty fingers ooze from the young girl's lips, doesn't see the vapor slither up Cyn's arms, creeping around her neck. Doesn't see it seep into Cyn's vision.

Paralyzing her.

Dragging her into the eternal gray where her soul dissolves. Where she becomes thinner. Transparent. Yet she still feels the gut-dropping fall, the endless collapse of her identity.

The falling.

Always falling—forever and ever—in the Nowhere.

"Cyn?"

Cyn jerks away from the hand on her arm, her chest pumping air that's thick and stale. Linda takes both of Cyn's hands, cradling them gently.

Miranda is motionless. Lips sealed.

"We all had the same dream." Cyn's mouth is dry. "Every night."

Linda patiently squeezes, staying present. Giving her space to work through what's coming to light.

Cyn tries to swallow and says, "We would walk up to a cliff and look down. But there wasn't a bottom. There was just...it was just fog."

She hesitates, thoughts freezing.

"What's in the fog?"

Tendons spring from her wrists. Fingers clenching. Memories push through a thick veil. She remembers what's out there, remembers stepping through the fence at the edge of the trees, falling into the gray dream where memories pounced on her like demons.

Her stepfather is out there. Dope. Violence.

Desperation. Loneliness.

"Fear," Cyn says.

Linda squeezes, reassuring her. Cyn doesn't really see her, just feels her. But there's something else out there, too. They are out there. The girls that were shoved from their bodies. The boys from Foreverland, too.

And Sandy.

Everyone that was pushed from their body was thrown into the Nowhere like fistfuls of ash, where they would eternally dissolve. Forever fall.

She remembers that. She remembers the falling.

Arms out. Tipping into the abyss.

Merging with the gray. Embracing the fear.

And falling out of the dream.

Cyn clenches Linda like a ledge. Feet dangling. Linda allows her to squeeze as if her life depends on it. Cyn looks away from the bed, breaking the trance. Indentions remain on Linda's arm.

They remain next to the bed, holding hands. Cyn's breathing

returns to normal. The fear recedes. Nothing escapes Sandy's lips; her eyes remain motionless. *This is not the dream.*

Jackie arrives to connect an IV. They help her turn the body, rubbing her sore spots with lotion. Even though she doesn't know Sandy, Cyn cares for her body. She deserves that much.

They leave the brick house and stand on the porch. The weather is warming. Cyn doesn't tell Linda what she remembers.

I know how I escaped.

126

THE SUN IS UP.

Linda quietly walks through the tent and pulls the curtain aside. She watches Cyn's chest gently rise and fall then grabs a few things off her desk. The door closes.

Cyn opens her eyes.

That's the second time Linda has checked on her. And the second time Cyn was pretending to sleep. Linda knows she isn't sleeping well at night and tells her to sleep in as late as she wants. The morning will get along just fine without her.

At night, the bed feels like a cell.

Cyn wishes for the nights of falling into dead sleep, even misses the gray dreams, standing on the ledge. Better than the dreams she's having now, waking in the night like a pillow has been pushed over her face.

Linda woke her up sometime in the night and said she was making noise. Cyn doesn't remember the dream, only remembers drowning in a sea of emotions. Her pillow was damp.

She had waited there, listening to Linda fall asleep before sneaking through the tent and gently closing the door. The wind harvesters were still.

The moon full.

A couple of guys were on the front porch of the dinner house, a cigarette cherry streaking from lap to mouth. Their chatter easily carried across the garden. She went back inside, where sleep came in bite-sized pieces.

Now she dozes in and out to the lullabies of trucks and generators, wondering how far she can go in an ATV with a full tank of gas. There's a bag of clothes under her bed that Linda doesn't know about. Cyn has an urge to escape, to get away from people before they discover her secret. She keeps her memories tightly sealed, away from Linda's prying questions. There are more secrets inside her, and she'd be fine if they stayed hidden from her. She's had enough of the truth; she just wants some peace. If they're thinking of sending her home, then she'll have to steal a fully loaded ATV.

Home.

That word is supposed to feel warm and fuzzy. To Cyn, it feels like drowning. She doesn't have many memories of home. There are giant puddles of ink on the fabric of her mind, blotting memories out of existence, keeping much of what's inside her hidden. Maybe those ink spots were there before the old women punched her with the needle.

Doesn't matter. She's not going home. She's not going anywhere before she fixes things.

Cyn sits up slowly. She looks around the curtain just to make sure the tent's empty. There's a mirror under Linda's bed; she saw her fussing with it the other day. She finds it in a plastic bag. It fits in the palm of her hand.

Her forehead looks normal except for the tiny black hole. It's still sore, but at least it's not red and swollen. She can't move her head too quickly or it throbs. She frames the hole with two fingers, tender to the touch. The stent is a tiny knot embedded in her skull.

A going-away gift.

Her green eyes are sunk inside the sockets. She pulls at her blonde hair, barely finger length. She touches her reflection.

Was the dream just another layer of reality in the mirror that I've peeled away? Is this just another dream inside a dream? Is there another layer of reality below this? Will I wake up and realize that this, right here, right now, is a dream, too?

How many layers are there?

"It'll go away."

Cyn drops the mirror. Linda is holding the curtain back.

"Feeling rested?"

Cyn doesn't answer and wants to hide the mirror under her foot. Feels stupid for getting caught gazing at her reflection. It's not why she was looking in the mirror.

"I'll let you get dressed."

Cyn's sitting there in panties and a tank top, no bra.

"You hungry?" Linda calls from the other side while rummaging through stuff. "I saved you breakfast in the mess tent. If you're not feeling up to it, there's a can of Ensure in the cooler. Make sure you drink that. The doctor wants to see you this morning. If you're not eating, they're going to put an IV in your—*crap!*"

She drops something. A number of things get stacked. A drawer shuts. Linda mutters to herself.

"I've got a meeting in a few minutes, but I want us to go for a little hike across the meadow today, get a little fresh air. What do you say?"

The curtain pulls back.

Cyn hasn't moved. Still half-naked. "Hike sounds good."

"You all right?" Linda sits on her bed across from her. "You want to talk?"

"No. Just waking up."

She puts up her best smile. The smile sucks, but it's good by her standards. Linda hesitates, but she buys it. She knows things aren't easy. Cyn's tough. Right now she's just hanging in there.

Linda has no idea what Cyn's thinking.

"Breakfast, then?" Linda asks.

"I'll get it."

Linda pauses, looking inside her. She can't see the thoughts, but she's satisfied enough to stand. She reaches for the curtain.

"How much time do you think has passed in there?" Cyn asks. "It's been a week since I got out—how long do you think it's been inside the dream? A month?"

"We don't know. Why?"

"Just wondering." She stares into space.

Again, Linda tries to look inside her. She waits to hear more. She's not leaving until Cyn spills a thought or two.

"They could be dead," Cyn says.

"We don't know that."

"I left them."

"It's not your fault."

Cyn shakes her head. She's thinking. There are thoughts she wants to spit out. But if she does, Linda will know what she's thinking. She can't have that. She bites down, swallowing the words.

"Hey." Linda sits on the bed. "You sure you're all right?"

Cyn focuses on her, faking another smile. "Just a dream I had last night, that's all."

"The gray?"

"No. It's nothing. I'll get dressed, grab some breakfast."

Linda doesn't want to leave. If she didn't have a meeting, she wouldn't let her out of her sight. She'll probably call someone as soon as she leaves, have Thomas or someone keep an eye on the tent. Watch where Cyn goes.

That's why Cyn dresses quickly.

The nurse is sitting in the back of the bunkhouse, poking at the tablet in his lap. He looks up, smiling.

"You're a little late to help, darling." He goes back to his tablet and says, "Stick around, the girls need to be turned in half an hour."

Cyn stands quite still, looking at the walls, the rafters and beds, taking a mental snapshot of what it looks like, how it smells and feels. Memorizing this layer of reality.

She walks around, stopping at each bed. The bodies still uninhabited. Kat, Jen, Roc, and Mad. All of them still somewhere else. Miranda's bed still empty.

Sandy, she reminds herself.

Cyn's bed is still empty. The sheets tucked under the mattress, the wire coiled on the small table. She slows her breathing, swallows, and walks to the bed.

Walk. Don't run.

She sits on the edge, sinking into the gel-infused mattress. It molds to her bottom. There's an indention in the pillow, waiting to cradle her head. She reaches slowly and picks up the glass vial.

The surgical steel needle, suspended in the clear gel, gleams.

"Honey, don't touch that," he says. "That needs to stay sterile."

Her fingers shake. She pinches the wire at the base of the needle. Her pulse flutters in her fingertips.

"Sweetheart." The nurse stands. "You need to put that down."

It slides from the rubber stopper. The tip is blunt. She brackets the stent with two fingers—

"Don't." Linda's at the door, hand raised. "Please."

Cyn opens her eyes. The needle lowers.

No one moves.

"I can get them," she whispers.

"I can't let you."

"You know what they're going through? If they're alive, they're cold and hungry. And I can get them out."

"There's time, Cynthia. We'll figure out how to communicate. They'll learn how to escape, just like you."

"You've been real good to me."

"Don't do this."

Cyn grimly nods. Their eyes engage. Linda only makes it half a step, hand reaching—

An icicle slides between Cyn's eyes.

Her head goes numb.

DECEMBER

Meet me at the edge.
  Where we all fall down.

127

CYN STUMBLES OUT of the trees, the white ground rushing towards her. She doesn't get her hands out, landing face-first in the white pluff. Doesn't bother clawing out of the drift, hunkering inside, protected from the wind.

Can't feel her legs.

Her hands.

Face.

The shivers are electric. She'll die out here, in the meadow, winter's hand wrapped around her throat. *No.*

She emerges from the snow dune, inhaling an icy breath dusted with crystals, chilling her from the inside. But there's something over there, across the meadow, over the barren white stretch. She wipes her eyes, but the world still sways like a storm-tossed ship.

She starts again.

Crawling. Eventually stumbling. Foot in front of foot.

Fall.

Up again.

The crossing is lost in time, but she emerges from a snowdrift. The cabins are there.

Her jaw chatters, her teeth chattering like frozen cubes. She wipes her eyes, trying to focus. *There are only two wind harvesters*, she thinks.

The bunkhouse...it's...*gone*. The blackened walls are sagging, spattered with icy white patches. The rafters poke through scorched holes. A white blade sticks out of the ground like a giant plastic knife.

The dinner house is on fire, too. Smoke blossoms from the roof. She's too late. It's all burning to the ground; the girls have nowhere to go.

I'm too late. This is my fault.

Her feet hit the ground like dead pegs. Four steps, maybe five, and she crashes into another puff of snow. Up again.

Little by little she crosses, she finds the other side. Discovers the dinner house isn't on fire; the chimney is belching a long white cloud. The bunkhouse, though, is still gutted, black and dead.

Cyn crawls onto the porch, fighting to breathe. She reaches up, hand shaking against the slick doorknob. Unable to feel the cold steel, unable to grasp and turn it. She collapses against the door, her head hitting the thick wood. She doesn't have the strength to raise her arm, afraid her hand will shatter if she knocks.

Thump, thump, thump. She bangs her head.

What if they're dead? What if everyone is gone? She may not make it out. She could be trapped here for eternity. And she was out, but she came back.

"I know you can hear me." Her lips hardly move. "Let us out, Patricia. Don't do this to us, please."

Thump, thump, thump.

"Please."

Thump.

"We don't deserve..."

Cyn closes her eyes. So tired.

So, so tired.

She doesn't feel the door move. Or the floor on the back of her head. But she hears the voices, feels the hardwood sliding beneath her.

And the warmth of a fire.

The ache begins in her legs.

Feeling is coming back. She still can't feel her fingers. Her tongue is a lump of meat.

She's leaning against the wall next to the stove.

Kat and Mad are knocking snowy crust from her legs and arms, rubbing her fingers, her cheeks. Their words are just sounds, no different than a dog barking or a brook babbling.

"Don't." Mad's voice. "Keep snow packed on that."

She's talking about the backs of her feet. Kat agrees.

"Mmmrggg." Cyn works her useless lips, her tongue not helping. She's met with a crushing embrace. Kat and Mad squeeze her at the same time.

"You came back," Mad says.

Cyn wipes her eyes, running her tongue over her gums. The girls come into focus. They're gaunt. Eyes set deeply. Open sores on Kat's cheeks. Mad's gums are receding. Roc is lying under the table behind them, wrapped in blankets, her bruised face peeking out. Blood caked on her bent nose.

They start asking questions. It becomes noise again. Cyn raises her hand.

"We've got to go. Now."

"It didn't work," Kat says. "When we grabbed the tree, it didn't work for us."

Pain is sneaking up Cyn's legs, spilling nausea into her stomach. She pulls her feet up so her heels aren't touching the floor. The snow on the back of her legs is pink. The shivering eases, lifting the veil on the cold fear hiding beneath.

"You saw the cliff," Cyn says, pushing the words out. "When you touched the tree, you went to dream."

"Yeah, but—"

"Don't run from it. You have to fall."

Kat and Mad don't answer. They know what's out there, what it feels like. They feel it every time they go to sleep.

"I know you're scared, there's fear in the unknown. Fear in the gray. Allow that. Fall into it."

Cyn shudders, biting back the urge to heave.

"Allow yourself to fall...and you'll wake up."

They're nodding. They don't mean it, but they're nodding.

"Trust me."

Roc throws the cover back and sits up. Her face is purplish, left eye swollen shut. But she's nodding. She knows.

We all fall.

Cyn looks around. "Where's Jen?"

The front door slams open. Winter howls inside.

Mad stifles a sob.

128

MIRANDA IS NO LONGER HORRIFIED.

Disgusted, sure.

She hides her face in her hands and pushes. The smell is of no consequence. Her olfactory senses have long been corrupted, the candles used up. Still, she closes her eyes and finishes her business, to get it over with. The lid snaps into place and she slides it next to the water heater.

She doesn't enjoy hovering bare-assed over a five-gallon bucket to move her bowels.

The furnace rarely turns on. The thermostat is in the hallway. Mr. Williams has control of that. He's conserving power. He also has a space heater out there to keep his bunions from freezing off.

Miranda has five layers of clothing. She only has to brave the elements when it's time to pull out the bucket.

Her food is stacked against the back door, the only room she still refuses to investigate. She cracks the lid on a bottle of water and takes a tiny sip. Not too much—just enough to keep from dehydrating. The food supply is dwindling.

And she's not leaving the back room.

Ever.

When the food is gone, she'll starve. She's sure of it.

She can't say she's accustomed to hunger. It's still there, twisting her stomach like a dishrag, wringing out every ounce of comfort. She thinks of it constantly, but still, it's not as bad as it used to be. Maybe when you see atrocity worse than hunger, it creates a sort of peaceful perspective.

Why are we still here? He said the dream would end when Patricia's food was gone.

That's when she stopped believing him, when she no longer thought this was a dream. Cyn is gone. They said she found her way out, just grabbed onto a branch and disappeared. All the rest tried, they grabbed it the same way and nothing happened. But Miranda is sure that something else went down. They killed her or something weird.

Mr. Williams did something.

Monster.

She saw what he did to Jen—she watched it on the security camera. Sid was right there with him, stood there like a lobotomized goon and watched, doing nothing.

Miranda did something.

She hauled food out of the pantry, as much as she could get before they returned. And then she locked the door. All it took was an override command on the computer. She'd been watching Mr. Williams operate the system, learning where to go and what to do. She acted stupid, like she didn't understand.

But he found out when he got back.

He and Sid banged on the door for hours. Mr. Williams begged and pleaded, promised he wouldn't hurt her. He just needs to use the computers, that's all. "Please, Miranda. This is hurting all of us."

Liar. *Monster*.

And when the promises didn't work, he proved it. He threw every name ever invented at her. Whore. Bitch. Murderer. A few others. None of them made sense.

He quit after a few days. But he left Sid to hammer the door with the back side of an ax. The clank of metal on metal drove deep inside her skull. It went on for weeks. If there were a button to end her life, she would've pressed it.

Finally, that stopped, too.

Miranda takes another sip and replaces the lid. She takes a package of ramen noodles out of a box and tears open a corner, saving the packet of seasoning for later. It will spice up the water and provide a dose of salt. The noodles are brittle, chalky.

She sits in the office chair, taps the keyboard, and leans back. The monitors come to life. The old man is in the kitchen, preparing tea, looking out the window at a bleak and angry world. Sid is vegetating on the couch. He probably wouldn't eat if Mr. Williams didn't put food in front of him.

The big monitor shows the view from the brick house across the garden, only hints of crops long since shriveled and buried beneath snowdrifts. Only one lump remains in the garden. It shouldn't be there.

She doesn't look at that.

Winter wind continues to scour the land, piling snow against the buildings and sides of trees. The charred remains of the bunkhouse are visible, skeletal and empty. Only two wind harvesters spin near the barn, the other a bladeless post pointing at the sky, rendered useless during a bitter storm.

Smoke puffs out the dinner house chimney. The girls are walking past the windows. They usually huddle around the stove, a stack of wood pilfered from the bunkhouse wreckage. The kitchen is nearly barren. They only move to keep the fire stoked. Or to do business in the corner.

They don't even have a bucket.

There are no footsteps in the snow. Winter wiped them out of existence. The sun went missing behind the steel clouds weeks ago. The forecast is easy.

Misery.

With one wind harvester down, power is limited. But that's not why it's so cold. Thankfully Mr. Williams can't shut the back room down from out there. He would if he could. And then Miranda would surely die.

Miranda learned the computer system. She could remotely lock and unlock all the doors, including the kitchen doors in the dinner house. That explained the electronic keycard locks.

In a fit of dreadful boredom, Miranda popped open the very back room once, her pulse bouncing in her throat, but when the smell oozed out, she kicked it closed with a definitive snap.

There are things worse than a bucket full of crap.

She even turned off the fence. It's a huge power hog. Roc isn't going anywhere near the brick house. Not anymore. And even if she did, she's not getting into the back room.

No one is.

Miranda nibbles on the block of noodles, stopping when it's half gone, wrapping up the remains for later. She chases it with a swallow of water and sits back to watch the cameras, the scenes rarely changing. Patricia looks like a dried apple, her lips puckered with radial lines. *Why won't she die?*

She puts her head back, closing her eyes.

Sleeping is hard. She tried to do push-ups and sit-ups to wear herself out, but got too weak. There's just not enough food to burn calories. But she's tired and figures she can get a couple hours of uninterrupted sleep. She crawls under the counter next to the computers where it's warmest, where there's a bed of coats to curl up in.

She drifts off. No dreams. Never a dream. Just sweet, sweet slumber. The only joy to be found in this dreadful world.

Bang.

She lifts her head, not sure if she heard that. Sometimes she hears voices when she's falling asleep, like someone is right next to her, whispering in her ear. Did she imagine it?

BANG.

The front door.

Miranda scurries out from under the counters and, getting down on her knees, taps the monitors awake. She cycles through the cameras...

Sid is running alongside the garden, forcing his way through the dinner house front door. Mr. Williams trudges along the path Sid left in the snow, walking as fast as a shrinking old man can walk.

Miranda punches a key.

The dinner house interior flickers on one of the smaller monitors. The girls are gathered around the stove. One is leaning against the wall. Her face is agony.

It can't be.

129

Sid's mouth hangs open. A tooth is missing.

Kat and Mad scramble to the corner and come up wielding broken table legs like crude swords. Each takes a side of the table, ready to cut him off. Roc stays put.

He doesn't come after them, instead acting more like a roadblock, letting the bitter chill steal warmth from the stove. Cyn chatters, looking for an extra club, something she can swing. Nothing's within reach, not that she could grip it.

Sid steps aside.

The old man climbs the porch, limping inside.

A ball of anger erupts in Cyn's belly, burning through the fear and hypothermia, a hearth trapped inside, artificially warming her will. If only she had the strength to stand.

He's weathered, like the sky leached gray into his flesh. A withering leaf. A decaying soul.

Sid closes the door behind him.

Mr. Williams rubs his hands, surveying the room. His dead gaze falls on Cyn. "Your stupidity is my good fortune."

"I know who you are," Cyn says.

"Your moronic friends could not find their way back to the gate. You will take me there now." He flicks his hand. "Pick her up."

Sid comes around Mad's side of the table. The club glances off his forearm. He snatches her by the coat and slams her into the wall. The club clatters on the floor. Kat comes over the table, but Sid wields Mad like a shield.

"Stop!" Cyn tries to shout. "Stop it!"

Sid charges Kat, using Mad as a battering ram. Kat jumps on the table with a club.

"Stop." Mr. Williams raises his hand.

Sid freezes like he pushed a button.

"He killed her, Cyn!" Kat points at Mr. Williams without taking her eyes off of Sid. "He killed Jen!"

Cyn sits up, but all the anger in the world can't help her stand.

"He took her out back and killed her, dragged her into the garden. I saw it. I saw her body."

Mad sobs quietly, the coat bunched around her face, hiding her tears.

"This is a dream; she is not dead," Mr. Williams says to Cyn. "You know that to be true now."

"She still suffered."

"And suffering will continue unless *you take me to the gate!*"

Blood vessels emerge on the old man's gray complexion. He paces at the front of the room.

"I am out of patience, girls. Your suffering ends when you get me to the gate. I will leave this world and you'll be relieved of your suffering."

"Kill me," Cyn says. "I'm not taking you."

"There's a problem with that, young lady. Death will not relieve you of suffering—you will simply be reborn in the dream to suffer again. You will forget, I will find you, and then here you'll be in the cabin again. But you have a choice. Take me to the gate and you will never see me again. It's your choice to suffer."

Cyn shakes her head. "Liar."

"*Use your head!*" He thumps his scalp with a single finger. "Why do you think there are so many marks on your wall? Our worlds were linked. You came to Foreverland, you interacted with the boys, but now Foreverland is dead and this godforsaken place cycles over and over and over. You wake up with no memories and I am sent back to the Nowhere, into the gray, lost until I can find my way back. I will not go back there, not again. This time it ends. I am leaving this world."

"Where will you go?"

He stops pacing. They share a knowing glance. *His body is dead. Where will he go?*

She knows.

He'll take one of their bodies. He'll wake in the bunkhouse in Cyn's body or Kat's or Roc's. Linda will be there and Thomas will ask him to remember how he got out and how the girls are doing...

And they'll have no idea.

"Sid," the old man says, "push her face against the stove."

"No!" Kat grabs the back of Mad's coat. Sid lets go with one hand and pops her in the forehead. Kat grabs Mad with both arms, pulling her back.

Roc grabs the table and stands.

"Stop it!" Cyn says.

"Where is it?" The old man holds up the fob, thumb on the button. *"Where is the gate?"*

"Call him off!"

"Tell me! Now!"

"Make him stop!"

Roc starts around the table. Mr. Williams points the fob at her—

"I'll tell you," Cyn says. "Make him stop."

Mr. Williams raises his hand. "This is your last chance. If not, I put all of you asleep. You will wake with half your faces melted to the stove. And I will continue experimenting with you until you do."

"It's due south—"

"No!" Kat shouts. "Don't tell him—he'll kill us once he knows."

Mr. Williams aims the fob at her like a weapon. The button clicks. Kat cringes.

Click. Click, click, click.

She opens her eyes. Still awake. Still standing.

Mr. Williams looks at the ceiling. "You little bitch."

"It doesn't work," Kat says.

"Sid, get over here."

Sid throws Mad and runs to his master's side. The girls pick up their weapons. Roc, too. The old man pockets the fob and lifts his chin, masking the doubt and fear quivering just beneath the surface.

"Girls," he says, "if you do not drop those sticks, I will have Sid beat them out of your hands. You know what he is capable of doing."

He nods at Roc.

"Stalemate," Cyn manages to say. Her legs are coming alive, waking in pain. "If that animal comes, girls, break his legs. Both of them. Without Sid, the old man is helpless. He'll never reach the gate."

The girls lift the clubs, each big enough to snap a bone, shatter a knee. He can't take all of them. They'll lose, sure. But so will the old man.

Stalemate.

The old man blinks heavily.

"I'm taking the girls to the gate," Cyn says. "I can't stop you from following, but if you interfere with us, then I'll stop and you'll never find it. We all die. We start over and you go back out to the Nowhere."

Mr. Williams's lips stretch over his perfect teeth. He calculates the offer. Without the fob, without Sid...there is no counter.

"Do we have a deal?" she asks.

He opens the door and says with his back turned, "If you attempt to lose us, someone will suffer greatly."

He goes outside, waiting on the porch. Arms folded. Sid follows.

"Can you walk?" Kat squats down.

No way she can walk. She closes her eyes, putting her arms up. Kat and Mad pick her up. Her skin burns with fever. The pressure on her legs is too much, like a thousand hot pins stabbing in and out.

The room dims. She loses a few moments of awareness, panting to stay alert. Yearning for the cold to take the pain back.

This body is almost done.

Just a mile, that's all. A mile and it's over. One way or another.

"Stop," she grunts, leaning against the table.

Mad gathers up the extra coats and sweaters they were using for bedding. The old man is still on the porch, huddled against the cold. He turns to see what the hell is taking so long. Roc is just inside the doorway, glaring back.

Her eyes are dead and buried in bruised flesh. She swapped out her club for a broken chair leg that's splintered and shaped like a blade.

"Don't," Cyn says.

Roc adjusts her grip, her knuckles white.

"Whatever happened, drop it. They're nothing. You understand, Roc? Nothing. You can escape."

"Here." Mad shoves gloves at them and wraps a scarf around Cyn's neck. Kat stretches another coat over the ones she's already wearing. Mad pulls a hat over her head.

Roc stares.

"You need to say it," Cyn says. "I need to hear it."

Her jaw flexes. Nostrils flare.

Roc puts gloves on. Mad hands her a wad of scarves and hats. Those go on, too. She nods once.

Good enough.

Cyn throws her arms over Kat's and Mad's shoulders. They prop her onto her feet. She can't support her weight. Just moving steals her breath. They drag her to the door.

"We need to get Miranda," Mad adds.

"No," Cyn grits. "She's dead."

"I just saw her in the window this morning."

"Not what I mean. Miranda's dead, she just doesn't know it."

Mad pulls back. "You serious? You really going to leave her? Kat? We can't do that; we ain't like the old man, Kat. We got our differences, but we can't leave her, you heard what he said—"

"That's not Miranda!" Cyn grabs a handful of Mad's scarf and hisses through clenched teeth, "Trust me. She's dead."

She lets go, lunging forward. Kat keeps her from falling and hauls her through the door. Roc follows, weapon in hand.

Mad eventually comes out.

130

THEY MARCH INTO THE MEADOW, a desolate stretch of snowy dunes. The figures fade into the blizzard, icy wind swirling, scraping the land, enveloping the small band of girls in its cold grip. Disappear.

Miranda pushes buttons, zooming the camera's view to maximum, focusing on the two figures that straggle behind them. The old man leans heavily on the boy, pushing through the snowy mounds.

The men fade in the swirling snow, too.

And she's alone.

This time, she's really alone. They're not coming back. They're escaping. Or dying.

Her hand shaking, she clicks through multiple screens. The door clicks. Miranda yanks it open, rushing into the hallway and through the house, pulling on the front door. The storm throws it open, the hinges groaning.

Barefoot, Miranda runs down the steps, snow pushing up her pant legs, reaching her knees. The world of white blurs, her eyes filling with water.

The wintry blast snatches the air from her lungs.

The cruel world grinds her pursuit to a halt. Even if she got dressed, if she traipsed over the frozen meadow, she wouldn't find them. The wind has already scoured their tracks from existence.

If they don't escape, they'll die. Either way, they're not coming back.

Really alone.

She begins shivering, her chin rattling uncontrollably. She runs inside and closes the door, sliding to the floor. Melting snow puddles between her numb toes.

The smell of death fills the house.

Cyn abandoned her. Miranda was the one that saved them. She was the one that disabled the zapper. If it wasn't for her, Mr. Williams would have knocked them out; he'd be doing things to them right now, like the things he did to Jen. And they couldn't stop them.

Miranda saved them.

And they left her.

Miranda is dead.

She said it, she knows something. Miranda isn't dead; she's sitting on the floor, holding the panic at bay. Staring down the hall, the metal door swung open.

The back door in view.

Cyn said it like she knew Miranda would hear it. She wanted her to hear it, wanted her to know something. Miranda looks at her hands, turns them over, runs her fingers over the bracelet and the name engraved on the gold plate like they're proof she's alive.

I'm alive.

But even she knows something isn't right. She's always known. Miranda pushes herself up, wiggling her fingers and toes to bring back sensation, wishing the cold could snuff out the fear squirming in her stomach. Wishing she didn't have to do this.

Wishing she wasn't alone.

She pauses in the back room. There's nothing holding her back now. No reason to wait. A few clicks with the mouse, and the lock on the back door whirs.

Snick.

The door moves but doesn't open. Waiting for someone to pull, to make the decision to go back there, to look, to see what's been hiding in the back all this time. For someone to summon the courage to see the truth.

Her hand quivers on the knob, but not because it's cold.

This time, she grabs it.

This time, she pulls it.

The moist odor of death hits her, filling her sinuses, sticking to the back of her throat. She gags before covering her face, her eyes tearing up. She uses both hands to filter the foul air.

It's dark.

A small green light glows on a monitor somewhere in the back. She doesn't search for a light switch, letting her eyes adjust, letting the smell seep out like a tomb that's been steeped in death for far too long.

Two examination tables are in the center, side by side.

A large metal lamp hangs from the ceiling directly over them. One table is empty. There's a bag on the other, brown vinyl. A zipper bisects the center. The corners bulge with liquid.

There are no clear windows to see inside.

She wouldn't look anyway.

She knows what's in there.

A white tag is attached to the zipper dangling at the top. She pushes through the dense air, adjusting one hand over her face, pinching her nose. She flips the tag over, bending over to read it.

Miranda Myers. Dispose.

The room tilts. Begins to turn.

She uses both hands to cover her face again.

Because it can't be. Because Miranda is alive, she's standing next to the table.

Not in that bag.

Something touches her hair.

She jerks back. A coil of wire dangles on a hook suspended from the ceiling, a needle attached to the end, pointing at the table.

Pointing at the bag.

She shakes her head, backing away. The room is dusty. The counters are covered with open journals and stacks of books, scattered pens and paper clips. A chair lies on its side. The computers are dead.

Except for the one across from the tables.

The one with the green light.

Her heart thumps in her throat. Ears ringing.

She's hardly breathing when she reaches down and touches the green light. When the monitor flashes.

Two photos appear side by side, separated by a column of data. One is an image of an old woman, liver spots on her puffy cheeks; her eyes, saggy. The gray hair is thin.

The other is a young girl with blonde hair and a fair complexion. It's Miranda. But that's not what the name at the bottom indicates.

Sandy, it says. *Crossover complete.*

The young girl is Sandy. And the old woman has a name, but Miranda doesn't read it. She knows what it says. She knows who she is.

What she's done.

"This is the Fountain of Youth," Mr. Williams had said.

For Sandy, the place is the River of Death.

Suddenly, the house feels like a coffin. The walls are tighter and thicker. The world, heavier.

She drops her hands, willfully inhaling the scent of death. Accepting it. Gagging on it.

Staggers into the hall.

Into the front room.

Hand on the window. The glass is so cold.

The empty world is cloaked in eternal winter.

131

TIME IS ERASED BY PAIN.

There were trees and rocks, hills and valleys. And snow.

Cyn is draped over Kat and Mad. At times she's limp, her feet dragging behind them, carving a line in the snow. Fever rages inside, making the shivering more violent. Her bladder swells with urine, but she resists the urge to let it go. *What does it matter now?*

Roc keeps an eye on the old man, who is following behind at a safe distance. Cyn guides them, but she's not sure. It's hard to think, her thoughts flowing like molasses. And everything is white.

The trees creak overhead, the branches waving, occasionally snapping. The storm batters the valley as they exit the forest. The girls sway like the trees but keep their balance. Cyn rests her chin on her chest, concentrating on each step, looking every so often.

She's just not sure.

"There." Mad says it. "Look at that."

They force Cyn to stand taller, pulling her arms across their shoulders. At first she only sees a canvas smudged with whites and grays. She blinks heavily, licking her lips.

A hill.

A tree.

The branches without needles. Without snow. An artifact, of sorts, resisting the winter storm, not of this world. A gate to another.

She tries to turn her head. The girls turn her to see the old man emerge from the trees, Sid at his side. Mr. Williams looks up.

He sees it, too.

He knows.

"Go," Cyn says. "Remember...to fall."

"We're not leaving you," Kat says.

"I can get out, don't worry." *Lie.*

The old man says something. Sid lets go of him.

And the girls are running, pulling Cyn up the hill. Roc plows ahead of them, hopping through the knee-deep snow. Kat shouts, but Roc doesn't slow down, bounding for the exit with a wolf at her heels.

The girls struggle to breathe.

Cyn's head bounces; the world falters.

She's slammed through the snow and into the ground beneath, the frigid fluff falling over her. The shouts are muffled. A dull thud of a boot on her back.

Her head cracks beneath another boot. Lights sparkle.

Pressure on top. Someone holding her beneath the surface.

Suffocating. Drowning.

The weight rolls off. She pushes up, her face in the wind, gulping air. The world is blurry. Spinning. An animal is devouring Kat and Mad.

Not an animal.

Sid.

His long arms are flailing. The girls covering up, screaming. They're too far away. Cyn crawls, but she can't reach them, can't help them, can't stop the animal thrashing—

Another crash.

Bodies tumble down the slope, slamming into her. Arms and legs, elbows and knees. Screaming. Roc growls like cornered prey, slashing at Sid's face. Sid rolls over to get leverage and falls into Cyn's lap.

She locks her arms around his waist.

She latches her hands together, clasping each wrist. She wills her arms to clamp her dead fingers down. Sid throws his weight backwards and they roll down the slope. She comes up for air.

"Gooooo!"

She can't see them.

But she feels them hesitate.

Feels them bolt for the top of the hill. For the gate.

And then she closes her eyes. She buries her head against Sid's back, avoids the wild elbows, resists the twisting and rolling. Her fingers slip but don't release.

Down the hill they go.

She only hopes that the girls fall.

All the way back to reality. To the truth.

Her arms are empty.

She doesn't remember letting go.

A shadow passes over her. She looks up, snow melting on her lips. Mr. Williams is looking down. Sid is holding him up, blood streaming from both nostrils and dripping from his chin.

Mr. Williams clutches his chest, leaning against the boy.

"Wait...until I'm gone," he wheezes. "Then finish her."

"You'll leave him here?" The words are long and slurred on her slow tongue. "He'll go back to the Nowhere."

He looks up the slope, trying to catch his breath. "He doesn't know any different. A blissful idiot."

The old man rustles the boy's hair, mouthing the words *good boy*. He starts the climb, falling twice. It takes great effort to get up, to find his balance. Cyn holds out hope he'll tumble down, that he'll lack the strength to reach up, that somehow he'll freeze to the ground like a stone.

He slips only two steps from the gate, resting on his knees. He looks up, a ghostly supplicant raising his head to a false idol, a dead tree, his only hope of escape.

One foot. Then the other.

He stands.

Grasps.

And becomes translucent. She sees the tree through his fading body. Sees sleet and snow blowing through him.

And then he's gone.

But so are the girls.

They made it. They're waking up. And so is the old man, but in whose body? His is dead.

She knows. "Finish her," he said.

Once again, a shadow passes over her. Sid kneels. His fingers are like cold steel on her throat. Her lungs burn, but she doesn't resist, even when all the oxygen is used up. She doesn't feel much as the world fades.

Warmth fills her.

And winter is gone.

Winter is gone.

132

SLEEP SO DEEP. Dreamless, beautiful sleep.

A place inside that's warm and cozy. Like an infant pressed to her mother's breast, curled up and safe. Melting in a loving embrace.

No boundaries.

No lies.

Everything exposed. Present.

Nothing rejected.

Mmmmmmm.

She's not aware she's sleeping. There is no "out there", no "me", and no "you".

No "this" or "that".

And she rests in that moment. That eternal moment.

Having been nowhere, there is nowhere to go. Just here.

She's not sure when she became this. There are no thoughts, no memories.

Images arise.

Nothing she sees; it's just pictures, like she is the dream. She is all of it. She is the hills and trees, the wind and snow.

There is beauty and joy, cold and pain. Warmth and pleasure. And great sadness fills the heavens, tears falling in great, salty drops, becoming snowflakes in the frigid loneliness.

It's all there, all contained in this perfect moment where it all makes sense. Where it's all perfectly flawed.

Nothing to be changed.

She is this. And she smiles.

She expands, feeling endless and eternal. But there are boundaries. There is a line at which she stops, a great circle that envelops the wondrous wilderness. There is a tree in the middle, one with barren branches, smooth and rippling, a tree splitting a granite boulder.

A boy sits on the hillside not far from it.

He's next to a girl. She lies so still, her vacant eyes staring into the gray sky.

Me.

She inhabited that body. She left it, became this...this...she became this. And the boy, he did it. He held her down, pressing his thumbs into her windpipe until her bladder released and her lungs contracted.

Her heart beat its last note.

This is all a dream.

The scenes shift, her focus turning to the north, soaring through the trees, beneath the hills, and emerging above the cabins.

Miranda sits in the brick house, one sock hanging from her foot. The other is bare. Music blares, but she doesn't hear it. She sits cross-legged, muttering nonsense.

The walls grow closer. The air thinner.

Outside, the snow ceaselessly piles atop the roofs, growing thicker and heavier. The remains of the bunkhouse topple beneath the weight. The dinner house door is wide open, winter's breath frosting the table, snow filling the corners.

The garden is summer's graveyard, the crops long dead and buried. It is the final resting place for another body, a lump in the middle, its brown skin hidden beneath winter's blanket along with the reprehensible things the old man did to it.

Where are you, Jen?

Safe.

It's a word. It doesn't echo. It's a thought permeating the land. Jen is safe, it says.

Jen is safe.

Deep in the woods there is a small cabin. Inside, an old woman is withered and dry. She won't die. She can't.

She is this world.

She is the one that holds them, the one that imprisons them.

Why won't you let us go?

There is no answer.

Only the slow rise and fall of the ancient woman's chest.

But images unfold.

She sees the old woman's life. She knows her past. Her life. She sees, she feels and knows what is Patricia Ballard.

She was not a happy child. She could not see the difference between thoughts and reality. She struggled with dense emotions, a contracted life, and tortured thoughts. She was diagnosed as mentally ill, her adult life immersed in the psychotropic haze, of dry mouth and dull eyes.

Numb emotions.

She cut herself to feel alive. She plucked her eyebrows to punish herself for being so broken. She cried and screamed. Laughed.

Her life frayed, the edges quickly coming undone.

In her sane moments, she demonstrated brilliance. She painted vivid portraits, wrote stunning poetry, and conducted tearful sonnets. But the malaise of insanity washed those moments of genius from her, leaving her empty.

Reality was harsh. She couldn't accept it.

She said no.

She was a vortex of emotions spiraling into itself.

Until her husband saved her. Her husband bent reality to fit her warped identity. He gave her a universe, made her a goddess. The memory of the needle piercing her frontal lobe is parched and faded. She hardly remembers it.

Patricia has resided within the confines of her own mind longer than the outside world. She created these landscapes, this world. She gave life to her own reality the way she wanted it to be. She developed stars, created Heaven and Hell, God and Devil, and all the entities in between.

She lived in a lush paradise, an endless beach with tepid waters. She savored the sun's kiss, the moon's caress. Eternity was hers, as she wished it to be.

But loneliness crept into her universe.

She craved another's voice, the touch of a stranger.

She created cities with buildings and streets, cars jamming intersections and cafés with coffee, bars with whiskey. She walked among the people who lived in the skyscrapers; she acted like them, talked to them. But no matter how many came to the city, she knew they were just illusions.

They were just thoughts.

And the loneliness howled like winter.

Until her son came for her. He took her away and linked her with his own mind. Her son! She was no longer alone. And soon there were others. Children came to play. They came to the island.

Foreverland.

There were boys on the island. And the girls went to see them, spending day and night with them, wanting so badly to escape the reality of the cabin, to go to Foreverland.

Forever.

Patricia's loneliness dissipated.

Joy reigned. Filled her like the sun.

But she knew what her son was doing to the children. She could feel their identities fraying into the gray void, coming apart at the seams torn from the fabric of their souls. They dissolved.

They never returned.

But there were always more. Always new children to experience. And she was so happy. She had never had this, not in the real world.

And when he disappeared, when her son blinked out of existence, the sadness, the loneliness returned like a scornful god. It struck her long and slow, a cold blade slinking deep into her soul, cutting her over and over.

Forever and ever.

Her universe became cold and isolated, absorbing the details of the real world. Her reality was as harsh as the outside world. There was nothing she could do to stop it. Patricia spiraled into madness once again.

Snow falls in frozen tears.

It piles onto the roofs. Buries the land.

Let us go, Cyn thinks.

And day follows night.

Day follows night.

The snow falls. The weight buckles the dinner house.

The wind harvesters fracture under the weight.

The solar panels become lumps in a frozen land.

Miranda is driven mad with loneliness and guilt. She no longer eats. No longer moves. Frost covers the windows. When the end arrives, she goes to the bedroom and dresses in shiny black shoes and a striped dress. Her foggy breath streams between her chattering lips as she applies eye shadow, smacking her lips with red lipstick.

She walks outside, into the bitter world.

No coat.

Just a wish for the end.

She's numb within minutes. Her skin blue. The snow up to her waist.

She makes it to the meadow, where she falls. Where the dimness creeps in.

She is the last of the girls, and she goes to sleep in death's eternal grip.

Let us go, Cyn asks again.

I'm sorry. Patricia's voice tearfully echoes. She answers, No.

Cyn experiences the warmness once again. The lovely embrace of eternity. Feels the old woman take her to her breast, their souls merging.

Loving.

And night falls on the world.

But she will live to see the sun rise again.

133

The rising sun on us, day beginning.
The sky collapses.
And consumes us all.

———————

THE ROOSTER IS CROWING.

He pulls her from a deep sleep. She struggles to open her eyes, the trace of the terrible dream still glowing.

The sky collapsing on a gray world.

Something vibrates in her throat, a moan escapes her lips. She doesn't recognize it as her own. Her eyes flutter open, her heart matching the alarm. *Wake up!*

It's dark. She can't see. But she feels the bed, feels the pillow cradling her head. She stares ahead, wondering where she is and how she got there.

There are rafters. There are beds with smooth blankets and empty pillows.

The rooster beckons.

She pulls her sheets back and slowly sits up, eyes fully open, searching. The scuffed floor is gritty and cold. She stands up, wearing a long T-shirt that reaches to mid-thigh and reeks of hard labor.

There's a small table beneath a window, an empty bed on the other side of it. Her reflection in the glass looks like an apparition. It must be very early morning; a hint of light illuminates massive white posts with churning blades. Horse hooves thunder in the distance.

She stubs her toe on a pair of worn boots, the tongues pulled out. Her feet fit snugly, the creases stiff and biting. They clop on the wood floor—

"Who's there?" someone says.

The girl freezes.

Something bangs the table. "Ow."

The girl stares into the back corner and sees a small figure bend over to rub her knee. She reaches out. The tip of a match flares, tossing shadows into the rafters. A candle holds the flame.

"Who are you?" the girl in back asks.

The girl in boots doesn't answer. The candlelight is reflecting inside a tin shield, directing it away from the girl holding it. The girl in boots lights a candle on the table in front of her.

The cabin glows warmly.

The girl in the back steps back. Her hair is black and shaved; her T-shirt down to her knees and smudged with dirt. Her skin is dark.

"Who are you?" the girl asks again.

"I don't know," the girl in boots answers.

She swings the candle around. There are boxes under the bed and slashes carved into the wall. She steps closer and leans over the bed. The marks are gouged into the wood, bundled in fives. The last several marks are thin and weak, like they were scratched with a fingernail or a butter knife.

There are voices outside.

"Dammit," someone says. "Hold still before I box you one in the ear." Long pause. "You said this ain't real."

The girl in back blows out her candle and shrinks into the dark. The girl in boots holds her ground, pointing the light at the door. She looks around for a club or something sharp. She can throw the candle at them if she has to, charge them.

The door flies open.

She steps back and crouches. Ready to defend herself.

Two girls look inside. They're wearing designer clothes that were dragged through the mud and tattered from long days. The white girl's hair is matted and knotty.

"Cyn?"

The girl in boots doesn't know what that means. *Sin?*

The smaller one steps inside, her skin black. She smiles and points at the back of the bunkhouse.

"Jen," she says.

Jen cowers slightly. The strangers approach her slowly, gently. They wrap their arms around her. She doesn't try to stop them.

The smaller one begins weeping. "We're so sorry, Jen," she says. "We couldn't stop him..."

The girl lets them hug her, lets them weep and apologize. Not that she can do anything about it; they've got her locked between them and aren't letting go.

"What the hell is going on?" the girl in boots says.

They wipe their eyes, laughing and crying, putting their arms around Jen and guiding her around the stove.

"We'd hug you," one of the girls says, "but you're dangerous when you don't know what's going on."

"Then tell me." She holds the candle up.

They shield their eyes.

"I'm Kat and this is Mad. We came to get you out."

"Where am I?"

"Later." Kat reaches out and squeezes her arm. "I'm so glad to see you, Cyn. We were afraid..."

She chokes on rising emotion.

Mad comes over and, despite her reservations, puts a hug on Cyn. They both do. Cyn stands there stiffly and lets them.

"You saved our lives," Mad says, squeezing tightly. "All of us."

Cyn doesn't know what any of this means. Neither does Jen. They watch the strangers go through another round of laughing and weeping. Mad stands back, wiping her eyes.

Kat reaches under one of the empty beds, blows her nose in a T-shirt, and throws it back under.

"Why can't I remember my name?" Cyn asks.

"You will, pretty soon," Kat says. "We need to get going. It's a little chilly outside. There are clothes under your beds—you should get dressed. We've got to walk a bit to reach the gate."

"What gate? What's going on?"

"Just trust us."

Cyn isn't trusting. She sure as hell isn't moving.

Kat keeps an eye on her as she pulls a box out from beneath the bed and gets out a few sweatshirts and some jeans. Mad does the same for Jen, and Jen goes along with it.

"Look, you got no reason to trust me, I know. But you're going to have to make that leap."

"I don't know you."

"You don't know yourself."

Kat holds the clothes in one hand, reeking of body odor. Cyn isn't reaching for those rags. But Kat's right: she doesn't know anything. These girls seem to know something.

"We know you, Cyn," Mad says. "I can prove it. Check those pants, the ones from under your bed. You read the tag on the inside of the waist, see what it says."

Kat throws them at her feet. Cyn bends down and picks them up without looking away from her. She flips the waistband and finds a white tag sewn to the inside.

Cyn.

"I know that don't prove anything." Kat holds up her hands. "But we're telling you the truth. You don't have to be near us, you just need to follow. And if you don't like what you see, you just go on your own way."

Mad starts to protest. Kat stops her.

"We got a deal?"

Cyn looks at the pants.

"You ain't got nowhere else to be, nothing else to do. And no one else to trust. You just got to fall with us, Cyn."

Jen is dressed and ready.

Cyn stares at the tag. She puts the candle down and slides the jeans on one damp, moldy leg at a time. Kat throws the sweatshirts at her feet, and she puts those on, too.

Fall with us.

Kat goes to the door, putting her hand on the knob. She takes a breath and opens it.

Cyn steps back. Alarms go off in her head.

An old man lies on the ground, his hands and feet tied with strips of clothing. He groans through a dirty rag tied around his mouth. His angry words are distorted, his eyebrows pinched. His scalp is red and ridged.

"We brought him with us," Kat says. "We didn't hurt him, Cyn. He was just taking up space he didn't need to be taking up."

"I don't understand."

"Don't matter. We'll leave him here."

The old man growls a string of words muffled by the gag.

"Why?" Cyn asks.

Kat looks at Jen. "He's a real bad man, Cyn. This is where he belongs."

Kat checks the bindings, making sure they'll hold long enough for them to reach the gate. Mad guides Jen outside, staying between her and the old man. Cyn comes out next, the old man cursing nonsense at each of them. But cursing for sure.

The morning chill slips down her neck. Cyn crosses her arms, shivering while staring at the helpless old man. He bites the cloth like a muzzled dog.

"Is that his house?" Jen asks.

There's a large brick house to the east where the sky is glowing, the sun still below the trees. A lamp lights up one of the front windows.

"Yeah," Kat says. "He lives there with his daughter. They helped build this place. We're going to let them have it all to themselves."

Kat, Mad, and Jen start walking towards a meadow. The old man begins another round of guttural, angry protests. A window lights up on the second floor of the brick house. The curtains part, and the outline of a girl appears, her hand on the glass. Maybe she'll come out for him when the girls are gone and untie him. He looks hungry.

The old man rolls into Cyn's leg. His eyes plead. The growls turn to whines.

"Come on!" Kat shouts.

Cyn walks around him. The grunts and cries fade behind her. Grass brushes her waist, the flowers tickling her outstretched hands. Mountains are on the horizon to her right. The brick house recedes in the distance, only the lit windows visible.

"Where you taking us?" Cyn asks.

"A mile due south." Kat says. "We're going to fall out of here, Cyn. I just need you to remember one thing."

Kat leans in and whispers in her ear.

Pain radiates between her eyes. A face hovers over her. Short brown hair drapes like curtains, framing an angular face and green eyes.

"Password?" Linda says.

Cyn's arms are pinned at her sides. Jackie stands at the IV, a syringe inserted in the tube, her thumb on the plunger.

"Password?" she asks again. "What is it? You know it—tell me."

Cyn shakes her head. She hasn't a clue what she's talking about. There's no password. She knows that, but maybe something has changed. She thinks, trying to remember where she was a second ago. She just woke up in the bed. But before that, she was...she was...

"Last time," Linda says. "Password?"

She closes her eyes, holding her breath. There was a tree and a rock. The sun was rising when she grabbed onto it.

When she fell.

When Kat told her to say—

"Sandy sent me." She opens her eyes.

"What's your name?"

"Cyn."

"Full name?"

She hesitates. "Cynthia."

Linda nods at Jackie. She pulls the syringe out of the tube.

Someone reaches over Cyn's head, her finger and thumb on the wire stuck between her eyes. A needle slides out of her head, a cold sliver that's been in far too long.

A drop of clear liquid streams across her forehead. The pressure between her eyes eases. Linda embraces her tightly.

"Welcome back, Cynthia."

And there's applause.

The bunkhouse is full of people. The youngest of them fall on her. Cyn is trapped by three girls and a grown woman.

Home.

134

THE GRASS IS KNEE-HIGH. Wildflowers sway here and there, but few are left as the mornings have gotten colder. Mad, Kat, and Jen wander up the slope, Jen with a fistful of white flowers from the meadow.

Jennifer. And Madeline and Kathryn.

"Those are their names," Linda reminded Cyn. The three-letter versions are the names inside the dream.

We're not in the dream anymore.

It's been weeks since she woke up. Weeks since Kat and Mad were brave enough to come back for her and Jen. It took a lot of work, though. Linda and Thomas wouldn't get duped again. There was a close watch on those needles. They weren't planning on the girls going back inside. Cyn had done it, and look what happened to her.

"She did it for us!" Kat had argued. "You ain't stopping us."

No good, though. They were just kids—they didn't know the risks. And Thomas and the important people did, and they weren't going to take them.

But then Kat and Mad got clever. They lied to Linda and Thomas, said that Patricia was about dead and that Cyn and Jen would be lost to the Nowhere forever. They had no idea the word "Nowhere" would sell it. Linda bought it and came to their rescue. She persuaded Thomas to let the girls go back inside the needle.

"We running out of time, Mr. Thomas," Kat had added. "We'll lose Cyn forever."

Besides, Cyn wasn't getting out until someone escorted Mr. Williams back inside the dream. Otherwise, she had no body.

Yeah, Cyn's body.

His body is dead.

He exited the dream into the one body he knew would be vacant. Cyn was still in the dream when he made his escape, opened his eyes as a sixteen-year-old female, which beat the hell out of spending eternity in the Nowhere. He could figure out bras and tampons. No one would know the difference.

But Thomas and the important people had done their research— they knew how things worked on the island. They knew there was a password. When an old man transferred into a young man's body, they were asked for it in order to confirm the identity, to make sure the right person was in the body.

Linda asked for a password the first time and Cyn didn't know one. The girls were asked, too. They had no idea.

But Mr. Williams had said, with a smile, "Foreverland."

After that, he was easy pickings.

They sent him back inside the dream to make room for Cyn to return. It was her body, after all.

She shivers at the thought of that old bastard sliding into her body. It was a good thing she couldn't remember him when Kat and Mad came back for her and Jen. She would've done something to him.

Something very bad.

Strangely, she feels sorry for him. A small part of her, deep inside, will miss him. She told Linda that. She decided it was time to start talking about things, to start digging through the memories and working them out. To start remembering.

When she said a part of her was fond of Mr. Williams, Linda called it Stockholm syndrome. Cyn doesn't like the way it feels—wanting to kill him and save him at the same time.

"Little by little," Linda had reminded her. "We heal little by little."

The girls climb the green slope toward a split boulder with a picturesque bristlecone pine nudging the fracture wider. The ancient-looking branches are loaded with seed-bearing cones and short needles.

Unlike the dream, it's full of life.

Why did Patricia choose this as the gate? Was it because it was so far from the cabins? Cyn doesn't think that's it. She couldn't keep them from leaving the dream, but used their fears to trap them. Ultimately, the girls could leave at any time. They chose to stay in the dream by refusing to face their fears.

In the dream, the tree was dead.

But it was so difficult to see through the illusion when they were immersed in it. Cyn hadn't slept more than an hour at a time since escaping, afraid she'd awake in the bunkhouse, marks on the wall. And how does she know this isn't a dream? What if dreams are endless layers, each another dimension of reality? Which one is real?

When they're all peeled away, what will be in the middle?

She looks at her hands, turning them over. Linda had said that will help to ground herself, remind her she's in the flesh. *In the dream, you doubt. Here, you know.*

But Linda wasn't there. She wasn't seduced by the sights and sounds. The suffering.

Cyn touches the sensitive hole in her forehead. The stent is still there. Maybe they can remove it one day, but she doubts it. It will be there forever, Patricia's parting gift, something to remember her by. Maybe that's not a bad thing. In the dream, there was no hole. She can always look at that instead of her hands.

The girls reach the top of the hill. Jen lays the bundle of flowers on the stone. The flowers from their earlier trips are still there, dry and crumbling, the seeds blowing on the ground, where they will bloom again. They'd done this several times over the last couple of weeks to honor all the girls that are lost in the Nowhere.

Sandy is out there.

Miranda forgot what she'd done. She woke up with no memories in a young body with blonde hair. Why would she believe that it wasn't her body? She brought Sandy out to the Fountain of Youth and

destroyed her identity so she could take the body. Whatever they are—
a soul, an identity, an essence—can be moved in and out of bodies.

Sandy was pushed out and Miranda moved in.

Maybe the Fountain of Youth program intentionally made her
forget what she'd done. Maybe it was easier that way, to forget what
she'd done to Sandy. To forget she's a murderer.

Miranda started fresh. Her essence, her soul, got a new body to
make more memories. *We are not our memories, that's not who we are.* Cyn
even suspects Miranda had some of Sandy's memories and convinced
herself she was innocent. She was using the stolen memories to ease
the guilt. How would she know? How would any of us know who we
really are if we get someone else's memories?

Doesn't matter. Whatever Miranda is, it's in Sandy's body.

So she's a murderer. And a thief.

All the girls, all their souls, are lost in the Nowhere, and Thomas
promised to find them and get them out. But how will they get out?
They don't have bodies anymore.

The distant thumping gets louder.

The girls look up. A helicopter banks to the east. Jen waves. They
can't see her, but that's not why she's doing it. The helicopter is
carrying Patricia to a lab far away. A universe is inside her, a world that
contains Sid, Miranda, and Mr. Williams.

Mr. Graham.

Somewhere in the real world his wife is hoping to find him. She'll
be expecting to reunite with her husband, expecting him to be inside a
young man's body, one that he sponsored.

She'll be disappointed. But at least she's not trapped in the
Nowhere.

A utility vehicle putters out of the trees. Linda steers it around a
dip in the ground. Roc sits in the passenger's seat.

Cyn avoids looking at her. They don't like each other any more in
the skin than they did in the dream. Roc would've killed them, and
Cyn can't forgive her for that. A part of her wants to send her back to
the dream with the old man and Miranda, because she's a piece of
garbage.

But that's how the old women saw all of them: girls that had wasted their lives. The old women were just taking a body that had already been abandoned by the mind. A body is a terrible thing to waste.

"Time to go," Linda says.

The girls come down the slope, their laughter ahead of them. Linda doesn't mean it's time to leave the hill. It's time to leave the camp. *Forever*.

Kat, Mad, and Jen have family. They have brothers or sisters, uncles, cousins...someone in the world who wants them. Roc, it turns out, is eighteen. She doesn't need family. She can go right back to her crappy life. They'll keep an eye on her for some time. Probably forever. Some government official had informed them that they would be compensated for their pain and suffering with funds confiscated from the Fountain of Youth operation.

We're talking millions.

Cyn's memories about her stepfather were legitimate. Evidently, she was removed from the home by Family Services and placed with a foster family. She didn't stay long, though; she was reported missing a month after she arrived. She doesn't remember much of that, and the memories are coming back slowly. She's not going back to Ohio, though. She'll go somewhere else that has the funds to support her.

For now, she's going back with Linda. Cyn hopes it's more than just temporary.

The girls climb into the back of the vehicle.

"Can we make a detour?" Cyn asks.

"Depends."

"It's not far." She points down the slope at a line of trees. "I just need to see something."

Linda checks her watch. "I think we can manage. Hop in."

The vehicle is weighted in the back, but they're going over smooth terrain, straight downhill. She taps Linda on the shoulder and points at the gap in the trees.

Cyn climbs out.

The short hairs on the back of her neck tingle. She's afraid to move, afraid that it will mean that her worst fears are true. But she finds the courage to take a step toward the opening. She holds her hand out, reaching for a feeling she'll recognize in the lump still in her neck.

Fear stiffens her arm.

She steps onto the road, the tracks still on the ground. The same road she encountered in the dream, where the world ends. She walks several feet down it and turns around.

Drops her arm.

The girls are watching her from the vehicle.

Cyn lets out a deep breath. Smiles. Nothing tingles, nothing stops her. And the gray is still in the dream. *And this is not the dream.*

She's ready to start a new life in the real world. She's convinced it really is out there. And she's in it. At least this layer.

"Looking for a dead body?" Kat shouts.

The girls don't get out of the vehicle. They stay in the back, chatting away. Cyn considers walking a little farther, wondering if she can stay out here a bit longer, maybe wander down the road and get lost for a while, just be with her thoughts and the promise of a brighter future. It just feels so good to be back in the flesh, in the real world.

"What was the name of the old lady that had the leather journal?" Kat asks. "The one that sponsored Cyn?"

There's discussion. Linda answers. "Her name was Barbara."

"Yes?" Cyn says.

But it wasn't that she was agreeing with her. It happened so fast, so naturally. No one heard her. Not even Linda. But Cyn knows what happened. She almost collapses with the realization that she answered to the name.

She answered to Barbara.

Oh, sweet Jesus.

BOOK 3

ASHES OF FOREVERLAND

SPRING

We all...

fall...

down.

135

ADMAX Penitentiary, Colorado

Tyler stepped onto the ledge.

The Italian marble was cold, his toes gripping the chiseled edge. The platform cantilevered from the roof a thousand feet above traffic. Taillights were strung throughout Central Park, starting and stopping, merging and turning, moving through the city like corpuscles.

He couldn't smell the exhaust from up there, couldn't hear the horns or the congestion, the shouts and whistles.

He held out his arms, Christ-like, tipped his head and inhaled the wind untainted by human grime, from the trash of selfish thoughts. Only the fierce breeze in his ears.

"Sorry to keep you waiting." Patricia crossed the portico.

Her loosely fit dress fluttered around her feet. The brightly lit glass walls of the luxury apartment—the only such apartment atop the Bank of America building—betrayed the layers of beige fabric that other-wise would hide her pear-shaped body. Her graying hair flowed to her shoulders.

"I can't stay long," he said.

She looked through him with those penetrating eyes, a smile reflecting somewhere in their depths. Her scent carried through the cutting breeze, her dress snapping like taut flags. He stopped on the bottom step.

"You don't have to leave."

"You know I can't stay, love."

A beige pile of fabric fell at her bare feet. Her naked body was without wrinkles; the sweep of her hips hypnotic. None of her curves were as alluring as the tight curls of her lips pushing into her cherub cheeks.

He watched her from the bottom step, watched her dive into the glass-bottom pool that was suspended over the thousand-foot drop. The water, crystal blue.

She hardly made a ripple, swimming beneath the surface to the other end. Her strokes were long, water beading from her fair skin. Tyler waited with a towel. He wrapped her as she stepped out, water dripping from her nose.

The taste of her filled his sinuses.

He pulled the towel over her shoulders. This time, it was he that turned away and climbed back onto the ledge. The night consumed the streets. Red lights flared; headlights glared. And there, on the horizon, between the stiff city edifices lining the streets like metallic offerings to an industrial God, just past the end of the road where the sun would rise in the morning, he saw the flicker of gray static. Nothing existed beyond that.

Stay? That would give me no greater pleasure.

But staying in this reality, this world that Patricia dreamed, would be so small. Despite her ability, she could dream up the city.

Stay, he could—he wanted to.

But stay and the human population would never know the true freedom of another reality—this reality.

Foreverland.

"The hosts?" he asked. "How are they doing?"

"You know your answer." Her shadow crept up behind him. "Hope is your albatross, dear."

Hope. It was indeed his bastard.

He was not so desperate to lay his future, his life, on the fragile ice of hope. But never had he thought he would be this old, this close to the edge of dying. He couldn't live forever. *Not in the flesh.*

Unless they found someone with the potential, the brain structure, to host a limitless Foreverland, one that went far beyond the city, past the horizon, one that replicated this planet.

This universe.

A new reality.

Patricia couldn't do it. Neither could he. Even Harold, their son, if he were alive, could only do so much. But someone out there could. There had to be. And that was why he asked, that was why he hoped.

Maybe they would find one before this flesh ended.

Her hands slid over his ribs, laced over his stomach. "I may have found one," she whispered.

"What?"

"A viable host."

"What do you mean? Why didn't you tell me?"

"Hope, dear. I didn't want to stoke it any more than you have. I'm taking a chance, but I've sensed her exceptional potential."

"You have her already?"

She nodded. "I've already had her. She is dreaming her own Foreverland and it is wondrous."

His chest fluttered. "She agreed to host?"

"No. She doesn't know...I had to take her, dear. She has no idea."

It was risky, but abduction was nothing new. "Why didn't you tell me?"

"I wanted to be sure."

"And you're sure?"

She kissed his chin. "A goddess."

Chance was a suspicious mistress, the harbinger of hope. And, try as he might to deny it, he was willing to gamble on a goddess.

Because a goddess is what we need.

"In order for her Foreverland to stabilize," she said, "we'll need her to sleep."

"How long?"

"A year."

A year? They had already squandered so much time on the other hosts. *Is this really our last chance to bring Foreverland to the world?*

He pulled her close.

Their lips met, warm and wet. The wind howled. He held her until it was time to leave her, to return to the physical realm, where his body of aging flesh waited. Her floral scent lingered in his nostrils, but a faint layer of decay sifted through it.

A year, he thought. *One more year.*

A point burned his forehead like a red-hot wire. He reached up, felt the slither, the sting of a wasp as the surgical steel needle slid from his forehead.

He stared through a blurry veil at a cracked ceiling.

A metal door clanged. Two prison guards stepped next to Tyler Ballard's bed and waited. He took his time, letting his feet touch the floor. He rubbed the thin spotted skin on his knobby hands for warmth.

The floral scent faded.

136

"Ladies and gentlemen, can I have your attention?" someone shouted. "The tour is about to begin."

Alex put her phone away. Her husband had texted, wondering how long this visit would last. If he timed his exit from the Guggenheim, he could pick her up without parking.

Journalists crowded to the front. Alex dumped her coffee and moved along the wall, hands still shaking. A cold wave vibrated inside her like a chilled metal coil, a set of eyes scanning her organs. Her teeth damn near chattered, but she wasn't cold.

Nerves?

Through a gap of photographers, she saw the Institute's PR person standing in front of heavy double doors. Like the rest of the lobby, they were forest green, imbued with a sense of calming and healing. She had a sense that beyond those doors it was quite the opposite.

"I would like to welcome you." The small woman's name was Ellen; that's what the badge said. She was in her early thirties, her teeth flashing a white smile. "This is a very exciting day at the Institute of

Technological Research. You were handpicked to see our work up close, to ask our scientists questions. It's through you the public will know what we're doing."

She made it sound like they'd found golden tickets in chocolate bars when, in fact, they gave select tours all the time. But it was by invitation. Alex's invitation came as a surprise. She wasn't a journalist anymore and didn't work for a major newspaper like the others. She squeezed between a young photographer and the wall. Her black hair fell over her face.

She rubbed her hands. Her lips, cold.

"Before we do," Ellen said with her flashy smile, "I want to emphasize a few items. You have all signed a release and agreed to the above-mentioned rules."

She held up a sheet of paper.

"Your enhancements, should you have them, will remain off during your stay."

There was a rumble of laughter.

"I know, I know. We're the pioneers of biomite research, but while you're inside the laboratory, we don't want to run the risk of interference."

The punchline wasn't *off*, it was *should you have them*. Every journalist on the planet had a certain degree of biomites—the recently invented and globally distributed artificial stem cells—seeded into their brain to help with memory, data processing and, for some, emotional regulation. And this was where biomites were manufactured. Alex had the maximum allowed by the government. They probably all did.

And that's why I'm cold.

She couldn't remember the last time she'd shut off her internal enhancements. In the last hour, it had become quite clear how much they helped regulate her emotions.

It sucked to be plain human.

"Your identification has an imbedded monitor." Ellen lifted the card around her neck. "Keep it on you at all times."

She added a few more pleasantries before pushing the doors open, leading the group down a stark white hallway. Alex worked her way to the end of the line. The smell of gourmet coffee was quickly replaced with sterilizing solutions and artificial clay—the distinctive odor of biomites. The place felt a bit too much like a 1940s asylum.

Scientists stood in doorways, wearing white lab coats, smiling and waving like they were extras hired to watch a parade.

"Alex?" The man in front of her had turned while walking.

"Oh, hey, Mason. Didn't recognize you."

"¿Come esta?" the balding man asked. *How are you?*

"*Muy bien.*" Being Latina, she often entertained bits of Spanish. "How have you been?"

"Soulless."

They had briefly worked together at *The Washington Post.* They caught up on gossip in between stops as Ellen briefed them on the function of the various labs—where new strains of biomites were being developed, how disease would be erased, how biomites would regenerate new limbs.

All the promises of heaven on Earth.

"What are you doing here?" he asked.

"Following the story, what else?"

She didn't want to tell him the truth, that she'd received an unexpected invitation to such an exclusive event. A man named Jonathan Deer. His name was a joke, but she'd done some research and discovered he was employed by the Institute and wanted her to see the new and exciting developments for herself. She was already writing about animal cruelty and was about to expose practices in all sorts of industries.

This wasn't even on her radar.

"Congrats on the book, by the way," Mason said. "Took balls to go into North Korea like that."

"That's what they say." Alex fiddled with her monitor badge.

"This your next project?"

She shrugged. "Maybe."

"Good luck, if it is. Getting inside information out of these people will make North Koreans look like old ladies. No offense."

"You calling me old?"

"Calling you a lady."

"That's a first."

His laughter was more of a grunt. Alex was in her mid-forties but turned heads like she was closer to twenty. Mason knew she was the furthest thing from a beauty queen. Those that didn't were quickly discarded.

They gathered at another set of metal doors. Ellen waited until everyone was crowded together. They were about to enter Wonka's factory, only there wouldn't be a chocolate river. Photographers held up their cameras; reporters lifted their phones.

"So far, you're disappointed." Ellen smiled and many of them laughed. "You didn't come all this way to be greeted by computer programmers and lab directors, or even get a history lesson on biomites, but it was part of the package deal. Now that's out of the way, we can get to the good stuff. I ask that you kindly find a seat in order for us to properly introduce the main thrust of our research. You will be allowed to explore once we are finished."

Someone raised their hand.

"Hold your questions," Ellen interrupted. "There will be time for that. I also want to remind you to avoid engaging in any degree of enhancement activity."

She paused, let that sink in, and then opened the doors.

There were exclamations of surprise, a storm of photography clicking and whirring. Alex could only see black walls above the group. They were reflective, like glass.

"You all right?" Mason was looking at Alex's chest.

She was holding the badge/monitor, but her hands were shaking almost violently.

"I'm cold." Her breath quivered. "Are you?"

He shook his head.

She rubbed her face. They shuffled ahead a tiny step at a time. Mason was the first to get a glimpse of what was around the corner and stopped. Alex bumped into him.

A scientist stood next to a lone table. His hair was unnaturally black; his face thick and square.

It resembled an operating table, but the surface was cushioned. An orangutan rested on it, his long orange hair contrasting with the green cushion, his weight sinking partway into it. There was nothing alarming about being so close to a sleeping primate.

It was the needle.

The long, surgical barrel was positioned in the middle of his forehead.

"Ladies and gentlemen," Ellen was announcing, "if you would kindly find a seat, we can get started."

It was a bit like herding kindergarteners away from an ice-cream truck, but the crowd eventually moved to a small block of chairs. Alex took the last seat in the back row, oblivious to the opposite wall's reflection.

"Good morning." It was the scientist who spoke, his accented English slightly broken. Russian, maybe? "I am Dr. K.P. Baronov, director and lead scientist at the Institute. I trust Ellen has answered your questions up to this point."

Ellen was sitting separate from the group.

"Very good. I know you have many questions, and I will answer them shortly. I also know you are very educated in this process, it was why you were selected for such exclusive tour, but I would like to update you on what we do here and why."

If he thought they were educated on needles in foreheads, he had been misinformed. Alex had seen pictures, but that was it.

"You understand, I am quite sure, that computer-assisted alternate reality, or CAAR, makes a direct connection with the organism's frontal lobe via a surgical probe."

He half-gestured to the orangutan.

"The subject's awareness, or identity if you will, is in some ways transported out of the body and into a dreamlike state. During the inception of such technology, the identity of the subject was put into a computer, but, as some of you know, that is no longer an effective means of creating an alternate reality."

"Why?" Alex's voice shook.

"Mrs. Diosa." Ellen half stood. "Hold your questions, please."

"It is okay," Dr. Baronov said. "It is very good question and why we brought you here. You understand that there are great many benefits that can occur through this method. We use orangutan because it is the smartest primate on earth besides humans. It is our hope that, with our research, this method will soon be accessible to all people."

"What about permanent damage?" Alex couldn't stop herself. Ellen's smile faltered, but the doctor nodded without hesitation.

"Of course, that is good concern," he said. "There was much to learn about this process and the obvious distress of the irreparable damage to one's psychology. It has taken much research to perfect the procedure, but I feel confident you will see the benefits today."

"How many test subjects did you kill? How many went insane?"

"We do nothing illegal at the Institute, Mrs. Diosa," the doctor said. "In fact, we have made tremendous strides in the process. For instance, it will soon be possible to link minds without the needle by harnessing the power of biomite-enhanced brains, like yourselves. Your brain biomites will operate like wireless computers. We strive to improve the quality of life in our test subjects."

Is that why our enhancements are off?

"In old method, the one discovered by Dr. Tyler Ballard, a computer was used to host an artificial environment, the alternate reality, if you will. The computer, though, is not efficient or suitable to respond to the soulful needs of a biological intelligence, like you or me. Or Coco."

He placed his hands on the sides of the orangutan's head.

"Coco is organic host, if you will. A network server, to borrow term from our computer friends. It is Coco that creates world in his mind for others to be transferred. He is host. It is his imagination that creates alternate reality."

"A dream?" Mason said.

"Of sorts." The doctor raised his hand. "Not anyone can become host. There is special quality to how the two hemispheres of the test subject's brain operate, a certain degree of openness and creativity that make him or her ideal candidate. It is this degree that will limit the world he or she can create. For instance"—the doctor waved his arms —"this room is extent of the world Coco can create. Beyond there is nothing, like limit of universe."

"And what do you hope to accomplish?" someone asked. "Some sort of virtual tourism? The animals, or test subjects, will pick up the tab of suffering for our pleasure?"

Ellen stiffened, but the doctor calmed her with an easy hand. "It is all right. I understand your apprehension. It is difficult to see organism with needle in forehead, but I assure you there is no discomfort. To answer question, what we have accomplished already is an improvement in psychological disorder. Test subjects emerge from altered states with increased intelligence and emotional stability."

"Is there really a need to network brains?"

The doctor smiled. "We are stronger and happier when we are united."

"In a new world?"

"Coco sets the rules of his world. It can be fantasy land or just like this."

"For who?"

"That is very good question, Mrs. Diosa." The doctor walked around the table and went to the wall. The black surface mirrored his expression as he reached up and knocked. It rang like glass.

The murkiness began to clear, revealing dark lumps.

The biting chill inside Alex gripped her whole body, pressing the air from her lungs.

Everyone reacted.

There were small cubicles on the other side of the glass walls, like boxes stacked to the ceiling of various sizes with test subjects laying still and prostrate—mice, rats, rabbits, chimps and gibbons. One large gorilla filled the square in front of the doctor. They all had one thing in common.

A needle.

"This is our community," the doctor said. "There is convincing data to show that while their bodies remain stable and alive, their identities are currently in Coco's world. And, more importantly"—the doctor raised his finger—"and this is very important for you to understand, they also contribute to Coco's world. It is like ecosystem, you see. They are integral to Coco and Coco to them."

"And Coco is god," someone said.

"Maybe." The doctor turned to face them. "We are still trying to understand how Coco creates the world's rules, if he even knows he has created them. In other words, are the laws of this virtual world locked into place as they are in our world? Or can he change them?"

"Can they go back to their bodies?"

The doctor chuckled. "Yes, Mrs. Diosa. They wake as if sleeping a wonderful dream."

"With no reality confusion?"

"There is some, yes. The dream state is very convincing. But that is the beauty, you understand. We have created a dream that is inseparable from reality, a dream where time is malleable, where time can go fast or slow. Imagine the possibilities to help soldiers suffering from post-traumatic syndrome? The handicapped can walk, the blind can see.

"The test subjects living in Coco's Foreverland, if you like to call it that, can experience entire lifetime in the span of one minute in flesh. Time, you know, is a dimension. We can live many lives this way, you understand."

"But they return to their bodies?" someone asked. "The right ones?"

The doctor glanced at Ellen, slowly nodding. "Yes, the correct bodies."

"But you said—"

"If you are referring to Foreverland body switches, I assure you there is nothing of that nature occurring at the Institute. It was unfortunate, indeed, that people have used it for such purposes, but such is the nature of many things. Bullets can be used for good and evil, yes?"

The doors opened. The scientists from the labs they passed earlier entered.

"And I think now would be good time to explore, yes?" He lifted his arms, staring at Ellen.

"You may look through the lab," she said. "You may ask questions. Please do not touch anything. As Dr. Baronov stated, this is a living organism."

The group moved slowly at first. Alex, too. Her leg muscles were stiff. She clamped her hands together to keep them from quivering.

The journalists spread out and, little by little, cornered scientists with questions. Photographers were madly capturing the scene.

Especially Coco.

Alex hovered at the end of the table, working her way near the orangutan's head. The primate smelled earthy and damp. The cushioned table hugged him. Occasionally, the whir of internal rollers massaged his body, reducing the probability of bedsores. Unless he moved, his muscles would atrophy, the blood would pool.

How many lives have they lived already? Maybe years have passed.

She couldn't help wonder if the doctor was right: this could be the next step in evolution, a new revolution. *The reality revolution.*

Security stood nearby. If she gave in to the temptation and reached out to stroke the orange hair, to touch the eyelids or puffy patch of flesh around the surgical needle, she would surely be removed.

A bead of saliva glistened on the corner of Coco's mouth.

Foreverland. The doctor dared to use that word with what they were doing, but it was probably inevitable. If the public was going to embrace this technology, they would surely associate it with that word. He would need to reinvent it, to purge it of past associations.

Alex had read of Foreverland, of the boys and girls forced to visit a virtual reality. It was an odd name since it was anything but forever, a reality that was limited in space and the imagination of the host.

Unless the right host is selected. According to the doctor, it would then become forever, indeed.

"So he's dreaming?" A photographer was kneeling to capture the needle at eye level. He looked over the camera at Alex. "How do we know *we're* not dreaming?"

"Limits," she said. "There wouldn't be anything outside this room."

The young man raised his eyebrows, seemingly unaffected by the grotesque subject matter. They were in the belly of the experiment, surrounded by victims of research. All the photographer could think about while capturing all of this was the potential of the dream, his youth, his resilience.

"Have you done any human trials?" someone asked.

The many questions and answers bouncing off the hard floor and glass walls lulled. Many of them turned toward Dr. Baronov, waiting for his response to this particular question.

"We have not. We follow the law."

"What about Patricia Ballard?" a journalist asked. "Where is she?"

"Yes, she is here." He addressed the room as a whole, an answer he wanted to be clearly heard. "She has been here for quite some time, but I assure you there has been no experimentation. We are only serving to support her life. I believe you would agree we are best suited for such purpose."

"No research at all?"

"I believe you know her story, so I will not repeat it. It is very unfortunate what she was forced to do and we are respecting her life, as we were asked to do. That is all I will comment, thank you."

Alex noticed doors on the other side of the room, not the ones where they had entered. Guards stood in front of them. Judging by the lock, the guards weren't necessary. But, perhaps, what was behind them wasn't meant to be seen at any cost.

Coco's nostrils flared.

Alex swore she heard something guttural beneath his chin. The photographer was too busy reviewing his shots to notice.

"What about reports that Patricia is still hosting a Foreverland?" someone asked.

"The doctor will not comment further," Ellen announced. "We would like the focus to remain on the process and the future of this technology."

A few more voices chimed in. The journalists had what they came for. Now they were going for the great white shark, the jewel of this story: *Patricia Ballard, the only living human to host a computer-aided alternate reality.*

"Is she currently connected to a CAAR network?" someone asked.

Something moved beneath Coco's eyelids. His eyes moved back and forth as if, for the first time, he was experiencing REM. The saliva spread into surrounding wrinkles.

"How do you respond to reports of using synthetic brain cells on Patricia?" another person shouted. "Could she reach out to other people with brain biomites?"

"Is that why we're not allowed to use our enhancements?" somebody else asked.

"Any alterations we have implemented," Dr. Baronov said, "have been within our code of conduct, the law, and for the good of Patricia Ballard."

"Are you monitoring her inner world?"

"Can you communicate with her?"

"What does her world look like?"

The walls went black and the lights dimmed. The scientists were leaving. Coco's eyes continued to dance.

Alex ignored the chill down her back and leaned closer. Her scalp began to tingle. Warmth trickled from the top of her head, down into her chest, pushing away the chills. She didn't notice that she had stopped shivering.

"We will continue the tour through the staging area, where you will get a glimpse into Coco's inner world on computer monitors," Ellen announced. "Please, everyone, exit to the left where—"

The eyelids popped open.

Dark brown irises stared up.

Alex saw her reflection in the engorged pupils. But behind her she saw not the fluorescent lights or the black walls. It was something entirely different, something she didn't expect, not in a million years.

Palm trees.

"Oh!" Alex jumped back. Her fingers trembled over her mouth. Her chest was buzzing.

Her thighs filled with icy water. Her knees came unhinged.

Mason caught her before she hit the floor.

The energy shifted in the room. Several people ran to her. Mason laid her on her back. A red light reflected off the black walls. Ellen directed traffic. The journalists were ushered out of the room. Mason was the last one.

The red light and buzzing were coming from the identity card around Alex's neck. The monitor had been activated.

Her enhancements were engaged.

137

NEW YORK CITY

The waiting room was nearly empty.

Alex sat in a row of thinly cushioned seats that were linked at the armrests, staring at a properly dressed young man sitting almost statuesque. He was reading a *National Geographic*, an odd choice, so it seemed, for a kid with shoulder-length hair and clothing he likely found at a resale shop. The color of his hair matched the trunks of the palm trees on the front cover.

Later on, she would remember that.

She watched the traffic crawl, from the sixth-story office. Forty-Sixth Street was worse than usual. She attempted to ignore how long it would take to drive home, but her mind kept doing the math. She thumbed through emails on her phone.

Another one from the Institute.

Her lawyer had made it clear for them to leave her alone, that any contact be directed to her attorney. This health screening she agreed to had already eaten a day out of her life. They said she had violated her terms of agreement by engaging her enhancements while on tour.

She explained the nature of her condition, that she was prone to seizures and her biomites had auto-engaged when one was coming.

But the thing was this: she hadn't felt one coming.

If she thought about it, the whole auto-engage incident was nothing she had ever experienced. Even if she hadn't agreed to see a doctor, to document the seizure-induced auto-engagement, she would've gone to see him anyway.

Coco opened his eyes.

He woke up, she was sure of it. But when she told the EMTs, they assured her everything was all right. They even brought the photographer out, the young man that was snapping photos when she *went ape,* as someone said. Not a single shot with the eyes open.

"He never moved," the photographer said.

Her phone rang. "Hey," she answered.

"Still there?" Her husband's voice piped through the Bluetooth cells implanted near her auditory nerve.

"Still here."

"Have you heard the results?"

"No, not yet." She checked the time again. "They're running late."

"Okay." There was a long pause. "How you feeling?"

"Good." She told him about traffic and the rude receptionist that still worked for the biomite doctor. If the doctor wasn't so good, she'd go somewhere else. And, oddly enough, it wasn't far from the Institute. She could see the front door from the lobby if she stood to the right.

"Thought you'd be done," Samuel said. "We're back at the car, suppose we could walk around."

He said *we,* but she didn't catch that. She did notice his voice was a little off; it sounded like he had a cold.

"I'll text when I know, but it could be another twenty minutes or, I don't know, twenty-four hours."

He chuckled. "We'll just double-park. I'm sure the parking fairies will understand."

"We?"

"Mrs. Diosa?" the receptionist called.

Alex stood slowly and paused before walking toward the receptionist, making sure the floor was steady. That was the other thing she didn't tell Samuel, just how unstable everything felt. If she stood too fast or walked too quickly, the world felt...unreliable. Like walking on thin ice.

"You realize it's an hour after my appointment?"

The woman behind the counter pointed at the door to Alex's left without looking, her fingernail tapping on the iPad's glass. She wrinkled her nose like Alex wasn't wearing deodorant.

"Dr. Mallard got called out."

"Then who am I seeing?"

She sighed. "Dr. Johnstone."

"Who?"

Alex continued to stare. The receptionist didn't look up, pointing at the door instead. A sharp letter to Dr. Mallard was in order.

Enhance Your Life.

That was written on the only poster in the examination room, attached to the back of the door, an elderly woman beaming at children on a playground.

Biomites.

The medical industry introduced synthetic stem cells as the cure-all to human suffering, engineered to replace organic cells in the body, to regenerate damaged tissues, immunize cells and heighten senses. And now the possibility of wireless communication.

Some people seeded their legs to become better athletes; some improved a faulty heart. Others used them to replace skin cells; there were even rumors they could change the way they looked. The government only let you have so many biomites, so seeding your skin to look younger seemed more than superfluous.

It was idiotic.

But, hey, enhance your life.

The old woman looked so happy with her white teeth and wrinkle-free smile, like she would live forever and love every minute of it. Because that was what people wanted, they wanted to live forever.

Alex touched the poster, leaning in as if closer inspection would reveal the deep-down dirty secret. She had seen enough dark corners in humanity to know we didn't deserve immortality.

No one wants to live forever.

The door opened. Alex jumped and, regrettably, went, "Eeep."

Dr. Johnstone didn't notice. He was young, athletic and handsome. His hair was brown and curly, a little longer than usual for someone in his profession. And he smelled clean. Almost too clean, as if that was possible.

He introduced himself and apologized for the last minute substitution. She kicked the tires and asked for qualifications. He gave her a rundown.

"Have a seat." He gestured across the table. "Let's talk."

"That sounds serious."

"Everything's fine, Alex. There's nothing to worry about."

He docked an iPad on a round table. The glass surface lit up with an image of a naked brain. Her brain. He swiped his hand across it and various colors appeared. He began explaining how things worked, referring to methodology and seeding rates and recent biomite strains.

"You had a full scan with some biofeedback after your incident at the Institute and there's nothing abnormal. The majority of your biomites seeds are in your brain and the proliferation is proceeding nicely." He touched a thicket of red cottony growth near the frontal lobe. It looked more like a tumor. "Your cognitive functions are at peak performance for a woman your age."

"My age?"

"Mid-thirties, I'm guessing?" He smiled devilishly. He was only off by ten years. "Have you experienced an increase in performance since seeding?"

This was starting to sound like an erectile dysfunction commercial. "So why did I auto-engage?"

He shrugged. "The biofeedback didn't provide an answer, but that's not unusual."

She mentioned seizures, but he was doubtful.

"Have you ever done meditation?"

"No."

"You'll realize that we typically entertain more thoughts than we're aware of. There's all sorts of static going on in our minds, usually just below the surface. The subconscious is deep and mysterious. It's possible you engaged them without knowing."

"Wouldn't biofeedback show that?"

"In most cases. Or maybe you just don't want to remember."

She frowned. She didn't like to mix existentialism with her doctor's appointments. Stick to the facts, and the fact was this: Coco opened his eyes.

"Is there any chance someone could engage my enhancements?"

"What do you mean?"

"Some sort of wireless chatter that crossed over."

He shook his head. "Currently, there's no evidence of person-to-person mindjacking, if that's what you mean."

"But biomites can wirelessly communicate."

"Within your body, that's the extent."

She didn't mention what they said at the Institute, that the needle might become irrelevant due to biomite connectivity. Doubtful he would even believe the needle part.

"Subliminal messaging and thought hijacking are in the movies, Alex. Biomites are meant to enhance your senses, to heal injuries, and prevent genetic disease. They're not magic. You've got to take care of yourself—sleep right, eat right, moderate caffeine and sugar, lower your stress."

"My lifestyle never bothered me."

"Spicy food never used to bother me." He'd used that line before. Something told her he had this talk with a lot of his patients. He scribbled on the iPad. "I'm writing a prescription for anxiety. Take it for a month. It'll help you sleep, calm you down. Let's see how it goes. Come back in a month."

She nodded, but that was a white lie. "Just so we're clear, all the tests were normal?"

"Correct."

"I need an answer for the auto-engage, Doctor. I didn't do it." The doctor shook his head. "Can you at least recognize that I have a history of seizures and that there is a possibility of auto-engagement?"

"It's already in my report."

"And would you also include that there is a chance that biofeedback would not necessarily tell you it was auto-engagement that occurred, that a subconscious thought beyond my awareness could be responsible?"

"That's a small chance, Alex."

"Still a chance."

He sighed. She was gearing up for a lawsuit. "I can do that, if you promise me something. Slow your life down. Biomites don't make you invincible."

He looked at his wristwatch, a round antique with two hands and a second hand ticking across the numbers. *Strange choice for a man steeped in technology.*

"I'll see what I can do."

He left before she could ask about the wristwatch.

The waiting room was empty.

She didn't hesitate leaving the office, the receptionist busy texting or posting photos of quitting time. The hinges on the glass door squealed at a pitch that could shatter diamonds. It was unnerving and unacceptable and that would go in her tersely worded letter to Dr. Mallard, along with her reservations to continue as a patient.

The elevator doors were open and waiting. She punched the button and texted her husband, watching the traffic lights and endless line of brake lights.

Her toe caught something.

It was the *National Geographic* from the waiting room, the one the kid was reading. The corners were bent; creases cut across the tropical island and reflective waters. She picked it up as the elevator opened on the ground floor and rolled it into a tight cylinder.

Fifteen minutes passed. A produce truck had sideswiped a taxi and nothing was moving. The buildings' shadows grew longer and brake lights brighter. Cars honked; people shouted. An ambulance threaded its way down the street.

An hour elapsed.

Alex walked down the street and found the white Camry in the intersection of Forty-Sixth and Ninth. Traffic was slow enough that she climbed into the passenger seat, tossed her stuff on the floor and kissed Samuel on the cheek. Just as she was turning around, before she had a chance to look into the backseat—

Two headlights blinded her.

The driver's door collapsed beneath the bumper of a delivery truck, crushing Samuel's head.

Glass rained down.

Blackness enveloped her. Horns bled into angry shouts and the tinkle of glass. She spun in the darkness like a stuffed animal tumbling in a clothes drier...over and over and over—

"Oh!" Alex snapped her eyes open.

"You all right?" Samuel's voice was distant, almost like he wasn't there. "What's wrong? Alessandra, what's wrong?"

The car was fine.

There was no broken glass. No blood.

Not even a truck.

She climbed out of the car. Traffic angled to get around her, drivers raising their hands or giving her the finger. She stumbled against the car and looked up at the tall buildings, the sky bruised and crumpled. Anxiety lit her chest with dazzling tendrils. At the very same moment, lightning flashed across the sky.

Later she would remember looking at her hands, balling them into fists, and the city rushing past her like a raging storm. She would remember her husband's voice calling through cotton stuffed in her ears, even though the traffic was sharp and clear. Eyewitnesses reported she fell on her knees and pounded the asphalt.

She didn't remember that. Or the flashing lights of the ambulance.

Or seeing her husband.

138

New York City

Pressure.

Her head felt like an overinflated balloon, the rubber skin creaking with each stroke. And voices. There were voices out there.

So many voices.

Each one blurred like a bad recording. Each time, it joined a smudge of color, like blackness streaked with glowing lights, vivid smatterings of pigments that lingered for a moment, just a moment, then were swallowed by the dark until the next one.

Her own thoughts flitted in and out of existence, like an art film splashing random images. A few made sense, but none belonged to the voices. Just before the last stroke of the compressor filled her head, she saw a pair of brown eyes.

Coco.

The balloon popped.

A bright flash swallowed it all.

Alex was spared the pressure and the voices and haunting thoughts.

The world fell into place, all the pieces reshuffled and fit where they belonged. And the universe existed again.

It just existed.

And she did, too.

"We'll be suing," Samuel was saying. "Negligence, pain and suffering."

Through a veil of crusted eyelashes, the flowers were blurry. Brightly colored balls bobbed over them. Alex blinked slowly and the balls turned into helium-filled balloons tied to colored ribbon. She smacked her lips; the corners of her mouth stung.

"Got to let you go." Samuel hovered over her. "Alex? You awake?"

"Water."

He rushed out of sight and returned with a cup. She tried to lift her head. He helped her reach the bendy straw.

"Little sips." He took it away. "Give that a moment."

The water rushed into her parched throat and cooled her insides all the way to her stomach. He stared at her while she looked around the hospital room. His black hair was pushed back, his whiskers casting a shadow over the lower half of his face. And his smile glowed.

She smiled back, couldn't help it, but winced when her lips cracked.

He helped her with two more sips before setting it down.

"Are you feeling all right?" His voice was soft. She couldn't remember the last time it was like that. So soft, so caring.

"How long...have I been asleep?"

"Almost three days."

She lifted her arms and stared at her hands. There were no bandages. Besides feeling a bit shaky—she always felt that way when she was hungry—there didn't appear to be a reason she was in the hospital. Or sleeping for three days.

"They reset your biomites." He ran his hand through her hair. "Do you remember anything?"

The first thing was the pressure and streaking colors. But then the memory of traffic slowly rose from obscurity, the impact of a speeding truck and blaring horn that wasn't there.

And Coco.

"What's your name?" he asked.

She smiled. "Alex Diosa."

"Your full name?"

"Alessandra Diosa."

"That's my girl." He kissed her forehead. "I'll get the doctors."

He gave her one more swallow of water and put it out of reach. The muscles moved beneath his T-shirt. She collapsed on the pillow and watched him go. She was already tired, fighting sleep. She wanted to see the doctors, to see Samuel again.

The ceiling tiles had tiny perforations, like a white slice of the universe. The helium balloons drifted back and forth, crashing like soft metal.

A wave of static passed through the room, like a radio dial turned through a space of nothingness. It wasn't static. It was more like a conglomeration of words.

Voices.

She was suddenly thirsty. It took considerable effort to reach the cup. Her fingers brushed over the surface, finally grasping it. She took large sips, noticing the tracks her hand had left on the table.

And a circle the cup had left in a thick layer of dust.

Alex checked her email and answered voicemail, followed by a nap. There were more doctors and a thousand explanations. She felt partly numb, but that would change.

"What about the voices?" she asked.

"Voices?" the doctor asked.

She waved her hand around, as if this explained her experience. It was like a crowd in a distance, a stadium miles away, the roar swelling, the sounds blending, the voices indistinguishable from each other.

"What about that?"

The doctor nodded. They would run some more tests. Eventually, the voices would fade.

The next morning, she waited to be discharged.

A nurse was supposed to come with a wheelchair. Alex's belongings were already in the truck.

Except a ragged *National Geographic*.

It took a moment; then she remembered. It was on the elevator floor. Someone was looking at it in the waiting room. She was compelled to pick it up. Samuel must've thought she was doing research and brought it up to the room. It had been years since she'd read a print magazine.

The pages flopped in her hands. The cover was a tropical island set in the middle of the ocean, with swaying palm trees and a setting sun. *Not a bad place to be.*

The nurse finally arrived. Alex kept the magazine on her lap and was about to give it to an orderly when she noticed a piece of paper stuck in the middle. The end was torn.

An "A" was written on the end in green ink.

Chills crawled around her neck and tightened, reminding her of the cold chills in the Institute, not like a cool breeze or frozen rain. More like someone watching her.

Alex opened to the centerfold and the bookmark fluttered onto the floor. The nurse stopped to pick it up and handed it forward. She flipped it over.

Alessandra.

Few knew her birth name. Even fewer knew how to spell it. And there it was, written in block letters and wedged into a worn magazine. It wasn't Samuel's handwriting. And he didn't have a green pen, not that she knew. Not that any of that was impossible.

So why did she feel so cold?

139

AN ISLAND off the coast of Spain

An espresso waited.

A shirtless young man walked barefoot onto the veranda. He stretched, ribs protruding beneath pale skin, a patch of freckles across his shoulders and upper chest. He flipped the shag of red hair from his eyes and took the cup to the railing.

A tiny sip jolted Danny awake.

Jet lag still tugged at his inner clock, swishing in his head like water in the ears. Rarely did he fly back to the United States, but there were times when the situation was unavoidable. He spent the weekend in New York City and slept so hard on the flight back—a nonstop red-eye —that he hardly remembered boarding.

The Balearic Sea was spread out below, the deep blue water nearly glassy, cutting the horizon sharply where it met the equally blue sky. Beyond was the mainland of Spain and the port of Valencia. Once a month, he took the boat over to walk the open-air markets and meet with people for lunch, maybe dinner.

Business. Always business. And unusual for a sixteen-year-old. But very few sixteen-year-olds owned a thirty-million-dollar villa in the Mediterranean.

His name would not appear in Forbes or any other lists. His money was hidden, dispersed amongst various accounts and names. Danny had good reason to remain anonymous.

He finished the espresso, but it did nothing to clear his head. Maybe yoga would help. He looked more like a skater than a wealthy acolyte of meditation: lanky and rail thin. His breath was slow and purposeful. He could feel the sea below him, the birds above.

A breeze cooled him, sifting through his thick curls, as if God breathed with him. Through him.

Lilac. I smell lilac.

Lying in the corpse pose—the final pose—he thought that was odd since there were no lilacs growing on his property, yet it pervaded the atmosphere, saturated each breath. He heard a bone-china cup placed on a marble table beneath the portico. Sweat beaded across his chest. He exhaled then retreated to the shade.

Another espresso waited.

He took a moment to listen to the birds, to bathe in the mysterious lilac scent before tapping the low-set table. The morning reports danced across the surface in high definition. Life on the island was peaceful, almost solitary. But technology made distance irrelevant.

He sat back and sampled his drink, rubbing the knot on his forehead while scanning the newsfeeds. It itched this morning. The hole had healed, but a scar reminded him of Foreverland. Even if he could forget the itch and ignore the scar, his dreams took him back to the tropical island, put him back in the dark and dank cell where the needle waited. Two years in his past and he still fought the temptation to reach for the needle in his dreams.

We never left the island, someone once told him.

He left the island. He just went back there every night.

He had escaped the island with the seed money to invest in the villa. For that he was grateful but, given the choice, would trade it all to erase those days from his past.

"*¿Quieres algo más, señor?*" Maria stood near the open doors.

"*No, gracias, Maria.*"

"*Muy bien. El correo está sobre la mesa.*" *The mail is on the table.*
"*Gracias.*"

She smiled and began to close the doors.

"Maria, wait!" Danny waved to stop her. He retrieved the colorful bag that he had placed beneath the sink a week ago. She shook her head while he held it out.

"*Para su hijo,*" he said. "*Feliz cumpleaños.*" *For your son. Happy birthday.*

As she stood with one hand over her mouth and the other over her chest, Danny hooked the handles over her fingers. Her son had been in an accident. Danny was paying the medical bills, but the boy might not walk again.

"*Gracias,*" she muttered. "*Gracias, gracias, gracias.*"

He returned to the kitchen. The veranda doors were still open, the curtains dancing as the breeze picked up. He searched the refrigerator for a late morning snack, cutting cantaloupe and pineapple into chunks. The wind scattered the mail across the floor. Danny took a bite and started for the basement, where more business waited.

A thick envelope rested between his feet.

Danny Boy was written on it.

He nearly dropped the bowl. No one had called him Danny Boy in years. Two years, to be exact.

Not since the island.

There was no return address, just a stamp in the corner. The handwriting was shaky, the ink bright green. He held it up to the light, as if it might ambush him. He could feel something inside it, something circular and heavy.

Danny tore it open.

It was a disc about the size and shape of a DVD but as thick as a slice of cheese. The edge was blue, but the reflective surface was scattered with a hundred pinholes. Maybe a thousand. He turned it at angles, watching his blue eyes cross over the constellation. A sticky note was attached to the back. *Build the bridge, Danny Boy.*

A single sheet of lined paper fell out of the envelope, the writing in the same green ink as the address and sticky note. It was four lines:

. . .

The Earth I tread
  Upon leaves and loam
  I fly alone
  Where the sand is home.

He read it at least a dozen times and promptly tore it up, and would spend the coming weeks trying to forget who sent it.

———————

Danny woke in heaven.

The clouds floated around him. His stomach rose into his throat, and then he remembered he'd taken a meeting in the immersion room —a hemispherical domed projection room—and fell asleep. He had been dreaming of, what else, the island. Just before waking, he was flying like they often did in Foreverland.

But now he was awake.

He wiped the drool off his lip and called the effects off. The polished wall went blank and he stared at his reflection in all directions.

It must be late; he was still tired. He'd gone for a swim that morning, maybe that was it. He started for the outline of the door.

A bundle of letters was on the floor.

Maria must've dropped them off after seeing him snoozing on the lone chair. This wouldn't have bothered him had his name not been spelled out in big green letters.

Danny Boy.

The foggy remains of sleep blew away, replaced by a shiver. He considered whether to open it or just throw it out like he'd done the first letter. He didn't want to be reminded of the island. He'd escaped that tropical hell with Reed and Zin, but they'd all split up soon after and hardly kept in touch.

To start new lives.

And now this.

The Earth I tread upon leaves and loam could be any of them. For a time, they'd all wandered around lost. *I fly alone* could be Reed because he was an introvert, a loner. When they were on the island, he didn't mix with the other boys, didn't do what he was told. Everyone on the island knew that.

Where the sand is home.

That was the clincher. Only three people in the world knew where Reed's body was buried—his teenage body, the flesh he was born into. That body was dead. But Reed had transferred his identity, his awareness, into Harold Ballard's body when they erased Harold's identity. They did so without guilt, without shame. He was the one doing it to them; he had it coming.

Reed was a teenager in Harold Ballard's old body.

Reed's bruised and broken teenage body was buried on the beach. *Where the sand is home.* Only three people knew that. Danny was one of them. Reed and Zin were the other two.

But why so cryptic? Why the handwritten letter?

Zin was unreachable. The last Danny heard, he was on a vision quest somewhere in India where phones and computers didn't exist.

Reed, though, had moved back to the States. It had been a year or so since he last saw him. Even then he was a little off, dealing with survivor's guilt. They all were. No one could survive the island and be normal.

Maybe someone from the island had located Danny and was preparing to blackmail him. This thought crossed his mind. After all, Danny, Reed and Zin escaped with Harold Ballard's money and left all the boys on the island to be rescued by the Coast Guard. Maybe someone wanted a cut.

Danny could let that happen.

If that was the case, he wouldn't arm himself with a battery of lawyers. He would just walk out of the house and disappear. Money could always be made, but freedom was different. Have that taken away and you realize money means nothing.

The island taught him that.

Danny slid his thumb under the envelope's flap. Another disc fell out, the same as before: a blue edge and reflective sides with hundreds of pinpoints. The holes, he noticed, weren't simply poked or drilled through the thick plastic, they were angled on the inside, conical but at different degrees.

A note was attached. *Build the bridge, Danny Boy.*

Inside the envelope, there was a tri-folded paper, one edge still had ragged tags left from a spiral-bound notebook. Four lines in green ink.

We all dream the same,
    A dream that feeds in the dark.
    My demons are different than yours,
    But we all have them, just the same.

He read it three times. He doubted no more.

We all have demons, Reed once told him. It was the last thing he said before leaving Spain. Zin went on a vision quest to vanquish his demons. Danny threw himself into innovation. But Reed was different.

My demons are different than yours, he told Danny.

"Maps." The immersion room came to life. "Find Reed's last known location."

Reed never left an address, but Danny had tracked the IP address on his emails, cross-referencing his point of access and snooping through his activity.

He was good at that.

The image of Earth rotated on the immersion room's spherical wall and floor until Boston was beneath him. His stomach lurched as the clouds soared up and the city zoomed toward him. His feet were directly over Holworthy Street in Roxbury, an everyday neighborhood with tall, narrow homes.

"Street View."

The details twisted and formed a three-story house, the siding beige, the door new. A white van with a missing hubcap was parked out front. Reed was living on the second or third floor.

Why here, in the middle of the city?

Danny walked near the still form of a man on the sidewalk captured by Google's roaming Street View vehicles. He was wearing a blue sweatsuit, white stripes down the legs. His pit bull was caught sniffing the curb.

"Zoom."

He pointed at the third-floor window and the view pixelated for a fraction of a second before enhancing. Danny clutched at empty space, turning the view to the side of the house. Nothing of interest there, he went up and down the street and got as far as four blocks before returning.

He might not even be here anymore.

He began to call the immersion room off, couldn't waste the day deciphering an amateur poem and wandering the streets of south Boston. But a small detail caught his eye. It was the second story. The curtains in the window were crumpled.

A small flash had been captured, like a reflection. But the angle was all wrong for the sun to be reflecting off the window.

Danny pulled the view closer. The window zoomed but pixelated. It took a few moments for the computer to process the details.

A jar.

He pulled the view so close that the window towered over him, warping across the domed ceiling's curve. He stepped closer. There was something beige inside the jar, hidden beneath the hot flash. At first, he thought it was blurring across from the house's siding. When the details finally crystalized, he recognized the contents.

Sand.

140

V*ALENCIA, Spain*

"*Por favor.*" Danny raised his cup.

A waiter arrived, minutes later, with another espresso.

Santiago, a plump Spaniard with bristled mustache and thinning hair, sat opposite Danny. Always dressed impeccably, he kept his collars unbuttoned, where a tuft of curly black hair emerged. His attention was buried in his phone, his thumbs busy. Another email to answer, another report to read. He would stop to rub the birthmark high on his forehead that resembled the state of Florida.

Danny cocked his head. There was something off about Santiago, something he couldn't quite place. *Did he trim his mustache? Dye his hair? Maybe he lost weight?*

He meant to ask him, but forgot. Much later, he would understand what had changed. And why.

From where they sat, Danny could smell the port and see the beach, the flat line of the ocean's horizon. It smelled different, more fragrant. Like a flower. Lilacs again. Children were laughing some-where. This was a good place to do business.

A good place to live life.

The Spaniard excused himself. Danny crossed his legs and watched a ship cross the horizon before pulling the reflective disc from his pants' pocket. It was too thick to be a DVD or a Blu-ray. There were no grooves or inscriptions. He tried inserting a pencil into the holes, attempting to turn the disc like a template but they were too small. He even compared the pattern to various constellations, but nothing matched.

All he saw when he looked at it was his reflection. *Build the bridge, Danny Boy*.

He couldn't build a bridge with a disc, unless it contained plans that he hadn't figured out. Maybe Reed would send a special disc reader, but why all the clues? He only needed to pick up a phone.

Santiago was across the restaurant. Danny sank the disc deep into his pocket. He was nearly finished with his drink when Santiago returned with a tall American woman. "*Señor Daniel*," he said, "*esta es María*."

Danny stood.

"Mary." The woman reached across the table. Her grip was strong.

She dropped the leather bag slung over her shoulder. The waiter was at the table before she could sit. In Spanish, she ordered a drink. Her words tumbled off her tongue like misshaped stones, as if she looked it up in a translator only moments earlier.

Santiago asked about her trip, how she like Valencia so far. She answered with a bright, white smile, looking at Danny more often than Santiago. Her blonde hair was short and smooth, the kind you'd see on a billboard. Danny found himself smiling.

She returned his grin. When she did, her eyes sparkled like a car was behind him, the headlights forewarning him.

"How old are you?" she asked.

"Does it matter?"

"My clients are about to invest a billion dollars with your company."

"I don't need their money."

Santiago laughed nervously. "Danny's record is well established," he said in his most affected English, an accent that was effectively sophisticated. "His age, I assure you, is of no consequence."

She nodded while smiling. She'd flown the better part of a day to negotiate when they could've met in the immersion room. *How do Americans say?* Santiago had said to Danny when he arranged the meeting. *We meet old school.* She wanted to sit in front of him, look him in the eyes and sway him with charm, perhaps nudge him and later bully him with facts.

The waiter returned with a drink.

"Danny Jones." She used his full name, the name he now used. Danny Jones owned a thirty-million-dollar villa off the coast of Spain.

Danny *Forrester* left the island.

"The wonder boy with no past," she said. "The boy with no family, a teenager that, according to Santiago, learned Spanish within months of arriving."

Danny looked at his companion. Santiago shrugged. He did become fluent in Spanish, but she had it wrong. It was two weeks.

"You've invested extremely well and managed to stay out of the spotlight for a sixteen-year-old. What was it you said, Santiago? He is the reincarnation of Einstein with a taste for technology instead of stars."

"I, uh..." Santiago rubbed his birthmark.

"He's right." Danny lifted his cup. "And would you do business with Einstein at sixteen?"

Her smile was less flashy, but genuine. Had she sized him up already? She lifted her coffee.

All three drank.

"I suggest you drop the name 'Danny'," she said. "Sounds like a kid I went to summer camp with."

Santiago filled the awkward silence with the wonders of Valencia while Señorita Maria nodded, occasionally flicking a glance at Danny. He was sixteen years old; she was right about that. And most sixteen-year-olds were full of hormones, enslaved by them.

Not Danny.

There was a famous study called the Stanford Marshmallow Experiment that measured children's intellect with a proposition. The experimenter put a single marshmallow on the table. If the child could wait fifteen minutes without eating it, he or she would get two marshmallows. Those that waited the longest had grown up to be more intelligent.

Danny would've outlasted them all.

"I would love to see your city," Mary interrupted Santiago, "but I'd like to discuss a few matters with Danny."

She launched into her presentation with ease—nonchalant and conversational. Her clients were aiming to become the largest manufacturer of biomites, not just in quantity but innovation. They saw the artificial stem cells as the future of humankind, the next step in evolution, the perfecting of the human body.

Immortality was in reach.

Danny watched her present the facts of cost and production and risk. He wondered how old she was. How many biomites had she already injected into her face, smoothing out the wrinkles and glossing over the rough spots, waxing her intelligence to become one of the world's best—and most beautiful—negotiators?

Her eyes were magnetic blue, the kind of blue reserved for the glassy sea on a clear morning. Her lips were perfectly painted, her teeth pearly white. Her eyelashes fluttered. It was hypnotic. Give her enough time, and perhaps every man would melt.

Eventually, there was a flicker.

It was a small change in the way the light danced in her eyes, like the headlights behind him turned on the high beams. He turned around. It wasn't a reflection. There was no light behind him.

It was as if a piece of color had gone missing, a pixel of blue absent from her left eye. This cancerous gray dot bled out to the surrounding iris just to the side of the pupil, bleaching the pristine color.

It continued into the white.

The gray pixilation oozed over her eyelid and consumed her eyelashes, up into the hollow of her eye socket and over the bridge of her nose. Danny slid his chair back and refrained from recoiling as it soaked outward like an inky stain of gray static, eating a hole through the smooth complexion, turning Mary's face into a mechanical face-plate spouting words that were just sounds, data that were just numbers.

She glanced at Santiago.

The gray spot wasn't eating her face. It was chewing a hole in the fabric of space. As if she wasn't there. As if nothing was there.

Nothing at all.

And it was nothing that howled inside him. He felt it in his gut, heard it deep in his subconscious, calling like wolves. Calling him to be with it. To be nothing.

To be Nowhere.

"Señor Danny Boy?"

Danny snapped back into the present moment. Santiago stared with wide eyes. Mary was beautiful again, not a spot on her cheek or in her eye, as if nothing had happened, the fabric of space just as it should be.

They were looking at someone next to the table.

"Señor Danny Boy?" a boy asked, then dropped a letter on the table. This was a standard-sized envelope, the kind that would contain a letter, not a disk. Danny was transfixed by the green lettering.

Danny Boy.

"Hey!" He shoved away from the table. "*¡Espera!*"

"Danny." Santiago swiped at his arm.

Danny jumped out of reach; the chair clapped onto the floor. He leaped over the stone wall onto the sidewalk. The messenger was already pumping the pedals on a beach bike, bouncing over the curb and around a building. Danny leaped around traffic, swinging his arms with the letter squashed in his fist. He was gaining on the young man, whose coarse black hair fluttered over his shoulders.

He cut down an alley.

Danny gave chase through a crowd and emerged on the road running parallel to the beach. His side stitched with stabbing pain; he struggled to breathe. The boy was gone.

He looked at the wrinkled letter damp with sweat. *What is happening?*

Had someone tracked him down? One of the old men, perhaps? They certainly would want revenge. Danny had taken everything from them. *Everything.* But if one of them had survived, managed to elude the authorities that arrived when Danny, Reed and Zin had escaped, they wouldn't bother with poems or clues; they would've come straight away, kidnapped him while he slept. And even if they did send letters, they wouldn't know what to write.

The sand is my home.

Danny sat on the beach, watching sailboats slice across the horizon, the gulls hover over the water. Children ran past. He tore the letter open.

Another four lines. Another poem.

He read it over and over, hoping repetition would ease the cold fear rising. Like those days on the island, trapped in the cold concrete room of the haystack when the needle dropped from the ceiling, when he felt like crying.

When sometimes he did.

He didn't go back to the restaurant, didn't conclude business. He walked to the port where his ship waited. His captain took him back to the house. Santiago would later call him, but he wouldn't answer, wouldn't return his messages. Mary would stay in Valencia another week before returning to the United States, and her clients would refuse to invest with an unstable teenager, no matter how bright and promising.

But none of it would matter.

Every question contains its answer,
   When the children sing and stare,
   When you look into the blue,
   And see the endless Nowhere.

Nowhere was the opposite of somewhere. But for those that survived the island, it was more than that. It was the place where existence ceased, where space became a maddening array of gray static, complete chaos.

He saw it in Mary's eye, felt it howl inside him. It beckoned; it threatened.

As Reed knew it would.

141

AN ISLAND off the coast of Spain

Danny swiped the bathroom mirror. Beads of condensation raced to the sink. His irises were blue with dark bands radiating out like spokes. No gray.

No Nowhere.

He held the note, the edges damp in his hand. *When the children sing and stare.* Just before someone was sent to the Nowhere, they had a blank stare. Is that what it meant? *When you look into the blue.* Did he mean the blue in her eyes? The blue on the edge of the disc.

What bridge?

He shook his head and took a deep breath. He was reading too much into it. The symbolism could mean anything.

Every question contains its answer.

"*¿Señor Daniel?*" Maria knocked on the bedroom door. "*Señor Santiago es aqui.*"

"*Un momento!*"

A small scar was centered between his eyes, an inch above his eyebrows—the mark was innocence lost. Danny knocked on the mirror and stared at his hands. Ever since he returned from New York, everything felt a little off. Was it his imagination? He had the sense of skating on a frozen pond when spring had already arrived.

And he could feel the ice thinning.

Danny got dressed to meet his mentor on the veranda.

A cloud of smoke hung around Santiago's head.

He was admiring the million-dollar view. Danny watched him from beneath the shade of the pergola. The smoke polluted the ever-present smell of lilac. He hadn't seen the Spaniard since he abandoned them at the café. Santiago sensed the eyes on him and turned.

"Cigar?" Santiago waved the Cuban. "You are too young to smoke, forgive me."

His laughter cut across the wind.

"Sit in the shade?" Danny said.

The heavyset Spaniard shuffled beneath the pergola, the cigar clenched between his teeth. Maria stood in the doorway. Danny asked for water.

"Scotch," Santiago said. "Neat."

They sat opposite each other. Santiago's laughter rumbled on for no apparent reason. He did this for one of two reasons: he'd been drinking, or he was nervous.

And one never occurred without the other.

"Danny," he said. "Danny, Danny. *¿Cómo estás, mi amigo?*"

"*Muy bien.*"

"*¿Huh? ¿Si?*" His laughter faded. He rolled the cigar between finger and thumb, the smoke hanging over the Florida birthmark. Something was off. It was like two images that didn't quite line up.

"I worry about you, Danny. I worry."

"*Pero innecesario.*"

"Oh, I think it very necessary, *amigo*. You are so young and the world so big. You grow up so fast, and I worry. You have everything ahead of you, Danny—whatever you want. *¿Comprende?*"

Danny nodded. *I understand.*

Maria brought their drinks and a bowl of fruit. Santiago took tiny sips, sighing. He worked the cigar like a child casually hitting a pacifier. Danny took an ice cube and ran it across his forehead. They spoke about the stock market, about potential investment opportunities as well as the current ones.

When lunch arrived, Santiago shook his empty glass. When Maria brought a second drink, he bit a grape in half. "There is the matter of Mary and her investors."

Danny winced. It took a moment to comprehend what caused it. His forehead tingled. He connected the sensation to a word.

Investors.

The Investors, they were the old men that brought them out to the island, the old men that meant to steal their bodies. That word would always sting. He put on sunglasses, the world feeling a bit too bright.

"You see, your escapade"—he waved his knife—"the running you did at our meeting has caused...consternation, Danny. It was childish. People do not care to give money to a child."

"I won't explain myself, Santiago. There will be other investors, you see. Entrepreneurs are interested in one thing—money. They don't care who makes it for them."

"May I ask, what was the letter?"

"A girl, in town." The lie seemed fitting, less secretive. He was grateful for the sunglasses.

"*¿Amiga?*" The laughter slowly rumbled. "This is what I mean, Danny. *Amigas* are for boys, not men."

"Then the world is run by boys!" Danny's laughter was louder than Santiago's.

"Perhaps this is so. But, lucky for you, I saved this meeting with your investors. Mary will meet again on the promise you wait to chase your *amigas* after lunch."

"How do you work such magic?"

Santiago shrugged. "They know me, Danny. They trust me. I tell them to trust you because I believe in you. Since day one, I believe in you."

"Why?"

"I know a jewel when I see one. I recognize talent."

"*¿Cómo?*" Danny pressed. "What talent do you see?"

"You always ask the right questions, that's what I like about you. You make good choices." He pointed with the knife, chewing with his mouth open. "You are one in a million, Danny."

When lunch was finished, Santiago pushed away from the table and lit a second cigar. He took a cappuccino from Maria and puffed blue rings.

"No more running, Danny." He pointed with the cigar wedged between his fingers. "The investor will meet us tomorrow at the same restaurant. No more letters and such, no interruptions or we meet right here, on the veranda." He thumped the table. "They want your ideas, Danny. You are visionary. You will help bring a new world into one that is tired and old. *¿Comprende?*"

New world?

This was a new pep talk. Santiago was always about enjoying the fruits of life. By fruits, he meant wine, he meant women. Not a tired world or a new one.

It was getting hot, even in the shade. Maybe it was the smoke. Danny rubbed another ice cube on his forehead.

"Everything is yours, Danny. And when you are old enough, we will enjoy cigars together and talk of our triumphs. We will drink good liquor and live very long. A new reality."

Reality? "You mean new world?"

"Same thing, Danny. You have everything you want. *¿Comprende?*" Santiago's laughter returned. He lifted his cup. "*¿Por qué nunca dejar?*"

Danny choked.

Santiago didn't notice. His head was back, a column of blue smoke streaming from his lips. It reminded Danny of something long forgotten, a chimney on the tropical island that belched smoke when one of the old men had successfully stolen another body. *Smoked* is what they called it. *Someone just got smoked.*

"What did you say?" Danny said.

"*¿Que?*"

"What did you say, just a second ago?"

Santiago thought a moment, dashing his ashes. "*¿Por qué nunca dejar?*"

It was an innocent phrase that sank its knuckles so far under Danny's ribs that it robbed his breath. He gulped small bites of air, tears brimming behind the dark lenses.

"The bathroom calls." Santiago excused himself.

Danny raised a hand but didn't wait for the Spaniard to return before going to the patio's wall. He ran the last couple of steps, vomiting over the edge. He rinsed his mouth, wiped his eyes and tried to appear normal.

Those words, the very same words, had been uttered before.

He'd heard those words on the island, long ago, to describe Foreverland—the imaginary land where he and all the boys were forced to go, where their dreams had come true, where they got everything they wanted so they would never return. They would leave their bodies behind, empty of awareness.

Foreverland was the trap they couldn't resist, so wonderfully everything a boy could want. The old men told them so. They said exactly what Santiago just said in Spanish.

Why would you ever leave?

"Lunch tomorrow, Danny?" Santiago waved from the house. "I come pick you up."

Danny agreed.

It was the second lie he told that day. He wouldn't be there when the Spaniard arrived. He wouldn't go to lunch. Reed sent those letters.

Now he had to find him.

142

Upstate New York

"*¡Hola! ¡Hola!*"

The front door opened, followed by rustling bags and heavy footsteps. Alex wiped her hands on an apron and turned just in time to see a petite woman come at her with arms wide open.

"Ooo," the woman dressed in brown moaned, clenching her daughter in a long hug that betrayed her inner strength. "*¿Cómo estás?*"

They hugged beneath a rack of stainless steel pots and pans, an embrace Alex tried to relinquish twice.

"*Bien, Madre. Bien, bien, bien.*"

Madre pulled back and stared at her daughter, searching for the truth. Alex took the old woman's hands and kissed them like she did when she was a child. Madre's eyes teared up. She held Alex's hands to her cheeks and kissed them over and over while muttering prayers.

An unsteady march came down the hall.

"Ah, there she is." Her stepfather, a retired farmer, limped into the kitchen, the uneven gait the result of a tractor rolling on top of him. He wore boots made for cutting wood because you never know when a pile might need tending. The only thing bigger than his boots was his belly and, of course, his personality.

"Can I get an autograph?" Hank asked.

Alex hugged him. His beefy hands were cut from bucking bales and manhandling ornery hogs. He lifted her onto her toes.

"*Bonita.*"

"*Gracias.*" She laughed. "You're early."

"No traffic," he said. "Your mother fell asleep."

"So you drove 100?"

"Not quite."

Alex took the paper bag and placed the bottle of wine on the island counter. Hank went to find a comfortable chair and a television because, as he always said, driving makes you tired.

"You are cooking?" Madre asked.

"I follow the directions on the box."

"But that's still good, you know. The apron and everything is good." Madre patted her hand like before, this time without the prayer.

Alex began cleaning dishes. She could only take so much of that look, the one Madre lovingly saddled onto her children. *Look what you do to me,* Madre would say when something bad happened. Her brothers, perhaps, deserved as much, but none of the guilt stuck to them. And Alex, the fallout of her older siblings fell on her like ashes of a well-tended fire that had once burned fiercely.

It took three years of therapy for Alex to unwind the weight of Madre's suffering. That was why Samuel didn't call her from the hospital, why Alex didn't contact Madre until she was home, when everything was normal. The old woman no longer said those words, not to Alex. But her eyes still spoke them, the creases on her forehead were very clear.

Look what you do to me.

Alex lifted her hand halfway to her head before stopping. She thought the voices were beginning to swarm, but it was just the lawnmower. That strange crowd of voices, young voices like children, still came in waves. If she listened for them, they were always there, in the distance. The doctors had no explanation, just to be patient.

Hank came back into the kitchen and asked for a corkscrew. Madre refused to let him open the wine. They argued while he pulled the cork out.

Cheese and crackers were served and nearly gone when Samuel finished mowing. Madre's worry lines had faded in the warm glow of red wine. Now there was just laughter, and a warm feeling infused the room, like sunshine beamed from the light fixtures. The last time Alex felt like that she was very young, before she was saddled with worry and declarations.

A sunbeam sliced through the window; a heavy cloud of dust danced in the light when she noticed the distant chatter, like a crowd on the other side of the fence, the garbled words muffled in the trees. She paused at the sink and looked into the backyard until the voices faded.

Samuel had turned the yard into paradise. Almost everything was blooming yellow, her favorite color. Butterflies and bees and dragon-flies came to visit and never seemed to leave. And the scent of her favorite shrub filled the kitchen, violet flowers in full bloom.

Lilac.

Hank dropped the last card on the pile and they added up the points. Alex wrote down the scores while Madre gathered the cards to shuffle. Samuel excused himself to find another bottle of wine.

"When are you going to start writing?" Hank asked.

"When I'm ready."

"Well, how long does that take?"

"I'll know."

"You know what they say about getting back on the horse?"

"Wear a helmet?"

Hank bellowed laughter like a distant relative of Santa. Madre arranged the cards all in one direction, tapping the deck on the table, and began the ritual of shuffling exactly seven times. She placed the deck in front of Hank.

"Whatever happened to the piece you were working on, the one on animal abuse?"

"Hank." Madre knocked on the deck. "More cards, less talk."

He nodded and dutifully cut the deck. Madre began dealing. Alex didn't answer. She didn't want to talk about writing or hospitals or accidents. She caught Samuel's cards before they slid onto his chair, and waited for his return.

"What's done is done, Alex," Hank said. "You can't fix the past."

A cantankerous old fart, Hank liked politics and drama. Not the usual modus operandi for someone that grew up in the country. *If you're not pushing buttons,* he once said, *you're not living.* Hank insisted that stones were not meant to sit and rest, but to turn over to see what was hiding beneath. Sometimes that meant you had to throw a few.

"I'm not trying to fix the past, Hank. Just leaving it where it belongs."

"But you're not writing. Sounds like the past is still in the present."

"Stop," Madre hissed. "Talk is over, old man."

"I'm just saying." He gave his patented shrug and leaned back with a slight smile. It was the equivalent of a boxer taunting an opponent with his chin. "Alex is a writer. She's not writing. So is she Alex?"

"Bones don't heal overnight," Alex said.

"Or maybe they're not broken."

"You still limp."

He patted his hip. "That's hard living, *chica.*"

Alex bristled. He only called her *chica* when he was bored, his way of saying she hit like a girl.

"You could get it fixed," she said.

"It's not broke."

"Then why do you limp?"

"Old men are supposed to limp."

"You're saying your past makes you who you are? Sounds like someone isn't present."

"I'm saying I'm exactly who I should be. Old men die and babies suck on mother's milk."

"Enough." Madre slapped the table. "No more talk of *niños*. Look at your cards before I take them."

Lines carved her forehead, but these were different than the ones

Alex feared. This expression Madre reserved for her husband, when he forgot to take out the trash or pushed arguments too far.

He scooped up his cards, adding a twinkling wink that said meet me out back later and we'll finish this. Samuel came back with a fresh bottle and filled all the glasses. The game resumed; cards were played.

Jazz streamed through the speakers and somewhere outside children were playing. Samuel began to whistle and Hank asked him to stop and Madre told them to behave themselves. The hand was almost over when someone said.

"Don't forget who you are."

"What?" Alex said.

"Your play," Hank said.

"No, what'd you say?"

The others looked confused. "It's your play, Alex," Samuel added.

"No, he said something else." *Don't forget who you are.*

Alex waited. She wanted to push more, but Madre's lines of impatience could turn to worry, so she dropped a card. Madre smiled, played her trump cards, and the hand ended soon enough.

Samuel corralled the deck.

Alex noticed the subtle tracks on the polished surface, a light dusting. She dragged her finger across the table, wondering where all the debris was coming from.

"Some things you can't forget," Hank said. "Or shouldn't."

But when she looked up, the old man was finishing his wine. And Samuel was eating a cracker. Madre tallied the points.

She didn't ask him to repeat it. Instead, she excused herself to the bathroom.

Madre didn't need to see her breakdown.

———————————

Alex went to the bathroom then hauled the recycling out to the garage.

She didn't explain why she felt compelled to do it before the card game was over, just called out from the kitchen and walked out before anyone could argue.

Hank got to me.

The old man never argued with Samuel. Maybe because Samuel was a lawyer, a damn good one, or a man. Or maybe because Hank knew Alex would give him a good fight but, in the end, he'd get the final word. She couldn't recall anyone ever winning a debate with Hank, whether it was politics or Chinese checkers.

But she'd never heard him pretend not to say things.

She didn't imagine that. He wasn't pretending. He couldn't have said it because *he had a throat full of wine.*

She took a deep breath, made a detour through the backyard, and cleared her mind. Despite the cloudless sky, it was brisk. She hugged herself against the chill and wished she would warm up. She needed to clear the clutter in her head. Maybe a nap. Sleeping had been doing her good lately. She always woke up refreshed and happy.

And happy wasn't a word she wore often.

She dumped the recycling and crossed the driveway. The neighbor across the road waved from his mailbox. Alex waved back and slowly made her way out to the curb.

The street was lined with mature elms that arched overhead. Despite the dappled shade, it was warmer out there, almost ten degrees. She already felt good inside and out. Must've been the fresh air. *Sometimes a short walk is the remedy.*

There was a wad of envelopes stuffed in the mailbox; she sifted through them on the way back, half of it junk. The garage door was still open. She tossed all of it into the recycling bin but noticed the address on a large envelope.

Alessandra.

A wave of gooseflesh raced down her arms. Alex looked around, even at the blue sky. She'd done a story once, when she first started as a journalist for *The Washington Post*, on paranoid schizophrenia. One of her subjects insisted there were cameras always watching, satellites that recorded everything. He described how he got this feeling when the spies were watching him, how his joints tickled and the back of his throat itched.

She never forgot that.

She tore the envelope open. Several glossy sheets fell on the concrete. It was from a travel agency. The fliers advertised package deals all over the world with illustrious beaches, endless sand and swaying palms on uninhabited islands.

She flipped the pages over, admired the views and, one by one, dropped them into the recycling bin. But they seemed familiar. *Where have I seen these?*

It was the last page.

White sand was on one side of the island and cliffs on the other. The view was from above, taken from a helicopter or a drone. *Maybe even a satellite.*

She'd seen this photo, seen this island.

"Alex!"

She dropped the photo. Samuel was on the back porch.

"You all right?" he asked.

"Yes, sure. Just...picked up the mail."

"You want to finish the game?"

"Yes, of course."

How long had he been standing there? Was that what she felt?

She wadded up the page and tossed it. Of course she hadn't been there. She'd never been to a remote island in her life. She'd seen a thousand photos of beaches. She climbed the steps and noticed the red tulips in the bed Samuel had mulched.

He stood with the door open. When she turned around, the tulips were yellow. Maybe she needed to schedule another appointment with Dr. Mallard or Dr. Johnstone. She wasn't just hearing things.

She was seeing them, too.

143

The tulips' petals had fallen.

They rested on the mulch in various degrees of yellow, faded by sunlight and age, signaling the end of spring. Alex snipped the tulip stalks. She had plans for the backyard. A row of fruit trees against the fence and a vegetable garden in the corner.

She entertained thoughts of moving to upstate New York or even western New Jersey, where they could purchase acreage. Samuel could still get to the city and, should she decide to write again, she could get to her agent.

For now, she just wanted to be home.

There was a hole in her glove and dirt was getting under her finger-nail. She went to the garage and found another pair, almost new, in the bottom of a bucket, but they were too small even for her hands. They were for a child.

Alex searched under the workbench for another pair of gloves. She noticed her briefcase stuffed inside a plastic bin. It was on top of a stack of papers, empty cups and sweaters. Samuel must've cleaned out her car.

It had been months since she drove her car. In fact, she hadn't even left their property.

The leather smelled like work. Life was smooth now, like gliding over black ice. She hadn't seen her briefcase since getting out of the hospital, hadn't even thought about it. Half-written notes and unsigned contracts were mixed with traffic tickets.

The small raincoat was at the bottom of the plastic bin. She pulled it out and something fell. It was the *National Geographic*, the one from the doctor's office. She hadn't seen it since the hospital.

The bookmark.

She'd forgotten about that. Her name had been written on the piece of notebook paper in green ink. It was rather shocking at the time. No one ever used her full name, not outside the family at least. Now it was gone.

She smoothed the wrinkles on the cover. The island was small and isolated in an endless ocean. A sense of déjà vu passed through her. The issue was a few years old, which would explain the wear. She licked her fingers and flipped to the cover story.

Places You'll Never Want to Leave.

The piece was dominated by photos of remote tropical islands. *Heaven does exist*, said one blurb. *It's just hard to get to.*

The photos were stunning, but the centerfold resolved the sense of déjà vu. That was the one from the travel agency, the piece of mail she'd opened when Madre and Hank were visiting.

The exact same photo.

There were no credits. She turned to the front, went through all the names where the photographers were properly recognized, but nothing was credited for the tropical island.

"There you are."

Alex dropped the magazine. Her heart thudded. Despite the clear sky, thunder faded in the distance. Spring showers were coming.

Samuel had the mail in one hand, a tall glass of tea in the other. He handed her the glass and shuffled through the mail, dropping most of it in the recycling after ripping the junk in half. One of them was a large white envelope addressed with green ink, her name in big block letters.

Alessandra.

"You all right?" he asked.

"Did you clean out my car?"

"Someone had to."

He began searching the shelves for car wax. Alex remained in the garage, staring at the recycling bin. The return address was a travel agency. She couldn't remember the name of the other one, but they had to be the same.

It was getting hot and stuffy. The afternoon heat was picking up fast. She pressed the glass of iced tea against her forehead.

"Where'd you get this?" Samuel held up the *National Geographic.*

"It was with my stuff."

He thumbed through it, frowning. His complexion turned a shade darker, eyebrows protruding. She felt the heat of his anger and took an involuntary step back.

"I didn't put that in there."

She shrugged. "I didn't clean out the car."

"Where'd you get a three-year-old magazine?"

"It was from the doctor's office. I had it with me in the hospital, remember?"

He fanned through the pages. The bookmark fluttered out from the last couple of pages. It landed on the workbench, her name staring up at him in green ink.

Green ink. The travel agency envelope was also lettered in green ink. Samuel grunted. Something twisted inside her when he made that sound, like predators were nearby.

"You do this?" He held it up.

Did he not remember the magazine? He had to bring it from the car to the hospital room.

But that didn't mean he read it, didn't mean he pulled the bookmark out. But the way he was holding it, the way his eyebrows protruded told her he didn't. And he really wanted to know who did.

"Yes," she said. "Just marking a spot."

"When did you start using your full name?"

"I was playing around."

"Playing?"

"Yeah."

"With your full name?"

"I don't remember a lot of what happened then, Samuel. Is something wrong?"

He was nodding. It wasn't her handwriting, and he knew it.

"Where'd you get a green pen?"

"It was at the hospital."

She avoided stepping toward the recycling bin. Half the travel agency's envelope was turned up. He'd obviously forgotten about it or wasn't paying attention when he ripped it.

"Just seems odd you would write this," he said.

"I'm a little confused. Is there something you should be telling me?" She found her footing, like she sometimes did in the middle of a debate with Hank. Sometimes a good offense is a good defense. "It's an old magazine, Samuel. Here."

She placed it in the recycling bin, perfectly covering any trace of green ink. "You keeping that for evidence?"

He was still pinching the bookmark. When he didn't move, she snatched it from his fingers and threw it away.

"Could you haul a bag of mulch to the tulip bed?" she asked. "My back is a little achy."

He thought about it, then smiled. It was a forced smile, one that never quite reached his eyes. She pretended to search for gloves while he took a bag out to the yard. She quickly grabbed the junk mail and hid it on a shelf of old paint cans, making sure the magazine stayed in the exact same position.

The spring shower that, minutes earlier, sounded nearby had cleared up.

The sky was cloudless and blue.

———

Alex quickly tore the large envelope open.

More vacation fliers. She quickly found the one she was looking for. It was the overhead view of an island with white sands on one side, cliffs on the other.

She could've held it next to the *National Geographic* centerfold; they would be identical. *National Geographic* wouldn't use stock photos. Unless the agency pilfered it, this was highly unusual.

The Land of Forever, the title said in the corner. *Why would you ever want to leave?*

Later that night, she and Samuel watched a movie with a bottle of wine. They slipped into bed. She waited until he was snoring, and then waited another half an hour.

The old wooden steps creaked on the way up to her office above the garage. She turned on the computer, the first time in months, and typed a search.

Land of forever.

The result was at the top, the number one hit.

A gust of wind hammered the house. The windowpane creaked.

She swallowed a hard lump, looked at the door and listened. A familiar sensation buzzed in the back of her head, sending up the small hairs on her arms. Her journalist instincts lit up. Something was about to happen.

She clicked the link.

Foreverland.

144

ADMAX P*ENITENTIARY,* *Colorado*

Gramm raked his fingers through his hair and counted the stray follicles. He always counted, sort of a way to show his respects to his receding hairline.

A former chemist, his hair used to be thick and wavy and fall over his ears, curled just above his eyes. He was known as *the surfer scientist.* But twenty years in the United States Penitentiary knocked the surfer out of him. Now it was thin; now it was gray. Now he watched the surfer scientist disappear one follicle at a time.

He started up the metal stairs, his footsteps clanging on the treads. Two pairs of footsteps trailed behind him. Gramm waited on the third floor.

Melfy, a short, heavyset African-American guard, carried a tray with a bowl of soup and a carton of milk. Her tight curly hair was cut close to the scalp, but there were signs of gray mixed in. Gramm noticed those things.

Drake, the second guard, pulled himself up the steps, his boots clobbering the metal treads. The six-foot-something, pasty-white male still smoked on his days off. He wheezed on the top step.

Gramm stared at the flabby piece of work, raking his hair five times. It would cost him twenty follicles. They passed through a checkpoint without pausing. Green metal doors were on each side, the paint chipping from the surfaces, white numbers painted below sliding slots. The stringent odor of cleaning supplies stung his nostrils.

They stopped at the last green door.

"Hold on." Gramm raised his hand.

He took several slow breaths. His heart rate only became more violent. It didn't matter how many slow breaths he took, it wasn't going to slow down.

He nodded.

Drake threw the door open, the scent of potpourri wafting out. Beneath the floral aroma was the smell of old skin and decay, like something dying a very slow death.

One that was thirty years in the making.

A cafeteria tray sat on a cluttered desk, the food cold and untouched. Gramm waved Melfy inside. She replaced the tray with the one she was carrying, the soup still warm and spilling over the edges.

There was a bed against the wall. It was thick and wide and humming. Gramm took the chair from the desk and sat down, facing the bed and the old man sleeping on it. Dr. Tyler Ballard looked to be one hundred years old, but Gramm knew he wasn't quite eighty.

The old man wore a gray uniform with a number stitched over the right breast. It was loose and wrinkled, oddly matching the thin skin that sagged from his cheeks and chin. Even his eyelids were paper-thin, the bulge of irises moving beneath them.

Gray and withered, only the slow rise of his chest and the fluttering of his lower lip suggested he was alive. Only the rosy flesh around the needle in his forehead was other than gray.

Drake, the fat guard, wheezed like a long-distance runner finishing a marathon, his lungs wet like a recovered drowning victim. He stepped forward with that rheumy gaze, the long-term effect of a mental hostile takeover, a man with a biomite brain that had been hijacked years ago. The imbecile was dull and trainable, which made it that much easier for Dr. Ballard to take over the fat man's biomite-laden brain and reprogram his thoughts to do whatever Gramm needed. Still, the oaf couldn't follow directions.

He reached for the old man and Gramm yanked him back. *You don't wake him.*

They watched and waited. Gramm raked his scalp. Twelve follicles were lost before the old man's chest began to swell, a long, deep breath. He smacked his lips.

His eyes fluttered.

His fingers began to crawl. The bed whirred, internal rollers kneading the aged body.

Dr. Ballard's hand rose like invisible strings lifted it. His hand hovered over his face and stalled like the puppeteer wasn't sure what to do next. Dr. Ballard focused on his fingers and the lines creasing his palm, then reached for the needle.

He pulled it out.

Gramm squeezed his hands together to avoid squirming, to keep from pulling his hair. That lone feeling of the needle plunging in or out of the brain was cold and foreign, tasted like metal, an inch and a half of surgical steel that glistened.

The old man propped himself up on one elbow and threw his weight to his side. Gramm and the two guards watched him slowly work his way into a sitting position. They didn't attempt to help. He had made that clear long ago.

The bed continued to thrum.

The old man leaned on his knees and contemplated the needle like script was written along the gleaming shaft. Then he broke it off and threw it away. Three deep breaths with his eyes closed, he hummed upon exhalation. When the paper-thin eyelids fluttered open once again, blue eyes with sharp edges aimed directly at Gramm.

Gramm's head hummed with a cold touch.

"Tell me," Dr. Ballard said, his words long and drawn, "why she is searching for Foreverland."

Gramm fidgeted. He couldn't help it. He uncrossed his legs, dropped both feet on the floor but didn't answer. It wasn't time to answer.

"What rekindled her interest, Gramm? Answer."

"I...I don't, don't know. No one has sent emails or texts or called. Samuel has been with her the entire time and, and given her everything she wanted."

"Hank's behavior didn't seem odd to you?"

"He was a little feisty, but that's been his personality, the way she knows him. If he changed, she'd notice."

"But we don't need him goading her back into writing, either. We need her happy, content. We need her to sleep, Gramm. Not motivated."

Gramm allowed his hand one pass through his hair.

Dr. Ballard didn't ask about the magazine and the photos of the tropical island. He would bring it up later, discuss whether this was another coincidence or a pattern. No need to pile on.

There's bigger news.

He rubbed his face with both hands and stared at the floor. Gramm could feel the old man's thoughts churning. Give him enough time and he would have a solution. But that was the problem.

Time.

The old man didn't have much. He insisted on letting his body wither like a husk of harvested corn.

"I don't like this." He raised his hands.

Drake and Melfy took them on command and helped him stand, waiting by his side to let the world balance beneath his feet. His elbows were bruised. Gramm suspected there were bruises on his buttocks and back as well, despite the specialized bed.

The old man shuffled to the desk and drank a bottle of water without pause, wiped his mouth with the back of his hand and stared at Gramm. The queer coldness was in his head again, starting in the core of his brain where a patch of biomites had been seeded. The sensation crept out like frozen tendrils.

Dr. Ballard sensed the worry. "What is it?"

Gramm could barely feel his legs when he stood. He didn't want to say it, not out loud. If he thought about it, concentrated on the image, the doctor would just know it as if it was his own thoughts. But the old man just returned from Patricia's Foreverland; he was still adjusting to physical reality.

Gramm would have to say it.

"The boy. We've lost him."

"Danny?"

"He...left the villa. Didn't tell anyone."

"Where did he go?"

Gramm shook his head. That was all the old man needed to know. It was obvious now that he said it out loud. Hank's badgering, the *National Geographic*, Alex researching Foreverland, and now Danny had disappeared.

This is no coincidence.

And there was no time for complications.

The old man dropped the spoon and pushed the tray away. Melfy guided him into the hallway. Drake and Gramm followed them out to the yard, where the doctor would spend the next half an hour walking and thinking and returning to the world of flesh.

He would decide how to address these changes.

And fast.

SUMMER

A snake sheds its skin.
To be born again.

145

"W*HAT DO* you have to offer, Mr. Deer?"

"Call me Jonathan."

Mr. Connick glanced at his notes and shook his head.

He blinked, his eyes closing an extra beat, considering whether he should throw Jonathan out of the office, have him arrested. His name was a joke, but in a meeting like this, no one showed their true face.

Jonathan reached into his jacket and revealed an index card sharply folded. The other sheet, the one with a list of names, would remain in his pocket for now.

"You can speak freely," Mr. Connick said.

The office was soundproof, tamperproof, completely isolated from eavesdropping. Still, Jonathan slid the card across the polished desk. They stared at the steepled note.

Mr. Connick bounced his fingers, perhaps considering, once again, throwing him out. He leaned forward and read what was written on the inner portion of the fold.

"This is what you want. I asked what you have to offer."

"Can you deliver?"

Mr. Connick tapped the rigid edge of the note on the desk, staring at Jonathan's eyes. They were green for this meeting, and slightly narrow. He'd *reshaped the bridge of his nose and extruded his brow. Only a few people in the world knew his true identity. But no one, no matter how much technological power they had, would be able to match Jonathan's identity with facial recognition.*

Not even Mr. Connick.

He got up and paced along the spacious window with a view down Chicago's Adam Street. The lake was visible between the buildings. The note bounced between his fingers, his hands clasped behind his back.

"Audacious, Mr. Deer." His voice reverberated off the glass. "What could you possibly have to offer me for this? Money? Information? Power? I assure you, whatever it is, there is not enough to get what you're asking. Nothing even close."

He flicked his wrist. The note skidded across the desk, landing on its side, open for Jonathan to see his own handwriting.

"What could you possibly offer us?" Mr. Connick said.

Jonathan leaned back. "Your very own universe," he said. "Foreverland."

146

The rental car was still running.

Danny adjusted the vents. The sun had moved behind him, the glare no longer in his eyes, but it was still blazing hot. No one was doing much of anything outside. Every thirty minutes, a stringy woman would come onto the porch to smoke. She'd stare at him until she finished, flick the butt onto the lawn and go back inside.

All the deals he put together in Valencia had fallen apart by now. Santiago would try to delay the inevitable and convince the investors their millions of dollars were in good hands. But Danny had turned off his phone and left everything behind when he flew out late one night.

The emaciated woman was coming out for another smoke, her tenth of the day, when Danny opened his door. Cicada song welcomed him to the summer furnace. He locked the doors and walked down the cracked sidewalk, feeling the eye of a neighborhood watch sign follow him to the corner house.

The neighborhood had the smell of trash—sour beer and rotting eggs. Beneath it all, he noticed the faint hint of lilac. It reminded him of his villa off the coast of Spain.

He climbed the porch and walked to the staircase built into the side of the house. The wood was relatively new, the steps leading up to a platform on the second floor and another on the third.

His heart rate grew louder.

The door on the second-floor platform was locked. There was a peephole but nothing for Danny to see inside. He looked around before lightly tapping with a knuckle. He waited a full minute before doing it again and thought about trying the third floor when he noticed the digital lock.

It was brand new.

He rapped one more time, staring at the distorted reflection on the numerical pad. Someone had scratched four letters into the gold-plated trim.

GRAD.

Danny punched the numbers that corresponded to the letters. Nothing happened. He rubbed his finger over the etching, the lines smooth and tarnished. Someone had done it quite some time ago. Assuming it was Reed, why would he put that there?

Was it a clue?

Grad was short for gradient, such as slope. That could be converted to a number, which could be the combination. Reed's letters led him here with clues from the island, but there was nothing that corresponded with slope—nothing on the island or anything since. He couldn't even guess.

Grad could also mean graduate. *Or graduating.*

Back on the island, when a transition was complete, when one of the boys had permanently vacated their body, the chimney would smoke. That was when the old men said someone graduated from the island, that they were healed.

They got SMOKED.

Danny punched the corresponding number: *766533.*

The lock whirred. Warm, stale air seeped out—

"What are you doing there?" A man stood on the bottom step. He was wearing flannel bottoms and no shirt, his stomach overhanging the drawstrings.

"Looking for a friend."

"And you just walk in?"

"He gave me the code." Danny pushed the door open.

"Don't mean you can walk in."

"I'm meeting him. He gave me the code so I didn't have to wait in the sun, you know."

The man pushed his fingers through oily black hair.

"Is there a problem?" Danny added.

"I don't know, is there?"

"My friend up here making noise?"

"Why?" The man's second chin jiggled.

"He doesn't pay his rent sometimes." Danny reached for his wallet. "Do I need to square up for him?"

"Yeah, sure."

"Look, is he paid up or not?"

"None of your business."

The man looked away. Reed was paid up, but it was hard to tell if he was the landlord or a nosy tenant.

"Have you seen him?" Danny asked.

"Not in a while."

"Like a week? A month?"

"Something like that."

"Which is it?"

"What do you want with him?"

Danny grimaced. "I'm worried about a friend, that's all. He doesn't feel good most of the time. If he's not here, which I don't think he is, then I'm just going to wait inside for a few, all right?"

The man rubbed his gut in a slow circle like he was comforting an unborn baby.

Danny walked inside, pulled the door closed and waited. When there were no footsteps up the staircase, he began to look around.

All the blinds were closed. A couple of the windows were covered with sheets, throwing the apartment into dim gray light. A fan rotated on a coffee table, the whirring blades pushing dead air around the room.

Danny turned on a short lamp. There was a couch and a couple of chairs. The pillows were perfectly arranged, almost intentionally, as if someone dressed the place up or never sat down. A kitchenette was to the left and a cluttered desk straight ahead.

Danny stood perfectly still.

It smelled like a vacation, like sand and sunscreen. Reed always had the scent about him, like he showered in the ocean. Danny sometimes wondered if there was a strange connection to the island, if somehow Reed had been infected with the false promises of Foreverland, saturated with the tropical allure.

A television blared from downstairs. The ceiling creaked from footsteps above him. Inside the apartment, ghosts of desolation dared him to come inside, to look around. Light sliced through a bend in the blinds.

He reached through the plastic slats and grabbed the Mason jar. It was nearly full of white sand, the kind that would sift through an hourglass. *Or found on a tropical island.*

A green ink pen had been stabbed into it.

All doubts fell away.

A jar of mustard was inside the refrigerator, along with a block of hard cheese, an egg and a bloated jug of milk. It had been expired for six months.

The bed was bare, the mattress thin and frayed. A round cushion was in the middle of the floor, a zafu for meditation. So he was meditating, just like Zin taught him.

A few clothes were folded beneath the bed. Danny pulled out jeans and T-shirts. He was braced to find a tropical shirt—something Harold Ballard wore on the island—but they were solid colors. That's when he realized one of his nagging fears: somehow Harold Ballard had returned from the ethers of the Nowhere and reclaimed his old body.

He folded the shirts and noticed a black cable. Danny fished it out, pulling something heavy from the dark corner. Straps were attached to the end. A cold chill shook through his arms. The leather straps formed a headset with a knob that would center over the forehead.

Inside was the needle.

The last time Danny saw the headset was on the island, when the needle would flick out like a stainless steel tongue, find the hole in their head and transport them away from the suffering.

To Foreverland.

But Reed never took the needle, not until they forced it on him. He was the only boy on the island that refused Foreverland. So why now? Even so, there was no host to create Foreverland. It was Harold Ballard's mind that created Foreverland. And he was gone.

Where would he go?

The other end of the cable had been cut. Whatever it was connected to was gone. And Reed had left the rest to be found, to let Danny know he was using it.

Just above the naked pillow, scratched into the wall with the same instrument used on the digital lock, were tiny letters.

Danny leaned closer.

Build the bridge.

He wondered if he left his home to follow the ramblings of a madman, an addict to the needle, a broken mind fighting to get back to Foreverland. Why would Reed go back to Foreverland? Even when they were on the island, when all the boys couldn't wait to punch the needle, he knew it was a trap.

Why go back now?

There was no computer or television, no sign of anything electronic. In the front room, the desk was buried beneath memos and office supplies. An article had been trimmed and taped to the paneling. It was the only thing on the wall, a printout from *The Washington Post* announcing the opening of the Institute of Technological Research in New York City.

That was Danny's last and only trip back to the States.

Spiral-bound notebooks were stacked in one drawer, their pages filled with poems and run-on sentences, no periods or commas, just page after page of words, like a prisoner trying to relieve his loneliness by spilling his thoughts.

With green ink.

A sketchpad was at the bottom. Every page was covered with a face drawn in pencil, shadows smudged for effect. It was a girl with short hair. Despite the grayscale, Danny knew who the girl was. She had bright red hair and green eyes.

Lucinda.

She was Reed's girlfriend, his love. If it wasn't for her, they never would've escaped the island. None of them could thank her enough, and none of them could forget her.

Especially Reed.

The folders stacked on the desk were organized in a way only Reed might understand. There were photos that appeared to be all the teenage boys that had been on the island and a list of names. *Incomplete list,* it said. As if there were still victims to be discovered.

There were meticulous notes on the back of each one, written in green ink, some describing their past and what happened to them. A photo of an old man was attached to each boy's photo.

The Investors.

Was he hunting them down?

It would be impossible to find them. The wealthy bastards disappeared after leaving the island in their boys' bodies. They might even get plastic surgery, hide in remote places. Money could get you lost and never found.

Danny knew that all too well.

There was another folder with teenage girls, accompanied by the same type of notes and similar Investors, these old women. This was the other Foreverland, the one with cabins in the middle of Wyoming. Danny knew about that one, too.

The Wilderness.

While the boys were on a tropical island, the girls were stranded in cold desolation. Harold Ballard's mother, Patricia Ballard, was the host. She was the one that created Foreverland for the girls, sucked their identities out and made room for the old women to steal their young and able bodies. But when Harold Ballard's Foreverland was destroyed, his mother began to malfunction.

The girls had it so much worse.

They lived in squalor, forced to wear rags and crap in the woods while the boys slept in dormitories and played video games. Reed had photos of the survivors shortly after the girls were saved. They were beautiful with short hair that had been shaved when they arrived, but the memories haunted their eyes. They would never forget.

None of us will.

The girl on top, Danny remembered her. She was the one, they said, that saved them all. She had somehow escaped Foreverland, woke up to pull the needle out of her head. But when the other girls wouldn't wake up, she volunteered to go back inside. She was blonde with blue eyes. He flipped the page over.

Cyn. Her name is Cyn.

It would take months to go through all Reed's notes. Danny couldn't carry them out without Flannel Pants seeing him. He couldn't risk anyone calling the police, either. He could come back in a week, go through them more carefully. There must be a clue hidden in the text.

He checked the other drawers, found several pencils and a new box of green pens. The lid was open. One of the pens was missing.

Only one.

Danny looked at the window, the green pen stuck in the sand like a cigarette butt. He sat down on the couch with the jar, pulled the pen out, and stirred the sand like thick soup. He went to the kitchen and brought back a bowl to empty it.

Nothing but sand.

Danny raked the contents, swirling it in circles, sifting it between his fingers. There were no prizes, no clues. Just fine particles of sugar sand.

He thought about things to take, ways he might stuff them down his pants, a notebook or stack of papers, take them to the hotel and study them. He began pouring the sand back into the jar. Something was inside.

My body lies beneath the sand.

That was in the first poem. Danny assumed it meant Reed's teenage body, but maybe it meant the sand in the jar, also.

A square of paper was glued down, grains of sand stuck to the bottom. His fingers were too fat to reach it. He used the pen to swipe at the edges until it broke loose. The folds were intricate and numerous. It unfurled into a narrow strip with tiny green letters. He held it up to the dim light.

It was an address.

147

CENTRAL PARK, *New York City*

Alex was tired.

In her younger days, she could go days on a few hours of sleep. Now she was always tired, napping at least twice a day.

She found an empty bench and sat back to record her senses. This moment—the green smell, the birds singing—was a keeper. She opened a new biomite function that would play the moment back with all these sensations on a later day.

Ever since the biomite reset following the accident—the accident that never happened, she reminded herself—life had been good and the weather perfect. She was truly blessed.

A couple jogged around a twenty-something college student. Her coat was out of season, along with her stocking cap. She approached with her head down, seeing only the concrete in front of her, carrying a to-go cup of coffee in each hand.

Exactly what Alex wanted.

"*Hola*," Geri said.

"Good morning."

"*Caliente.*"

"You read my mind."

Geri dropped her bag between them. "How are you?" she asked with a trace of Chicago nasal.

"How are things at the magazine?" Alex asked, tired of responding to Geri's inquiry, a question everyone asked her nowadays. It was never in a flippant manner, like *hey, hi, how are ya?* It was very serious, very concerned. Like they all knew about the breakdown, the reset.

"Good," Geri answered. "Seven years of college and a ton of student loans might get me minimum wage."

"But you love what you do."

"Can't get enough."

"And Jeff?"

"A pain in the ass."

Geri looked over her rectangular glasses at Alex, studying, looking for an answer to her first question.

Alex touched her hand. "I'm fine. Thanks for asking."

It had that *Let's move on* tone. Geri got the message, unzipped her frayed bag, coffee stains down the side, and dropped three folders on Alex's lap, each an inch thick.

"There's everything on the Foreverland projects. I can dig up more if you plan to write about it. Which I don't think you should."

Alex frowned. *Enough, already*.

The plain folders were unlabeled and loaded with printed photographs and documents with tiny font. Most of it was public knowledge, but some of it was exclusive stuff that Geri was good at finding. It's why Alex paid her to do the preliminary work. Sorting through the chaff was tedious.

"There are two documented cases of Foreverland body snatching. One was somewhere in BFE, where a bunch of girls were kept in dirty cabins with a wood-burning stove and candles while rich old ladies lived in luxury. Their host was a comatose woman." Geri looked over her glasses. "I think you know her."

Alex opened the folder and saw a photo of mountains and rolling hills and an old cabin. It could be the middle of Montana or Wyoming. She was familiar with the story, knew the girls were teenagers. The wealthy women kidnapped them, used Foreverland to suck their identities out of their bodies and then, voilà, an old woman moved in. It was like buying a new car—a young, healthy car with smooth skin and perky breasts and another sixty years of life.

Alex lifted a photo of an old woman that looked like a shrunken version of a full-sized person, like God left her in the oven too long.

Patricia Ballard.

"The other folder has to do with the first Foreverland, the one on the tropical island. They were doing the same thing, the body-switch stuff, only with boys. They had it way better than the girls." She grunted. "Figures."

There were photos of the boys and old men, of the buildings and grounds. It was more like a resort.

"What happened to the kids?"

"What do you mean?"

"Was it like their brains were erased and reformatted? Where did the personality go, I guess is what I mean?"

"That's a good question." Geri flipped through the pages and pulled a photo out of the stack. "The survivors said there was some gray cloud beyond the sky, like outer space. That's where their minds got shredded and mixed together."

Dios mío.

"They called the gray space the Nowhere. But here's where it gets weird." Geri put down her cup and slid the bottom folder out. "The guy that ran the tropical island Foreverland was Harold Ballard. He made a zillion dollars and went missing when the whole thing collapsed, probably sipping mai tais in a Mediterranean bungalow somewhere. He was, or is, the son of Patricia, the host of the wilderness Foreverland."

Harold looked more like a vagrant with a tropical shirt than a mai-tai-sipping zillionaire. There was a smile behind the dull gray beard, she could see it in the squinting eyes.

"Patricia Ballard is married to Tyler Ballard," Geri said. "Or was. Are you still married if your wife is a vegetable? I don't know, maybe she's not in a coma anymore, who knows where she is. In fact, I don't think anyone knows."

"At the Institute."

"Did you see her?"

I felt her. Alex flinched. That thought slapped her hard. *She was at the Institute when I was there, when I was looking into Coco's eyes.*

"I'll bet you didn't see her," Geri said.

Alex shook her head. No, no, she didn't.

"That's what I mean. They say she's in the Institute, but no one ever confirms it. You ever hear of her husband?"

Again, Alex shook her head.

"He invented the whole computer-aided alternate reality thing."

"Foreverland?"

"Yeah. He used it to experiment on his wife, turned her into an overcooked vegetable and went to prison. And then guess what happened? Harold followed in daddy's footsteps and started experimenting on anyone he could get his hands on, pretending like he was healing minds when he was just buying property and tropical islands to serve the insanely wealthy. The bastard put his mother in the wilderness and they played their messed-up alternate reality games while they made billions."

"What happened to the money?"

"What?"

"After the rings fell apart, what happened to the money?"

"Authorities got it, mostly. Used it to set up a Foreverland fund to help the survivors. They're a little cuckoo with the hole in the head and everything."

Geri put a finger gun to her forehead.

"Where's the rest of it?" Alex asked.

"Rest?"

"You said 'mostly'. Where's the rest of the money?"

"Some of it went to fund the Institute." She avoided looking at Alex, knowing that was where things got weird, and flipped through the pages on her lap. "I got it noted in there somewhere. There were also a number of accounts that went missing, which they figure was moved when Harold disappeared."

"How much?"

"Millions." Geri flicked the photo on Alex's lap. "Twisted pups, right?"

Alex heard the rumors, she knew the story about the Ballard family, but no more than the general public. Most of it sounded like science fiction and the family no more than characters with split personalities. If pressed, she didn't believe most of it. It was tabloid fodder.

But now it was sitting on her lap. There were documents from reputable sources, things no one would know, from people she trusted.

A quiver of fear shot through her midsection and lit up the nerves in her arm. Her hands began to shake, coffee spilled through the lid. She pretended to sneeze, clasping her fingers together.

Geri looked at her phone and explained freelance work was picking up. She threw her bag over her shoulder. "I can still do some research for you, if you need me."

"I need to pay you."

"I'll bill you with PayPal."

Alex looked at the folders, careful not to release her hands. They would shake if she let go. *What's wrong with me?*

The trees began to quiver. A rogue breeze swept through the park. Alex slammed the folders down before the papers ended up littering the park. A crowd roared somewhere, but she knew better. There wasn't a crowd.

She closed her eyes.

Geri sneezed as the dust rode past them.

Alex was staring down, waiting for the wind to die, but losing track of time. Time seemed to be doing that—speeding up and slowing down. Had she been staring at her lap for one minute or one second?

"What happened at the Institute?" Geri was still there. "If you don't mind me asking."

"Getting old. I don't recommend it."

"I heard a rumor about you. Want to hear it?" She waited, but continued without Alex's consent. "Rumor is you tripped out, tried to activate some enhancement during the tour that short-circuited your senses. Like pushing 240 volts through a hair drier, you know."

Alex chuckled. She didn't respond because it was stupid. But then the time lapse thing happened again and she lost track of how long she'd been chuckling, how long Geri had been standing.

"Why do you want to do this?" Geri pointed at the folders.

"What do you mean?"

"This is heavy. Why do you want to get involved? You're getting old, like you said."

There was a time when that would've pissed her off. Now she couldn't disagree. She was sitting in the park trying not to let someone see her hands shake. *Why am I doing this?*

"You ever feel an untold story?" she said.

"What?"

"It's a journalist's gut feeling, a sort of sixth sense you develop when there's more to a story than what's being presented, a piece that wants to be told, that wants you to know it. That wants you to tell others."

"That's what this is all about?" Geri tapped the folders.

"Yes."

"Seems pretty open and shut to me. Old people with money and poor people with something they want. A tale as old as time."

Alex wasn't sure about that. She was letting her instincts lead the way because something was out there, an untold story that even the secrets didn't know. She felt it at the Institute, a wave welling up in the ocean, something just below the surface. A monster in the deep and she was sitting directly over it in a little boat.

The wind had died.

Geri said goodbye. She was running late for another appointment. Alex sat with the folders on her lap until her coffee was cold. She opened her briefcase and placed all of Geri's research on top of the torn travel agency photo and *National Geographic.*

She stopped.

It took a moment to find the photo in Geri's folder. She placed it on the bench, side by side with the travel agency photo and *National Geographic.*

The exact same island.

The monster in the deep.

148

The backyard felt like carpet. Deep, lush green carpet.

Alex slid her shoes off, wiggled her toes, turned her face to the sky like a sunflower and listened to her call go to voicemail.

"This is Shane Lee, director of photography at *National Geographic*. I can't take your call right now. Please leave your name and number. Thank you."

This time, she decided to leave a message. "Shane, this is Alex Diosa. We have a mutual friend, Amy Ferris at *The Washington Post*. I had a question about a photographer in one of your back issues. I won't take much of your time, please give me a call."

She continued her walk to the vegetable garden while thumbing a text to Mr. Lee. If she didn't hear back by the next day, she'd call again. Some folks never returned a call until after the third message.

How did he get that shot of the Foreverland island? And why was a travel agency using it, a travel agency that wasn't returning her calls, either?

First, find the photographer.

The lilacs were spent but still fragrant. Weeds choked the garden. A month ago, it was as clean as the driveway. That was before Geri delivered a gold mine in Central Park.

Alex rolled her shoulders. Knots were bunching up beneath her shoulder blades and a perennial ache took root in her spine, keeping her awake when she did make it to bed. She didn't need a chiropractor. She fell on her knees and sank in the composted soil; puffs of organic dust filled her nostrils.

Just a little horticultural therapy.

The weeds easily came out. She crawled to the next row and recalled playing in the garden while her mother pulled weeds, setting up dolls and rolling cars between the stalks. She'd sit in the shade of sweet corn and pretend it was a forest.

She was halfway down the third row when she noticed something yellow tucked between the tomato plants. Sweat stung her eyes. She wiped her face with the bottom of her shirt, but everything seemed a little out of focus.

Samuel's car rolled up the driveway.

"Hey." His tie was loose, his collar open. He dropped his leather briefcase on the ground. "What are you doing?"

She got up and wiped her hands on her thighs.

"Got a call from the Institute today," he said. "Know anything about it?"

"What?"

"They said you were dropping the lawsuit."

"I...I told you, Samuel, I don't want to sue."

"Nah, nah, nah, that's not what this is about." He tugged the knot on his tie. "You're angling."

"What?"

"What are you up to?"

"Samuel, I don't like the way you're talking to me. I told you in the hospital I didn't want to sue."

"You're trying to go back there."

She stepped out of the garden and pushed all the weeds together. The ground swayed. *Am I dehydrated?*

The Institute wasn't supposed to tell him she was negotiating an interview with their executives. *We drop the lawsuit, I come back for another tour. And this time I see Patricia.*

It was a long shot.

"We're not doing this," he said. "You're not going back. Write whatever you want, you're not going back to the Institute."

"Don't tell me what to do."

"I'm worried." His hands were on his hips, jaw set. The words didn't match the body language. For a second, he looked like someone entirely different, like a man ready to break something in half.

"I need some water."

She went into the shade of the garage. Samuel came out with a bottle of water. He set up a chair and watched her drink until she waved him off.

"I'm all right. Get out of your suit; we'll talk later."

He paused, unsure if she would be all right. Or just didn't trust leaving her alone. Eventually, he went inside. Alex finished the water but still felt wobbly.

Her phone buzzed. Alex took it on the third ring.

"You busy?" Geri asked.

"No, I'm fine. What do you got?"

"I got more weird for you."

Something squeaked. Samuel was rolling the wheelbarrow into the backyard, the axles squealing for oil. He loaded the mound of weeds, significantly more than she thought. *Have I been out there this long?*

The sky had cleared, clouds on the horizon. Everything was back in focus and she felt good again. Normal. Just needed water.

"I'm sending over more notes," Geri said. "This Ballard family is a bunch of dysfunctional geniuses. You should consider writing a book on them. At the very least, a novel. They're like characters out of a science-fiction movie."

Alex had been through her notes. She was having the same thoughts.

"The father's been in a maximum-security prison for over thirty years. He was only sentenced to twenty years."

"Twenty?"

"Yeah, twenty."

"So, why is he still incarcerated?"

"It gets a little murky there. Best I can find is that his sentence was extended twice, but there's no reason."

"Even bad behavior doesn't extend your sentence."

"See what I mean?"

"Can I get an interview?"

"I made some calls, talked to a few people, but it doesn't sound good. He doesn't take visitors."

Samuel stepped into the garden to grab another pile of weeds. He waded to the end of the row and stepped between the tomatoes.

"You want me to submit a request?" Geri asked.

He picked up a yellow object, the one that was nestled in the weeds between the tomatoes. He kept his back to her and quickly threw it over the fence into the neighbor's yard.

"Hello?"

"Yes, yes," Alex said. "File a request. I want to interview him as soon as possible. Tell them whatever you have to. I'll sign whatever, promise whatever. Let's get it started."

"Done."

Samuel stepped out of the garden and dumped the wheelbarrow in the back before going into the house, sweat stains on his shirt.

Alex stared at the fence.

Those neighbors were good people. They had two dogs, but no kids. Alex swore she saw him throw a plastic truck.

A little yellow plastic truck.

She was feeling dehydrated again.

149

ADMAX Penitentiary, *Colorado*

Tyler stood in front of a wide window, watching inmates play basketball and walk the track. The threat of rain sank into his joints like cold drips of mercury.

The door opened behind him. A middle-aged man in a starched white coat stepped into the room and docked a tablet next to a computer. Harvard educated, perennially optimistic and a believer in reform, he was a good man. A good doctor.

"Body of an old man," he said. "Engine of a teenager."

The good doctor patted the exam table. His eyes were sleepy, whiskers a few days old. He washed his hands, humming as he dried them, gently inspecting Tyler's forehead. The hole appeared to be an empty blackhead, but the surrounding flesh was puffy and red. Gramm was concerned about infection. The stent had been in place for over twenty years and there had never been a problem.

But his body was twenty years older.

"You need to stop with the needle," the good doctor said. "You don't need it."

"Don't lecture me."

"Your current brain biomites are fully capable of digital transmission. There is a new biomite strain with improved frequency. It would only take a little training to make your...*connection*...without it."

The good doctor always stuttered on the topic of Foreverland, as if the word only surfaced in his consciousness long enough to leap off his tongue.

Tyler winced when he touched the stent.

The good doctor apologized, but that's not why Tyler reacted. He liked the needle, had grown accustomed to it in the same way a long-distance runner enjoyed the burn.

Or a junkie craved the spike.

The good doctor tapped the tablet a few times. An image of Tyler's body—slightly hunched and crooked—illuminated on the wall monitor. The good doctor stared while tapping his lower lip.

He began to say something. Then froze.

Caught with an awkward expression, like a sneeze was coming, a sneeze flash-frozen on his face while his biomite-laden brain seized. It waited for a command.

Waited for Tyler.

The old man closed his eyes, drew a deep breath and let his thoughts sink into the good doctor as if he was clay. Tyler's thoughts were the fingers of an artisan penetrating his canvas. A violent shiver vibrated between his ears, an electric arc that made his brain itch. This always happened when he synced up with one of his people.

My people, he thought. *The people that run this prison, the people that voluntarily seeded themselves with biomites. The people I own.*

My people.

Tyler had hijacked them one at a time, recoded their brains like programmable processors, left suggestions in their subconsciousness, secret words that turned them catatonic, that opened their minds and allowed him to pick their thoughts like fruit. Afterwards, they had no idea a thief had run through them.

Life was so much easier when people did what you wanted.

The new biomite strain the good doctor mentioned was experimental, more research was needed to assess their stability and function. And that would take time.

Tyler didn't have time.

He didn't like experimenting. He was old and vulnerable. He was also nearing the maximum biomites allowed by the government. *No human being could be composed of more than 49.9% biomites, lest they be considered more machine than human.*

The penalty was swift and eternal.

He didn't need the government sniffing around the prison. There were rumors of illegal biomites, ones the government couldn't monitor. These could be used to go over the 50% mark. In fact, an entire body could be made of them. But they were rumors.

There was no time for rumors.

"Seed a microliter of biotype Q into the brain," Tyler said.

"Seed a microliter of biotype Q into the brain," the good doctor repeated.

"Bypass brain-blood barrier via mucosa."

The good doctor waited, eyes wide like a car accident was happening. "Bypass brain-blood barrier via mucosa."

Tyler turned his attention to the wall monitor and focused on the colorations filling the brain. The right hemisphere, the creative half, the land of imagination—where Foreverland was born—was vivid and varied.

"Program a 100 ppm proliferation in the right hemisphere."

"Program a 100 ppm proliferation in the right hemisphere."

The good doctor turned to prepare one microliter of biotype Q that would increase Tyler's brain capacity. He inserted the seeder up his right nostril.

Hot tracks remained on Tyler's cheeks.

The good doctor sat on a stool, staring at the window. The wide-eyed shock was gone, but blankness still haunted him.

Gramm waited at the foot of the table.

Tyler lifted his hand. Gramm helped him sit and gave him a few minutes to sit quietly. The new seeding would need a few days to integrate. He expected more efficient wireless transmission of his thoughts, a more seamless transition into Foreverland. Still, he wasn't ready to give up the needle.

Rain streaked the window.

The good doctor maintained a glassy-eyed stare, his zombification proof that, little by little, Tyler was carving away his identity. The good doctor would return to normal, regain his own self within the hour. But there was always a little missing.

Tyler didn't hijack Gramm. He enjoyed the old-fashioned camaraderie. At the very least, he didn't want him to end up an empty glove like the good doctor.

"Alessandra has requested an interview," Gramm said.

"What?"

"She's moving forward with her research."

"I thought we took care of this, Gramm."

"Her assistant keeps providing research, keeps her interested."

"Where's she getting it?"

Gramm shook his head.

"Put a stop to it."

"Certainly." Gramm cleared his throat. "In the meantime, the interview..."

"Deny."

"I think you should reconsider—"

"Deny her, Gramm. I don't want her coming here, not now. We need her to focus on normality. Acceptance. Once she realizes how happy she is, how perfect her life has become, then she'll sleep. That's all I care about."

He trusted Gramm. His assessment was always unfiltered, unbiased and accurate. But this wasn't the time for Alessandra to know Tyler. More adjustment was needed. More acceptance.

She's our last hope, the one person capable of hosting a new reality, an endless Foreverland. Humankind will give eternal thanks for her sacrifice.

The gray sky was a smear of charcoal. A thunderhead was crawling over the distant mountain range. The men returned inside.

"Danny is going to Minnesota," Gramm said.

"Duluth?"

"Yes."

He turned at the shoulders. Gramm stood like a noble soldier. The good doctor remained on the stool, lower lip glistening with saliva.

"Interesting," Tyler said. "He's looking for Cynthia."

Gramm nodded.

"Why would he be doing that?"

"I...I don't know. I suggest we stop them both."

"Stop them?"

"Permanently."

"You want to terminate them?"

Gramm raked his hair and stammered. "We don't need them. Keeping them alive can only be trouble. Cynthia is, you know...contaminated."

Tyler watched the former chemist pull the stray hairs from his fingers, watched his lips silently count. Uncertainty pained him. He was a scientist at heart; he liked control. Having the ability to eliminate Danny and Cynthia at will was too much temptation.

Tyler knew better.

Those two kids had potential. They couldn't host a Foreverland like he and Patricia wanted—certainly not like Alessandra—but they were not useless. And despite Tyler's willingness to sacrifice with callous decisiveness, he was not a cold-blooded murderer.

"No," he said. "We'll not end them, Gramm."

That moment of compassion would eventually be his undoing.

"Where did you find Danny?"

"He arrived in the States undetected," Gramm said. "But we located him at Reed's last known residence."

"Interesting. Why is he searching for Reed all of a sudden? Why now? Why in secret?"

"He spent an hour and a half inside the apartment. When he came out, he began driving and hasn't stopped."

"How do you know it's Minnesota?"

"He programmed Cynthia's address into the GPS."

"Where'd he get her address?"

Gramm stuttered without an answer.

Tyler turned at the sound of thunder. The skyline was hazy. "He found something in the apartment," Tyler muttered. "Has he been in communication with anyone?"

"Nothing out of the ordinary. Every email, text and phone call has been verified, nothing to suggest a secret code or otherwise."

"Reed?"

Gramm hesitated. "Reed is gone, sir."

He wanted to say more, to argue there was no way Reed could be behind this. They knew that the boy named Reed, the one that took Tyler's son's body, no longer existed. Reed was dead.

Tyler had the proof.

The sinus on the right side of his face was beginning to throb. He was already feeling the euphoric effects of the new seeding. His thoughts felt crisper, his body thrumming with good intentions.

"Someone is guiding Danny," Tyler said.

"There's no evidence—"

"He leaves his home, breaks communication with Santiago and goes directly to Reed's apartment? That is all the evidence we need; someone is guiding him. The young man does not take an interest in a long-dead friend out of the blue."

"We need to stick with facts, sir. Reed is nonexistent; we have verified that. There must be another explanation."

"Or we've missed something."

Underestimation was not the mistake Tyler wanted to make. It seemed impossible that Reed was alive, but so did hijacking this entire prison. *My people.*

"Why would he go to Cynthia?" Tyler mused.

Gramm offered suggestions, but the old man wasn't interested. This hardly seemed threatening. It might even be beneficial. Cynthia was the girl that survived Patricia's Foreverland; she had trouble acclimating to normal life. Danny might be exactly what she needed. Maybe she would become an asset after all.

Still, why is he going? Why now?

Tyler started for the exit.

His newfound stamina was not to be wasted on pointless arguments. They would watch Danny and Cynthia, not let them out of their sight again. But now, real work needed to be done. Gramm followed him to the elevator.

They descended to the basement.

150

DULUTH, Minnesota

Cyn didn't open letters.

There was a stack next to the coffee machine and another in a wicker basket. The bills were taken care of through a trust fund established by the Foreverland Survivor Fund, assets acquired from the old women that kidnapped them.

Cyn wasn't a survivor. She was a fighter.

But she was tired of bleeding.

The curtains were drawn, blotting out the afternoon sunlight. The television droned in the background, electric light dancing on the ceiling. She hardly watched the programs, just wanted the sound to drown out the chatter in her head.

Not chatter. Just a voice.

She had thoughts that she called her own. But she also had someone else's thoughts in her head. That was the voice she was attempting to mute.

She dropped her foot on the floor, a sandbag thudding on the carpet. It took a minute to pull herself out of the swishing slumber.

The cracks of light streaming around the front door told her it was daytime. The clock told her to get going. A meeting started in twenty minutes. And if she wasn't there, someone would come for her.

It was better, she learned, to act like a normal addict than someone with a special affliction—an identity crisis that no one would understand, that no one knew existed.

Then just kill yourself, the voice told her.

Cyn pushed her short hair from her eyes. In the dusty light, it looked more muddy than blonde. She shoved a magazine off the low table, found the plastic prescription bottle under a newspaper and tapped out a white pill. A tiny pill.

A voice-dulling pill.

Shut up.

The voice had a name. It wasn't a name Cyn gave it because it wasn't just her imagination. The voice was someone that had a name, a name Cyn refused to acknowledge. She tried to ignore the ghost that lived in her subconscious, the identity that, without the pills, would rise to the surface like a leviathan, an old woman distorted by her nightmares, a demon with a massive maw, with row after row of teeth that wanted to devour Cyn whole.

I have a name.

Cyn wasn't bipolar. Not crazy, not unstable. The voice in her head was the old woman that kidnapped her, that dragged her out to the wilderness to steal her body.

Barbara.

It was bad timing that put the old woman in her head. But Cyn was a survivor.

Barb, Barb, Barb.

Living in the ashes of Foreverland.

The chalky pill stuck to her tongue. She washed it down at the kitchen sink.

"Now shut up."

She pulled the towel from the window and squinted in the daylight. The postal truck was at her mailbox.

The pill bottle slipped from her fingers and bounced on the

linoleum. She bent over and picked it up near the oven, the glass door covered with three layers of wax paper to obscure any reflections.

Pull the paper off, Barb whispered. Her voice was fading in the pill's haze. *Look at my reflection.*

Her arm ached to rise; her hand itched to do what she said. Cyn never did, but hated the compulsion to do so. Barb was confused. The old woman thought this was her body.

Cyn's cell phone vibrated somewhere in the front room. She found it beneath a pizza box. A text from Macy.

Meeting in 20. Picking up in 10.

Cyn chewed at the side of her thumb, nibbling off a fresh lump of skin before working on her fingernail, staring at the text. The prescription haze settled around her, picked her up and carried her to a place where she didn't care about anything.

A place where she could survive.

Where she didn't hear Barb.

She could stand there for a half hour if she let the haze have her, until she was ready to sleep again. But then Macy would knock on the door, force her way into her life and save her again, like she did six months ago.

And then she'd have to explain the pills.

She'd have to explain she wasn't really clean, that she couldn't live without the little white saviors, the slayers of Barb. She would have to explain something that no one would understand.

I don't hear voices. I have an old woman inside me!

She chuckled, despite the fog.

Quickly, she picked up the empty sacks and pizza boxes, filling three trash bags that went out the back door. She went to the fishbowl and noticed Teddy doing the backstroke.

Teddy got flushed while the shower ran.

The water pushed away the fuzzy veil.

If she could live in the shower, where the guilt would be washed away, where her tears circled the drain, she would never step out. She would let her skin pucker, she would scrub away her sins, let her mind be clean.

New again.

But nothing is ever new again.

The doorbell was ringing.

Cyn watched the last of the water seep into the drain, listened to the showerhead drip. The ringing turned into thumping. Cyn stepped out, her flesh soft and pink. She dried off in front of the sink; three towels covered the mirror.

Teddy was still floating. She forgot to flush.

"Cynthia?" The voice was muffled.

More knocking.

"Coming!"

Cyn answered the door in a robe, hair still dripping. Sunlight knifed across her face. Macy was on the front step, arms crossed, skin as black as her tightly cropped curls.

"You just wake up?"

"Shower. Be ready in a sec."

"Better make that half a second. I don't like being late."

"Sorry."

Cyn left the door open and ran to the bedroom to get dressed, pulling clothes from a pile. She pinned her hair on top of her head and brushed her teeth, bending over a small corner of the exposed bathroom mirror, where she saw her teeth.

But not her eyes.

She walked out to a bright front room, sunlight streaming through all the windows. Macy pulled aside the last curtain, her black skin flawless, smooth.

"What'd I tell you about the windows? Relapse lurks in dark corners."

There are other things in the dark.

"Your mail." Macy tossed a bundle in the wicker basket. She palmed a glossy flier and shoved it in her back pocket, sort of hiding it.

Cyn didn't need to see it to know what it was. The same flier came every week. And Macy took it every week.

Biomites.

The evil advert for biomedical technology, here to cure hormonal imbalance, heal your pain. Here to save the human race.

Biomites, the scourge of addicts everywhere.

Feel how you want to feel? Think how you want to think? That's just another drug, Cynthia, only this one is on the inside, one you can't turn away from. This one turns you into a drug.

Live life on life's terms, Cynthia.

Let go. Let God.

There were a hundred more lines she could quote from the Big Book—Macy beat them into her head like ten-penny nails—but none of that wisdom could exorcise the demon from her head.

Can biomites make you new again?

Cyn knew the answer.

In the spring, she'd gone to New York City to find out. She'd been invited to participate in the new healing at the Institute of Technological Research. She didn't remember much about the trip; those were the using days, soaked in alcohol and popped by pills. She got so hammered that she'd fallen off a curb and cut the back of her hand. Blood was dripping off her elbow. The people at the Institute took her to the hospital and got her stitched up.

She didn't remember much of that either, but the scar on the back of her hand was proof. She did remember the biomites, though. They had those. She didn't get any, but they had them.

That was almost five months ago.

She remembered that because the day she got home was the first day she went to a meeting, the day she got clean, the day she met Macy.

The first day of the rest of her life, Macy told her.

Macy held the door, tapping her toe, staring at her blank wrist because late addicts were relapsing addicts. Cyn grabbed a banana, noticing the envelopes in the basket, the one written in green ink. She hardly noticed the name on the front. It wasn't addressed to Cynthia.

Later, when Macy dropped her off, she would scramble to find her pills when she picked up the thick envelope and read the name no one had called her since leaving the wilderness.

Cyn.

Recovery happened in the back of a bowling alley.

When addicts opened up their lives, displayed all the warts, the wars, the bleeding souls and unhealed wounds, they did so to the rumble of pin setters and rolling thunder.

Cyn swam to the front row.

Macy took one look at her and whispered, "We got to talk."

Her eyes couldn't hide the pill's haze. Cyn was drowning in it. How could she explain the pills weren't the water filling her lungs, they were the lifesaver she clung to.

Cyn. It was addressed to Cyn.

It was a bulky envelope containing more than a message. It was thick and round, maybe a DVD. But she didn't find out. It went straight into the trash.

She received another one a week later. A third one arrived a week after that. Both of those went into the trash, unopened. She doubled down on the pills to dull the voice, but the little white saviors couldn't stop the envelopes from arriving.

Let go. Let God.

Several regulars of the bowling alley AA meeting told their war stories about the days in the trenches with the drink, the drugs, the high. They listened without response, nodding as the details rolled out. They all knew how the stories went. And how they ended.

Cyn nodded, only to blend in.

She often made up reasons for why she turned to drugs and alcohol, things like abusive parents and uncontrollable boyfriends. Maybe they weren't too far from the truth, she didn't really know. She didn't really trust her memories. Maybe what she remembered really did happen to her.

Maybe not.

Didn't matter.

The pain was real. And that was what she talked about, the pain. That was what everyone nodded along with.

The ache.

That was real.

"Anniversaries?" Josh took the podium. "Anyone?"

Macy raised her hand, waving it on her way to the front. Maybe she didn't know about Cyn's pill haze that day. If she did, she wouldn't be holding an anniversary chip, wouldn't be smiling down on her.

"I want to recognize six months, y'all. Six haaard-earned months to a brave girl that fights the fight each and every day, here and now. Eighteen years old, you're the youngest recovering addict in this room, congratulations, girl. Six months."

Macy started the applause.

The room joined in.

Some stood up.

The love cut through the numbing pill haze and reminded her why she got up every morning, why she fought the fight, that when clouds covered the sky, there was still a sun behind them, shining its light on everyone. The good and the bad. The unclean.

The broken.

You should kill yourself, Barb whispered in her head.

Cyn took the chip, squeezing it like a lifeline, clinging to it like a rope dangling over a pit that had no bottom. Drugs and alcohol had thrown her into their depths once before, plunged her into the cauldron of despair.

It was these people, this chip, her loving sponsor that reminded her pain was inevitable, suffering was optional.

If only Barb would die.

I die, Barb whispered, *you die.*

"Anyone else?" Josh asked.

Cyn didn't hear the next round of applause, just realized the world was out of focus from tears burning her cheeks. She wiped her eyes to see the newcomer.

"One day clean," Josh said, shaking the boy's hand. "Looks like Cynthia's no longer the youngest."

Long red hair, the body of a skater.

"How old are you, Danny?" Josh asked.

"Sixteen."

"Welcome to the rest of your life."

There was a standing ovation, a long line of recovering addicts shaking his hand, hugging him, patting his back. The boy was all smiles, the glowing grin of newfound redemption. She remembered what that was like, the smell of hope, the promise there was more to life than the high.

Fred, the three-hundred-pound security guard, a longtime sober member of the bowling alley chapter, applied his welcome hug: a vicious embrace that lifted the new member off his feet amid a chorus of laughter and good cheer. He squeezed the chip from Danny's hand.

Fred dropped him. Danny bent over to pick it up.

Cyn froze.

She had stood to welcome him in a much less dramatic fashion than Fred when the long red hair fell away from the back of Danny's neck.

A lump over the fifth vertebra.

The plastic chip dug into her palm. She backed away, resisting reaching up to massage the lump on her own neck, the same size and shape that covered the fifth vertebra. It could be coincidence, but there were no accidents in this room. Everything happened for a reason. That lump could only mean one thing.

Through the pill haze, through the love, through all the happiness in the room, a cold chill filled her legs.

He's been to Foreverland.

The leash.

The clamp, the lump, had been surgically installed to bite the nervous system should any of the girls go where they didn't belong. It was an invisible fence for humans.

The doctors said they couldn't remove it, that it was too risky. But it was safe; it was deactivated. Nothing would happen.

Except remind her of the wilderness for the rest of her life.

Cyn stopped going to meetings.

The windows were covered, the doors locked. Macy called, texted, hammered the windows. Cyn feigned illness, insisted she hadn't relapsed.

Just pills. But I need these. You don't understand.

The days were bleached in the haze. She stopped checking the mail, but Macy left it on the front step. Through the window, she could see the green ink, the name on the envelopes that kept coming.

You should kill yourself.

Meeting adjourned, Cyn watched the bowling alley chapter leave through the back door.

Skater boy was there.

He would have a one-week chip by now. Or was it a month? The pills had smudged time into one long blur.

She watched them get into their cars, watched cigarette smoke stream out cracked windows. Danny, however, walked past the front doors of the bowling alley and went to the diner at the end of the strip mall.

From a safe distance, she saw him sit in a booth. The summer asphalt baked the cold chill from her chest. She paced behind a McDonald's, wiping the sweat from her face.

He ordered.

The waitress arrived with two coffee cups.

He sipped from one.

The diner's air was cold.

The waitress didn't ask to seat her. "He's over there," she said.

She could see him across the room, sitting in a booth, eyes cast down as if he was reading. A cup of coffee was in front of him, the other waiting for her.

The noisy kitchen competed with the chatter in her head, Barb rushing out of her subconscious, whispering in her ear with that deep, scratchy voice scarred by a lifetime of smoking.

Get out of here, Barb whispered. *Go home. Be alone.*

She closed her eyes until colors splashed in the dark, tears seeping through the cracks and wetting her eyelashes. The floor beneath her disappeared.

And she was falling.

Get out.

"Hon?" The waitress was drying her hands. "You all right?"

"Yeah."

"You're looking for the boy over there, right?"

Cyn nodded.

"Well, he's waiting. Unless you want me to tell him you didn't show. I don't think he's seen you."

She could walk out, go back to the house and close the windows, hide in a scalding shower until she couldn't feel the emptiness, take pills until the falling stopped and she just hovered over the pit.

"That what you want?"

"No."

She fell once before and found her way out. She could do it again.

"Who are you?"

He didn't look up.

There was a folder to his right, a stuffed manila folder with ragged corners. He was clutching the table, his knuckles white. She thought he was having a seizure, but then he let go and slid the folder across the table, next to the cup of coffee. That was her cup, cream already stirred in.

Just like she took it.

She could ask him again, but he wasn't going to answer. The answer, it seemed, was in the folder. He sipped at the coffee cup, eyes cast not at a phone or an iPad but the blank slate of a cheap diner tabletop, breath streaming in and out like a metronome.

Do I know you?

There were photos in the folder. Glossy paper and dark colors. She didn't sit in the fake red leather bench across from him. Not yet.

She dragged her fingers across the table, let them rest like twigs on the coarse folder before pulling it closer. There was a stack of about twenty photos inside, all printed on full pages. She didn't need to see them all.

Just the first one.

The rolling hills and a dilapidated cabin.

She knew the inside of the cabin, the beds and the marks on the wall she had scratched to count the days where she woke up—where all the girls woke up—with a shaved head and no memories.

Foreverland.

"I've been there," Danny said.

A tear streaked over her cheek. Because she knew what he meant. He knew. He hadn't been to the cabin or the wilderness. But he had been *there*.

He'd been to Foreverland.

Silence, for once, filled her head. Barb receded into the darkness of her subconscious.

"I was on a tropical island," he said. "We all woke up without our memories, were told we were sick, that we would be healed. Old men gave us everything we wanted, as long as we took the needle."

He looked up, his blue eyes clear, placid.

"We never thought about where the girls came from, but it only made sense that you were coming from your own Foreverland, but not from a tropical island."

He spread the photos on the table.

The luxurious brick house where the old women lived. The garden where Jen's body was buried. The little cabin where Patricia slept. It was nothing like a tropical island.

Nothing but suffering in the wilderness.

"We were the ones that crashed Foreverland," he said. "A few of us escaped the island, left the old men for the authorities. We didn't know there was another Foreverland. Didn't know you were still in it."

"Do you remember me?" she asked. She searched his face, begging for recognition.

"No."

"But we went there? With you?"

"I don't remember much." Weakness trailed in his voice. "I try not to. It brings back too much..." He shook his head.

"How did you find me?"

"A friend of mine—one I escaped with—he told me to find you."

"Why?"

"We might be in trouble."

Despite the ominous tone, the dire warning, the threat that Foreverland might still be out there, she didn't shake or shiver. Not a quiver touched her insides or hummed in her head. For the first time she could remember, she felt alive and present.

Because he was there. He knew the suffering.

I'm not alone.

Cyn dropped into the seat.

She came eye level with the fair-skinned redheaded boy, a ginger with a slight build and an unshakeable presence.

"What kind of trouble?"

"It might not be over."

"What?"

"Foreverland."

"How...how is that possible?"

The little bell over the diner's door rang. Danny looked over her shoulder. He said without taking his eyes off the front, "He wrote me, told me to find you."

"A letter?"

"Yes."

Finally, she shuddered. She didn't have to ask the color of the ink. "Why?"

"I don't know."

Danny gathered the photos and dropped them on the seat next to him, out of sight.

"There you are." Macy stood at the table. "I'm worried about you, girl. Why aren't you taking my calls?"

Cyn didn't look away from Danny. His gaze lingered. *Keep this quiet.*

"Sorry, Macy. I got a little mixed up in the head."

"You all right?"

Did you relapse? Are you using? Do you need me to run this punk out of town? Because you've been acting strange ever since he arrived.

"I'm good, yeah."

There were pleasantries passed back and forth, thank you for the coffee and the conversation. Danny really helped clear her head, get back on track. Macy hummed and nodded. That wasn't his job, not without the group, not when he had less than a month clean.

Cyn left him at the table. When she reached the parking lot, the whisper returned.

By the time she got home, it was more than a whisper.

You will kill yourself.

151

The coffee tasted like dishwater.

Danny cradled the mug, staring at the brown swirls as the tingling faded from his arms and legs. He'd never felt it that strong before. When she sat down across from him, it was like inhaling a steady stream of nitrous. He had been clutching the table to keep from floating away.

Now that she was gone, he sank into the red leather bench.

When he saw her the first time, he'd experienced something like that, but it was faint. He'd chalked that up to the new environment and nerves. He always sat in the back of the room, never got closer than ten or twenty feet to her. But when she sat across from him, within arm's length...

Wow.

It wasn't until the initial rush settled that he noticed the fragrance, a scent that clung to the back of his throat. He assumed it was something she was wearing, an essential oil or something. Even now it hung over the table thicker than usual.

Lilac.

She was beautiful, no surprise. She was stunning, even from a distance. She had the gait of a cat, lithe and dangerous, but fragile at the same time. If she missed a step, he was afraid she might shatter. He got lost in her blue eyes, suppressed the urge to reach out and take her hand. When their fingers brushed, a tingle sent him toward the ceiling again.

It made no sense, but this was the right place.

He thought the photos would jar something loose. Maybe she could explain why Reed sent him. It was just a guess. But there was nothing. All he saw was the ghosts in her eyes—the same ghosts that haunted his dreams.

The memories of Foreverland.

He ordered another coffee and read the newsfeed. He caught up on daily events, counted all the missed opportunities since leaving the villa. He'd stay in Duluth until he figured something out. There was only one certainty: he wasn't going back to Spain.

Not until something makes sense.

The diner's bell rang as the door opened. Danny was thumbing through a story on biomite halfskin laws when he sensed Santiago, could smell the Spaniard's musky body odor, the trace of a cigar.

A strong, slim figure was walking toward him. The backlit glare obscured her features. A slight sense of vertigo turned the table as Santiago's presence got stronger.

Macy dropped into the booth.

He rubbed his eyes. The smell of Santiago didn't match up with the glaring dark-skinned woman. It took a moment for his senses to reset.

Her eyes were almost all pupils, the irises dark brown. Unblinking, she folded her bony fingers on the table. The waitress stopped by. Macy dismissed her without breaking her deadlocked stare.

"What are you doing?" she asked.

Danny didn't answer. She was asking something else.

"Huh?" she grunted.

"Living one day at a time."

"Cute." She nodded. "You drive a rental into town and shack up in a hotel and decide to clean up in the back of a bowling alley like our chapter is some holy grail."

Danny stiffened.

He'd been careful to keep quiet, never went directly to the hotel that he'd booked several miles away. He hadn't sensed anyone watching him, no one waiting in the parking lot or following him.

"You come for her?" she asked.

"You know who I am?"

"I can spot an addict a mile away. You ain't no addict, son."

A chill raced beneath his ribs. *Son*. That's what they called each other on the island, it was their slang. They didn't say *man* or *boy* or *dude*. Everyone was *son*.

"Give me the folder."

The photos were still on the seat. He didn't move. She already knew too much.

"I will tear this place apart and beat you with a table leg if you don't get a move on." She leaned over the table, never breaking eye contact. "Give me the folder."

Someone once told him that you didn't have to be stronger or meaner than your enemy, you just had to out-crazy them. He didn't stand a chance.

He put the folder on the table.

"Is this a joke?" She spread the photos out. "You trying to make her relapse? Push her over the edge?"

Danny didn't respond.

"Who sent you?"

That was the question she wanted to ask. That's what she wanted to know the second she sat down. She was trying to disguise it in all this concern for Cyn's sobriety, but the subtle change in expression—the slight shift from hard rage to hopeful curiosity—told him she was angling for something else.

"I'm going to ask you again." She leaned in. "Who sent you?"

"No one."

She looked around, perhaps considering trashing the place to beat him with a table leg.

"Out of the blue you travel across the world to get clean? Is that what you want me to believe, that you just got a wild hair to leave your life to ruin my girl?"

"She's a Foreverland survivor. You know about Foreverland, right?"

"I know about survival."

"There's not many of us left."

"Maybe she doesn't want to remember."

"None of us do," he said. "But we can't forget."

"I don't care about you or any of the others. Only one survivor I do and you can bank on this." She shoved the photos into his lap and stood up. "You break her and you better keep running, son. *¿Comprende?*"

She hovered over him. Her breath was humid with a faint trace of smoke and lilac. Danny met her challenging gaze.

"*¿Por qué iba yo a dejar?*" he asked.

She began nodding, a dangerous smile touching her eyes. Cold fear clenched Danny's chest. Macy shoved away from the table and backed toward the front door before turning to leave.

His coffee was cold.

He needed to find out why Reed sent him here. *They* knew he was here. And Danny didn't know who *they* were, but Reed was sending cryptic poems and planting clues along the way. So there had to be a *they*.

Why would I leave? Macy knew exactly what he said in Spanish.

There was definitely a *they*.

152

DULUTH, Minnesota

A slick of sweat.

The air conditioner running, the ceiling fan blowing. The heat coming from inside her, a furnace churning hot coals.

Get up.

Electric light swam through the fan's blades, shadows flickering over textured ceiling. Shadows painted the corners while a late night pitchman demonstrated a waterless mop.

Wake up, darling.

Cyn's elbow sank into the cushion. Her head a dead weight. Mouth stuffed with cotton.

You're nothing. You don't exist because you're nothing—

"Shut up." She weaved her fingers through her hair, squeezing the sides of her head. "Shut up!"

It was better not to engage, not to recognize her. It only made her real, gave her substance. Brought the old woman closer to the surface.

She searched a pile of clothes, swiped papers off the coffee table— photos of the wilderness fluttered in front of the television, photos she wanted to ignore but couldn't escape. A glass of water soaked a *National Geographic* crumpled on the floor, the cover photo a puckering tropical island. A magazine that just showed up in the mail.

Her prescription bottle wasn't there.

You're nothing. Stop wasting my time and kill yourself.

"Shut up!"

It didn't make sense that Barb would want Cyn to kill herself. Where would the old woman be without the body? They were both in it. If Cyn killed herself, they'd both be dead. *Right?*

Laughter echoed.

These were the dark moments Cyn thought about suicide, to just end all this, to get it over with. What was the point? She lived alone. And every night was a battle with sanity.

With no end in sight.

But it was these dark moments when Barb came so close, when thoughts of suicide rose up that Cyn chose life. Because she knew the moment she swallowed enough pills to end this, Barb would win.

And Cyn was a fighter.

You silly girl. Silly, silly girl, Barb whispered. *You are a mistake, a hapless floundering mistake. You always have been, and always will be. You cling to nothing—*

"You did this!" Cyn kicked over the table. "You should've died! You lived your life, you old diseased bitch! Your life was over. You lived it! This is my body; now get out!"

You were nothing when I found you. A broken young girl with so much potential, wasting away while your body—your young and able body—was trashed and scorned. You didn't want it, so I took it. Now...let...GO.

"This is my body. My life."

Your life? And who are you?

Cyn crawled into the kitchen, searched the cabinets, pulled spices out of the cupboards, fumbled through empty containers and old prescription bottles.

Memories? Is that who you think you are...memories? Silly girl.

She searched for an answer, told herself not to engage, not to answer the old woman. But if she wasn't her memories, then what was she? She couldn't answer.

Memories were all she had.

She woke up in the Foreverland cabin, sixteen years old and a shaved head. She struggled to survive with no identity and none of her memories. It wasn't until her memories returned that she felt real, that she regained her youth and innocence. Even the memories—the abusive parents, the drugs and homelessness—they were better than none at all.

She went to the bathroom and searched under the sink. The towels hung off the corners of the mirror, a slice of her reflection looked back.

A wrinkled cheek.

Bright red lipstick.

"No."

Her lower lip quivered. That was her reflection. *But how...*

You wasted your life, didn't you?

Thoughts bubbled to the surface.

Cyn stood under the harsh light of a bare LED bulb, staring at the beige towels hanging over the mirror, recalling memories of a young girl that got a horse for her tenth birthday.

Of being elected high school president.

Graduating Princeton cumma sum laude.

Vacations. Marriage. Children. Grandchildren.

Yachts.

Cancer.

"Sweet Jesus." The words slipped out.

She hated it when that happened. That wasn't what she would say, never in her life. That was *Barb's* displeasure forming on her lips. Those were Barb's memories, that was her standing on beaches, living in mansions, wearing diamonds—

"No, no, no." She pulled her hair. "Get out of my head. Get out!"

The memories poured in like sewage.

Shhhh. Just close your eyes, darling. Just go to sleep. That's what you want. That's what the pills are for. Just sleep.

Her back ached. She did want to sleep, wanted to close her eyes and drift into bliss and never wake up.

You were never meant to be here.

Barb had taken her body. She had expelled Cyn into the Nowhere, cast her identity into the nothingness, into the eternal grayness, never to inhabit a body again.

But she did. Cyn came out of the Nowhere to find her body that they now shared already inhabited by Barb.

"This is my body."

Not for long.

"Get out."

Just sleep, darling. Shhhhhh.

A cold rush of fear gushed through her. Her grip on this moment was slipping.

"No!"

She slammed her fist into the towel, felt the mirror spider beneath it, the satisfying crackle of shards across the sink.

She ran into the front room, turned up the television and covered her ears, singing along to an infomercial that promised everlasting peace with one dose of biomites. She sang all her favorite songs.

And realized she'd never heard them before.

Shhhhhhh.

An old woman was watching her.

Wrinkles across her face, lips bright red. Jagged pieces missing from her torso.

A chunk of time was missing. *How did I get in the bathroom?*

The mirror was shattered; the fractured reflection of an old woman looked back, hypnotic eyes snaring Cyn, the truth swimming in their blue depths.

Barb was in the mirror.

A bottle rattled in Cyn's hand. The lid was off. Thirty pills inside. She had the impulse to pour them in her hand, to tip her head back and swallow.

"No."

Invisible strings tugged her hand. The jagged reflection watched her empty the bottle into her left hand and smiled. Cyn's jaw felt pried open, her head pulled back. Pills danced on the floor.

Most of them landed on her tongue.

Close your eyes. It'll all be over shortly.

Her cell phone was on the sink. She had no memory of putting it there.

You can't kill me, Cyn thought, *without killing yourself.*

Shhhhhh.

You can't kill this body without killing yourself!

The invisible strings pulled her arm, this time toward the phone. She felt herself reaching for it, sliding her thumb over the glass. She would call for help after she swallowed.

And help would come. Help would come.

No, please.

Barb was close to the surface, her thoughts slipping into the light. Paramedics would pull her back from the brink of death; they would save the body. But Cyn would be unconscious. Barb would rise from the deep and snatch her up, would shove her into the dark subconscious where no one would hear her again. When the paramedics revived the body, Cyn wouldn't open her eyes.

Barb would.

Please don't throw me into the Nowhere, Cyn begged.

She hated herself for giving up, hated herself for letting Barb win, but she was willing to trade places with Barb, to be a prisoner in the dark subconscious if she just promised. *Not the Nowhere.*

Cyn swirled her tongue and managed to get three pills to fall out. A fourth stuck to her lip. The rest continued to melt.

Why are you doing this?

Barb didn't answer, just watched her slide down the glass door of the shower—phone still in hand—meeting the cold tile floor.

Danny, Cyn thought. *It was Danny.*

The old woman remained quiet, feeling the saliva pool under Cyn's tongue. It was in the diner, when Cyn was near Danny, that Barb went quiet. Somehow Danny's presence pushed her deep into the dark subconscious. He was a threat.

Barb knew it.

Danny! Cyn thought.

Her thumb slid across the phone. Numbers glowed beneath the glass. She attempted to throw the phone, but her elbow barely flinched.

No, you don't, Barb said.

She pushed the pills against the roof of her mouth, chalky residue squeezing between her teeth, saliva dangling from her lower lip. Cyn squeezed her eyes until sparks danced, and focused on her arm.

This time the phone bounced across the floor.

It hit the door jamb and ricocheted into the front room. The screen cracked. The numbers cast an eerie glow on the back of the couch.

She was kicked by an invisible boot. Her face slapped the floor. Half the pills were involuntarily spit out, but the rest were stuck inside her mouth. Her hand, moving on its own, scooped the slimy white mess back into her mouth.

The slurry began to slide down her throat.

She was forced to crawl into the front room. Her tongue swelled. She collapsed on one elbow. Her knees continued moving, sliding across the floor, hand extended, fingers stretching for the phone.

Closer, she moved.

Her legs lost feeling. Her hands tingled. Cyn willed herself to give into the numbing. She was quitting. Her body heard the white flag of surrender and answered.

Her hip thumped the floor.

The strings were cut. Barb pushed it, but she only squirmed like a poisoned animal. The phone was a mile away.

Get up, Barb hissed. *Get up, damn you.*

Half a smile curled on her lips. The pills would eventually go down. But without the phone, the paramedics wouldn't arrive. Cyn would die.

But so would Barb.

153

DULUTH, Minnesota

The foliage was thick and dewy.

The edges cut Danny. He ran blindly through the thicket. The tickle of hot breath was on his neck. Something crashed through the canopy. He didn't look back.

Nails dug into his back.

Leaves and dust swirled in the air. Despite the pain, there were no talons piercing his flesh, no predator above him. Just an invisible force lifting him into the clouds. He knew what would come next, what always came next.

Pelting sand.

Voices.

No sun above the clouds, no blue sky or stars. Just the endless gray of the Nowhere—

Danny!

He surged awake, jumped off the sweat-soaked bed, chest heaving, pulse thumping.

The hotel. He was in the hotel room.

Someone had shouted his name. There were people outside his room, but that's not where it came from. Someone called for him in his sleep. But the dream was always the same, never interrupted, never changed.

Someone needed him.

Heart still racing.

The moon illuminated his faint exhalations. Danny hesitated in the driveway. Cyn's house was nestled in the dark, the windows dark, a television splashing light from the corner.

Danny didn't believe in fate, didn't believe destiny was predetermined. He didn't believe in soul mates or the alignment of stars. Danny believed in free will.

But she needs me.

He cupped his hands to the window, risking looking like a complete creep. The porch was dark, the shadows hiding him from the street. The couch was empty. The microwave threw faint green light across the kitchen. If he rang the doorbell, how would he explain what he was doing there after midnight?

It already seemed like he was stalking her. Because he was. This would make it all too obvious.

He was about to turn around when something caught his eye. He pressed his face against the window. The microwave light revealed a sickly green arm from behind the couch.

Danny burst through the front door.

Cyn was curled up on the hardwood, convulsing, clutching an empty prescription bottle. A shiver shot through him.

She's laughing.

It gurgled in her throat. A hoarse, gravelly laugh crawled out of her. Her cheek lay in a pool of saliva; a white pill stuck to her lip. He hooked his finger under her tongue and pulled out a lump of half-melted pills. There were more. He dug deeper and she gagged.

Panic.

Did she already swallow them? Should I make her puke? Call for help?

She planked against the floor, vibrating like a bare wire pumping voltage through her legs. Something was grinding, like two stones under tremendous pressure. Her jaws were clenched.

He had to call someone, but in the rush out of the hotel he'd forgotten his phone. He had to do something. Run outside, pound on the neighbor's door, scream in the street...*something!*

A phone!

He scrambled over Cyn and grabbed the cell phone. The glass was shattered, but it lit up. He didn't need her code, just needed to press the *Emergency* icon.

No!

Her eyes snapped open, the whites on full display.

Danny crawled over to her. He took her hand, a long scar bright and raised across the back of it. Her fingers were stiff, her arm a rigid bar. He slid his palm against hers and cupped her hand between both of his hands. That sweet feeling he experienced in the diner returned, melting through his arm, lighting him up with peaceful warmth.

And something broke. Cyn fell limp.

He felt it when he squeezed her hand, like he'd triggered something. He felt it flow through his arm. Her eyes closed; her head rolled to the side.

"Cyn?" She stiffened when he started to let go. "Can you hear me?"

She panted. Hair plastered to her forehead. He brushed it aside and noticed the small scar where a needle had long ago carried her into Foreverland.

The phone began dimming. He debated. If she swallowed the pills, there was still time to pump her stomach. But when he took her hand, something stopped. He stroked her cheeks, flush and damp.

She squeezed back.

Her fingers tightened, just once. Like someone calling from the other shore, waving a flag. He squeezed again. Moments later, she squeezed back, a bit tighter, a little longer.

He leaned against the couch and pulled her head on his lap. She was so limp, burning hot. He wanted to get a damp rag to cool her, but every time he loosened his grip she would go rigid.

He couldn't explain why he didn't call for help. It was just a hunch.

He didn't believe in soul mates, didn't believe in fate. But he believed
—for now, right now—she needed him.

<hr>

Sunlight cut the outline of the front door.

A morning chill crept inside the house. The furnace kicked on, but
the floor was cold. And hard.

Danny woke with a start, pain stabbing his neck. He'd slept on his
side without a pillow. His hip and shoulder were bruised; his fingers,
still laced with Cyn's, throbbed.

She breathed easy.

Her temperature was normal. They made it through the night. If
she'd swallowed the pills, she wouldn't look so normal. But if he was
wrong... *Why didn't I call for help?*

Slowly, he slid his hand away from her, folded her hands over her
stomach and waited. She rolled her head, moaning. He almost reached
back when she fell back to sleep.

Quickly, he went to the bathroom.

Towels were piled on the floor, shards of the mirror lay across the
sink. Pills were scattered around the bathroom. It looked like suicide.

But why would the pills be everywhere?

It looked more like someone poured the pills down her. And what
magic did Danny possess? He held her hand and it stopped. Then he
realized what had happened to him.

No dreams!

He had fallen asleep and didn't dream. He couldn't remember the
last time he wasn't cast into the nightmare. Each and every night he
ran for his life, sometimes across the sand, sometimes through the
jungle.

Always on the island.

Danny brought pillows and blankets to make her more comfortable. He'd stay until she woke up, make her breakfast. They could talk,
really talk about what was happening, what all this meant and what
they were supposed to do. Reed sent him for a reason.

He began picking up trash and cleared a place on the couch. If he could pick her up without disturbing her, she could sleep on the cushions. He noticed the envelopes. It was a stack of unwanted mail in a basket. It was mostly junk, and Danny wouldn't have given it a second thought had he not seen the green ink.

There were three large envelopes. Two more were under a pizza box, another one halfway beneath the couch. They were the same size, same thickness. The stiff outline of the disc was evident. All unopened.

He looked at her sleeping soundly.

She knew what was inside, knew that Foreverland was coming. And she wanted to forget.

But Foreverland came calling. He didn't know how or why, he was just glad he'd reached her in time.

Danny ripped the flap open.

The disc rolled out. The pattern of pinholes looked the same as the one he'd received. The only difference was the thick edge. His was blue, hers yellow.

A folded sheet of lined paper fell out.

Danny picked it up and held it to the light. There was nothing about building a bridge, just two lines written in green.

43.58039085560786

-107.24716186523438

He recognized the numbers. They were coordinates.

Raised letters had been pressed through the paper from the other side. He flipped it over to see the poem.

He put it in his back pocket.

Danny put her on the couch. He lay next to her, reciting the poem, dissecting and examining every word. He had to be sure.

Half an hour later, he backed the SUV into the driveway, loaded it with blankets and winter clothing and all the food and bottled water in the house. It was still very early when he carried her to the SUV and laid her in the passenger seat. No one saw them drive away.

Danny passed the hotel, but didn't stop. There was nothing he needed. He was thinking about the poem.

. . .

Where once there was light on a dusted rim,
When day followed day, now a night-filled sin,
Turn back your sight to where your steps begin,
And return to the root and fall again.

He programmed the coordinates into his GPS. That's why Reed sent him, to take her back to where her steps began.

To fall again.

154

The trees were turning.

It was still early September, but fall had begun showing its colors.

The waiting room was filled with children. Most were there for physicals, a little biomite boost to maximize their ability, to make them better athletes. Better students.

Just better.

A trail of taillights lit up the street, another day in traffic hell. The Institute was down the street on the corner of Forty-Sixth and Seventh. Tourists walked past without a glance into the prestigious research center, no clue that the world was being changed inside those doors. She considered making a surprise visit, tapping the intercom and asking for Dr. Baronov.

Today's not a day I want to be escorted away by security.

After her appointment, she'd call Kada. She used to be an editor for Penguin before becoming a freelancer. Kada took on a project here and there, even consulted with Alex, because she loved the business as much as she loved the city. And if she wasn't working, she was on Broadway.

And a show sounds good.

Someone yanked on her pant leg. "I think she wants you."

A little girl pointed across the room. The receptionist stared at Alex, eyebrows pinched, waving her over. Alex took her time.

"Anything wrong?" the receptionist asked.

"Just a checkup."

"I called your name five times."

She'd been doing that more often, getting lost in thought, losing track of time. It was just a few minutes here and there, but when she'd blanked out for an hour, she decided to make an appointment.

The receptionist tapped her computer screen with a long fingernail. "The doctor is waiting."

Alex went to the back room and stared at the inspirational poster of a grandmother watching children at play because biomites make life better.

She checked her phone, sat back and stared at the poster again, remembering a time when she was younger, when her parents would take her to the park and she'd play on the equipment for hours. Summer smelled like cut grass and tasted like sweet tea.

Ah, summer.

"*Hola.*" Dr. Johnstone opened the door.

Alex dropped her phone. She looked for her bag, but she'd left it in the waiting room. There were no new messages, but another time lapse occurred. Twenty minutes gone.

Damn it.

He washed his hands. Long curls of brown hair hung over his eyebrows. "How's the book going?"

"It's in a holding pattern."

"A little delay?"

"Something like that."

Her interview requests with Dr. Tyler Ballard had been rebuffed. Interviews with his doctors, lawyers, investigators and grocery store clerks had been denied, too. The Institute not only denied her access but filed a restraining order, citing her prying had damaged their research and if she was caught on or near the premises she would be arrested. Samuel wanted to restart the lawsuit, but Alex held out hope. If they sued, she'd never see the inside again.

"Well, you can't work all the time." The doctor checked his wristwatch. "Got to save some time to smell the flowers."

"I suppose."

"Just another day in paradise. Why would you ever want to leave?"

"What?"

"Mmm?"

"What did you say?"

He looked up. "Pardon me?"

"I'm sorry, I don't mean to sound defensive. You said something that sounded familiar."

"Another day in paradise?"

"The other one."

"Why leave?"

She nodded. It was something like that. *When life is so perfect, why would you ever want to change it? Or leave it?* Everything was perfect— perfect house, perfect marriage, perfect job. Perfect life.

Why would she ever want to leave?

Has it always been this way?

She didn't think so. Didn't her marriage suffer? Didn't Samuel have an affair or something? Those things sounded familiar, but what did any of that matter?

And isn't there something missing?

She wondered that every day, like there was an enormous hole below her, covered by the thinnest of materials, a cap that creaked with each step. She didn't want to know what was down there. If she did, she'd fall.

And everything was perfect.

"You having any problems?"

"No."

"No more episodes like last time?"

"No."

"Any unusual events, such as phantom car accidents?"

"Nothing."

"Anything suspicious?"

"Suspicious?"

"You know, out of the ordinary. Anything that might strike you as odd."

He doodled with the image on the desktop, of her brain lit up. There was a lot more red than the last time, most of it still in the right hemisphere. In fact, the entire right hemisphere was enflamed.

"Alessandra?"

"What?"

"Are you all right?"

"What did you just call me?"

He frowned.

"You called me Alessandra."

"I think I said Alex. Is there something else you prefer?"

Her knee was bouncing. She kept it hidden beneath the table. Maybe she should let him see it. If she was going to have an episode, this was a good time. She suddenly had her doubts about him, not sure she trusted him.

Then why am I here?

"So anything unusual?"

"I'm sleeping a lot."

"How much is a lot?"

"Twelve hours." *With naps, it was more like fourteen.*

"That's more than usual?"

"I think it's more than usual for anyone, don't you?"

"Not necessarily. Everyone's different. You said you weren't writing as much, you're working in the garden more often. Maybe your body is just catching up."

She didn't remember telling him about the garden.

"Listen," he said, "everything looks fine, Alex. In fact, your numbers are perfect. If I wasn't in the biomite technology field, I'm not sure I would even suspect you were seeded, that's just how perfect you are."

Her phone vibrated. A text arrived.

"How happy are you?" he asked.

"What?"

"On a scale from one to ten, how happy are you?"

"Eight."

She had no problems, no irritations. She had everything she could ask for. Isn't that what life was supposed to be? Shouldn't that be a ten? *Why did I say eight?*

"There's a biomite update available, if you're interested." The doctor began washing his hands. "Nothing invasive, just a sync treatment to prevent any potential mutations. Not saying you're susceptible to a malfunction, it's just good to stay on top of things, stay preventative. All the trials for this new strain have been excellent. I fully recommend it. It'll take five minutes and then you're out of here."

She nodded. Her life was an eight. She wanted it to be a ten. *Doesn't everyone?*

He squeezed her shoulder and left the room with an adios.

Alex checked her phone. *Geri?*

For a moment, she couldn't recall the name. Then she remembered and it was clear. How could she forget her free-soul assistant? She hadn't heard from her all summer. Geri hadn't returned most of her messages, and when she did, she was too busy.

"Got something for you," the text said.

Alex texted back, "What?"

A minute later. "You in the city?"

"Yes." She stopped from texting back, *How did you know?*

"Meet at Bella's Deli at 4."

That was right down the street. She could walk there. In fact, Kada's apartment wasn't far from that. She could leave the car in long term.

A nurse arrived.

Alex leaned back and let her insert the seeder into her right nostril.

"Mrs. Diosa!" The receptionist held up a handbag.

Alex stopped at the door. That was her bag, the one she left in the waiting room. She was careful to watch her step on the way back, still a bit woozy.

The receptionist smiled. "Thank you."

Alex wasn't sure why she was being thanked. Everything had that double-vision feel, like the lenses were still being focused.

On the elevator, she checked her phone. It was past five. She'd been in the back room almost two hours. She thumbed her phone and Kada answered on the second ring.

"Come on over," she said.

There was something else she was supposed to do, but there were no voicemails or texts. In fact, the only text she'd received that day was from Samuel. She decided to call him.

She really missed him.

Alex saw five Broadway shows that week.

She went by herself to see *Wicked* a second time. It was night when it ended. A drizzle wet the asphalt and beaded on the hoods of taxis. Despite the chill, she decided to walk back to Kada's, maybe catch a cab on Forty-Eighth.

She enjoyed the lights, especially the way they stretched over the wet pavement, the way they sparkled on the buildings. It was the sound of cars honking, people shouting, the smell of exhaust that tingled her bones. It was all around.

It was the city.

My city.

She felt like she owned it. There was a connection deep in her core, a feeling that everything tugged at her heart, emanated from her soul; a connection that was seamless and unbreakable.

Even when someone coughed from a doorway and began following her, she was unshaken. She felt the gap in his teeth, the wet hair beneath his hood, the withdrawal shaking his hand. He didn't harm her, didn't ask for change or a handout. He just stopped following her at some point.

She should've found that odd, but she was connected. Didn't everyone feel this?

This must be a ten.

She left Friday morning.

The traffic wasn't bad and it wasn't long before she was cruising through the hills. The phone rang.

"Where are you?" Samuel asked.

"Not far."

"I miss you."

She smiled. It felt much longer than a week. She foraged in her handbag for chapstick while steering with her knee. A manila package slid out, spilling its contents on the seat and floorboard.

"I'll leave work early," he said. "See you for lunch."

Alex waited for the next stoplight, glancing every so often at the cache spread across the floor mat. There were folders and photos and paper-clipped reports. Mail, too. When she caught a red light, she unbuckled her seatbelt and grabbed a handful.

The reports were from Geri.

There was a vague memory of wanting to meet her in the city. *Wasn't I supposed to be at a deli?*

A quick skim revealed loads of inside information, photos of a young Tyler and Patricia Ballard, stuff Alex could only dream of finding. *How does she do it?*

She'd have to give her a bonus when the book published.

The mail, though, wasn't addressed to Alex and it didn't belong to Geri. It wasn't a letter, it was a flier. One of those small glossy cards. It said, *Have you seen this boy?*

There was a photo.

A car horn blared. The light was green.

The postcard slipped from her fingers and fell to the floorboard. She drove the rest of the way home, reading random sheets of paper pinned to the steering wheel, whatever she could grab while driving through the countryside, occasionally driving off the road or crossing the center line.

Tyler Ballard was a young neuroscientist. Patricia was a psychologist. Both were tenured professors at an Ivy League university, career-minded people intent upon helping the world.

Then Patricia was diagnosed with early onset Alzheimer's. The story of the couple was well documented. The public empathized.

Until the holes appeared.

Tyler was researching his controversial technology that involved brains, computers and needles in the brains of rats and mice, but was not given permission for human trials. The couple attempted to cover the evidence, but was quietly placed on leave with pay.

He took his research to the basement.

There were pictures of Patricia in the basement with a needle protruding from her forehead, Tyler in his basement lab with eyes that hadn't slept for days.

And a photo of them lying in bed, holding hands.

If she didn't know how the story ended—Foreverland kidnapping youth—her heart would ache.

Alex threw the papers on the kitchen table and shuffled through them like gold coins.

The postcard was on the bottom.

She held it up as if it was hard to see. Even under the light, it felt dim. It was a picture of a twelve-year-old boy. He was Hispanic with short black hair, his eyes large and brown. His smile sly and knowing.

The back door slammed, but no one was there.

The room began turning.

She needed water. Dehydration caused room spins. She stood at the sink, downing a tall glass of water when the music began.

It was upstairs.

"Hello?"

It wasn't a radio. It was more bells and tones, something more soothing, like a lullaby.

A crib mobile.

"Samuel?"

She put one foot on the bottom step and the room suddenly turned her toward the couch.

There was a box of crayons on the floor, paper on the end table, but not the papers from the car. These were pulled from a coloring book with bright faces and purple lips and yellow eyes.

She threw herself against the wall and followed it through the kitchen, made it to the back door in time to puke over the railing.

The petunias were a mess.

A car pulled up as she heaved round three, this one squeezing her gut like a wrung towel.

Samuel jumped out. He was by her side for a moment, running inside the house. She sat down and closed her eyes, the acrid taste of vomit in her sinuses.

The Tilt-O-Whirl began to slow.

"What happened?" Samuel put a wet rag on her forehead.

She didn't know, explained the room-spins, the sudden nausea. She thought he was home, that he was upstairs playing...*music?* What the hell happened?

The biomite sync.

She'd been fine all week. Better than fine, in fact. She'd been perfect.

A ten.

When she was ready, when she trusted her body to stand up, she made it inside the house without assistance. The floor didn't spin, the walls didn't turn. She just wanted a warm shower and a nap.

On her way past the dining room table, the papers were neatly stacked. The front room was clean, no coloring book pages scattered on the floor. And no music.

It was later she thought something was missing.

A postcard, or something.

155

ADMAX PENITENTIARY, Colorado

Tyler's bed didn't creak, just gently squished under him.

He reached beneath the mattress and stared at the surgical steel needle encased in a tube of gel. He broke the seal—his arthritic hands knobby in the joints, the thin skin spotted—and admired the perfect symmetry of the needle, the silver gleam and dangerous point.

Anticipation wet his mouth.

Pins rolled beneath the mattress, massaging his legs, back and buttocks. He positioned the tip of the needle near the stent. The leathery flesh began to throb. Sometimes, he rammed it into his head and his consciousness would be slung into another dimension.

He kept his eyes open, breathed deep the musty odor of the prison's painted walls and slid it slowly into his forehead. The cold spike sank its fang.

The ceiling swirled into the sky, the walls fell apart.

There was no sensation of travel, no illusion of space. *The needle's kiss.*

His reflection looked back from a ticket kiosk. He was wearing khaki pants and a navy blue blazer. He ran his hand through thick wavy hair the color of honey and straightened his open collar, a gold ring glinting in the theatre's lights.

The city smelled like a cleansing rain. There was no exhaust, no trash—just the sterilized version of a perfect society. *A perfect reality.*

The usher opened the door.

A few people milled through the lobby in tuxedos and long gowns. Beyond another set of doors, a tenor bellowed opera.

An escort led him to a grand tier box with two seats. Below, *Phantom of the Opera* unfolded. He sat next to Patricia, reached into her lap and took her hand. She held him tightly, her other hand holding a tissue to her chest.

She would sob when it was over.

She always did.

Patricia slid her hand over the brass rail.

The theatre was empty. The crowd had dispersed, leaving in their cars or calling cabs, heading back to their supposed homes. In Patricia's Foreverland, they were just illusions of her own mind, but he often wondered if she replicated them from actual people in the city.

The details of the theatre, the opera singers and the custodians sweeping the stage were flawless. Her ability to absorb these details from the space around her physical body, as it lay in the Institute, and project them into her Foreverland was as uncanny as it was unexplainable. Her mind was an ethereal sponge.

Is the physical world any more legitimate than Foreverland? Under what pretense is physicality the gold standard?

That was the question he begged all of humankind to answer.

"Tyler? Are you listening?"

"I'm sorry, lost in thought. You were saying?"

"I'm concerned."

"And what are your concerns?"

"Your body, for one. I was looking at the results of your latest physical."

He didn't want her to worry, frequently hiding the dire conditions he encountered in physical reality, but it was difficult to hide his thoughts or emotions when he came here, where all was on display.

"I want you to consider using the good doctor's new biomite strain. It will stabilize your health, guarantee longevity."

"It's too much risk."

"Your health is far too fragile to argue. If you lose your body at the wrong time, then where will I be?"

"I fear government intervention is more to be worried about than my health. Abusing biomites will set off alarms. We don't need the authorities watching us too closely."

"What about undetectable biomites, the ones Gramm spoke of?"

He shook his head. "You speak of things far more risky. My body is old, yes. There are aches and pains, but it will last as long as we need it to last. And when the time comes, we will cross over into Alessandra's eternal Foreverland. Don't worry yourself, please."

She drummed her fingers on the brass rail, watching men push brooms across the stage. "Perhaps you should stay here, then. We'll cross over when she's ready."

She didn't look at him when she said it.

He could feel her loneliness when he was gone. Living in this Foreverland, within her own mind, knowing these were merely reflections of people in the physical world and not actual beings was distressing. No matter what shapes and sizes and colors she looked at, no matter how human they seemed, they were all projections of her mind.

She needs me.

"I can't leave my body," he said. "Not yet."

"But she is almost ready."

"That's not it. I need to be here, in the prison. There are still matters to attend."

"And Gramm cannot do them?"

He trusted the former chemist, but he was weak. His mind was too open, his taste for biomites too strong. Tyler feared his assistant could be overwhelmed by the wrong person too easily. And that he could not risk.

"Perhaps it's time to abandon the prison," she said. "It's always been a risk. And now that the Institute is fully functional, there's no reason for you not to come here."

He cocked his head. "What's really bothering you, dear?"

She wiped her eyes and stuffed the tissue in her purse. Perhaps the opera jarred loose long-held emotions she didn't want to face, or didn't know were there. *There is so much in the subconscious that a thousand lifetimes could not uncover the secrets we keep from ourselves.*

"I don't think Alex will sleep," she said. "There have been too many disruptions."

"Anomalies."

"More than anomalies, Tyler. Someone is purposefully enticing her to remember."

She refused to name him, as if uttering *Reed* would somehow summon him into being.

"She won't remember her past. And even if Reed is behind this, he won't succeed. Her life is perfect, darling. She'll soon forget everything and sleep."

He floated a thought into this world. Unlike physical reality, a thought here could become a wish that, falling into the right context, was fulfilled. Tyler envisioned a man dressed in black and called him to the stage.

Moments later, a man dressed in black strode across the stage, his face partially obscured by the white mask. The custodians continued sweeping as he lifted an arm and his voice carried into the empty theatre.

"Think of Me", he sang all alone.

It tugged at the emotion welling just beneath Patricia's eyes.

Tyler held out his hand. There was no more talk of biomites and host, no more worry about the future. Everything was going near enough to plan that Tyler pulled her close for the remainder of his stay.

In the grand tier box, they danced.

He opened his eyes, a concrete ceiling above him, a dull wall beside him. And all the aches and pains, the stiffness of eighty years surrounded him.

He extracted the needle.

It slithered out and left behind an antiseptic sting. Tears involuntarily welled up. He hated to leave her, to come back to this plane. If hell existed, it was in the physical world, not some distant make-believe. He no longer doubted that.

The opera still echoed in his head.

He wiped his eyes. The throbbing continued.

An infection was setting in. Soon, it would alter the function of his brain and, in turn, the quality of his mind. Even if he avoided the needle and went to wireless brain biomites, the infection was already there.

Have I already failed you, dear?

He blinked away the tears. More had pooled against the bridge of his nose. Patricia trusted him. It was her vision to create Foreverland, to build a new reality. She was the one that conceived of it in the very beginning, not him. She knew, long before biomites were ever conceived, that all the minds in the world could be linked, that human singularity was possible, that the illusion of separateness could be dispelled.

And peace would reign.

While astrophysicists searched for new worlds in faraway solar systems, she knew that a new reality was not light-years away, but the distance of a thought.

It's here. We are the new reality. We are the endless possibilities. We are heaven, we are hell.

And she trusted him to bring her vision to fruition, trusted his technology, trusted him to plug her into the needle first. It nearly killed her. Had it done so, he would surely have taken his own life, not strong enough to bear the guilt, not brave enough to go on without her.

But now there was little sand left in the hourglass for him. Time was the god that meted out each grain with methodic timing and refused to sell more. Time was a cruel god that promised eternity.

But delivered only the past.

His bare foot found the floor. Slowly, he slid his feet into slippers and opened the cell door. Moonlight cast his shadow. He passed a guard holding the elevator open at the end of the hall, and pressed a button on the panel.

Tyler's stomach dropped all the way to the basement.

The smell greeted him.

Sunrise was still hours away. His guards were at home, sleeping next to their spouses. He was alone. If he fell, he would call them. Despite his confidence, he managed to keep the depth of his concern hidden from his bride.

Reed is more than an anomaly.

Tyler went down the hall and put his hand on a metal door. Death and decay slammed into him like a hot cloud, licked his face with a humid tongue.

Tables were lined up.

Their metal edges dull and curved, their surfaces soft—each held a nude male. Tubes ran from their thin arms, trailing over their protruding ribs. Some of them were connected to respirators.

All of them had a needle in their forehead.

A lamp was positioned over each table, exposing each body with the spectrum of sunlight to stimulate vitamin D. They were a much higher form of plants. The bodies were necessary for the mind to exist.

One day that would change.

Tyler idly walked amongst his people. Green lights glowed at the head of each table, splashing the floor with an eerie effect. Some of the indicators were yellow instead of green, indicating stress, whether mental or physical. A few were red.

These were the ones that smelled the worst.

They would need to be disposed of in the furnace like annual flowers that had reached the end of their life cycle and fulfilled their duty.

These were his people. They were willing to send themselves into Foreverland, to sacrifice themselves to create a new reality. They were willing to die for him. Some did so consciously, others he convinced.

The justice system thought they had sentenced Tyler to prison. This was to be his punishment. But he chose to be here. Where else would he find so many lives that didn't matter? Where else would he find so many men that wouldn't be missed?

Men to build the next Foreverland.

———————

Gramm rose from sleep.

His awareness floated to the surface like a hand gently lifted him from the sandy depths, a whisper that commanded he wake. His senses clouded, he nabbed the webbing of flesh between his finger and thumb and twisted until cold flames lanced into his palm.

He tasted the pain. And that was good. It was real.

Too often, he had awakened to find himself in the throes of reality confusion, not sure if he was indeed in the flesh or Foreverland. It was difficult to trust life when he didn't know where he was. Or who.

Pain, he had learned, tasted different in the flesh. It was immediate and fresh. It grounded him. Made him real. If he didn't taste the cold burn, he knew he had awakened in Foreverland.

Did that matter?

The cell door was unlocked. Gramm was still dressing as he skipped down the hallway and took the waiting elevator to the pool.

Chlorine stung his nostrils.

Gramm raked his thinning hair and watched Tyler swim another lap in the Olympic pool. His strokes were long and methodical. Gramm waited with a towel and an open robe. The old man climbed out of the water, his flesh soft and puckered, like soaked leather. It was gray and patchy, moles dotting his hairless chest.

Only his forehead was red and puffy.

"Thank you." He took the towel.

A pool of this size and quality was unheard of in a correctional facility. But the warden seemed to see it Tyler's way.

We all do.

An inmate met them at a small table against the wall, placed two mugs in front of them, poured coffee and slid a plate of fresh fruit toward Tyler. They watched three other men begin maintenance on the pool.

Tyler chewed like he swam: slow and methodical. "You are aware of what has happened?" he asked.

"Yes."

Gramm sipped the coffee, watching the men untangle the hose and test the water. He didn't meet Tyler's eyes, but felt the tension emanating from the old man's chest, felt the twist in his gut. Felt his pain, his fear.

It had been that way ever since Gramm had received biomite remediation. It was experimental, the state's attempt at rehabilitation. He volunteered and would get time off his sentence by taking biomites. Days later, he sensed thoughts that weren't his own, moved his fingers when he hadn't wanted to.

Felt the probing of another mind.

And then the barrier between Tyler and Gramm dropped like a curtain. The illusion of their separation—that they were individuals—evaporated. Like fingers, they belonged to a hand.

The hand of God.

Tyler had synced their brain biomites. Gramm watched him do the same to the guards, the staff and even the warden, watched him slowly take control. The takeover happened years ago. *Seems like yesterday.*

"Alessandra is on schedule," Gramm said. "She'll sleep, I promise. She will become the host."

Tyler hummed. Alessandra was happy. She was satisfied, drifting toward a blissful state of open awareness. Soon, she would be sleeping. She would become the unknowing host of Foreverland.

"And Danny and Cyn?" Tyler said.

He wasn't asking. He knew what had happened. Gramm had promised that it wouldn't. And now, for a second time, the kids were gone. He didn't know how. Or why.

They need to be terminated. He wanted to say it. Instead, he let the thought linger for Tyler to see.

"There is an infection in Foreverland, Gramm. A virus."

Tyler wiped his mouth thoughtfully.

"I've assured Patricia that everything is under control, that these complications were not unexpected. I don't want her to worry, you see. But Alessandra has received information she should not be receiving.

She saw a photo of the child, you see, so let's not be naïve. Is that understood?"

"Yes."

"Good. I believe it is Reed; let's accept that. He has been communicating with them."

"But there's been no communication, I assure you. No email, phone calls, or texts. His presence has been nonexistent since his death. There's just no evidence he exists. It's just not possible. He's dead, sir."

"And mail?"

"Pardon me?"

"You've been monitoring the mail, as well?"

Gramm hadn't thought of that. A letter wouldn't be detected, it would have to be intercepted. That wouldn't be difficult to do, he just hadn't thought of it.

"Alessandra has been receiving dubious mail and photos of the island through magazines and false advertisements, correct?"

Gramm nodded.

"Our perpetrator is using outdated means. Surely he knows we've discovered it by now—a very audacious move to send her a photo of the child. He wanted us to know that, I believe. He wanted us to know that his pieces are in place. The question is, where is he? Mmm? Where is Reed?"

"I just...I don't see how he could be anywhere."

"You mean you don't see him?"

"Correct."

"So what you don't see doesn't exist?"

"That's not what I'm saying. It's just, there's no evidence he exists."

"The evidence is right in front of us, Gramm. Let's move past the doubt and accept that we've been outplayed and answer the question. If you can't see him, does that mean he doesn't exist?"

"Not necessarily."

"If you can't see him, then where could he be?"

The old man chewed the last cube of cantaloupe and waited for an answer. Waited for Gramm to say it first.

If you can't find someone in Foreverland, they can only be in one place.

"The Nowhere doesn't exist," Gramm said. "Not anymore."

"There is always a Nowhere. We can't be so arrogant to think that we have obliterated it. There will always be a boundary, a perimeter outside the realm of knowing, where nothing exists. And where nothing exists, everything exists."

Gramm felt nauseous. "I don't believe it," he muttered. "There is no Nowhere."

"What we believe does not shape reality."

"I beg your pardon?"

A wry smile curled the corner of the old man's mouth like the dry twist of a senescing leaf.

"What we believe doesn't shape reality?" Gramm stammered. "I thought..."

Belief was the basis of the new reality, the creation of Foreverland. The inner reality that Harold, Tyler's son, had created was based on his imagination. The inner reality that Patricia, Tyler's wife, had created was the result of her imagination. What she believed came true. The Foreverland she hosted was her mind; she made the rules of its existence. She invented the physics by which all of life had to abide.

What we believe becomes our reality!

"There are other forces at work, Gramm. In this case, I believe that other force to be Reed. And while our reality is shaped by our convictions, it cannot bend the unbendable truth, the true nature of existence, that Reed is throwing chaos into our well-laid plans. We need to deal with it. We cannot close our eyes and wish him away. In this case, we deal with life on life's terms."

"But how could he exist?"

"Ah, yes. How?" Tyler pushed his plate away. An inmate swept it up and replaced it with a fresh cup of coffee. "You recall how Reed was introduced to Foreverland when he was first brought to the island?"

Of course. Reed was the boy that refused to take the needle, the one that stole Harold's body.

"But Reed didn't destroy Foreverland." Tyler picked up Gramm's thoughts. "Who destroyed Harold's Foreverland?"

It was Reed's girlfriend. Lucinda.

That was the true anomaly. Her memory escaped Reed when he

was brought to the island. That memory was intact, a fully embodied awareness that woke up in Foreverland. She went from being a memory to a conscious being.

In Harold's mind!

She fled to the Nowhere, the gray static where nothing survived. She lived out there and watched the boys and girls arrive in Foreverland to play their games before they were sucked into the Nowhere themselves, where they were pulled apart, their skins left behind for the old men and women to inhabit.

"Is it not a coincidence, then," Tyler continued, "that it is Reed that haunts us?"

"What are you saying?"

"Maybe Lucinda didn't escape his memory in the first place. Maybe he was capable of sending her there, whether he was aware of it or not. And we underestimated him, Gramm. All this time, he was the one that ruled the Nowhere, not Lucinda."

They always thought Danny was the intelligent threat. Now there was the possibility that Reed had somehow survived in Foreverland without a physical body.

Could survive in the Nowhere.

If it is Reed, we have indeed been duped.

"The next question," Tyler said, "is what is he planning?"

"Revenge."

"Too shallow. Vengeance is for children, and a child cannot play this game. There is something larger at stake, a whole new universe. No, these are calculated disruptions. He's patient. And there's a pattern, I believe."

"Perhaps we're not looking at it from the right angle." The words spilled from Gramm's mouth as if they were not his thoughts.

"Precisely. We are not seeing the pattern because we are not looking at it the right way."

They finished their coffee.

The table was cleared. The pool was clean. Just the hum of the pumps filled the silence.

"What would Reed want, if not vengeance?" Tyler pondered.

"Lucinda."

The old man snapped his fingers, nodding with a smile. "True love is quite a motivator, yes. But what else would he want?"

"Justice."

"Yes, justice. His perception is that a great injustice has been done and he is the equalizer, that he will right the wrong."

"What injustice is he after?" Gramm asked. It was obvious, but he had asked it, the words tumbling out as if they did not belong to him, once again.

"Sacrifice, Gramm. Revolution requires sacrifice, it has always been thus. And who perceives injustice more greatly than the ones that have been sacrificed?"

"The children."

In the making of Foreverland, children had been forced to leave their bodies and were sentenced to the eternal Nowhere. *But don't they realize we are creating a new universe, an entirely new reality? Even the physical universe demands a price for its creation. There are black holes that gobble light, there are volcanoes and asteroids and predators and prey. Sacrifice is the nature of creation. Even children.*

"Bring her to me," Tyler said.

"Alessandra?"

"Yes. Grant her the interview she requested."

"Is that a good idea?"

"I want to make contact with her, see where she is, feel her out. See her from another angle. The sooner she sleeps, the sooner she is ready for Foreverland. We don't know where Reed is, Gramm. We don't know what he's doing, and time is not on our side."

"When do you want to see her?"

The old man stood. "Soon."

That was all he said. His guards appeared, the two he most relied on. His personal attendants.

"What if we fail?" Gramm said. "Contacting her could make her unravel into madness. Maybe Reed is planning that you'd do this."

"Maybe."

A cold chill passed through Gramm. It didn't emanate from the old man this time.

Tyler eschewed the wheelchair Melfy was pushing and shuffled away holding her elbow instead, like he had all the time in the world. But if time were currency, the old man was nearly broke. Yet he walked like a prince.

A prince that would become a king.

The old man stopped at the door. "Maybe we're already in Reed's Foreverland and don't know it yet."

He was joking, of course. They couldn't be in a Foreverland without knowing it. Certainly not in Reed's mind.

Gramm twisted the webbing between his finger and thumb.

The pain was good.

156

ADMAX PENITENTIARY, *Colorado*

The table was metal.

Cold.

Alex rubbed her hands on her thighs. But it wasn't the table or the metal chair that drove a shiver deep inside. It was the white light. It was the putty walls with hairline fractures. It was the smell of suffering.

This was the Alcatraz of the Rockies.

She'd been in federal prisons before, even the extant Russian gulags and Nazi gas chambers, where ghosts tugged at her soul. But this...this felt colder, like apparitions floated around the table, taking turns sitting in the empty chair across from her.

She'd flown out of New York the same day she got the invitation, and stayed in the nearest hotel for two days. Now she tapped her toe and rubbed her thighs for warmth.

She spread the folders on the table to get her mind off the chill and organized two stacks of photos that still smelled of new ink. In one stack, there were photos of a tropical island, the palms tall and bending, the grass green and lush. The other stack contained desolate hills and harsh living and gray skies.

The walls shuddered.

Momentarily, the floor jiggled like gelatin, the colors smeared. Lately things had been a little off, like a camera constantly trying to autofocus. She rubbed her eyes. When she opened them, a door was open in the anteroom.

Through the wire-mesh glass, Alex watched a guard enter, his belly filling the doorway. He was followed by an old man dressed in a saggy blue shirt and loose-fitting pants. The hunch between his shoulders caused him to look at the floor. He was followed by another guard, this one female. She held the old man's elbow.

Alex stood. The legs of the chair raked the concrete.

The big guard held the interview room door open. The old man's slippers scuffed the floor. He paused at the empty chair, wheezing. The guards remained until he waved his knobby hand.

As if dismissed.

"Dr. Ballard?" Alex said.

The old man blinked slowly, lazily. The gray eyes rested on her. His nostrils flared. He tipped his head, examining her as a collector might evaluate a new possession. His eyes appeared to smile, but his lips remained a grim slit beneath a lumpy nose.

"I'm Alex Diosa. Thanks for agreeing to meet with me."

She knifed her hand over the table. Dr. Ballard never took his eyes off of her. Neither did he move his hand.

Alex looked through the wire-mesh window. The guards sat in chairs as bare as the ones in the interview room. She wondered if Dr. Ballard could hear her, if maybe dementia had taken hold. She'd heard strange things about him, that he preferred long bouts of solitary confinements—sometimes weeks at a time. *Did I read that or see it on* 60 Minutes?

"Can you hear me?" she asked.

"Yes, Mrs. Diosa."

She had the urge to run, to leave the briefcase her father gave her twenty years ago for graduation, to abandon her notes and belongings like rubbish and flee through the wire-mesh glass. It was his voice, the way it resonated inside her. She'd heard it before. *No. I've felt it.*

Alex fumbled with the pictures, pulling the paperclips off of bundles Geri had assembled for her, bundles Alex took apart over and over late at night, reshuffling and reorganizing. She'd memorized every photo, every note, but now aimlessly looked through them.

Deep breath.

He was smiling—the corner of his mouth curled like a hook. He cocked his head curiously.

My grandfather used to do that. Alex jerked at the sudden realization, felt the warmth of familiarity soothe her flailing nerves. He didn't look anything like her grandfather. Still, she couldn't help but smile.

"I'm an investigative journalist," she started. "I wrote for *The Washington Post* as well as *The New Yorker*, *60 Minutes* as well as producing several documentaries. I've written books on crimes against humanity in North Korea. You might be familiar with some of my work."

She mentioned a few. He smiled.

"And what do you want?"

"I'm researching the Foreverland crimes."

"Is that what you really want from me?"

"I'm looking for the truth, yes."

"And what is truth?"

He didn't say *the* truth. He just said *truth*, like a Buddha searching for deeper meaning. She looked at the photos. Her hands were steady, but her heart fluttered. "I want to know how all this started."

"Is truth relative, Mrs. Diosa?"

"Let me be clear, I'm looking for facts."

"Ah, facts. That's different than truth."

"I don't believe so, Doctor."

His eyes flickered upward, looking just above her eyes, right in the middle of her forehead. A shiver raced beneath her scalp, a tingly net that wrapped around her head, microwaving her brain. There was a circular scar on his forehead, about the size of a chicken pock, where a hole used to be, where a needle used to go.

Now healed over.

"You're the inventor of computer-aided alternate reality," she said. "It was your technology that spawned Foreverland."

And your son.

His right eye twitched, as if he heard her thinking. He drew a deep breath and coughed into his fist. "I've been in prison for thirty years," he said. "What do you want from me?"

"I know you didn't have anything to do with it, but—"

"Then why are you here?"

He asked that question as if it had nothing to do with what she was saying, like a Zen Master asking his pupil what the true nature of reality is.

No, no. Why are you HERE?

She found a photo of a group of old women standing in a patch of dead grass. Young women, ranging in ages from twelve to eighteen years old, were behind them. "This was the second Foreverland, I'm sure you know. Your wife helped these wealthy women acquire the young bodies of the girls behind them. Your wife erased the identities of these young girls so that they left behind their living bodies."

He was nodding but looking at her in that examining way again.

"It's body snatching, Dr. Ballard. Murder. It never should've happened."

"Why is that?"

"Why is...it's *murder*."

"We are still human, Alessandra. We evolved to survive."

"We're talking about teenagers."

"Children die every day. In underprivileged countries, they die by the thousands. And you're concerned with a few?"

"I'm concerned that privileged men and women are kidnapping neglected children instead of accepting their own death. We're still human, Dr. Ballard, yes. Not immortal."

He stroked the tabletop, blinking slowly.

She hesitated before reaching for the briefcase and dropped a manila folder on the table and displayed newspaper articles dating back decades.

"Your wife, Patricia Ballard, suffered from schizophrenia. You invented CAAR in an attempt to stabilize her mind. You continued to do so even after you were arrested the first time."

He didn't look at the articles, didn't see the photo of a younger Dr. Ballard in his basement laboratory wearing a striped necktie, his thick wavy hair combed to the side. He didn't see the picture of the beautiful woman, either, or read about their only child, Harold Ballard.

"What did you expect to happen?" she asked.

The tone of her question came out all wrong. She only wanted to ask why he would take such a risk by sticking a needle in his wife's head. Instead, it sounded like she questioned why he would invent an alternate reality.

He sniffed briefly; his nostrils, like before, flared momentarily. He slightly craned his neck toward her.

"What," he asked carefully, "is love?"

"I'm sorry?"

"Love, Mrs. Diosa. What is love?"

"You're saying you did it because you loved her?"

"What would you do for someone you loved? Would you not have compassion? Would you not sacrifice everything for that person?"

"You loved her?"

"True love, Mrs. Diosa, has many faces. Some not so pleasant. Would you agree?"

"I'm afraid I'm not following."

"What would you sacrifice for someone you loved?"

"That's got nothing to do—"

"Would you sacrifice yourself? Would you?"

She shook her head. "Dr. Ballard—"

"Answer the question, please." His smile was as gentle as his words. "Yes."

"Of course you would. And what if your sacrifice would save millions? Would you?"

She looked through the wire mesh. The guards looked asleep.

"Why are you asking me this?"

"I'm curious." Soft smile. "Would you give yourself to save millions of people?"

"You're talking about a biblical savior."

"Not necessarily. It could be any reason, perhaps a blood type or an antibody that makes you special. But you had to give yourself entirely, unconditionally. Would you?"

She shook her head. "Could you look at these pictures?"

He covered her hand with his. It was papery, but warm. He blinked slowly. "Answer me honestly. That's all I ask."

She wanted to put the newspaper articles back, wanted to shove everything on the floor, sit back and listen to him. His voice had a soothing quality, a vibrato that resonated somewhere between her eyes. In her chest.

"Yes," she whispered.

"Of course you would." He sat back and folded his hands in his lap. "Have you ever heard voices?"

"What?"

"In your head, have you heard voices? The chatter of another mind inside your head, arguing with you about everything, whispering to you at night? Have you?"

"I..." She clasped her hands under the table, swallowed and lied. "No."

"Have you ever scratched yourself until you bled, hoping if you dug deep enough you would let the voices out?"

Alex shook her head.

"My wife suffered, Mrs. Diosa. And nothing was helping her. I would do anything to help her. I believe you would, too."

"You're saying your wife was schizophrenic?"

"Have you ever wished for a better place?" he continued. "Have you ever closed your eyes and dreamed of a world where there's no pain, no suffering? A place many people call heaven?"

She swallowed spastically. Suddenly, she was sleepy.

His eyebrows pinched together. Lines wrinkled his forehead, the circular scar, the size of a BB, bulged on a crest of old skin. Sadness dripped inside her, as if emanating from across the table. So many emotions she couldn't explain, this interview was a carnival ride whirling through the night.

"Your son," she whispered, cleared her throat and tried again. "Did you teach him how to do it?"

He looked disappointed and clucked his tongue. *Who is interviewing who?*

"He must've seen you doing it," Alex continued. "Went down to the basement, saw Mommy with the needle in her..."

The wind ran out of her. Her throat constricted. Not another word could fight through it. The doctor looked at his hands, nodding while he recalled.

"He was still a child," he said, "when I was sent to prison."

"Then how did he know how to do it?"

"He was always bright. And he loved his mother."

"He loved her so much that he left her in the wilderness."

Something triggered inside her, a stone pulled from the bottom of the pile, a landslide beginning to tumble.

"You don't understand what he created—"

"He destroyed children." She slammed her fist on the table. She jumped at her own anger, while he merely sat back.

"The death of children," he said, "was not intended."

"Just an unfortunate side effect?"

"I was in prison."

"But you could've stopped him."

"Mrs. Diosa, unfortunate events happen every day. We call them unfortunate because they bring suffering. Now I asked you if you wanted to know truth."

"You haven't told me anything yet."

"God allows the world to suffer, would you agree?"

"You don't strike me as religious, Doctor."

"And yet God allows torture and death. Criminals savage their victims—"

"What defines a criminal, Doctor?"

"Storms strip people of their homes, natural disasters wreck their lives, disease takes away loved ones. This is the nature of the world we live in, Mrs. Diosa. Would you agree?"

Her throat tightened.

"Good and bad, Mrs. Diosa, are part of life. One event is deemed good if we favor it, bad if we don't. Without our interpretation, it is just life. Just God. And God allows it all to exist; He accepts the world as it is, allows it to exist. Can you be like that, Mrs. Diosa? Can you allow the world to exist?"

"They were children…"

"Can you be like God? Can you allow reality to be as it is?"

He blinked so slowly she thought she'd entered a time warp.

"What if you can do better than God?" he asked. "What if you can create a world without suffering, would you do it? The children wouldn't suffer anymore, Mrs. Diosa."

"What are you talking about?"

The slightest curl twisted the corner of his mouth. "What would you sacrifice to end the suffering? Would you climb upon the cross?"

She shook her head, tried to swallow.

She wouldn't say it out loud, wouldn't give him the satisfaction. Would she sacrifice herself for the world? Would she give up her family to end all suffering? Would she create Foreverland?

Yes.

He closed his eyes, nodding, as if savoring a moment, the taste on his dry tongue. It sounded like something was stuck in his throat. He was humming.

The interview door opened.

The female guard placed a glass of water on the table. Dr. Ballard drank as he looked through the tropical pictures.

A glass in prison?

This was all wrong. Paperclips, pens and glass were being passed around like Office Depot, not a supermax federal prison.

Alex felt depleted. She let her eyelids fall for a long moment. When she opened them, the old man had already reached the end of the pile. Both guards helped him stand before he made an effort. His right knee was stiff.

"Would you care to walk, Mrs. Diosa?"

"A walk?"

The ground was damp and the air crisp, the sun above the distant mountains. It had recently rained. The roads were dusty on the drive in. Now everything was clean.

How long were we in there?

The doctor stood on a concrete slab with a cane, his right leg still stiff. But he wasn't hunched over anymore. In fact, his complexion wasn't ashen, either.

Maybe it's the sunlight.

There were no guards at his side. Beyond, the inmates played basketball or sat on picnic tables. If someone meant to do them harm, there was nothing they could do. But none of them looked at Alex, the only female in the yard. As if she didn't exist.

"And how are you feeling now?" he asked.

"A little nervous."

"You looked a little pale inside. I thought a walk would do us good. You came so far to see me."

He gestured at the track that circled the chain-link fences and barbed wire. Guard towers with black windows were stationed in the corners. He patted her hand.

"I wasn't expecting this," she said.

"What were you expecting?"

This was supposed to be a hard-hitting interview, her one chance to unearth details the world had never seen about the man behind Foreverland. She felt like a little girl seeing the mountains for the first time.

The wonder.

"Are you happy?" he asked.

He was looking through her, like he'd done inside. His eyes were x-rays, seeing her thoughts and feelings. *What is he asking? Does he want to know about the hallucinations? The malfunctions? The nervousness? The vomiting and the uncontrollable grief that sometimes shakes me at night?*

"Are you disappointed in your son?" she asked. "For starting Foreverland and using it the way he did?"

He let go of her hand. And they began their walk. Her guilt for asking such a question was measured in small breaths. Dr. Ballard's steps were quiet, not once shuffling. The inmates on the track gave them a wide berth. He stopped and looked up.

"What do you see?" he asked.

"What?"

"Above us, what do you see?"

"Sky. Clouds."

"And why is the sky blue?"

"The atmosphere scatters more blue light than red."

"So you see blue?" Dr. Ballard smiled. "Your perception tells you that it's blue."

"I don't understand."

"You came here to know truth, yet our senses determine our reality. Perception is not truth, Mrs. Diosa."

"The presence of that spectrum of light is blue whether I perceive it or not. A tree that falls in the forest makes vibrations whether I hear it or not."

"You labeled it blue; therefore it is blue."

"Blue is just a word."

He raised an eyebrow. She shook her head. He was twisting words, molding facts, playing a head game, and she was losing.

Have I already lost?

"How do you feel about your son, Dr. Ballard?"

He raised a finger. "Is the sky blue?"

"Of course."

He didn't move, only smiled with finger raised. They weren't going anywhere until she answered the question, like a Buddhist monk required to answer a koan before entering the temple.

What is blue?

Alex learned to surf when she was younger. She lived on the West Coast until she was twelve and her cousins would take her out to Hermosa Beach and connect with the spiritual nature of the wave. *The wave is the wave and we cannot change that*. It was her responsibility to ride it.

Dr. Ballard was the wave.

"Perception is not the same as truth," she said.

"Very good."

"Therefore our reality is not truth."

"And why is that?"

"Because our perceptions determine our reality. And perception, by its very nature, is flawed."

"You're saying we create our own reality?"

"*You're* saying that," she quipped.

"Perhaps I am." His smile brightened.

They began walking again. She had passed the koan. She was exhilarated, like a little girl receiving her father's approval. Or a dog thrown a bone.

A misty cloud filled her head. It was light and cool and intoxicating. She wanted to close her eyes and lay down on it. Somewhere in that pleasantness, she was nagged by the queer nature of this conversation, like the words she spoke didn't belong to her, as if she was cheating on an exam or being fed lines through an automated teleprompter.

What she said made sense. *But this isn't why I came here.*

They stopped at a group of picnic tables and the inmates calmly left. Dr. Ballard fell on one of the benches with a satisfied groan and rested his hands on the crook of the cane. The flat ground beyond the fence was thick and grassy.

"A father," he said, "always loves his child."

Alex nodded, giving him plenty of space to reflect. He was answering her question from a few minutes earlier. *Or was that an hour ago?* The sun was so much lower.

"What he did with your technology, were you disappointed?"

"My son is dead, Mrs. Diosa. Dead or alive, that does not change my love for him, not one bit. He will always be my son. I will always love him."

"But were you disappointed?"

"He did his best to understand. That's all I could ask."

"So you approved?"

"Does it matter?"

"You knew it was possible, that Foreverland could be used to switch bodies?"

He pondered. His blue eyes seemed to glitter. *I thought his eyes were gray.*

"Are we our memories?" he asked. "Or are we our body?"

"That's irrelevant."

"You asked about switching bodies, who is switching?"

"Don't twist words, Doctor. Those boys and girls were taken against their will, forced to give up their bodies."

"They gave up their bodies, you say? So you agree that who we are is not our bodies."

"Who they are, Doctor, was thrown into something called the Nowhere."

His eyebrows pitched. He threw a hard glare at the ground, squeezing the cane until his knuckles were bone white. He nodded, tipped his chin to her and winked.

"You've done your homework," he said.

"Did you know what he was going to do?" A sudden realization trickled through her. "You wanted him to create Foreverland."

The air around them cooled, an invisible cloud falling over them like a chilled hand. He minced unspoken words, staring into the distance.

"What if we could live without the body?" he asked.

"You mean in Foreverland?"

"If we are not this body, Mrs. Diosa, then we must be something else. Something more essential."

"You mean a soul?"

"Perhaps."

"And Foreverland is heaven?"

"Foreverland," he said, grinning, "is just a word, Mrs. Diosa."

"Foreverland was built with the *souls* of innocent boys and girls, remember. And you approved of it."

"Lack of disapproval is not approval."

"Then your crime is inaction."

"I'm in prison, Mrs. Diosa." He stood with a groan. "How could I have stopped him?"

"Did you want to stop him?"

"I believe that is irrelevant."

The walk continued. His footsteps were still quiet and carefully measured. Occasionally, he would look up at the sky while she asked questions and he would answer distantly, as if the conversation had grown stale. The conversation was going in a circle.

Because she was chasing her tail.

They were on the far side of the yard, alone on the track. The distant shouting of a basketball game was small compared to the wind rushing through the barbed wire, blowing through the open field, carrying fragments of voices from beyond the fence. She closed her eyes, pinched her nose. When the static of voices frayed her attention, she had learned focusing quieted them.

The voices fell on her like pellets, pricking her cheeks and neck. She searched the sky. *The sky is blue.*

He took her by the elbow and silence returned. The thin skin of his fingers slid the length of her forearm until he held her hand. "I need to ask a question, Alessandra."

"How do you know my name?" She wanted to shout, but it came out as a whisper.

The words broke the downward spiral of thoughts, the eddy of confusion, and rooted her in the present moment with the wind on her face and the sky—the blue, blue sky—above and the smell of sweat and fear and suffering.

"Why do you care about Foreverland?" He waited for an answer. It was a formality, really. *He can see inside me.*

"The children..."

"Yes, the children. You care about the children. You care about all people, the old and the young, the innocent and the powerful. Why do you care?" His eyelids grew heavy but unblinking. "Why?"

She shook her head.

"Because you love, Alessandra. You love deeply, truly. And you have so much to give. You love."

She nodded. *Yes. I love.*

"Are you happy?" he whispered. "With all the justice and injustice in the universe, with the lion eating the antelope, cancer ravaging bodies, black holes trapping light?"

His hand was so warm on her arm.

"God allows the good and bad, the pleasant and the suffering."

She shook her head.

"Good and bad are just words, words that God allows. He allows it all to be as it is because He loves. And your love, Alessandra, is as big as His."

"How do you know my name?"

"Can you be a god?"

"I don't believe..."

"Something gave rise to all of this." He spread his arms. "Allows it all to be. Can you do that?"

The air was dense, like breathing water. The ground was soft and the sky—the blue, blue sky—was down and the mountains were up and the wind in her lungs—

A tear fell.

A raindrop smacked the dirt.

"It's the answer you came for. It's truth, Alessandra. You have truth. You can be truth. Only true love has space to allow for the saints and the sinners, the heroes and the villains. You are the truth and the reality."

His face was blurry through brimming tears.

"You are the words."

She was crying, but this time the tears were different. They sprang not from a mysterious emotional hole inside her, but from the wind and the sky and the gentle hands cradling hers.

And knowing that she could be all right with everything. Just as it was. She could be everything.

Everything.

The rain splattered around them. Spots darkened on the old man's shirt. A cart pulled next to them. The big guard, the man at the interview, was driving. The old man fell into the passenger seat and propped his hands on the cane. He looked straight ahead. The cart remained still. Alex felt the heat of a thousand eyes.

The inmates were staring at them.

The basketball games had stopped, the card games frozen. Their clothes were wet; the cards rain-soaked.

The cart moved forward, turning onto the track, slowly grinding its way back to the building. Alex remained at the far end of the yard, but she wasn't afraid. She wiped her eyes, sniffed a final time and walked back as they watched her. She felt their eyes, their hunger and fear.

Saints and sinners.

She could be with the saints. But the sinners...yes, she could be with them, too.

She walked to her car and drove down the road. When the hill ascended in her rearview mirror and the prison was no longer in sight, she stopped in the middle of the road and began to cry. A deluge smeared the world into blurry colors, pounding the hood, snapping on the window.

Alex cried tears of joy.

Because she loved.

157

ADMAX PENITENTIARY, *Colorado*

Gramm was waiting. There were tears in his eyes.

"Temper your enthusiasm." Tyler sat on the edge of his bed, twirling the wet needle between his fingers. His head throbbed, an electric spike pulsing through his forehead. He dared not move until his heart rate settled.

The mere thought of speaking caused it to rise. In spite of the pain, even he couldn't suppress the smile. *Alessandra is the one.*

He knew what she looked like. Patricia had sent stills and video of Alessandra. He had heard her talk, saw her quickened pace when she was agitated, the furrowed brow when she concentrated, the tip of her tongue dragging over her teeth when she was curious. But to finally meet her, to be with her, all of her, was stunning.

She's beautiful.

He'd meant to calm her down, to sway her with dialog like a mythical siren. Half of what he said flowed out of him spontaneously, as if her beauty gave rise to inspiration. She was a beautifully tortured soul, full of pain and pleasure, suffering and joy. He spoke nothing but the truth—*she is love.*

And that's why they needed her.

Regardless of the disruptions, Reed couldn't stop the inevitable—Alessandra Diosa would close her eyes and dream a new reality. Humanity would join her.

Tyler and Patricia would lead the way.

He wished to immerse himself right then, to see his wife on the inside, in her mind, to meet her at the opera or walk the streets of her city, to share the good news and celebrate, but pain spread across his face.

The stent was done.

He had pulled the needle for the last time. The hole was swollen, nearly closed, like he'd used the prong of a pitchfork. Raw fingers scratched his brain. He would have to make the change; his next leap into Foreverland would be through biomites.

"Call the guards." He couldn't feel them out there, couldn't feel Gramm in front of him. To expand his mind would exhaust what little strength he still had and ignite the brain storm that had finally passed.

The rubber wheels of a wheelchair approached. He reached up and took Melfy's hand. He wanted to sit in the yard, feel the sun on his face before the good doctor injected more biomites up his nostril.

"Sir," Gramm said, "there's a problem."

The yard would have to wait. It would have to wait much longer than Tyler realized.

They went straight to the basement.

Yellow and red lights everywhere.

The guards dry heaved when they entered. Melfy splattered the floor before she could get out, the acrid smell of vomit steamrolled by the smell of death.

"What happened?" Tyler asked.

Gramm held a cloth over his face with one hand, spastically raking his hair with the other, hair follicles wedged between his fingers. "The health indicators," he said, "all started dropping."

"When?"

"When Alessandra left."

Tyler was too weak to stand. He waved forward until Gramm pushed, pointing when to turn. Half of them were still green, the ones he deemed most important. He didn't need them all. And when Alessandra was asleep, when she gave herself to hosting Foreverland—completely and eternally—he wouldn't need any of them.

He just needed her.

Tyler covered his face and had Gramm turn right at the fourth table. He raised his hand. He grabbed the edge of the nearest table, his fingers brushing the cool flesh of its occupant—a bald white man from the Arian brotherhood, his chest a canvas of ink.

The light was red.

The occupant was fat when he first took the needle, an obese man sent to the penitentiary for double murder. Now his ribs were showing beneath olive-colored skin. Wisps of remaining hair stuck to his balding scalp, swirling around a purple birthmark distinctly shaped like the state of Florida.

Santiago.

"What happened?" Tyler asked.

"He had flown to the United States this morning and arrived in Minneapolis. He met with Macy. That afternoon, just after lunch, he stopped breathing." Gramm stopped to rake his hair. "I can't explain it. There was no reason for them to...it was like they were just turned off."

Tyler held the Spaniard's hand. It was colder than usual.

Death usually is.

This was a time to rejoice, not mourn. Alessandra had nearly gone to sleep during their interview. It was only a matter of time, and now this.

"What's the biofeedback?" Tyler asked. "The cause of death?"

"Preliminary reports suggest...it's just..." Gramm pulled at his graying hair.

"What?"

"He stopped breathing."

"That's not an answer, Gramm! Goddamn it, it can't be nothing. No one stops breathing for no reason."

Gramm's breathing became shallow. He pursed his lips and took short stabbing breaths like a woman going into labor. If Tyler was twenty years younger, he'd snatch the pansy by the earlobe and drag him down to the table, shove his worried face into Santiago's clammy stomach and let him smell death until it was burned into his palette.

The pounding started again; this time his forehead was being stabbed with an ice pick in time to his heartbeat.

"The good doctor needs to see your stent," Gramm said.

Tyler clenched his teeth, driving the ice pick deeper into his gray matter. *Reed did this.*

It was a slap to the face, an insult. A warning. Santiago was a good soldier. He was meant to guide Danny, but when it was clear that the boy wasn't capable of supporting a Foreverland on the level Tyler wanted, Santiago watched after him.

But now that Danny was missing, it was irrelevant.

Damn him.

"The good doctor," Tyler said, "will perform a full autopsy—"

Beep-beep-beep...

The lamp next to them dimmed. The monitor was red lights.

Tyler reached for the table—the man's chest sweaty, pale and still—when another warning chimed. The next table, red lights signaling another loss.

And then another. And another.

Like dominos falling.

"Do something!" Tyler shuffled around the table. "Damn it, Gramm, stop this!"

Gramm's hands fluttered at his sides. He looked around like a bird sensing a predator, his brain stuck in a panic loop. His hands went to his scalp and locked onto his hair, gray tufts between his fingers.

Tyler took several short steps and grabbed a handful of the former chemist's shirt. "Puh the pugs," Tyler said, the words slurring past his swollen tongue. He wet his lips and slowly enunciated, "Pull... the...plugs."

More warnings joined the chorus.

Six tables had been lost, and now a seventh. They were dropping one after another. Tyler looked down the long row, looked for the one table they could not afford to lose. If the man in the back stopped breathing, all would be lost.

Alessandra would not sleep.

Tyler shoved off and began sliding his feet. When he reached the end of the table, he made a three-step lunge to the next table, and then the next.

The red lights were behind him, but they were gaining. The room was dimming. They were going to lose them all. Tyler kept his eyes on the back.

Three more tables.

His breath shortened. Darkness bled into the fringes of his vision.

His knees shattered like glass. Warmth spilled into the crown of his skull, spread over his head and face like oil, washing away the throbbing pain, and trickled into his burning chest.

One more.

He could barely feel the edge of the table beneath his cold fingers. The beeping was behind him. He reached out, focused on the table against the back wall, when warmth bled through his hips, into his thighs and knees, taking all his strength with it.

The floor began rising.

He took one big step and closed his eyes. The impact was dull, but a sharp crack cut through the numbing fog as his hip shattered.

The beeping was a distant warning. The red lights were still coming.

The table was above him, the lights on the panel still green. He reached up, his senseless fingers finding the buttons. He pushed randomly, pushed them all.

With every bit of strength, he pecked at the monitor, hoping to hit the button that would pull Samuel offline.

We can't lose him!

All at once, the beeping stopped. The room was quiet.

His wheezy breath scratched the silence. He tried to swallow.

"Doctor?" Warm hands were on his cheeks. "Doctor?"

Gramm was squatting in front of him. The good doctor was with him. Tyler's eyelids were so heavy, so tired. A green haze shaded Gramm's worried expression. Tyler barely moved his lips. Words would not fall off his tongue.

He tried to whisper his wife's name, but he couldn't feel his lips, couldn't feel his body. He'd run out of time and could only send out a thought and hope it would reach her.

I'm sorry.

AUTUMN

Dreams are strange.
Some never-ending.

158

THE ELEVATOR DESCENDED WITH PURPOSE.

The smell of manufacturing gave way to what was below ground: a distinct odor of burnt plastic and clay.

Jonathan pushed his hair back. His distorted reflection—his eyes still green, the bent hump on his nose—split in half as the elevator doors opened to reveal a long empty hall and an attractive young woman in a white lab coat.

"Welcome, Mr. Deer."

"Jonathan."

"Of course." She extended her hand. "My name is Dr. Jones. You can call me Julie. Watch your step."

The hairs on his head stiffened. An electrified field slowly rode down his neck, over his shoulders and arms until all the hair on his body was rigid.

"It'll take just a moment," she said.

"Aren't you certain by now?"

"Redundancy ensures our security, Jonathan."

The scan sank through his epidermal layers, vibrating through subdural layers until it reached his core, examining every cell that composed his body.

Julie paced around him, her eyes crawling over him like he was on display in the Smithsonian. "Remarkable," she whispered. "Simply remarkable."

They didn't know who he was. What *he was, though...they knew what he was. They were in the business of biomites.*

She took his hand, traced the veins forking over his knuckles, leaned close enough that he could smell toothpaste. He held his ground while the scan penetrated his chest. She looked at his eyes, his bent nose.

"You altered your face," she said.

"Anonymity is my ally as much as yours."

"Where were you done?"

He sighed. "Are we finished?"

Julie turned down the hall. There was no end in sight. The subsurface laboratory felt cool and damp. If he was correct, they were at least one hundred feet below the manufacturing plant. They passed heavy lab doors where vibrations leaked out.

"Can I ask a question?" she said. "Why come to us? Why on earth would you come here when you can have anything you want in one of those Foreverland worlds?"

She stopped at a set of double doors. Her hand hovered over a scanner.

"You have the secret to creating a Foreverland reality, why would you want to toil in the physical world?"

The doors opened.

The room was the size of a warehouse. They stepped between two long rows of glass cubicles that resembled side-by-side shower stalls, the glass black and reflective. The cold air settled around him and he shivered. He would count the stalls to make sure they were all present, they were all functional.

"To balance the scales," he answered her question. "I came to balance the scales."

159

THE WILDERNESS of Wyoming

Her sleep was endless.

She swam in the ether of unconsciousness, where dreams came in fragments and images blurred into colors and sound smeared the background. There were snippets of waking, of seeing the landscape slur past her, of night falling. For the most part, her eyelids were too heavy and she remained in dream purgatory.

Until all was quiet.

She rolled her head off the glass, her chin wet with saliva. She rubbed the sleep from her eyes.

It was a truck.

She was in an SUV. It took a moment to notice the person in the driver's seat, a boy with long red hair. His name limped out of the fog.

Danny.

That was all she could remember. They were parked on an incline, surrounded by trees. Senescing foliage, in the grip of autumn's approach, was among needled evergreens. A single tree stood before them, one barren of life, wedged between two halves of a boulder, a tree with silver-gray branches, dead and gnarled.

She knew this tree. *Impossible.*

"No." She slammed her fist into her leg. Pain radiated across her thigh. This was no longer a dream.

"No, no, no..." She fumbled with the handle.

"Cyn."

"Don't touch me!"

"Let me—"

The door popped open. She tumbled from the SUV and slammed into the ground. A thousand memories rose to the surface.

There was snow here.

I was buried in the snow. The boy, Sid, on my chest, his hands around my throat.

The driver's door slammed. Cyn scrambled on all fours and stumbled through the thicket, away from the hill. Around the back of the SUV, she ran in the opposite direction. Away.

Away, away, away...

Run, Barb's voice whispered. *Run, run away.*

Cyn's throat hurt, her chest burned. She missed steps, fell and got back up, racing down the long slope, sprinting for the trees at the bottom.

She fell one last time, her palms scuffing through long grassy reeds, raking the rocky ground. She crashed hard, losing all her breath, rolling over with pain deep in her stomach.

She was here once before. She was here again.

In the wilderness.

Give me the body.

Cyn closed her eyes and wished it would all go away, that this was all over. She couldn't do this again, couldn't face the wilderness.

"Not again," she muttered. "Not again."

Barb's presence began to fade.

It receded into the background, far below the surface of her awareness, deep into her subconscious where Cyn no longer felt her, no longer heard her.

A shadow fell.

Danny reached out. She considered it. He brought her out here, took her to the last place on earth she ever wanted to see again, and now he wanted to help her stand. If he thought she would enjoy this, that she would follow him back to the SUV so they could tour the countryside and reminisce about the old women in their brick house, about their shaved heads and the cots and the needles in their heads, about waking up in an endless Foreverland loop without memories...

She raised a limp hand and let it fall into his hand.

He latched on and tugged. When her dead weight didn't budge, he relaxed.

And she pulled.

Danny's weight yanked forward, the toe of his boot catching her ribs as he tried to stop. She snatched his coat and pulled him over her as she turned, bringing his weight crashing down.

She hooked her leg around his waist to mount him, but the slope carried his momentum away from her. He was on his hands and knees. Too lanky and strong to take down, she threw herself onto his back and wrapped her arm around his neck. With the inside of her elbow over his windpipe, she secured the choke hold with her other arm and rolled.

All his weight fell on her.

He flailed like a flipped turtle, grinding jagged stones into her shoulders. She ducked her head, hooked her legs over the top of his and applied more pressure. Wildly, he tapped her arm. A few more seconds and the restriction on the carotid artery would black him out. She kept her head down.

His arms thrashed through the tall grass.

Paper began to rustle. He stopped prying at her arm and waved a piece of paper. She couldn't read it, but she saw the lettering.

Her hold relaxed.

He dropped the note and gasped for air. Cyn bucked him down the hill and spun in the opposite direction, sweeping the paper up as she jumped to her feet. Danny stayed on his hands and knees, choking a string of drool to the ground.

Green ink.

That was the color of the letters on the envelopes she never opened. The envelopes she stacked in a wicker basket, envelopes she threw in the garage.

"What is this?"

He put his hands on his hips, still on his knees. His cheeks were red; a scuff on his chin was finely lined with blood.

"Did you write this?" She shook it in his face. "Are you the asshole sending me letters?"

He shook his head.

"Then who?"

"A friend."

"Is this a joke? You were in on this sick joke the whole time?"

He didn't answer.

"What...what does this even mean?"

"I don't know."

"What do you..." She balled up the note and fired it into his face.

She regretted letting go of the choke hold and stormed up the hill, her thighs burning as she climbed. Not even halfway to the top where the dead tree waited, she stopped.

Pressure was building. *No, not pressure. Presence.*

Barb was rising from her subconscious like something lurking beneath the water. She ignored it, pumping her arms until she was halfway—

Give me the body.

Cyn turned around. Danny was on his feet, opening the wadded note, smoothing it against his thigh. Barb whispered in the dark.

She took a step back down the hill. Her head swirled with panic as Barb tried to find a handhold. With each step toward Danny, she faded away, disappearing like an apparition.

Danny was catching his breath. Blood was smeared across his chin and the back of his hand.

"Why do I feel...*different* around you?" She wouldn't talk about Barb, would never admit to it.

"We survived Foreverland."

He feels it. Does he have someone inside of him, too? "Why'd you bring me out here?"

He held up the wrinkled paper. When she narrowed her eyes, when the thought of ripping that page into little pieces crossed her mind, he began to read.

"Where once there was light on a dusted rim, when day followed day, now a night-filled *sin*." He emphasized the last word and paused.

Sin is the homonym of Cyn. But sin could mean Barb: the demon in my head.

"Turn back your sight to where your steps begin," he continued, "and return to the root and fall again."

He dropped his hand and, once again, paused. "This is about you," he said, "going back to where Foreverland started."

He nodded up the hill, at the dead tree.

"Where you fell," he said.

"You kidnapped me, dragged me out to hell because of a poem? A goddamn poem?" She grabbed two fistfuls of his coat and swung him around. "We're going back to the truck; we're getting the hell out of here."

"You feel different. You said so."

"I don't want to be here."

"Reed is how I found you. He sent me. I don't know why, I just know that something feels different when I'm with you. And he's telling us to be out here."

"Why?"

"I don't know yet."

"He told you to bring me back to my nightmare, to hell on earth? Are you out of your mind? How would you like to go back to the island?"

"I do." He turned his head and swallowed. "Every night. Except when I'm with you."

The pain was in his eyes. *Are we all doomed to relive the nightmare?*

"How old are you?" she asked.

"What's that matter?"

"You don't belong out here."

"But you do?"

"I didn't say that. Neither of us should be in the wilderness."

"You think we're too young for this? You think that's how it works?" He chuckled. "Age is relative. There's a time dilation between

Foreverland and physical reality; they're not synced up. Time goes much faster in Foreverland."

"I know."

"Think about how long we were in Foreverland." He spit blood and thumped his head. "I look young, but that's an illusion."

"I'm just saying we're over our head out here. You don't know anything about surviving in the wilderness and neither do I."

"We don't have a choice."

"I didn't choose this life."

"None of us did." He rattled the letter. "Something's happening, and this is all I got."

A chill wind streamed down the hill. Cyn wrapped her arms around herself. Her fingers were nearly numb, her nose leaking.

"So what then?" she asked. "What now?"

"There are supplies in the truck. We set up camp."

"And what? Search for another note?"

"We wait. Something will come up." He sounded too confident.

"You know how cold it gets out here?"

"Yeah."

"And you want to camp?"

"That's the plan."

"There are cabins." She pointed at the hilltop. "Over there."

He looked around, nodding. There was something else on his mind. She knew what it was. It was the same thought lurking in her mind, one she wanted to ignore before the vertigo of reality confusion dropped her stomach.

She followed him up the hill, past the dead tree, staying close enough to him that Barb didn't surface. By the time they reached the SUV, her legs were numb.

How do I know this isn't Foreverland?

———

They stopped in an open field.

The headlights grazed dying wildflowers. Beyond, in twilight's gray shade, scrubby trees and thick undergrowth were swallowing the remnants of three buildings: two log cabins on the left, a brick house on the right.

Somewhere between them was a lump of earth where Jen was buried. *No, that was in Foreverland. Jen died in Foreverland, not in real life. We all died in Foreverland.*

They all woke up in their bodies, but the memories of those deaths remained. Somewhere in the ethers of the universe, imagined or not, it happened.

"I can't go," she muttered.

If they were going to stay out there, the house would be more suitable than a tent. But there were memories in there. Memories, she feared, that were worse than the cold.

Danny turned around.

When night had fully arrived, he had set up two tents and stacked wood. He'd stopped for supplies somewhere between Minnesota and Wyoming, and stocked the back of the SUV while Cyn slept in the front seat. There was enough for months. She shivered at the thought of staying that long.

He heated tea and something to eat. They sat in silence and listened to wolves howl in the distance. A quarter moon hung over the mountains. Exhausted, she climbed into her tent.

She didn't stay long.

Afraid that Barb would return, she went to the only place she knew would keep the old woman quiet. Danny looked up from his sleeping bag when she unzipped the flap and crawled in. He watched her shove her sleeping bag inside. She could feel his arm between the layers of fabric.

"This doesn't mean anything," she whispered.

Barb didn't visit her dreams that night.

Cyn opened her eyes to the smell of smoke.

It was well past sunrise. Danny sat on a fabric chair with a stack of broken limbs beside him. A cup of coffee waited on an empty chair.

They drank in silence.

She felt foolish for crawling into his tent and couldn't look him in the eye. He was younger than her. Maybe sixteen? Cyn was eighteen, or nineteen. She wondered about the accuracy of her memories, and that included her birthday, a day she hadn't celebrated, ever.

But he was right: age didn't matter.

"How long are we staying?"

"I don't know." He kept busy breaking wood.

Cyn cleaned the plates in a bucket of ice-cold water.

"Can I show you something?" he asked.

"Depends."

"It's just something someone taught me. It helped me through, you know, the worst of it."

He didn't need to elaborate. The days that followed Foreverland were *it*.

"When I couldn't take it anymore, someone taught me that pain is unavoidable, but suffering is optional."

"Cute."

"What he meant was the thoughts, how I identified with them, believed them, let them spin stories in my head, take me out of the present moment where I didn't want to be. The present moment is all that exists."

He crossed his legs and closed his eyes. He didn't call it meditation. "Be here," he said. "Let the thoughts rise, let the thoughts go, and count your breaths without prejudice."

He didn't know her thoughts.

As long as he was near her, her thoughts were ordinary thoughts. But when he went to fetch wood or get water from a nearby stream, other thoughts surfaced.

Was there a method to meditate with another person living inside your head, someone that could pour a bottle of pills down your throat?

In just over a week, the nights were too cold to crawl out to pee. They slept together, always in their own sleeping bags. Sometimes she woke in the night to find they were holding hands. It was always his arm that hung out from the sleeping bag, as if he'd reached out.

She tried going back to the cabins, but the sight of the brick house racked her fear. Danny never pushed, giving her space.

Occasionally, they'd see something move in the trees. Just over the ridge, one morning, they saw the wolves that kept them awake at night. Five of them stared across the field before trotting into the forest.

"We need to be careful," Danny said.

There were nights she swore she could hear them walking around the tents.

It was mid-afternoon when he left with a towel over his shoulder. Tired of clinging by his side, she decided to stay at the camp. Ten minutes later, Barb began to whisper. The old woman's voice was weak and scratchy, almost exhausted.

Cyn didn't wait for her to reach the light.

She followed a path into the trees and up to a ridge. She saw a cliff ahead and hid in the trees. Down several granite shelves was a shallow stream. Danny was in the middle of it, his underwear clinging to his skin.

The water had to be just above freezing. His ribs jutted from his sides. He wasn't shivering, yet. His skin was fair, his shoulders freckled. He scrubbed his head with shampoo and rinsed it in the slow current.

"I know you're there," he said.

She ducked behind a tree.

"You should come in, rinse off," he said. "You won't regret it."

It had been weeks since she bathed—her clothes would testify— but she was already shivering, a cold that reached her bones, one that started on the inside, ignited by fear.

She didn't join him. But she didn't go back to the camp. She huddled against the tree, arms crossed, sitting on a bed of moss.

Barb was quiet.

Danny climbed the granite shelves and squatted next to her, fully dressed with the towel around his shoulders. Steam was rising from his head. She noticed the scar, the tiny starfish in the middle of his forehead.

Branded by Foreverland.

"How'd you do that?" Danny ran his finger over the raised scar on the back of her hand.

She jerked it away. "It wasn't suicide."

"I didn't think that."

He took her hand, his fingers icy cold, and tenderly traced the white line that went from her knuckle to the knob of her wrist. His touch tingled up her arm, embraced her heart, almost brought her to tears.

"Did it happen out here?"

She closed her eyes, remembering the big city, the tall buildings. She arrived at the airport alone, feeling so small and insignificant. Before she arrived at the Institute, she got so high that the sidewalk rocked like the deck of a ship and almost threw her into traffic when she fell off the curb.

Those days felt so distant and foggy. Almost like they weren't real.

"It was the last day I used. I was so messed up." She chuckled and shook her head. "Unlike now, right?"

"So what made you stop using?"

"This new recovery program paid for by the Foreverland fund. Hurray," she said flatly. "I didn't plan on cleaning up, really. It was a free trip to the city, and I wasn't doing anything, so..."

"What city?"

"New York."

He stiffened. "The Institute?"

"Yeah. How'd you know?"

"When?"

"Like, last spring."

He looked away, calculating; his lips moved slightly until he shook his head. "I was there, too, about the same time. I received an invitation from the director."

"Mr. Deer?"

He nodded slowly. Thoughts churning.

"What's that mean?" she asked.

"I don't know. Maybe it's just a coincidence."

He didn't sound like he believed that. Nothing, so far, had been a coincidence.

Danny pulled a stocking cap over his damp hair and gloves over her hands. "We should get back to the fire."

"How do you know?"

"Because it's cold."

"No. I mean, how do you know this is real?"

His smile faded, but didn't disappear.

"I mean," she added, "how do you know this isn't still...you know..."

Cyn's Foreverland looked exactly like the wilderness. There was no difference. That tree on top of the hill, the one they saw when she woke in the SUV, was in Foreverland, too.

The scar on their foreheads would always be there to remind them, but the real scar was the question they asked themselves every day for the rest of their lives.

How do you know this isn't a dream?

"I don't."

"What if we're dreaming again?" she muttered.

"I don't know how that would be possible."

"Of course it's possible." She woke up every day in that Foreverland cabin. Only when she woke up did she know it was the dream.

He fell against the tree, their shoulders touching. "Does it matter? Wherever this is, we can only be here. It's all we can do."

Her chin quivered. She clenched down, hated showing emotion, hated her weakness. It was something she couldn't control, couldn't throw on the ground and choke. She felt his hand reach for her, felt his fingers lace between hers.

"This is real," he said.

They held hands that way, listening to the stream until the cold chased them back to camp. They sat by the fire, warming their hands without letting go. Their clothes were saturated with smoke. Perhaps it was the wood they were using, but there was an odd hint of something fragrant. It wasn't cedar.

It was lilac.

160

THE WILDERNESS *of Wyoming*

My demons are different than yours.

Reed wrote that in one of the poems. Danny remembered that every time Cyn ventured off into the trees alone. She'd return with a wide-eyed look and stare into the fire, rocking back and forth.

It had been weeks and she never left his side; then one morning she climbed out of her tent and took a walk. She didn't go far, just up and went. Her hands were quivering when she returned, but then she did it the next morning, going out a little farther.

Her demons are different than mine.

When Foreverland crashed, a lot of the old men died. They got what they deserved. But now he realized those bastards got off easy. They didn't have to deal with the demons that haunted dreams, the nightmare sometime lurking in Cyn's eyes. The ashes of Foreverland would never dust over them.

Death was too good for them.

And the ones that escaped—the old men somewhere out there in their young, new bodies—left the survivors with the bill, a debt Danny,

Cyn and others paid every day. He could only hope the old bastards would come back to wipe the slate.

The old women, too.

"I'm ready."

Danny looked up. Cyn's arms were stiff, fists balled against her hips. She'd left to fetch water from the stream and was gone longer than ever before; he was about to go looking for her, afraid the wolves had gotten too close.

Steely tension ridged across her brow. She sat in the passenger seat.

He didn't ask what happened, just got in the SUV and began to drive. *She's ready to face the demons. And the demons live just over the hill.*

It was early afternoon.

The sun was breaking through a cloud fracture, sunbeams gliding over the meadow, but darker clouds shrouded the three buildings ahead. The log cabins peeked through the overgrowth like relics from another era. The brick house was obscured by evergreens, as if hiding from shame.

Dilapidated wind harvesters leaned near the partially collapsed barn, blades locked in place.

Cyn's breaths had become clipped and punctual. Unblinking, disbelief filled her eyes. *The boogeyman really did live under the bed.*

"We woke in there," she said.

She pointed at the cabin on the left. And then she said it two more times, then nodded.

Danny put the SUV in drive and idled over the hill. She was still nodding and pointing when they stopped in front of the cabin and opened the door.

Six beds.

Steel shafts of sunlight came through the clouded windows, exposing abandoned spider webs. The mattresses were faded and frayed, soiled from a leaky roof or bodily fluids.

"We woke up." Her voice bounced in the exposed rafters. "And couldn't remember anything."

Danny remembered that feeling, of waking up on the island and not knowing who he was, where he came from. They told him he'd been in an accident, that he was going to be healed.

Did the old women tell the girls that, too? Or just feed them to the needle?

The wood planks were spattered with bird feces, their footsteps echoing in the crawlspace beneath. She stopped at the wood-burning stove. The clouds, for a moment, parted and a dusty spotlight cut across the room. A rogue gust of wind hit the building. The walls creaked and splintered. Outside, one of the wind turbines squealed for a moment.

She looked at the bed in the corner. The wall above the mattress had been clawed into lines. Cyn sank her knee into the mattress and dragged her fingers over the markings like Braille.

They were gouged in bundles of five.

She had been counting the days.

She woke up scared, alone and confused; she began counting the days when it would all be over, when someone would come for her, take her away, tell her it would be all right. That this couldn't be happening.

That someone loved her.

An enormous patch of weeds had grown next to the brick house. Dried sunflowers peeked above the fray like dying sentinels.

A slate of rain slid over the sky, casting a gray pall over Cyn's complexion. Her eyes darkened. The big bad wolves had lived inside the brick house.

She walked toward the sunflowers, disappearing into the thicket of weeds. The weeds had lain down where she walked, but he lost track of her. He exited near the brick house. He stood and listened, heard her scrambling like a rodent for cover.

Something began thumping.

It sounded like a bat dully pounding a bag of rice.

"Cyn?" He listened. "You all right?"

He marched back into the fray, plowing through the thickest parts, where thorny vines raked his hands and cut his cheeks, sharp grassy edges slicing at his forearms. Memories of the jungle jumped into his head and his heart beat as loud as the thumping.

There were whimpers.

"Cyn!"

Panic dumped into his veins. Nothing could happen to her. He brought her out here, nothing weird could happen, it would be all his fault. *Please, not to her.*

She was on her knees, as if praying.

Her fists were smudged with fresh earth. She raised them above her head and hammered the ground, again and again and again.

The first patter of rain touched the ground. The drops were cold. Danny knelt next to her and put his hand on her back. Welts were slashed across her arms from the weeds.

"I hate who I am," she said.

She said it after slamming the earth. Again. And again.

He put his arms around her. She hid her face on his shoulder.

"I hate who I am. I hate who I am."

He didn't know why she chose that spot to punish. But he thought he knew why she hated who she was, who the old women turned her into. At some level, she blamed herself for being dragged out here. If she just didn't run away from home, if she didn't use, didn't lie. If she was just a good girl, her parents wouldn't have hated. Wouldn't have left her. If she just wasn't bad to the core, none of this would have happened.

Danny knew why she cried and shook, knew what was inside her; the guilt she carried was the same as his. It didn't make sense, it wasn't logical. But there it was.

I deserved it.

The rain came down in icy bullets.

Danny ushered her out of the weeds. The SUV was parked in front of the cabin, but the wolves had arrived.

It was a pack of ten.

Their noses to the ground, they circled the truck. The pack leader trotted between them and urinated on the front tire. He locked eyes with Danny. The pack stood their ground, as if guarding the truck.

"This way," Cyn said.

She pulled him in the direction of the brick house. Danny held her hand and kept looking back. The predators watched their retreat through a blurry curtain of rain.

The trees in front of the brick house gave them some cover. Danny stood on the bottom step, still watching for the wolves. Despite shivering, Cyn took the stairs one at a time, laying both feet down before taking the next. The railing creaked in her hand.

Vines trailed from the soffits, moss clung to the brick. Somewhere under a tangle of vines was a porch swing. He followed her up onto the porch and out of the rain.

"You hear that?" she asked.

Danny remained still. Had he missed the crunch of a paw or the snap of a twig? He looked back and counted. They were all there, but what if one had been hiding?

The wind raked the trees and a swirl of leaves tumbled past.

He realized there was a chance they might be stuck out here for a while. Until the wolves moved, they weren't getting back to camp. But the brick house was a fortress, a rock-solid castle with security cameras and metal shutters that could withstand a military assault. Stones were scattered on the sloping porch. If the door was locked, they could throw one through a window.

It was a Southern-style porch that was wide and accommodating. Ceiling fans were above, their blades wilting from decay; small tables were surrounded by cushioned chairs, the stuffing ripped out and stolen by vermin.

There was even a tall glass on the far table, one that would hold a cool sip of tea on a summer day when the old women would sit and watch the girls blister in the sun. The napkin was still beneath it, the edges curled and shrunken.

Cyn twisted the knob. It took a boot to the bottom half to open. The house sighed a stale breath of rat turds and damp fabric. She stood in the doorway.

A breeze sprayed rain over the floorboards. The napkin fluttered beneath the tall glass on the table. He had assumed it was a napkin, but it sounded more like paper. He ducked beneath limbs and cleared heavy vines to reach the table.

It was an envelope.

The paper was warped with mildew, tainted green. He turned it over. The ink was the same color as algae.

Danny Boy.

He tore it open without hesitation, without questioning how it had gotten out here. *Had it been out here all this time?*

A single sheet inside, folded once.

Once the past uncovered,
And the demon cast out,
Only then forward you move,
To live without doubt.

The door slammed.

The porch was empty. Danny ran to the door, turned the knob and kicked at the bottom. It was jammed in the swollen frame.

"Cyn?" He pounded with his fist. "Cyn!"

He put his shoulder into it without luck and found a stone near the steps. The rain had stopped. It took both hands to raise it above his head and crush the doorknob. The door flew open on the third attempt, as if it had been open the entire time.

The house was silent.

He screamed her name and searched the house. All the doors were locked, all the windows shut. The house was empty. She was gone. Danny ran outside and discovered something else.

The wolves had also disappeared.

161

THE WILDERNESS of Wyoming

She had reached the end.

The bottom.

There was no chance to give up the drug of choice until you bounced off the ground floor. Problem was, what you thought was rock bottom could be a false stage—you crashed through to find there was more falling to do.

But this is the end, she decided. *No more running.*

She had beaten the earth where Jen was buried. Even though it happened in Foreverland, even though Jen didn't really die, not in reality, not in the flesh, she still felt the old man's hands around her neck in Foreverland. Still fed the worms, in Foreverland.

Did that make it any less real?

Cyn had been hiding in fear ever since she left the wilderness. Now that she was back, she was still hiding—from the pain, from the voice in her head. And nothing was working. She was ready to face this. And she knew where the big bad wolves lived.

No more.

She walked up the steps of the brick house and heard music, something classical, cellos and flutes. "You hear that?" she asked Danny.

She twisted the handle and kicked the door open. She expected the smell of death to barrel its fist into her nose. What she saw was impossible.

The house was immaculate.

There was an oval carpet in the center of the room, credenzas to the right and left, a television directly ahead. The grandfather clock was tucked in the corner, the pendulum dutifully keeping time.

Scented candles burned on the coffee table.

The cabins were still dilapidated, the garden still a tangle of weeds. All was as it should be. But inside the brick house, dreamland waited.

Foreverland is alive.

Beethoven floated on the scent of vanilla-cinnamon. A shadow appeared at one of the doorways. Nerves tightened along Cyn's arms, across her chest. Cold fear gave way to a furious storm. Her fingers curled into her palms; fists clenched at her sides. An old woman stepped into the hall.

Barbara.

Her clothing was expensive, a brand Cyn couldn't name and didn't care if she could. A loose scarf—zebra print—was bunched around her neck where, undoubtedly, folds of skin hung loosely. Her gray hair curled around large earrings that were outsized by the rings on her fingers.

And her lipstick, bright red.

It was her. Only this time she wasn't looking in the reflection of a shattered mirror. She walked into the hall, a separate person. Their eyes met and they stood like cowboys waiting for a move.

The music ended.

The silence was meted out by the grandfather clock. Barb turned her back and walked into another room down the hall. Coffee cups clinked from a cupboard.

Cyn looked around.

She could break the leg off one of the end tables or shatter the glass on the grandfather clock, wrap a shard with a blanket off the couch.

The coat rack.

She wedged it against her hip, the polished pegs aimed forward like a rack of manufactured antlers. Barb returned with two cups and stopped.

Cyn's knuckles whitened.

"Piss and vinegar." A smile touched the old woman's painted lips. "That's why I chose you."

"I should run this through you."

"Sweet Jesus, child. You don't know where you are."

"I know who I am...I'm not you."

"I didn't say *who* you are. I said *where*."

With that, the old woman sat on the wide sofa littered with throw pillows of the same floral print. She sank into the center, placed the mugs next to a thick binder on the table, and slid one toward Cyn.

"What's that mean, I don't know *where* I am?"

Barb sat back to sip the coffee, smudging the rim with lipstick. She indulged in another taste before leaning forward to open the binder.

With a steel grip on the burnished coat rack, Cyn could see the collection of photos of beaches with blinding white sand, impossibly long yachts, and tropical resorts. She kept her eyes on the old woman, waiting for her to fling scalding coffee in her face, or pull a weapon from the cushions. Instead, she leisurely flipped the pages over, one at a time.

As if she had just arrived.

"Your life was miserable before I found you," Barb said. "A street rat, a rag doll. A little sex toy for drugs. For you, death would be easy. You were already killing yourself, you just didn't have the courage to do it all at once. For me, it was quite the opposite. I worked hard to succeed at life, you see. I had a career and a family and a wonderful marriage."

The plastic pages crinkled.

"If you think I was born with a spoon of sterling silver, you're wrong. I was like you, Cynthia—beaten by my stepfather and hated by my mother. I made myself, I rose above it. I earned it, you see. And I wasn't about to give it up to death without a fight."

"*Where* the hell are we?"

"I had an opportunity to beat Death, you see. To start again, to keep what I earned. There would be one less homeless child causing trouble in the world, one less tick on the mane of society." She nodded at her, unaffected by the battering ram pointed at her head. "You didn't want the gift of life, child. I did."

"So you took it."

"I took it."

There was nothing for her to argue. Everything she said was true. Cyn was worthless. Long before Barb was in her head, little voices told her so. She had nothing to live for.

If you would've just asked for my life, I probably would've given it.

"No, you wouldn't." Barb answered Cyn's thought.

Of course she did. Somehow she was still in Cyn's head. *She's inside me, part of me. So is this room, this house...it was too real, the colors vivid, the touch, the smell. Where am I?*

"You're a fighter, Cynthia. Just like me, you refuse to let anything be taken from you. And that's why we're here, right now."

"*Where?*"

"I put a needle in your head and sent you to Foreverland, where you were tossed into the Nowhere and your empty body left behind for me to rightfully have. I put a needle in my head"—Barb rubbed a tiny scar on her forehead—"and left this cancer-ridden body to move into your body, child—your beautiful, healthy unwanted body. It's what you wanted; you wanted to die. And I wanted more life. We both got what we wanted."

"You know that's wrong."

"But then Foreverland crashed and I hadn't fully crossed over into your body. That was me that woke up in the cabin, in your body, I just didn't know it. That was me that suffered through Foreverland's endless cycle of birth and death because Patricia refused to let us wake up in physical reality. That was me that went to the edge of Foreverland and peered into the Nowhere. And that was you that came out of it, your memories, your soul that came back to *your body!*"

She slammed the binder closed, a moment of finality. Or acceptance. Those photos—her husband, her family—represented her life. And she would never have that life again.

"You're the only one to have survived the Nowhere, as far as I know. You should've been shredded and dissolved, but somehow you fought your way out of it and took your body back. Do you know what happened to me, where *I* went when you returned, mmm? I was plunged into your subconscious. It's dark in there, child. And very lonely."

"Then get out."

"That's what I'm trying to do." She sipped her coffee. "Maybe I was wrong, I should've chosen a meeker girl, a coward. But then I don't think I would've been at home. It is what it is, no arguing over spilt milk."

She was wrong. There were others that survived the Nowhere, that walked out of it. She was forgetting her husband, how he was caught crossing over when Foreverland crashed, how he walked out.

But it wasn't like that. I didn't walk out of the Nowhere. Something pushed me out. Or someone.

She remembered those memories being forced back into her body. No, more than her memories. Her soul.

"This is *my* body."

"It's *our* body, child."

Cyn slammed the coat rack on the binder; the table cracked and the pegs splintered. She swept the book into the television; photos fluttered out.

"That's why I like you." Barb didn't flinch. Her laugh had wicked notes, the husky crackle of tumbling cigarette butts. "Put that down before you hurt yourself. Sweet Jesus, have the coffee. I didn't poison it."

Cyn heaved the coat rack into the wall like a spear.

Outside, it was sunny and the weedy patch gone. The garden was back—straight rows of beans and beets and corn.

Am I dreaming?

"Of course you're dreaming," Barbara said. "But you're not asleep. And that's the problem."

"Then *where* am I? Tell me, goddammnit! Why the hell am I in the house like this, and the world is back to the way it was?"

"You can thank your boyfriend." She cleared her throat. "There's some connection with him, something that pushes me deeper into your subconscious when he's around. He forced me to discover parts of you that I'd never seen before, things that you don't even know exist."

"What are you talking about?"

"Beliefs, thoughts, the things that make you tick. Your psychology, child. I understand you far better than you ever will. Let's say I've discovered some truths that needed to be learned. And now I understand what I've done."

"What truth?"

"I can't tell you the truth. You'll have to see it."

"What do you want?"

"Peace. I want peace."

"Then go away."

The old woman's smile was grim. She stood with a slight groan and walked to the window, leaving a trail of expensive perfume. Birds fluttered around the corn.

"What is real?" Barb asked.

"Not this."

"And how do you know?"

Cyn started to answer, but nothing would come out. Everything that defined reality—eyes, ears, nose, mouth, touch—was all here. To her senses, the garden, the music, the candles were all real.

"Where am I?" she whispered.

"You're lost, Cynthia. Like so many in the world, you're lost. But we can find our way back. We can find the truth."

The old woman faced her. Her steeled eyes had softened. She looked kinder. There was no smile, but there was no resistance. No more *you should kill yourself.*

No more separation.

Barb had been in her subconscious. She knew the underworld of Cyn's thoughts, whatever was in there. What else did she know?

"Why now?" Cyn asked. "Why are you friendly now?"

"I told you, I learned the truth, down there in the dark subconscious. I suppose I have your boyfriend to thank for that, for forcing me down there and facing it. Let's say I know how to solve this standoff between us. I've had a change of heart."

"Tell me what to do."

A kind smile brushed her lips. Barb walked softly across the room, stepped over scattered photos and reached for the door. The music, the candles, the grandfather clock faded as she pulled it open. Outside, the wind howled across a gray landscape, branches scratching the weathered railing and the slumping steps.

"Remember how to fall."

"Fall?"

"Open your eyes, child. See what I see. Know what I know. I bring you the truth of where you are."

Barb offered her hand.

Cyn hesitated. It could be a trap. The old woman had fought her all these years and still lived inside her. Maybe this was a new attack: woo her with kindness before shoving Cyn into the dark subconscious.

As long as it's not the Nowhere.

Cyn was tired. With one fist clenched, she reached out.

She accepted Barb's hand.

Her body seized like she'd grabbed a hot wire, voltage gripping her nervous system.

"Open, child. Open and fall."

This was the moment of standing on the precipice, looking into the chasm of the unknown. This was how she escaped Foreverland the first time, by surrendering to the present moment.

By falling.

Cyn unclenched her fist.

She let go of the hatred, the piss and vinegar, the clinging to what was rightfully hers. She wiped away the separation in her mind so that there was no *Cyn*.

There was no *Barb*.

No *us*.

No *I*.

Just *Am*.

In that moment, Barb's thoughts rose to the surface, titans surging from the dark. They didn't have teeth or claws, didn't consume her. They simply told her where to find the truth.

The door slammed.

Cyn stood inside a dilapidated room with rotting furniture and a broken clock, the smell of mold and neglect. There were no pictures on the floor or coat rack stuck in the wall.

She opened the door and took the steps one at a time to find Danny. She knew where they needed to go, what they had to do.

You are the bridge.

(162)

THE WILDERNESS of Wyoming

Danny woke up shivering.

The windshield was frosted. The rain had stopped sometime in the night. He heard sniffing and leaned against the driver's window. A thick mane of fur was investigating the crease of the door. The pack circled around the SUV. The pack leader stood in front of the brick house. One by one, they trotted around the house.

Danny looked through the brick house for the tenth time. He went back to the camp and sat inside the SUV until he stopped shaking, then started a fire.

What if I'm all wrong?

Doubt had punched him in the throat, convinced him that his delusion brought them out here to die. He read through the letters, held them up to the sky to reveal any hidden messages, imprints he may have missed.

Once the past uncovered,

And the demon cast out,
Only then forward you move,
To live without doubt.

He'd brought her to the wilderness to fall again, to face her demons. *But where the hell is she?*

The house was empty. There were no open windows, no back doors for her to escape. The door slammed like the house had swallowed her whole.

Danny examined the two discs that had been sent with the poems. His disc had a blue edge; Cyn's was yellow. Other than that, they were identical. They reflected the firelight across the beige fabric of his coat, the pattern mottled from the arrangement of pinholes and strange angles at which they were drilled.

Build the bridge.

That was the message, yet the discs didn't contain any directions on how to build anything. There were no images or messages in the reflection, no grooves that contained data. The pinholes could be some rudimentary code, some altered form of Morse code.

Or maybe they draw code.

He found a pencil in the glove box. Using a manual as a straight edge, he stuck the tip into one of the holes and rotated it like a wheel, producing a scribbled mess. He reached for Cyn's disc, the one with a yellow edge, and the discs magnetically stuck together. They were easy enough to pull apart. He rotated them until the holes were aligned.

The patterns were exact matches.

"What bridge?" His voice echoed in the distance. "Build what bridge? Tell me where you are, Reed! What the hell are we doing?"

He stomped around the fire, kicked up clods of mud, and heaved logs as far as he could. The pressure of survival weighed on him like stones. Somehow he'd lost Cyn, there wasn't much food left, and winter was almost on them. He had to keep moving to avoid letting the weight pull him deeper.

Pretty soon he was running.

He ran in no particular direction, zigzagging across the field, coming back to the fire, then up the hill, pumping his arms until his ankles burned and his thighs were numb and his chest was blowing up.

He fell on his knees.

The cabins and brick house were just over the hill. He wanted to throw the discs into the great wilderness, lose them in the obscurity of nature. If Reed wanted a bridge, he could mail plans next time. Danny curled his finger along the blue edge of the disc, tested the weight, imagined the sun flashing off the silver surface as it twisted into the gray air—

A wolf howled.

It was long and lonely, rising from over the hill. Danny turned for the campsite when the pack answered. They were striding around the SUV, all of them except one.

The alpha male howled from over the hill again.

Danny stayed on his knees, his heart thudding in his throat. There would be no running. No hiding. He had given in to a moment of weakness, took the bait, threw a tantrum. This was the end. He dropped his chin.

This is where it ends.

At least he found her. At least, for a moment, when he held her hand, he slept without guilt. In those moments, he left Foreverland behind and dreamed of a better life. He hoped Cyn felt that, too.

Wherever she was.

The howling had stopped. They were coming for him. The alpha male came into view and stopped at the crest of the hill, looking down on him while the pack snuck up from behind.

Danny closed his eyes. *I'd rather the wolves take me than the needle.*

The alpha male sniffed the ground. Eyes still closed, Danny felt the weight of the pack circling. Their footsteps grew louder.

A shadow fell over him.

"Danny."

She stood in front of him—short, ragged blonde hair and a baggy sweater billowing in a sudden breeze. She was calm and deep, as still as a midnight pool, yet he sensed the tension of a predator, one that could spring without notice.

"Is it you?" was all he could say.

She reached out and took his hand. Warmth flooded his arm, filled his mind. Her presence was as large as the distant mountains.

Doubt was vanquished.

She touched his face, dragged her fingers down his nose, over his lips, and drew him close. She smelled of sweat and things old, but her kiss was sweet. There was something else, something so intense that it tingled in his sinuses, something wafting out as they held each other near the crest of the hill—fragrant and floral, richly permeating everything that was her.

Lilac.

Somewhere, the wolves howled.

They slept in the SUV that night.

Danny did not dream, not of tomorrow or today. It was just a long blank dream canvas where all his hopes rested in complete silence. They woke with hands clasped, saints in prayer.

They packed the camp before the sun rose, left no trace of their existence.

"Where are we going?" he asked.

"To make a delivery."

She wouldn't tell him where she had been or what happened. She told him to set the GPS. The wolves stood across the meadow and watched them drive out of the wilderness forever.

Toward New York City.

WINTER

To have everything,
   Is to have nothing.
   The opposite is true.

163

JONATHAN SAT AT A ROUND TABLE.

The man across from him was overweight and sweating. His eyes were set too close. He stared at Jonathan, unblinking, as his fingers rapped against the desktop like the tips of ten-penny nails.

Monitors were mounted side by side. Video, which Jonathan could only assume was streaming from other labs, was on display with bar graphs and dynamic charts and scrolling numbers.

The door opened. Neither Jonathan nor Beady-eyes looked up, holding each other's gaze. A man in a gray suit, jacket open, leaned over the table, red tie dangling. Beady-eyes spun in his chair and the two proceeded to whisper, occasionally looking over the table.

Jonathan waited patiently while Beady-eyes pointed at the screens and pecked at various keyboards. The suit stood back, arms folded, and watched. Beady-eyes turned his small eyes back on Jonathan.

The suit pulled up a chair.

"Mr. Deer." He sighed. "This is all very complicated."

"I understand."

"I'm sure you do." That was sincere. "You understand there is no room for error in what we're doing? We can't estimate, not one single item. Vagary will *leave the result up to chance, and neither you nor we have the right to guess at what you want us to do. You understand?"*

"Of course."

"So when you say you want to use your memory, we have a problem."

"I didn't say memory."

Beady-eye's knuckles whitened, fingers interlaced like a wrecking ball.

"I'm capable of carrying the data," Jonathan said.

"For two hundred and four fabrications?"

"I've given you the physical specs for each one."

"But not the personalities."

Jonathan nodded slowly. "I don't have them yet."

"And you want to start production without them?"

"I'll have them."

"Timing is critical, Mr. Deer."

"I understand."

"I don't think you do." Beady-eyes pounded the table. "When fabrication is finished, there has to be a personality matrix uploaded immediately. If you're late or there's a problem, you'll stand by and watch them rot."

Obviously, Beady-eyes had seen this before.

"I understand the timing," he said. "And I'll be there."

The suit and Beady-eyes argued some more. In the end, they couldn't stop Jonathan. He'd paid for the service, their bosses accepted. Jonathan would make the delivery.

Or die trying.

164

Drip. Drip. Drip.

Liquid sunlight dripped onto a desert in steady, even strokes. Like a clock. A metronome.

A heartbeat.

The beat measured the seconds of the day. But it wasn't sand that caught each golden drop. It fell into Alex.

Heavy, heavy Alex.

She floated in a dream, not knowing it was a dream—a nowhere of sweetness—until she neared the surface, close enough to taste real life.

Her eyelashes cracked.

She stared at a popcorn ceiling. Up there in the catacombs of her misty mind was her name, but she couldn't see past the fluffy grit, the swirly texture. It was just a ceiling.

There was no name.

There was a warm place beneath the covers. She reached under the downy comforter, expecting to feel a dark spot spreading across her midsection where she had wet the bed. She was nude, but dry. Her bladder, full.

The blinds in the window were dark. She began drifting beneath the surface again where nothing mattered, where her dreams would cradle her in a warm embrace.

What's my name?

When the bedroom door opened, she didn't recognize Samuel at first. It took a few seconds to recognize her spouse, then a few more to remember his name. He appeared fuzzy. Even after she blinked several times, he still appeared to be a double image out of focus.

"Hungry?" He placed a tray on the dresser.

He had gone away for a few weeks.

She seemed to remember a sudden business trip and complications, something to do with the government and CIA, top secret service that required his anonymity. He texted and emailed, but didn't have the service to call.

But now he was here, every day. He appeared when she woke up, always with food and a smile. Steam rose from a teacup; the scent of chamomile mixing with her body odor rising from beneath the covers. It wasn't a bad smell, but it made her wonder when she showered last.

Samuel sat on the bed; his musky scent, his manly allure pushed into her senses. He took her hand and massaged her fingers one at a time, kneaded her palms, rubbed her arms until her eyes began to roll. She smiled. It was impossible not to.

"What time is it?" she asked.

"It's about that time."

She looked around. *Where are the clocks?*

"I got to pee."

"Want a pan?"

"What?"

"Joking."

Samuel made shushing sounds, rubbing and stroking and caressing. If there wasn't pressure in her midsection, she'd have pulled him under the covers and let him do things to her.

She peeled herself away and urinated in the bathroom for what seemed like hours. Her head, resting on her knees, was a sandbag.

Thoughts and memories trickled through the fog, things she should be doing but no longer wanted to.

There were interviews and drafts to write, chapters to edit. Deadlines to meet. *It could wait. It could all wait. Even,* she thought while flushing, *personal hygiene.*

Samuel was under the covers. His shoulders were bare and bronze; muscles bunched along his arms. She slid next to him, fell into his embrace and forgot about those deadlines.

Life was too damn good.

Samuel was gone.

Sunlight cut between the blinds.

That side of the house faced west, which meant it was afternoon. Judging by the angle and length of the dusty sunbeams, it was late. Had she slept an entire day?

It was impossible to know.

She wrapped a robe around her nudity and bent a single blind. It was clear and sunny, the window chilled. A school bus rolled down the street, followed by laughter.

A pang of guilt struck her. *Or is it sadness? Or both?*

Somewhere in the endless blue sky, thunder rumbled.

The bed is new.

She couldn't remember ever sleeping in a king with comforters that thick. And she slept right in the middle, like it was all hers. She couldn't remember falling asleep, just remembered the rhythm of Samuel's embrace. Now it was mid-afternoon and there were things to do, but the thought of sitting at the computer, of punching those keys and staring at the screen was empty. She wanted to sleep, to sink deep into the mattress and into a dream where nothing hurt, and nothing bothered her.

Pots and pans rang downstairs. Samuel was cooking.

The front room was spotless. All the shelves had been dusted, the carpet cleaned, the throw pillows just the way she liked them. Samuel was stirring a warm pot of stew. She loved stew on a lazy winter day.

"Don't you have to work?" she asked.

"Working at home." He sampled the pot and stirred. "Skyping a conference a bit later. Thought we could watch a movie tonight."

The laptop was on the kitchen table, a background photo of Alex on the screen, her eyes closed, a slight smile. She couldn't remember that picture—maybe Samuel took it while she was sleeping.

It was strange to see contentment on her. Her photos were always intense, all business, get the job done. Even their wedding photos, like she was imitating joy.

A bad actor pretending to be happy.

But that picture on the computer—that was the real deal. She felt it in her toes.

A ten.

"Where you going?" he asked.

She had her hand on the back door. There was a little blank spot between staring at the laptop and going to the door. She couldn't remember that short little walk.

"Getting some fresh air," she said.

The leaves had fallen, but Samuel had picked them up. The flower beds had been put to sleep, the grass neatly trimmed. A squirrel or something squabbled in the bushes.

She pulled her robe closed, but the winter air rushed up her legs. It felt clean, the deck boards hard on her feet. She took a long deep breath through her nostrils and closed her eyes.

Somewhere a child laughed.

It wasn't far away. There were kids in the neighborhood, but this sounded like it was right in front of her. The backyard, though, was quiet, still and empty. A wave of voices passed overhead, like a speaker mounted on a passing drone—those fragmented pieces of language all mixed together like a pot of stew.

Thunder rumbled in a blue sky.

Her toes had become stiff. She wandered deeper into the backyard, walking like a monk, thinking about Tyler Ballard. She had never gotten around to transcribing her notes. It was probably the best interview she'd ever done. At the very least, the most revealing. And yet, she couldn't bring herself to pick up where she left off.

Not the best interview...the most satisfying.

She couldn't quite put her finger on it, though. *What had been so gratifying? Was it what he said?* But as she dragged her feet across the lawn, she couldn't remember anything he said.

Or was it the way he said it?

A door slammed.

Alex was on the driveway, the concrete colder and harder than the grass. Her knees were sufficiently numb, her fingers and nose aching. A brown truck had pulled up to the curb.

UPS.

The deliveryman stepped out of the open door. He rushed up the driveway with long strides just short of a trot with a box under his arm. It was wrapped in brown paper. He smiled at Alex.

"Bit cold today," he said.

There was writing on the box.

She didn't have to sign for it. He just handed it to her.

Her name was on the front. It was written in green ink. *Alessandra Diosa.*

"You're going to freeze." He took the box away. But it wasn't the UPS guy. Samuel put his arm around her. The truck was gone. How long had she been standing there?

Long enough that she couldn't feel her lips.

They went inside. They ate stew. They watched a movie. Later, they made love.

When Alex woke late the next day, she tried to remember her name and the day. She eventually did. But she never saw the package addressed in green ink again.

Never even remembered it.

She just wanted to sleep.

165

ADMAX Penitentiary, *Colorado*

A headlight.

One bright locomotive.

Tyler was on the tracks. He tried to move, to look away, blink, but it only got brighter, only got closer. The ground didn't shake; the wind didn't blow.

Everything was silent.

The light went away and came back twice. It was after the second time he saw shapes. They emerged from the glow like Polaroid snapshots. A white coat.

A white man in a white coat.

The good doctor.

He put the silver pen in his white coat and stepped back.

Tyler saw spots. Tears rolled down his cheeks. His forehead was inflated and hard like the shell of a tortoise. His pulse thumped just above his eyebrows.

Sensation came back to his hands and feet first. His whole body vibrated with pins and needles, the kind that felt like a giant hand squeezing a lemon.

More tears.

Someone else was in the room. Tyler could feel him without turning. Gramm was off to the side, his arms folded, observing the good doctor. Tyler remained a solid object mounted on the examination table, but his mind was expanding like a net, capturing Gramm's thoughts like minnows. There were too many to make sense, silvery flashes that darted about in the ethereal mindspace.

But Tyler's mindnet went beyond the room.

It went out to the prison yard, where inmates squared up on the basketball court, walked the track or read books. He heard them all simultaneously.

Hundreds of them.

They chattered like the roar of a sporting event, the crash of a waterfall, a thunderstorm smashing across a flat rock. He covered his ears—

"You had a stroke."

Tyler turned his head. Gramm was near the doorway.

"Wheh?" Tyler slurred the word.

"Almost three months ago."

Three months?

"The good doctor saved you. I thought we lost you." Emotion strained the last couple of words. Gramm cleared his throat. "He maximized your biomite content and injected you with a new strain to repair the damage and restore your identity."

Tyler closed his eyes, working his finger and thumb around the bridge of his nose. Too much, it was too much. He closed his mind, withdrew until he only heard his own thoughts.

"Whah..." He worked his tongue and lips. "What happened?"

"A clot had formed around the stent." Gramm paused. "The good doctor thinks."

"Thinks?"

"That was the biofeedback. It was a miracle we saved you."

Again, the emotion in Gramm's voice.

They couldn't take Tyler out of the prison. If a doctor besides the good doctor were to see Tyler, the entire operation would be compromised.

Tyler agreed.

"From what we understand, the clot formed from overuse. Your last session was extremely long and stressful. And when we began to lose the basement network..."

Tyler lifted his head too quickly. Stars flitted through his eyesight. Memories reported for recall. He had just seen Alessandra for the interview, then went to the basement, where his carefully selected network of volunteers—all wired into Foreverland, all lending Tyler their minds to support the cause—began to fail.

All that red.

Gramm handed him a glass of water. "You're infused with maximum biomite capacity. Your body is now 49.9% biomites, as close to artificial as we can make it without the government coming for you."

The government's halfskin laws denied humans the right to exceed 50% biomites. At that point, the lawmakers claimed, people were more machine than human. And machines, the government decided, didn't deserve to live.

As long as he was breathing and thinking, Tyler didn't care how many biomites kept his heart ticking.

"There are special biomites we can use," Gramm said, "ones the government can't detect, if we need to increase your levels. There are advantages, Doctor."

Doctor? Who's he talking to?

Gramm was addressing Tyler, not the good doctor. It was confusing.

"It would halt some of your health concerns, but it'll take some time to locate—"

"No, thank you, Gramm. This is just fine."

Tyler caressed his forehead. It was senseless and leathery, without the deep wrinkles that once carved horizontal tracks from temple to temple. There was something missing.

"The stent was removed. No more needle, Doctor."

"Why are you calling me that?"

Gramm looked to the good doctor with concern. "Do you know your name?"

"I know my name, damn you. Why are you calling me 'doctor'?"

"Please tell us your name."

"Tyler Ballard."

"You are *Doctor* Tyler Ballard."

That wasn't it. He was calling him doctor. He never called him that. *Or maybe I don't remember it.*

"The stent," Tyler said. "You removed it completely?"

"Yes."

Tyler's sense of emptiness was confirmed: he was now a junkie without his needle.

"Reed was coming through the needles."

"Reed?"

"The volunteers. We determined it was Reed that killed them."

Tyler rubbed his jaw. Numbness was slowly fading. He was riding a wave of dull sensations into awareness, his thoughts becoming sharper and cleaner.

"The biofeedback suggested a termination command was initiated," Gramm said. "Someone or something simply told the bodies to just...turn off."

"We lost them all?"

Gramm shook his head. "No, we saved one. You saved him, actually."

Tyler had run to the back of the room. Samuel was the only one he needed to save. The rest he could lose, but that one volunteer he had to keep alive.

Alessandra depends on it.

"The Institute?" Tyler blurted. "Were they—"

"No, the volunteers at the Institute were unaffected. We took Samuel off the needle, increased his brain biomites, and converted him to wireless connectivity like you. He was offline for a short spell, but Alessandra didn't notice. Even if it's not Reed causing these problems, something's out there, Doctor. We can't risk you using the needle. We're too close."

The emotion got to Gramm this time. He rubbed his eyes and apologized. It seemed genuine.

"It's all right," Tyler said. "I understand."

"I thought we lost you, that all of this was...that Foreverland would just..."

"Now, now, Gramm. You did good. You and the good doctor, you both did good."

The good doctor, in a brief moment of clarity, nodded.

Perhaps Patricia was right: he should cross into her Foreverland and leave his body behind. Gramm and the good doctor would watch over it until Alessandra was ready.

Tyler held out his hand. They helped him stand. His legs were weak. Blood rushed to his head, thumped in his forehead. The guards appeared with a wheelchair.

"No, thank you." He waved them off. "Let's go to the basement."

"I don't think that's wise, Doctor."

"Nonsense. Time is short."

"You need rest."

"Apparently, I've been resting for months."

He made it to the elevator before succumbing to the wheelchair when the fuzzy static of the random voices buzzed in his head again. He assumed these were thoughts from the inmates, that the new biomites were spontaneously connecting with other minds, but they crackled in his inner ear like a stadium of angry spectators.

Gramm pushed him to his cell, where he closed his eyes and laid back on his bed to rest. The basement would have to wait.

Tyler spent weeks sweating on his mattress like a heroin addict gone cold turkey. The voices of static had become fingernails clawing through his scalp, pulling his brain apart a neuron at a time.

And Patricia...she was a snowflake in a blizzard of thoughts. If he couldn't find her, if he couldn't go to her, be with her, then none of this mattered.

He sat up and squeezed the sides of his head, as if that would quell the voices, but the vertigo caused him to vomit. Gramm assured him this would end, that he would return to normal. Occasionally, Tyler heard Patricia's voice rise above the din.

She was out there, waiting for him.

"Do something, Gramm." His voice scratched his throat.

It was another week before he was able to leave the room. The static of voices faded. Gramm and the guards came for him and took him to the basement.

The room was dark.

The lights had been turned down. The tables were empty slabs, red lights casting enough light to illuminate the aisles. The bodies had been removed and disposed of, all done while Tyler was in an induced coma.

Despite the emptiness, he opened his mouth to breathe, the heavy odor of decay and infection saturating the walls, clinging to the ceiling. Nearly a lifetime of work wasted in a single day.

These were the volunteers, the inmates that readily gave themselves to the needle. Their deaths would go unnoticed. They were lifers without family, men forgotten by the world.

It took great effort to make them disappear from the system—creating false documents, trails of paperwork, deleted notes. It had been over twenty years and no one had come looking for a volunteer.

And volunteer, they did.

Once Tyler showed them a way out of their suffering, a simple means of closing their eyes and going to a new reality, a way to leave their life, go where they could be anything they wanted, do anything they desired. They would never be imprisoned as long as their minds were free.

And Foreverland was the doorway.

Tyler's son, Harold, had learned this lesson from his father. He discovered that people would do anything to escape their suffering and they would take the needle willingly.

Harold found an island, found investors and collected the lost children that would never be missed. Their bodies would not go to waste, and neither would the minds of the elderly men that didn't deserve to die.

Harold made a great sum of money and funneled it back to the prison, where Tyler expanded his empire of volunteers. In a perverted way, Harold helped build the basement, helped bring his mother and father closer together. It was all in the name of science, a means of discovering a new reality. All the volunteers were potential candidates to become a permanent host of a boundless Foreverland.

But now they were gone.

As long as the volunteers at the Institute survived, none of that mattered. *And Samuel.*

All the lamps were off except one. It shined on a bleached and sickly body, like that of a drowning victim. His once olive-colored skin, the genetic trait of his Hispanic heritage, was pasty. Teardrops were tattooed on the side of his face; an enormous crucifix on his chest was etched in fuzzy blue lines.

Samuel was one of the first volunteers.

He'd renounced his affiliation to gangs and crime, had taken up a life of solitary study in the library, of assisting other inmates in their spiritual study. He taught himself law at night, reviewing case notes. Serving a life sentence, he would never practice, but his advice was often sound.

Next to Gramm, he was Tyler's most important soldier. Samuel was caring for the new host.

Alessandra's husband.

Tyler's last trip through the needle was to meet Alessandra for the interview. She was in her own Foreverland and didn't know it. And Samuel was making sure she stayed there.

"He's stable, Doctor." Gramm stepped through the green light. "Because of you."

Tyler touched Samuel's arm, the veins still pulsing.

"Samuel discovered Reed is behind this," Gramm said.

"How?"

"He intercepted a UPS package addressed to Alessandra. It was written in green ink. It's why we haven't been able to locate him. He's done nothing electronically—no email, no texts, phone calls or video conferencing. He went completely off grid. I suspect he's been communicating this way all along." Gramm cleared his throat. "Clearly, he's alive somehow."

"What was in the package?"

"More reminders of Alex's past and a poem of sorts. Cryptic. I assume he wrote that way in case we saw it. We could go back and search Danny's and Cyn's belongings, even Reed's old apartment. I still don't understand how he's doing it—"

"It doesn't matter now."

"It appears he's trying to jar her memories loose, create a disturbance in her acceptance pattern. If she remembers certain events, it'll set her back. I think he knows our time is limited. He's just trying to stall."

"We have more time than he thinks." Tyler lifted his hands above the body. In the bright light, they looked twenty years younger. The biomites bought him all the time he needed.

But with the noise in his head, did he want to?

"It's time to relocate, Doctor."

"What do you mean?"

"We need to leave the prison."

"Move?"

"Alessandra is nearly asleep. It's almost time."

Tyler felt dizzy. "No need to leave; I can do it from here."

"You need to be closer to Patricia."

"Distance isn't a problem, Gramm."

"We'll need to be out—"

"We can't be hasty!" He bridged his temples with finger and thumb, the voices spiking with his anger. "I need her fully asleep; there can be no instability."

Gramm knew this. If Tyler committed to the host, if he crossed into Alessandra's Foreverland and she woke up, there was the risk of being thrown into an expanding Nowhere. He had already taken that risk once when he went inside her Foreverland for the interview. To be sentenced to the Nowhere...that was worse than death.

"The feds are investigating the prison," Gramm said.

"What?"

"There have been inquiries by the FBI into abuse and lack of response by the warden."

"Why didn't you tell me sooner?"

"You were in a coma."

"Now, damn you!" He backhanded him across the table. "I've been awake all this time, and you tell me this now?"

Gramm dabbed the bead of blood swelling on his lip with the tip of his tongue. "We've been holding the authorities off. The trail of missing paperwork, missing prisoners is unmistakable. They suspect the warden has been involved in a ring of money for escape. They came to investigate a month ago, but the warden kept them out of the basement, kept you hidden. They're scheduled to come back in a week."

Fear radiated in waves. Gramm always cringed in the presence of Tyler's intense emotions.

He didn't flinch.

"There was no need to hamper your recovery, Doctor."

The feds were coming. All of these tables wouldn't matter, empty or not, when they stepped inside. The trail would quickly lead to the Institute. They had contingency plans, they could relocate all essential personnel out of New York within the day.

But Alessandra is too close. It could disrupt everything!

"We'll disassemble the basement, Doctor. They won't know what happened. All data can be erased and reprogrammed. Evidence can be planted to set the warden and guards up. We'll keep Samuel in sick bay. He'll continue his mission until its complete, and then we'll pull the plug."

When Alessandra is asleep.

Tyler pushed the black curly hair from Samuel's forehead. A red welt remained where the stent had been removed. Tyler had killed the connection just before his stroke.

Reed was coming through the needle.

"We transitioned him while you were out, brought his biomite levels up while he was still unconscious. We were able to explain his disappearance to Alessandra until he crossed back over."

"How?"

"I went in, placed a few calls. Explained he was recruited by the government based on his past service with the CIA. I implanted a few vague memories in Alessandra that he'd served in the military before she met him."

"It worked?"

"She's almost asleep, very open to suggestion. Now that Samuel's back, she's almost out."

Tyler rubbed his face. He had to check with Patricia. She would be worried; he hadn't seen her in months. Gramm would've kept her updated, but he needed to see what she thought.

But how do I connect without the needle?

He looked inward and the voices cranked up like the knob on a radio.

"I can show you the way, Doctor. I guided Samuel back inside, I can do the same for you."

Tyler's chest fluttered as he paced around the table, his hands against his head. It was all coming so fast.

Why didn't he wake me earlier?

"I've already arranged for your transfer to Attica in three days. En route, we'll detour to the Institute. We have time, Doctor."

Gramm put his hand on Tyler's shoulder. Peace and calm flowed around him.

"I'll show you the way."

The voices went quiet and still. As if they heard him.

And listened.

In the middle of the prison yard, the afternoon sun fell on Tyler's face, warm and radiant. He sat on the frozen ground, legs crossed, Gramm beside him.

The inmates wandered. *Breathe in.*

Birds overhead. *Breathe out.*

Snow on the mountains. *Breathe.*

There was only breath, only this moment.

Perfectly still.

He closed his eyes. In the darkness, the breeze whipped broken grass around his knees. Men shouted and birds called. The voices no longer haunted his mind. Across the great silence, one voice called softly.

And warmed his heart.

Without movement or effort, the cold vanished and the men fell silent. The breeze died. He crossed the vast space in an eternal moment of absolute perfection.

The breeze returned, warmer. The clatter of cutlery, the murmur of conversation.

He opened his eyes.

Gramm stood in front of him. Instead of the gray prison garb, he wore casual khakis and a loose-fitting white shirt unbuttoned at the top. His front teeth were still slightly crooked, but his hair was thick and past his ears. The surfing chemist was back.

A waiter cradled a padded menu, gold letters emblazoned on the side: *The Press Lounge.* Over his shoulder, the New York skyline glittered.

"This way, sir." The waiter gestured.

Patrons were just beginning their evening at the rooftop bar. The waiter pointed at a table near the edge. A woman sat alone, swirling a glass of white wine while she drank the city's view. Her dress seemed to flow despite the stillness.

Glowed, despite the darkness.

She turned. And smiled.

She fell into his arms, her essence melting through him, her floral scent swirling around him.

So warm, so soft.

All of this, everything was Patricia—the people, the buildings, the setting sun. This was her Foreverland. Perhaps he should forget Alessandra, live here the rest of their lives so that, when she died, they would go together. If death came at this very moment, he would not be disappointed.

But Alessandra could do so much more. Her Foreverland would be endless. She could network people into her Foreverland, bring all of humanity together. Alessandra would be the hub that established an immortal Foreverland, one that didn't rely on one person, one host.

The human population would become the host.

We would become heaven on earth.

With Alessandra, there would be eternal happiness, not just the fleeting moments of joy. It was what Tyler and Patricia had worked for all these decades.

He wanted the world to have this joy, too, wanted the world to believe that if death came in this moment, it would not be disappointing.

They swayed back and forth, dancing on the rooftop. The city light blazed like stars.

166

Bing.

Alex had to go through a mental catalog to figure out what that sound was.

Doorbell.

That recognition lifted her from sleep, pulled her from a lifetime beneath the sand. Her eyes were open, but she didn't remember opening them. She was staring at an object.

Ceiling fan.

Her throat burned, her lips cracked, but the allure of the bed was greater than her thirst. Sleep was warm like the sun, those first few minutes on the beach before sunburn really set in, warmth that seeped through her, saturated every pore, tugged her beneath the sand—

Wake up.

There were voices. One of them was Samuel. The other was a stranger that told her to wake up. *Did I dream that?*

At first, they were downstairs. The front door was closed and muffled sounds were just below her window. She would've been content to lay there and let them lull her back to sleep, but this time her thirst won.

Her robe was piled on the floor.

She tied it closed, but not before seeing her hips jutting out at her waist, her ribs pronounced beneath her breasts. The window was a sheet of ice. The lawn was buried under snow, a fresh set of tracks carved to the front porch.

Everything so foggy.

Alex shuffled to the stairs, grabbing the walls and furniture for support. She couldn't quite straighten up, and her feet hurt. Her fingers were stiff. It wasn't until she reached the bottom of the steps that she moved less like an old woman.

Samuel had his hand on the glass door. He was talking to a kid all bundled against the cold, ice crystals coating his ski mask. A lock of red hair had escaped through one of the eyeholes. Large snowflakes, the biggest she'd ever seen, hissed behind him.

Snowflakes don't hiss.

The distant buzz of the voices was back, a radio playing static between her ears.

Samuel started backing into the house, waving the kid off, thanking him for stopping by, wishing him luck to find a house he could shovel, when Alex heard the tapping.

A fingernail on a pane of glass.

It came from the back door.

167

Upstate New York

Danny rolled in the snow, getting legitimately cold before walking down Park Street, to the address Cyn gave him. Even though they didn't dare drive past it, she described it in great detail like she'd been there before. Like she knew exactly what to do.

"Just keep him busy for five minutes," she had said.

"How do you know all this?"

Ever since leaving the wilderness, that's how she answered questions: like she didn't hear them.

"You going to tell me what happened?" he once asked.

"I will."

Her unperturbed posture and her unblinking gaze were intimidating. She knew exactly where they were going, what they were doing. She didn't say how, one look was all he needed to know. *Did Reed come to you? Did he tell you how to build the bridge?*

When Danny's confidence wavered, the few moments his thoughts carried doubt into the foyer of his mind, she took his hand. As if she knew.

"We'll find the truth, Danny," she would say. "It'll set us free."

And doubt would be extinguished.

"His name is Samuel," Cyn had told him.

"What are you going to do?"

"Meet me at the truck."

He left the house on Park Street, a teenager in search of driveways to shovel. Danny walked down the sidewalk, a brand-new snow shovel over his shoulders. The truck was around the corner, the tailpipe huffing a steady cloud, the tires half-buried in the unplowed street. Cyn was turned in the passenger seat looking into the back.

The back windows reflected the drifting snowflakes and gray sky. Danny cupped his hands against the tinted glass. They had laid the backseats down before parking, and used their pillows and blankets to make a bed. She didn't say why. When he left her, it was unoccupied.

Now someone was in it.

We need to make a delivery, Cyn told him when they left the wilderness. And the *package* they were to deliver was lying in the back.

The woman's eyes were closed. He hoped she was sleeping and not dead. Cyn was holding her hand. Danny opened the driver's door.

"Take my hand," Cyn said.

The smell of lilacs was overpowering. His eyes began to water. Danny climbed in and did what he was told. He took her hand—

Blinding light.

A spotlight beamed through the windshield. It was like looking into the sun. A jolt of energy fired from her hand, pure sunlight beamed through every pore in his body.

He melted into ecstasy.

There was no separation.

He merged with everything around him. The silky essence of the universe flowed without friction, without boundaries, without resistance—

"She must stay asleep."

Danny was back in his body, back in the truck, the steering wheel in front of him. "What the hell just happened?"

"Don't let go."

"Who is she?"

"I don't really know, just don't let go," Cyn added. "They can't see her if she's asleep. Go now."

"Who are *they?*"

"Drive, Danny. And don't let go."

The GPS was set for New York City.

He didn't ask how she got the woman into the truck, or who she was or where they were taking her or why. But this was about Foreverland. It had always been about Foreverland, ever since he escaped the tropical island.

The faces might change, but there was always a *they*.

New York City

The snow had been cleared from the Brooklyn Bridge.

Traffic was unusually sparse. Danny drove with one hand on the steering wheel. His other hand was clammy; his fingers ached in Cyn's grasp. In the hours it took to get this far, her grip had tightened. She never looked away from the sleeping woman.

Lilacs were pasted to the back of his throat. It had never been this strong, as if the woman sleeping in the back was the essence of lilac.

"Alessandra Diosa," Cyn told him. "Her name is Alessandra Diosa."

Diosa? Danny had cringed. *Goddess.*

"Go faster," Cyn said.

He crossed the Brooklyn Bridge. The first light was green. So was the second one. They were all green, as far as he could see.

And traffic was thinning.

Cars were turning off Fifth Avenue, clearing a path for them to speed through the green lights. Even ambulances didn't get respect like that.

Alessandra moaned.

Cyn squeezed Danny's hand, their fingers grinding together.

"As fast as you can," she said.

Earlier, she told him to go the speed limit. They didn't want to attract attention. Besides, the roads were slippery and with only one hand on the wheel, they could just as easily have wrapped around a tree. But now they had a straight shot through the middle of the city.

And everyone, somehow everyone, knew they were coming.

But someone doesn't. We're hiding from someone with an all-reaching eye, someone that's looking for Alessandra.

"Do *they* know she's missing?" he asked.

"Not yet."

Danny flattened the accelerator.

The truck bounced over imperfections in the road, tossing them in their seats. Cyn's grip tightened. He couldn't feel his fingers anymore.

The flag on the GPS came into view. The destination was close.

Buildings towered over them, their shadows dissolving into the night. Broadway billboards looked down on them. The street was nearly empty. Only a few cars waited for them to pass; pedestrians watched from the sidewalks and inside brightly lit storefronts.

They turned on Forty-Sixth Avenue. There, on the corner of Seventh Street, the windows were brightly lit. The door stood open.

"Stop in front," Cyn shouted.

"There's nowhere to park."

"Just stop!"

He mashed the brake with both feet. The truck slid sideways before jerking to a stop. Alessandra slid forward, but her eyes remained closed. Danny opened his door.

"Don't let go!" She pulled him back. "You can't let go, understand?"

She crawled into the back and he followed. They moved slowly and methodically, keeping their fingers laced. He reached the latch and the back door whooshed open.

Headlights glared inside.

Traffic had resumed closer to normal and was starting to back up. People were shouting as they passed, windows down, fingers out. Whoever had cleared the roads and turned the lights green had waned.

Or maybe they were focusing on other things.

"Sit her up."

Danny pulled her into a sitting position. Alessandra's head wobbled. Drool glistened on her chin. *Are we committing a crime?*

The time to ask that question had passed.

"Take her hand." Cyn let go of Danny.

"You sure?"

"Take her hand!"

Danny grabbed Alessandra's free hand. It was limp and cold.

They held her up and took half-steps, her bare feet dragging across the pavement. She weighed as much as a grade-schooler. Danny could carry her with one arm.

Horns sounded off, cars stopped.

"Alessandra?" Cyn leaned in. "You don't have to open your eyes, but take a step."

Her head rolled from left to right, mouth open. They didn't slow down, but kept moving toward the open door on the corner of the building beneath bold letters, *The Institute of Technological Research.*

They reached the curb when she took her first step, flopping her bare foot onto the sidewalk, skin scuffed from her toes. Her eyebrows arched, but her eyelids were too heavy.

Car doors slammed behind them. Red and blue lights swirled across the building. Someone told them to stop.

"Don't turn around," Cyn said.

They were going through that door, even if shots were fired.

The police lights reflected off the letters above the door. Sirens came from the other direction.

Three steps left.

Two.

One.

A man in a white lab coat blocked the entrance. There would be no fight, not with a barely conscious woman in their possession.

Cyn looked at him, unblinking. And like the wolves, he stepped aside. They went inside the lobby. The man locked the door. Seconds later, a fist hammered it.

"Unlock this door!" a cop shouted.

The man in the lab coat crossed the lobby and pushed open the swinging doors. A harsh antiseptic smell rushed out. The soles of their boots squeaked on the waxed floor. Alessandra slid her feet until her knees buckled. They caught her before she crumpled.

"Alessandra?" Cyn shook her. "You can wake up now. We're here."

Her eyes fluttered but didn't open.

"Where are we taking her?" Danny asked.

"Just don't let go."

"Tell me where we're taking her!"

"Follow him." The man in the lab coat led the way.

"Why are we here?" He couldn't ignore the fear pounding in his chest. "Why are we bringing her to this place?"

"The truth is down there, Danny."

"But why Alessandra?"

Cyn stopped midway down the hall, clinging to Alessandra's thin arm. She panted like a cornered animal. *She feels the quiver, too.*

"It's the only way out of this?" she said.

"Out of what?"

"This mess, Danny. She told me she'd leave me alone if we did this."

"Who told you?"

Desperation pleadingly pried her eyes wide. "Just trust me."

She gently shook Alessandra until her eyelids fluttered again. An unfocused gaze peered through slits.

"We need to walk," Cyn said.

They took one step, then another. Alessandra's feet dragged and flopped. They held her hands like parents guiding their child to a very scary place.

The hall was long, the doors open and offices empty. The man in the lab coat waited at a metal door. Alessandra was walking on her own when they arrived, her eyes almost completely open. The man in the coat tugged the metal door.

Danny had been to the Institute in the spring, but none of this was familiar. He didn't remember the hall or what was beyond the metal door. He only had a vague memory of arriving. When the metal opened and the funk of wet fur and dung hit him, he remembered.

Coco.

The orangutan lay on a table, long arms at his sides, a needle in the forehead.

The walls weren't walls. They were dark, but he could see through the reflections, could see the cubicles with smaller animals strapped down.

And the wire. All the wires.

"She has to go back there." Cyn pointed at another set of doors across the room. The man in the coat waited.

"Why?"

"I don't know! We just have to go back there, Danny." She swallowed the lump cracking her voice. "We go back there."

"Why?"

"We have to fall."

Her voice faltered. She was tired of falling, and that's what scared him. He thought the falling was over. The way she emerged from the brick house, the confidence that brought them here had evaporated. They were two kids that kidnapped a goddess that someone would be looking for very soon.

But the man in the coat continued leading the way. Someone was expecting them. Expecting the goddess.

Cyn reached for his other hand. Even when he didn't take it, she left it out there. They were two steps from the doors, the man in the coat latched onto the handle. The sirens were still audible, the police still at the front door.

We have to fall.

He took her hand and nodded. They would fall together.

The man in the coat opened the doors.

They took the last two steps. Alessandra shuffled between them. Cyn's breath caught in her throat. There were two tables back there. A very old woman was on one.

Alessandra was on the other.

Alessandra crushed Danny's hand. She was standing between them, but she was on the table, too. Unless that was a twin.

That can't be her.

"You promised," Cyn said, "you would leave!"

Danny pulled Alessandra close to him, but he wasn't holding Alessandra's hand. He was holding Cyn's hand.

Alessandra was gone.

168

Upstate New York

Alex hardly ate.

When she did, Samuel nuked a small bowl of soup. He'd spoon in a couple bites before her eyes started to roll, then dump it back in the pot. He did that for two weeks, same pot of soup. He never bothered to even put it in the refrigerator.

She never knew the difference.

Husbandry is easy.

Alex was a first-class bitch in the beginning. The old man had warned him. "She's a little difficult."

Difficult. Bitch. Same thing.

But Dr. Tyler Ballard promised him a reward no fool would turn down. He put the needle in Samuel's head and gave him a taste of heaven. "Get her to sleep and you can have that," the old man said. "Forever."

Samuel didn't understand how this world was in Alessandra's head, what it meant that she was a host or how she could dream something so real, a dream he was in.

He also didn't give a damn.

He punched that needle in his head and went to work. He smiled when she gave him that condescending look, turned away when she laughed at him. Where he grew up, you didn't walk away from that. He just had to keep his eyes on the prize.

He hadn't heard a peep on the baby monitor all afternoon. That was his idea and it was genius. He found the monitor in the attic, buried behind boxes where no one would find it. Instead of hauling his ass up and down those stairs, he just listened for her smacking those lips.

That meant she was waking up.

He ordered a pizza and decided to smoke a bowl. His stash was above the stove, tucked behind a jar of pennies. Just in case Sleeping Beauty came downstairs, he went out to the back porch. He only needed a puff or two because his stuff was potent. Everything in a Foreverland world, the old man said, was potent.

As potent as I want it to be.

He stepped outside without a coat. The flame flickered near the end of the pipe.

Footsteps.

Someone had been on the back porch. A second set of steps had followed. Those were bare feet.

He dropped the lighter.

Samuel ran upstairs three steps at a time. The bed was empty, the covers thrown back, the robe gone.

"Alex!" He went room to room. "Alex! Where are you?"

He leaped down the steps and crashed through the front door. Samuel raced down the center of the street without a coat. He shouted until his voice gave out, ran until his legs went numb.

Looked until the world turned dark.

And then he found himself nude on a table, staring at a bright light. The smell of death was all around.

He'd never see Foreverland again.

169

The Institute of Technological Research, New York City

"You promised," Cyn said, "you would leave!"

"Patience, child," Barb said. "It's been a long trip."

She dragged her fingers along the edge of the table, her bracelets ringing. Barb was in the back room, as if she'd been waiting. She looked the same as she did in the brick house—the red lipstick, the thin scarf and large oval earrings with shiny stones.

She ran her fingers over the very old woman's bent knee, across her knobby hand and up to her hunched shoulders, where the thinning hair—like that of a doll from a bygone era—spread out. Her body sank in a thick cushion. The simple white smock was bunched around her like a potato sack.

"Patricia," Barb muttered.

Cyn recognized the very old woman—the curling body, the smell of old skin. How could she forget? She'd hosted the wilderness Foreverland that imprisoned Cyn and the girls. And now, with the needle in her head, she was hosting it again.

Cyn's fist clenched involuntarily.

"You said if we brought Alessandra here, you'd get out of my head."

That was the deal. When she took Barb's hand in the brick house, her thoughts merged into Cyn and told her where to find Alessandra, where to take her, and where to find the truth.

And that she would leave.

Cyn wasn't concerned that Alessandra disappeared, but a small pang of guilt tugged at her. She didn't know where Alessandra was. When they stepped into the back room, there were two Alessandras—the one on the table similar to Patricia's, wearing a baggy green gown. There was also the one they brought to the Institute and disappeared. *What if we delivered her to the Nowhere?*

"You tricked me," Cyn said.

"We trick ourselves, child." Barb traced the wrinkles in the old woman's forehead, around the protruding needle. "When I first met Patricia, I had serious doubts that any of this Foreverland crap was true. I'd heard through social circles there was a way to cheat death, circles that only people like me are privy to, you know. Circles that run on money. I didn't believe it, of course."

She sighed.

"But stage 3 cancer will make you listen to anything."

Barb didn't look like a cancer patient. She'd abandoned that diseased body long ago. The image in front of her was a concept built on memories that only Cyn could see.

Barb flashed lipstick-stained teeth in a joyless smile.

"I wasn't excited about taking your body. I know you find that hard to believe, but it was murder, I knew that. But I was addicted to life, Cynthia. I wasn't willing to give it up cold turkey and told myself I was doing you a favor. How's that for rationalization?"

Barb raked the old woman's hair to the side and combed a part down the middle with her fingers. She smoothed the wrinkles on the white gown and stroked her cheek—a cheek so gray and thin that Cyn was afraid merely touching it would tear it like wet tissue.

"Do you remember your first taste of Foreverland?" Barb asked. "The freedom? The joy? I went there a few times, sort of practice for crossing over when your body was ready. I knew, right then, Patricia had bigger plans than swapping bodies for rich people like me. This body-switching business that she and her son had been doing was just practice for something much grander."

Barb looked at Alessandra's body.

"I was right."

Alessandra was set up exactly like Patricia. Was she her replacement? Was she already hosting?

Were there already boys and girls trapped inside?

Cyn squeezed Danny's hand, afraid if she let go, he'd take off running. He was watching her talk to empty space. Barb looked at their clenched hands and smiled—genuinely, sweetly. It reminded her of someone. Cyn sensed Barb's memory. *Her husband.*

Cyn's memories of that man were not so sweet—an old man that murdered Jen and buried her in the garden. He did it in Foreverland, but she woke up with the memory of the things he did to her.

"He murdered, but don't judge," Barb said. "He was a good man."

"He was worse. You know the things he did."

Her smile turned hollow. "You're too young to understand."

"Why are we here? You promised to tell me *where* we are."

"I promised to *show* you."

Barb looked across the room, over the tables, past Alessandra to the heavy curtain drawn across the narrow room. A stack of white boxes was on the floor and mail crates overflowed with envelopes. The Institute had been abandoned in a hurry.

The curtain that separated Patricia's and Alessandra's tables had been pushed aside. Cyn felt the room spin, confusion swirling beneath her. The truth was lurking just beneath the surface.

There are more tables back there.

"Why are we here?" Cyn muttered.

"Because I and others made a mess, child, but there's a young man that's going to fix all of it. He's going to balance the scales."

Cyn grabbed Danny's arm.

"I'm not talking about your boyfriend," Barb said.

Danny began spouting questions and tried to let go, but she wouldn't let him. He'd been patient with her talking to an empty room, but panic was setting in. The crazy train was at full throttle.

"Reed sent the letters," Barb said.

"Reed?"

Danny yanked her off balance. "What the hell is going on?"

She stilled him with a look, but it wouldn't last for long.

"Why send letters?"

"So *they* wouldn't see," Barb said.

"*They*...who are *they*?"

"Reed sent Danny to find you, child. There's a connection between you two, something that calms your minds, has something to do with your shared experiences, I don't know how. All I know is that when you were together, I was pushed deep in your subconscious. And Reed was waiting for me."

"You saw him?"

"I saw the truth."

She looked down, her expression sagging, her shoulders slumping. An emotional weight had been slung over her like a blanket of chains. *Was that guilt?*

"I am no longer blind to my blindness, child. I know what I've done, and what I need to do to balance the scales."

Barb looked up and half smiled.

Cyn hadn't noticed that Danny let go. She stood alone facing Barb. He went to the stack of boxes and began digging through the mail crate.

"What's back there?" Cyn asked.

"I think you know." She glanced at the heavy, plastic curtain. "I think you've always known."

"Reed showed me the folly of our situation, you and I. Even if I managed to possess your body and stuffed you into the dark subconscious, our fight would continue. One of us has to go." Barb held out her hands. "And it's your body, child."

"So you're leaving?"

Barb smiled.

"Where?"

"To visit some old friends."

This didn't make her feel better. She had the sense that Barb was going to haunt someone else's mind, that leaving only meant she would no longer be inside Cyn. After all, her cancer-ridden body was gone.

She had nowhere to go.

And she wasn't keen on dying.

"I don't understand."

"It's all very complicated, child." Barb slipped her hand into Patricia's curled fingers. "You'll understand once you pull the curtain."

The boxes crashed. Danny stood in a mess of papers and large beige envelopes. Cyn trembled and wished he was next to her. The truth felt like a monster.

"If you don't want to know the truth, that's up to you. You'll be lost until you do. But that wouldn't be fair to Danny, now would it?"

"Fair?"

Her smile faded. Who was she to speak of fairness, the old woman that refused to die? But Barb's face was so heavy, her eyes slumped with guilt. A thief was no judge of fairness. Barb continued holding onto Patricia, and reached out her free hand and wiggled her painted fingernails for Cyn to take it.

"I'm sorry, Cynthia. This wasn't your fault."

Hesitantly, Cyn began to reach out but stopped. It could be a trick, all of this a bigger plan to throw her into Patricia's mind. Or Alessandra's.

"You didn't deserve this," Barb said.

Sadness stirred in Cyn's chest. To take her hand was to risk it all.

To fall again.

Barb let go of Patricia and offered both her hands.

"You won't hurt me?" Cyn's voice sounded as childish as the words, a little girl afraid of what an adult would do to her again. She hated the mist filling her eyes.

"You've hurt yourself enough."

Cyn finally slid her fingers into Barb's palm. Jewelry jingled.

Just like that, her hands were empty. No grand explosion, no insights of truth or fireworks. Barb just disappeared.

And the weight that held her down all these years had been lifted. She threw her arms around Danny and began to weep.

Alone, at last.

170

THE INSTITUTE OF TECHNOLOGICAL RESEARCH, *New York City*

She collapsed like a windless sail.

Cyn had been speaking to herself, arguing with her imagination and pausing to listen. Danny let it play out, afraid an interruption would kick the legs of her sanity. She had been so stable since leaving the wilderness, so confident and powerful. But her sanity was a slippery slope. All he could do was watch her slide.

Lilac overwhelmed the medicinal scents and animals in the next room. It made no sense.

He tried to peel off her dead weight. He couldn't hold her up anymore. His knees were getting weak and the floor was spinning. He locked his knees and leaned against the door. The walls jittered, but the tables never seemed to move. He gulped at the thinning air.

"Breathe, Danny."

He focused on her face, expecting to see the haunted emptiness of a broken soul. Instead, the unblinking confidence was back. Her eyes, still puffy and red, cheeks slick with tears, were relaxed; the pupils large and calming.

The room flickered.

Sometimes it would turn then stop. Occasionally, an overlay of the same room was slightly askew. That's how Santiago sometimes felt, like a projection, an illusion.

A mask.

"What the hell is happening?" he asked.

"Foreverland messed me up, Danny."

"It messed us all up."

"My demon was different than yours."

Danny abruptly grabbed the table, his fingers accidently brushing against Patricia's arm, the skin like brittle paper. *My demons are different than yours, but we all have them, just the same.*

They were surrounded by beige envelopes with preprinted labels. He was holding one in a fist. He'd seen it from across the room when Cyn was ranting. It was beige, also. But there was no preprinted label.

Large green letters.

"What is it?" Cyn asked.

He held it up to the bright light. *Danny Boy, Cyn and Alessandra.*

It was addressed to all three of them, as if waiting for them to arrive. This entire experience—the traffic lights turning green, the empty Institute, the man in the lab coat waiting for them—was warped.

But nothing had made sense since that first letter arrived.

He slid his thumb under the flap. Three discs fell out. They were the same discs as before—weighty and perforated. The edges were different colors. There was the blue one and yellow like before.

The third disc was forest green, the exact shade of Alessandra's gown.

"Three discs," he muttered. "Three discs."

"What do they mean?"

He shook his head. He never figured it out. And now three of them had been mailed to the Institute. *What does he want us to see?*

A tremor inside him, a fault line breaking loose a current of fear. They were in danger. "Cyn," he stammered, "I think we should go..."

"We can't."

He could feel her pulse in his hand, could feel her chest rise and fall

like the long easy strokes of the ocean. She looked at the heavy plastic
curtain.

"Why?"

"We have to look."

"We can come back." He held the discs up. "I need some time to
think."

"It's why he sent us."

"Who?"

"Reed."

"When did you..."

The tremor returned. This time he felt it below his feet, not inside
his chest. The building shook like something very large fell on Fifth
Avenue. *Was she talking to Reed?*

"What's back there?" he asked.

"We have to look."

"You know, tell me."

"I don't know."

But she did, she knew what was back there. Some part of Danny
knew, too. He knew the truth was back there. That's why Reed sent
them here. He didn't want to know the truth; it would be too much.
He also knew that if they didn't look, if they didn't know, they would
continue searching for it.

And it's right there.

Another tremor rattled items on the wall.

"It has to be now." Cyn reached out. "Because only now exists."

He took her hand.

Cyn clutched the curtain. She waited with her knuckles white, the
heavy plastic bunched in her hand. Danny placed his hand over hers.
Together, they pulled it aside.

The rings slid in the metal track.

Two more tables.

171

SOMEWHERE OUTSIDE PHILADELPHIA

Tyler!

The old man snapped upright.

He had fallen asleep in the transport van. The straight-back seats were rigid, but he hadn't slept in days. Exhaustion ran him down within an hour of leaving the Colorado penitentiary.

He wiped the spittle from his chin, using both hands since they were bound with plastic ties.

His head roared. *The voices*.

Someone had shouted his name above the fray.

Gramm was across from Tyler, his head leaning against the wall separating them from the drivers. His eyes were closed, lips parted.

Tyler heard a voice, though. A familiar voice.

He sat upright, his backbone rigid, and closed his eyes. He took a deep breath and, like Gramm had taught him during the days before the transport van arrived, reached out to find an Internet connection he could ride through the ethers to find Patricia. They were just outside Philadelphia. The voices wreaked havoc on his concentration.

The static roared.

A small wave of panic tossed him head over heels, like a surfer crashing through the undercurrent.

TYLER!

"Take the next exit!" Tyler slammed his fists on the wire-mesh window. "The next exit!"

Gramm jumped. "What's wrong?"

Tyler squatted in front of the window. He had agreed to the transfer orders that would take him to Attica, agreed to be shackled like any other prisoner in case they were inspected. All the papers were in order, nothing would stop them from getting close enough that he could make a detour into New York City.

He would lay his body in the Institute and, when the time was right, exit it for good.

"What's wrong?" Gramm asked again.

Tyler braced himself on the seat as the van took the exit. He locked eyes with Gramm. Their biomites synchronized, their thoughts mingled like salt in the ocean.

It was Samuel's voice.

Tyler never felt the transport van pull into the rest stop, didn't feel it jerk to a stop. He didn't bother releasing the driver's mind from his control. As a result, the driver sat like a mannequin. The authorities would eventually find him sitting in a puddle of piss, with his stiff hands on the steering wheel.

Tyler lay on the bench, eyes closed.

He pined for the quick slip of the needle, the direct pipeline to his beloved. But Gramm was there. He was already an expert at navigating the wireless connections. He carved through the cloud of voices like a missile guiding him through black cyberspace to find Patricia.

She was still in her own Foreverland, waiting for Tyler.

When he arrived at her side, she frowned.

Something was wrong.

172

The air had become gritty. It scratched Alex's throat.

Somewhere, sirens were singing.

She felt warm, felt full. She was almost asleep when the voices returned.

Hundreds of them.

Someone carried her through the white noise that stuck to her throat, crashed in her lungs. It was the breath of the universe.

I am the universe.

And that thought gave her comfort.

She was everything and wanted nothing more.

Just to sleep.

In bliss.

I love.

Perhaps it would have all ended there, she would've gone to sleep forever had the visions not come. She hadn't even realized that her senses were gone, that sight, smell, touch and sound had been replaced with the endless field of static, this amniotic world of voices.

It started with antiseptic—a distinct flavor of evergreen pine that clung to her tongue and sinuses beneath the ever-present smell of lilac. It reminded her of something, of somewhere.

There were halls. Long white halls.

Hard floors and open doors.

Wet fur.

The Institute.

Her eyes snapped opened. The white static evaporated in the present moment where two people, one on each side, held her hands.

A boy.

A girl.

They led her through the animal lab, past Coco splayed on the center table to the door on the other side, the door she had seen once before...

Pressure hardened between her eyes, in the center of her forehead. Pressure that condensed and hardened like a collapsing star.

The door opened.

She saw the table.

She saw the very old woman, saw the needle.

But on the other table.

The other table.

She saw.

The pressure burst between her eyes, filled the universe with scorching light, radiated pain to the hundreds of voices that cried out, that shrank into silence. The explosion released memories.

She knew everything there was to know. She knew the truth.

Alessandra was awakened.

Times Square.

Lights sparkled. The streets empty.

The buildings punched the gray sky.

Rain fell like heavy drops of mercury, snapping on the asphalt, pressing her shirt against her skin; rivulets raced down her face, dripping from her nose, tasting warm.

Salty.

The giant screens that advertised Broadway shows were blank, overlooking the heavy rain that filled the street, raced down the gutters. Trash drained into the storm sewers.

Thunder rumbled.

The screens came to life, flickering like lightning.

Images flashed in a blur of colors. She stood in the middle of the empty street, rain pouring down, watching the images slow like a roulette wheel. They weren't advertisements for Kodak or Virgin Records or a Broadway show.

They were memories.

Memorial Day. She was six. They were in the park, having a picnic. She was flying a kite with her cousins, holding the string as the plastic wings rattled in the wind, climbing into the sky. She was sucking on a Popsicle stick, watching her parents argue.

Watching her dad leave.

Drive away.

Forever.

Graduation day. She finished college at the top of her class, gave the honorary speech, and received offers from a dozen companies, one of which she accepted.

The Washington Post. *Where she met Samuel. He was short and stout, prematurely balding. Smart and funny. They married two years later.*

Lightning shredded the sky.

Samuel doesn't look like that.

They got married at Martha's Vineyard. They were career-minded, ready to change the world. They lived in Washington, DC. She covered politics for the paper. He was a lawyer.

But Samuel doesn't look like...

Alex worked ten years for *The Washington Post.* Samuel took a job in New York and they moved again. Alex continued investigative reporting. She wrote books, toured the country.

She got pregnant.

But Samuel...

They hadn't planned it, but things happen. Her career had always come first, but the pregnancy changed her.

Pregnant?

She never wanted to be a mother. She had seen too many bad things to bring a child into this world. But when she gave birth, everything changed.

Her world suddenly had meaning.

Rain gushed into the sewers. The heavens opened and dropped rain like a bucket, obscuring the birth of her little boy. He had a name. They were holding him.

Smiling and holding him.

Her little boy had a name.

He had a name.

Lucas.

A shiver ran down her back, kicked her legs. She fell on the dashed crosswalk, punched in the gut. Lightning splashed the gray sky that engulfed the skyscrapers, temporarily blinding her.

A solitary car was coming down the road.

The blurred headlights moved slowly down the side of the road, the reflection stretching over the asphalt. A streetlight turned red. The car stopped.

Alex stood.

Blood was smeared on her knees. Her hands.

Her leg began throbbing. She'd only fallen on her knees, but her whole body suddenly ached. She looked up; the car was still waiting on the light.

All alone.

You need to move, she thought. *Move!*

Despite the empty roads, panic gripped her. She wasn't thinking of herself. The car had to move. *It has to move!* She sprinted with her hand out, her bare feet slapping the pavement. On the screens, the memory reels displayed the present moment.

The car's at a stoplight.

She didn't watch the images, because she already knew.

The stoplight turns green.

She remembered.

The car eases into the intersection.

"No," she cried.

A truck blew through the red light; its front bumper crushed the driver's side door. Glass shattered.

The car spun away from the delivery truck.

The radiator hiss cut through the crashing rain. Steam poured from the grill. Fluid dripped to the pavement; glass scattered like ice chips.

The headlights askew, one working.

Samuel was trapped, the steering wheel wedged deep into his belly. There was blood on his bald scalp, his eyes blank.

Alex put her hand to her mouth and tried to stop the tears.

She tried to open the door, but the handle had been sheared away. She reached through the window and grabbed her husband's shirt, muttering his name as if she could wake him up because this couldn't be happening.

Because she forgot this was a memory.

It was happening again.

So consumed by Samuel—broken ribs poking through the shirt, the empty eyes—that she'd forgotten about the backseat.

Until she saw a yellow dump truck.

And a small shoe.

She backed away from the car and closed her eyes.

Lightning struck one of the buildings. She was on the ground. She'd fallen. Her legs too weak to stand, she pulled herself up the steel carnage to see into the backseat.

To see the little body.

"No."

Lightning struck again. It filled her with rage. The memory had settled in place. She remembered now. Remembered leaving the Institute, remembered it was Samuel that picked her up with Lucas in the backseat. They'd gone to the museum while she was touring the facilities. They were going to drive around and wait for her so they didn't have to park.

Coco opened her eyes.

She'd gone to the doctor, but the accident wasn't a hallucination.

"No. No, no, no, NO, NO, NO!"

Lightning. Thunder.

The creak of metal, the tinkle of glass.

She tore the back door off its hinges, flung it like a plastic toy, pulled her son from the backseat.

His body so small, so fragile.

The rain washed the hair from his eyes.

She cradled him while tears flowed. And the rain fell harder, muting her sobs, her cries. Her anguish.

The screens were blank.

She cried for the loss of her son and husband, but more than that, she wept for forgetting them. How could she let this happen? How could she go on with her life without their memory?

How could I forget his name?

The screens flickered and began to play forgotten memories. They played out what had happened after the accident, how she had survived, had gone home, how her parents cared for her, brought food to her bed, took her to physical therapy, moved into the house. Did everything a parent would do for their child.

But Alex couldn't carry the pain and loss. Life no longer had meaning and she wanted out. She wanted everything to go away.

The Ballards did that for her.

She'd gone back to the Institute and never left.

The images on the screens proved it: Alex on the table, a needle in her head.

Her past rewritten. The accident erased.

Too risky to ever remember having a child. She loved him too much. It was best to forget him. They erased it all.

Entirely.

Forever.

How could I?

The rain continued. She wouldn't let it stop.

Alex curled over Lucas's body until her back ached, her knees throbbed. Her eyes swelled. Her grief had no sense of time. Her tears flowed for eternity.

Shallow rivers coursed down the gutters, falling below the street. The city was still empty, cars parked at the curb. The accident was still in the intersection, the engine no longer steaming.

"It doesn't have to be this way." The screens were filled with faces. An older woman, her hair gracefully gray, cheeks rosy and plump and dented with a comforting smile. "Those are just memories." Her voice echoed down the empty street. "Thoughts."

"You're so much more than memories." It was an older man—handsome, genteel, hair graying like the woman. He looked so familiar. "You are much more than any man, woman or child. You've given birth to a universe, Alessandra."

"You are a goddess," the old woman added.

"We chose you because you are a strong woman that loves deeply; a woman with the potential to create new worlds, give rise to a home for millions of souls where suffering no longer exists."

Alex squeezed her son. He was so cold, so still. "Why did I forget?"

"He's not dead," the old woman whispered. "In your new world, he lives. Love, Alessandra. You are so filled with love. Even now, you can feel it swelling inside you. The memory of your pain only serves to hide that love. Put down your suffering, Alessandra. And be your love."

Thunder rumbled in the distance.

"This is your Foreverland, where anything can exist," the old man said. "Only you can bring heaven to earth. You, Alessandra. Only you."

Alex couldn't let him go. She would never put him down; she would hold him in her arms until her life ended. She would never forget him again.

"Don't end your life over a memory," the old man whispered. "You *are* Foreverland."

They weren't here; she could feel it. They were in another world. That's why they were on the screens—they were projections.

They did this to me.

They were the ones that put the needle in her head, rewrote her memories, made her life perfect. They were the Ballards. She hardly recognized the younger versions of their elderly selves. She was seeing their idealized forms. They wanted her to be here.

They erased Lucas.

And they needed her.

I am Foreverland.

She was the buildings, the pavement, the rain. When she was sad, it rained. When she was happy, it was sunny. The sky above, the air she breathed, the food she swallowed...*this is all me.*

But something was out there, something above the sky, far beyond the atmosphere. The noise was out there. The static.

The voices.

She had heard them ever since she woke up in this Foreverland, but now she could feel them. Out there—where the voices were calling from—that was where true suffering existed.

But this is my lilac world.

"Yes," Patricia said. "You are this world, Alessandra. You are the Foreverland no one could be. You have given rise to all of this; it is you that has sacrificed so much for so many. Even your son, your only son, will find life again in your world. He will live again."

There was nothing she could do to save them. She couldn't bring them back, not on earth. But here, where she was a goddess, where she, Alessandra, was the universe, where it would be her laws that physics obeyed. It would be her will that determined reality.

She could bring them back, will them into existence.

"Yes." Patricia's face loomed larger. "No more sadness."

"No more suffering," Tyler said.

"Only love."

"Love."

"If you sleep," Patricia said. "Sleep and give your love to the world."

Alessandra began to rock her boy. His face so perfect, so peaceful. She sang to him, promised she wouldn't let anything hurt him, ever again. If she had to sleep, she would sleep for him.

"Mama's here," she whispered. "Mama's here."

Her eyes grew heavy.

The weight began to lift from her. Lightness filled her heart. The gray sky parted. A beam of light fell on her like she was the only thing in the world that existed.

Because I am the world.

"Mama's here."

She would sleep for her son, for her husband. For the world.

A shadow fell over her.

Two strong hands gripped her shoulders. They coaxed her to stand and lifted her to her feet. The old man and old woman raged, their voices echoing throughout the city.

Alessandra wanted to sleep, wanted to take away the world's suffering, to soothe her baby boy. But she let the hands pick her up and put her on her feet. They held her upright and shook her until her eyelids —her impossibly heavy eyelids—became slits.

The voices grew louder.

"Wake up." A woman held her steady, jewelry jingling on her wrists.

Lips painted bright red.

173

NEW YORK CITY

Tyler paced around the rooftop pool and splashed frigid water on his face until his shirt was soaked. He kneeled on the concrete deck. Water dripped from his nose, shattering his reflection in the pool.

It's over. Just like that.

A lifetime of work had come undone in a matter of hours. Was it Reed? Was he that far ahead of them?

He wanted us to see it.

It wasn't enough to destroy everything, he wanted them to see it unravel. Tyler and Patricia peered like voyeurs into Alessandra's world from the safety of Patricia's Foreverland. They watched her walk down the street, watched her memories come to life. They watched her wake up. She was going back to sleep, this time willingly. She would give herself to Foreverland, for her boy, for her husband.

And then Barb arrived.

"How the hell did she get there?" he said.

"It's over," Patricia said.

"I want to know how the hell she got there!"

"Don't raise your voice to me."

"One of your Investors, Patricia, waltzed into Alessandra's Foreverland like a goddamn revolving door!"

"Isn't it obvious? She was sent to wake her."

"I want to know how she separated herself from Cynthia!"

He ripped the sodden shirt from his chest and slammed it into the pool. It floated like a dead body.

How could Barb separate herself from Cynthia? And why? Barb shared that body; why would she leave it? It didn't make sense. At the very least, she should be helping the Ballards, not tearing down a lifetime of work. She would know the potential of Foreverland, would know that she could be immortal. It's why she went out to the wilderness in the first place, why she kidnapped Cynthia. If Alessandra went to sleep, Barb could have anything she wanted.

So why is she there?

On his hands and knees, he stared at his rippling reflection—the younger version of Tyler stared back. "Why?" he said. "Why is she helping him?"

Patricia shook her head. She didn't know. Didn't care. *Did it matter?*

She turned her back on him and went to the rooftop's ledge. The folds of her angelic dress fluttered. She laced her hands and sighed. Deflated of hope, she overlooked the traffic in the streets below, all the simulated people rushing to nonexistent jobs, to meaningless families.

They were alone. But it was more than that.

On the horizon, just past the setting sun, the crinkle of the Nowhere, the limitation of Patricia's Foreverland, shimmered. In comparison to Alessandra, this was a shoebox.

Patricia was feeling the claustrophobia.

Even with Tyler, they would be alone.

He went to her and stood on the ledge. "It's not over," he said. "We can still intervene. We'll have to bridge into Alessandra and throw Barb into the Nowhere. It's not too late, but we have to do it now."

"We can't."

"I'm not going to let a lifetime of our work go away. A lifetime, Patricia! This is our dream. We owe it to humanity. We can't turn our backs—"

"We can't risk it!" She spun around, her heels hanging off the ledge. "We can't go inside her world, Tyler. We'll invoke her rage and never leave. She has to be asleep!"

"We can still manipulate her thoughts, change her memories..."

She shook her head. A smile crept over her face, one of joyless acceptance. "She knows what we've done. She won't forget this time."

"There's still time."

"We walk away. We start again."

His physical body was doing well. With the new infusion of biomites, he could continue another five or ten years. If he could find the special biomites that Gramm spoke of, it could be longer.

Where is Gramm?

But it wasn't his body that made starting over impossible. They abandoned the prison. Federal agents would be looking for him very soon. They would discover his ability to transport his awareness. They would change that, make sure he never connected with Foreverland again.

He would never see Patricia again.

They had to abandon their bodies, exist in Alessandra's Foreverland. Their bodies were just vehicles. Their identities, their souls, were free to roam.

Reed had done it. So can we.

The breeze rose up the side of the building, chilling his bare chest. Patricia closed her eyes and breathed it in. He did the same.

His hand found hers.

He couldn't be a god without his goddess, couldn't live without her breath. The Institute was funded to operate in secrecy for another hundred years. Patricia's body would survive. He would abandon his body in the back of the transport van and stay with her until they found a host.

If not Alessandra, then another.

He wrapped his arm around her waist, lifted her hand and swayed his hips into hers. Soft music came up on the portico, a tune from the year they were married.

He inhaled the essence that was Patricia.

She laid her cheek against his chest. He rested his chin and closed his eyes. They danced that way—slow, close and loving.

Let Alessandra's Foreverland burn. Let Reed have his victory. Let them all wake up and go about their lives.

Tyler and Patricia would dance.

They danced until the sun set and the city lights speckled the streets and buildings. The pool glowed blue. All was perfect, all was happy. They ignored Alessandra, let their lifetime of work fall apart and swayed in each other's arms. They could live this way for quite some time.

Nausea crept in.

Tyler felt it in his gut. A queasy sensation, like he was falling.

No, not falling.

About to.

Like he was leaning over the ledge, his balance tipped too far, committing him to the fall. It was that feeling, just before it began, that he felt tugging his stomach.

Patricia pulled away. She felt it, too.

Her eyes went wide. She was looking at the monitor they used to peer into Alessandra's Foreverland. It was still projecting Times Square. The city was falling apart. The street had cracked open, the buildings were crumbling like rock slides, cratering the asphalt and concrete in clouds of dust and debris.

Alessandra was still there. She stood in the crosswalk, the enormous monitors scattered around her. Barb was at her side. None of this surprised him; they were literally destroying Tyler and Patricia's work. Reed had likely wanted them to see Rome fall.

What bothered him were the others. They were on the sidewalk, the wreckage all around.

And they were nude.

Where the hell did they come from?

They were old men and women, and tried to cover themselves, looking around in confusion, unsure of how they got there and why. Tyler didn't know, either. But he recognized them.

The Investors.

It was all the Investors from the island and the wilderness, the old men and women that Harold and Patricia had dealt with. With the exception of Barb, they were completely naked. It was as if they were pulled into Alessandra's Foreverland against their will.

If she could pull them...

And like a fish on the line, the hook was set.

The pool, the rooftop, the city floor blurred past them.

Tyler and Patricia would never see her Foreverland again.

174

The Institute of Technological Research, New York City

Two tables, two bodies.

Danny clung to the plastic curtain, the eyeholes straining to rip through the metal clips.

"What does this mean?" Cyn muttered. "What does this mean, what does this mean, what does this mean..."

Danny's emaciated body was in a blue hospital gown, the cheek-bones sharp, the lips swollen and cracked. It was sunk in the table's cushion. The complexion was pasty beneath the bright lamp, the needle in his forehead gleamed.

Cyn's body was on the other table, dressed in a thin yellow gown. Like Danny's body, it was too skinny, the eye sockets deep, the cheeks sunken. She picked up the hand and touched the forehead where the needle protruded.

Thunder rattled the walls. The lights flickered.

Danny walked around the lab, far away from the body, near desks crowded with stacks of folders, computers, centrifuges, and other machines to the curtain on the other side. He threw it open, the metal hooks scraping along the ceiling rail.

Another table, another body.

Another curtain.

He pushed past it. Table after table, body after body, men and women in various states of atrophy, all dressed in plain white gowns, all surrounded by desks, notes and instruments. Some with needles, some without. The ones without needles were dead, the light above them turned off like a plant no longer needed to photosynthesize. Danny could see the last body in the dim darkness of death. It was in a vibrant red gown instead of white.

The kind of red that spilled life.

"What does this mean?" Cyn asked.

He looked at his hands and felt the room shift below his feet, the ground surging through his stomach like he'd fallen off an unexpected step.

"But I left the island," he said. "I left the island."

"What does this mean, Danny!"

The room jittered, the overlay of reality faltering, the dream shaking. He'd experienced this before, when he saw Santiago like that he knew. He just didn't want to remember, didn't want to see the truth.

And now the truth lay in front of him.

He knew where they were.

But how did I get here?

Danny shoved a pile of folders off a desk. Papers spilled across the floor. He kicked them across the room, then pulled a computer over and cleared the desk with his arm.

Who the hell am I?

He heaved a chair through a plastic curtain.

Are these even my memories?

Smashed a monitor with his heel, flung a plastic mail basket against the wall.

Did I ever live in Spain?

Rain pummeled the outside of the building.

He stood over his own body.

Sweat trickled down his cheeks. He put his finger and thumb

around the needle. This was a replicated reality. This was what Patricia did in the wilderness; when the girls woke up in a cabin, the surroundings looked just like the physical reality.

This was the Institute; this was New York City.

This is Foreverland.

The needle was firmly planted in the body's forehead. That meant his physical body was lying in the Institute—the knees bent, the fingers curled, the ribs protruding—while he was here, standing over the replication. He could pull the needle out, but that wouldn't matter.

"I left the island." His fingers quivered. "I left the island."

Cyn put her hand around his. He let her gently pull it away. Her lower lip quivered. She knew, too.

"You left the wilderness," Danny said. "How did we..."

He remembered escaping the island, remembered Spain, remembered his life in the villa. His memories couldn't be trusted, but he remembered coming to the Institute last spring.

So did Cyn.

"We never left the Institute," he said.

Cyn nodded.

"They're experimenting," he said blankly. "The animals and all the bodies, they're looking for a host."

"Where are we now?"

He shook his head. *If this is Foreverland, who's hosting it? Patricia? Alessandra? Coco?*

Another round of thunder shook the building.

"Where did Alessandra go?" Danny asked. "The person we brought here, she disappeared. Where did she go?"

Cyn swallowed spastically.

"Why did we bring her here?" He grabbed her shoulders. "Why?"

"I don't know."

"Who told you to bring her here?"

She was shaking her head, quivering all over. "I think it was Reed."

She was hiding something, but it made sense. The envelope was waiting for them. He wanted Danny and Cyn to see their bodies. *To shock us into knowing the truth?*

Then the same would be true for Alessandra. He wanted her to see her body, for her to see the truth. But why? So that she'd wake up?

Lilacs. He could still smell lilacs, but it wasn't nearly as intense, not like it was when Alessandra was near. *This whole world smells of lilacs.*

The lights flickered for several seconds. The ceiling had fractured, debris showering the room. A light coating fell across the tables.

"We should go," Cyn said.

Danny spread his hand over the blue gown covering his body. "Where?" he whispered. "Where do we go?"

Cyn's grip tightened on his arm.

She pulled him away, dragging him through the papers and overturned boxes, around the plastic curtain when the next tremor hit. They braced themselves against the wall. A box spilled from the nearest bench, spilling envelopes across the floor. They were all addressed with green ink.

Danny Boy, Cyn, and Alessandra.

Thirty envelopes, some with the flap open, shiny discs peeking out. A lined square of paper was stuck between them.

Danny picked it up and unfolded it.

Where one to another is three,
    In the dark there is now light to see.
    Climb not the mountain nor the ridge,
    But look inward, for you are the bridge.

"You are the bridge." Cyn read. No poem this time, just a statement. "That's what she told me, *you are the bridge.*"

"Who told you?"

"I don't...what's it mean?"

Danny stared until another tremor hit, this one mild compared to the others. *You are the bridge.*

That was different than *build a bridge,* but it didn't make any more sense. *How am I the bridge?*

It had something to do with the discs. He held one of them up to the overhead lamp that was still swinging. Thin filaments of light fired through the pinholes and drifting dust.

He shook his head. There was nothing different about these. They were the same weight with the same colors. His reflection was perfect, like polished steel; his eyes looked back through a galaxy of stars.

An oval of light raced over the ceiling. The disc's reflection danced on the dark ceiling. The outline was spotlight sharp, the tiny holes twinkled like stars. Danny held the discs side by side, beaming three spots on the ceiling. They were identical, the artistry and craftsmanship astounding, but told him nothing.

We're supposed to be here. He mailed those packages so we would get them when we arrived, after we saw the truth, once we knew where we were.

The next tremor hit.

"Come on." Cyn tugged at him. "Look at them later."

Now he says 'you are the bridge'.

He turned the reflections onto different parts of the wall, overlapping them in hopes that a symbol or words would appear. Cyn pulled more forcefully. The noises were getting louder, the building felt like it would come down any second. Foreverland or not, the pain of a collapsing skyscraper would be real.

He stepped away from the light and, at the last second, looked down instead of up. His shadow was sharply cast on the floor.

But the shadows of the discs were fragmented.

The light didn't pass straight through the holes because the holes were drilled at slight angles. As a result, the shadow was hazy. Instead of three sharp circular shadows, each disc cast a fuzzy shadow.

The floor lurched. The lights bounced on their cords. Cyn fell down. Danny hit the table and dropped one of the discs on the blue gown of his body.

"Danny!"

It was the exact color of the gown. And Cyn's body was wearing a yellow gown.

The same yellow on the disc.

He didn't need to compare the third one to the gown on Alex's body. They were both green.

Three discs. Three matching colors.

Where one to another is three, in the dark there is now light to see.

The walls didn't stop shaking. Large objects toppled in the dark end of the room; framed pictures slid off the walls. Cyn pulled him past Alex, past Patricia before he stopped. Her shouting was blotted out by another cataclysmic crash, this one knocking out the power.

"I need a light!"

"We have to get out!" she answered.

They went left to feel their way back through the animal room, past Coco and down the hall. Just as they reached the lobby, a generator kicked on. Emergency light shined from the ceiling.

Danny fumbled with the discs. He knelt on the floor—grit grinding into his knees—and stacked them on top of each other. The weak magnetic forces snapped them in place.

Cyn yanked him to his feet.

They lost their footing as the foundation cracked. Danny leaned against the wall, turning the discs until the holes lined up, and held them to the emergency light.

He looked down.

There's no shadow!

There was the shadow of his hand, but the space between his fingers and thumb was empty. The refracted light obliterated the shadow, as if the discs had disappeared.

Climb not the mountain nor the ridge.

The discs looked like galaxies, maps of the universe. But when lined up, they refracted light to leave no trace of a shadow, as if they didn't exist.

For you are the bridge.

"Danny!"

The front door was askew, the glass shattered. Danny kicked through it and ran as the building buckled and moaned.

The street was a war zone.

The buildings had fallen like metal boulders. I-beams poked out of the rubble like crooked fingers; craters pocked the uneven road. The pavement was still wet, but raindrops were rising off it like dewy drops of condensation, floating skyward like rain falling in the wrong direction.

They ran down the street wherever they could find an opening. A building fell behind them, the quake throwing them to the ground, a cloud of dust engulfing them. He was coughing on his hands and knees when Cyn dragged him to his feet.

A block later, they emerged from the cloud.

She pulled him down Seventh Avenue. The destruction seemed to be less frequent in that direction.

The sky was collapsing, but only faint wisps of smoke circled the crumbling skyscrapers. Above the clouds was a grinding white pall. It sounded like a mass of metallic insects, a roiling cloud of static that was deafening, that vibrated in their chests.

Danny knew what it was. He'd seen it before. So had Cyn.

The Nowhere is coming.

Something shattered.

Monitors were crashing in a heap of glittering glass and smoke. Times Square was coated with a thin layer of ash that fluttered like snowflakes. The ensuing sound of destruction was quickly swallowed by the grinding buzz.

The sky had morphed into a gray, gritty texture. It wasn't anything from this world; it was the absence of everything, a void in the fabric of existence. The closer it got, the more the sound transformed. It wasn't static or the buzz of some otherworldly insects that filled his head and hammered his chest.

Voices.

The last monitor fell, but the road through Broadway was mostly clear.

The discs were vibrating.

Something was missing, he hadn't unlocked the mystery. But he was close. A bridge connected two points of land, usually over a body of water or a chasm or steep drop.

Climb not the mountain nor the ridge.

A bridge allowed someone to go from one island to the next.

But look inward.

In other words, from one land to the next.

For you are the bridge.

"Cyn!"

She was running toward Times Square, ashy puffs splashing with each step.

Danny barely heard himself. His voice was absorbed by the great homogenous hum that cast a dull glow over the broken street and swirling dust.

A single beam of light cut through the falling ash and smoke, high-lighting someone in the center of Broadway—severed marquees hung from the walls, streetlights bent, scaffolding scattered like broken toys. It was a dystopian Christmas.

Alessandra.

Her head was back, arms out. The sky was falling and the city collapsing, but the chaos didn't touch her. The closer they got, the stronger the scent of lilac.

She's the air we breathe, the ground we walk. And she's destroying it.

Now there is light to see.

But Alessandra wasn't alone. There were others huddled beneath the remnants of awnings and crooked doorways. And they were nude, not a pair of socks or a shirt among them. Ash settled on their shoulders and hung from their frayed hair.

Old, wrinkled, and saggy, they clung to each other. Some appeared to be shouting, but most were wide-eyed and frightened. He recognized one of them. His hair was the color of black that only came from a bottle.

Mr. Smith. Danny stopped running. *The Investors.*

These were the perpetrators, the thieves, the old men and women that refused to die. They were the ones that threw them into the Nowhere.

The Nowhere that now hovered over them with a menacing boil.

Somehow, Alessandra brought them here.

"Cyn!"

Someone intercepted her—an old woman, the only one clothed, grabbed her before Cyn reached Alessandra. She wrapped both arms around her and dragged her down, jewelry sparkling on her wrists.

Cyn struggled to get away.

Danny twisted the discs to keep the holes lined up as he ran. The vibrations quickly numbed his fingers. Alessandra wasn't standing in a beam of light.

She is the light.

Her light beamed through the discs' tiny holes like infinitesimal wires. With each turn they began to line up. With each turn, the wire of light became less intense. The circular shadow cast across his stomach became more opaque.

And then vanished.

The discs were aligned—blue, yellow and green. All three solid objects left no trace in the presence of light.

They didn't need to find a bridge, didn't need to build a bridge. The last package was addressed to all three of them. Danny misinterpreted the message—it wasn't *you* are the bridge.

We are the bridge.

175

Foreverland

Monster.

They sought to create a new Foreverland, one for every living soul. Instead, they created a monster.

A black hole.

Alessandra could've ended their lives like meaningless ants. Instead, she bridged into Patricia's Foreverland and yanked them into her world, put them on the curb to watch the annihilation of Foreverland.

They thought they were safe. No one could bridge Foreverlands like that. *No one is like Alessandra.*

One moment, Tyler was standing next to the pool, dancing with his wife, and the next he was without clothes, shivering on the sidewalk, gravel digging into the soles of his feet, old age aching in his hunched spine.

What have we done?

It was hard to breathe, the air hot and gritty, thick with floral essence that coated his lungs. It was snowing, the remnants of a distant volcano drifting down from a gray sky.

The noise was worse. He didn't hear the pillar slam into the street, didn't hear the cracking asphalt. It was lost in the pervasive buzz, the sound of static that drowned everything, that scratched his ears, his eyes. The buzz drove a ticklish fever beneath his wrinkled, spotted skin.

Tyler put his arm around Patricia and attempted to cover her nudity. Alessandra could strip him of his dignity, but not his wife.

Not like this.

She hid her face. Her hair had thinned and grayed, her flesh hung from her shoulders. She aged the moment she was pulled from her world, no longer graceful. No longer angelic. She was a dried husk of a human being.

And the noise grew louder.

It was a jackhammer inside his teeth, picking at his organs and chiseling apart his joints. It shook loose his bladder. Urine ran down his legs.

There were others.

One by one, they fell out of the sky and landed with bone-breaking force—men and women just as nude, just as old. They emerged from a cloud of gray fluff, uninjured, and covered their ears.

Their shock was all too apparent.

They struggled to breathe the thick air, attempted to speak. Eventually, they backed away from the beam of light. Alessandra glowed like an angel.

Destroyed like a demon.

Patricia covered her mouth. Tyler felt her breath on his shoulder, her words against his ear. He couldn't understand her, but knew what she was saying. She recognized them, too.

The Investors.

These were the men and women that funded Foreverland. They were the ones that went out to the island, the ones that lived in the wilderness. They had moved into younger bodies, yet they were here.

They were old again.

Did she pull them out of their stolen bodies, just reach into the physical world and snatch them up like she'd done to us?

The biomites, of course.

The Investors had likely been seeded with biomites that allowed them to network with other biomites. Just like Tyler. Alessandra was reaching across all networks and grabbing their true identities.

Tyler could feel Patricia's tears against his arm. He moved to shield her from the others as they continued to fall. A puddle formed around his feet. Patricia's bladder let loose.

Don't do this to Patricia. She's given so much.

Alessandra could take Tyler, do what she wanted: embarrass him, ridicule him, march him naked in front of the entire world. He deserved it. But not Patricia. She was too loving.

Too good.

Tyler stepped off the curb and shook his fist to get Alessandra's attention. An invisible force pushed him back. His words were crushed in the heightened grind of static. He fell back, struggling to breathe. All he could do was mutter a prayer that never made it past his fluttering lips.

God, help us.

But their goddess wasn't listening.

All he could do was hold his wife. If it was the last thing he could do, he would hold her, protect her from the falling sky until the vibrations reached his bones.

The beam of light intensified.

Tyler shielded his eyes. Alessandra was a bleached, blurry figure. Barb was out there. Somehow that guilty bitch escaped the goddess's wrath. She stopped Cynthia from reaching Alessandra.

Reed sent her. She showed Alessandra the extent of her omnipotence. She should be on the curb.

The buildings no longer crumbled, but the blizzard of ash continued. The dark sky closed on them.

The hair on his arms stood up.

The grind of static popped his ears like hot needles. The old men and women covered their ears, mouths agape in agony. In silence, they screamed.

The static was inside him now. He felt it grind the inside of his body. His eyes filled with tears.

He looked up.

Please no formed on his lips.

In his liquefying bones, he heard the true nature of the tortuous sound. It wasn't static after all.

Voices.

Hundreds of scared and lonely voices, scattered like dust. They were coming for them.

We threw them out there.

Those were the voices he heard when he woke from the stroke, when Gramm saved his life.

Where are you, Gramm?

Alessandra wasn't just ending her world. She was making them pay for it. And the sins that built it.

The shadow collapsed around them.

The buildings disappeared.

The road.

Ashes filled the world.

Only a shaft of light remained, Alessandra a blurred vision.

Tyler whispered a plea that would never become more than a thought.

I love you, he whispered and wrapped his arms around his wife as the voices exploded like a sandstorm inside him.

His body went fuzzy.

The air corroded his lungs and softened his flesh.

He pulled Patricia closer and felt his arms merge into her as if she were dissolving.

Their molecules were letting go, spreading out.

Her heart beat into his chest. Her screams, silent.

With the last movement of his mind, the last thought that would ever be experienced by the human being known as Tyler Ballard was formed. It was a realization.

He saw the real monsters.

They burst into subatomic particles, the fabric of their minds stretched across the universe. The agony was unforgiveable.

This is the Nowhere.

176

Foreverland

Alex pulled down the Nowhere.

Barb had calmed her, got her to breathe, to feel just how big this world had become.

How big *she* had become.

This was all a product of her mind—these buildings and streets, the sky and clouds and insects crawling along the sidewalks. The realization was overwhelming, but Barb was there to guide her through it, to help her see the truth, that this reality—what Alex had become—was not solely the product of her mind.

They used children to build it.

And Barb was one of the guilty ones.

"I know." Barb closed her eyes and nodded. She was aware of what she'd done. That's why she was there. *To balance the scales.*

"I was an Investor," she said. "There are more like me."

The Investors lived in these younger, stolen bodies. In today's era of biotechnology, they all had biomites.

"And biomites interconnect minds."

Alex could network through biomites. And that's what she did. She created connections, starting with the Ballards. She found them in Patricia's Foreverland, a tiny universe in the ethers of existence. Having already established a connection, they were easy. The others took some time, but like an electromagnetic claw, she found them in the physical world and pulled them from their thieved bodies.

She brought them into Foreverland.

The Investors witnessed their true forms and were forced to see each other for what they were: naked, ugly and alone.

Alex closed her eyes and lifted her face to the sun.

It was not the sun that beamed down. She was the sun, the source of light, the center of this reality. She was a star that willingly collapsed like a black hole.

The warmth cleansed her of anguish, shed the sorrow and the pain. Her sadness transformed into acceptance.

And the rain rose off the ground and the ash fell.

The buzz of the Nowhere raged like a lumber mill, the voices becoming clearer. *The children...the children were fed to the Nowhere to build this. To support me.*

"Shhhhhh," Barb said, soothing the voices in the Nowhere. "Soon. Your suffering ends soon."

Alex drew the life force into a beam of light.

She let go of the guilt, the shame and sorrow. She let go of her past.

She looked out at the Investors, naked and alone in the shattered world. They were dim forms, vague figures lost in the blizzard of the approaching Nowhere. Their cries were endless and silent. Their anguish as deep as the Nowhere.

The Nowhere pulled them, cell by cell, into its entropic void. They fed the insatiable hunger with their being. Even Barb.

And the voices stopped, the ashes gracefully drifting to the ground until all was quiet, all was still.

The children hushed.

She didn't know where the children went, how they escaped or how the Investors took their place.

The scales were balanced.

177

Foreverland

The Nowhere hummed at Danny's heels, ate through his ears and burned in his chest. The asphalt, once unforgiving, now softened beneath his steps like melting clay. Amidst the charred wreckage, the smell of lilac could not be stronger, as if the buildings were built of it.

He clutched the discs.

Alessandra was pure light, only a faint outline still visible. Barb had thrown Cyn to the ground. Hardly visible through the thickening ash, they rolled in puffs of dusty gray until they were coated. Barb saw him coming and yanked her to her feet. Cyn's hair stood out like fire. An aura encircled her as he neared.

The city had been swallowed.

The light burned Danny's eyes. He shielded his face, the discs glowing. Barb let go just as he grabbed Cyn's hand. The road turned to quicksand, eating their steps as they charged the beam of light.

Their fingers snapped together.

The Nowhere closed around them; the voices ate the ground, the air, the inside of their bones.

He didn't feel his last step as they reached for the light, lunged with all their weight and collided with Alessandra—

No sight, no sound.

Not even the ring of silence.

Nothingness.

SPRING (AGAIN)

Death is a doorway.
   To exit.
   To enter.

178

THE OFFICE WAS SILENT.

Distant vibrations and damp, cool air were reminders of the subterranean laboratory. Production never stopped. There was always a need, always a want. As long as people could pay the price, they would.

They did.

Jonathan sat back in the chair. He focused on his breathing, harnessed his attention, brought his awareness to the right here and now.

The door opened.

Julie and others walked into the spacious office. Outside those doors, the warehouse was silent. Jonathan bolted upright. No one took a seat. He looked from face to face, searching for an answer. He'd given everything for this moment.

"We're ready," Julie said. "They're dressed."

Jonathan could hardly feel his legs.

The team of technicians was all present, all twenty-seven of them from different parts of the world, all sworn to secrecy, to operate in anonymity. They were compensated handsomely.

They walked into the warehouse.

A few words were said by the team leaders, this being the largest and most ambitious project of its kind. One of them held an object about the size of a cell *phone. Julie handed it to Jonathan. His hand was shaking. She wrapped her fingers around his hand.*

"You do the honors, Jonathan."

A single icon shone beneath the glass. He put his thumb on it and looked around. On eyes on him. Two hundred and four latches simultaneously thrummed. The doors released.

Movement stirred.

Jonathan didn't feel Julie take the control from him. He didn't see the team spread out and watch the doors, one by one, slowly open. No one moved, everyone waited, collectively holding their breath.

The warehouse grew quiet again.

Water dripped.

And then the first door swung open. A pair of large eyes peeked out. A child, a girl about the age of twelve, blonde hair damp and matted, stepped out.

179

Foreverland

There was sky.

Danny didn't recognize it as sky. He was on his back, looking into the endless blue canvas. It could've been the glassy ocean at daybreak, but his mouth was dry and the air warm.

Pain flashed across his forehead.

He closed his eyes until the tension relaxed. His skin was warm and damp with sweat, tight where the sun had turned it pink. The grass crunched as he lifted his arm.

His elbow struck something hard.

It lay in the tall weeds, a half-buried circle with raised numbers. He pulled the grass aside and scraped the algae and matted leaves away.

A sundial.

The pain returned when he sat up, almost dragging him back into unconsciousness. He rode out the splashing white flashes inside his skull. Birds scuttled in the trees behind him. The briny scent of the ocean was strong.

Something is missing.

A three-storied dormitory was across the field, the windows punched out, vines clawing the walls. Beyond that, just above the trees, the cylindrical outline of another building was set against the cloudless tropical sky. The windows, once reflective, were now dull and chalky. It listed slightly to the left.

He knew where he was. *How did I get here?*

Something rustled in the grass.

Danny jumped up, regrettably, and fought the spots stabbing his vision, the pain lighting up his head as he scanned the trees and sky for predators. The tall grass was still matted where he was lying, the edge of the sundial—weathered and cracked—still exposed.

A path led away from it.

The sun reflected off the trampled grass. Danny bent down to pick up a disc—just one disc, the side smooth and reflective and perforated with a galaxy of tiny holes. And then the memories surfaced.

The three discs, the ash-covered world, the final beam of light. And then this.

The island.

A shiver trickled down his back, clinked in his stomach like cold cubes. It was just like he remembered when he woke up that first day with the old man telling him he was somewhere special, that they were going to help him. It smelled green and new. White birds soared with promise.

But the buildings were abandoned, the field overgrown. There were no old men, no boys being marched to the haystack. And something else was missing.

The lilac is gone.

The ever-present scent of lilac that had followed him for the past year had been replaced by the ocean.

He turned the disc over. The pattern of holes was the same as the others, but he didn't expect to find them. They wouldn't be hiding in the grass. This disc was different. The edge was red.

A moan behind him.

Danny spun and saw a depression ten feet away, the curve of a bended knee. Cyn lay on her back, her head cradled in a nest of bundled grass, her skin slightly pink. He fell on his knees and took her hand. Her repose was undisturbed, her hair fanned over the ground.

Her eyelids fluttered. Eyes unfocused, she gazed into the cloudless blue for several moments.

"Hey." Danny squeezed.

Her breath came in long, cool strokes. She started to sit up and scrunched her eyes. Folds wrinkled across her forehead. Danny could still feel a dull ache between his eyes, but the pain had faded. Hers was fresh out of the box.

"Where are we?" she asked.

"An island."

"How..." She swallowed. "Island?"

She lay still, eyes closed, breathing through the settling ache. He could see the subtle hints of memory returning, the details of Times Square covered in ash, running at Alessandra...*and then the light.*

"How'd we get here?" she muttered.

He held up the disc. She shook her head. Confusion clouded her pained eyes.

"*Where one to another is three, in the dark there is now light to see,*" he said, quoting the last poem found at the Institute. "The discs he sent, they were colored on the edges; each one matched the gown we were wearing."

A touch of vertigo swirled in his belly, the jiggling trapdoor threatening to drop him into a pit of reality confusion. They were in a Foreverland world looking at their bodies in the Institute that he presumed were representations of their *real* bodies.

"*Our bodies,*" he said, "were wearing those gowns: blue, yellow and green. Three of us, just like the last poem said, *where one to another is three, in the dark there is now light.* And Alessandra was the light."

He held the disc above her, the shadow falling on her stomach, a small galaxy of pinpoints.

"When the three discs were together, they vibrated. And then I noticed that these little holes dispersed the light in a way that made the shadow disappear, like the discs were just an illusion, like they weren't really there. Like the poem said, *look inward, for you are the bridge.* Only it meant all three of us. *We* are the bridge."

Cyn sat up and rested her arms on her knees. Her hair hung over her face like curtains. "But we were together before that."

"There is now light to see."

Alessandra wasn't the light when they walked into the Institute. That was the missing element. The pieces were in place so that when the time came, when Alessandra pulled down the Nowhere, when she'd brought the Investors back and transformed herself into a beam of light, there was a way for them to escape.

"She saved me," Cyn said.

"She saved all of us."

"Barb." The blonde curtains shook. *"Barb* saved me."

Danny sat next to her and gave her several seconds.

"Barb was...she was an Investor."

He thought so, but couldn't understand why Cyn was hiding her face from him. Why her voice quivered. The old woman had helped them become the bridge. She stopped Cyn until Danny arrived. Like she knew.

But she was the only Investor clothed.

"We all had an Investor," Danny said.

"Mine was different." She sighed heavily. "I never told anyone this, but something happened in Foreverland that was...different than everyone else when, you know, the time came for her to take my body."

She swallowed. Hard. *My demon is different than yours.*

"That cloud in Times Square," she said, "the gray coming down, I remember that, Danny. I remember the Nowhere. I know what it's like to be out there and pulled into a billion pieces. I remember having no body, no mind, just this...this shattered something...spilled all over the place like a...like a nothing."

She sniffed.

"And then I just got pushed out, like someone pulled me back together and shoved me back into my body. All of the others were still in the Nowhere and I was back, but..." She exhaled. "Barb was already there—I'm sorry, I don't like to...it's all weird and confusing. I know it sounds all, you know, impossible but, it's just...no one ever came out of the Nowhere except for me, I think. And, I don't really know why."

She quivered and stifled a sob. *Why me?*

She'd been in the Nowhere, tasted it. Danny was there, too, as a tourist. He didn't feel the separation, didn't dissolve. Maybe it would all sound impossible if she didn't say someone had *pushed her out.* Danny knew someone that survived the Nowhere, someone that could come and go as she wished.

Lucinda.

Reed's girlfriend came to Danny when he first went to Foreverland. She was the one with candy red hair, the one that knew the Nowhere, the one that took Danny out there to see and hear. She destroyed herself when Foreverland crashed.

But not before she found Cyn.

"Was Barb the one you were talking to?" Danny asked. "At the Institute?"

She nodded. "I'm not crazy, Danny."

"I know."

"She's been in my head since Foreverland ended. Every day was a battle. Until you showed up."

He remembered how it felt when he held her hand the first time, the way his body shook with relief, how his nightmare went away.

"When you showed up, she just went away, sort of. For the first time, I couldn't hear her voice. But she didn't disappear. When you were gone, she came back, she poured the pills down my throat, tried to take back my body. If you hadn't showed up that night..."

She took several cleansing breaths.

"But then she changed," Cyn said. "Said Reed was behind it all."

"Told you about Alessandra."

She nodded. "And when I saw Times Square and the sky falling, I thought she was sending us all to the..."

She sighed and didn't finish.

"I don't think that's what she was doing."

"That was the Nowhere. She was pulling it down, I could feel it. I can't go back there, Danny. I can't."

"We're not going back. I promise."

"How do you know?" She looked up, eyes wide, red and glassy.

He didn't want to lie to her, not ever. She didn't deserve that. He didn't know where they were going; he could only tell her what he thought Alessandra did, what made sense.

She destroyed Foreverland.

It was more than that. Somehow, Alessandra brought the Investors back and made them pay. How she did it, he couldn't explain. He even wondered if they were real, maybe they were just illusions. It was impossible to tell if anything was real.

Their fear, though, that was real. They stood with wide-eyed panic on the sidewalk as the ashes fell around them, cries lost in the descending static that ate up the world. And all those voices intermingled with that tortuous noise, all those fragmented voices that haunted the Nowhere. And just before Danny and Cyn hit Alessandra, just before the light swallowed them, he heard the voices go silent.

"You all right?" he asked.

"Head starting to hurt again."

Danny's forehead had settled, but there was still a throbbing knot between his eyes that he massaged with his thumb. Her headache appeared to go away, too, but now it was coming back. She rubbed tiny circles between her eyes.

"Where is she?" Cyn asked. "Where's Alessandra?"

Danny eyed the path. Maybe she woke up before they did and went exploring. Judging by their pink skin, he and Cyn had been lying in the sun a while.

"Where are we, Danny? If Alessandra destroyed Foreverland, where are we?"

"We're not awake."

"Why?" Her eyes pleaded, still wide, panic on the rims, reality confusion nipping at her heels. Thoughts of the Nowhere lurked behind her eyes.

He exhaled sharply, searching the sky.

If Alessandra was no longer a host and this wasn't reality, then where were they? Who was hosting *this? And why the island?*

A warm breeze rushed over the field. The grass rustled and brushed against them. Blonde strands stuck to Cyn's damp cheeks. Danny brushed them away, her face warm.

Once again, the smell of the ocean was strong, like they were bathing in it, breathing the salt spray, the taste lingering on his lips, stinging his eyes. And yet they weren't close enough to hear the waves.

And not a hint of lilac.

He searched the blue sky in the disc's reflection, the pinpoints dotting his eyes. The blood-red edge on his fingers. It wasn't blue or yellow or green. It was a different color.

Then he realized.

Something about the ocean, something about the red edge told him where they were.

Like we're breathing the ocean.

The path led to the beach. That was where Reed spent all his time when they were on the island. That's where they buried his body. *And this is what he smelled like.*

Maybe Alessandra didn't walk away from the sundial after all. Or maybe someone led her away while they slept. Danny knew where the answers would be.

"Let's go this way." He walked several steps down the trampled path. "I think we'll find something on the sand—"

She was gone.

Danny ran back. The grass was still matted, the bundled pillow still in place. There was no path leading away from it, no footsteps or broken stems. Cyn was just gone.

His smile faded, and he took a deep breath.

He walked in a large circle, looking through the grass like she was an object that fell out of his pocket. He tripped over the sundial.

This was the center of Foreverland when they were on the island, where everything started. Danny pushed away the debris and placed his hand on it. There was no tingling, no surge of power.

It was cold and dead.

Danny's head began to throb. The sky was still blue, the air still salty. If this was still a dream, if his physical body was still in the Institute, then he hadn't awakened. *And maybe Cyn's opening her eyes.*

"She's all right," he told himself. Then, "Please let her be all right."

He waited in case she reappeared. He couldn't stand the thought of her coming back alone. When the sun was directly above him, he decided to follow the path to the beach. He crossed the dunes out to the hardpack, where a set of barefooted tracks still dented the sand, slowly melting in the sliding waves.

The footprints walked straight into the ocean.

Danny stared at the crisp line of the horizon, remembering a time when he sat with Reed, when everything was bleak and hopeless, wondering what was out there. He took off his boots and socks, dug his toes into the ground, the water cool around his ankles.

Pain hammered a beating rhythm across his forehead.

He went back to the soft sand of the dunes, sat down, and turned his face to the sun that was still high, still hot. He closed his eyes, letting the salty air fill him. The thrumming pain shrank until it was a spot between his eyes going boom-boom, boom-boom.

The smell of the ocean faded.

The water went silent.

And Danny opened his eyes to a bright light.

180

A thorn.

It was wedged between her eyes, probably no larger than a sliver. Felt like a railroad spike.

She blinked. Colors smeared across the landscape. She distinctly remembered seeing everything, being everything. She didn't need eyes. There was no separation. She was the city. She was everywhere.

The light.

But now she lay in a sterile room, the smell of antiseptic mingled with the rank odor of wet fur and mucus.

She blinked again.

Pain flashed between her eyes. The sliver was a double image, a gleaming rod extending somewhere between her eyebrows. Each breath sent it deeper into her head.

She lifted her hand.

Fire ignited her elbow, muscles screeching along her forearm. Her fingers hovered above her face, careful not to bump the metal sliver, pinching it between finger and thumb.

A deep breath.

It slid from her like an icicle, tickling her inner ears, raking the back of her eyes. Tears pooled. She turned her head and let them roll over the bridge of her nose.

Another bed.

It was on a white stand. An old woman was sunk halfway into a green cushion. Her arms and legs were bent. Her hair as white as the stand. She was a mummy pulled from the belly of a pyramid, her flesh wrinkled like ancient leather. Her mouth was slightly open.

The beds hummed.

Roller pins massaged the back of Alex's legs, buttocks and shoulders. Pain radiated all over. It took three efforts to get up. She sat in a hunched position, catching her breath, waiting for strength to return...

When she remembered who she was, where she'd been.

What she did.

The room began to turn. It was too much—the dream, the reality —and the walls began to shrink. She wished for the peaceful light that swallowed her, that eternal existence where she rested after bringing back the old men and women.

After silencing the voices.

Peace.

She ended their suffering. She sat in the middle of the empty street, bemoaning her own fate, when the woman named Barb showed Alex her destiny. She was the one that would bring peace to the children.

You will balance the scales, Barb told her.

Alex let one of her bare feet touch the floor. It was hard and cold. Pins and needles crawled up her leg as if struck with an aluminum post. She let the other one down and rested. There were tubes in her arms that burned when pulled out, clear liquid dripping on her toes.

Images were scattered over two computers.

She reached out and took one large step to the one nearest her. Data scrolled along the margins. A picture of her was set in the upper left-hand corner. None of the script made sense except one flashing word.

AWAKE.

She was no longer dreaming, back in her body, her flesh. It seemed so obvious she wasn't asleep, now; the density of her body was like a shrink-wrap of flesh, her identity contained within.

The image fractured into static. Data blazed over the screen and then went black. A single line appeared on a blue screen.

DATA CORRUPT.

Something broke.

Her reflection looked back from the blank screen—frizzy black hair, dark eyes. A red spot glistened on her forehead. She brushed clear liquid from the hole. It ached with each pulse.

The room resumed a slow spin.

She latched onto the computer and closed her eyes. *I'm awake now. I'm awake now.*

The monitor nearest the old woman showed a different status. Alex stumbled over to it. The photo hardly matched the shriveled husk behind her. It was a younger version, a healthier time.

Patricia Ballard, it said.

And the word below it brought the room to a standstill.

DECEASED.

She remembered her on the oversized monitors in Times Square, an image that more closely resembled the picture on the computer. But on the sidewalk, she was naked and old and hidden in the arms of her husband. Her husband, Tyler Ballard, the man she interviewed at the prison, was enraged.

That was in the dream. I interviewed him in the dream.

He had shouted at Alex, but the voices—the poor, distorted voices, the children that had been thrown into that gray static—filled the air, blotting out the crashing buildings that fell in plumes of ashes. Tyler was responsible. They both were.

Patricia wasn't angry. She was sad, resigned. Accepting.

She knew her fate. And when the Nowhere collapsed, she went willingly.

Of course, Alex hadn't meant to murder anyone. She only brought the ones responsible for the crimes she witnessed. Patricia and Tyler had kidnapped Alex like all those old men and women had abducted the children. The Ballards inserted Alex into her own dream. They wanted her to be the sleeping host that would keep Foreverland alive.

And they had already hurt so many.

But now there was silence. No more voices, no more pain. No ashes.

Machines began beeping on the other side of a curtain. Alex needed to leave. Her gown was loose, her feet bare. She needed to be less conspicuous and pulled open all the drawers and found a box of bandages. Gently, she covered the oozing hole in her head.

Her clothes were beneath her bed.

She ran past Coco, down an empty hall, all the offices open and vacant. She stopped at the front doors. Outside, it was dark, the streets empty. A light rain fell in slow motion.

Two cabs were waiting.

She pulled a hood over her head and ran. It was late, the city asleep. But the night was warm. Winter had ended. She could smell the green of new growth.

And no lilac.

Alex jumped in the first cab, lay back and watched the city pass by. The streets were slick and shiny. It was perfectly quiet, beautifully silent.

The voices no longer cried.

181

The Institute of Technological Research, New York City

Thirst came in waves.

It was a pebble, a tiny stone that rose and fell. Cyn was reaching for something to stop it from rising and falling, rising and falling. But it wasn't a pebble, not something she could touch.

It throbbed.

Something beeped just out of reach, auditory spikes between valleys of silence, reminding her of a rooster that woke her after long, dead nights in the cabin.

Her eyelids cracked.

The light was harsh, slapping her into the cold tight ache of her body. She blinked back the fluorescent light and smacked at the thirst on her lips. Something was between her eyes.

She yanked it out too quickly, throwing a switch on an internal tuning fork. When the room stopped spinning—her head still singing —she was looking at a boy with red hair, sunk halfway into a green cushion. His arms and legs were slightly bent.

"Danny," she croaked.

She sat on the edge of the strange bed, her feet dangling just above the floor. Her knees, exposed below the hem of the yellow gown, ached. So did her fingers and elbows. Most of all, her hand throbbed like her forehead. It was wrapped in gauze. She peeled off the tape, exposing a slice across the back of her hand, thick whiskers of black stitching poking out.

I cut myself so long ago. Why does it still look like that?

The time dilation.

Danny was right: time went much faster in Foreverland. If she still had stitches, that meant—

Her knees buckled when she leaped, catching herself before coming down hard. Pins and needles shot through her feet. She lowered herself to the floor and crawled. The curtain that separated their beds had been pulled aside. She passed an open cabinet and noticed the box of clothing as she pulled herself up to Danny's bed.

She grew faint.

Closing her eyes, she slowed her breath. It came back to her now— where they were, where they'd been.

This is real.

"Danny?" she whispered. "Wake up, Danny."

His lips were parted; his breath shallow and warm. She pressed her ear to his chest.

Another computer beeped.

It was against the wall. Each step burned; the muscles and tendons contracted. Danny's photo was in the corner. The status flashed below it.

WAKING.

The cardiac monitor began to spike.

She stumbled back to his side and clawed at his shoulders, held his cheeks. His eyes moved beneath the eyelids.

"Come on, Danny." She looked around, hoping no one would hear her, no idea if someone was just beyond the curtains. She just knew they needed to get out. "Wake up."

If she pulled the needle too soon, would he be trapped in Foreverland? His eyes continued dancing. She squeezed his hand, fingers weaving together.

His eyes opened and stared into nothing.

"Danny?"

Tears welled up. She hovered over his face, stroking his cheeks. He blinked several times. Cyn pinched the needle and waited.

Waited for focus to return.

Waited for him to see her.

And when he did, when he blinked, when a tiny smile bent the corners of his mouth—

She yanked it out.

He bolted upright and couldn't catch his breath, huffing like he was dumped into a bucket of icy water.

"Danny." She rubbed his arm. "We've got to go, Danny."

He looked around, the pieces of reality falling in place too slowly. She pushed him up and pulled his legs over the edge.

"Easy."

She held him while he slid his weight onto his feet. He stared down and looked at his hands, turning them over like she'd seen him do before, his barometers of reality.

"We're back, Danny. This is the skin."

He was nodding, but still turning, needing to believe it, not just hear it. She retrieved the boxes of clothing while he sorted out this layer of reality. *Is he wondering the same thing I am, wondering if this is the last layer?*

She was only wearing panties beneath the gown. Danny grabbed a sweatshirt and a pair of sweatpants, tenderly walking around the curtain. She quickly pulled on a pair of pants, tucking the gown inside them and throwing the hoodie over it. Danny was still dressing.

Cyn peeked around the opposite curtain. Patricia lay still on a bed. She didn't appear to be breathing. The other bed was empty.

The building was silent.

"Danny?" she whispered. "You all right?"

His bare feet weren't beneath the curtain. A dreaded wave settled in her chest. Cyn shuffled around the tables.

"Danny?" She tugged the plastic curtain.

Several curtains were pulled back. Danny was ten tables back, still dressed in the gown, clothes in hand. He stared at an older man, his beard shaggy, hair wild. There was a hole in his forehead, but no needle.

"It's him," Danny said hollowly. "It's Reed."

She thought Reed would be younger, then remembered that wasn't his original body. Reed migrated into Harold Ballard's body when they overthrew Foreverland and escaped the island.

Reed's original body was dead. *So is that one.*

"I thought he sent us the letters," Cyn said.

"It was him. It had to be. It just..."

He started to sway, reality confusion tilting the floor. She let him take his time, but more computers were beginning to beep. They needed to go. They could figure this out later. Besides, it didn't matter who sent the letters.

"Danny, no. This way."

He slid his bare feet over the floor, went to the other side of Reed and pulled back the curtain. An overhead light flickered to life.

Another bed, another body.

"Oh, man, no," he moaned. "No, no, no...not you, Zin."

Cyn read the name on the computer. *Eric Zinder.*

He'd escaped the island with them. Now he was there, in the Institute, a hole in his head but no needle. He wasn't breathing.

There were more curtains.

Danny rushed through them, tearing them off their hooks, dropping them on the floor. The lights turned on one after another, bed after bed.

Body after body.

The first three were boys. She wasn't sure he recognized them all. The fourth one, though, was a dark-skinned woman.

Macy. She was helping them. She was working for the Ballards.

This time the floor tipped beneath Cyn's feet.

"They were searching for a host," he said. "They were bringing us here, searching for a host."

"She's gone." Cyn looked back toward the front. "Alessandra's bed is empty."

"Zin's the one that saved me," he said. "Kept me from going insane on the island."

"We have to go." She clutched his elbow.

He resisted. "They lured us into the Institute, somehow put us back here and then, they manipulated our memories so that we didn't remember...we didn't know we were..."

The room was spinning on him. He hung onto the bed.

"Danny! We have to go!"

He tried to yank away from her.

"Don't do this. We can't help them now. We don't know what's happening, someone might come back, we're not supposed to be awake, they'll put us back in...we have to go now!"

Danny was shaking his head. He went back to Zin, took the boy's hand, and continued shaking his head as if he just couldn't take it anymore. No more layers.

No more lies.

Cyn gently wrapped her hand around his. Danny remained unfocused as she took the clothes wedged under his arm and began dressing him. She put her hands on his cheeks.

"We're alive, Danny. And we need to leave. Do you understand?"

She pressed her lips against his, her body against his body.

"We have to go."

He nodded.

There wasn't time to lament, no time to understand where they were or why. There was only time to escape. She pulled him away, but Danny paused at Reed's body, his head cocked to the side. His thoughts, like hers, were obscured in the fog of waking.

He clutched Reed's gown and shook it. It was red.

"Come on."

They made it past the beds where they woke, past Patricia Ballard. The last time Cyn saw her was in a small cabin hidden in the woods. There was a monitor with Patricia's picture in the upper left-hand corner. *DECEASED.*

Danny was in front of another computer, this one near the empty bed. The cabinets below it were open. There was an image of an attractive Hispanic woman. *AWAKE.*

She made it out.

They passed through the animal lab and paused at the front door.

Brake lights glowed in an otherwise black and empty street. Rain drifted in tiny droplets, throwing red halos around the back end of the car. The driver stared at them through a blue cloud from an electric cigarette.

The back door was open.

Instinctively, they pulled their hoods up and walked out. It was late, the city still asleep.

"Wait." Danny held the door. "We don't have money."

"Fare's already covered," the driver said. "Get in."

"Who?"

"Somebody called, paid in advance. Come on, already."

"Where we going?"

"JFK."

Cyn and Danny traded empty stares, trying to cut through the mental fog, to calculate whether this was a good idea. Maybe they should walk until things cleared up.

Cyn saw the envelope on the backseat. She reached inside and pulled out two tickets. "Spain?"

Danny ushered her inside the cab.

182

New York City

It unfolded below.

The third-story window was spattered with tiny droplets that, over the hours he had stood there, coalesced and eventually ran in jagged lines. The man pushed brown curly hair off his forehead and checked his wristwatch. Thirty-two minutes past four.

The taxi pulled away.

It was the second car to pull up to the Institute of Technological Research, this one instructed to take an envelope taped to the front door and wait for two people. The driver would later be interviewed by police. With their hoods up, he wouldn't be able to help them with identifying the boy and girl other than remembering they were young.

The first car was different. That was a private driver, someone Reed paid handsomely for confidentiality. He took her to a home in the suburbs.

There would be no trace of Alessandra.

Rain continued drifting into the empty street. Occasionally, a car passed below, but no one noticed that the door to the Institute was open, that all the lights were on.

He took a deep breath and closed his eyes.

At 4:45, he reached into the front pocket of his white lab coat and pulled out a phone. The glass was cool against his thumb. He touched several icons, then sent a message. He waited for confirmation that all relevant data had been downloaded from the Institute.

It's done.

Even he was surprised by the weight falling off his shoulders, like a beast stepping off. It had been such a long journey, so many people had been hurt. He didn't plan it to happen like this, but the Ballards had already been so powerful.

But it was over. It was finally over.

Reed took off the white coat and placed it on the receptionist's counter. He punched a code into the phone and placed it on top like a paperweight as the self-destruct code erased all trace of the biomite doctor.

At the glass doors, he set the alarm and stepped out as the countdown beeped. The elevator doors squealed open. He pulled a hood over his head and stepped onto the sidewalk, drizzle beading on his hunched shoulders. The early morning chill cut through layers of clothing as delivery trucks began their morning routes.

He walked nearly two city blocks when the first police car passed him. They were heading for the Institute. The eerie news of the empty research facility would be all over the world by lunch.

By then, Reed would be far away.

183

Alex grabbed for something, a ledge or a rope or a helping hand, but nothing, black nothing slipped through her fingers—

Asleep again. This time at the computer. Had her Madre seen her jerk her head off the desk, she would've fretfully wrung her hands. *"¿Otra pesadilla?"*

Si, Madre. Another nightmare.

It was those moments just after she woke, when she wasn't sure if the dream had ended or was just beginning, that disturbed her most. Her forehead always reminded her. She parted her black bangs and touched the tiny hole.

This is real.

Something was dripping.

The coffee cup lay on its side, a brown stain spreading over a mess of papers. She must've knocked it over when she lurched into wakefulness.

"Damn!"

She pulled old papers and tissues from the trash but stood too quickly and grabbed the desk to keep from falling. That was the second time in a minute she was glad Madre wasn't around. When the vertigo settled, she dabbed up the mess.

The doorbell rang.

She looked out the window. The lilacs had faded. Spring had passed. The neighbor was mowing his front yard. Spring blossoms had completely fallen from the cherry tree, replaced by foliage that blocked her view. The taillights of a black SUV were barely visible.

The front door opened. "Yes?" Madre said.

The voices were muffled, but Alex heard the word "agent" somewhere in the exchange.

Surprised it took so long.

She dropped the sopping papers. Coffee bled through the photo on top, the image of the white transfer van had been found in Pennsylvania, en route to New York.

The catatonic drivers made full recoveries. They were transporting one passenger to Attica Correctional Facility when they pulled into the rest area with no recollection of why or how long they'd been there.

Dr. Tyler Ballard.

It wasn't long before a full-scale Foreverland operation was discovered at the prison. Dr. Tyler Ballard had just left. He'd arranged the transfer, but the investigation suspected he was planning to be discharged at the Institute, where a similar Foreverland was in full swing. That's where his wife awaited him.

She was found dead, too.

Tyler Ballard was still in restraints, alone in the back of the van. The drivers claimed he was a little loco. When he wasn't sleeping, he talked to himself. "What was really weird," one of the drivers said, "was when he'd pause, like someone was answering him."

No one in the prison remembered anything. They were all fully loaded with brain biomites that had been rebooted. The only exception was an inmate named Gramm Hamilton, a former chemist serving a life sentence. He claimed to have been trapped in his cell by an intruder, that he had nothing to do with Tyler Ballard's escape and subsequent death.

The coroner couldn't explain how Tyler Ballard died. It was eventually written up as "old age and biomite complications."

"Right on the line," the coroner said. "He had the most biomites allowed by law, and they were experimental, too. I suspect this had something to do with his delusions."

The press eventually concocted an image of Dr. Tyler Ballard the mad scientist that hijacked a prison and tortured inmates with delusions of Foreverland.

Alex knew better.

In the months since she'd walked out of the Institute, no one had called or come knocking. Even when the investigation revealed a cab taking two unknown people, a young man and woman, from the Institute shortly before the alarms went off, no one ever contacted Alex.

There was no mention of a cab that picked up a middle-aged Hispanic woman.

Alex went to the top of the steps and listened.

"I'd just like to speak with her, ask a few questions," a young man said.

"Unless you have a warrant—"

"Mrs. Diosa is not a suspect, ma'am. I just have some questions about one of her previous visits to the Institute."

"I don't appreciate your implications," Madre said.

"Any information she could give me—"

"Bring a warrant."

She's been watching too much TV. "What's going on?" Alex stopped on the bottom step.

"Mrs. Diosa?" he called through the screen.

"You don't need to talk to the police," Madre said.

"What does he want?"

"It doesn't matter." It would take a crane to move her.

Three months earlier, the cab had dropped Alex off at a dark and empty house. Exhausted, she fell asleep on the couch and didn't call her parents until that afternoon. Madre shouted at her on the phone, but they drove over to the house immediately. They were both sick with grief. She'd disappeared for two weeks.

Only two weeks.

Alex later learned of the time dilation between reality and Foreverland. *But an entire year?*

Her parents noticed the wound on her forehead, but never said a word about it. Even when the story broke about the Institute and Tyler Ballard—the story about all those bodies, all those people networked into a computer—they pretended not to know that their daughter had gone there. And they never mentioned needles.

Madre moved into the spare bedroom. She had already lost a grandson and son-in-law, she wasn't going to lose her daughter. Alex didn't argue.

"I just want to talk," the man shouted through the door.

"Madre."

She took Alex's hand, pressed it against her cheek and kissed it. Then she went to the kitchen to make some coffee.

Alex leaned closer to the mirror and pulled strands of black hair over her forehead. The hole had healed, but she preferred to keep her bangs just in case someone looked too closely.

When she came out of the bathroom, Madre was sitting at the kitchen table with her cell phone. The agent stood at the back door, admiring the garden where Alex spent most of the summer, sometimes getting lost in the weeds, expecting to find a forgotten yellow truck.

"I'm recording this." Her mother put the cell phone down.

"That's not necessary, Madre."

"You never know."

"All right, okay. You never know."

Madre remained at the table like a mediator.

"Beautiful backyard," the agent said. "You do it all yourself?"

Alex pulled a chair from the table. "Want to sit?"

"Okay." He raised his cup. "Thanks for the coffee, Mrs. Diosa. Better than I deserve."

Madre nodded once.

"So what can I do for you?" Alex asked.

"Right. You're familiar with Foreverland?"

"Yes, of course. I'm writing a book. You know that."

He smiled sheepishly. *Let's cut through it.* "Like I said, you're not a suspect."

"Why would I think that?"

He eyed the phone. "If there's any way you can help, anything you can say, we'd appreciate it. I know you're well aware of the children involved."

The voices.

She heard them at night sometimes, woke in a sweat to silence. Dreams, that's all they were, memories of that dreadful event. It seemed like years ago, but the voices were nails that had scratched grooves into her memory.

"I don't know any more than you," she said.

"Right."

"The Ballards started all of this, correct? You found their bodies. What else is there?"

"You were at the Institute."

She clutched her hands. They were below the table, but the tension extended past her shoulders. "I've been there, yes."

"When?"

"In the spring. A group of journalists were invited. I can get the exact date..."

He shook his head. "That's all right. You went to a biomite doctor across the road shortly after that?"

"Some time after that, yes."

"He's missing."

"I think he left the practice."

He grimaced. "Leaving your coat and phone on the counter isn't how most people retire."

"I don't know where he is, if that's what you're asking."

"No one has been able to locate him."

"What do you want me to say?"

He paused for a long sip, swirling the remains. "You went to see him because of the incident at the Institute, right?"

"More coffee?" Alex asked.

Madre began to stand. Alex stopped her, went to the coffee pot and poured a cup. He looked at her forehead when he asked that. Not just a glance, but a question with his eyes.

"Why are you asking questions you already know the answers to?" she said.

"Helps me keep my thoughts straight."

She put the cup in the microwave and watched it go around.

"I lost my balance while I was there. The smells, the lab…you know, it wasn't what I was expecting."

"What were you expecting?"

"Not that."

"I understand you were in a car accident. I'm very sorry for your loss."

"Thank you."

He muttered condolences to Madre, talked about how proud she must be of her family and she had every right to be. The death of a child was a terrible loss.

"Have you sought treatment for your grief?"

"I'm sorry, what?"

"Since the accident, have you done anything to process your emotions?"

"What are you suggesting?"

He cleared his throat. "Have you gone back to the Institute?"

They stared for a long moment. "No."

"Not even to research for your book?"

"No."

"What happened with Coco?"

"The orangutan?"

"Yes. There are reports you said Coco opened his eyes."

"When did this turn into an interrogation?"

"I'm just following trails, Mrs. Diosa. Anything that will help."

"Look, I don't think I can help you. The Institute was performing illegal research. They were kidnapping suitable hosts to create an alternate reality and, thank God, someone stopped them."

"How do you know someone stopped them?"

"Don't play that. Those facts are all over the Internet. Someone woke up the hosts and wiped the computers clean. Some of them escaped before the alarm sounded and a car was recorded on a nearby security camera picking up two kids."

"Kids?"

"The footage is on Youtube."

"No one said they were kids."

"If you can't tell those are kids by the way they act, then you should turn in your badge."

He grinned and shrugged.

"I'll tell you what I don't know," Alex said. "What happened to all the employees that disappeared?"

"What have you heard?"

"The place was empty. And what about Mr. Deer?"

He cocked his head curiously.

"He was the one that organized these tours and invited the journalists," she said. "We heard he was a major part of the operation."

"I can't share that with you."

"And Patricia? Is she really dead?"

He nodded.

Alex sat down, cradling the warm mug for comfort. "And the unidentified hosts, the ones that woke up. Did you find out who they were?"

"Why do you ask?"

"I'm concerned, hope they're all right."

He leaned forward. "I thought this wasn't an interrogation."

"I just want to know that the children are safe."

She flicked a knowing glance at his forehead. It was unblemished, apparently untouched by a needle. But he knew the depth of the crimes committed in Foreverland. Maybe he didn't hear the voices, but he knew that children paved the way to Foreverland. Alex wanted to be sure she wasn't imagining she had quieted the voices, that she took away their suffering.

That she ended the Nowhere.

"They're safe," he said, unblinking. The tone suggested he answered the unspoken question, the real question.

"Safe?"

He nodded. "Thank you."

"For what?"

He held up his mug. "For the coffee."

That felt like a lie. The *thank you* meant something else.

A grin broke across his face. Madre's arms were crossed, her head hung down. Soft little snores rattled in the back of her throat. They got up quietly and left the kitchen without disturbing her or the phone recorder.

"Tell your mother it was nice to meet her." He stopped at the door. "It must be nice having her here."

She nodded suspiciously. He seemed to know more about her than he should. Or maybe he was just a better detective than she'd thought.

"Be careful," he said.

"What?"

He held out his hand. They shook. "With your book."

"Yes, of course. The book." She cocked her head, careful not to disturb her bangs. "Are you telling me not to write it?"

"Not at all. The world needs heroes."

"Is that what you think I am?"

He cupped her hand with both of his and gently squeezed. His tone softened, his eyes relaxed. He said, "I'm very sorry for your loss, Mrs. Diosa. I truly am."

She watched him get into his SUV, watched him drive away. She'd never seen him before in her life, she was sure of that. But he seemed so familiar.

Madre was rinsing the coffee pot. Her phone was still on the table. Next to it was a business card. It looked legitimate, an agent from the Biomite Oversite Agency. It was just his last name.

Johnstone.

She'd later remember that name and call the number and get the office of her biomite doctor, the one that mysteriously left the practice. But she right then, as Madre took chicken from the freezer, as children laughed somewhere in the neighborhood and birds squabbled at the feeder, she turned the card over.

Her breath caught short.

The agent had written something on the back.

She pinched herself, hugged her mother and wept.

The sky was clear blue, not a cloud in sight. She wept and the birds continued to sing and the sun continued to shine. She wept because it didn't rain.

"Thank you" was written on the back of the card.

In green ink.

184

AN ISLAND *off the coast of Spain*

The sea breeze blew through the house.

Danny slapped the papers against the table. Santiago rushed to close the doors, the curtain fluttering around him.

"Just close one," Danny said.

The portly Spaniard hesitated, knowing one door would only make it worse. But Danny smiled, and Santiago nodded. Danny didn't like the house closed up. *The breeze should always blow through the house,* Danny said. *I want to smell the water.*

The smell of this ocean was different than the Foreverland scent. This was more authentic, natural. And it reminded him where he was. *I am here.*

Santiago stood in the doorway, as if his rotund frame would block the wind. He held his mesh hat down, tufts of black curly hair escaping his open collar, the breeze carrying his musky scent into the room.

Santiago, the overweight Spaniard with crooked teeth and always a shadow of whiskers. How could I forget?

His compatriot. His business partner.

The Foreverland imposter resembled him, could pass as a twin. But he didn't have the mannerisms, not in the flesh. And now that Danny was back, it was all too obvious. The integration into Foreverland had been so seamless, his memories so well manipulated that Danny couldn't remember at what point he had been inserted.

The Institute.

That was the turning point. Something happened when the scientists brought him into the lab, when they had explained the experimentation. Danny had shuddered, appalled at their disregard for the animals' suffering. Mr. Jonathan Deer, the man that had invited him, the man that arranged for Cyn to visit, wasn't there during that trip. He was going to hear from Danny, though.

Danny remembered flying home, remembered crafting a tersely worded email on the plane, remembered landing in Spain and Santiago picking him up at the airport.

The other Santiago.

There was no plane ride, no coming home. They inserted Danny right then.

"Daniel?" Mary tapped the table with her fingernail, a clear coat of polish and tailored business suit revealed her impeccable taste. "Everything all right?"

"Yes. Sorry."

Danny turned his attention back to the contract, a stack as thick as a roll of dimes. He signed where there were Xs, taking the time to read sections he could understand, jotting notes in the margins. Santiago eventually looked over his shoulder, grunting each time Danny scratched out a line or made a comment.

It feels so good to be back.

Danny had returned to the villa after mysteriously disappearing for almost a month. The Spaniard didn't ask why or where Cyn came from or why they had covered their foreheads; he simply explained the state of his affairs.

Normality returned.

Danny tabbed each page he edited. When he reached the last page, the margins were littered with plastic strips.

"*Jorge tendrá que leer a través de él de nuevo,*" Danny said. *Jorge will need to read through it again.*

"Of course." Santiago patted his shoulder.

Someone crossed the open doorway, the curtain dancing around her. A lithe young woman was squeezing water from her hair.

"Is everything all right?" Mary asked.

Even Mary looked familiar, the client he'd met at the diner, when the Nowhere oozed out of her left eye. Danny still couldn't understand how it was all accomplished, how Alessandra could absorb the details of the physical world and build a Foreverland world. Her mind was like a substance, a sponge that permeated the planet.

We were even discussing the same deal at the café. Or maybe my memories are corrupt and I only think she looks familiar.

He couldn't reason his way through the experience. In fact, the memories (false or not) put him at ease, like he'd practiced this negotiation already. Still, he was tempted to ask her if they'd met before.

"Daniel?" she asked.

"You will have to excuse us," Santiago said. "There have been late nights."

Danny was watching Cyn on the portico. "I changed some of the language that I'd like my attorney to look at. If you'd like, you can look it over first."

Danny slid it to the man on Mary's right. He efficiently scooped up the brightly flagged document.

"We can have it back to you in the morning," she said. "I'd like to conclude business before flying out tomorrow night."

"I don't see why not."

"Well." They stood. "Thanks for meeting us in person. It's not that we don't trust projection rooms. We'd rather meet face to face before investing in people."

"Ironic, don't you think?"

They didn't trust the very thing they were investing in: technology. *I don't blame them.*

"The irony's lost when you're giving millions to a seventeen-year-old."

"Time is relative." Danny smiled. "Einstein proved that."

"We're not flying through space."

They shook hands across the table. He could've sworn she glanced at his forehead.

"We prefer to shake hands," she added. "In person."

"Even that's not reliable," Danny said. "Not if we both have biomite-created hands."

"If the government continues restricting biomite technology, we might be looking for work."

"It should be none of the government's business," Mary's companion said. "If a man needs more than 49% biomites to save his body, he should have the right to do so."

"Can't have people turning into robots," Danny said.

"Halfskin," Mary said.

"What's that?"

"It's what they've termed the condition when the body is more artificial than human."

"Arbitrary, if you ask me." Her companion snapped his briefcase and dropped it on the table. "Man gets two prosthetic arms, two prosthetic legs and he's just fine. Make those prosthetics out of biomites and the government wants to turn him off. You know the story about the diver? He found an illegal strain of biomites, ones the government couldn't track."

Danny had heard of them and wanted no part of it.

"He dove to the bottom of the ocean, almost three miles below the surface, and came back unharmed because his body was almost entirely biomites. You know what the government did when they found out, right? Turned him off, like a light." He snapped his fingers. "Imagine what we could accomplish."

"That's the world we live in," Danny said. "So let's change it."

"Let's do so." They shook hands again. Mary caught him glancing at Cyn and smiled. "I'll let you get back to your business."

"It's been a long year," he said.

"I understand."

She has no idea.

Cyn was tone and tan, one leg pulled onto the lounger while she painted her toenails bright red.

Danny stood beneath the portico with two glasses of iced tea.

"Meeting adjourned?" she asked.

Her skin was perfect, barely a scar where the needle had pierced her flawless forehead. The cut across her hand had healed nicely, a white slash that would always remind her of the Institute.

He was grateful she woke up first, that he didn't see her with the needle in her head. It would've hurt to see her so helpless, so prone.

She stopped painting. "What?"

"Nothing."

"We going back to the States?"

"No, not yet. Best we stay here a bit longer."

A year, he was thinking. *Maybe more.*

The ripples from the Institute were still moving. Several months had gone by and the investigation was ongoing and would be for some time. Nothing had been solved. The Ballards had been found, but they had to have had help. An operation that expansive required men and women in high places.

Jonathan Deer disappeared. And Zin, Reed, and all the other victims in the Institute...they no longer have a living body.

There was nothing he could do for them. Cyn wanted to do something, but what? All they could do was follow the case from a safe distance. When things cooled down, maybe then they could find who was helping the Ballards.

Danny felt like it was his fault, the survivor guilt returning. He was convinced Reed had written the notes, that he was the one that put the pieces together. But Reed was dead. Was it possible to untether from the body and live in Foreverland?

That's what happened to Lucinda.

Cyn held out the sunscreen. She pulled her hair forward. Danny rubbed the lotion on her shoulders and across her back.

"What are we going to do?" she asked.

"We stay, maybe a year. Maybe longer. We can improve biomite production and efficiency, fund lobbyists to ease government restrictions, help those that really need it."

"No. I mean what are we going to do right now?"

"Oh, you mean now? As in now-now?"

"As in now-now." She wrapped her sun-warmed arms over his shoulders. They swayed like the ocean was an orchestra, paradise their dance floor. She nuzzled into his neck and sighed, her hair pressed against his cheek. It was an intoxicating mixture of the roses and ocean.

"Do we just live happily ever after?" she asked.

"Was there ever a doubt?"

They danced until their skin was hot, their bodies thirsty.

They swam in the sea, the water warm and buoyant. Danny floated on his back, staring at the blue sky, looking for the gray static to eat a hole through it, to fall on them. It would take some time to get out of that habit.

No more lilacs.

Somehow that fragrance pervaded Alessandra's world. The lack of that scent, oddly enough, kept him grounded in the physical world. Because of her, the Nowhere was no more. The children were quiet. No more dreams. No more suffering. They helped her with that.

And that eased the survivor's guilt.

Cyn swam into the deep and stayed under for a full minute. She emerged next to him and wrapped her arms around him. He thought about the diver, the one with the biomite body that went to the bottom of the ocean. He was the man that converted his body into biomites.

Like he built it.

And despite the bathwater temperature of the ocean, Danny felt a chill. He'd been missing the obvious.

That night, he found one of the invitations he'd received from the Institute, the one that lured him in to be captured. It was from Jonathan Deer.

Danny held it up to the mirror and read the last name.

And began to laugh.

EPILOGUE

ANOTHER DOOR OPENED; *this time a boy about the age of thirteen stepped out. One by one the children of the Nowhere stepped out of the fabricating tanks, their eyes wide with wonder. Born again into the physical world, their bodies just like they left them on the island or in the wilderness.*

Only now they were better.

They were made of biomites, no different than flesh. Special biomites the government couldn't see. The same biomites that composed Jonathan's body, the body he fabricated himself so he could leave the body of flesh he despised. This one, the fabricated one, the body of biomites, felt more like his body than Harold Ballard's body ever did.

And Jonathan could use this body to look like anyone he wanted. Become whoever he wanted. He had morphed his face and body to look like many different people, had taken on many different names to make this day happen.

But inside, he had never changed.

The technicians went to the children, welcomed two hundred and three children to the world. Jonathan remained in place, eyes on the last tank at the end of the line, the door still cracked and unmoving. His heart thudded like falling stones.

He drifted through the crowd, not hearing, not seeing, watching only one tank, the only one not to open.

His legs had become numb. He locked his knees to keep from falling, afraid to reach out, to look inside and see the failure. Of all the fabrications, this was the hardest. This was the most difficult one to piece together.

She'd been through so much. So fragmented.

She was the one that saved the children, that kept their existence in the Nowhere bearable. She was the one, of all of them, that deserved to step out of that tank.

He swallowed and reached. The door swung open.

He fell back half a step and saw only her, standing inside, head bowed.

Candy red hair.

Damp gown stuck to her perfect skin.

Her eyes closed, he watched. He held his breath, vowed never to take another until she—

The eyelashes fluttered.

Big green eyes, vivid in color, sharp in contrast, looked upon the world. Big green eyes seeing it for the first time in what seemed like forever and fell on the young man in front of her.

Jonathan Deer was no longer the green-eyed stranger with the bent nose. He let his true features return, showed his true face. His hair brown, long and curly.

She stepped out and reached up. Her fingers brushed his cheek.

The world blurred through his tears. "Lucinda," he said.

She whispered in his ear what he'd longed to hear since the day he woke on the island.

"Reed."

WHAT TO READ NEXT?

What are biomites? Where did they come from and where do they lead?

Continue the Foreverland journey.

HALFSKIN

An Underground Reviews 2015 Best Books

bertauski.com/halfskin

REVIEW FOREVERLAND!

If you enjoyed this ride, please drop a review on your favorite vendor. It doesn't have to be long and complicated. Throw some stars on it and write *Loved it!* or *It was really, really okay!* or *Meh*.

Reviews make the difference.

BERTAUSKI STARTER LIBRARY

Get the
BERTAUSKI STARTER LIBRARY
FREE!
Click link below

bertauski.com

ABOUT THE AUTHOR

TONY BERTAUSKI

My grandpa never graduated high school. He retired from a steel mill in the mid-70s. He was uneducated, but a voracious reader. As a kid, I'd go through his bookshelves of musty paperback novels, pulling Piers Anthony and Isaac Asimov off the shelf and promising to bring them back. I was fascinated by robots that could think and act like people. What happened when they died?

Writing is sort of a thought experiment to explore human nature and possibilities. What makes us human? What is true nature?

I'm also a big fan of plot twists.

bertauski.com

CPSIA information can be obtained
at www.ICGtesting.com
Printed in the USA
LVHW010316080720
660051LV00015B/1183

9 781951 432454